The
Collected Papers
of
Sherlock
Holmes
Volume IV - Narratives
(19 Holmes Adventures)

New Sherlock Holmes

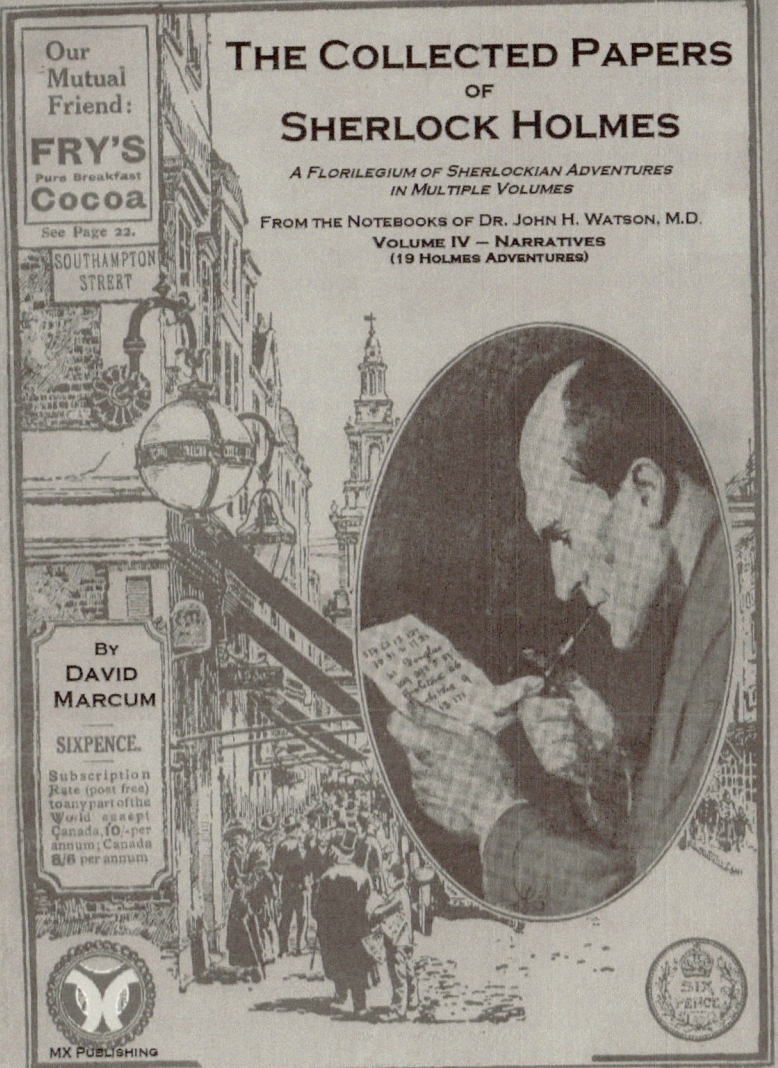

THE COLLECTED PAPERS
OF
SHERLOCK HOLMES

A Florilegium of Sherlockian Adventures
in Multiple Volumes

FROM THE NOTEBOOKS OF DR. JOHN H. WATSON, M.D.
VOLUME IV — NARRATIVES
(19 HOLMES ADVENTURES)

BY
**DAVID
MARCUM**

MX PUBLISHING

Published by MX PUBLISHING, 335 PRINCESS PARK MANOR, London, England.

"Watson's Descendants" ©2021 by Nicholas Meyer. All Rights Reserved. First publication, original to this collection. Printed by permission of the author.

ISBN Hardback 978-1-78705-911-5
ISBN Paperback 978-1-78705-912-2
AUK ePub ISBN 978-1-78705-913-9
AUK PDF ISBN 978-1-78705-914-6

Published in the UK by
MX Publishing
335 Princess Park Manor, Royal Drive,
London, N11 3GX
www.mxpublishing.co.uk

David Marcum can be reached at:
thepapersofsherlockholmes@gmail.com

Cover design by Brian Belanger
www.belangerbooks.com and *www.redbubble.com/people/zhahadun*

Internal illustrations by Sidney Paget

CONTENTS

Foreword

Narratives

Sources

"The London Wheel" **The MX Book of New Sherlock Holmes Stories – Part IV** *MX Publishing, 2016*

"The Two Different Women" **The MX Book of New Sherlock Holmes Stories – Part VIII** *MX Publishing, 2017*

"The Coffee House Girl" **The MX Book of New Sherlock Holmes Stories – Part XIII** *MX Publishing, 2019*

"The Regressive Man" **The MX Book of New Sherlock Holmes Stories – Part XVI** *MX Publishing, 2019*

"The Gordon Square Discovery" **The MX Book of New Sherlock Holmes Stories – Part XIX** *MX Publishing, 2020*

"The Secret in Lowndes Court" **The MX Book of New Sherlock Holmes Stories – Part XXII** *MX Publishing, 2020*

"The Sunderland Tragedies" **The MX Book of New Sherlock Holmes Stories – Part XXV** *MX Publishing, 2021*

"No Good Deed" **Further Associates of Sherlock Holmes** *Titan Publishing, 2017*

"The Dorset Square Business" **Sherlock Holmes: The Ultimate Smoking Companion** *Cunning Crime Books, 2019*

"The Brook Street Mystery" **Sherlock Holmes: Adventures Beyond the Canon – Volume III** *Belanger Books, 2018*

"The Colchester Experiment" **Sherlock Holmes and Doctor Watson: The Early Adventures – Volume III** *Belanger Books, 2019*

"The Keeper's Tale" **Sherlock Holmes: Adventures in the Realms of Edgar Allan Poe** *Belanger Books, 2019*

"The Village on the Cliff" **Sherlock Holmes and the Occult Detectives** *Belanger Books, 2020*

"The Tuefel Murders" – *Previously Unpublished*

"The Unpleasant Affair in Clipstone Street" **After the East Wind – Part III: When the Storm Has Cleared (1921-1928)** *Belanger Books, 2021*

"The Lincoln Street Minister" – *Previously Unpublished*

"The Tea Merchant's Dilemma" **The Strand Magazine** *Issue LIV, 2018*

"The Dowser's Discovery" **The Strand Magazine** *Issue LVIII, 2019*

"The Triangle of Death" **The Strand Magazine** *Issue LXI, 2020*

These additional adventures are contained in
Volume I – Tales
(9 Short Stories and a Novel)
The Papers of Sherlock Holmes (9 Short Stories)
The Adventure of the Least Winning Woman
The Adventure of the Treacherous Tea
The Singular Affair at Sissinghurst Castle
The Adventure of the Second Chance
The Haunting of Sutton House
The Adventure of the Missing Missing Link
The Affair of The Brother's Request
The Adventure of the Madman's Ceremony
The Adventure of the Other Brother
and
Sherlock Holmes and A Quantity of Debt (A Novel)

Volume II – Records
(5 Short Stories and a Novel)
Sherlock Holmes – Tangled Skeins
The Mystery at Kerrett's Rood
The Curious Incident of the Goat-Cart Man
The Matter of Boz's Last Letter
The Tangled Skein at Birling Gap
The Gower Street Murder
and
Sherlock Holmes and The Eye of Heka (A Novel)

Volume III – Accounts
(22 Holmes Adventures)
The Adventure of the Pawnbroker's Daughter
The Problem of the Holy Oil
The Trusted Advisor
An Actor and a Rare One
The Unnerved Estate Agent
The Cat's Meat Lady of Cavendish Square
The Hammerford Will Business
The Farraway Street Lodger

(Continued on the next page . . . .)

November, 1888
Some Notes Upon the Matter of John Douglas
The Adventure of the Old Brownstone
The Doctor's Tale
The Treasures of the Gog Magog Hills
The Inner Temple Intruder
The Cambridge Codes
The Adventure of the Retired Beekeeper
An Actual Treasure
The Manipulative Messages
The Civil Engineer's Discovery
The Girl at the Northumberland Hotel (A Simple Solution)
The Austrian Certificates
The Adventure of the Home Office Baby

Volume V – Chronicles
(20 Holmes Adventures)
The Stolen Relic
The Helverton Inheritance
The Carroun Document
The Reappearance of Mr. James Phillimore
The Keadby Cross
The Rhayader Affair
The Cliddesden Questions
The Affair of the Mother's Return
The Painting in the Parlour
The Two Bullets
The Coombs Contrivance
The True Account of the Bushell Street Killing
The Polmayne Puzzles
The Curious Cardboard Boxes
The Bizarre Affair of the Octagon House
The Peculiar Persecution of Mr. Druitt
The Service for the American Colonel
The Rescue at Ypres
The Problem of the Hindhead Minister
The Edinburgh Bankers

As always, this is for Rebecca and Dan, with all my love

"It's all one case."
by David Marcum

It's all about playing The Game.

That's the bottom-line reason behind these stories. And what is The Game? For those who don't know, it's reading the Sherlock Holmes stories with the firm belief that he and Watson were real historical figures. That Dr. Watson wrote the stories, and Sir Arthur Conan Doyle was his Literary Agent. That Our Heroes actually lived in Baker Street (for a couple of decades, off and on, and not forever) and solved real cases for real people, even if names and places and dates were changed and obfuscated to protect the innocent, or maybe because Watson's handwriting was bad, or because of some hidden agenda that the Literary Agent needed to fulfill.

By acknowledging that Holmes and Watson were real, living, breathing, functioning people, then it's a given that were born, lived, and died. (No magic immortal detectives need apply!) And if they were born and lived and died, then these lives occurred across a fixed period. These men aren't Time Lords who can be picked up and dropped into other eras, or supernaturally gifted monster hunters in a world where such things exist, and they cannot be remade into a plethora of completely different people to fit whatever agenda some current reader needs to project upon them.

No, the stories in these books are about the same Sherlock Holmes and Dr. Watson that one finds in the original Canon – those pitifully few sixty stories that were published from 1887 to 1927.

I've enjoyed the notion that Mr. Sherlock Holmes was real from nearly the same time that I discovered him – as a boy of ten in 1975. Before I'd even read many of the Canonical adventures, I found two other books that reinforced this idea: William S. Baring-Gould's biography *Sherlock Holmes of Baker Street* (1962), with its chronology of the events in Holmes's long and amazing life (1854-1957), and also Nicholas Meyer's *The Seven-Per-Cent Solution* (1974), in which Holmes meets historical figures such as Sigmund Freud. How could one read those books, especially at that age, and not be convinced that Holmes was real?

In the decades that have passed since then, my interest in Mr. Holmes has only grown. While I read and collect a great many volumes about my other "book friends", as my son called them when he was small – and there are a great lot of them besides Holmes – I've always had a special interest in the consulting detective in Baker Street and his Boswell. Since obtaining my first Holmes book in 1975, I've managed to collect and read (and create a massively dense chronology for) literally thousands of traditional Canonical adventures. I've worn a deerstalker as my only hat, all year long and everywhere since age nineteen. I've been able to make three extensive Holmes Pilgrimages to England and Scotland (so far), wherein I pretty much visited only Holmes-related sites. So it was probably inevitable that, in 2008, I started writing Holmes adventures.

I'd always wanted to write, all the way back to when I was eight years old and intensely reading about The Three Investigators and The Hardy Boys. Not satisfied with just the official publications, I wanted more new stories too. I spent quite a few Saturdays of my young boyhood tapping away on my dad's typewriter to create new "books".

As I grew, I dabbled with writing little short pieces, mostly humorous, just intended to make family members laugh, because I loved to write, and it always came easily to me. By the late 1980's, I was a U.S. Federal Investigator employed by an obscure government agency, often sent away from home for long periods, conducting investigations that lasted anywhere from five weeks to three months. Once, when I was sent to Albuquerque for several months to conduct extensive field investigations, I impulsively stopped at a local Walmart and bought a hundred-dollar typewriter and a big pack of paper with some of my *per diem* money. (This was the early 1990's – a long time before personal computers or laptops.)

It was there that I sat down for my first real effort at being a writer – and before I departed I'd finished most of a 600-plus page Ludlumesque novel. (One can get a lot of writing done night after night in a bleak hotel room.) The book was coincidentally about a heroic federal investigator – not unlike myself – who stumbled into a vast Russian-led conspiracy in the American southeast where I'm from. I still have that book – *Civil Servants* – stored in my old federal investigator briefcase, pushed underneath my bed. Its plot is mired in the early 1990's when it was written, locked to the aftermath of the Cold War, but it isn't half bad, and it taught me the valuable lesson that other writers also know: *The secret to writing is to put your butt in the chair and do it.*

After that particular trip, I went back home, finished up what was left of my epic adventure novel, and then settled back into writing the occasional short piece for our private amusement – but it was inevitable that at some point I would write a Holmes adventure.

In the mid-1990's, the federal agency where I'd been employed was abruptly eliminated, a victim of the end of the Cold War and a move to reduce the size of government. (After all, the higher-up wise men thought, who needs security now? We won!) Over the next few years, I went back to school and obtained a second degree in Civil Engineering. Then, in 2008 at the start of the Great Recession, I was unexpectedly laid off from my engineering job. With time on my hands, and a desire to try my hand at Sherlockian pastichery, I began writing each morning after the daily job searching was finished.

I ended up with nine of Holmes pastiches, written over several weeks, and then . . . I did nothing with them. That's right. Simply satisfied that I'd written them and that they existed, I put them in a binder labeled *The Papers of Sherlock Holmes* and shelved them with the rest of my Holmes Collection, happy with my secret collector's item.

But eventually I began to wish for other Sherlockians to see them. I shared one with a Sherlockian friend here and another one there, and the response was very positive. Finally I became bolder and wanted more people to see them, asking myself: *Why not put them in a real book of my own?*

I communicated about it with a Sherlockian publisher from whom I'd bought books in the past. He immediately offered to publish *The Papers*, and after a great deal of back-and-forth, my first book eventually appeared. For those who have had that experience – Opening the newly delivered carton to see *your book!* – there is nothing like it. It's a satisfaction that cannot easily be described.

That was in 2011. Over the next couple of years, I became aware of MX Publishing. I saw that an acquaintance of mine who'd also had his first book published with the same original publisher as mine had switched to MX, and I reached out to him. He informed me that he was happy to have switched to MX. With that in mind, I sent an email to Steve Emecz, Sherlockian Publisher Extraordinaire – and that was truly life-changing and improving decision.

In 2013, Steve republished my first book, *The Papers of Sherlock Holmes*, and he made the whole experience so painless that I set about writing a Holmes novel, *Sherlock Holmes and A Quantity of Debt*. That same fall, I was making my long-planned first Holmes Pilgrimage to London, and Steve arranged for me to have a book-signing in The Sherlock Holmes Hotel in Baker Street, where I was staying (when not traveling about to Dartmoor, the Sussex Coast, Edinburgh, and other locations). I was able to meet Steve for the first time on that trip, and found him to be one of the nicest, most supportive, and most thoughtful people around – and that hasn't changed a bit.

Jump ahead a little bit: In early 2015, I woke up early from a dream in which I'd edited a Holmes anthology. Instead of rolling over and forgetting the idea, I arose and started thinking about authors whom I admired and that I might want to invite to write stories. I ran the idea by Steve, and he was willing to publish it, so I began sending invitations. I hoped that I might get a dozen stories (at best) for a modest paperback volume. Fearing a lack of response, I kept sending invitations to everyone that I could think of – and then, amazingly, people started signing up. New Sherlock Holmes stories started to arrive in my email in-box – which quickly becomes addictive. More and more authors heard about it – some that I didn't even know about yet – and before we knew it, the little idea had grown into a three-volume hardcover behemoth of over 60 new Holmes stories – *Parts I, II,* and *III* of *The MX Book of New Sherlock Holmes Stories*, the largest collection of its kind ever produced to that point.

Early on, Steve and I had decided that the royalties from the project would go to support the Stepping Stones School for special needs children, located at Undershaw, one of Sir Arthur Conan Doyle's former homes. The books were a smashing success and received a lot of attention, and I was able to go to London in the fall of 2015 for the release party – what turned out to be Holmes Pilgrimage No. 2. There I was able to meet a number of the contributing authors in person – and to my everlasting regret, I was so thrilled that I barely remembered to take any photos!

After I returned home, I began to receive more emails, now asking when the next book was planned – *Good grief! A next book?!?* – and also stating that many authors (both returning and new) wanted to contribute.

I'd had no plans to do any more books, thinking that the first three were lightning in a bottle that couldn't be recaptured . . . but then I realized that the heavy-lifting in terms of decision-making and set-up and formatting and process-building had already occurred, so Steve and I decided to keep going. (I think I said to him "Let's do one more . . . .")

Part IV came out in the spring of 2016 – and after that, more people kept sending stories for *the next books* and wanting to join the party. We came up with the plan to have yearly books. But we received so many stories that it grew to twice a year. We now have an un-themed spring collection – the yearly *Annual* – and also a fall collection with a specific theme, such as Christmas adventures, seemingly impossible crimes, Untold Cases, etc. As more and more stories kept rolling in, it became necessary for each season's particular set to grow to multiple simultaneously published volumes. That's how, in just a few short years, we're now up to *Parts XXVIII, XXIX,* and *XXX* (to be published in Fall 2021), and as I write this, I'm already receiving stories for the *Spring 2022 Annual, Part XXXI* (and *XXXII* and *XXXIII* too . . . ?)

4

So far the books have raised over $85,000 for the school, and it's my hope and expectation that they'll go over $100,000 within the next few months of writing this foreword.

As part of editing these books, I couldn't let them pass by without adding my own stories – editor's prerogative. Thus, that helped to motivate me to sit my butt in the chair and write more about Mr. Holmes. By way of these books, I've met some really incredible people, including the incomparable Belanger Brothers, Derrick and Brian. Derrick initially contributed short stories, while Brian – a truly gifted artist – became the MX cover artist after the original artist passed away.

At one point, the two Belangers wrote a series of Holmes books for children. Eventually they formed Belanger Books – another amazing Sherlockian publishing venture. Between MX and Belanger Books – both of which cooperate beautifully with one another – the Sherlockian publishing field is amazingly well covered, providing an opportunity for so many people to be Sherlockian pasticheurs when they would otherwise be excluded by those who happily and aggressively seek to squash that aspect of the Sherlockian experience.

In 2016, the Belangers asked me to assemble and edit a Holmes story collection for them. I did, and as it also consisted of traditional and Canonical adventures, and had many of the same authors as in the MX anthologies, I formatted it the same way. After that, I edited another one for them, and another, and those also grew to simultaneously published multiple volumes. This extra editing also served to motivate me to write more Holmes stories for each of those collections as well – because I didn't want those trains leaving without me being on them.

From there, I began to receive invitations to write still more stories for other editors' anthologies and magazines. Along the way I published a couple more of my own books – *Sherlock Holmes – Tangled Skeins* (2015) and *Sherlock Holmes and The Eye of Heka* (2021) – but most of my stories that I wrote over those years remained uncollected within the various anthologies and magazines in which they had originally appeared. All along, I stayed too busy with real life and family and my dream job (as a civil engineer working for my home town's public works department), along with writing more stories and editing various books, to take the time to properly collect them all into my own books.

But within the last few months, I looked up and saw that (as of right now) I've now written 86 Holmes pastiches, (along with 20 pastiches about Solar Pons, "The Sherlock Holmes of Baker Street" – but that's another story and another hero.) Thus, the idea of this collection was born.

These initial five books of *The Complete Papers* contain 77 of those 86 stories. The others are still in the pipeline to be published elsewhere. Right now (as of mid-September 2021), I also have five more Holmes stories promised to be written for various editors before the end of the year, and all of these, plus whatever I'm able to write in 2022 – with a plan to reach Pastiche No. 100 – will be published in Volume VI of this set in later 2022 . . . *Fingers crossed!*

Many people have sports figures or musicians or actors or (curiously) politicians as heroes. My heroes have always been my book friends and authors – all the way back to when I was eight or nine and wondering about why I couldn't track down satisfying biographical information concerning the brilliant and prolific and mysterious author Franklin W. Dixon. I've always admired writers for what they accomplish and create while spending great chunks of their lives self-imposed isolation – something which I now understand. And at least if I had to set aside all that time to put my butt in the chair, I've been very fortunate that all of these stories almost told themselves. I almost never outline or plan. Instead, when I write – when I find that it's time for another story – I simply open a blank Word document on the computer and then wait for Watson to begin whispering to me. It's scary, but I trust the process now, and when it works – and it always has so far – there's no feeling quite like it.

Through these stories, I've achieved two important personal goals: In my own small way, I've become a writer, and I've also added to *The Great Holmes Tapestry*, a phrase I coined several years ago to describe the massive collection of narratives about the true Holmes and Watson – novels, short stories, radio and television episodes, movies and scripts, comics and fan-fiction, and unpublished manuscripts – that tell the complete and entire course of their lives from beginning to end. The Canon serves as the supporting structure – the wire core of the rope, the heavy steel girders of the skyscraper – but the thousands of traditional post-Canonical pastiches provide essential depth and color, filling in all the spaces around The Canon, and adding important information about The Whole Lives of Our Heroes.

I've long described myself as a missionary for The Church of the Traditional Canonical Holmes, preaching that the bigger picture of both Canon and the traditional pastiches should be seen and supported. This means giving respect and value to additional Holmes adventures, and not just those original sixty because they were the ones that came across the first Literary Agent's desk.

Ross MacDonald – (Real Name: Kenneth Millar, another of my authorial heroes because of his incredible private eye, Lew Archer) – said

"It's all one case." In other words, a *Great Tapestry*. He meant that even though he'd written eighteen Archer novels and a number of short stories from the 1940's to the 1970's, they were never meant to stand alone. They were all part of one overall arching story – Lew Archer's story – spanning across multiple narratives.

It's the same with the Holmes adventures – *all* of them, Canon and traditional pastiche, mine and everyone else's. They fit together to tell the *entire* story of Sherlock Holmes, and with the stories in this collection, I'm incredibly proud to have added my own contribution.

* * * * *

"Of course, I could only stammer out my thanks."
– The unhappy John Hector McFarlane, "The Norwood Builder"

At some point during the foreword-writing for the various MX anthologies, I began to use the quote shown above from Mr. McFarlane in regard to Thank You's. It's fitting – I can only stammer out thanks, and never adequately express how grateful I am for all the help and encouragement I've received over the years in all aspects of my life – not just the writing and editing of Sherlock Holmes stories.

First and foremost, I am always overwhelmed at how incredibly fortunate I am to have my wife and son in my life. In all aspects, my wife – of 33 years as I write this – is the kindest and wisest and most beautiful person inside and out I know, and she has been there throughout with complete support and encouragement when we went through such things as some terrible jobs and the grind of my returning to school. We have pushed through together, and anything that I can ever accomplish I owe to her. And equally amazing is our son, so incredibly funny and smart, and truly an amazing person in every way. I enjoy every minute spent with him, and it only gets better. I love you both, and you are everything to me!

Then there are my parents and sister, who put up with me during those first couple of decades – I probably don't even realize how bad that was for them. My parents did everything to encourage me – music lessons leading to a piano scholarship in college, all the books that I could read, and generally anything to help me grow as a person, so that it never occurred to me that I couldn't do whatever I wanted. And my sister was my best friend then, patiently listening as I rambled about whatever interested me. Even then, she probably heard more about Sherlock Holmes than she'd ever bargained for!

There is a group that exchanges emails with me when we have the time – and time is a valuable commodity for all of us these days! As the

7

years have gone by, we've gotten busier and busier, and I don't get to write as often as I'd like, but I really enjoy catching up whenever we get the chance. These people are all wonderful writers, and I recommend them highly as both friends and authors: Mark Mower, Denis Smith, Tom Turley, Dan Victor, and Marcia Wilson.

Next, I wish to send several huge Thank You's to the following:

- *Steve Emecz* – When I first emailed Steve from out of the blue back in 2013 – *Only eight years? So much in eight years!* – I was interested in MX re-publishing my first book. Even then, as a guy who works to accumulate *all* traditional Sherlockian pastiches, I could see that MX (under Steve's leadership) was *the* fast-rising superstar of the Sherlockian publishing world.

    The re-publication of my first book with MX was an amazing life-changing event for me, leading to writing many more stories and then editing books, along with unexpected Holmes Pilgrimages to England. By way of that first email with Steve, I've had the chance to make some incredible Sherlockian friends and play in the Holmesian Sandbox in ways that I'd never before dreamed possible.

    Through all of it, Steve has been one of the most positive and supportive people that I've ever known. He works far more than a full-time week at his day job, and he still finds time to take care of all aspects of MX Publishing, with the help of his wife Sharon Emecz, and cousin, Timi Emecz. (That's right – MX is just the three of them who get all of this done!)

    Many who just buy books and have a vague idea of how the publishing industry works now might not realize that MX, a non-profit which supports several important charities, consists of simply these three people. Between them, they take care of running the entire business, including the production, marketing, and shipping – all in their precious spare time, in and around their real lives.

    With incredible hard work, they have made MX into a world-wide Sherlockian publishing phenomenon, providing opportunities for authors who would never have them otherwise. There are some like me who return more than once to Watson's Tin Dispatch Box, and there are others who only find one or two stories there – but they get the chance to publish their books, and then they can point with pride at this accomplishment, and how they too have added to The Great Holmes Tapestry.

From the beginning, Steve has let me explore various Sherlockian projects and open up my own personal possibilities in ways that otherwise would have never happened. Thank you, Steve, for every opportunity!

- *Derrick Belanger* and *Brian Belanger* – I first "met" Derrick Belanger when he graciously reviewed one of my early books, and we quickly became friends. Then he interviewed me several times for his online blog, and when I had the idea for the first MX Holmes anthology in 2015, he quickly joined the party and contributed a fine pastiche. From there he's written a number of others, and then he formed Belanger Books with his brother, Brian. It's turned into a Sherlockian powerhouse, working in tandem with MX Publishing, supporting each other to produce more and more wonderful Holmes adventures. I've very grateful to have had this additional opportunity to further contribute to The Great Holmes Tapestry by editing and writing stories for their different anthologies. Derrick continues to write, but he also stays quite busy as a noted aware-winning teacher, husband, and father, as well as running Belanger Books with Brian.

Over the last few years, my amazement at Brian Belanger's ever-increasing talent has only grown. I initially became acquainted with him when he took over the duties of creating the covers for MX Books following the untimely death of their previous graphic artist. I found Brian to be a great collaborator, very easy-going and stress-free in his approach and willingness to work with authors, and wonderfully creative too. His skills became most apparent to me when he created the cover for my 2017 book, *The Papers of Solar Pons*, which was one of the most striking covers that I've ever seen. Later, when the Belangers and I began reissuing the original Pons books in new editions, and then new Pons anthologies, Brian's similarly themed covers continued to astound me. He truly deserves an award for these.

9

In the meantime, he has become busier and busier, continuing to provide covers for MX Books, and now for Belanger Books as well, along with editing and occasionally writing.

I finally met both Brian and Derrick in person in early (pre-pandemic) 2020 at the annual Sherlock Holmes Birthday Celebration in New York City, and they're just as great in person as they were by way of email. I immediately felt like I'd known them both forever. I cannot express to either one of you just how grateful I am.

- *Roger Johnson* – I had known of Roger for quite a while, having seen his name connected with the "District Messenger" newsletter of *The Sherlock Holmes Society of London Journal.* I could tell, even then, that he represented the finest kind of Sherlockian. When I wrote my first Holmes book, I sent him a copy – out of the blue, as he had no idea who I was – as a thank you, and with the timid and dim spark of a hope that he would review it, because having him do so would mean (to me) that what I had written was legitimized. He did write a wonderful review, and we began to correspond. When I was able to get to England for my first Holmes Pilgrimage in 2013, I made arrangements to meet with Roger and his wonderful wife, Jean Upton, in person, and I discovered that what I'd already known by email was true: They are both the very best people!

Later, in 2015 on Holmes Pilgrimage No. 2, they invited me to stay with them for several days in their home, and that was one of the best parts of all the trips. They gave me tours, they showed me their incredible collection, they let me see life in a real British household and not just from a hotel room, and we had some wonderful conversations along the way. I was able to see them again in 2016, Holmes Pilgrimage No. 3, when we attended the Grand Opening of the Stepping Stones School at Undershaw.

I'm more grateful than I can say that I know Roger. His Sherlockian knowledge is exceptional, as is the work that he does to further the cause of The Master. But even more than that, both Roger and his wonderful wife, Jean, are simply the finest and best, and I'm very lucky to know both of them – even though I don't get to see them nearly as often as I'd like, and especially in these crazy days! In so many ways, Roger, I can't thank you enough, and I can't imagine these books without you.

- *Nicholas Meyer* – I started reading Nick Meyer's Holmes books before I'd even read all of The Canon, and for that I'm eternally grateful. It was through his first two books, *The Seven-Per-Cent Solution* and *The West End Horror* (the latter of which is still one of my favorite pastiches to this very day) that I firmly understood that The Canon wasn't the be-all end-all of Sherlockian story-telling. I obtained Nick's first book as part of a free book give-away at school, and I found the second not long after when my mother took my sister and me to buy school clothes and I spotted it in the mall bookstore. (I sat cross-legged along an out-of-the-way wall in a Sears while my mother and sister shopped and started reading *The West End Horror* straight out of the bag.)

    After those first two books, Nick went on to have a very successful career in film. (More about that in a minute.) But he has continued to dip in an out of Sherlockian pastichery with *The Canary Trainer* (1993), *The Adventure of the Peculiar Protocols* (2019), and *The Return of the Pharaoh* (2021). He is a Sherlockian legend, and it's an indisputable fact that the publication in 1974 of *The Seven-Per-Cent Solution* – a pastiche, mind you! – was the beginning of the Sherlockian Golden Age when has grown and grown, and has never stopped, all the way to today.

    If it was just that, Sherlockians – and especially pasticheurs – would owe him an unpayable debt. But then there's *Star Trek*, which he also saved. As mentioned above, I have lots of interests besides Mr. Holmes, although he does demand more and more attention as my years pass. But I've been a Trekkie (or Trekker, or whatever the correct term is) since I was a wee lad in the late 1960's, when my babysitter happened to watch one of the original prime-time episodes. After that, I grew up seeing the original series in re-reruns, and then I was among those who saw the first Star Trek film in 1979 (and truthfully felt mightily disappointed. I do like it better now.) But it was Nick Meyer's *Star Trek:*

The Wrath of Khan (1982) which electrified the Trek Universe, jump-starting it into motion in a way that – like the Holmes Golden Age – has only grown. And how it's grown! Hundreds and hundreds of Star Trek novels and comic books, multiple films and television shows, with more in planning and production all the time, and fan interest around the world at an all-time high. As a nearly life-long Star Trek fan, who loves it nearly as much as The World of Sherlock Holmes, I credit the origin of this original escalation entirely to Nick Meyer.

I generally despise social media, but it's a very useful way for Sherlockians to connect. Imagine my thrill when I began to see occasional online posts from Nick Meyer – and when I dared to respond, sometimes he would respond back! I've learned that if you don't ask, you'll never know, so I connected with him a bit more often, and eventually I boldly asked him to write a foreword to one of the MX anthologies that I edit, and he most-generously agreed. After that, we've stayed in touch off-and-on, and that still never ceases to amaze me.

I met him in person at the 2011 *From Gillette to Brett* conference in Bloominton, Indiana, where he was the featured guest. I took my Holmes book, asked him to autograph them, and asked – like everyone does – when he'd write his next Holmes book. He certainly doesn't remember that, but he was the main reason I chose to attend that event.

One of my greatest regrets is that, while attending the 2020 Sherlock Holmes Birthday Celebration in New York, I was almost able to meet him in person again – and this time he'd know who I was – but I didn't get to speak with him, and it was my own fault. We had emailed ahead of time, planning to meet, and that day I entered the famed dealer's room and saw him seated at a table near the door, surrounded by many fans. I wandered away, intending to return in a just a very few minutes and dive into the crowd, hoping that it might have thinned a bit. But when I got back over there, he'd already left! Hopefully I'll get another chance, sooner rather than later, where I can thank him in person for so many things . . .

. . . including generously writing a foreword for these volumes. When I was considering who could write a foreword, I couldn't think of anyone more fitting. Through Nicholas Meyer I found pastiches, which have been so important to me over the years. Nick, thanks from the bottom of my heart for taking the time to be part of these books!

And finally, last but certainly *not* least, thanks to **Sir Arthur Conan Doyle**: Author, doctor, adventurer, and the Founder of the Sherlockian Feast. Honored, and present in spirit.

As I always note when putting together an anthology of Holmes stories, the effort has been a labor of love. This time the labor and love have been mine. These adventures are more tiny threads woven into the ongoing *Great Holmes Tapestry*, continuing to grow and grow, for there can *never* be enough stories about the man whom Watson described as *"the best and wisest . . . whom I have ever known."*

David Marcum
September 8th, 2021
A most important day,
for all kinds of reasons

Questions, comments, or story submissions
may be addressed to David Marcum at

thepapersofsherlockholmes@gmail.com

A Note on the
Modern Publishing Paradigm

For the longest time, publishing something was mostly impossible for most people. The Great Publishing Houses – which sounds like something from *Dune* – are giant machines, with carefully calculated formulas to know just how many books they need to sell to make a profit. It's no different than selling cereal: Many of the boxes of cereal on grocery store shelves won't be sold, and they were never meant to be sold, and the manufacturers are okay with that, because they've calculated the amount that they do need to actually sell in order to stay profitable while figuring in just how much can be discarded.

It used to be the same with books. Publishers would create a print run of a certain number of copies, sending out so many of them to bookstores across the country. Some would be sold – enough, hopefully, to cover costs – while many copies would just sit there, unsold, forever. Then, after a certain amount of time, they would be removed – either destroyed, or "remaindered", to be sold at rock-bottom prices in bargain bins.

It's an investment by the publishers to go to the trouble and expense to create all of those physical books, hoping to make their money back on enough of them to justify the waste of the others. That's why they're so restrictive about what they publish: They must meet the razor-thin edge of profit. But that makes the path to being published a very narrow needle's eye.

Several years ago, the paradigm began to shift. Online sales began to disrupt the physical bookstore model. And as people ordered online, some publishers figured out that they didn't have to have back rooms and warehouses jammed full of physical books sitting around waiting for a physical customer to enter a store or a dealer's room, examine it, and possibly buy it. Instead, when an online order arrived, the manufacturing of the book could commence right then, only as needed, and not months or years earlier.

This print-on-demand idea had been around for a while. (When I was going back to school for my second degree in civil engineering, the campus print shop did the same thing for certain locally produced text-books, printing them as they were purchased on fancy copying machines.) Publishers and authors began to take advantage of technological advances to produce their own books – straight from author to reader, happily eliminating the giant publishing middlemen.

Steve Emecz of MX Publishing brilliantly took advantage of this, building his business and allowing authors who would have never had a chance otherwise – like me – to create and connect.

But there are certain legitimate complaints.

In the olden days, the giant publishers slow-walked books through the process, so that it sometimes took literally years for a book to actually be published. Authors could actually die before ever seeing their work excreted at the far end of the giant publisher's process. The print-on-demand process, by comparison, is nearly immediate. As part of the large publishers' slow walk, there were battalions of editors who went through books forwards, backwards, and upside down. With the new technology, where a file can be loaded with the book manufacturer with very little effort and time spent, there is clearly less editing . . . and mistakes slip through.

Some readers continue to expect flawless and perfect works, as if legions of editors were behind the curtain as in days of old, still involved in the process. For this type of reader/consumer, the new format of publishing will always be pain they just can't ease. That's why, with this set of my stories, I want to apologize up front to those who will find typos – *because in spite of every effort, there will be some typos.*

In my own case, I love to write and edit, and I spend a sizeable amount of time doing both, but I also have a very busy and rich life doing other things. I spend time with my family, and I work more-than-full time as a civil engineer, fitting in these Sherlockian writing and editing projects during lunch hours, evenings, and weekends. It's a high wire act with no safety net. I'm the writer and sole editor of the stories in this collection. My wife, with a Bachelor's Degree in Journalism and two Master's Degrees in English Literature and Library Science, and with a first job as a copy editor, used to go through my stories and catch what I missed – because you never *ever* see your own mistakes – but she works way more than full time at her own job, and she just doesn't have any extra time to spare for playing uncredited editor on these projects. So they're all on me.

It's the same with the anthologies that I edit – any mistake that slips through in the end is my fault, because there are no other editors. When assembling a Holmes anthology, I receive the stories, format them to the "house style", print them on 8½ x 11-inch paper, edit and revise, go back and forth with emails to the author – sometimes a lot of emails – and then plug them into a giant Word document for more editing and revision. But from the time I get the story until I send the final file to the publisher, there isn't anyone else to edit, and no time to work one into the process. It's the new publishing paradigm.

As a print-on-demand publisher, MX does not have squadrons of editors. The business consists of three part-time people who also have busy lives elsewhere – so the editing effort largely falls on the contributors. Some readers and consumers out there in the world absolutely despise this – apparently forgetting about all those self-produced Holmes stories and volumes from decades ago with awkward self-published formatting and loads of errors that are now prized as collector's items.

These critics should recall that every one of these new volumes by various authors – even those that have typographic and formatting errors – are the very best efforts that can be produced by very sincere people who don't have professional full-time editors to help, and who would never ever have had the opportunity to publish otherwise, and because of these authors, there is thankfully more Sherlockian content in the world.

I'm personally mortified when errors slip through – ironically, there will probably be errors in this essay – and I apologize now, but without a regiment of editors looking over my shoulder, this is as good as it gets. Real life is more important than writing and editing, and only so much time can be spent preparing these books before they are released into the wild. I hope that you can look past any errors, small or huge, and simply enjoy these stories, and appreciate the effort involved, and the sincere desire to add to The Great Holmes Tapestry.

And in spite of any errors here, there are more Sherlock Holmes stories than there were before, and that's a good thing.

David Marcum

Watson's Descendants
by Nicholas Meyer

It is generally felt that the short story was Sherlock Holmes's best venue. The novellas, by contrast, are judged to be . . . lesser. Even the fabled *The Hound of the Baskervilles* suffers from the detective's absence for many pages. Though *A Study in Scarlet*, *The Sign of the Four*, and *The Valley of Fear* remain deliciously absorbing, it is in the short stories that Holmes and Watson truly flourish.

As Michael Chabon has observed, all fiction is fan fiction. Almost from the beginning, Sherlock Holmes has prompted imitators of his creator's creation. Arthur Conan Doyle wrote sixty Holmes cases in all – fifty-six short stories and four novellas. When they ended, boys and girls, men and women of all ages mourned Watson's silence and the series' cessation. But it wasn't long before others took up – or attempted to take up – Sir Arthur's pen.

Writing a full-length Holmes novel has always posed a challenge, even for Doyle himself, to say nothing of generations of later writers and filmmakers. Short stories, on the other hand, pose problems of their own. A good short story must compress action and character. It must – obviously – be short. The gift of writing compelling short fiction remains in a class by itself. Poe, Doyle of course, Twain, Saki, and Hawthorne are among the masters of the form from the Victorian and Edwardian eras, but over the years, the short story has produced many masters.

I alas am not among them. Even as a kid in art class, my paintings were so huge the murals I attempted had to be unfurled in the hall, not the studio. And so it comes as no surprise that writing a short Holmes story does not come easily to me. In fact, it does not come at all.

I retain nothing but admiration for those writers who *can* create short fiction, and a special respect for those who can bring off simulacra of Doyle's charming and distinctive Holmes tales. There many practitioners, including some whose efforts, unfortunately, resemble nothing so much as taxidermy. But among the best I must number David Marcum, who, by this point has written more Holmes stories than Doyle himself. Characterized by unflagging imagination and ceaseless ingenuity, along with felicitous prose, these tales continue to provide what we all crave: More Sherlock.

All Sherlock Holmes stories, (except Doyle's), are of course forgeries. And it's the rare forger who can resist signing his own work. See if you can spot David Marcum's fine Italian hand.

Enjoy.

Nicholas Meyer
Los Angeles, 2021

Sherlock Holmes (1854-1957) was born in Yorkshire, England, on 6 January, 1854. In the mid-1870's, he moved to 24 Montague Street, London, where he established himself as the world's first Consulting Detective. After meeting Dr. John H. Watson in early 1881, he and Watson moved to rooms at 221b Baker Street, where his reputation as the world's greatest detective grew for several decades. He was presumed to have died battling noted criminal Professor James Moriarty on 4 May, 1891, but he returned to London on 5 April, 1894, resuming his consulting practice in Baker Street. Retiring to the Sussex coast near Beachy Head in October 1903, he continued to be associated in various private and government investigations while giving the impression of being a reclusive apiarist. He was very involved in the events encompassing World War I, and to a lesser degree those of World War II. He passed away peacefully upon the cliffs above his Sussex home on his 103rd birthday, 6 January, 1957.

Dr. John Hamish Watson (1852-1929) was born in Stranraer, Scotland on 7 August, 1852. In 1878, he took his Doctor of Medicine Degree from the University of London, and later joined the army as a surgeon. Wounded at the Battle of Maiwand in Afghanistan (27 July, 1880), he returned to London late that same year. On New Year's Day, 1881, he was introduced to Sherlock Holmes in the chemical laboratory at Barts. Agreeing to share rooms with Holmes in Baker Street, Watson became invaluable to Holmes's consulting detective practice. Watson was married and widowed three times, and from the late 1880's onward, in addition to his participation in Holmes's investigations and his medical practice, he chronicled Holmes's adventures, with the assistance of his literary agent, Sir Arthur Conan Doyle, in a series of popular narratives, most of which were first published in *The Strand* magazine. Watson's later years were spent preparing a vast number of his notes of Holmes's cases for future publication. Following a final important investigation with Holmes, Watson contracted pneumonia and passed away on 24 July, 1929.

Photos of Sherlock Holmes and Dr. John H. Watson courtesy of Roger Johnson

The
Collected Papers
of
Sherlock
Holmes
Volume IV - Narratives
(19 Holmes Adventures)

The London Wheel

Sherlock Holmes glanced up from the papers spread before him when Lestrade vented a disgusted sigh. From my position at the side of the inspector's desk, unable to easily examine the documents that were the reason for our visit, I watched as our friend's irritation grew.

Lestrade stepped to the doorway, calling out to someone unseen for tea. Then, closing the door, he returned to the window, looking toward the Thames. He sighed again.

Holmes, previously lost in a comparison of two yellowed sheets covered in spidery handwriting, as well as the various confiscated ledgers and letters associated with that matter later referred to in the press as "The Foster Obligation", smiled. "Is something vexing you, Lestrade?"

Lestrade did not turn, answering, "It's that bloody wheel, Mr. Holmes. You've seen it, over on the other shore? Something like that has no business cluttering up the landscape."

Although I knew of what he spoke, I rose and joined him, Holmes doing the same on the other side. From that high window in the south wall of New Scotland Yard, we could see the Embankment and the pier down below us, and then the Thames, currently at high tide. A number of craft plied the waterway, and all would have seemed very normal indeed, if not for the object that had aroused Lestrade's ire.

On the opposite side of the river, not far from where the bank was touched by Westminster Bridge, was a cleared space teeming with people. I knew from newspaper reports that the area was currently occupied by some sort of circus, making use of a space that had been left vacant by a fire in the past year or so. After the debris was cleared, and with no new construction yet planned, the owners of the property had allowed the circus to set up there temporarily.

There was nothing unusual in this. What was it, then, that could affect Lestrade so keenly? Could it truly be the mere presence, in the middle of the surging throng, of a Ferris Wheel?

"It seems harmless enough to me, Lestrade," I said. "What offends you so by its presence?"

"It doesn't fit," he replied. "Within sight of Parliament, for heaven's sake. It just isn't right."

"Surely," said Holmes, "it is far more pleasant, for instance, to see something devoted to recreation and pleasure than those buildings just to the south of it. They, too, are within view from our government buildings, including this one, and they stand as a silent accusation and a reminder of a great deal of unfortunate poverty, separated by only a waterway and a bridge from the wealth that rules them."

"I see your point, Mr. Holmes. Yet, I still cannot help but resent that my view is spoiled by that monstrosity."

I suspected that it was more than that.

Holmes smiled. "Seeing as I've finished with my examination of Mr. Foster's papers, a singularly unrewarding effort I might add, I feel that a walk in this rare sunshine could be quite refreshing. What say you, Lestrade, to joining us as we stroll over and take a better look at this wheel? I can't recall having been able to view one up close before."

Lestrade clearly had no interest in seeing the thing any closer than he already could from his current vantage point, but I could tell that he understood Holmes's friendly offer. He canceled the order for tea, and within moments we had made our way through the busy hallways of the Yard, down the steps, and out through the gate. Big Ben in the clock tower was just chiming two, but the early spring sun was already quite past its highest point in the sky.

Along the way, Holmes entertained us with a surprising amount of knowledge regarding the object of our expedition. The original wheel, designed and constructed by Ferris, had been erected just seven years earlier for the 1893 Chicago World's Fair. Holmes intimated that he had some personal experience with that event, which I did not doubt, since I knew that segments of his roaming during that period when he was believed to be dead had incorporated stops in the United States, including Chicago.

We were in the center of Westminster Bridge when Holmes gestured vaguely to the west, indicating that another similar structure to Ferris's creation, The Great Wheel, had been in operation at Earls Court since 1895, when it first graced the Empire of India Exhibition. Both Lestrade and I had seen it in passing, but only from a distance. "Unlike this eyesore, I don't have to look at that one in Kensington every day," grumbled the inspector.

Upon reaching the circus grounds, we found that the crowds were surprisingly thick for the middle of the week. For the most part, they consisted of men and women of the working class, either as couples or families with small children. The smells brought back memories of childhood from similar circuses where I walked hand-in-hand with my father, unable to see a great deal for all of the adults around me in every direction. The noise was almost a force unto itself. There was a singular one-man band who seemed to rely most heavily upon a cymbal affixed to his bass drum. An unseen calliope was wheezing from nearby within a tattered tent. Barkers yelled to attract our attention, and as we passed each one, Holmes would scan him quickly before looking to the next, no doubt reading each man's entire life story in a glance.

I was loudly trying to tell Lestrade about my boyhood dream of running away with a circus that had visited near my childhood home in Scotland, after finding myself infatuated with a lady bareback rider, when Holmes came to a stop. Without my realizing it, he had led us unerringly through the throng and to the great metal wheel, turning slowly above us.

There were shrieks of enjoyment as the passengers, particularly the women clinging to the arms of their men, would rotate down the front side of the wheel, before rising again along the back with each revolution. I was shielding my eyes to look up at the carriages affixed to thing, noting that each held several passengers, when my attention was pulled back down to ground level. Before me were two men, arguing. They stood near a third smaller fellow in the area where passengers would entrain or depart from the wheel. This man seemed to be cringing away from the other two, whose disagreement was escalating. The gentleman on the left, small and thin-shouldered, raised his stick in anger, causing the other man, taller and with a long face, to take a step back.

"I won't stand for it, Green!" cried the smaller man with the stick, in an unmistakable American accent. "I've suspected that you've been cheating me somehow, and the lease for this Wheel which you have foisted upon us is simply the last straw!"

Sensing impending violence, Lestrade pushed forward and took the arm of the smaller man. "Here, now!" he cried. "We'll have none of that."

The smaller man tried to shake him off. "Let me be! What right have you – ?"

"I have every right. Inspector Lestrade! Police! Now calm down, and let's see if this can't be discussed like gentlemen."

The man gave one more shake of his arm, firmly in Lestrade's grip, and then seemed to release his anger as if turning loose of a rope. He relaxed into a defeated slump, and Lestrade freed him. "Here," said the inspector, "what's your name?"

"Bouchard," said the American, sullenly. "William White Bouchard."

"Well, Mr. Bouchard, I don't know what your disagreement is with Mr. Green, here, but violence is no way to settle it."

"You're a policeman, you say?" countered Bouchard. He gestured toward Green. "Then arrest this man. He has defrauded me, and I will not stand for it!"

"Careful, my friend," drawled Green, his eyes half-shut. "That's slander, you know. That statement, in front of witnesses, might be enough for me to take everything you have."

Holmes smiled and said, "I don't think it would be as cut-and-dried as all that."

Green glanced toward Holmes, and then seemed to truly see him for the first time. A look of recognition widened his eyes.

"Sherlock Holmes, isn't it?" he said. He stepped forward suddenly. "It is! You're just the man to settle this! I want to hire you!"

Holmes laughed. "For what, Mr. Green? I'm a consulting detective, not a solicitor or bookkeeper. I'm afraid a tedious case of possible fraud, or a defense against such a charge, is of little interest to me." His eyes glanced over the two men, and then toward the smaller fellow lurking behind them.

Bouchard also took a step closer, an interested expression on his face. "It's more than that, Mr. Holmes. I didn't mean what I said about Green, here. What you observed was the result of a great deal of stress creating friction between two old friends."

"He's right," added Green. "Our circus may be small, but we've always been very successful. That is, until recently. There have been a series of accidents – "

"It's more than that," interjected Bouchard. "There have been deliberate attempts to drive us out of business!"

I could tell that Holmes was becoming intrigued. "What sort of attempts?"

"We had a fire a few weeks ago," said Green, "not long after we set up here along the Thames. It destroyed a tent and also one of the supply wagons. Since then, equipment used in performances has been found broken in ways that could have only been intentional. Just last week, one of the animals in our menagerie, Walter the Lion, was poisoned to death in a most horrible and painful way. None of these things are enough in themselves to drive us out of business, but circus folk are a superstitious lot, and the word has spread quickly through our little family that we might be unlucky."

The inspector barked a short laugh, causing Holmes to state, "That is a very real concern among circus people, Lestrade. One whiff that there is something wrong with the enterprise, and the performers will flee to a different operation that is considered more safe and acceptable."

"Exactly, Mr. Holmes," said Bouchard. "We've been quite successful until now, having recently completed a very profitable tour throughout northern England. It was only after we arrived here, at this site, that our luck seemed to change. It's amazing how quickly the feelings amongst the performers can shift from a sense of safety and stability to one of unease. We were once like a family, but now my partner and I are being looked upon as enemies."

32

"If you are both concerned that the incidents are part of an attempt to drive you out of business, then what was the conversation that we interrupted, in which you, Mr. Bouchard, were accusing Mr. Green of cheating you? I believe that you mentioned that the lease for the Wheel was 'the last straw'?"

Bouchard looked uncomfortable, but replied, "I was angry, and take back what I said about being cheated. But the fact is that the lease for this poor man's Ferris Wheel was negotiated without my knowledge. Following our last stop in Easingwold, I traveled down to Colchester for a few days to visit with a friend who has been ill. During that time, the circus was packed up and moved here, as planned. We've negotiated an open-ended arrangement with the owners of this property, who had no objections to our setting up here, as it has been vacant land since a fire destroyed several buildings last year, or so I understand.

"While I was away, Mr. Green was approached by the gentleman who built this wheel that you see behind us, offering to lease it at an exorbitant rate – "

"It is not exorbitant!" interrupted Green, showing more emotion than I had seen from him since our arrival. "Our business has doubled – even tripled or quadrupled! – since we installed the London Wheel. Word of mouth alone, as people share the fact that one can obtain a new and different view of London, a bird's-eye view as it were, will only continue to increase our visitors."

I had my doubts that the Wheel, considerably smaller than the Great Wheel at Earls Court, would provide any sort of bird's eye view of the capital, or even of nearby Westminster across the river. Green continued, "If we hadn't begun to have other difficulties, you would never have complained about the lease."

"Not true!" countered Bouchard. "I do not believe that we should be turning away from what has made our circus so successful over the years, in favor of mechanical contraptions that cause a mere momentary sensation, only to quickly leave the patron jaded and expecting some other machine to provide and even bigger and better thrill. There is nothing wrong with traditional circus acts, thrilling feats of skill and danger, and the possibility of something new and unexpected in each and every performance!"

I glanced at Holmes, watching the argument with some amusement. "This wheel is the future!" stated Green, his voice rising, taking a step toward his partner.

"Such a device is beneath us," countered Bouchard. "We've had great success for years with a traditional circus, featuring traditional performers. But you, my friend, had your head turned by talk of doubling our business.

33

You made the arrangements to lease Charters' Wheel without my knowledge or approval, because you knew I would never give it otherwise."

"Charters?" prodded Holmes.

"Lester Charters," said Green. "He is the man from whom we leased the Wheel. He built it."

"As partners, Mr. Bouchard, how was Mr. Green able to make such a deal without your approval?"

"Our arrangement," said Green, somewhat righteously, with a dark glance toward Bouchard, "is one of trust, allowing us to make decisions without the other's approval. Granted, this has usually been in the form of hiring or firing performers as needed. When one or the other of us isn't available, we don't have to wait on the other to take care of something urgent. In this case, I was able to recognize the opportunity and seize it during the time when my friend was away."

"You knew I wouldn't approve!" Bouchard cried. "It cheapens our enterprise to feature such an attraction. Soon, people will only attend circuses to take a turn on machines like this. Traditional performers will be ignored or forgotten. Why bother to have performers at all? We can simply buy a piece of property and erect row upon row of risky automata, each bigger and more dangerous than the last."

"Would that be such a bad thing?" Green asked grimly.

"What do you know about it?" responded Bouchard. "Your strong suit has never been the business side of things. You didn't even understand the nature of the lease that you signed. I've just returned from a meeting with our solicitor, who explained an interesting clause in the lease agreement that *you* seem to have missed. And I also found that Charters is the subject of a lawsuit by the Ferris people, as he built this wheel using their design, but without any arrangement or accommodation with them – "

Before he could continue, a rough voice behind us interrupted. "Oi!" It came from a fellow at the front of the line of people waiting to board the wheel. "That fella there doesn't look well at all."

The man who spoke was rough-looking, a laborer sporting a billycock pushed back on his brow. Beside him, clutching his arm, was a small woman, clearly his wife. Both of them were looking past us, toward the wheel, and even as I started to turn from them to observe what they had seen, the wife buried her head in her husband's sleeve with a slight cry.

The small man who had been standing near Green and Bouchard when we first approached had since moved back toward the wheel. He had his hand on a lever, which apparently controlled the machinery driving the great structure. The wheel had stopped so that one of the cars was level with a small ramp, allowing passengers to enter or depart from the carriage seats. Sitting alone in the lowermost of these was a heavy-set man, slumped to one side with his eyes wide and staring.

Pushing past Lestrade, I moved up the ramp. There was a buckled leather strap fastened across the man's ample waist, no doubt a safety precaution, and I spent a useless few seconds trying to open it before the man at the controls stepped up, his nimble fingers quickly tossing it to one side. I glanced at him, and saw that he was pale with shock. Afterwards, he stepped away, stumbling over his own feet. My quick examination of the man in the carriage, his face horribly contorted, confirmed what I had suspected, and I turned back to my companions.

"This man is dead."

"Impossible!" cried Green, stepping forward. "He was perfectly fine when he waved to me, not five minutes ago!"

"You know him then?" asked Lestrade. "Who is he?"

"That is Lester Charters," said Bouchard. "He is the man of whom we have been speaking. It was from him that we leased the Wheel."

"I stopped it," said the small man who controlled it, "to let him off. I thought he might want to join in the discussion. But then I saw that he was ... was ...."

"Doctor," said Lestrade, glancing back my way, "can you tell how he died?"

"There are no obvious wounds. However, from the red coloring of the skin, the slight foam about the mouth, and the faint smell on his lips, I would venture that there is a possibility, in fact almost a certainty, that this man has been poisoned."

Holmes raised an eyebrow and moved toward the body, while Lestrade stepped to one side and blew his whistle. Within a moment, a constable had joined him. After receiving a series of terse whispered instructions from the inspector, the constable left us in a hurry.

Above us, men and women in the other carriages were craning their heads, attempting to see what was happening below. The ones immediately above us had apparently heard my diagnosis, for they were passing the news up from car to neighboring car, yelling the words "murder" and "poison" several times. Meanwhile, the crowd on the ground waiting to board the Wheel was pressing forward, while Lestrade attempted to keep them at bay. "Doctor," he cried. "A bit of assistance, if you don't mind!"

As Holmes continued his examination, I left him and joined Lestrade, holding my arms wide. As a defense, we would have been quickly overrun, but Lestrade's authority temporarily asserted itself, and the crowd moved back. Between us and the Wheel, Bouchard and Green stood closely and whispered, casting glances toward the dead man and the crowd in equal measure.

The masses has continued to accumulate as more and more people noticed something unusual was afoot, and wandered that way out of simple curiosity. Lestrade and I were starting to be pressed once again when a clatter of constables' boots was heard approaching us. Within a moment, the crowd was under control, and soon after was being dispersed.

Lestrade and I rejoined Holmes, while the calls and cries of those above us became more strident. After Holmes stated that there was nothing more to be learned from the carriage itself, we quickly decided to remove the body, thus allowing the other passengers to be released from their temporary bondage.

A pair of constables assisted us in carrying Charters into a nearby tent, while several others corralled the Wheel's passengers as they disembarked until they could be identified and questioned.

Inside the tent, Holmes called us to the table where the body lay, illuminated by a lantern hanging above it. Turning, he opened his hand to reveal a pair of wrapped candies, along with a great number of similar wrapping papers, now empty.

"These were in Charters' waistcoat pocket," he said. "Watson, what do you think?"

I took one of the pieces and looked at the paper, which indicated it was a well-known brand of chocolate-covered almonds. I raised it to my nose. The smell of bitter almonds was very faint, and not what one would expect from a simple candy.

"Cyanide," I said. "No doubt."

The empty wrappers also held the same smell. While Lestrade confirmed the fact for himself, Green and Bouchard pressed closer. "That is your favorite candy," said Bouchard to Green. He looked at Holmes. "He eats them constantly."

Green glanced at the small American with a sour grimace. "Thank you for that, my friend." Turning toward Lestrade, he stated, "That is not an unpopular type of candy, Inspector. Surely you don't believe that I had anything to do with this?"

Lestrade, who had been watching Holmes examine the body, said, "Early days yet, Mr. Green. As you can see, we're only beginning to gather our facts."

Holmes sniffed around the dead man's mouth, and then pulled back the fellow's lips. Nodding me over, I could see traces of chocolate still around the man's gums and in the crevices of his teeth. "He must have eaten them very quickly."

36

Our examination was interrupted by a commotion at the entrance to the tent. A burly constable pushed his way in, pulling the small man who had been operating the Wheel. "After he let everyone off, I caught this fellow trying to slip away," he said.

"Here now! What's your name?" demanded Lestrade, when the slight man was placed before him.

"Edward Meeser," he replied in uncertain tones, as if he were not sure of the fact.

"One of your employees, gentlemen?"

"Not exactly," replied Bouchard. "We acquired him, so to speak, when we leased the Wheel. He is an employee of Charters'."

"Indeed," said Holmes, joining us after completing his inspection of the dead man. "And what are your duties, Mr. Meeser?"

"Well, as you saw, I run the Wheel. I help load and unload the passengers, and keep track of how long each group has been on it, so as to make sure everyone gets a fair ride. There's a slow rotation where each car is loaded, and then I run it a spell before stopping it a few minutes later, rotating it slowly again to unload. I make certain there isn't any horsing around when the Wheel is in motion. And I check the machinery and connections every day as well."

"You do not look so well," said Holmes. "Perhaps it is the shock of encountering Mr. Charters' body?"

Meeser nodded earnestly. "That's the truth, sir. I never expected to see something like that come around."

"I understand that Mr. Charters built the Wheel. Can you tell me where his workshop is located?"

"Down Stepney way. In Exmouth Street."

"And what can you tell me about the accusation that Mr. Charters built the Wheel by using Ferris's plans without permission?"

The small man's eyes flashed in anger for just a moment. "Nonsense! This wheel is much better than anything that Ferris ever came up with. Or the one at Earls Court, for that matter. There are a number of improvements with this design that are far more advanced than what has been seen before. The mechanical works alone have many unique improvements that can be applied to a number of other machines."

Meeser seemed to realize that his passion was unusual for someone in his position, and he took a breath and stepped back. "You seem rather defensive of your employer's work," said Holmes. "How long have you been associated with Mr. Charters?"

"Just a few months," he replied. "But I know how much effort went into building this wheel. I can assure you that nothing was stolen or borrowed from any other inventor."

"Except for the very idea of a giant wheel," murmured Lestrade, bringing a scowl to Meeser's face.

"Why was Mr. Charters riding the Wheel today?" asked Holmes. "Surely he's ridden it before, probably many times."

"I believe I can answer that, Mr. Holmes," said Green. "Mr. Charters stops by several times a week to check on the condition of his machinery, and part of that is to see how the Wheel is operating."

"He just liked to ride it," muttered Meeser.

"What's that?" queried Lestrade.

"He always wanted to have a go when he stopped by. No harm in it, was there?"

"Be that as it may," said Green, "he also visited us regularly to go over the accounts and verify the number of people who ride on the Wheel. Meeser here keeps track of that. Charters' agreement is to receive a certain percentage of our revenue, based on the number of riders."

"Ridiculous," muttered Bouchard. "I would never have agreed to such an arrangement if I had been here."

"But I *did* agree to it!" returned Green, his tone threatening to return the two men back to their earlier disagreement.

"You have no idea what you agreed to!" countered his friend.

"Gentlemen, please!" thundered Lestrade, clearly fed up with the both of them.

"This agreement," said Holmes. "I would like to see it, if possible."

"Certainly," said Green, gesturing toward the tent exit. "Right this way. It's in our office."

"It's in my pocket," countered Bouchard. "I took it to show the solicitor."

Green appeared ready to explode, but Lestrade intervened, motioning both men to the exit. "Let's discuss it in your office."

The two owners acquiesced, and Holmes, Lestrade, and I moved to join them, leaving a constable to guard the body. Then, Holmes stopped suddenly and said, "Oh, Lestrade." He then whispered to the inspector for a moment before joining the rest of us outside. The inspector, who returned to have a brief word with one of his officers, was quickly back by our side as we strolled toward a brightly painted caravan at the rear of the circus, on the far side of the lot away from the river. Painted red with gold trim, its roof was peaked with an elaborately scripted sign stating, "Green & Bouchard's Circus Extraordinaire".

"What did you tell Lestrade?" I asked softly, so that only Holmes could hear.

"Simply that he can release the other riders of the Wheel, after making sure that we have recorded their names and addresses, as well as

38

establishing in which car they were riding, relative to that of the dead man. And also that he should make sure Mr. Meeser does not eel away from us too soon."

Before we reached the rather gaudy wagon, Holmes stopped abruptly, venting a quiet "Ha!" that only I could hear, and turned perpendicular from our path and into the crowd. Lestrade sensed this and stopped in puzzlement. Craning my neck, I could see that Holmes was approaching a big man who was standing stationary like a stone in a moving stream of people. Almost immediately I recognized the fellow as Barker, Holmes's friendly rival detective from here on the Surrey side of the river. The man's dark glasses, even in the middle of the day, were unmistakable. He looked just as imposing now as he had that evening in '94, when I had seen him expressing theories in Park Lane on the walk outside the home where young Ronald Adair had been murdered.

Holmes and Barker, both tall men, were nearly the same height, and it was easy to keep them in sight, with Holmes in his Inverness and fore-and-aft cap and Barker with his glasses, while the crowds divided and reformed around them. Holmes gestured toward the Wheel, and then toward the wagon where Bouchard and Green kept their offices. After a few more words, Barker nodded and slipped away, heading quickly toward Westminster Bridge.

Lestrade and I stood a little apart, while the two owners waited by the caravan steps. Rejoining us, Holmes said, "It was a bit of good luck to notice our friend Barker. He is here on a completely unrelated matter, tracking a gang of pick-pockets. When I explained my preliminary conclusions, he immediately grasped what I needed, and has gone to follow up on a few conclusions.

"You have formed conclusions, then?" asked Lestrade. "Already? And might I ask what they are?"

"Ah, Lestrade, you know that I am loathe to reveal anything ahead of its time. Either I will be proven right, or not, and we shall move forward from there. For now, let us examine this contentious agreement."

We all climbed the narrow, steep steps attached to the side of the caravan, finding the interior surprisingly roomier and more pleasant than I would have anticipated. A couple of desks lined the walls, and there were several comfortable chairs scattered around them.

When we had situated ourselves, Bouchard pulled a document from his coat, unfolded it, and laid it upon one of the desks, clearly his own, while Green seated himself at the other. "As you can see," said the American, placing a rigid finger firmly on the paper, "there is a clause here, buried in with the legal mumbo-jumbo regarding payment, which our lawyer says will give a half-share of the circus to Charters, the owner of the Wheel, should anything happen to one or the other of us. Or if to both of us, he will get *both* shares."

"What?" cried Green, half rising to his feet.

"It's true," said Bouchard. "You certainly have a gift for running the day-to-day needs of a circus, but you have no skill whatsoever in matters of business," he said coldly.

"Here now," asked Lestrade. "How would something like that work?"

"As it was explained to me," responded Bouchard, "the clause outlines that the owner of the Wheel has a legitimate vested interest in the income from the thing, and therefore the success of the circus in general, as it helps attract business to the Wheel, and vice versa. If for some reason one of us were to die, or become unable to manage the circus, then it would cause a negative and unplanned-for effect to the Wheel owner's income. Therefore, through this agreement, he has the right to step in and take over the incapacitated owner's share of the circus, in order to keep things up and running, thus preventing any loss or decrease of his own income."

"Is that right?" asked Lestrade. "Can someone do that?"

Holmes, meanwhile, had been looking at the paper. He raised his head and nodded. "I believe that what the lawyer told you is correct, although I do not know if such an agreement would truly stand up in court. I assume this is not a normal clause in a document of this type."

"Absolutely not," said Bouchard. "He had never seen anything like it before."

Holmes tightened his lips and thought for a moment while the rest of us remained silent. Then, "Do you also have a copy of your agreement for this property where the circus is currently located?"

Green nodded and stood. "Certainly. It is right here on my desk, under these papers – Wait! What's this, then?"

He shifted some of the sheets piled on his rather untidy desk to reveal a dark brown box, about one foot square, of the sort that contains candy. Reaching for it, he said, "Chocolate covered almonds? Now how did that get there?"

Before he could place his hands on the box, Holmes stepped closer and prevented him. "Gentlemen, please do not move," he said softly.

I was instantly on alert, fearing that there was some danger in the box, perhaps even a hidden swamp adder, poised to spring when the lid was removed. "What is it, Holmes?" I whispered. "Should I summon one of the circus's snake handlers?"

My friend smiled. "No, Watson, I don't believe that will be necessary. I only I wish to make a better examination before any of us move around more than we already have, possibly destroying evidence."

We all remained where we were, except for Green, who collapsed back into his chair. Holmes carefully shifted the box loose from the surrounding papers and lifted the lid. Holding it up, we could see that there was a card attached. "'To my friend'," read Holmes. "And it's signed, 'Bouchard'."

"What!" cried Bouchard. "That isn't my handwriting! I did not provide that box of candy!"

"I have no doubt of that," said Holmes. "You would not be that clumsy. I expect that after the contents of the box took care of Mr. Green, it was supposed to be discovered, thus implicating you in your business partner's murder."

He leaned down to sniff the candy. Before he replaced the lid, I could see that there were a number of empty places where candies had been removed. "There is the same faint bitter almond smell," stated Holmes, "indicating that other pieces, if not all, of the candy in the box are also poisoned with cyanide."

"I don't smell anything," complained Bouchard.

"You wouldn't necessarily," I explained. "Only about four in ten people can actually smell cyanide in small doses. Holmes and I, and the inspector as well, have come across this before, and know what to expect."

"That's the truth," agreed Lestrade."

Holmes turned. "It would appear that you have an enemy, Mr. Green. And you, too, Mr. Bouchard, as someone is apparently trying to kill one and frame the other. Have either of you seen this box here before?"

Green shook his head, while Bouchard said, "Certainly not!"

"Can you think of anyone who might have gained entrance to your caravan, in order to place the poisoned candy on the desk?"

"No," said Green. "The door is usually left unlocked, but this part of the circus is well away from the public, and the company knows to keep an eye on the wagon to make sure that strangers do not enter."

"Charters ate those poisoned candies," I said. "He must have been in here, seen the box, and taken some, accidentally becoming the unintended victim."

"Exactly, Watson," said Holmes. Glancing toward the owners, he asked, "Is it unusual that Mr. Charters would enter the caravan?"

Green nodded. "It is possible. He has done so before. He visits the circus a few times each week, and if one of us is not easily found on the grounds, he knows to check this caravan."

"Did he come in here today?"

"He may have, but I cannot know for sure." said Green.

"He must have," said Bouchard. "After all, he ate some of the poisoned candy."

Green responded, "I don't know. I suppose he came here first. I initially encountered him near the Wheel. We talked for a few moments about the ongoing success of the enterprise, and then he took his ride. He said he never got tired of riding it. While I was standing there waiting, Bouchard returned from the solicitor's office and discovered me there, where you found us."

"After you returned, did you visit the caravan before proceeding to the Wheel?" Holmes asked Bouchard.

"No," said Bouchard. "I was angry, and looking for Green, but I spotted him as soon as I entered the grounds and walked right up to him."

Holmes glanced left and right across the floor. "Stay still, gentlemen," he said. "This should only take a few moments." Then he proceeded to throw himself upon the floor, crawling here and there, from door to desk and back, all the while muttering to himself and venting a series of whistles, clicks, and tight-lipped mmm's. Lestrade and I had seen such things many times over the years, but Green and Bouchard were surprised, to say the very least.

Finally, Holmes stood and brushed off his trousers. His face held the flicker of a smile that I recognized after many years. I suspect that Lestrade saw it too. "It is fortunate that it rained this morning. Now, may I examine the agreement for this location, Mr. Green?"

Wordlessly, Green handed him a document from his desk. Holmes scanned it quickly before finding something in the middle of the page that interested him. Calling Mr. Bouchard to his side, he asked, "Is this your standard agreement?"

"It is," said Bouchard. "We provide it whenever we set up at a site. The public has the idea that a circus randomly stops in some farmer's field or empty lot and performs until the urge arises to move on. It's much more complicated than that. Future sites are scouted, sometimes months in advance, and careful arrangements are made with property owners. We never simply stop and set up where we do not have both permission and a signed agreement. I don't know how some smaller circuses work, but that's the way we do it here."

"And this clause? Where you cannot be evicted while in operation?"

"For our own protection. It's set that way so that we cannot be forced to leave before we're ready, as packing and moving is quite complicated, as you might imagine. Additionally, the place where we are going next might not be ready for us."

"This is an interesting clause, then, especially in conjunction with the one contained in the Wheel agreement. Has no one ever questioned it?"

"No," replied Bouchard with puzzlement. "Why should they? It's always been a matter of straight forward business."

"Indeed." Holmes reached for the Wheel agreement, and folded it with the property document. Placing both into his pocket, he said, "There's nothing to be done, then, until Barker returns. Lestrade, are your men still holding the fort outside?"

"Of course," replied the inspector.

"Excellent. Then might I suggest that we wait patiently until there are further developments." He pulled out his watch. "It shouldn't be too long."

And so saying, he seated himself near Bouchard's desk, while the two circus owners looked at each other with confusion. Then, Green pulled open a drawer and removed a bottle of whisky. "Gentlemen?" he asked.

Holmes sat up a little straighter. "I wouldn't, Mr. Green. The same person who left you those candies might have added something to that bottle as well."

Green suddenly looked ill and gently replaced the bottle in the drawer. Holmes glanced at me with a mischievous light in his eye, and then looked at Bouchard, saying, "Tell me, sir, do you perhaps have a lady bare-back rider amongst your company?"

And so the conversation proceeded. Lestrade remembered my earlier mention of just such a woman in my distant past, and I was prompted to tell the story, which had no doubt been Holmes's plan all along. From there, the conversation proceeded along similar lines, although everyone was aware of the odd and artificial nature of the situation as we waited interminably for the return of the bespectacled Surrey-side detective, bringing whatever it was that Holmes had dispatched him to find.

On a number of occasions when the conversation would falter, Holmes would revive it with questions about the workings of the circus. The two owners provided several amusing anecdotes, strangely incongruous with the fact that we were sitting by a box of poisoned chocolates and awaiting additional information about a murder. At one point, Holmes managed to get Lestrade to admit that his dislike of the circus's Wheel was related to a nervousness that he felt whenever he pictured himself riding it. "I understand, Inspector," said Bouchard. "It is for that reason that I myself have never been up on the accursed thing."

Several times Lestrade stepped to the door to make whispered inquiries of one of the constables. Finally, conversation lapsed into awkward silence, although it did not appear to affect Holmes. Then, after a period of time that felt longer than it actually was, there was a forceful knock on the door.

"Ah," said Holmes, rising. "That will be Barker, I expect. Excuse me for just a moment."

43

He stepped outside and shut the door behind him. I listened idly to see if I could hear any of their conversation, but all that I could pick out was the tired calliope, wheezing in the distance.

After just a couple of moments, Holmes returned, followed by Barker. I nodded, and Barker returned it. I hadn't seen him since nearly a year before, when he and I had waited in the stables of Lord Burchem's manor, while Holmes and Inspector Gregson forced Willoughby Clayton to flee with an accusation constructed of pure bluff. Holmes had known that Clayton would not depart without his great horse, Fury, and he had placed Barker and myself in the stables to catch him. It had worked, but Barker had received a nasty blow before all was said and done.

Holmes did not return to his seat, but rather stood near the door. Barker found a chair and sat down, his dark glasses aimed intently at Green and Bouchard. I expected Holmes to speak, but he remained silent, until there was another knock on the door.

"Forgive me, Lestrade," he said, reaching for the door. "I took the liberty of having one of your men bring the final player for today's drama."

The door opened, and a constable led Edward Meeser into the wagon. Only now did the place start to seem crowded. Holmes pointed to one of the empty chairs, and the constable placed the small man in front of it, before taking a place to the rear. Looking back and forth like an animal in a trap, Meeser finally dropped into the seat.

"I believe," said Holmes, "that I have enough amateur legal training that I can get a sense of the implications of the clauses in question in both of these documents." He retrieved the folded pages from his pocket. "I thought about sending a message to my protégé Thorndyke in Kings Bench Walk for his opinion, as he could have been here very quickly, should he be at home at all and not out on his own business. However, I don't believe that will be necessary.

He placed the papers beside him on the corner of Green's desk. "As Mr. Bouchard explained, his attorney noted that there is an unacceptable clause in the agreement to lease the Wheel, wherein the owner of said object can obtain an ownership stake in the circus. The levels of this acquired ownership vary – if both owners are removed from the picture, then the Wheel's owner takes over all shares. As I said, I don't know if it would stand up in court, and shows a certain optimistic ignorance on the part of the man who constructed it, but it was a bold effort nonetheless."

He briefly smiled at Meeser, who continued to try to shrink into his chair.

"The other document," continued Holmes, "between the circus proprietors and the owner of the property where we are now located, also has an oddly phrased clause, essentially stating that the circus cannot be evicted as long as it is operating. I understand why this clause was included, but I'm surprised that no property owner has objected to it, as it is quite open-ended."

"It was never a problem," said Bouchard. "It is the nature and cycle of our business. Eventually attendance starts to dwindle, and we move to the next town. Our possible eviction has never even been an issue."

"I'm sure you're right, Mr. Bouchard. But these two documents together were a motivation for murder."

"I begin to see where you're going with this," said Lestrade. "But I'm still not sure why. You seem to be saying that it would be in the interest of the Wheel's owner to incapacitate one or both of the circus owners to get their shares, and you have also stated that Mr. Bouchard did not leave the poison candy for Mr. Green. Therefore, it must have been the Wheel's owner who left it. But if Charters did that, in an attempt to poison one and frame the other, then why would he turn right around and take some and eat it, thus killing himself?"

"Barker?" said Holmes, turning to our silent companion.

"Because Charters wasn't the owner of the Wheel." He hooked a thumb toward Meeser. "He is."

"What?" cried Bouchard, rising from his chair. Green stood more slowly, looking with confusion at the man in question.

"Impossible," said Green. "I've met with Charters multiple times over the last weeks. He was the owner and builder of the Wheel, without a doubt."

Barker shook his head and rumbled, "No, he wasn't. Based on what he observed, Mr. Holmes directed me to go to the workshop in Exmouth Street and ask a few questions. It didn't take long to winkle out that Meeser here was the true brains behind the operation. He owned the Wheel. He's the one that designed it and built it, too. From some things he let slip to his neighbor, a widow named Mrs. Crabtree that he fancied bragging in front of, he was a bit worried that it was too close to Ferris's design, so he hid behind Charters, a man he hired to be the face of the business."

Meeser lowered his head, but made no move either to defend himself or deny Barker's statements.

"Barker," said Lestrade, "you said 'based on what he observed'." Turning to Holmes, he twisted his head and raised his eyebrows. "Mr. Holmes?"

Holmes smiled. "When I examined Charters' body, still reclining in one of the Wheel's carriages, I found the candies and empty wrappers, as well as the evidence that Charters had recently eaten them. I could smell the poison on his breath and later in the uneaten candies. That part was clear. But I also observed that Charters' hands were very soft and had no callosities whatsoever. His nails were quite clean, with no indications of dirt or grease that might be associated with one who builds and works with mechanical devices. In short, his hands did not appear to be those of a working man or an inventor. When I heard that he had supposedly designed and built the Wheel, I did not believe it.

"I also noted that Mr. Charters' shoes were a notably large size of a very common and rather cheap style. At that point, it was only a fact to be docketed. Later, we were able to speak with Mr. Meeser. At that time, I already disbelieved the statement that Charters was the builder of the Wheel. But here was a man who *did* have a workman's hands. Now, that is not unusual or unexpected, since he took care of the daily maintenance and operation of the Wheel. However, during our conversation, it became apparent that he was rather defensive against criticisms of the machine, especially when the statement was made that the design had been copied from that of Ferris. But most important, his shoes, of a much smaller size, were very well made indeed, and though worn, quite expensive. A closer examination of his clothing revealed that, while it is well used, it is also of excellent quality, and quite likely tailored. I believe, in fact, that his garments were made by Tundell's, off the Strand. Again, a fact that by itself was only curious, but something to be retained for later consideration.

"I had thus decided that Mr. Meeser might well be the true designer and builder, and therefore the owner, of the Wheel, although I had no idea why he would conceal the fact and hide behind the straw man, Charters, and it was not my business to reveal it at that time just for the satisfaction of confirming it. But I did want to learn the truth, since the supposed owner of the contraption had just been murdered, and perhaps there was a connection. When I luckily observed friend Barker here, I sent him to confirm or deny my hypothesis regarding Mr. Charters' status. As you've heard, he has done so."

"But the poisoned candies, Holmes?" I asked. "How does it all connect?"

"Surely it is obvious, Watson. The first clause gives some degree of ownership of the circus to the Wheel's owner if something were to happen to either Mr. Green or Mr. Bouchard. That might be extended and interpreted to cover what would happen if one or the other chose to sell out, should the operation lose its profitability. The second clause means that the circus could stay at this location indefinitely as long as some part of it were still functioning, since it could not be evicted while still in operation. It was a clear motivation for the Wheel's owner to try and gain control of the circus, thus giving him both ownership and a perpetual site in which to run his wheel.

"After managing to get the agreement signed, with the naïve belief that it would hold up legally, our killer set about trying to sabotage the circus, hoping that one or the other of the owners would become dispirited and decide to sell out, or forfeit the shares per the agreement. Then, becoming impatient when that didn't seem to be working, he tried something more desperate, proving most certainly that his mechanical genius does not extend to planning a murder."

At this, Meeser raised his head, with a look of defiance on his face that was quite different from the meek persona that he had shown so far. "It's true that I am the Wheel's owner," he said. "But you have no proof that I poisoned any candy. I don't know why Charters killed himself that way, but you can't pin it on me."

"My examination of the floor of this caravan," continued Holmes, for the moment ignoring the small man and revealing his evidence point by point, "confirmed that Mr. Charters was in here earlier today. I know that it was today because his large shoes were obviously damp from walking outside after the rains this morning. On the floor, his prints are underneath all of the other recent tracks that we have made since entering. He came in earlier, looking for either of the two owners, before leaving again and encountering Mr. Green by the Wheel. While he was here, he noticed the big box of chocolate-covered almonds on the desk, and he couldn't resist taking some, probably thinking they wouldn't be missed. Even if he was one of the people who *can* smell cyanide in this form, he would have likely believed that it was simply part of the strong flavoring of the almonds.

"If he had eaten them as he walked from here to the Wheel, or even while he stood at this desk, he would have died sooner. But he waited to enjoy them while taking his regular ride on the Wheel."

"That still doesn't connect anything with me," said Meeser.

"I believe," said Holmes, "you said that it would not be unusual for Mr. Charters to stop in here to look for either of you?"

Bouchard nodded, and Green said, "That's right."

"Would there have ever been any reason, any reason at all, for Mr. Meeser to have entered this caravan?"

"None whatsoever," said Bouchard definitely.

"Not even to lean in the door?"

"No."

"Never," added Green.

"And certainly he would not have been allowed or expected to walk up to Mr. Green's desk, for instance."

"Certainly not."

Turning to Meeser, Holmes said, "I did neglect to mention one important fact, Mr. Meeser. Along with the footprints of the deceased, Mr.

Charters, on the floor, and those that came later from the owners, the inspector, Dr. Watson, and myself, there was one other, earlier, set. They were underneath and overlapped by those of Mr. Charters. They were *your* size, very good quality, and made by shoes carrying a distinctive design, also of Tundell's off the Strand. You left those prints, Mr. Meeser, when you brought in the box of poisoned candy, labeled with a false card to frame Mr. Bouchard, and deposited it here on Mr. Green's desk in order to kill him.

"Finally, it should be noted that there is a grease mark on the candy box that corresponds to that made by a left hand. The grease itself seems to be the type associated with machinery. And I note that, while the fact that the mark was made by a left hand is eventually inconclusive, as there are a great many left-handed people in the world, the only left-handed person in this room right now, a man who happens to have that same mechanical grease on his hands, is you, Mr. Meeser."

The small man was silent, his eyes dropping slowly from where they had been fixed on Holmes to his own hands, fingers twisted in his lap. Finally, he spoke.

"That idiot wasn't supposed to eat the candy. It was an accident. Granted I left it here, and you can try and prove why, but Charters' death was an accident. You can't charge me for an accident. It was his own fault for taking candy that didn't belong to him."

Holmes's eyes widened in amusement. "How," he asked, changing course, "did you know about the property clause that would allow the circus to stay on in perpetuity without being evicted?"

Meeser hung his head and shrugged as if surrendering. "After I built the Wheel, I couldn't find anywhere to set it up. I owed money for loans I'd acquired while constructing it, and I'd heard that Ferris was coming after me for stealing his design. Which I didn't!" He looked up then, turning his head from side to side, his gaze fierce, and his breathing increasing for a moment, before he resumed in the earlier defeated tone. "I went to the owners of this very property to see about putting the Wheel here permanently. They weren't interested. They said there was already a wheel at Earls Court.

"Something the property owners said made me curious about who *was* going to be occupying this site, and I broke into their offices to find out more about it. That's where I saw their copy of the lease, showing that the circus could stay here as long as it wanted. I recognized right off how powerful something like that could be. If I could somehow get my Wheel established at this circus, with that clause in the agreement, I would never have to leave. Because once I got it up and running, I wouldn't have to stop, as long as I could make the circus stay there too. I could make enough money to pay off my debts, and I could use the ideas I'd developed while building my wheel to construct other machines here, amusements that the public will also want to ride. Bigger wheels, and vehicles that give the feeling of great speed or vertical drops."

"But that was only the first part of the plan," prompted Holmes. "The next was making yourself a part-owner."

"Based on what I had read of the wording of the property agreement, I designed my own document so that I could end up with at least part ownership of the circus. Then, since we couldn't be evicted, I'd slowly switch from a traveling attraction to something permanent, a destination for people to visit who wanted to be thrilled with mechanical wonders, and not the same old trapeze acts and animal tamers.

"After I had identified this circus from the copy of the agreement in the owner's office, I traveled north for a few days to Easingwold and hung around, learning what I could. I found that Mr. Green was the one that would need to be approached. It worked out well that his partner was away for a few days. I schooled Charters in what to say, and got him to fix up the agreement. He'd been a salesman at some point, and a good one, too, and it worked well in convincing Mr. Green."

Green looked down, while Bouchard snorted.

"Surely the document was non-binding, as it was signed as if Charters was the true owner," said Lestrade.

"I had a separate arrangement giving him limited authorization to conduct such agreements in my stead."

"And then, hoping that one of the owners would get discouraged, you began to create the accidents, giving the impression that the circus was now unlucky."

Meeser nodded and said softly, "I thought if it became financially unsound, I could convince one of them to sell out to me."

"But that didn't work," said Holmes. Meeser shook his head.

Bouchard started to speak, but Holmes interrupted him. "An interesting vision, this mechanical carnival you planned. But you became impatient."

"Mr. Bouchard had been arguing to have the Wheel removed."

"So you decided to force the issue with the poisoned chocolates. Rather foolish, to try to kill Green, who actually seemed to agree with you regarding the use of amusement-related machinery. Surely you see now that it wasn't worth committing murder."

"But this wasn't murder," whined Meeser. "Whatever might have been intended *didn't* happen. This was just an accident. Charters killed *himself*, you see. It's no different than if he'd been playing with a loaded gun he'd found and shot himself."

"An interesting defense," said Lestrade. "It might save you from the rope, but I doubt it." The inspector stood up. "I'll be very interested indeed to hear how it plays at your trial, Mr. Meeser. Come with me."

He took Meeser's arm and pulled him up. At the door, the small man turned suddenly, looking toward the two owners. "I'll be sending someone else to keep track of my machine," he said. "The arrangement still stands, you know, whatever else happens here. Whenever you run it, a part of the proceeds belongs to me. I suspect that I'll be needing them."

Bouchard looked at Green, who looked back and then dropped his eyes. "The Wheel is closed," said Bouchard. "Effective immediately." He glared at the little man. "There shall be no more proceeds!"

Meeser looked stricken. "You . . . you can't! You can't do that! We have an agreement."

"We have an agreement to give you a share from the operation of the Wheel. We do not have to agree to keep operating it. And I can assure you that the agreement will be dissolved altogether before the day is over, if I have *my* way!" replied Bouchard. "Good day, sir."

We all followed Lestrade and his prisoner outside. With our thanks, Barker departed. The inspector placed Meeser in the custody of several constables, who began to march him toward Westminster Bridge, and so on, across to the Yard. Meanwhile, Holmes was speaking with Bouchard and Green. In a moment, he turned and said, "Lestrade?"

"Yes, Mr. Holmes?"

"It seems as if you get your wish, and the Wheel will be coming down, nearly immediately. But I've convinced these men to run it just one more time, so that you can have a ride on it, and conquer your fears before it's gone."

The inspector froze, with a look on his face as if he were a stoat suddenly illuminated by a gamekeeper's lantern. "I . . . umm, I would rather not."

"Lestrade, how often will you have this opportunity? Don't pass it up. How else can you confront this aversion and defeat it? Shall Watson and I ride with you as well?"

"That won't be necessary, Mr. Holmes," said Green. "I believe that my partner, Mr. Bouchard, who has also never had a go on it, would benefit from a last spin of the London Wheel."

So it was, a few minutes later, that Green, who had learned how to operate the machinery weeks earlier, shifted the lever that sent the contraption into motion one final time. Lestrade and Bouchard were buckled in together, and shrieking like terrified children with every revolution. I could get no sense through the entire voyage whether our

50

friend the inspector was enjoying himself, or if each trip around and over and back down was as bad as the very first.

As for myself, I refused to pass up the chance to take a ride upon the contraption, and was seated alone in an adjacent carriage. The sensation was certainly somewhat thrilling, and the view was interesting, although not the bird's-eye vantage that had been promised. Still, I suppose that I would not have missed it. However, I did wonder at Holmes's last minute indifferent decision not to join us, as he stood down below us at some little distance, arms resolutely folded beneath the caped shoulders of his Inverness, while he watched speculatively, his eyes shadowed by his fore-and-aft cap.

The Two Different Women

As his gaze shifted to something beyond me, I saw my friend's eyes narrow with the slightest indication of irritation. Having known Mr. Sherlock Holmes at that time for nearly a quarter-century, I had long ago learned not to twist like a new constable and attempt to see what had provoked that most subtle of reactions.

Holmes, being who he was, had of course noticed that *I* had noticed his glance, and he didn't need to evince his uncanny skills, sometimes mistaken for mind-reading, to understand my unspoken question.

"A pesterment, Watson," explained. "Nothing more." Then, as almost an afterthought, he added, "Give me your opinion."

Free now to pivot in my seat, I laid down my fork and turned slightly, looking across the common room at the man and woman seating themselves at a nearby table. The woman was concentrating on getting situated in her chair, and I realized that she was, in fact, well into her second term. The man paused beside his own chair, caught in the act of looking rather despairingly in our direction. Turning my attention his way caused his focus to shift slightly from my friend to me, and our gazes met. Then his eyes dropped, rather nervously I thought, and he settled into his own seat beside his companion.

I took another moment to frankly study him while he gestured, almost angrily, toward the bar. I noticed that he had a head that was much too large for his narrow shoulders, before realizing that it was actually normal, and that it was his body that was smallish. His lower lip, underneath a Bismarck moustache waxed at the tips, rested above an average chin and was pursed with a natural petulance. This didn't not improve when a large whisky was set before him. Although he appeared to be in his mid-thirties, his high forehead was quite lined and topped by thin brownish hair, parted on his left and already going gray at the temples. Those same eyes which had looked my way were underscored with dark circles, along with an underlying shiftiness that would certainly have been there before whatever was worrying him now had begun, and would still be there in future days as well.

"His wife?" I asked rather foolishly, turning back to my own dinner, a magnificent piece of roasted pork with a thin layer of flavorful fat forming an outer layer, crisped and awaiting my further attentions. I suspected that, as the friend of Sherlock Holmes, I was being rewarded. Holmes, with a similar slab upon his plate, seemed indifferent.

"Obviously. But what else did you see?"

I shifted my eyes, gazing into the distance and concentrating a moment before replying. "Moderately wealthy," I began, recalling the excellent quality of the couples' clothing – at least what I could see across the dim dining room.

"The clothing," agreed Holmes, nodding and following my thinking, still serving as something of a teacher after all these years. "And?"

"American," I added as I envisioned the peculiar cut of the garments that suggested ostentatiousness without a corresponding level of class. Holmes began to pounce, but I held up a hand. "Wait. The clothing was *purchased* in America, I should say. It has something of the western styles that I saw in San Francisco years ago. But it wasn't obtained recently, as it seems rather worn. Based on that fact, along with the man's moustaches and gestures, and a few other random indications from his lady, I should say that they are actually of German descent, having moved to America at some time in the past, where they had enough money to the purchase moderately expensive clothing. But for some reason they haven't purchased new clothing since traveling here."

Holmes dropped his napkin and clapped with a smile and a rather loud, "Ha!" which caused an elderly man at the adjacent table to start and drop his spoon with a clatter. Holmes ignored the resulting scowl and replied, "Really, Watson, that was excellent. If I wasn't already retired and rusticating here in my self-imposed apiaristic seclusion, I would have to consider leaving things in your capable hands!"

I snorted, replying, "We both know that your 'retirement' has ended up being almost a hobby, as you still become involved in nearly as many cases now as when you lived in London. You have your brother to thank for that, if not your own curiosity. Else, why would I be down here?"

We both knew the answer to that, as I had arrived only that afternoon from the capital on the Eastbourne train, carrying with me the final evidence that would prove the guilt of Vincent Berne, the False Parson of East Dean. It was a tragic tale, spiraling out from one of Holmes's long-past cases, and set into motion by the untimely death of Berne's own son who, upon learning what his father had done to his mother, had tragically jumped over the high cliff of Beachy Head, directly across from Holmes's own retirement villa.

"I should point out," continued Holmes, "that the gentleman and his wife, both of whom are actually both from the Kingdom of Bavaria, did live in the western United States for several years before returning to the German Empire late last year, apparently choosing to retain their American clothing throughout the trip rather than purchase something new in their native land.. They have one daughter, less than a year old, currently upstairs in the care of a nurse. They are now returning to the United States, but have inexplicably stopped in this little inn in this out-of-the-way village, where they seem determined to stay for an indefinite period of time."

I was beginning to feel that usual amazement when Holmes meticulously revealed all the hidden layers of anyone that fell under his scrutiny. And then I remembered his short statement referring to the man as a *pesterment*. "You've met him before," I said.

"Indeed. Three days ago. He introduced himself and attempted to solicit my services. As he had been here for nearly two weeks at that point, and as my reasons for 'retirement' include being aware of all things German, I had already become curious about – and wary of – him. I naturally wonder about any Germans who stay around here for too long, and for no apparent reasons. Therefore, I instigated some inquiries through my brother, and also with friends across both the eastern and western seas. In short, this is not a man with whom I wish to associate."

Having known Holmes for so long, I realized that he would reveal nothing more. However, circumstances were such that I was soon to be introduced to the traveler and his wife, although by an unexpected source.

For at that moment, our table was approached by Tom Keller, the proprietor of the Tiger Inn where we supped. At the time of this narrative, mid-June 1905, I had known Keller for a little under two years. Not long after Holmes announced his retirement from active London practice in October 1903, with the intention to settle east of Birling Gap (which I have referred to in some of my notes as "Fulworth" – something of an inside joke), I had travelled down to visit. During the course of that first stay, Holmes and I had naturally walked the mile or so from his "villa" (as he liked to call it), across the fields to the Tiger Inn on the East Dean common. It was an old smuggler's inn, like so many others dotting the landscape of these seacoast hamlets, dating back half-a-thousand years or more – although that was still young compared to some of the nearby churches, now approaching their first millennial birthdays.

Holmes, as a nearby resident, made the trip from his Sussex home to the common regularly, as he had an arrangement with the village estate office to serve as a mailing address. It was at that same building, west across the green and visible through the window where we now sat, that we had confronted Vincent Berne only a few hours earlier. After that unpleasant encounter, it had been only natural to repair to the inn. Stepping through the low door, clearly built for men of another age, we had been greeted by the owner and shown to a fine table near the window. The late afternoon sun had long since disappeared, leaving only massing clouds behind the brick buildings lined across the far side of the green.

Keller had recommended the pork, and had also brought us ale. "On the house," he added, in a tone that brooked no argument. As he walked away, I raised my eyebrows.

"A benefit related to little service that I performed for him several weeks ago. A trifle."

Realizing that this was another of Holmes's investigations that I would likely never add to my notes, I instead questioned him about some more details from the Berne affair, which I hope to publish in due course, as my restriction against placing narratives of Holmes's adventures in *The Strand* was lifted upon his retirement. The food arrived, excellent as expected, and we proceeded through the meal to the point where we had observed our fellow diners, the Bavarians, and so on to Keller's arrival at our table, asking, "Is it all right, then?"

"Excellent!" I beamed.

Keller nodded and turned his head towards Holmes, who added with a more leveled enthusiasm, "Indeed."

The proprietor nodded, as if he expected no other response, but his eyes didn't seem as if he were truly listening. He appeared distracted, and he said in a lowered voice. "A word please, Mr. Holmes? When you and the Doctor are finished?"

Holmes, long accustomed to surreptitious conversations, simply nodded. "I'll be in my office," Keller added, turning away and gesturing toward his daughter Katy. She went into motion, resulting in her smiling appearance beside us a moment later with two fresh ales standing beside our plates.

At that point, Holmes began to finish his meal, but in a steady workmanlike way, rather than savoring the brilliance of the preparation. I turned toward the window, observing with some uneasiness the piling clouds in the west. There was a storm coming.

Within moments, Holmes had finished and, seeing that I had also concluded my portion, he arose and walked towards the foreign man and his wife without casting either of them a glance, whereas both of them were clearly watching us. I tried not to look at them either, but instead followed Holmes around the end of the bar, and so into Keller's small office behind it.

"What can we do for you, Mr. Keller?" asked Holmes as we found our seats. The big man didn't answer for a moment, and then he ran his hands over his face in a curious washing motion before releasing a sigh.

"I hate to ask it, Mr. Holmes, especially so soon after what you did to help Katy." Holmes waved a hand in dismissal, but Keller continued. "No, it's true. I'll always be in your debt, and have no right to be bothering you again, and especially so soon. And during your dinner, no less. But he's been pestering me about it for a couple of days, and I told him no, but then you and the Doctor walked in, and . . . and I decided to go ahead and ask anyway."

"The *he* that's been pestering you," said Holmes, "is surely *Herr* Siegen, now in the dining room with his wife."

"It is. He told me how he spoke to you the other day, and that you turned him down. Rightly so, I might add. If doesn't like it, he can go somewhere else. I don't know why he stays, to be honest, if he's that unhappy."

"I asked him the same question," said my friend. "He had no good answer. That, and what I already knew about him, led me to turn down his initial request."

"Excuse me," I said, interrupting as I had a thousand times before in an attempt to find the trail. "What would Mr. Siegen's problem be, exactly?"

Holmes's lips tightened. "He feels that he is being persecuted by a ghost."

By now, nothing surprised me, and knowing Holmes, I understood why he had declined the case. Keller interjected, "The White Lady wouldn't persecute anyone. She was a healer in life."

"The White Lady?" I asked, as the door opened, allowing Katy Keller to slip inside.

"That's what we call her," answered Keller, glancing toward his daughter. "We don't know what her real name was."

"She's been here for several hundred years, at least, or longer," added Katy, taking a seat beside her father. "All the stories agree that she was a nurse, or at least someone who cared for the ill and wounded. There are stories that she first worked for the Estate as a servant, but that she also tended to the injured who were placed in the houses just next door during the wars with Napoleon. Others think that she has been here much longer than that – since The Plague in the 1600's."

"And like all of these spirits," added Holmes, with a touch of sarcasm, "she would rather stay here than move on."

"She *can't* move on, you see," said Keller. "Whatever she saw in life – the suffering, the pain – affected her in some way, and now she stays." He looked from one to the other of us as if that explained it. "We've all seen her, you know. At different times. In the hallways or on the stairs. In the kitchen, or in the bar when it's late and closed and when there's no bright light to obscure her."

A sudden burst of wind outside rattled the window, causing me to start involuntarily. Keller and his daughter also looked unnerved, and Holmes smiled slightly to himself.

"Sometimes I wake up, and she's standing by my bed," said the young lady softly. Keller nodded, as if this didn't surprise him.

"I've seen her since I was a little girl," continued Katy. "I . . . I used to think it was my mum." She glanced at her father, whose eyes dropped, and then continued. "But now I know better. Mum . . . Mum has let me know in other ways that she's watching over us. The White Lady is someone else. She watches too, but in a different way. She's good – I can feel it. She never does anything hurtful. Sometimes she just moves things, or shuts doors or windows."

"The usual ghostly forms of amusement," added Holmes, with just the hint of sarcasm. I knew that he could say more. Often in days past, he and I, along with our friend the spiritual investigator Alton Peake, would sit in Baker Street, sharing a glass and telling tales. It was always one of Holmes's sticking points that a spirit, free from the body and physical obligations and limitations, and with a world – nay *a universe* – to explore, should instead choose to remain in one location and drop books and slam doors to get attention. Peake would shake his head with a tolerant smile and give us yet another example of why such a behavior, in his experience, was caused by a torment that the poor spirit could not overcome. Peake had debunked many a false claim, but he also insisted that he had seen the real thing, and he told us that in many cases he had exorcised these souls, allowing them to finally achieve peace. Holmes was a skeptic, but he also respected Peake, and therefore he – usually – held his tongue.

Now, he was clearly doing the same in Keller's office. "This is what Siegen asked you about?" I said to Holmes. "To protect him from the Tiger Inn's ghost?" He nodded, and I added, "I understand why you declined, but why did you not refer him to Peake in London?"

"Because I didn't want our friend to have to deal with this man any more than I wanted to." Holmes shifted his gaze to Keller. "You know something of my background," he said. "I am a cautious man, and part of that is to be aware of my surroundings, and those who populate them. Word reached me through the usual local gossip – your cook by way of Mrs. Hudson – that this man Siegen was staying here for quite a long time and for no apparent reason, and that he seemed to be unhappy while doing so. It wasn't sinister *per se*, but it was a bit unusual. I sent a few messages here and there to learn more about him. He is . . . unsavory.

"His name, loosely translated, means *triumph*, but I find his history anything but. He is originally from Kallstadt, in Bavaria, near Mannheim. When he was in his teens, he moved to the United States, where he lived with relatives for a number of years in the East. At some point, apparently related to the gold discoveries in the West, he traveled, and when settled he began to scramble, revealing his true character. He was able to worm

57

into a series of questionable shipping investments and land deals, and he began to build a modest fortune. However . . . ." At this point, Holmes paused for just a moment, glancing at Katy before continuing, ". . . However, his greatest source income came from establishing a sizeable bordello along the routes to the gold fields. Upon this shaky ground, his wealth multiplied exponentially.

"At some point, he became a citizen of the United States. Returning to Bavaria for a visit a few years ago, he ended up marrying a woman who is a number of years younger than he. Then they returned to America, where they have lived until last year, before returning to Kallstadt for a visit. After only being back there for only a short while, there was some sort of scandal, and Siegen was ordered to leave. Rather than returning directly to their home, they traveled, first to France, and then on to London, before eventually washing up here – to your consternation, Mr. Keller."

Keller ran a hand over his whiskers and nodded. "Consternation is right, Mr. Holmes. I had no idea about his past until now, but I've never liked him much anyway."

"Then why let him stay?" I asked. "Surely you can find a way to turn him out."

Keller dropped his eyes, and then glanced at his daughter, who smiled. "It's the money, you see," she said. "He's rented all of the upstairs rooms – the whole floor – and is paying twice the normal rate to keep them."

The innkeeper glanced back up. "We've made some improvements in the last year or so. You can't see them, as they relate to the piping and the drains and so forth. But there was some expense involved, major expense, and I'm still paying for it. The extra money . . . well, I can't lie and say that it doesn't help."

"*Twice*?" said Holmes, fixating on Keller's earlier statement. "He is paying twice your rate?"

"He is. He made the offer when he first arrived, without prompting. And as Katy said, that's for all of the upstairs rooms."

"His own, one for the nurse and the baby . . . ."

"And one for his wife too. They are not lodging together. The rest stand empty"

"Twice the rate," muttered Holmes to himself. "That is significant in and of itself." Looking back at Keller, he asked, "Why would he do that – why would he wish to stay here, especially as he seems to be suffering under the illusion that this White Lady is tormenting him?"

"I cannot tell you," said Keller, even as his daughter spoke at the same time: "I can't believe that she would do that!"

"The Lady has always been gentle," added her father. "Although I will say that since Siegen has been here, she's been acting up quite a bit. She's agitated. And more of her mischief has occurred than usual. Katy and I have seen her often of late." The girl nodded in agreement.

Holmes shook his head, as if annoyed by a gnat. "And what do you want me to do for Herr. Siegen?"

"Well, it's this way," said Keller. "He has asked me . . . he . . . asked me to ask *you* to speak to him once more. To have mercy and see if you can't give him some assistance."

"Battling the supernatural does not fall within my purview," said my friend shortly.

"I understand. I appreciate that. But as a favor to me – to us – " I could see that the man hated being put in this position, but he also would do what was needed to keep the added funds flowing toward relieving his debt.

Holmes scratched his forehead and then cupped his chin in thought. Then, tapping his forefinger, he seemed to reach a decision. "May we use your office to speak with him?"

Keller seemed relieved, standing abruptly. "Of course. We'll go and get him. And . . . and thank you, Mr. Holmes."

As they left us, I glanced at my friend. "What changed your mind?"

"The Kellers, of course. They wouldn't have asked if it were not important to them. Otherwise, I have no interest in proving or disproving the existence of a White Lady, and certainly not in helping *Herr* Siegen."

He had made no effort to lower his voice, and he concluded this sentence even as the man in question was being shown into the office. He must have been waiting, poised on the edge of his seat to see if he would be summoned. As he walked in, the little man clearly heard Holmes's declaration, and his eyes narrowed. Siegen's wife, who had accompanied him, quite frankly looked rather angrier than her husband at this sleight.

Keller introduced me, and Katy slipped past him, setting down a tray with a full bottle of brandy and glasses. Then they both nodded and backed out, closing the door behind them.

Holmes and I had stood in deference to Mrs. Siegen. "My wife, Berta," said our prospective client, providing us with the lady's heretofore unspoken first name and clearly trying to be as charming as he knew how. He still had something of an accent, which his recent sojourn in Germany had likely sharpened.

Up close, I could see that Mrs. Siegen was quite a bit younger than her husband, as reported. She had classic Bavarian features, but they were marred by a cold and calculating expression that would only harden as she aged.

59

We found our seats, and Siegen reached for the brandy. He was already exhibiting the early signs of inebriation, which was no surprise, as he presented unmistakable indications of alcoholic tendencies, which were quite obvious up close. After pouring himself a tall measure, he remembered his manners and looked at Holmes and me, gesturing toward the other glasses. We declined. He made no such offer toward his wife – rightly so, I thought, for a woman in her condition, although I douted if that was his reasoning.

Holmes began in a curt tone. "Mr. Siegen, I only agreed to speak with you again at the request of my friends, the Kellers. As I explained to you the other day, I do not waste my time on pointless investigations of the supernatural."

Siegen started to speak, but he was interrupted by his wife, allowing him to take a deep swallow of the brandy. "*Gott in Himmel, Friedrich!*" she hissed. "*Du machst dich selbst zum narren!*"

Holmes's German was excellent, and mine passable. Her criticism of him, telling him that he was making a fool of himself, caused his eyes to narrow, and he slammed the empty brandy glass onto the table.

"I am an American, now," he said in English, "and my name is *Fred*, not *Friedrich*." And then he filled the glass, raised it to his lips, emptied it, and proceeded to fill it again.

His wife turned to us. "I have tried to tell him! He is only imagining this White Woman that torments him so. He stays in his room all day, brooding and only coming out for meals. He drinks too much – " and she glared at him, where his own actions seemed to be proving her point " – and he is having problems sleeping. He has heard these innkeeper stories about a ghostly woman walking the hallways and causing mischief, and he has started to imagine that he's seeing her."

"I *have* seen her," muttered Siegen in a surly tone.

"After what happened in Kallstadt," continued his wife, "it's no wonder that he's upset. When we return home to New York, all will be well."

"And what happened there, in Kallstadt?" asked Holmes, having noticed, as did I, that Siegen winced when his hometown was mentioned.

The downtrodden little man cleared his throat. "It . . . well, you see, my brother died while we were there." Another swallow. Then, before the glass was emptied this time, he topped it off again.

"Really," said Holmes blandly. "Was he murdered?"

Siegen's eyes widened. "What? No! Don't be absurd. He had a bad heart, and it finally caught up with him."

"And that is why you are upset?"

"Of course."

"Ah. I had heard differently, you see. My information was that there was some scandal there, necessitating your hasty departure. Perhaps, as I need to have an understanding of *all* of the relevant facts to determine why this spirit is harassing you, you will share that story as well."

Siegen scowled and looked at his wife, who returned the expression. Then, with a nod, she released him to speak.

"It was determined – falsely, I would add – that when I first moved to the United States, it was to avoid service in the military of the German Empire. Nothing could be further from the truth. Upon my return last year, this was . . . discussed with me by the authorities, and based upon that, I was told to leave the country."

Holmes nodded. "And then, instead of returning to America, you have buried yourself here in this English village, specifically within this establishment, where I'm told you have reserved the whole upstairs floor and pay above the going rate, in spite of clearly being unhappy and feeling as if you are being victimized by a dead woman." His skepticism was palpable. "Why would you do that, Mr. Siegen?"

Holmes's tone had sharpened as if he were a prosecutor interrogating a lying witness. Siegen looked again to his wife, but she seemed to have no advice or direction for him this time. He swallowed and said, "When I first departed for America, twenty years ago, my brother – the one who has just died – went with me. We had plans to make our fortunes. He was a carpenter, and I, while having no special skills, was willing to work hard. We left home and began to make our way in a leisurely fashion, eventually reaching England. With no plan in mind, we explored a bit, and almost by accident we ended up in this village, staying in this very inn. We had a bit of money at the time, a gift from our grandmother for the journey, and those were happy days – at least at first. But my brother quickly became homesick, and we fought while we were here. Finally, he decided to return home and we parted – he to go back to Kallstadt, while I journeyed onward.

"Last year, my wife and I were both missing our old home after all those years away, and I especially wanted to visit and spend time with my brother, whom we had learned was ill. I tried to regain the closeness that we'd had when we were young, but it seemed as if we couldn't rebuild the bond from twenty years ago. There were too many different experiences between us since then. He had grown to regret his decision to return home, and hearing about my adventures in the west had only fed his resentment. He was very ill during our entire visit, often unconscious, and when he died, there was no understanding between us. Then, soon after, we were asked to leave Germany, and we wandered a bit before I had the idea that if I stayed here, in the very inn where he and I had parted, I might obtain some sort of comfort."

"Instead," said Holmes, "you find yourself, not making peace with the shade of your brother as you'd hoped, but rather being visited by a stranger, an English woman dead for hundreds of years."

"It is not just me," said Siegen, with something of a whine creeping into his voice. "Gerda has seen her too."

"Gerda?"

"The nurse," snapped Mrs. Siegen. "She has mentioned something of the sort. But she is a simple-minded girl, and cannot be trusted."

"Nevertheless," said Holmes, "I shall want to speak to her. Is she available?"

"She is not," said the wife firmly. "She is with the baby."

"Ah. Perhaps tomorrow, then." He turned back toward Siegen, who was pouring yet more brandy into his glass. "Does the nurse's account agree with your own experience?"

Siegen nodded and took a drink, and his wife snapped, "It is foolish. I have seen nothing of this *geist*. Friedrich is hoping for a message from his brother, and instead his imagination creates some woman moving about his room."

"Is that what she does?" I asked. "Appear in your room and move around?"

"She does," answered the man. "Each night, my sleep is troubled. I fall asleep without incident, even when I try to stay awake, but I always become aware that she is there. I don't know the exact time that she appears or leaves. It is as if I am paralyzed, but I can see her, glowing, as she moves from here to there about the room, intent on something, but often pausing to turn her gaze toward me, frowning in disapproval. Eventually, I fall back to sleep, awakening in the morning exhausted, as if I've had no true rest."

"Then again I ask you: Why stay?" asked Holmes. "You've been here for several weeks now. You have been ignored by your brother's spirit the entire time, and yet you continue to place yourself in a situation that only disturbs you."

Siegen nodded. "You are right. I can only say that I feel that my business here is not yet finished, and if I must face this White Woman to do so, then so be it. But I would feel better if you could advise me, Mr. Holmes, and perhaps find a way to make her leave me alone so that I may rest."

Holmes shook his head, and I thought that he was going to refuse, but he said, "I'm not clear on what exactly that I can do, as I know nothing about exorcising spirits, but I will make some sort of effort, if only because

62

my friends the Kellers have requested it. However, I will need to do a bit of research, and the hour is late. May I call on you again in the morning?"

Siegen seemed to have a moment of emotion, possibly as he considered that night was approaching, and that he was facing another encounter with the inn's resident phantom. But he nodded, rising and lurching slightly from the quantities of alcohol that he had just consumed in such a short time. "Thank you, Mr. Holmes. Doctor. I believe that my stay here will conclude successfully soon, but in the meantime, I will hope that your intervention can make the remaining days more tolerable."

He turned to his wife. "It is as I've told you, Berta. Mr. Holmes can see things that others cannot. If anyone can get to the bottom of this, it is he."

Mrs. Siegen simply frowned and nodded at our wishes for a good night. We let them proceed us out of the office, and I was amused to notice Siegen reach out for his wife's hand. With a flick of her wrist, she swatted his fingers away before they could touch her, leaving him slumping as he shambled forward, attempting to retain his drunken balance. In a low voice, she began to berate him with a nearly continuous string of guttural billingsgate as they moved away from us.

We exited into the common room, now considerably emptier than it had been a half-hour earlier. In fact, Tom Keller was in the act of sending one last patron out the door and into the windy darkness. The Siegens also made their way to the front door, which opened onto a small vestibule. There, as was curiously the way in the construction of these old buildings, a separate doorway opened to the stairs leading up to the upper floor, wherein their rooms were located. We watched them open that door and begin to climb, the woman's complaints never ceasing. As the door to the common room shut, we turned to Keller, who was now standing behind the bar.

"Can you help them?" he asked.

"Possibly. I told them that we'd be back tomorrow morning."

At that moment, the wind rose afresh, throwing small pebbles against the front window. "Well, then," said Keller. "I won't hold you up. It promises to be a right night of it, or so the old fellows at the bar were saying before they scooted off home."

I nodded in his direction and moved toward the entryway, taking my coat from the hook as I did so. Pulling the door open, I looked back to see that Holmes had moved in the opposite direction, leaning toward Keller and saying something quick and quiet and short. With a puzzled look on his face that quickly turned canny, Keller nodded. Then Holmes joined me, grabbing his own coat and hat as we ducked our heads, stepping into the vestibule. The area was shallow, just a few square feet across, with the

63

doors to both the common room and the upstairs pressed close beside us. I started ask a question, but Holmes, in the act of adjusting his fore-and-aft cap, put a cautionary finger to his lips. Then he led me out onto the village green.

As we had perceived from inside, the wind had steadily risen, and dark clouds were moving with great speed across the sky toward us. In the distance I could see lightning. There was no thunder yet, as so far this was only some electrical disturbance in the high atmosphere. But I knew that it would arrive soon, along with the rains that undoubtedly follow.

"We should hurry," I said, "or we're going to be drenched."

"No need," said Holmes. "We want to stay here and see what happens."

I understood. "So you told Keller – "

" – to join us in five minutes."

"And your promise to return in the morning . . . ?"

"As you will have realized, old friend, that was simply a way to make sure that whatever has been happening on previous nights will also happen on this one. As soon as it is perceived that we will be taking a more focused interest in the matter, ostensibly in the morning, the conditions will change. I want to give the impression that there will be one more night wherein things can proceed as they have been doing before our further involvement skews the matter into a different direction.

"In science," he continued, leading me across the green toward the estate office, "sometimes the simple act of *observing* a reaction is enough to *affect* the reaction. For instance, measuring an electrical current with a voltage meter necessarily diverts some quantity of that current, no matter how minute, to power the measuring device, causing a slightly false reading of the true current. A thermometer must use some energy, thermal converted to kinetic, in order to move the mercury, again taking energy away from the thing being measured. Even checking the pressure in an automobile tire causes some air to be inadvertently released, resulting in a slightly inaccurate reading. Thus, the introduction of the two of us as variables into this situation will change the conditions of the experiment, and before that is expected to happen on the morrow, we need to allow it to play out tonight, as it has every night."

I was about to make a contrary and less-scientific statement about "*A watched pot never boils*" when the door to the inn opened, and Keller slipped out. He looked around, spotted us in the dim light, and walked across to where we stood in the shadows of the estate office. "It's going to be a raw night for sure," he said, handing each of us Mackintoshes that he had thoughtfully gathered. Although both Holmes and I were wearing

64

overcoats, for the day had been cool, we gratefully put on the waterproof coverings.

"I think that I understand the upstairs layout," said Holmes, gesturing back the hundred or so feet toward the inn. "There is, unfortunately, nowhere to hide within the hallway itself, or I would have suggested it. The steps leading up from the entryway there in the vestibule open at the top into the hallway, which then leads along the front of the building where behind those windows there. The rooms in question are each situated along the backside of the building. Do they also have windows?"

"Of course. They look down on the courtyard."

"Excellent. Then I'm afraid there is nothing to do but wait. I have a key to the estate office, and if the rains begin we'll certainly step inside, but for now we'll be able to see much better from out here. It shouldn't take long. Mr. Siegen is already quite inebriated, and will no doubt be asleep very soon."

"What do you expect to see?" asked Keller, glancing back and forth from the inn to Holmes.

"Why, your White Lady, of course. With the knowledge that our investigation begins in earnest tomorrow, things will have to intensify tonight. No doubt she will appear. Eyes sharp, now."

And in truth, it did not take very long at all before we saw signs of something in the hallway windows. On the left a light suddenly glowed, near where the stairs down to the outside door were located. "Ah," said Holmes. "She is confident enough that there is no need to put out her own bedroom light when she opens her door."

"Who?" asked Keller. "Mrs. Siegen?"

"Indeed. Watch."

It was hard to see, but there was some movement across the windows as the woman moved down the hallway from our left to right. "Mr. Siegen is in the last room?" asked Holmes.

"He is. Their rooms are separated by that of the nurse."

The light vanished to the right, apparently as the woman entered Siegen's room. After several moments where nothing happened, I was moved to ask, "What do we expect to see?"

"That, for whatever reason, Mr. Siegen's specter is really his wife, as just indicated by her visit to his room."

"Surely," I countered, "it isn't completely unusual for a wife to visit her husband's room – even such an unpleasant couple as the Siegens. Perhaps he is ill, and she is checking on him."

"I suppose so," replied Holmes, "But we must be certain. Keller, is there a ladder near the back courtyard, long enough to reach the first floor windows?"

"Mr. Holmes, I – " He swallowed whatever objection was about to be voiced and said, "Yes. In the open shed."

"Excellent. I shall return momentarily." And with that, he vanished into the ever-growing darkness, leaving Keller and me looking at one another with puzzled and somewhat uncomfortable expressions. It didn't surprise me that Holmes would leave no stone unturned, no fact unverified. In the meantime, I was aware that the wind was increasing, and the first hints of rain – those fine, almost non-existent drops that brush one's face or the back of one's hand and might only be imagined – seemed to be increasing.

We had stood there in silence for nearly five minutes, and I was considering leading us to a more sheltered location, when Holmes reappeared, a smile barely visible upon his face. "As I expected. Siegen is lying on the bed, still fully clothed, flat on his back and apparently passed out – no doubt helped down that path by whatever was slipped to him by his wife. You didn't see it? Well, you were facing the wrong direction. While he was turned to request yet another whisky at dinner, she passed a hand over his glass. I could just see something drop from it. At the time, it was none of my business. But now? It becomes amazingly relevant. As of just a few minutes ago, she is frantically searching his room. She must be looking at night for whatever it is that he has been seeking unsuccessfully during the day. What a pair! The promise of our involvement and interest has motivated her to try even harder than before."

"Wait," said Keller. "You're saying that she's been drugging him, and then going into his room at night to look for something hidden there?"

"Undoubtedly. Siegen probably learned of whatever it is that they seek from his dying brother, who must have hidden it there in that room twenty years ago when they first stayed at this inn. That's why he came back here now, and why he rented out the whole upstairs, and why he's been spending his days in his room. He's searching for something – and his wife also wants to find it – apparently without his knowledge. But time is slipping away from him – from both of them. And no doubt Mrs. Siegen has been drugging him with something of an evening to render him unconscious – thought not enough so that he is completely unaware of when she is moving about the room. His fogged mind has convinced him that what he sees, combined with the induced paralysis, is the result of the ghost that he has heard inhabits the place."

While Keller and I considered Holmes's conclusions, the storm began to arrive in its entirety. The lightning, so silent and distant earlier, was now nearly on top of us, along with the related thunder. The light raindrops had begun to solidify into larger pellets. Holmes glanced up and said, "We've let this go on long enough. I shall gather Mrs. Siegen, and we'll discuss the matter in the common room." And once again, as he had just a few minutes earlier, he vanished into the darkness.

At that moment, the storm broke in full force, and a flash of lightning revealed that Holmes had already covered the thirty yards or so to the inn door and was stepping into the vestibule, pulling open the door of the stairs leading to the upstairs rooms. Keller and I stayed put for a moment, reluctant to venture out of the protection of the estate office and into the now-driving rain. We saw the dark shadow of Holmes pass in front of the first floor hall windows, left to right, and then after a moment or so, return more slowly along the same path, now lit by Mrs. Siegen's lantern as he moved with a light-shaded bulk that could only be the lady in question. Seconds later, the hallway returned to darkness and the door at the bottom of the steps opened, revealing the two of them in the vestibule, pulling open the second door to the common room.

Realizing that it was time to join Holmes, I took a deep breath and prepared to spring through the rain, only to be stopped by Keller's oddly quiet voice. "There she is," he whispered flatly, pulling at my arm and pointing toward the inn.

I followed his gaze and saw her, standing in the window to far right, the side located near Siegen's room. She was tall and thin, nearly reaching the top of the window, and nothing like the dumpy silhouette of the woman who had just passed that way. There is no other way to describe it – she was illuminated somehow from within, not throwing any light of her own, but possessing light nonetheless. It was a cool glow, slightly greenish in cast but not unpleasant, and it seemed to pulsate with faint regularity, although that may have only been from the beating of my own heart, as my pulse was suddenly throbbing anxiously.

"The nurse," I whispered, my voice raspy. "It must be the nurse."

"No, it can't be," said Keller, an edge to his tone. "She's a tiny girl, no bigger than Katy. See how tall this woman is?" His grip tightened on my arm, and I realized that I hadn't noticed that he'd never let go from before. "She's there. It's her. *It's the Lady*. But I've never seen her so clear before."

And clear she was. Although a hundred feet separated us from that window and where we stood, I felt as if I could see the very expression upon her face. It was one of great beauty, and infinite sadness. The features were visible in that greenish glow, although they shouldn't have been at that distance. Her eyes were each a black abyss, framed in pain and wisdom, yet mysterious nonetheless. Even as I watched, she gestured, indicating in some way that gave me an instinctive understanding that I was needed. Yet, I was paralyzed, continuing to watch her while my feet remained locked to that patch of ground by the estate house doorway. Only

67

when she gestured again, this time sharper and with what almost looked like urgency and impatience, did I gain the impetus to break free and move.

"Come on!" I called to Keller, and set off running.

There was a blinding crack of lightning, and that, along with the sudden shock of the freezing rain instantly soaking through my clothing, left me gasping. I ran blindly, and as my vision cleared, I realized that I was already about half the distance to the inn. Looking up at the window, I saw that she was gone. That window was now as dark as the others along the same hallway, as if it had always been so.

Reaching the alcove, I wrenched open the door to the common room, seeing Holmes and Mrs. Siegen standing there facing one another, both with attitudes of tension. They turned their heads in my direction, and I summoned my breath to cry, "Holmes! Upstairs!" And then, letting that door swing shut, I opened the adjacent one and pounded up the steps, aware that Keller was right behind me.

Swinging around at the top, I ran along the hallway, sparing a glance as I passed the window where I had observed the woman, yet realizing without pause that there would now be nothing there to indicate her presence. I turned to the nearby door and was immediately joined by Keller. Thinking we would need a key, I reached for the knob, only to find it unlocked. I pushed open the door and entered.

The now nearly continuous lightning illuminated the room to reveal a low ceiling, crossed by ancient wooden beams, their bare unfinished appearance in contrast to the shadowed plaster bracketing them. Stepping closer to the bed in the center of the room, I perceived a foul smell hovering nearby, indicating that someone had been ill. And as there was only one person in the room, there was no question as to whom.

"Light a lantern," I snapped to Keller, moving toward the bed, where Siegen was lying on his back, as Holmes had described. I reached and turned his head toward the window, revealing the *vomitus* running alongside his mouth, down one cheek to puddle on the bed covering. Was it possible that he had aspirated it, too drunk or drugged to do otherwise? I was feeling his clammy forehead when simultaneously Keller lit the lamp and Holmes arrived.

"Mrs. Siegen?" I asked.

"She isn't going anywhere."

I could see that Siegen was in a bad way. His breath was quite shallow, and his eyes rolled up into his head. There was a distinct brandy-like odor wafting from his lips, along with a sour smell that could be anything from simple illness-related matter to poison.

"Keller," I snapped. "Black coffee. Not too hot – we have to get it into him as fast as possible. And find someone with an automobile."

68

"I have the remains of today's last pot beside the stove," said the innkeeper, moving toward the door. "And I'll wake up Clayton at the tobacconists across the way. He has a car."

"Have him go to Holmes's cottage. Bring my bag."

"Right."

"And send up Katy."

"I'll wake her."

After he left, Holmes helped me turn Siegen onto his side, instinctively understanding that the man was suffering from some likely combination of a narcotic and alcohol. "I don't believe that she intentionally poisoned him," I muttered as we effected respiration techniques. "This was likely an accident, spooked into using too much of what she's been giving him, combined with the increasingly large amounts of brandy and whisky that he consumed tonight. His respiration is dangerously suppressed."

"Agreed," said my friend. And then, "How did you know? To check him?"

I continued my efforts in silence for a moment before glancing up. "You won't believe me when I tell you."

In just a moment, Katy looked in, alerted by her father as he departed to seek an automobile. When she asked if there was anything that she could do, I sent her next door to check on the nurse, Gerda. Soon she reported that the girl was sleeping heavily and could not be awakened – "I pinched her!" – no doubt drugged, as had been Siegen, but she appeared to be in no danger.

Nearly half-an-hour was to pass before Keller finally returned, carrying my bag. I fished around for a stimulant, and used my stethoscope to verify what I'd already tried to hear without it – namely, whether the man's lungs were filled with any fluids from when he was ill while unconscious and on his back. They appeared to be clear, but I knew that he wasn't out of the woods yet.

It was touch-and-go for a while, but eventually he began to rally, and the stimulants brought him further around so that he could sit up and drink the cold coffee. Soon we had him up and walking, although he was not yet coherent at all.

When Siegen was somewhat better, I went next door and checked on the nurse, finding that the tiny figure was as Katy had indicated. Gerda might feel terrible in the morning, but for now she was in no danger.

I returned to Siegen's room to find that, in my absence, Anderson of the Sussex Constabulary had arrived, and that Holmes was apparently examining one of the low beams crisscrossing the ceiling with great satisfaction.

Even as I entered, he slipped something into his pocket, unseen by Anderson and Keller, who were both looking at Siegen, now slumped and groaning on the side of his bed, his hands on his head.

"Watson, you might give a short sketch of tonight's events to Anderson. In the meantime, I must tie up a few loose ends. I'll return with a full explanation shortly."

And with that, he slipped past us and out the door, leaving Anderson looking my way expectantly.

I pulled out my watch to discover that it was already approaching five in the morning. Where had that time gone? Glancing at Siegen, and not wanting to reveal too much in his presence, I nodded toward the hallway. Anderson joined me and, after pulling the door shut, I gave him a short *précis* of the night's happenings, from the time we were asked to meet with Siegen and his wife, to the observation of Berta Siegen going to her husband's room and Holmes's subsequent revelation of her nightly searches, followed by the discovery of Siegen's condition. Thankfully, Anderson didn't ask how I knew to check on the man, and I didn't volunteer it. "What are they looking for?" was his only question, and I had no answer for him.

We checked on Siegen one more time. He was still very sleepy, but as his condition had improved, letting him go back to bed now and sleep normally would only help his recovery, as he was out of danger. Downstairs, Keller and Katy had prepared coffee and an early breakfast, and we ate at one side of the common room, while Mrs. Siegen sat alone at the other. No one attempted to question her, or otherwise engage her in the least. At one point, she stood, indicating that she wished to check on her baby, but Katy quickly said that she would, and Mrs. Siegen could see that Anderson would accept no arguments otherwise.

It was nearly eight before Holmes returned. He bounded in, looking fresh and energetic as he crossed the room to the cold left-overs and made up a plate. Eating it quickly while standing, he watched us all with amusement, occasionally turning his gaze toward the glowering woman sitting by herself.

"Mr. Keller," he said, "would you and your daughter summon Mr. Siegen and the nurse? Thank you."

There was no conversation in the twenty minutes or so that we waited while the drugged individuals readied themselves. Eventually they entered, each looking befuddled and confused. They were led to seats near Mrs. Siegen, where they watched with puzzlement. Katy cuddled the baby, still sleeping, to her shoulder.

Turning to Mrs. Siegen, Holmes said, "Did you also drug the child?"

The woman looked startled. "No!" she said. "*Mein Gott*, no! She's always been a good baby, sleeping through the night."

"For your sake, I hope that's the truth." Then, "Mr. Siegen!"

His sharp tone focused the little man's attention. With a cough, he said, "Yes?"

"I want you to know that prevarication is useless. I have found the jewel. So far I believe you to be innocent. Now all I need from you is the truth."

"The . . . the jewel? What do you mean? I cannot think . . . ."

"The jewel that was stolen from Countess Brazelton in Bad Dürkheim in 1885. Your brother was a suspect, but there were others, so he was never seriously investigated. When you and he left the country at approximately the same time, it was considered suspicious, but when he returned alone a few months later, with no signs of increased wealth, it was finally decided that he was innocent, and the search focused elsewhere. The jewel has never been found."

At that point, he placed a thumb and forefinger in his waistcoat pocket, pulling out a sizeable emerald that winked in the morning light as he turned it this way and that. "Until now."

"The . . . the jewel," said Siegen, now more alert. "But . . . how did . . . how did you . . . ?"

"Yes, how?" snapped his wife, her harsh tone shocking us."

"It was inserted into one of the beams crossing the ceiling over the bed. Considering that your brother had been a carpenter, I assumed that whatever you were searching for would be cleverly concealed in some wooden object, but apparently that fact never crossed your minds. Or it did, but your imaginations were limited to articles of furniture, and you were unable to see the tell-tale marks that gave away the previous work when your brother opened a cavity in the beam.

"As for my deciding an object was concealed in the room in the first place? Last night, I considered why you were spending so much time in that room, in a place that you hadn't visited in twenty years. Your story of attempting to achieve a closeness with your deceased brother was, frankly, poppycock. I considered seven separate possibilities, but the most likely was that something was hidden there. But not by you, or you could have retrieved it on the first night. No, you didn't know where it was – thus, your continued stay, and willingness to reserve the rooms at double the rate to ensure that you would not be turned out. Clearly whatever you sought was worth more than whatever you were paying to keep the upstairs rooms free.

"You gave me the rest of the explanation when you explained that your brother, who had been here with you, had recently died. What else

71

could it be, but that *he* was the one who had hidden the item here on his earlier visit, failing to return over those long years, and had at the last told you where it was – but not *precisely* where."

Siegen nodded sadly. "When we left Kallstadt as boys, I didn't know that he had taken it. He had been in Bad Dürkheim, making a repair at the spa, and discovered that the jewel was left unsecured. He walked out with it, and though he realized that no one suspected him, he decided that it would be a good time to go to America, something that we had long discussed. Our grandmother gave us some money, and we decided to see the world along the way. Arriving in England, we traveled along the southern coast, intending to work our way to Bristol.

"But here in the inn, a random stop on our way to see some of the nearby white cliffs, Otto revealed the jewel to me, and how he had obtained it. I was appalled, and certain that we would be arrested immediately. By then, he also regretted taking it, but he was afraid to return it, and unwilling to completely abandon it. Unknown to me then, he hid it somewhere in our room, where he could sever his association with it, but find it again in years to come if he changed his mind. We continued to argue, and finally agreed to part ways.

"I proceeded to America, and gave only passing thoughts to the emerald over the next twenty years. Even when I visited Kallstadt a few years ago, and married Berta, Otto and I didn't discuss it – unwilling, I suppose, to open old wounds. But then I heard that he was sick, and Berta was missing the old country, so we went back again. This time, Otto wanted to tell me what had happened to the jewel, but the cancer had almost overwhelmed him at that point. He was only conscious long enough to relate that he'd hidden it in the old room upstairs, but was unable to share any other information.

"I should have let it go. But . . . but since selling out my business interests in the west and moving to New York, my finances have been . . . precarious. The possibility of getting the jewel became tempting. And . . . and I had told the story to Berta, and she was most anxious that we should find it."

His wife glowered by said nothing. However, Holmes addressed her.

"Mrs. Siegen. You gave the impression during our conversation last night that you were ready to leave for New York as soon as your husband could be convinced. And yet, you were actually as anxious as he to retrieve the jewel. Why argue to leave when you also wanted to stay?"

"Because," she snapped, "I knew that he would stay regardless of what I said. And I didn't want it to seem as if I was too interested in finding it."

"Because he might get suspicious at your interest, of course, if it was actually greater than his." She didn't answer, and he continued. "What were your plans if you found it?"

"Why, to sell it, of course. We can always use the money."

"Ah, but if it was to be used for the both of you, the 'we' to which you refer, then why did you feel the need to search in secret? Why not help your husband during his daytime searches? Why drug him at night, so that you could search on your own, if not to find it on your own, keeping the knowledge to yourself."

Siegen looked at his wife, shocked understanding crossing his features. "Berta?" he said, his voice small. "You . . . you drugged me?"

She stood up abruptly, her voice cutting like a whip. "Of course I drugged you, *dummkopf*! You, who were too stupid to take the jewel when you had the chance! You, who would have gone back home without trying to find it!"

"But . . . but I was trying to find it for us. Why would you try to keep it for yourself?"

"Why not? What have you ever done for me?"

"The house? The business? They were always for you."

"You spineless *kretin*! What kind of business do you have now? You had the chance to be a rich man and threw it away!"

"But I sold the . . . the club out west because I didn't want you to be embarrassed."

"You fool! That business would have made us rich! And now you won't even consider starting something similar in New York." She stood and rested her hands on her mid-section, where Siegen's unborn child rested. "This one, and Etta upstairs, are all that I need. If I could have found the jewel, I would have been able to leave you and find a real man!"

Siegen unexpectedly sobbed and lowered his head into his hands, while the rest of us looked on in mortified silence. He muttered something about the raging woman being "his life", to which she said, "Do you think that I don't know about the others? *Heuchler!* The lawyer's wife? Mrs. Allyn next door? *This one!*" And she flung out a hand toward Gerda, the nurse, who turned bright red before standing and fleeing from the room. Siegen made no reply.

"Mr. Siegen," said Holmes, his quiet voice cutting through the tension. "Your wife has been drugging you to search your room each night. Doubtless is it some opiate that didn't quite put you to sleep, but caused you to hallucinate that it was a ghost moving about your room, when in reality you were seeing her search. Last night, a combination of several things nearly resulted in your death: Your greater-than-normal drinking and her decision to use a higher dosage level, as her search had become more urgent, knowing that Dr. Watson and I would be investigating today, possibly finding some indication of her involvement, or even the jewel itself.

"I do not believe that she intended you any true harm . . . *this time. But I must warn you – this is a dangerous woman.* Should it suit her, and if she believes that she can accomplish it without consequences, *she will kill you.* Possibly not this year, or even this decade, but should the need arise, you will die, and likely in a way that seems natural and above suspicion."

He turned to the woman, who had sat back down and was hunched like a cornered beast. "After I had some idea of what had happened, I sent telegrams early this morning to Kallstadt. The wires sizzled between Germany and Eastbourne. Sorting through their records, they provided information that allowed me to narrow down what had likely happened twenty years ago, giving me a direction to search. But along the way, a great deal of information, madam, was sent this way about you too. It is their contention that you, as they say in America, are *a piece of work.*

"I will have my eye on you," he added. "And, as much as I dislike Mr. Siegen, he is now under my protection. Should something happen to him, I will know the reason why. Do you understand me?"

Of course, she made no acknowledgement. But I could see in her eyes, now stripped of all pretense, the dangerous animal lurking underneath, like some venomous lizard moving in and out of the light. So could Siegen, who was looking at her with raw fear.

"I can't tell you what to do, Mr. Siegen," concluded Holmes, "and I suspect that you'll return to New York with this woman. You are a weak man. But have a care, sir. Have a care!"

Of course, as the world now knows, Siegen did indeed come to a bad and unexpected end, and Holmes kept his promise, although things did not end quite as either of us expected.

I never saw the White Lady again – at least, not until last week, when I received an urgent message requesting my presence from Katy Hollander *née* Keller, still at the Tiger Inn, and fast approaching the date of her confinement. I was honored that she would contact me, in London, before even reaching out to Holmes. I rushed down to her aid . . . but that is another story.

Later in the afternoon following the recovery of the jewel, after the Siegens had been left in one another's custody and Holmes and I had returned to his villa, we found ourselves sitting in his study, discussing the recent events. My own questions had all been answered, and I sensed that we were circling closer to that matter which still puzzled him and of which I had yet to speak. Without making him ask, I explained.

"It was the White Lady," I sighed. "At least I suppose that it was. If I can make myself believe in such a thing." I went on to relate, as best I could, how she had become visible to both Keller and me from our vantage in the storm.

As expected, Holmes scoffed. "Nonsense," he said, lighting his pipe. "You somehow connected all of the alcohol that the man had been drinking with my report that his wife had drugged him, and you feared the results."

I shook my head. "It was Keller who drew my attention to her."

"Then it was the nurse," he said confidently.

"Not possible," I said. "She was also drugged."

"Perhaps she drugged herself after signaling to you from the window."

"Now why would she do that? And in any case, Mrs. Siegen has confirmed that she gave the opioid to the girl an hour or so earlier. There is no way that, at that dose, that she could have been up and walking by the window, let alone signaling for help. And soon after we found Siegen, Katy confirmed that the nurse was asleep."

"Katy, then," said Holmes, clutching at straws. "She was the one at the window."

"She said she wasn't, and you and I both know she wouldn't lie. The woman that Keller and I saw was too tall for Katy – and also for the nurse. And in any case, what business would Katy have had up there, in a hallway where you and Mrs. Siegen had just passed by seconds before?"

"Then it was a flash of lightning – your eyes were affected by the glare. Or a reflection on the wavy window glass."

This time I didn't answer at all, and Holmes fell silent. We both sipped our whisky. Then, to my great surprise, Holmes murmured, "When you have eliminated the impossible . . . ."

I lowered my glass. "Holmes! That is the last response that I would have expected from you."

"Good to know that I can still surprise you after all these years," he smiled. Then his smile failed. "How sad," he said.

"What?"

"If one admits the existence of a ghost – and do not mistake this conversation for such an admission on my part! – then why doesn't this nameless woman who spent her life serving others – a nurse or something like that, we're told – merit some sort of special dispensation for her soul, rather than being compelled to exist, year after year, century after century, in that place in-between, by whatever means that we do not understand – a phantom, prevented from going to her deserved rest? Is she somehow punished for having such a good and generous heart that she must remain to provide further help when needed, even across the generations?

"And yet, a creature such as Mrs. Siegen will barrel onward through her own misbegotten life, shedding misery around her in every direction, and no doubt poisoning the lives of her children and her children's children. Who can tell how far her evil influence will spread, and how much pain and suffering it will cause?

"Two women," he finished after a moment. "So different, and both with such very different fates."

I tried to think of some response. I knew that Holmes could occasionally find his way down these existential rabbit holes, and I was determined to prevent it. I took a deep breath, not knowing what to say, but trusting that I would think of something. But before I could begin, I heard the sound of a motorcar arriving. I raised my eyebrows.

"Just in time," said Holmes with a smile. "When I divined what might have happened to direct your attention to Siegen's bedroom – what you *think* might have happened – I took the liberty of inviting Peake down, in order for him to hear your story. He might have some valuable insight."

Soon our old friend had joined us, and it turned out that he did.

NOTE

It is claimed that The Tiger Inn in East Dean has been haunted by a figure known as *The White Lady* for several hundred years. Accounts vary as to her identity, with one possibility being that she was someone who was once employed by the family that owned both the village of East Dean and the surrounding estate. Another is that she was a nurse in a nearby hospital that was set up in the three buildings located immediately adjacent to the inn. At some point in the past, either during the Plague Years or the later Napoleonic Wars – accounts vary – her experiences were such that she has been unable to find any peace, even to the present time. The staff at The Tiger Inn reports slamming doors, falling pictures, and occasional appearances by the Lady.

In September 2013, I was able to make my first (of three so far) Holmes Pilgrimages, with a stop in East Dean to see the country around Holmes's retirement villa, nearby Hodcombe Farm. I stayed overnight in The Tiger Inn, having no idea at that time about the inn's connection with The White Lady. Coincidentally, I stayed in the same room that, from its description in this narrative, was used by Friedrich Siegen in 1905. During the night, I had one of the three (so far) supernatural occurrences that have happened to me in my life. I awakened from my sleep to find the room extremely cold, objects knocked to the floor, and flickering lights. I saw no shapes and heard no noises, but I felt that I wasn't alone. I wasn't scared, and after a few minutes, the incident ended, although I still felt as if I were being watched. Still, I eventually drifted back to sleep.

Sadly, I was too exhausted from my rambles over the Downs the day before to wake up further and investigate when the incident occurred. I did, however, mention the affair to the inn's owner and staff downstairs at the bar the next morning, asking them innocently if they had a ghost. They were strangely reticent, which puzzled me, as I would think they would be proud of their ghost. It was only later, after coming into possession of this Watsonian manuscript that it occurred to me to verify through further research whether The Tiger Inn is known to be haunted. Unsurprisingly, I learned that The White Lady has been a long-time resident of the inn.

I only wish I had known that before I stayed there. I might have been better prepared to pay more attention when she was carrying out her shenanigans . . . .

D.M.

The Coffee House Girl

In those early days in Baker Street, when my friendship with Sherlock Holmes was still relatively new, tolerating his eccentricities was always balanced by the belief that, once my health was recovered, I would be finding lodgings elsewhere, and those things, both large and small, that had vexed me would be relegated to the past – becoming amusing anecdotes for friends or family, and certainly fodder to my need to write, which had been with me as far back as my earliest memories.

On a particular morning in early 1882, I came downstairs to enter a sitting room that had been ill used, and certainly with no consideration by one lodger for the other. Even before I had opened the door, I had a fair idea of what to expect, as the fumes from my friend's latest chemical experiment had permeated the entire building.

"Holmes!" I coughed as I made my way vaguely in the direction of the windows. My eyes were stinging from the combination of some acrid smell that was bound up in a swirling fog of pipe smoke. Throwing up the sash resulted in a gasp from the icy outside air, reminding me of when my father and I had plunged into the sea when I was a boy. Yet the sudden shock was worth it, as the noxious vapors were soon pulled from the room. The thought crossed my mind that when I did find new lodgings, the memory of these would never be far away, as everything I owned would now be permeated with this smell.

"If the matter is that urgent," I told him while shivering, "I believe that the laboratory at Barts is open at all hours. Perhaps in future . . . ." There was no response.

"There is a reason," I continued, turning towards my friend, who was hunched on a stool, leaning over his deal chemical table and intensely observing the bubbling retort before him, "that real chemistry laboratories have ventilation systems. I'm sure that at some point in the past, after an employee or student was found dead beside an experiment, it was worth the extra effort to provide breathable air."

Holmes didn't move, but at least he spoke, which indicated that he was still among the living. "I suspect that Mrs. Hudson would not be agreeable to constructing the elaborate ductwork system that would be required."

The room now reasonably clear, I lowered the window, thinking that there were simpler ways to circulate air than what he suggested. Moving to build up the fire, and hoping that whatever fumes remained weren't volatile, I noticed by the mantel clock that it was later in the morning than I had thought. "Has Mrs. Hudson been up yet?"

"Hmm? Possibly." He moved then, making a note in the small journal that he kept to carefully record all steps and conclusions from his experiments, no matter how insignificant. Then, having transcribed the results of this particular olfactory offense, he leaned forward to shut off the Bunsen burner. "The bitumen in the samples scraped from Vicar Denis's bedroom floor show conclusive signs of Welsh origin. I believe that I have enough evidence to force a confession from Welwyn – if I don't spook him. We'll have to go carefully, and warn Gregson to do the same."

Only then did he spin to face me. His face looked weary, and I could see that he had been up all night. "I do have some sense that Mrs. Hudson opened the door earlier this morning," he said with a tired grin, "but then she immediately departed. At least," he added, rising and stretching, cat-like, before pivoting and settling in his armchair, "I assumed it to be her. A bit early for an assassin – or late, as they usually prefer to strike around midnight so as to get home to their well-earned rest."

I continued attending to the fire, considering whether to question his own personal knowledge of that assertion. However, before I could comment, he had risen again, his nervous energy preventing him from tarrying for too long. He went into his bedroom and shut the door.

I rang for breakfast, which wasn't long in coming. Mrs. Hudson opened the door rather cautiously, as if fearing that she might be overcome by billowing fumes. After ascertaining her safety, she entered and placed bacon and eggs on the table, wrinkling her nose in distaste.

It was a wonder to me how, in those early days, she didn't turn Holmes out into the street, and me along with him for simply being a passively complicit bystander.

For a number of years, I regularly pondered just why she let us stay. At times Holmes could be charming, but he countered that just as often with an impatience that could border on rudeness. Both of us were timely with our rents, even when we sometimes had to do without food or tobacco when Holmes's cases were few and far between, or when my own expenses exceeded my wound pension. However, Mrs. Hudson could have found countless other people who would also pay the rent on time – there was nothing special about the way that we simply met our required and agreed-upon obligations for shelter and meals.

It was only much later that I learned the truth from the lady herself, during a conversation that occurred during those bleak months of mid-1891, following Holmes's supposed death in Switzerland. I had stopped by to say hello, and talk had turned, as it must, to that most unique of individuals. She smiled, even while wiping away a tear, and explained that there were two reasons why we hadn't been turned out after the destructive incident when Jefferson Hope attempted to throw himself through our sitting room window following his capture in early March of '81. While Holmes often vexed her, Mrs. Hudson had explained, she had known him when he was a teen, some years before that last day of 1880 when a chance encounter between them had led to their reacquaintance and made him aware of her intention to rent the Baker Street rooms, providing an opportunity for him to move from his lodgings in Montague Street, if only he could find someone to go half on the rent. His mention of that fact the next day to our mutual acquaintance, Stamford, had resulted in my introduction to this most unusual fellow.

The other reason was that Mrs. Hudson was worried for *me*. She knew that my resources were limited and my health shattered, and that splitting the rent with Holmes gave me a chance to live in much better accommodations than I might otherwise have been able to obtain. And she also perceived quickly that my interest in Holmes's affairs, and then my participation in them, as rambunctious as they often were, did more to heal me in those months after my return from Afghanistan than anything else that might have come my way.

Not for the first or last time did I bless the good fortune that had led me to 221 Baker Street.

But on that icy morning in January 1882, with none of that knowledge in my head, I wondered again if I should not be seeking a different arrangement.

As the day progressed, I became more and more impatient. There was nothing in the newspapers. None of my books interested me. I didn't feel like writing. I would stand and wander to the window, or pause before my desk and see various sorted stacks of papers which awaited my attention. Then, without doing anything about it, I would return to my chair by the fire, aware that the day was slipping by.

When I was young, my brother and I called these spells "The Deadly Wanderings", wherein our toys and books, or distractions in other forms as we grew older, would suddenly hold no interest at all. Through the passing years, I came to understand that this temporary *ennui* would pass, and that the favorite things that meant nothing to me on a certain bleak day would again hold my interest on the next. Sadly, my brother never quite grasped this fact and, as he aged, he assuaged his boredom with certain destructive habits that darkened the rest of his attenuated life.

As I sat in my armchair, I considered Holmes, who had returned to his chemistry table sometime before noon, resuming his experiments but, thankfully, without generating the noxious fumes. I'd seen signs in him over the previous year of these same "deadly wanderings", but fortunately he seemed to work it out rather quickly for himself, either in the form of working on some new monograph, or research to gain a bit of finely focused knowledge to aid him in his profession, or when a new client would fortuitously seek his services. I was also aware that my own spells of boredom had also now been conditioned to dissipate when presented with one of Holmes's cases.

But there was nothing like that today, and I felt the walls of the sitting room closing in.

It was then that Holmes, without looking my way, said, "Why don't you adjourn to that coffee house you've favored over the last couple of months? You've been pacing like a caged tiger all morning."

My first response was to toss aside that suggestion, as it seemed as pointless and unfulfilling as anything else. But then I vaguely realized that the change of scene might do wonders. And I had come to enjoy visiting the shop upon occasion.

It took me a bit to work myself around to it, but I was eventually well-wrapped in hat, scarf, and coat, making my way down Baker Street, stopping not too far from Marylebone Road at a tidy building on the corner of the lane leading to the Portman Mansions, and so into East Street. In recent months, the building's ground floor had been refurbished into an atmospheric little coffee house, and one could smell the roasting beans for nearly a block in each direction.

I stepped inside and the old wooden floors creaked beneath me in welcome. I passed through a small alcove, as always never certain if the place would reveal itself to be empty or crowded. I always hoped for it to be quiet, but even on a busy day I enjoyed my visits.

Upon entering, I found it to be somewhere in the middle, with a number of tables occupied by my fellow Londoners in quiet conversation, some with coffee, and others with the more traditional tea. I saw that my favorite table was available, so I walked over and placed my hat upon it, as well as several of my journals, containing the records of a few of Holmes's recent cases that I planned to revise over coffee and pastries. I'd found that I was able to accomplish quite a bit while here, in spite of the buzz of conversation and the movement of patrons, as sometimes attempting to do the same thing at home led me to recall too many other necessary distractions that got in the way of completing my tasks.

Now considered something of a regular patron, I followed the prescribed routine and stepped to the counter, where I ordered a small cinnamon-filled cake and received a large empty mug. Following the appropriate exchange of coin, I shifted a few steps to my left, where several urns of coffee stood upon the counter, each roasted and brewed to various degrees of strength. Filling my mug with a moderate blend, I carried my comestible back to my table, arranged items to my satisfaction, and lost myself in my notes.

At some point in my labors, I realized that my unsettled mood had passed, as I knew it would. I was fortunate to understand that this would happen, without falling into a greater malaise. I'd just returned from refilling my mug when I became aware of someone approaching my table, taking a direct and unmistakable path toward me, rather than that of someone simply weaving his way to the urns.

Looking up, I saw that it was Jennie, the manager and daughter of the owner. She was in her mid-twenties, and had always greeted me with a twinkle in her eye. I cannot say that it went unnoticed. Though still recovering from my wounds of nearly eighteen months before, I was in my twenties then too, although I had thought more and more of my approaching thirtieth birthday, now just months away instead of years. Though still unsure as to what my greater future held, I was certain that marriage would be a part of it. And while I had no such intentions toward Miss Jennie Gains, I was a young man that was always open to possibilities.

"Excuse me, Doctor," she interrupted, a slight lilt of a Derbyshire accent in her speech. "I don't mean to bother you, but might I have a word?"

I stood and nodded toward the opposite chair at my small table for two. She smiled and I stepped forward, pulling out the chair for her. She then sat and then placed her own mug of coffee before her, while I returned to my own seat.

"I see that you enjoy your own wares," I said, nodding toward her cup. "I know of certain cooks who can no longer abide those things that they produce."

She shook her head. "I have to be careful," she replied, "or I'll be drinking it all day long. That happened when we first opened the shop. I fairly had the shakes every afternoon, and then I couldn't sleep, until I was able to limit myself." She leaned a bit closer, her voice lowering a tad. "I'm sorry to bother you, especially when I can see that you're busy." She cast her eyes toward my journals.

"Not at all," I said, pushing them aside and closing the ink. "How may I help you?"

She smiled, and a dimple appeared in her left cheek. I noticed for the first time that, with the light behind her just so, her hair – which might tend to curliness if not worn so long and kept wound in a fashionable manner – had most unusual rosy highlights. After just a second or two of hesitation, she continued. "I understand that you're friends with Mr. Sherlock Holmes, the detective-man from up the street."

82

I nodded. "We share rooms." I cleared my throat and added, "I've been fortunate enough to assist him on several of his cases."

"Oh, that's fine, then," she said. "I wanted to tell you about something that has happened, and see if you thought that he might have any advice."

"Certainly," I replied, a bit disappointed that my own experience wouldn't be sufficient.

She took a sip and related her story. "You probably didn't know, but we've – that is my father and I – have had several businesses here before the coffee house. There was a small used furniture store, with some storage upstairs. That's what it was for most of the years when I was small. Then, in the mid-seventies, my father tried to make a go of it with a shoe repair business. He'd found some of the necessary machinery for sale and purchased the lot of it. I think that he was tired of the furniture. He didn't know what he was doing at first, but he was always clever, and he learned quickly. But then, last year he had his stroke, and I didn't know what we were going to do.

"We've always had some money put aside. I believe that my father inherited it before I was born, and he's always been careful with it. That was how he bought the lease on this building, when I was very small, not long after my mother died. After his stroke, he couldn't work, and I thought about hiring someone to carry on with the shoe business, but I longed for something else – maybe I was as unhappy with shoes as my father had been with furniture. In any case, the father of one of my friends' owns a coffee house in Bloomsbury, and he gave me some advice. He was very gracious and never seemed to worry about me setting myself up in competition, as we're located quite a distance away. I sold the shoe equipment, as well as all of the stock, and with what I made from that, along with using our savings, which were quite a bit more than I had believed, I remodeled the building into the coffee house. Additionally, we import and roast our own coffee beans upstairs. In the months since we opened, we've been doing quite well.

She leaned closer and became even quieter. "I don't tell anyone, Doctor, but I actually run everything." Her lovely face had a glow of pride, mixed with sadness. "I still have to give the impression that father is making the final decisions, because the idea of a woman managing a business would be shocking to many, and there are people with whom I have dealings who wouldn't hesitate to cheat me otherwise. I make a show of consulting with father, but truth be told, he isn't any help. He can't be any longer."

I nodded, and realized that I wasn't particularly surprised. I had often seen her father in the shop – he was there that day, as a matter of fact – carefully placed in a comfortable chair in a back corner near the fireplace.

Once I happened to pass nearby when the two of them were there and the old man was coughing. I had offered my services as a doctor, but Jennie had smiled and politely declined, indicating that she had the matter in hand. It had been the start of our very limited acquaintance.

Nearly every time that I'd been there, her father was located in his spot, an elderly and enfeebled wreck of a man, slumped down and collapsed upon himself, and seemingly disconnected with his surroundings. And yet, I recalled any number of instances when Jennie had gone over and whispered to him, seemingly having some sort of conversation. While the man gave no indications of making any responses, she would nod as if receiving an answer before giving him a kiss and then returning to her place behind the counter. Now I understood that it was all theatre.

"I had no idea," I said. "I've seen you speak with him on numerous occasions."

"All mummery," she said, rather matter-of-factly. "I don't know if he's there or not. But when a question arises that seems to require more than my own authority, I make a show of asking him before providing my own decision.

"The business has been doing well," she continued. "We're making a profit. I'm in the process of hiring a new cook, and there will soon be more food on the menu. Father and I lived in some of the upstairs rooms for years, but after his stroke, we've moved down to this floor, through that door over there. Because there is only so much space here on this floor for the public, I'm considering opening up the additional rooms upstairs. Things seem to be going well – and yet, recently things have taken an unusual turn.

"It started late last year, just a month or so ago, really, when one of the walls in the cellar collapsed. It's in one of the rooms at the very front of the building. Like most of them here, it extends a bit under the pavement and out beneath the street. We don't have an areaway in front, so there are no windows down there and the cellar is quite dark. My father always claimed that there had been some structural damage back to when they installed the Underground, and that it still causes problems, but the station and the lines are a block away, so I'm not sure why he believed that. I just know that for as long as I can remember, he would periodically inspect the cellar, looking for problems.

"I'd pretty much ignored this as an eccentricity, but just before Christmas, I happened to be down there for another reason, and decided to take a look around. I was more than a little surprised to see that the brickwork under the street had crumbled, and that a void had opened up. Afraid that the pavement above would collapse and that I'd be somehow liable, I summoned a building contractor that we know. He said that it didn't seem to be a problem, as long as it was repaired quickly. The opening under the street was only a cubic foot or two, or so he told me after measuring it, and he packed it with bricks and cement. Then, he set about repairing the cellar wall. I was down there watching as they were clearing away the old rubble, and I noticed that he tossed something odd into the canvas bag they were using to carry the waste up to the street. It didn't quite look like a brick, and I stepped forward to ask about it. He seemed surprised, but I reached past him into the bag, pulling out a small metal box, not much larger than a brick. It was made of a heavy gray metal, and had a little lock through its hasp.

"This builder, who I've known since I was a child, seemed a bit perturbed, and said that he didn't realize in his hurry to clear the rubble that he'd picked up something other than a brick. I theorized that it must have been buried in the wall, and he agreed. And then he reached out to take it from me! I stepped back, clutching it and looking at him with surprise. For a long moment, we simply stood there, no words spoken, and for the first time in my life I was a little afraid of him. He's long been a friend to my father, and that was why I had called upon him to begin with. Now, I felt as if I'd never seen him before. He was quite terrifying in that moment, his eyes wide and his nostrils flaring as if he were a bull about to charge.

"I'm not sure what might have happened next, but I turned and dashed up the steps. Without stopping in the shop, I went up to the next floor, to the roastery, and looked for a place to hide the box. No one was around just then, so I was able to place it behind a piece of the baseboard along one wall which I knew to be loose. The box just fit between the lower part of the wall and the flooring, and when the baseboard was replaced, no one could tell anything at all. Then I went downstairs to the shop and resumed my duties.

"Later, my father's friend, Mr. Chesham, came upstairs and told me that the work was finished. He acted as if nothing had occurred, but there was still a tension between us. When he asked if I'd like to accompany him downstairs to inspect the repairs, I declined, telling him that I was busy and would check it later. That seemed to irritate him, but what could he do? With a scowl toward my poor father, he turned and left.

"Of course, my curiosity got the better of me, and even though I tried to put it off, it wasn't long before I'd climbed back upstairs, retrieved the box, and gave it a closer look. It was apparently made of iron, quite smooth, and well fashioned. Of course, I had no key, and no skills to open a lock. I retrieved a tool from the roastery and began to pry at it. The old lock gave way before the hasp did, and soon I had it open. Inside, curiously, was a single sheet of paper. It was in my father's handwriting, and signed by him. All that it said was, '*I owe you*' and his name, '*Will Gains*'.

"What was there about this box that had made Mr. Chesham try to sneak it out with the rubble – for I have no doubt that is what he intended to do. Did he think there was something else in there – or at least did he hope for something valuable, as I had? If so, he would have been as disappointed as I was. And why had my father taken the trouble to hide it down there in that odd place? I was greatly saddened that I couldn't ask him what it all meant. It was probably his work in digging out a spot behind the cellar wall that led to the weakness there that resulted in the collapse.

"Convinced that it would forever remain a curiosity, I re-hid the box behind the roastery baseboard and went back downstairs, wondering often about the curious paper and why it was worth that much trouble.

"I should mention that, ever since the shop has been open, we've been fortunate enough to be supported quite well by my father's old friends. There is Mr. Chesham, of course, and Mr. D'Abitot, who sells wine from his shop in Bingham Place, near the cripples' home. Mr. Brent sells knitted goods from Scotland in the Bazaar, and Mr. Stadhampton works as a clerk for one of the banks. They've all been like second fathers to me, and offered more good advice than I could have ever expected when I decided to open the business. They stop in frequently, sitting with my father and keeping him company, in spite of the fact that he likely doesn't know that they're here. One of them – Don't look! – is with him now. Mr. D'Abitot usually comes by in the middle of the day

"After Mr. Chesham found the box, things changed. Each of them still comes by, but their behaviors have changed – or at least it seems that way to me. They seem more guarded, and they talk with me in clipped tones and with narrowed eyes. Mr. Chesham has only been in once, and even though neither of us spoke of the matter in the cellar, it's clearly something that isn't forgotten.

"Then, last week, I came back from an errand, and as I entered from the front door, I looked over and saw Mr. Stadhampton stepping into the shop through the doorway to our apartment in the rear, pulling the door closed behind him. He was acting in a most suspicious manner. He didn't see me, and he returned to a seat near my father, where Mr. Brent was waiting. There were two cups of coffee on the table, one for each. I can assure you that Mr. Stadhampton had no business being in our rooms.

"After that, I became more careful, and I've seen subsequent signs that there have been intruders, as if our things were searched. Although I trust my employees, there are none that I can ask to help keep watch without some sort of explanation – it would simply start too much gossip, and I sense that this affair, whatever it is, should be kept quiet.

"Last night, after the shop was closed and father was in bed, I had put out the light and retired to my own room. However, I couldn't fall asleep – the curse of working in a coffee house where my own product is too tempting! – and I simply lay awake for quite a while. It was then that I heard footsteps – slow and careful – moving across the roastery in the floor above my bedroom!

"I am not a fearful woman, Doctor. My father didn't raise me that way, and starting and running a business has made me bolder than many. But I assure you that the sound of that intruder, passing just a dozen feet above my head, paralyzed me with terror. How had this person entered the shop? What was he looking for? And did it somehow relate to the mysterious iron box that was revealed several weeks ago? Somehow it seems that it must be connected, for only when it was found had my father's friends begun to act so suspiciously.

"After a while the sounds stopped – whoever it was had left. Later, I found the courage to go upstairs and check. The box and the note were still hidden where I had left them. I didn't know what to do, and then," she smiled, "it seemed as if fate has brought you here today.

"I'd thought of making the trek up Baker Street to visit with Mr. Holmes, but perhaps you can intercede for me, and see if my story suggests anything to him. It is said the he sees light where others only perceive darkness. My friend, Alice Cumnor, still recalls a time five years or more back when Mr. Holmes visited their house at the invitation of her father and located a painting hidden in plain sight, as well as pointing the finger of guilt at her own uncle as he attempted to defraud the family of a much-needed heirloom. Would you be willing to repeat for him all that I have told you?"

Of course I was willing, and I earnestly assured her of that fact. She laid a warm hand on the back of my own, and my heart beat a bit faster as she looked into my eyes and thanked me. I looked for the dimple, but it had vanished with the concerns of her tale. Then, removing her hand, she pushed back her chair, lifted her cup, and walked behind the counter.

I looked at my own coffee, now grown cold while I had listened to her strange tale. It was a small series of happenings, and yet, in her world, it was proportioned to fill the horizon. How could I not offer to help in any way possible?

I considered rising right then and asking if I might examine the scene of these matters myself, but then I recalled that one of the men in question, her father's friend Mr. D'Abitot, was currently in the room, and I decided that it wouldn't do to seem too curious. I turned in my seat and leaned down, untying and then retying my shoe, allowing me to see across to the fireplace where Jennie's father slumped in his chair. Beside him was a small, dark man of approximately the same age, sipping coffee and reading a newspaper. At any other time, I would have disregarded him as simply another face in the background of any other day, but now I saw him with a new perspective: One of a suspicious group who had some common secret, the existence of which had led to them causing fear in the heart of this admirable girl. Watching him, sitting there unaware of my interest, made me feel as if I were an agent on a vital mission, or a knight on a quest.

Then I realized that there was nothing that I could accomplish at that moment. I therefore sat upright and pulled my journals back to the center of the table. Opening the first, I began to read through, making notes and corrections as needed, but I found that my interest simply wasn't engaged any longer. Instead, I puzzled over the strange box and its meaningless message, and what could have brought about the sudden change in the behavior of these old family friends. It crossed my mind that Jennie might well be imagining it, but I quickly dismissed that notion. She didn't seem that type of woman at all, and to even those thoughts felt like some sort of betrayal of our new alliance. She had asked me for help – although it was really a request for me to obtain the help of someone better qualified – and as such I had to be her advocate, and not her doubter.

After a few minutes, I found that I could focus on my journals as planned, and I had several more productive hours as I recalled matters that I'd felt merited memorialization. Some had been quite serious, such as the terrorizing of Lucius Kintner at Old Radford, while others had drifted toward being quite ludicrous. Here I refer to the Prancing Minister of Dunchurch, and his unique marriage proposal to the Old Widow Ditton, and the singular misunderstanding that had provided him with a ducking in his rival's pond.

Recalling that affair, and how Holmes had held his tongue for so long before revealing the truth, forcing the minister to blurt out his true feelings, left me in a much better mood than when I had arrived. When I reached that point where I instinctively knew that it was time to go, I gathered my various materials, nodded toward Jennie, and walked toward the door. Along the way, I saw that D'Abitot had departed during the time my memories had been turned towards Dunchurch. Now her father, old Will Gains, was left sitting alone. Who knew what he could have told his daughter, if only he'd been given one more chance?

Stepping outside was like launching one's self into icy water. With a gasp, I pulled my coat tighter and faced toward home. Within moments, I had briskly covered the distance and entered and closed our front door behind me. Mrs. Hudson heard my arrival and came from her domain in the back, informing me that Holmes had departed an hour or so before without saying when he would return. I thanked her and, in spite of the prodigious amounts of coffee consumed during my time down the street, agreed when she offered to bring up tea. The pure taste of it, I felt, would cleanse my palate from the bitterness that currently washed over me, seeming to smoke from my very pores. Anyone who drinks coffee to their limit will understand.

Upstairs, I returned my journals to their proper place and then made myself more comfortable, with no intention of vacating the premises again that day. Mrs. Hudson soon arrived with the tea, and as I settled in my chair before the fire, I felt that all was right with the world. The Deadly Wanderings of the morning had been vanquished, as they always were. Reaching for and finding my place in the sea novel that was currently holding my attention, I settled back with a sigh and began to read.

I have no memory of emptying my tea cup or setting aside the book and falling asleep. Upon waking, my first thought was surprise that I had been able to do so, especially after consuming so much caffeine. However, it must be recalled that, even in those days, I was still recovering from my injuries, and I tired rather more easily than might be expected.

Not long after, Holmes came in, removing his Inverness and fore-and-aft cap. Hanging them behind the door, he rubbed his hands briskly and informed me that Welwyn had confessed with an almost grateful urgency as he attempted to free himself of the guilt which was consuming him. I was still rather sleepy, and knew that I'd need to question Holmes about the specific details later, should he be in a mood to relay them.

In fact, after dinner I was able to obtain how he had seen his way to a solution – a narrative which I will record elsewhere. It was only when he was finished with that narrative that I remembered to share with him Jennie Gains's tale from earlier in the day. As I spoke, he progressed from casual interest to a much more intense curiosity, leaning forward with his elbows upon his knees, sometimes waving his fingers as if to make me tell it faster. Then, something he heard seemed to please him, because the tension released, and he leaned back with a smile before immediately rocking forward again to stand while I was finishing my thought. He walked around me to the shelf holding his commonplace books, pulled one loose, and returned to his chair. Opening it carefully across his knees, he turned sheets until he found what he sought. Then he sat back and explained.

"You've heard me lecture the Yarders upon the history of crime?"

"Indeed. You've often commented on the fact that you are generally able, by the help of your knowledge of the history of crime, to set them straight."

"It is a valuable tool towards earning my bread and cheese. My researches started early, as I recognized the importance of identifying criminological patterns. During those bleak stretches when I first set myself up in practice, and clients were few and far between, I made good use of my time researching the old cases – both solved and otherwise. And one such was what the newspapers called 'The Duntisbourne Jewel Theft'."

"I've never heard of it."

"I would be surprised if you had. It occurred in 1858, and more accurately it took place in Perrott's Brook, rather than in nearby Duntisbourne proper. You may read the account here – " He tapped the page before him. " – but in short, a box of jewels – an iron box, mind you! – was stolen from a manor house, the hidden accumulated treasure of the manor's owner. Five of the servants were suspected, but nothing was ever proven. The jewels were never recovered, and the five men were sacked, disappearing into the fog of history. Or so I thought, until today. Here, read this."

He passed me the awkward book, with clippings threatening to spill to the floor and pages heavy with pasted news articles pulling loose from the feeble binding. Adjusting it toward the gaslight, I saw that the five listed servants of one Dr. Edward Benton all had very familiar names: Will Gains, of the stables; Arthur Chesham, the handyman; Richard D'Abitot, the butler; Jonathan Brent, the valet; and Clark Stadhampton, Benton's private secretary.

The case was quite simple: The jewels, kept in an iron box poorly secreted in Dr. Benton's bedroom, had been found missing. The eccentric doctor had summoned what passed for the law in those times and had accused his entire staff, including several of the maids, whose names were not listed. When the jewels weren't found, despite searches of the staff's possessions, they were all turned out. A final clipping showed that less than a week later, Dr. Benton had died naturally, succumbing to a wasting illness.

"In my youthful research," said Holmes, "the matter was interesting, but hardly instructive. No solution was ever discovered. I corresponded for a bit with a local vicar, presenting a few sincere questions, and he was quite willing to reply, but he had nothing useful to add. He told me that all of the accused had long since departed from the area, and that old Dr. Benton, who was eccentric in the best light and probably mad in an accurate light, had died without any heirs, and that his small estate had

90

been finagled and quickly absorbed by the locals in a most shocking manner, with the land being taken by a wealthy neighbor through passage of a special ordinance. And so the matter ended . . . until today, when you bring me a tale that effectively shackles all of these men together once again by their presence at another common location, and the reappearance of an iron box that holds their apparent fascination. But for this girl's story to you, as brought to me, it's unlikely that this connection would have ever been noticed."

I closed the book and sat back. "So . . . so Will Gains had the jewels, then, all this time? And the others knew of it, and now their interest has been aroused. That's what is implied by the iron box hidden in his cellar, with a note written in his own fist. But what of the note? '*I owe you.*' What does he owe? And to whom?"

"Why, surely that is clear. He owes the jewels – or at least an equivalent payment. And who to but the other men, his cohorts in the crime, all of whom shared in the original theft, and have since found London jobs and residences and lives near one another, staying in touch through the intervening years. It doesn't sound as if there was any animosity during that time. Your coffee house girl spoke of the men as being 'second fathers' to her, and there is no sign that they weren't her father's close friends throughout."

"She is not my 'coffee house girl'," I informed him. "Is she in danger?"

"I think not. If she considers them to be second fathers, then they certainly see her reciprocally as a daughter. It was only when the box was found that Chesham seems to have shown an unexpected covetous side. He has obviously spoken to the others, and they have since started to display this sudden grimness and suspicion. They don't know that the box is empty, save for the note. They only know that the jewels have been brought to light, and with Will Gains effectively out of the picture, their interest in their share has apparently been awakened."

"What shall we do?" I said. "The jewels must be gone. Will Gains was keeping them, but he's instead left a note of debt in their place." I stood up. "Should we arrange to hide in the coffee house, tonight perhaps, and give these men another chance to break in and be caught red-handed?" I took a step forward. "I can pop down the street and notify Jennie – that is to say, Miss Gains – of our intentions."

Holmes smiled and waved me back to my seat. "No need, Watson. I believe that I shall ask a few questions here and there on the morrow, and perhaps borrow that box from your Miss Gains. Then we shall have a little gathering here and settle this matter."

I nodded and walked to the shelf, returning the book to its place. It was curiously labeled "*L*", which as nearly as I could tell, had nothing whatsoever to do with the names of any of the principals or locations involved with the missing jewels. I doubted that I, or anyone, would ever understand Holmes's curious filing system.

The following morning proved to be possibly colder than before. I had awakened to discover one of those days when an unseasonable plunge in the temperatures had combined with a thick fog, making it quite unpleasant to step outside. The freezing mist had coated every surface – building and tree and pavement – with a thin rime of ice that resembled fairy tracery. As I dressed, I looked from my bedroom window at the bare yard behind our house to where the ice had limned the branches of the plane tree, delicately illuminated by light from the windows of the adjacent buildings. There was no sign of the sun.

Downstairs, I called for breakfast, observing that Holmes was already curled in his chair, seemingly fascinated with some textbook. I spoke a greeting but received no response. When Mrs. Hudson carried in my rashers and eggs, we exchanged glances of understanding.

Within the hour, Holmes had set aside his book, risen abruptly, and vanished into his bedroom. He soon returned, *sans* dressing gown, and fully dressed for the outside world. He confirmed that I would be at home in the early afternoon, and then he departed, wrapped well to face the bitter temperatures.

All morning and well past lunchtime, I fiddled with this or that distraction, but curiosity as to Holmes's actions, as well as what he might be arranging in connection to the matter of the Duntisbourne jewels, kept me from doing anything constructive. Several times I considered walking down to the corner at Portman Mansions in order to report on what Holmes had revealed to me the previous night, but I sensibly remained inside, knowing that I might cause whatever edifice he was constructing to fall apart by some inadvertent action on my part.

It was mid-afternoon when the doorbell rang, and after some murmured conversation downstairs, I heard light footsteps seemingly dancing up the stairs. In seconds the door was thrown open to reveal a rather effete fellow, accompanied by a much burlier youth, carrying a basket and a large flat box. "Mr. Holmes?" asked the first, and then ignoring the shake of my head, he snapped, "Fortnum and Mason." Then he and his assistant quickly and efficiently laid out upon the dining table a pheasant, a couple of brace of cold woodcock, what turned out to be *pâté de foie gras*, and a couple of tidy bottles of a respectable vintage. I became aware that Mrs. Hudson was standing in the door, watching with a mixture of amusement and skepticism, as displayed by a tolerant smile and two vertical lines between her brows. Without further explanation, the two men departed, leaving me to ask the reason for this surprising intrusion.

"I don't have the faintest," said our landlady. Then, with a muttered comment concerning hope and the expense of such victuals when the rent was due soon, she departed, while I tried and failed to find the words to explain that Holmes had recently received a very handsome reward for the recovery of Lady Drake's missing maid and the tiara she had taken with her.

Not long after, Holmes returned, noting with satisfaction the various items upon the table. Then, humming to himself and ignoring my requests for an explanation, he began to drag chairs around, making up something of a semi-circle before the fireplace. Counting the seats, I realized his intention. "You have invited the four old friends of Mr. Gains."

"Excellent, Watson."

I nodded toward the deliveries from Fortnum and Mason's. "This doesn't seem to be planned as an unpleasant afternoon of accusations and denials."

"Indeed. I have a proposal for them, and there is no reason for it to be contentious."

As he stood, seemingly satisfied with the room's arrangement, the doorbell rang again, and soon four men were shown into the sitting room.

D'Abitot, whom I had seen the day before, led the way. His past position as the butler of old Dr. Benton's household apparently still made him the *de facto* leader. He was a smaller man than the figures that followed, but he looked around, almost belligerently, as if he were a terrier seeking something to shake to death.

Behind him was a big individual whom I would learn was Chesham, the building contractor. It was easily deduced by his clothing, which was more worn than that of his compatriots. Next was Brent, a dark and solid fellow whose face, by inadvertent construction, seemed always to be smiling with a secret. His profession as a salesman of Scottish knitted goods was belied by rather colorful wool coat. At the rear was Stadhampton, the bank clerk, a thin faded chap who would disappear into the background if one wasn't careful.

D'Abitot glanced my way but then turned his attention to Holmes. "We're here," he snapped, obviously advancing with the idea that an immediate aggressive stance would place them on a better footing. "You have no leverage, sir. The events to which you referred in your invitation were long ago, and never proven. Still, we felt that it would be better to discuss it with you and nip this business in the bud now, rather than let you start asking questions where you shouldn't."

93

"Peace, Mr. D'Abitot," replied Holmes with raised hands and a smile. "Please find seats, and I'll tell you what I know for certain and what I've concluded. Then perhaps you'll find that there isn't as much need to worry as you might have believed. "

They looked at one another and then seemed to come to a common agreement, for they moved into the circle of chairs and the settee and arranged themselves. Holmes introduced me, and let me know the names of the four men. D'Abitot glanced my way, Chesham and Stadhampton nodded, and Brent flicked an indifferent glance my way before again focusing on Holmes.

"I had to be somewhat mysterious when issuing my invitation," explained Holmes. "How else to convince you to join us?" He nodded my way. "It was Watson who brought the matter to my attention, following a conversation with Miss Gains yesterday at the coffee house."

D'Abitot nodded. "I saw her speaking with you." He frowned. "We try to keep an eye on Jennie."

"In case she happened to reveal the existence of the iron box to a stranger?" I asked, rather more hotly than I'd intended.

The wine merchant was taken aback. Suddenly he seemed less angry, and more like a rather weary middle-aged man. "Why . . . why no. Simply to make sure that she's safe. Since her father's illness, she's done quite well, and demonstrated an impressive amount of strength and ability. And yet, each of us makes sure to regularly stop in and verify that all is well."

Holmes nodded. "That's what my own little researches have concluded. Miss Gains stated to Watson that the four of you are like second fathers. It's difficult to believe that you would suddenly reverse that position and pose a threat to her. While it is possible that any one of you might harbor greedy thoughts regarding the contents of the iron box, together you serve to check one another. However, Mr. Chesham – " Here he turned his attention to the contractor. " – you caused a bit of a fright the day that you reacted at seeing the iron box revealed in the cellar. As did whomever it was among you that got into the building the other night to search the premises for the box's hiding place."

Brent cast his eyes down. "That was me. Will had given me a key long ago, and I used it to look around, hoping to discover where Jennie had hidden the box when she removed it from the cellar. I thought that I was being quiet, but I suppose something gave me away."

"She was in the room below," I explained, "and heard your footsteps. I gather that she was quite terrified." Perhaps this was putting it on a little thick, but I wanted this man to feel ashamed.

"Be that as it may," said Holmes, again taking control of the conversation, "we are here to put that behind us. I have a general sense of

94

the events at Perrott's Brook nearly a quarter-of-a-century past. Several years ago, in my studies of the history of crime, I became aware of the unsolved jewel theft, and corresponded with Vicar Dill. I was happy to learn that he is still among the living, and a wire to him this morning confirmed my hypothesis – specifically that your employer, Dr. Benton, was a rather cruel and unpleasant individual while he slid through dementia toward death. In fact, he refused to help treat Mr. Gains's wife, who was the housekeeper, during her long and eventual fatal illness – making life rather more difficult for that family than it needed to be. I suspect that this led to a feeling of ill will, at best, toward him during his final days."

They men looked at one another, and then nodded in unison.

"You don't have to confirm anything, of course," said Holmes, "but I suspect that my understanding of events hews close to the truth. Knowing that Dr. Benton was not long for this world, and that he had no heirs, and also likely realizing that the local community in that remote area had already made plans to absorb his estate by whatever means – legal or otherwise – you probably saw no harm in taking his box of jewels, little realizing that he might rally long enough to discover that they were gone and thus summon the authorities. But fortunately, he chose to simply dismiss you *en masse*, allowing you to depart unhindered to new lives. You gravitated to London, where your shares were used to establish yourselves in new professions."

D'Abitot cleared his throat and decided to acknowledge Holmes's assumptions. "True enough, for the most part. But we didn't split the jewels equally and separate as strangers, never to see one another again. We were all good friends, like brothers really, and have remained so. Will convinced us that after the jewels went missing we might be watched, perhaps for a long time, and that it would be best if we kept our true names, lived innocent lives, and made use of the funds realized from the jewels gradually, rather than each suddenly spending an unlikely amount and making a fast leap to a substantially higher station. Thus, only a few jewels at a time were carefully sold and the profits divided. The rest were kept hidden by Will, to be divided gradually as the years passed."

"I helped with the banking side of things," explained Stadhampton.

"And I used my own skills to make improvements and expansions at our homes and businesses, as needed," added Chesham. "By paying me for repairs, I was able to charge what they were really worth, and it helped keep the money in the family, so to speak."

"But then," Holmes said, "Mr. Gains had a stroke, and you all realized that he'd neglected to tell you exactly where he hid the remaining jewels."

They nodded, and D'Abitot said, "It's a measure of the trust that we had with one another that we never needed to know."

"I never meant to frighten Jennie," added Chesham. "I recognized the box as soon as I saw it in the rubble. I tried to slip it out with the broken bricks, so that we wouldn't have to explain to her what it was or where it came from, but she saw it. I'm afraid that my surprised reaction scared her."

"It did," I explained. "She felt that all of you acted differently toward her after that."

They had the good grace to lower their heads. Then Holmes continued.

"I fear that your trust in Will Gains may have been misplaced after all. I stopped to see Miss Gains this morning, and she gave me this." He reached into his waistcoat pocket, pulling out a folded sheet. "It is what she found in the box – not jewels, but rather a simple note in her father's handwriting: '*I owe you.*' I expect that you understand his meaning." He handed it to D'Abitot.

The other's half-rose, leaning over to see before returning to their seats. Brent still had the half-smile on his face, which would likely be there if he were angry rather than pleased. Stadhampton had no expression, a skill likely learned in his position as a bank clerk. Chesham was surprisingly indifferent, while D'Abitot only shook his head. "Poor Will," was his unexpected comment.

"Indeed?" responded Holmes, who was clearly as unprepared for this reaction as I was.

D'Abitot looked over at him with a sad expression on his face. "You may not know that our friend Will had several unlucky occurrences in his life. He was the only one of us to marry, and then she died. When we set up in London, we all found – if not riches, then at least security – in our new lives, but he continued to struggle. Oh, he was able to obtain the lease on the building, but whichever venture he tried there never seemed to find its footing. His most recent – the shoe business – likely did much worse than he let on. I can only imagine how desperate he must have felt to have violated our trust and used the last remaining jewel for himself. And for Jenny."

"The last jewel?" I asked. "They had all been sold over the years?"

Stadhampton nodded. "There were never that many. Dr. Benton had greatly exaggerated the amount when he reported the theft, and how could we disagree with him? We only converted a few at a time every few years to supplement our incomes, and when we last met to make a 'withdrawal' two years ago, there were only three left. We determined that selling two of them would meet our needs, and that the last one – the finest of the lot

– should remain in the box. There was some mention of a tontine arrangement, wherein the last survivor would have it, but nothing was formalized – and how could it be? In the end, the box was closed with the final stone – a ruby – still inside. Poor Will," He said, shaking his head. "He must have been feeling quite pressed to have been forced to take from his friends in that way. I wish that he had come to us. It must have shaken him terribly to use the jewel."

The others seemed to share this sentiment, and I was impressed at how this band of men had stayed linked together during the intervening years, willing to think the best of their friend who had been forced to breach their agreement and trust.

"It seems," said Holmes, "that there was still enough left for Miss Gains to renovate the building into a coffee house. Some of these funds must have been paid to you, Mr. Chesham, for your labors."

"It's true," said the contractor. "She said that she realized a profit from selling the shoes and equipment, but I should have realized that paying me, along with buying the coffee roasting equipment, probably took more money than she would have rightfully had. The rest must have come from Will's account, where the proceeds of the last jewel rested."

"And further," said Holmes, "you have all benefitted from the arrangement in other ways. You have had a place to go, keeping your friendship alive in yet another way, and additionally your support has allowed a young woman who thinks of you all as second fathers to find both success and a firm footing."

"You're right," said D'Abitot. "None of us have families, other than each other really, and Jennie is truly like a daughter to all of us."

"Then she should know it and be certain of it," said Holmes, "rather than feeling unsettled, and now even a bit fearful towards all of you. Which is why," he said, glancing at the clock upon the mantel, "I've invited her to join us, so that you can explain the old bond shared between all of you and her father – and I trust let her know that his '*I owe you*' should be considered paid in full."

In a most timely fashion, the doorbell rang.

"That will be Miss Gains," noted Holmes. "Shall I instruct our landlady to let her in?"

D'Abitot said in a rueful tone, belied by his smiling face, "You don't give us much choice, Mr. Holmes."

"It's best that the truth be known," said Holmes, rising from his armchair. "I've researched each of you in the short time since I learned of this affair, and I learned that you are all honest, respected, and honorable. You have led good and useful lives, and now you can do some good in another way. You and Miss Gains have much to discuss. I'm certain that,

97

with the now open assistance of all four of you, the coffee house will became even more successful than it already is, ensuring that your informal daughter will be quite secure."

And such was the case. Jennie entered the sitting room to find the six of us standing in greeting. She seemed nonplussed, although she explained that Holmes had informed her beforehand that she was invited to discuss his findings related to the iron box in her cellar. As the history behind it was revealed, and then elaborated upon, Jennie went through a variety of emotions before finally succumbing to joyful tears, revealing in a quavering voice how much more difficult the preceding months had been than she had ever dared to let on, with her father's illness and the uneasiness of operating a business that each day might suddenly veer into failure, despite every effort and indication otherwise. Gradually we made our way across the room to the table and its fare, filling plates and glasses, and letting the little family – which is what they were – become known to each other in an entirely new way.

With the enthusiastic support of the four men, the coffee house went from success to success, and in the years since, it has become hard to recall when it wasn't in business at that corner. Jennie's father died not long after that little party in our sitting room, but she confided in me sometime afterwards that she was certain her father somehow knew that she was well cared-for, and that he had turned loose of life without any worries left.

I continued to go there for a few of those early years, finding it a convenient haven when an escape from our quarters for this or that reason became a necessity. I was intrigued by Jennie, still occasionally referred to by Holmes as my "coffee house girl", but nothing ever came of it. Within a year or two, she had been introduced to some fellow that was an acquaintance of Brett – a tall, dark, and rather gangly chap that didn't seem as if he would be her type at all – and they eventually married. I eventually frequented the place less and less as my own interests turned elsewhere, and as I instead spent more time involved with Holmes's investigations, along with visits to my club, and then later at my own hearth with my wife. But I never yet walk down the street in front of Jennie's coffee shop without thinking of that space in the cellar stretching out under the pavement, wherein the iron box of jewels was hidden, and wondering how many other similar treasures are scattered around, unknown and just underneath one's feet.

The Affair of the Regressive Man

Part I: A Short Series of Deaths Rooted in the Past

Sherlock Holmes's investigations were never as limited in real life as those presented in my published versions, wherein the beginning and middle lead to a resolved ending. Instead, we would occasionally hear more of former clients, sometimes arriving on our doorstep with a new problem, or presenting some aspect of continuation to their original investigation.

The matter which I will now recount seemed to be routine when it occurred – if a matter of murders can ever be called that. And yet, there was a loose end that led to a most unusual epilogue, and possibly the strangest story that was ever narrated to us in our Baker Street rooms. It resulted in our remaining awareness of this case even to the present, and while I consider it to be the merest moonshine, I would be remiss if I didn't make some record of it, although it will rest in my dispatch box like so many others, as one of those for which the world is not yet prepared.

The audience laughed, as did I, at the antics of the commanding figure upon the stage. The play was clearly a success, with the promise of a long run, and I was glad that we'd received tickets – however mysteriously that they had been sent to us. Once again the audience reacted with great amusement as the lead actor, in his role as Petruchio, twisted the ears of Grumio, his manservant. Clearly this interpretation of *The Taming of the Shrew* was intended to emphasize physical humor in addition to the clever plot.

As the business continued on stage, to the immense pleasure of those around me, I glanced toward my left to see that my friend, Sherlock Holmes, was not sharing the same sentiment as those surrounding him. I wondered if he, with his great knowledge and experience with the works of The Bard, had some objection to the presentation, or if he was still vexed by the manner in which we found ourselves at the Lyceum that night.

That afternoon we'd received a sealed envelope, delivered by a messenger that we knew slightly from a previous matter. It simply had our names written on the front, with no other information provided, and contained two tickets to that evening's performance. It was quite puzzling,

I knew, but I felt fortunate, as this was the most popular event in town at present. While I understood that it was possible that we were being lured to the theatre for some sinister purpose, I also felt that we had simply been gifted with the tickets by a former grateful client who wished to remain anonymous.

Holmes had been intrigued as well, and any suspicion that there might be an ulterior motive was simply one more reason for him to elect to attend. And yet, now that we were here and the play had begun, I saw that he wasn't going to allow himself to simply enjoy the performance. Rather, he was even more alert and watchful than usual.

That evening, as we were conveyed by hansom from our Baker Street rooms to the theatre in Wellington Street, his lips had been pursed, and I had initially taken it for simply a peevish mood. "They are billing this as the three-hundredth anniversary of the play," he'd said, in a rather irritated tone, "but there is no evidence that it was actually written as early as 1888. It's much more likely to have been initially performed in the early 1590's."

"Leave it to Irving to discover an unusual aspect that will sell tickets," I said, rather feebly, not knowing how else to respond. "There's talk of him receiving a knighthood, you know." When this elicited no response, I tried a different tack. "The reviews have been tremendous. This actor playing Petruchio – Myrddin, I think is his name. Sounds Welsh. – has seemingly appeared out of nowhere, and they say that he *becomes* the part – an amazing skill for one so young. And Jenny Sheridan, who plays Katherina, brings an amazing reputation with her back to England from all those years spent in America." I faded away for good, as I saw that Holmes wasn't listening.

Now, as I considered this, I wondered if I had let myself sink into the performance just a bit too easily. Perhaps, like Holmes, I should watch and enjoy, but observe a bit as well.

On stage, there was a long bit of dialogue between Hortensio, Grumio, and Gremio, while Petruchio stood a step or two away. I noticed that his attention seemed to be elsewhere, as if he were listening to another conversation instead of the one directly before him, which should be claiming his full attention. I found it rather distracting, and wondered if this was a choice that he had made as a performer. If so, I decided that it was a poor one from an actor who had been so fulsomely praised by the critics.

Just in that short time my mind had wandered, I had lost the rhythm of the actors' quickly paced lines, and leaned forward a bit, listening more intently, trying to find my way back. Grumio was saying, "O this learning, what a thing it is!" when I heard a woman scream.

We all heard it, as a matter of fact. It was muffled but shrill, and came from somewhere backstage. It was unmistakable, and the actor speaking seemed to physically stumble for a second as his voice lowered and then paused. Then he tried to resume his lines, but stopped again after only a few words. A couple of people in the audience twittered nervously from different parts of the house, for the scream had been so unexpected, and so very real. I knew that nothing like this was written into the play, but many productions chose to add unusual aspects to make their version different. Perhaps the Shrew was meant to be heard screaming off-stage. But no – this was clearly unplanned, as the actors suddenly lost character and appeared to be nonplussed.

I looked from right to left, noting the confusion on a number of faces in the audience. Holmes was sitting forward on his seat, as was I, his expression like that of a hound about to be released for the hunt.

The curtains at the right side of the stage billowed and moved, in that curious way that they do when someone behind them is trying to find his or her way onto the stage and cannot locate the correct space. Then a middle-aged woman – decidedly in modern dress and not representing sixteenth-century Verona – stepped out and peered toward the audience, her eyes nearly squint shut. "A doctor," she said, her voice low and hopeless. "Is there a doctor?"

At that point, Petruchio – or rather, the actor playing him – took a step forward and seemed to look directly toward me. "Dr. Watson," he called in a commanding voice, to my great surprise. And then, "Mr. Holmes. You are both needed. Please come backstage."

Without a second thought, Holmes was on his feet. Since he would have to pass by me to reach the aisle, I stood as well, although my thoughts were still vainly trying to catch up with the events that were unfolding. Together, he and I approached the stage and, finding the entryway to the right, went up the short set of steps and into that mysterious and decidedly unromantic area that is the backstage of a theatre.

After the brightly lit stage, supposedly representing a sunny plaza in Verona, the darkness behind it required a moment of adjustment. I had been backstage before at many theatres over the years, sometimes as part of Holmes's investigations, and other times on my own business, so I wasn't surprised, either by the shabby spaces filled with props, the hanging flats and myriad ropes running up into the darkness, or the smell of slightly unwashed bodies and makeup suddenly clustered around us, mixing with the general odor of the building – a cellar-like smell, augmented with the scents of canvas, paint, and freshly cut wood.

We were caught up short by the crowd of people, and as my eyes adjusted, I could see that they were various cast and crew members who had apparently been standing in the wings, watching the performance. To my left the bright lights of the stage were visible, with the four actors and the woman standing there, peering in our direction. Even as I looked that way, I saw the great curtain beginning to swing shut, cutting off the audience's view. Turning back toward the dark recesses of the theatre, I was aware that the mutterings of the seated crowd became more muted when the curtain closed.

A tall man stepped forward and the crowd of actors and stage hands parted around him. Gesturing us forward, he said, "I'm Grimley, the stage manager. Are you the police?"

Holmes shook his head. "I am Sherlock Holmes, and this is my associate, Dr. Watson. We were called forward from the stage by one of the actors – "

"I've heard of you," the man interrupted. He was tall and thin, with thick wild eyebrows combed upwards across his forehead. He was blessed or cursed with unusually broad and prominent cheekbones. He had an excessive amount of Macassar oil on his head, laying his hair straight back and giving him a rather Mephistopheleseian appearance. "This way."

Holmes glanced at me with a curiously amused expression. I knew what he was thinking – how quickly life could turn.

We were led deeper into the building, to the row of dressing rooms. One with a star affixed crookedly on the door had a large stagehand standing in front. Grimley waved him aside and threw open the door.

From the wafting smell of perfume that rolled our way, it was easy to determine that this was a woman's room. That was confirmed by the view through the door of various gowns and related accoutrements and appurtenances tossed about – on the backs of chairs, on stands, and on the floor. However, all of this was of no significance when compared to the body of the woman slumped in a chair before a dressing table.

After knowing Sherlock Holmes for so many years, and having been involved in the examination of so many scenes of violence – both in association with my friend's investigations, as well as sometimes doing occasional work for Scotland Yard as a part-time police surgeon – I was well aware of the importance of causing no disturbance to any of the evidence. And yet, my oath as a physician required that I step forward to ascertain whether any signs of life could be coaxed from the poor woman's body. I stepped carefully into the room, aware that my movements could obliterate some fingerprint or speck of ash that might provide Holmes with the solution to the mystery. But I had no choice.

I leaned over the woman, but it was immediately clear that she was beyond my aid. There was no pulse and the pupils of her open eyes were fixed and dilated with that flat sheen on their surface that only manifests

102

itself for the dead. Her skin was cool, and clearly the scarf knotted around her neck was so tight that the end had come quickly.

She had been beautiful once, but the bloom, as they say, was rather off the rose. Up close, it was easy to see that Jenny Sheridan – and it was certainly her, the famous actress who had traveled from England to America as a girl, finding fame and fortune, only to now return in triumph to the long-abandoned land of her birth before encountering a violent death – had known that her beauty was fading. Her hair was just a little too black, and her make-up – even for the stage – was a trace too thick.

I moved back with a shake of my head, and Holmes carefully shifted forward. He seemed to waste very little time on the corpse, other than to look closely at her face, hands, and clothing. He did examine the knotted handkerchief at her throat, and made a soft exclamation at something he discovered in her tightly curled right hand. Then he turned his attention to the floors and strewn items around her.

I don't know how much time passed, but surely not a great deal. It seemed almost immediate that there was a rustle of shifting bodies outside the dressing room, and then the door was filled with our old friend, Inspector Bradstreet. It was no surprise to see him, as he was normally located just a few blocks north at the Bow Street Police Station.

Holmes straightened at that moment, a look of disgust on his face. "Bah! Too many people in and out, all of them but the killer having legitimate business, most likely. There's no easy way to determine who the murderer might have been." He glanced toward the newcomer. "Good to see you again, Inspector. I thought that you'd have been around to Baker Street by now regarding that Haverley business."

"Planned to at the first of the week, Mr. Holmes."

"Let me save you a trip. Confront the groom about the house in Cavenagh Street – specifically the mews. Don't act as if you don't know – let him believe that you already have the whole story."

Bradstreet nodded. "That makes sense. I know just how to handle it." He stepped forward. "What's this, then? Is that Jenny Sheridan? I was here for a performance not a week ago."

"It is indeed. She's returned from America to meet a bad end." He looked toward the door. "Do you have any help?"

"I do," nodded Bradstreet. "Knowing that it's a theatre job, I brought a full passel of constables, and Inspector Jones is on hand as well. He's with the audience, making a list of names and finding out what they saw or heard, and if anything was strange on that side of the footlights."

"An excellent task for him," smiled Holmes.

At that time, March 1888, it was still several months before I would formally meet Inspector Athelney Jones, so Bradstreet's grin at Holmes's comment held no significance for me.

Bradstreet nodded. "What do we know?" he asked.

"Not much. During the early part of the performance, there was a scream. Then a woman came on stage and asked for a doctor. Watson and I were summoned – by name – by the leading actor. We hadn't been here long when you arrived."

Bradstreet took a moment to examine the body before turning back our way. "I suppose we should question the primaries – although at this point we won't learn a lot, I fear."

Holmes nodded and walked to the door. He opened it, calling, "Mr. Grimley? Come in here."

The stage manager appeared, entered, and shut the door behind him as directed. In the brighter light of the room, he seemed less intimidating and more nervous than in the mysterious shadows behind the stage.

Holmes introduced him to the inspector and then said, "Who discovered the body?"

"Her dresser, Mrs. Wick," was the reply. There was a nervous tremor in his voice. "Jenny – that is, Miss Sheridan . . . ." His eyes cut toward the dead woman – for the first time since he'd entered, I noted. He swallowed noticeably and said "Miss Sheridan was due for her first scene soon."

Holmes frowned. "To your knowledge, did anyone have a reason to kill her?"

"None at all. She's been a delight since her arrival." His words were belied by his tone, which implied that she had been anything but pleasant.

Bradstreet caught it as well. "No need to refrain from speaking ill of the dead," he said. "What did you really think?"

Grimley blew out a breath and seemed to collapse a bit. "She was every bit the shrew that she portrayed on stage. Demanding. Critical. Impatient. Arrogant. Hateful to the others. I regretted that she was chosen for the part, but my advice was ignored."

"You are allowed a vote on such matters, then?" asked Holmes. "Very democratic of Mr. Irving." He looked around. "Where is he, by the way? And his business manager, Mr. Stoker?"

"I am not allowed a vote," said Grimley with a frown, "and they are both out of town. Neither likes to be away, and never at the same time, but they are meeting with a new playwright in York who refuses to travel." He lowered his voice. "I'll never hear the end of this."

It seemed that Bradstreet might have had a few more questions, but Holmes interrupted. "That will be all for now, Mr. Grimley," he said. "If you'll send in Mrs. Wicks."

"Certainly," said the tall man, giving a second and final glance to the dead woman. Then, without further comment, he stepped outside.

"You have an idea, Mr. Holmes?" asked the inspector.

"Nothing definite," he replied. "The room is a mess, but I believe that the dresser, Mrs. Wick, will confirm that to be the normal state of affairs. There is nothing that can be determined from footprints on the floor – too many people have been in and out of here, as would be expected in a leading lady's dressing room."

"No footprints left by Persian slippers of two different sizes this time, eh?" grinned the policeman.

"Sadly, no," replied Holmes with a smile. "Sometimes we aren't that lucky. There is something to be determined however, from the scarf that is tied around her throat, and more importantly, from what she has curled in her left hand."

I hadn't noticed anything there, but reminded myself that I had been more interested in seeking any remaining signs of life. Bradstreet stepped forward and leaned down, reaching to uncurl her fingers. Clutched there was bright golden button.

Bradstreet lifted it to the light, turning it this way and that before handing it to me. It was oversized, constructed from some sort of gilded metal, and looked rather cheap. The stylized figure of a Paladin was stamped into it. I returned it to Bradstreet, and he tucked it into his waistcoat pocket.

Holmes spoke. "The button is from a costume. More about that in a bit. The handkerchief is tied in a common knot, pulled tight while she struggled, and then knotted after when she was still. There is something additionally sinister about the emotion that would cause someone to tie off the scarf when the deed was done, rather than simply carry it away. Please take note of the color."

While Bradstreet and I did so – seeing a dull and vaguely familiar plum hue – there was a knock, and then a constable opened the door to allow a small woman to pass him. She was the same who had fumbled so when trying to get through the stage curtain to announce that a doctor was needed. From my seat in the audience, she'd seemed shaken and distraught, but now she was quite composed, her mouth fixed in a tight scowl that ran along deeply grooved lines, surely set in place by that expression over many unhappy years.

"Mrs. Wick," said Holmes, stepping forward, using a sympathetic tone. "We're so sorry for the loss." When necessary, he could be the most polite of men, especially to women. It often worked to calm them, or gain their confidence – but this one was having none of it.

"It means nothing to me," she snapped. "I knew when I met her that she'd come to a bad end. Never satisfied with anything. Always complaining. Always trying to set one person against another, just to keep something stirred up."

I was torn between surprise at her speaking of the dead in such candid terms, especially in the very presence of the recently deceased, and a bit of admiration that she was apparently completely willing to express her mind.

Her accent was of a decided Liverpudlian cast, and I asked, "You are obviously British. Did you know Miss Sheridan previously in America?"

Mrs. Wick shook her head. "Not at all. I was hired two weeks ago, when she arrived here and began rehearsals. Her American dresser had refused to come with her – no surprise, I'm sure."

"Having known her for a fortnight," Holmes interjected, "you seem to have formed a strong opinion."

"Indeed I have. She wasn't ever happy unless there was some kind of trouble going on. Insulting the costumes. Complaining about the food. Turning the men against one another."

"Really," said Holmes with a conspiratorial smile. "How so?"

That seemed to be the key to unlocking her confidences. "She flirted with all of them – from Grimley to Myrddin, to Mr. Irving himself. Of course *he* had no part of it, being smart enough to see through her type, and she realized that she was wasting her time. But she seemed to enjoy teasing Mr. Grimley, who was very interested in her, with all the time she spent with young Mr. Myrddin – and her more than twice his age!"

"And how did Misters Grimley and Myrddin take that?"

"Grimley was angry at first," she replied. "I often saw him watching the two of them from darkness as they would leave together. But about a week ago, she threw over Myrddin and began dropping crumbs to Grimley again. He's followed her like a dog since then – but oh he hated her for it!"

"And what did Mr. Myrddin do when he was supplanted?"

Mrs. Wick looked confused, and Holmes amended his question. "When he was replaced by Mr. Grimley?"

"Truthfully, he didn't seem to care one way or the other – which bothered *her* more than she wanted to let on." And she nodded toward the body.

"Do you have any idea who could have done this?" asked Bradstreet, cutting to the bottom line, like the steadfast policeman he was.

"Not at all," the woman snapped, her willingness to gossip slamming shut.

"You were the one who found her?"

106

"I was. It was time to make sure she was ready for her first entrance."

"You screamed," stated Holmes.

"I did." She said it rather defiantly, as if admitting a weakness. "It's not what one expects to find, is it?"

"Why didn't you find someone backstage to ask for help?" I asked. "Why come out front onto the stage?"

She seemed a bit puzzled. Then, "I knew this lot. There's no one back here who could help. I thought that she might still be alive."

Bradstreet then asked, "Did you see anyone else nearby when you went into her dressing room? Or right after you came out?"

She shook her head. "They were all crowded up front, watching the stage. There's a lot of funny business worked into the part where Petruchio first arrives, and they all like to stand there and watch it. And I suppose a lot of the girls want a look at Corvidien – he takes off his shirt then, you see."

I raised an eyebrow. Clearly the modern interpretation of Shakespeare was different than it used to be.

"Did you see any strangers backstage?"

"Not a one."

At the mention of strangers, Holmes interrupted. "The man at the stage door would know if anyone was here that didn't belong. What is his name?"

"Amos," she said. And then, "He's a drunk. He can't tell you anything."

Holmes nodded toward the door. "Thank you, Mrs. Wick. Would you please have the constable summon Amos?"

She nodded and then took a single step toward the dead woman. She stood for ten or fifteen seconds, just looking, before making an impatient noise like one hears from the lips of a cab horse forced to stand too long in one place. She opened the door and stepped outside.

"Could she have done it?" I asked when the door shut. "She had a reason to be in and out of the dressing room. After the murder, she could have screamed to divert attention, knowing that someone could walk in at any second."

Holmes shook his head. "I doubt it. She's too small to have held the scarf tight enough to kill. If there had been a wound on the head, perhaps, to knock the victim unconscious first, I might have entertained the notion, but as it is . . . ."

"Do you have any ideas yet, Mr. Holmes?" interrupted the inspector.

Holmes shook his head. "These are early days, Bradstreet. But I suspect that before it's over, we'll need to know more about Miss Sheridan."

107

The door opened to reveal Grimley once again, now leading in a shabby old man in worn but clean clothes. He looked as if he would have been tall sometime in his past, but he was now bent and downtrodden. There was a distinct smell of alcohol about him. His hair was shaggy, and he kept his gaze toward the floor as the stage manager stopped him before us.

"This is Amos Lee," he said. "He sits at the stage door." He glanced at the man beside him with distaste. "Mr. Stoker hired him. I thought that I should come along – in case I can help answer any of your questions."

I was uncertain as to why, until the old man lifted his head, revealing a tracheostomy centered at his throat where his Adam's Apple would have been. I had seen a few such patients in my career, left with an opening to breathe when their larynxes had been removed due to various types of cancer. I was surprised that Amos left his uncovered, as most patients chose to mask the open hole to their trachea with a small cloth affixed to their collar.

I glanced to one side, where Holmes looked upon the man's neck with scientific interest, while Bradstreet tried not to look at all.

"Amos, is it?" asked Holmes. The man nodded. "How long have you worked here?"

He held up two fingers, and Grimley translated. "Two months." He sniffed. "He is apparently some sort of veteran with a background in the theatre, and he had a letter of reference for Mr. Stoker. I don't know what it said."

"Very good," replied Holmes. "Did you have any dealings with Miss Sheridan?"

The old man shook his head vigorously. I realized that he'd never once looked toward the body.

"And did you see any strangers backstage tonight?"

Again he shook his head, but not with such intensity.

"If I may," interrupted Grimley. "Amos sits by the back door, but his duties are minimal." He gave a look of frank disgust toward the man beside him. "He . . . falls asleep, you see, and is sometimes derelict in carrying out his responsibilities. Mr. Stoker has been informed about this – " Again he turned toward Amos, to see if his words were having any effect. " – but so far to no avail. Therefore, I've taken to keeping the stage door keys with me, and locking the door during the performances. We've had a problem backstage with petty thefts, you understand, and I don't trust that Amos is the man to make secure the premises."

"You lock the door?" asked Bradstreet, turning his head. "Isn't that a bit dangerous in case there's a fire?"

I knew what he was thinking. He had been with us at the tragic burning of Exeter's Theatre Royal the year before, when scenery, ignited by a gas burner, led to the death of nearly two-hundred people. Holmes, Bradstreet, and I had been there on other business when the fire broke out, and it was only chance that had placed us near the scene. Without Holmes's extreme bravery, leading the panicked people in the theatre to safety through the smoky darkness, and Bradstreet's great strength in prying open the stage door from the outside, the death toll could have been much higher. The true story, involving the facts that Holmes uncovered afterwards, may never be known, but their actions there that night should be.

"Sir," replied Grimley, affronted at Bradstreet's reaction. "We don't discuss that word here. It's bad luck. And in any case, if such a thing *were* to happen, then I would simply make my way to the stage door and unlock it. And that," he added, "will continue to be the procedure until we have a more responsible doorman."

Throughout this castigation, Amos simply stared at the floor without comment. Holmes had been looking at him, certainly cataloging countless details, but I saw nothing more than a broken old man.

"Amos," said Holmes. The old fellow looked up at the sharp tone. "You've let this man speak about you and for you. Do you have any knowledge of the lady's murder?"

Amos did a curious thing. He seemed to be swallowing, his throat working and his mouth open. I had seen this before from others who'd had the same surgery. By literally swallowing air, these people were able to *belch* words. Bradstreet's eyes widened when Amos rattled an emphatic and frog-like, "No!"

With nothing further to apparently be said, Holmes nodded and waved a hand toward the door. Grimley led the old man out.

Bradstreet shook his head. "What to do, gentlemen? There must be hundreds of people out there – "

"Oh, many more than that," interrupted Holmes.

Bradstreet rolled his eyes. "One way or the other, it's too many. Jones may spot something, but we'll likely have to question each and every one, and still we might not turn over the right leaf."

"But lest you forget, Bradstreet," said Holmes with a smile, "we have yet to meet one of the primary players in our little drama – the owner of the button and the handkerchief."

The inspector smiled grimly and said, "Let's do that, then." Holmes stepped to the door, opened it, and said something quietly. In a moment, a constable appeared in the door, ushering in the leading actor, Myrddin. The officer then backed out and pulled the door shut.

He was even taller and more broad than he'd appeared on stage. He was quite handsome, and had a most commanding presence for one so young. He was in his mid-twenties, although his eyes seemed older, as if he had seen much that had given him some sort of additional wisdom. Unlike Grimley, who had only looked twice with discomfort toward the dead woman, Myrddin stared frankly at the corpse with no signs of squeamishness. Rather, his expression seemed markedly sad.

However, in spite of the young man's confidence, what was noticeable to both Bradstreet and myself was the fact that his costume contained several pieces that perfectly matched the coloring of the murderous scarf, and missing from his waistcoat was a golden button, seemingly identical to the one found in the dead woman's grasp, if the others were any indication.

The actor looked toward the woman and then back to the three of us, facing him. He shook his head. "A terrible loss," he murmured, his voice deep and rumbling. Like many who have trained for the theatre, he projected clearly even when speaking in soft tones. His voice filled the room in a way that somehow seemed somehow disrespectful.

"We understand," said Holmes, "that you've had a somewhat special relationship with the woman since she arrived here."

Myrddin shook his head. "Nothing so special," he said. "In the theatre, people are simply ships that pass. From what I understand, she has most recently been associated with Mr. Grimley. Perhaps you might turn your attention that way."

"We shall," said Bradstreet, clearly disliking the man. "These is simply a preliminary to the larger investigation." He took a step closer. "Myrddin. That's unusual. What's your first name?"

The man smiled. "I have no other name. No need, really. I find that 'Myrddin' suffices for the present – and isn't living in the moment the secret of life?"

"I'm always looking backwards," said Bradstreet with a small laugh.

"What a coincidence," said the actor. "So am I."

Bradstreet frowned. "I'm certain that somewhere, your real name is recorded – likely along the lines of Ernie Smith, or something similar. Can't blame you for taking a stage name – but you *will* tell us the truth."

He reached toward his waistcoat pocket, and then paused, his fingers resting there. "Where did you lose your button?"

Myrddin didn't bother to look down. "I don't know. I realized that it was missing before the performance – too late to have it repaired. I'd hoped that it would add to the notion that Petruchio is a traveler arriving weary in a new town." He glanced toward the dead woman. "If you ask, there must be a reason. I take it that it was found here? On the floor, perhaps?"

"In her hand," said the inspector, pulling it finally from his pocket. "I believe that it is a match for the others that you're wearing – as is the scarf that killed her, which is clearly another piece of your costume."

Myrddin nodded. "I saw that." He smiled. "It looks bad for me, doesn't it? But I know that it all turns out all right in the end."

His indifferent attitude surprised me, and it irritated Bradstreet. I glanced toward Holmes, who was oddly silent, watching the actor carefully.

"Your accent intrigues me," he said. "I hear traces of London, but there are parts I cannot place."

"I am originally from London. I have traveled a great deal."

"Indeed. And I see that you write a great deal?"

Myrddin smiled again. "You observed this, perhaps, from the rubbing on my cuff?"

"Not at all," replied Holmes. "You are in a costume – nothing could be determined from that. Rather, you have ink stains on your fingers – some quite old, and a lot of them."

The man didn't bother to look at his hand. "So that's it. I thought that you'd made a rather clever deduction."

"And you are a writer?" Holmes asked. "Fiction perhaps? Or plays of your own?"

"Something like that."

"Do you have anything to add," interrupted Bradstreet impatiently, replacing in his pocket the button that he'd twirling in his fingers throughout, "about the murder?"

Myrddin shook his head. "I did not kill this woman." He turned toward my friend. "Mr. Holmes, I assure you that I did not. Please use your powers to clear me."

"Can you then provide any other information that will assist us?" asked Holmes.

"I cannot, other than my belief that this was due to something in Miss Sheridan's past – most likely connected to America."

"And why you think that?" asked Bradstreet.

"It simply seems likely. She has spent her whole adult life there, and she was only here for a few weeks."

That seemed to be enough for Bradstreet. Calling the constable, he had Myrddin taken into custody pending further investigation. When they had gone, he turned to us in a strangely explanatory manner. "I have to hold him," he said. "The button and the scarf. Possibly he's been framed, but that type – those actors – might flee at the drop of a hat."

"Oh, no doubt," said Holmes in a way that indicated he didn't actually agree. "In the meantime, you can continue organizing your data here, while Watson and I pursue a few other paths of interest."

Clearly Bradstreet wanted to ask further questions, but Holmes was obviously and suddenly finished with whatever he hoped to accomplish at the theatre, and ready to move on to something else.

Taking a last look at the dead woman slumped in her chair, and wishing Bradstreet a good evening, I followed Holmes outside. In the hansom back to Baker Street, he made no comments, and after our arrival, he set about sending a number of telegrams before sinking into his chair by the fire, smoking and staring into the distance. I murmured good night and went up to my room.

I had no rest that night, having trouble falling asleep, and then dreaming not of the dead woman, but rather the strange and compelling presence of the actor, Myrddin. As I slept, my mind seemed to see what I had missed while awake – he had an odd manner when questioned, as if he knew much more than he had told. I wondered if his arrest would serve to make him reveal his whole story.

It was very early – a subsequent verification of my clock showed that it wasn't quite six – when I was shaken awake by Holmes. "Hurry, Watson. Bradstreet has sent a cab. There has been another murder."

I knew better than to ask, and sooner than I would have liked, we were rattling back to the Lyceum. Holmes informed me that the cleaning women, who arrive at the theatre quite early indeed, had found a body lying in the center of the stage – Mrs. Wicks, the dresser of the dead actress. Her throat had been cut.

"And," said Holmes, "Bradstreet hinted at a further complication – something that he didn't share in his wire."

The cab pulled up in Exeter Street, at the stage door. A constable met us and then left us to find our own way to the stage. Bradstreet, as well as several other members of the force, were standing around a small body piteously highlighted by the stage lights.

She was staring straight up, with a terrible surprised expression on her face. Except for one great splash across her thin chest, there was surprisingly little blood.

Holmes looked back and forth, an expression of irritation on his face. "There were no footprints, Mr. Holmes," explained Bradstreet without preamble. "At least nothing of note. She was just lying here when the cleaning women turned on the lights. They all clustered around her, as did the passing bobby they called inside."

I could see that Holmes wanted to disagree, believing – and almost certainly correctly – that he would have been able to see some clue. "If you don't mind," he said, and then he proceeded to prowl around, sometimes upright and sometimes on his hands and knees, in ever-widening circles around the corpse. Finally he stood and rejoined us, commenting, "You indicated that there was something unusual."

Bradstreet put a hand in his pocket and withdrew a metallic object that shone in the high lights. "This was wedged in her mouth."

He handed it to Holmes, who looked at it front and back before passing it my way. It was a coin, rather sizeable and solid. Quite worn and faded, much of the imagery was rubbed away over the passing years. On the front was a woman facing to the left, her hair pushed back by a band stating *"Liberty"*. The back, much more worn than the front, had the remnants of something at the top that was just readable as ". . . *States of America"*, above a shield surrounded by an olive branch and a stalk of grain. The shield contained seven stars at the top, and seven vertical stripes at the boom. Something like a bee-hive capped the shield, while along the bottom were the words *"Twenty Dol."*

"States. Dollar," I said. "An American has done this thing."

Holmes smiled and shook his head. "In a way. In spite of the initial similarities, this is *not* a United States coin. Rather, it's a twenty-dollar gold piece from the Confederate States of America – the word 'Confederate' being what's worn away at the top there. The seven stars and the seven stripes represent the seven traitorous states that seceded from the Union 1861. Apparently they were unoriginal enough to come up with coinage that was too different from that of the true United States to the north."

He took back the coin and handed it to Bradstreet, saying, "Of more interest is that it was found in her mouth."

The policeman nodded. "She was trying to blackmail someone."

"The killer," I agreed. This was not the first time that we had encountered a coin left in a victim's mouth.

"I regret this," said Holmes. "I had received several wires very early this morning from America, but chose to wait until daybreak to act. Possibly this could have been prevented."

"I doubt it," said Bradstreet. "She probably didn't wait long at all before approaching the murderer. Clearly she knew more than she told us."

"At least," I said, "this clears Myrddin. He is in jail." I glanced at Bradstreet. "He is, isn't he?"

"Yes," agreed Bradstreet. "In the cells just up the street." He looked at Holmes. "You say that you can put an end to this?"

"I can. Let us proceed to Seven Dials, where all will be revealed."

Bradstreet had a constable go down to the Strand to procure a growler. Then we set off, up Bow Street and then along Long Acre to Mercer Street. There was no activity that early until we passed the brewery, where the workers were beginning to arrive for the day, and deliveries were already going out. The air changed as we crossed Seven Dials – a literal smell of decay and corruption that held even as we continued into nearby Lumber Court. Stopping before a shabby old building, half-collapsed upon itself, I felt a hundred angry eyes upon us from the surrounding dark and broken windows, and was glad that I had brought my service revolver, and also for the presence of the constable who had traveled with us.

As we stepped down, a wiry boy of ten or twelve approached. It was young Edwin Hopper, one of Holmes's more bold Irregulars – a lad who wouldn't have been fearful of spending the night in such a neighborhood. "'E's still here," was his announcement, while cocking a thumb toward the structure behind him. Without further comment, he melted into the shadows, and Holmes led us inside the filthy building, advising us to climb carefully and stealthily to the third floor.

What followed was accomplished without drama. Bradstreet easily forced the indicated door to find Amos Lee, the keeper of the stage door, asleep on a filthy pallet on the floor. He blinked in confusion, and then reached under his stained pillow, pulling out a straight razor while simultaneously struggling to his feet. Holmes brushed past Bradstreet and kicked with his foot, sending the weapon flying to the far side of the room. The constable then took charge of the man and led him outside. "He's stronger under these old loose clothes than he looks," he grunted.

A search of the room revealed a number of interesting items, including various clippings and theatre programs relating to Jenny Sheridan going back twenty years or more, to when she was a rising star on the American stage. On top was the news story that had appeared in the London newspapers when her triumphant return was announced.

"But why would he have had such an interest in her?" asked Bradstreet as we carefully made our way down the quivering staircase.

"Because he was her husband," replied Holmes.

We were outside before he could elaborate, and only after we were at the Bow Street Police Station did he explain.

"I agreed with Mr. Myrddin that this crime had its roots in the victim's American past," explained Holmes. "Last night I sent messages to several men that I trust in the United States, with instructions to quickly obtain a broad biography of Miss Sheridan. While you slept, Watson, I kept vigil as their various responses trickled in, and subsequent replies were made. A picture was quickly painted of her life – from when she had

114

arrived in the United States as a young lady not long after their Civil War, and through her rise in the American theatrical world. One thing that was mentioned was that she'd been married to another actor – a reprobate Southerner named Calvin Tyrell, considerably older than she. Their relationship would burn hot and cold from year to year, but she never seemed to shake him. Then, his fondness for drink, as well as a terrible throat cancer, seemed to be the necessary wedge to separate them – at her insistence. She made it clear that she would not be playing the part of the doting wife to nurse him back to health.

"The husband was known to have survived his illness, but he apparently vanished from the scene. However, my interest in him did not diminish, as I was aware that he might have been involved in this current matter.

"When we spoke to Amos Lee, I could see that his worn clothing was clearly American in cut and design, although it had certainly seen better days. Here then was an American, although I couldn't confirm it by hearing him speak. I had believed that the roots of the crime lay in the actress's American past. After receiving more specific information regarding Jenny Sheridan's former husband, I realized that his illness matched that of Amos Lee's affliction. Fortunately, I had set some of my Irregulars in place to follow various principals when they departed the theatre last night, so I knew where to place my hand upon him.

"Sadly for Mrs. Wicks, it didn't occur to me that the interior of the theatre needed to be watched as well. If she never left, she couldn't be followed. She must have seen Amos Lee, as Calvin Tyrell calls himself now, commit the murder – or at least she knew that he was in the vicinity when it occurred. Possibly she had seen or heard something that revealed his past connection to Jenny Sheridan. Later, after she discovered the body, she likely believed that she could make something from the situation, and informed Tyrell of what she had seen or knew. Late last night, they met in the theatre – she thinking to be paid for her silence, and he intending to eliminate her threat. Theatrically, he left the coin – a souvenir of his days in the Confederate Army – in her mouth signifying that she was a blackmailer. Then he departed, where he was followed by young Edwin Hopper, who had sent word where the man lived.

"When I saw the coin found in Mrs. Wick's mouth, I knew that this southern American, Calvin Tyrell, living as Amos Lee, had killed to protect his secret. It was really quite simple, but finding the solution wouldn't have been possible without making use of modern communications."

"Not quite so simple as that," rumbled Bradstreet. "Noticing the American clothing, for instance . . . ."

115

Later, through much tedious questioning as Amos Lee – Calvin Tyrell – attempted to communicate, Holmes's conclusions were verified. He was Jenny Sheridan's former husband. Knowing that she was coming to England, he'd arranged to travel there first, bringing with him a letter of reference in order to obtain employment at the Lyceum through the business manager, Bram Stoker. Then, his appearance much changed from when he'd known her, he'd settled in to wait for his chance to plead his case.

However, when he'd finally revealed himself, she'd treated him with great disgust. This he might have been able to take, as it was nothing new, but she began to fraternize with both Grimley and Myrddin, with the seeming intention of throwing it in her former husband's face. He'd confronted her several times, but she'd only laughed – clearly, in spite of their years apart, there was still some connection between them wherein she gained some twisted joy from getting a reaction out of the old actor. He realized that no one knew their connection, and he resolved to kill her – and to frame Myrddin in the process.

It was a simple matter to slip in during the performance, when everyone was gathered at the front to watch Petruchio. Jenny Sheridan never suspected his intent until the scarf stolen from Myrddin's dressing room was pulled tight around her throat. Then Calvin Tyrell knotted the cloth and slipped the unusual button, obtained in the same way, into her hand. He stepped out, unaware that he'd been seen by Mrs. Wicks. Soon after, he heard her scream – the body had been discovered. He waited around the theatre the rest of the night, as was his duty, and he was most surprised when Mrs. Wicks – who normally would have left much earlier – found him and said that she knew what he'd done. She demanded payment for her silence and he led her to the stage – the curtain was pulled, and it was as private as anywhere – and before she had a chance to elaborate, he killed her, placing the coin in her mouth – the only coin that he had with him at the moment, and one with great sentimental attachment, but a necessity, he indicated, when taking care of a blackmailer. "It was . . . a matter , , , of honor," he croaked.

He said that last statement in his curious and unusual way of speaking – a labored and painful thing to watch. After we had finished interviewing him, the entire distasteful situation became rather too much, and Holmes and I excused ourselves, wishing Bradstreet a good day and then returning to Baker Street.

Part II – The Past is Relative

The case had ended and the guilty man was discovered. And yet, I have debated whether to include what occurred next. Nothing is added in terms of the investigation by what I am about to relate – there was no additional killer, or fact whatsoever that added anything to what we already knew. But I would feel the matter incomplete if I didn't record the singularly unique narrative that was subsequently shared with us by one of the participants in the seamy Lyceum murders. The reader may, after reading the rest of this account, simply choose to disregard this addendum and instead accept only the first part as the whole and complete narrative, dispensing with this segment as pure speculative fiction, grafted onto my notes by some well-meaning but misguided and supernaturally obsessed literary agent. But to be complete, the entire tale must be told.

The following morning, Sunday, I awoke to find that the spring rains had set in. My bedroom window, which normally provided a rather bleak but unobstructed view of the buildings to the rear of our house and of the small yard where our lone plane tree eked out some sort of existence, was instead replaced by a constantly varying pattern of runnels of water, thrown there by the unceasing squalls. Occasionally the window would rattle under a fresh assault of wind, to be immediately followed by spattering of drops that sounded as if someone had tossed a handful of shot against the glass.

I dressed warmly, thankful that there were no plans afoot for me to leave the comfort of my fireside chair. Picking up the Clark Russell novel from my bed stand where I had lain it the night before, I made my way down to the sitting room.

After a satisfying breakfast, I steered my way for my chair, as according to plan, carrying the book, a handful of newspapers, and a refilled coffee cup. Settling in, I had just unfolded *The Times* when the doorbell downstairs rang.

Holmes, who had yet to make an appearance, briskly opened his bedroom door. I saw that he was fully dressed. As he purposefully stepped to the door at the landing, he said, "I have invited a visitor." Then he was descending the stairs, while I refolded my newspaper and set it aside with a sigh, vowing that my planned day would not be altered.

In moments he had returned, and with him was Myrddin, whom I had first seen little more than thirty-six hours earlier, when he made his initial entrance as Petruchio. Since then he'd been through a harrowing experience, spending a night in the Bow Street cells suspected of murder, but now he seemed little affected. Smiling and shaking my hand as I rose

117

to greet him, he gratefully accepted our offer of coffee and seated himself where directed in the basket chair before the fire. Then, while the storm raged outside, one of the strangest conversations that I was ever to witness in those Baker Street rooms began.

"Thank you, Mr. Holmes," said our visitor. "And you too, Doctor. I've been admirers of you both for so long – since I was a boy. I'm simply thrilled to be able to make your acquaintance now, even under such terrible circumstances." He lowered his head. "I knew that you would clear me of the charge."

I muttered something about being glad that it had worked out, and then Myrddin looked toward Holmes, who was silent for a moment as he fussed around, getting his pipe satisfactorily lit. After taking a long draw, he pulled it from his mouth and, using the stem as a pointer, directed it toward our guest. "It was you that sent us the tickets."

Myrddin raised his eyebrows, with surprise and seeming delight. "You knew? May I ask how?"

Holmes frowned. "I was inclined to credit you with the act immediately after the murder was announced, when you turned toward the audience and requested our assistance. I didn't mention it Friday night, as the inspector was already suspicious, and this was our business. It was possible, of course, that you had simply seen and recognized us from the corner of your eye while on stage – particularly as you had a bit of time while the other actors conversed without any lines required from Petruchio. I was an actor once myself, for a time, and I know that casting covert glances toward the audience is unavoidable, even if not good form. Still, someone had sent us anonymous tickets, and why not you? If you already knew that we were there due to your efforts, then asking for our assistance when Mrs. Wick screamed was no great trick. I confirmed with the ticket office that you had requested those particular tickets for complimentary use, although you chose not to have the theatre deliver them, or for them to be held at the box office until the performance. The question is, *why* did you want us there, before the murder diverted our attention?"

Myrddin continued to smile, but it had become faintly brittle, as if he were thinking furiously while continuing to present an easy-going front. Finally the silence became awkward, but both Holmes and I knew the value of such as that – often someone would nervously try to fill it, revealing more than they meant to. It was a useful tool.

"I invited you both," Myrddin finally said, his voice now lower, and rather strained, "because I already knew that I would need you to clear me of the murder."

118

Holmes's eyes narrowed, and I asked, "You *knew*? That you would be charged with murder before there *was* a murder? You knew that there *would* be a murder?"

He nodded.

"Then for God's sake, man," I cried, "if you knew, why didn't you do something to prevent it? Had you already seen some indication that Miss Sheridan was in danger? Some implied violence? Some overheard conversation?"

"No, Doctor. Nothing like that." He took a deep breath. "I didn't really know any details of the crime until I read in this morning's newspaper that you had both unmasked the killer on Saturday – yesterday."

"Did the police not explain what happened when they released you yesterday morning?" I asked.

He smiled. "I won't know for sure what they tell me until yesterday."

For a moment I thought that I had misunderstood, but his statement was clear enough. "Yesterday? You won't know . . . until *yesterday*?"

"That's right," said Myrddin. "Saturday is your *yesterday*, Doctor Watson. For me, it's my *tomorrow*."

Holmes looked intrigued, as if a chemical experiment that had been performed a thousand – nay, a million – times, had been repeated yet again, this time producing a much different and unexpected result. I was becoming irate, attempting to understand the actor's riddle.

"What are you trying to tell us, Mr. Myrddin?" asked Holmes.

Myrddin drained his coffee cup and set it aside. Then he pushed back into the basket chair, carefully placed his hands on the arms, and looked from one to the other of us.

"I live with a secret, gentlemen. A vast and complex and dangerous secret. I sometimes share it with others. I have decided to share it with the two of you. I . . . You see . . . ." He licked his lips, and then retreated. "I sometimes tell this to people – those that I have learned that I can trust. Those that I know will help me in the future – *their* future. My past, you understand." He looked at Holmes, and then me. "Ah, I can see that you don't. Not yet. You have helped me already, Mr. Holmes – in addition to clearing of Jenny Sheridan's murder . . . yesterday. That is, you *will* help – over twenty-five years from now." He suddenly appeared nervous, the first time I'd seen such a reaction for the normally steady young man. "It's very confusing."

"Go on," said Holmes, watching him closely.

"It's . . . it's difficult to explain. And difficult for others to comprehend," he said. "One would think that by I'd know by now how to relate the strange circumstances of my existence – "

"And those would be . . . ?" Holmes pressed once again, a touch impatient.

Myrddin nodded and cleared his throat. "Yes. Right. The fact is, gentlemen, that I knew there would be a murder before it occurred, Mr. Holmes, and that I knew you would clear me."

"You *knew*," I asked, still trying to grasp the implications of his outrageous story. "*Past tense*? You say that as if . . . ." I leaned back, fascinated to see such a sincere but mad conceit up close from someone who had initially appeared so sane. "You . . . you believe that you can see into the future? That you can predict events before they occur?

"Not exactly *before* they happen, Doctor," said the young man. "Instead, I prepare myself for what has already happened. *Your past* is *my future*. For I am living my life backwards through time."

Needless to say, a silence fell across the room. Myrddin's gaze pivoted from one of us to the other and back again. I settled back with a frank snort of disbelief while staring with fascination at the sincerity of the man's expression when making such an outrageous statement.. Meanwhile, Holmes looked at him as if he were facing a predatory animal that might make an unexpected move. Finally he spoke.

"You say that you have shared this before with others. Perhaps if you begin at the beginning, your . . . *interesting* experiences will make more sense to us."

Myrddin nodded, and seemed to relax a bit. "I don't expect you to believe me. There's no reason that you should. But I'll tell you anyway, because . . . because I know that you and I will meet again. We *have* met again, Mr. Holmes, from my perspective, although you don't know it yet – it hasn't happened to you, and won't for years to come – and you will remember me then.

"Today is Sunday. Yesterday – Saturday, *your* yesterday, and *my* tomorrow – you won't yet know this story that I'm about to tell you yet, because you're moving *forward* in time, and on Saturday, this conversation will still be in your future. But after I tell you today, from this day forward, you *will* remember it as you go into the future, and recalling me from today, and this conversation now, will be of benefit when we meet again, and when I need your help in your future – which is my past."

I closed my eyes, trying to order my thoughts. Myrddin saw my confusion.

"Imagine, Doctor," he said, looking at me, but speaking to both of us, "that time is like a series of fence posts, one after another, stretching from far to the left, out of sight – that's the past – and just as far to the right. That's the future. Time, as you and almost everyone else knows it, walks

120

along those fence posts, steadily from left to right, one after another, moving from the past into the future, minute after minute, day after day, year after year. Each post represents a minute, or a year, or a century, or however you want to view it. But nearly everyone inexorably follows that path from left to right."

"This is a given of the universe," said Holmes. "It is entropic. Time flows forward. Order declines into disorder. As time progresses, entropy controls. It increases – that is Newton's Second Law. Levels of high energy decrease and dissipate – that is the essence of the Third. What is uphill works its way down, slowly or quickly. Mountains are worn down and out into the sea – not the other way. Stars burn and send their energy into the cosmos until they are extinguished. The process doesn't work in reverse. Wood doesn't *un*-burn. An egg dropped on the floor does not suddenly rise back to the countertop and reassemble itself.

"And yet," Holmes continued, with a gleam of interest, "*you* assert that you are walking in the opposite direction along the fence, contrary to the unwinding of the entire universe. A most original conceit."

Myrddin nodded. "I do so assert it. I am *doing* it. It has been my whole life. How old do you think that I am?"

I felt that I could answer this with confidence. "No older than twenty-five."

"I am fifty-three years old," said the actor. "I was born in 1941, here in London. For the first couple of years of my life, I believe that I grew as any child would, both physically and mentally. When I was two, there was an . . . an *incident*, here in London, and my parents were killed."

"When you were two," interrupted Holmes. "So by your statements, you would assert that you were two years old in 1939 – two years *before you were born in 1941?*"

"That's correct," Myrddin agreed.

"Fascinating," muttered Holmes. He leaned back, thinking furiously. I didn't know if the idea itself was of such interest, or if – like me – he was intrigued at the elaborate beliefs of the man and the calmness that was exhibited by someone so clearly mad.

"How can you be fifty-three?" I asked, a tone of skepticism creeping into my voice that I tried unsuccessfully to hide. "You are clearly in the midst of your third decade – no more."

"I know that I am fifty-three, Doctor, in the same way that you know your age. You count the years that have passed from the date of your birth. I was born in 1941, and – living backwards – have passed through fifty-three cycles of the earth around the sun to reach this date, here in March 1888, when we are all now together in this room, having intersected in this place and time to carry on this conversation."

121

I waved my hand, a feeble gesture as if warding away an insect, not knowing what argument to make. He continued. "I know that I don't look my age. It's a curiosity of my condition. I seem to have reached a certain point and stopped aging altogether – or at least the process has been so significantly slowed that I can't tell the difference. I suspect that – barring an accident or illness – I'll continue living into the past for quite a long time before I eventually become an old man." He looked around. "Might I have something a little stronger than coffee?" he asked. "I have a great deal to carefully explain."

I arose and offered brandy or whisky, and he chose the latter. I poured one for myself, despite the early hours. Holmes declined.

Back in my seat, I took a sip, as did Myrddin. Then he began share his curious story in greater depth.

"As I said, I was born in 1941, the only child to my parents. I know very little about them. They were from somewhere north – if not actually in Scotland, then very close. As I said, there was an – *incident* – in 1939, when I was two years old, resulting in their deaths. More than that you don't need to know. I was placed with a friend of my mother's – a morose woman who felt it was her duty to raise me. It turned out that I was supposed to go with her when my parents died – they *knew* it was going to happen.

"This woman – we'll call her Margaret – was curiously reticent when relating facts about my past – thus my ignorance about my parents. If your parents had died in such a way, and you knew nothing of them, you could do research on the incident that killed them, and then back-track to find out their identities and their origins. I didn't have that luxury. When I was old enough to understand my backwards journey through time, I had no way to do any such research. By then I was living in the early 1930's, and then after that the late 1920's, and the incident would not occur for years. How could I search the newspapers for facts about their deaths when it hadn't happened yet?

"Margaret didn't send me to school, but rather taught me at home – and surprisingly well. I learned mathematics, and literature, and a number of other subjects, some rather advanced. Philosophy, for instance, and religion. The more complex sciences weren't ignored either – physics and chemistry. But *history* – that was the most important subject of all for someone like me, as I walked backwards into it.

"For several years, that was my only existence – Margaret and me and our little cottage. We lived far from any town or village, and I saw no one else. Early on, with memories of my own parents so hazy, I'd thought of this woman as my mother, but she was quick to point out that she was not. Of course, by then the nature of my curious existence had been revealed to me, and I found that Margaret was making the same backwards journey. My parents had been the same – that was how they knew when they would die – and that there was no avoiding it. It was set history, you see, and they expected it – and believed that they couldn't change it.

"There are others like us who swim upstream through time – the ones who don't go mad because of it and end their lives early before they really even begin – and we are known to one another. Some of us, anyway. There are probably more who never reveal this gift – or curse. We generally try to keep our existence a secret, even from each other, because there are some among us who never stop trying to profit from this unusual ability, and they are jealous and fearful of the rest of us who might do the same.

"I have no idea how old Margaret was – whether she was like me and had aged very slowly, or if she was progressing at a normal rate. She looked to be about seventy when I was ten or twelve, which would place her date of birth around the year 2000, I suppose. But if she was aging very slowly, she could have been born much further in the future – perhaps hundreds of years from now. She died of a sudden illness when I was ten years old, without telling me much that I still needed to know.

"But before she passed, she taught me a great deal about how we moved through time, and how to comprehend the seeming paradox of it, and tricks to survive it. She showed me how I could leave hints for myself from within the present, buried in the past like guideposts as I moved in that direction. Margaret explained how to devise a code that only I could understand. When she was certain that I understood it completely and would never forget it, being able to read it as easily as you do the English alphabet, I learned that I could leave messages for myself – in hidden diaries where I know to look, written by myself in the past to be discovered in the present, or as coded lines in the *Personals* column of a newspaper.

"I also found that I could think of some date in *my* future – *your* past – and in that way send myself a message of sorts. For example, say that in 1920, after having done research as to what present banks were around in 1900, I could *think* of that bank and a certain date in that year with great intensity, until it was unforgettable to me. Meanwhile, time flowed, and I would keep reminding myself of it, year after year. 1920, 1919, 1918, and so on. When I reached 1900, twenty years older and two decades into the past from when I made that initial memory, and having remembered that date and bank specifically for so long, I could go there and obtain a safety deposit box, placing vast amounts information in it about what had occurred over the last twenty years – extensive diaries and notes of things that I would need to know about my own life. Meanwhile, back in 1920, in the present where I was still twenty years younger and had just spent so much effort to think of that date and place, I could then go to the bank,

123

access the safety deposit box (which would have been maintained for all of those twenty years) and open it to find the information that my older self had placed there in 1900, sharing what is going to happen to me over the next two decades between 1900 and 1920 – people that I needed to remember, jobs that I would hold, and so on. I knew that it *would* work because it *did* work!

"In the meantime, having been able to read the history books and old newspapers along the way, I would know the greater world events as I went into them. That was where my trained memory was so useful. Obviously once I had seen today's newspaper and moved a day into the past, I could not go back and recheck it to confirm some fact, as you would in that pile of papers over there. The newspaper I had just seen was now lost in tomorrow and doesn't exist yet, and I was going the other way. Therefore, I practiced recalling all that I could. As I learned to remember more and more, and as I absorbed history from the books and newspapers, and from actually *seeing* it occur, I began to understand the patterns, and how it all flows and weaves together."

I cleared my throat. "How does this work? How does one move back into the past? How can you go through this day now, in the right order from morning to night so that we can sit here and converse with you in the same direction, and yet wake up yesterday?"

Holmes nodded. "Good, Watson!" he murmured.

"That's an excellent question, Doctor, and it's hard to explain," Myrddin replied. "I believe that it has something to do with the earth rotating on its axis, and portions of it passing through darkness and facing away from the sun – or so it seems. I do live each day forward, from morning to night as you both do, but something about passing through night moves me one day into the past. It's not a sudden snap from today to yesterday. Rather, as each new day begins, reality seems to coalesce and I realize from various clues – calendars and newspapers and seasons moving in reverse – that it's yesterday now instead of today."

He paused to take a sip of whisky, and I couldn't help remarking, "Good Lord, man! With such a . . . a gift, you could make a fortune. You could rule the world!"

He smiled. "One would think so, Doctor," he said. "But it isn't that easy. To become rich, I would need to do certain things today – place an investment, for instance – and reap the benefits tomorrow, and so on into the future. Instead, whatever I do today is lost to me as I go in the opposite direction. I've tried what you suggest – sending a memory message to myself in the past to place an investment that I can reap now. When the investment matures, I may have something extra today, but then I'll be one more day into the past, where the investment is diminishing, and I'm

124

moving away from the direction where it grows. I can leave notes for myself telling me where to go when I wake up yesterday – something like '*You are still working at the Capitol and Counties Bank on Wednesday, March 9th* – so that, on Thursday, March 10th, I'll know where to go, instead of awakening yesterday to find my immediate future a mystery.

"Since I'm *not* rich now, apparently I've yet to send a successful memory message to myself about some wise investment. My past self does hide some money in the past in my safety deposit boxes, or my other hidey-holes, that I can access now – a gift from my past self to my present self, in the same way that you set aside money for the future. But I'm careful not to take too much, as spending a lot today will leave less for the version of me who might need it tomorrow – *my yesterday*."

I groaned, barely able to follow this convoluted explanation. I glanced at Holmes, who appeared to be fascinated. "Thanks heavens," he murmured, "that Professor Moriarty doesn't know about this," he said, adding to the amazement that I was already feeling from our client's story. "He would find a way to turn it to his advantage."

"Or with such a thing to ponder," I added, "he might have never felt the need to turn to evil at all."

Holmes realized that his pipe had gone out and he set it aside. "You've explained how knowledge of the past – your *future* – is of no use toward your own acquisition of wealth, but what you do know of what's to come – and that's if I tolerantly accepted the authenticity of your tale! – would surely be of use to the British Government, which is always involved in preparing Britain for upcoming future conflicts, which some of us are certain cannot be avoided. If you truly had information about the next forty or fifty years, it would be your duty to share it."

Myrddin shook his head. "That isn't a good idea. Suppose I were to tell your someone within the government of an important battle ten years from now – and that is purely hypothetical. At first it's simply on the edge of his awareness, something vague, like a birthday months from now that he needs to recall in order to buy a gift. But as it gets closer, he begins to see how the events of history are unfolding, leading inevitably to that moment in time. He begins focus on it, however little at first, and his own interest begins to emphasize and even accelerate events, making it not only certain, but possibly worse than it would have been otherwise – because of my initial influence.

"His own interest in that event begins to have more and more of an unintended effect on *other* events. He convinces other men in positions of power to prepare as the battle approaches, before they should even know about it, and to direct resources in that direction which might have gone another way – possibly from somewhere that can't afford to lose those resources. This information might give that man a reputation for wisdom or prescience that he might not otherwise deserve, causing people to grant him more relevance and influence than he's supposed to have. Perhaps along the way, some new weapon is developed to end the battle more decisively – something that might not have appeared quite so soon if this man had never known so early about what to expect. The new weapon could itself nudge history in yet another wrong direction.

"And as I travel *away* from that future – my *past* – in ignorance, might it not change behind me, reweaving in a different way from how I remember it because of what I revealed?"

"But," I interrupted, caught up in his idea, "how do you know that your revelation of the foreknowledge of the battle, given to England in order that we might prepare, isn't the way that history and time are *supposed* to unfold? Perhaps it is part of the overall plan that you were able to intercede on our behalf and tell us what you know."

He shook his head. "Margaret was adamant in teaching me just how much or how little that I could attempt to nudge history. She always believed that time is like a river in a deep channel – no matter what temporary diversions impede the true flow, it will always correct itself – sometimes violently. What has happened *has* happened. But I'm more fearful. I think that it *could* be changed, and what I had observed as I passed backward through the future might have come undone and reknit itself into something else. Perhaps something that I've already done – some inadvertent and seemingly small action – has already changed what happens, and since I'm going the other way, I'll never know.

"It's one thing to for the older version of me, somewhere in the past, to write a coded message back to myself, left in a safe deposit box or other hiding place, about something that has already happened to *me* so that I can be prepared – about what to expect concerning an ongoing task at whatever job I'm walking into, or that I should learn Petruchio's lines because I'm going to be in a play at the Lyceum, and on what date I'll attend the audition and be hired. But pulling at larger threads in Time's Tapestry either fails, or might be a very bad idea. Possibly time might correct itself in ways that we cannot imagine." He took a final sip of whisky and set the empty glass down beside him. "No," he said. "I don't think that I'll be offering any advice about your future."

"'*Your* future'," I noticed sarcastically. "Is it so different than your own?"

"It is, Doctor. My future lies the other way. 1887, and then 1886, and so on."

"Can you foretell just how far you will be going?" Holmes asked. "Have you tried to determine just how far you exist into the past? A mention of yourself in the historical record, for instance?" I tried to see any emotion in the question – belief or skepticism, or anything in between – but there was nothing. "Have you foreseen the records of your own death, as you said was the case for your parents?"

"I have not. Every one of my attempts to 'remember' something, and send a message to myself farther and farther into the past, has been successful, no matter how far I push. I've left messages as far back as I can at businesses that were in existence in the deep past – a few banks and financial institutions, for instance – but I must wait to explore further. In the meantime, I've left myself increasingly comprehensive notes about yesterday, and the days past that. I know where I will be in a few weeks, before I obtain the job at the Lyceum, and what name I'll call myself. And beyond that, and beyond and beyond, versions of myself have left very detailed records of what I'm to do. The information continues to grow, and the tiniest of details are being painted in. My path is set. As I progress into the past, I'll keep leaving more detailed messages, filling in the blanks – I know this because I receive so much information now, so I must be taking a great deal of time to send it to myself, and I must be very good at it. And if I have questions, I simply think of a date in the future and remember it when I get there, and then I find out the answer, write it down, and leave it for me to come across here in the present.

"Acting is just one thing I will try. I know that I will become a doctor, and an engineer. And in spite of what I said about sharing information now about the future that lays behind me, I begin to see that I may be the one who *causes* history to happen along the path that it's already occurred. I've already seen some signs that I've done so."

"Indeed? In what way."

"Perhaps you've heard of the Confederate battle plans found by the Union forces, wrapped around three cigars, before the Battle of Antietam in 1862?"

I had. Holmes had not.

"Finding the plans allowed the Union to decisively defeat the Confederate forces at that battle. Would it surprise you to learn that I have been told in a message from a future version of myself (in the past) that I will be the one responsible for wrapping those cigars with the plans and getting them to the Union Army's attention?"

"So, along those lines – assuming any of this to be true," said Holmes, "you've already been trying this on a more limited scale, by sending a message to the version of yourself last Friday, to make sure we attended the theatre by arranging for our tickets."

Myrddin smiled. "That's right. It occurred to me to 'remember' it last Friday.

I tipped up the last of my own whisky. "Outrageous," I muttered.

Holmes, meanwhile, simply smiled tolerantly. "Have a care, Mr. Myrddin – or is that your true name?"

"True enough for now." He smiled.

"Your interest in affecting history," continued Holmes, his tone darkening, "sounds suspiciously arrogant. Power corrupts. And if you wish to enlist my aid for whatever it is that will assist you years from now, you're not leaving me with a very favorable impression today."

The smile seemed to wash from our visitor's face, as if realizing for the first time that his actions as described – or as he believed them to have occurred, at any rate – were bordering on something more malicious – or omnipotent – than the simple study of history while passing through it. He sat quietly for several minutes, and then nodded thoughtfully.

"You are right, of course. And you *will* give me more good advice when we meet again – in Chicago, in 1915. You will be surprised to see me again – but you will know me. Please recall this conversation, so that I can confirm to you then that I listened."

I was still trying to comprehend this story, and wondering if Myrddin were a danger to himself or others, and whether I should seek a constable in order to have him committed. He looked at me knowingly. "I am not insane, Doctor, I assure you. I am simply living something beyond your comprehension – until now. After this, you will know something about the way the world works that is hidden from most men. I don't understand it either, but I assure you that it's true."

"You say that others with this condition sometimes go mad," I said. "How do you know that you aren't already?"

He smiled. "I was fortunate to receive a good understanding and a solid grounding. And my quest for knowledge as I move back through time only expands my comprehension of the overall *patterns* of time."

"Surely knowing everything that will happen must become vastly boring. What will you do as you go back to keep things fresh, where there are no surprises?" I asked, curious to see how elaborate a structure he had constructed to support this madness.

"I have a theory," he said. "So many legends from the past – from all cultures around the world – hold a common belief in some sort of magic. And peeling away the froth on top reveals a great similarity in the stories, no matter what part of the world they originate. I believe that in the past, magic – *true magic* – existed, and that the farther one goes into the past, the more there was. Perhaps it was a substance of limited quantity, and in 1888 is has been nearly depleted, and any that remains will vanish entirely in the near future. But I'm going the *other* way, upstream *toward* the source – should it actually exist." He stood. "Knowing that it might be there and with the benefit of 'hindsight' and research along the way, I hope to find it, and learn it, and understand it – *and maybe master it!*"

He fell silent. What he had to tell us was finished. Holmes and I stood then too. "I only know some of what happens on Friday night – the theatre and the murder – from the little that I've read in today's newspapers and my notes to myself from yesterday when I was released. For you it's already a memory. For me it has yet to happen – the murder is two days in my future. I wish you both well – until we meet again last Friday, and also when you and I will continue this conversation in 1915, Mr. Holmes."

With that, Myrddin – or whomever he truly was – bowed and shook our hands, and walked out. We made no effort to follow, and in a moment we heard the street door close.

Holmes looked at me with a quizzical smile. I knew that he was asking what I thought.

"Utter rot," I said. "The man is insane."

"More likely an author," countered Holmes. "You'll recall that I did note the excessive ink on his fingers. He would have had us decide that it comes from constantly writing notes and diaries to himself and hiding them in safety deposit boxes for discovery yesterday and yesterday – or from his perspective, tomorrow and tomorrow. In fact, he's no doubt concocting this and other fantastic tales in the hopes of some sort of literary success."

"It will never happen," I said. "His premise is too confusing."

"Amen to that, Brother Watson," replied Holmes, and we both laughed.

I settled back in to my chair, turning my attention to the newspapers. And yet, my thoughts continued to return to Myrddin's amazing tale, and I found myself pondering various versions of him at different places along the fence posts of time, leaving hidden messages to be found decades later, or making memories for himself to be recalled when he was much older – in the past – requiring a certain action to be carried out. I tried to picture myself on such a fence, various versions of me in the past, present, and future, communicating with each other. At times I could almost understand – a version of me the week before had bought cigars and left them on the mantel so that I might find and enjoy them today – a thoughtful little gift from my past self to the present version. If such a person as Myrddin could travel backwards through time, mightn't he, and others like him, develop, by sheer necessity, just such a complex system as he'd described?

Throughout the day, I would glance at Holmes, ostensibly working at his chemical bench, but instead he was motionless, lost in thought. I knew without asking that he was pondering the same questions as I.

We never spoke of the matter again, but it still occasionally haunts my thoughts. And every once in a while, when I see Holmes studying the personal columns as he so often does, I wonder if he's trying to spot a coded message placed by the version of Myrddin on that particular day to be found days or years from now when a younger version of himself searches through an old newspaper in order to gain valuable information along life's journey.

But of course Holmes isn't looking for anything like that. To do so would be to acknowledge some sort of validity to Myrddin's ridiculous tale, and neither Holmes nor I are that foolish.

The Gordon Square Discovery

Many of Sherlock Holmes's investigations were handled quickly, but that never made them any less interesting to the student of his methods. Today I was reminded of this after reading in the newspaper of the untimely passing of someone who was peripherally associated with one of his past cases. This led me to reminisce about those days before my marriage when I was still residing in Baker Street, and I was moved to pull down my journal for that year. However, rather than immediately refreshing my memory concerning that specific series of events, I found myself lingering over recollections of this-and-that other previous adventure, glad that I had made such extensive notes when I had the opportunity.

Turning the pages, I recalled the vivid dilemma related to the disquieting observations of the funeral mute, and Holmes's quick thinking which had saved an old woman from an unhealthy marriage. And then there was the curious narrative of the four-fingered Methodist, which featured so widely in the press of the time. Holmes's demonstration of the charlatan's Bible and what was hidden in it had been a sensation – and both objects ended up going straight into Scotland Yard's unofficial Black Museum.

Each of these were solved within hours of being brought to Holmes's attention. Another, that related to the mystery associated with Lord St. Simon's marriage, was started and finished within one rainy October afternoon and evening, and that case led to a second investigation that (for the most part) also took little more than a day – although with more tragic results.

It had been after nine o'clock the previous night that Holmes had returned from his investigations into the missing wife of Lord St. Simon. His efforts had proceeded quite quickly. Holmes's involvement began in mid-afternoon when the nobleman had arrived to seek my friend's help in relation to the mystery that had been upon everyone's lips for the previous week. That day I had remained indoors, as heavy rains were being thrown against the window and the strong winds were occasionally finding their way down our chimney. I see from reviewing my journal that I was suffering particularly from my Afghan wound, in spite of it having occurred over half-a-decade earlier.

Holmes, however, had been quite active, as he had six or eight matters on hand at the time. His preferred to let some of them cook slowly, so to speak, while others progressed at a naturally accelerated pace. He had made mention that one such was complete, involving a curious furniture van associated with Grosvenor Square, and that he would be ready soon to reveal the true facts to the authorities. From this, our conversation moved to a letter that he'd received that morning from Lord St. Simon, regarding his new bride, the former Hattie Doran, American heiress, who had vanished during their wedding breakfast on the past Wednesday. Now a full week later, suspecting foul play and disgusted with the failed efforts of the official police, the groom requested – nay, *required* – an appointment with the private consulting detective.

Lord St. Simon arrived at four o'clock and told his story within a few minutes. The small marriage had gone off as planned. Later, during the wedding breakfast at the bride's father's home near Lancaster Gate, the new bride, following some conversation with her maid, had walked across the street into Hyde Park and vanished. She had last been seen then in the company of one of St. Simon's former female acquaintances, Flora Miller, who was now being held by the police, but it was uncertain as to whether the woman was actually involved in the bride's disappearance. Upon questioning, the nobleman could only add that his new wife had been in good spirits until immediately after the ceremony, when she suddenly seemed distracted. In fact, a change had come over her as she was leaving the church, when she curiously dropped her bouquet, which was then retrieved for her by a man in a nearby pew, apparently one of the many loiterers who turn up to watch strangers' weddings and funerals as a form of entertainment.

After Lord St. Simon's departure, we were joined almost immediately by Inspector Lestrade, in a pea-jacket as a concession to the terrible weather outside. He had been investigating the case with the idea that the bride, somehow lured from the wedding breakfast, had been murdered. He exhibited a wedding dress and appurtenances that had been found by a park-keeper, floating in the Serpentine, whose upper end was near the bride's father's house. Inside one of the dress pockets was a card-case that identified the owner as the missing Hattie Doran, along with a note stating *"You will see me when all is ready. Come at once. F. H. M."* on one side and *"Oct. 4th, rooms 8s., breakfast 2s. 6d., cocktail 1s., lunch 2s. 6d., glass sherry, 8d."* on the other. Lestrade felt that the initials added further evidence against the woman in custody, Flora Miller, but Holmes seemed to find great interest in the note for other unexplained reasons, to Lestrade's vexation. My friend was amused at some of the official policeman's notions, while Lestrade – who hadn't yet learned to trust Holmes in those days quite as much as he would in later years – left thinking that Holmes was on the wrong track. After the inspector's

132

withdrawal, his evidence bundled under his arm, Holmes also departed around five o'clock, and I didn't see him again until after nine.

However, those four hours did have a bit of excitement when, less than an hour later, a caterer arrived, laying out a meal fit for a nobleman, if not a king. Cold woodcock, and a pheasant. A *pâté de foie gras* pie – never my favorite – along with a grouping of bottles that seemed to be of very dear vintage indeed. Mrs. Hudson had followed the confectioner's man up the stairs, alternating between curiosity and a few comments of her own about sensible cooking being good enough for anyone. Then they were both gone, and I had several hours to fill, attempting to read both the newspapers and a recently acquired novel, but finding instead my thoughts returning again and again to Lord St. Simon's problem, and Holmes's seeming understanding of the solution based simply upon hearing the specifics of the events. (Additionally, the pervasive scent of the food was an ongoing distraction.)

At nine o'clock Holmes returned, looking approvingly at the little supper and seemingly happy to have arrived before the guests that he'd invited while he was out. I commented that he must have done so nearly first thing, as the food had arrived within an hour of his departure. He waved a hand dismissively, stating vaguely that the solution had been obvious to him before he left, and that his efforts since then had simply been to verify a few specifics – such as where to offer his invitation. I was about to ask who else would be joining us when Lord St. Simon arrived, sinking into the same chair that he'd occupied just a few hours earlier and bemoaning his misfortune in a most un-Lord-like manner. Apparently he had received a message from Holmes relating the solution to the problem – although I myself was still in the dark.

Yet all was soon revealed when there was a ring at the bell, and within a few moments a man and woman entered our modest sitting room.

Introduced as Mr. and Mrs. Francis Hay Moulton – the *F.H.M.* of the note found in the abandoned wedding dress – it became quickly apparent from the lady's solicitation as to Lord St. Simon's welfare that this was his missing bride, the American girl that he had met and married after traveling to the United States earlier that year. She was beautiful, in a rather coarse way. Clearly she had spent a great deal of her formative years out-of-doors, and she moved with a confident power that indicated she'd had no hesitation at helping her father with the physical labor that had been required as he made his fortunes in the gold field. She offered her hand to me in a forthright and modern American way, and I was surprised to find that her grip was strong and her palm rough, and covered with not-a-few callosities.

Moulton seemed just as toughened as his wife, although he was shorter than her, and wiry. He had a sharp face and darting eyes, looking quickly from person to person. He was clean-shaven and burned by the sun – quite unusual to see during a rainy October in London.

Mrs. Moulton quickly explained that two years before, long before she'd ever heard of Lord St. Simon, she had impulsively married the man at her side, but had later believed that he'd died after reading in the newspaper that he'd been killed in an Indian attack while on a prospecting trip. In fact, Moulton hadn't died, but instead had been grievously wounded. When he was finally able to return to civilization, it was as a rich man, but only to learn that his new wife of only a few days, believing herself to be a widow, had since agreed to marry a British nobleman. She and her father had come to England the previous summer, and Moulton had followed. Uncertain as to his wife's feelings after his prolonged absence, he didn't immediately reveal that he was still alive, but rather sat in the pew at her wedding. She had seen him and was momentarily startled, dropping her bouquet. Moulton retrieved it for her and slipped a note inside. Afterwards, she had abandoned Lord St. Simon during the wedding breakfast, walking into Hyde Park. She had been momentarily approached by Flora Miller then, the woman currently under arrest, but they'd only had the briefest of conversations before Miss Doran had joined Moulton, her true husband and love.

After tracking them down, Holmes had arranged the little supper in the hopes that hurt feelings could be mended, but Lord St. Simon was having none of it, instead preferring to depart immediately, with no wish to celebrate the reunion of the apparently happy couple. And who could blame him? He walked out with all the dignity that he could muster, leaving Holmes and me to share the meal with the Moultons.

It was quite interesting, especially hearing of Moulton's adventures in the American West. Holmes and I had travelled there in days past, both separately and then later when involved in various investigations, so some of what was related to us wasn't unknown. Moulton finished up one of his anecdotes and took a sip of wine. He had maintained a certain reserve throughout the evening. His wife, however, had treated the little gathering as something of a celebration. She clearly felt that the revelations were liberating, and she made free use of the contents of the various bottles.

Early on it was apparent that she was becoming rather inebriated, and Holmes had stopped offering to refill our glasses. However, that was meaningless to an American heiress raised in the rough western gold fields. She simply stood and opened the next bottle for herself, and proceeded to finish it on her own over the next hour or so as the rest of us declined.

It was after some comment related to one of Holmes's past cases that she said, "Of course, we've had own little mystery as well."

Moulton frowned and made as if to speak, but Holmes leaned forward and said, "What sort of mystery?"

Moulton waved his hand dismissively at what she'd said, a look of irritation on his face. His wife, seeing his expression, frowned slightly, and then, in what seemed to be typical willfulness, continued to pursue the matter. "The letters," she prompted. "Tell him about the letters."

Moulton's lips tightened. "It's nothing. Hattie, you're drunk."

She turned up her glass and finished what was left before reaching out to the bottle beside her. Finding it empty, she said, "I suppose that I know what is and isn't *nothing*." Then she looked at Holmes. "There was a problem at the hotel. After I walked out on Robert and joined Frank, we went to his house in Gordon Square, but after a day or so, I felt like the walls were closing in, so we went to the Metropole, where Frank had stayed when he first came to London. At first we had no reason to complain, but we returned from an outing one night to find that our room had been searched, and some of Frank's papers were missing."

"What sort of papers?" asked Holmes. I kept my eye on Moulton, who was poised as if he might spring to his feet to silence his wife. And yet, he did nothing except watch her intently.

"A few letters," she continued. "Nothing important, but Frank dearly hated to lose them. It was obvious that his case had been tampered with. I saw it as soon as we came back. We called for the manager, and he agreed with me completely, but Frank begged that he keep from involving the police."

Holmes turned to Moulton. "Is that true? You didn't summon the authorities?"

The American's mouth was tight. "Of course. As much as I hated my letters being stolen, Hattie and I didn't exactly want to come to the attention of the officials. Instead, we packed up and moved back yesterday morning to the house that I'd already leased in Gordon Square – where you tracked us earlier today. Since then, I've been considering what to do about getting my letters back, as I don't trust the hotel's efforts." He took another sip of wine and set the empty glass on the table.

"But Frank," said his wife, with a rather vindictive smile on her face, as if she had found a way to frustrate him. I had to question the future success of this marriage if it was already so important for her to score points off of her husband so soon. "Maybe it's luck that Mr. Holmes came knocking on our door. He can help us now, and after all, we don't have to be cagey anymore about who we are." She looked at Holmes. "Would you look into this for us? I'd be very grateful if you could retrieve Frank's letters." Then her eyes darted toward Moulton again to see his reaction.

Her husband's face darkened and he started to speak – he clearly didn't like the idea. I could see that the letters themselves had ceased to be important. Instead, they and Holmes's involvement were being used to see who would have leverage in the marriage. I doubted that this couple would remain happy for very long.

Holmes was certainly aware of this, observing what I had seen, but he apparently found no need to soothe these troubled waters. He nodded. "I'll be happy to look into it," he said, "but more information will be useful. Was anything else taken? Any other papers? Or jewelry or other valuables?"

"No," said Mrs. Moulton. "Only the letters."

Holmes looked toward Frank Moulton. "Do you have any idea why the letters would have caused any special interest?"

"None," he growled. "They're simply routine correspondence. There is no need to pursue this."

"Did the hotel manager have any explanation?" asked Holmes, ignoring the man's objections. "Any suspicions as to how your room was entered, or who could have been responsible?"

Moulton looked at his wife. "It did seem as if the manager had an idea about that. Hattie noticed it."

She nodded. "He called in his assistant, and they whispered for a minute. The assistant said something about 'Vernham' being on duty earlier that afternoon, and the manager nodded as if that made some kind of sense to him – as if they'd expected something like this to happen, and now here it was."

"And did they summon this Vernham to be questioned?" asked Holmes.

"He'd apparently already gone for the day," replied Moulton, somewhat surly, but relaxing a bit now that his resistance to Holmes's involvement had been overcome. "They assured me – us – that they would follow up, and that they would send Vernham a message immediately."

"And what happened? Did he respond?"

"We asked late that night, and there hadn't been an answer. He isn't due back to work until tomorrow, so the manager said that nothing more could be done until he could be questioned. I asked why they hadn't sent someone to his house, but they acted as if that weren't possible. Then I wanted his address so that I could go around and see him myself, but they wouldn't give it to me.

"At that point, I became disgusted with their handling of the situation, and that's when I decided to decamp back to Gordon Square. I sent a message around to the hotel this morning, asking if there were any developments, but they were vague – just that they still hadn't heard from Vernham. Then you came knocking at our door, so I haven't had a chance to see if anything else has happened."

Moulton leaned forward. "What Hattie said – about you investigating . . . There isn't any need. You understand? It's just some missing letters. I'll take care of it."

Beside him, his wife started to speak, but Moulton had had enough. He stood and turned quickly toward her, moving with the foot-work of a nimble bare-knuckle fighter. She started, leaning back in her chair, and with a suddenly sober – and rather wary – expression on her face. She seemed to understand that she was dangerously close to pushing her husband too far.

I stood, intending to prevent the American from further threatening the woman. I was already worried for her during the rest of the evening after they left our presence. Holmes rose smoothly to his feet, taking a step forward to diffuse the situation. "I understand, Mr. Moulton. I'm sure that the hotel staff will resolve the situation. And now, I wish you both a very good evening. I understand that the weather will be clearing tonight, so tomorrow should be a more pleasant day for all of us."

Moulton looked over his shoulder, as if for a short period he'd forgotten where he was, or that Holmes and I were there. For a moment, he and his wife had shared a look that conveyed volumes.

But soon after that they departed, with the couple considerably and curiously more tense than they had been upon arriving to face Lord St. Simon. After they were gone, I expressed my concern to Holmes, and he nodded in agreement. Then I asked if he wanted something else to drink, and he opted for a small whisky. I joined him, feeling the need to cleanse my palate from the rather unpleasant couple.

We sat for a while, and Holmes spent the first few minutes explaining to me how he had traced them, based on the writing on the back of the piece of paper found in the card case. The prices shown had clearly been from an expensive hotel which turned out to be the Hotel Metropole in Northumberland Avenue, which Holmes had found after just a few tries. He had learned at the front desk that they'd recently moved back to their rented lodgings at 226 Gordon Square in Bloomsbury, and it was there that he'd gone and convinced them that it would be better to tell the truth about what had happened to the unfortunate bridegroom.

Recalling Lord St. Simon's departure after he heard their story, I remarked, "His conduct was certainly not very gracious."

"Ah, Watson, perhaps you would not be very gracious either, if, after all the trouble of wooing and wedding, you found yourself deprived in an instant of wife and of fortune. I think that we may judge Lord St. Simon very mercifully and thank our stars that we are never likely to find ourselves in the same position." He set aside his pipe and said, "Draw your chair up and hand me my violin, for the only problem we have still to solve is how to while away these bleak autumnal evenings."

He played for a while, something mournful to fit the rainy night, reflective of the turn which the evening had taken, and perhaps as well the sad ending for Lord St. Simon's hopes of marriage and dowry. Then he allowed the instrument to fall silent. I could see that a thought had occurred to him. "It doesn't quite ring true," he said in response to my query.

"What?"

"Something about Mr. Moulton's reaction."

"They are two strong-willed people who barely know one another, and haven't seen each other in years – after an impulsive and secret mining-camp wedding. He didn't like it when she asserted her own ideas about asking you to look for the letters."

"No, that isn't it. I mean his reaction towards the hotel."

I frowned. "I would be upset if I found that my possessions had been searched and looted while supposedly safely secured in my room at a noted hotel."

"And yet, why depart? Why not stay there, where you could more easily harass the management to investigate the matter?"

"He felt that they could no longer be trusted."

"Possibly. But if he was worried about protecting whatever else he has that might be of value, he could have found a way to lock it up in a better way than simply leaving it in his room – placing it in the Metropole's safe, for instance, or even by making a temporary arrangement at a local bank. No, there's something about these letters that goes beyond a man simply being angry that he was victimized in this way. And then there's the question of the Gordon Square house."

"What do you mean?"

"They were supposed to be in hiding. Gordon Square was a better choice than a busy hotel. As you know, the Square consists of rows of rather standard houses surrounding the park, north of the University. There's nothing special about them – why not remain there? Yet they returned to the Hotel Metropole soon after their reunion – even as all of London speculated as to the woman's mysterious disappearance and her current whereabouts. She had become quite well-known in recent weeks as interest in the wedding of a British Lord to an American heiress reached a fever peak in the press. Her image has appeared in a number of journals. Surely there was the danger that she would be recognized."

I laughed. "Clearly you aren't taking into account the persuasive ways of a woman. And incidentally, as I recall, you asked me to brief you this morning before St. Simon's arrival, claiming that you knew nothing about the matter, and stating that you only read the criminal news and the agony columns. It seems that you knew enough after all to be aware of the capitol's rising interest in Hattie Doran."

He smiled in return. "Perhaps I did have somewhat more knowledge of the affair then I let on – although I didn't pay too much attention as the weeks leading to the wedding went by, little realizing that we would be peripherally involved. In any case, my point is that a great many people *did* know about Hattie Doran, and what she looked like, and later about her disappearance. The papers have maintained speculation as to her fate at a frenzied level for nearly a week now – and yet, I repeat that Moulton had no hesitation at returning with this notable woman to a very public hotel for several days – dining and shopping with her, and generally doing the opposite of hiding until they could arrange to leave the country. Only when his supposedly unimportant letters were taken did they move, the very next day, back to Gordon Square. Before his letters were taken, he apparently had no concerns about traipsing all over London with his noteworthy bride. Yet this afternoon when I knocked on the Gordon Square door, he answered with a pistol in his hand."

I raised an eyebrow. "Indeed."

"I simply put it down at the time to him being an American from the same rough life where his wife originated. As we learned, that was true – they had met in the same mining camp where Mrs. Moulton was residing with her father. I could see from the second that Moulton opened the door that he was a toughened American. Of course you noticed that he was armed tonight as well?"

I had to confess that I had not observed it.

"It was a small weapon, but effective nonetheless. Now possibly, but not very likely, he came here with a gun because he feared some sort of violent reaction from Lord St. Simon, although I doubt it. He would have sized him up as being no threat. He was already nervous when he answered the door in Gordon Square this afternoon, but he was comfortable and confident when he arrived our sitting room tonight. Clearly he was worried about something out there, and not what he'd find in here – including a jilted bridegroom. I wonder if he's gone about armed since his arrival in London. From what I was able to ascertain, he didn't seem to show any fear *before* his letters were stolen . . . ."

His musings trailed off, and I could only assume that he was considering what might be in those supposedly innocent letters. Seeing that he intended to think – and likely smoke – for a goodly portion of the rest of the night, I wished him well and went upstairs to my room, hoping that both the weather and the pain from my old Army wound would be more agreeable in the morning.

The new day promised to be much different than the previous one, when we had been beset by the equinoctial autumn gales. The sky was a brilliant blue, and there was a decided coolness to the air, encouraging one to feel both brisk and vital. I found that despite the change in the weather, the pain from the Jezail fragment still resting in my shoulder, a constant souvenir of my time in Afghanistan, remained in evidence, although greatly lessened.

I descended from my bedroom to find that Holmes had already started his breakfast. He nodded in my direction without speaking, his attention focused on one of the morning newspapers. This silent companionship lasted until he he rose, remarking "Your shoulder is still bothering you, I see."

It was no great deduction upon his part, as he'd observed these symptoms many times before. I had long ago given up trying to hide my pain, when it occurred, behind some sort of false pride. He had no doubt noticed that I reached for the salt and pepper in the awkward manner that presented itself when the ache returned. I was frankly grateful when he indicated that he planned to carry out his initial investigation of Moulton's problem on his own.

After his departure, I hauled the accumulated morning newspapers to my chair before the fire and settled in to see what was new in the world. The events were singularly uninteresting, which I suppose was good news for the masses as a whole, although there were certainly the usual tragedies and injustices occurring on an individual scale. I lost interest rather quickly and tried to immerse myself in a novel by a Scottish author of my acquaintance, loosely based on one of Holmes's former investigations, but I found myself becoming somewhat irate at certain liberties that had been taken. For the hundredth time, I vowed that one day I would make use of the voluminous journal entries that I regularly recorded of my friend's investigations and work them into some sort of material worthy of publication. With that in mind, I rose and resettled myself at my desk, moving aside the fossilized jawbone of some ancient lizard that had been used to kill a blackmailer and proceeding to polish my notes related to several of Holmes's more noteworthy inquiries.

Mrs. Hudson checked on me quite a few times, and I was surprised in the early afternoon when she asked about any preferences that I might have for lunch, having been unaware of how quickly that time was passing. After that question was determined and then the meal subsequently consumed, I continued at my labors, vaguely aware as the afternoon passed that my shoulder had finally started to feel better once again.

I was just finishing up my account of the events concerning the hideous visitant to the grounds of Deddington Castle when I heard the front door open, followed by Holmes's spry steps as he climbed to the sitting room. I was surprised to see that the day was fading away, and that it was later than I'd realized.

The door opened and he glanced toward me as he entered. "Ah, Watson – feeling better, I see. Are you game for a bit of burglary?" Then, before I could answer, he stepped to the shelves containing his scrapbooks, where he spent several minutes checking through various volumes while I made ready for departure.

And so it was that half-an-hour later we found ourselves settled at a table at Naples in Charlotte Street, an Italian restaurant that I'd discovered a year or so earlier. Holmes had eschewed bringing some of his more elaborate burglary tools, instead relying on the comprehensive lock-picking set that he usually carried with him. While eating our dinner, and waiting for a certain amount of time to pass until our excursion could be carried out with some degree of discretion, Holmes recounted the events of his day, sometimes waving a piece of bread like a baton as he cheerfully went, step-by-step, through his gradual understanding of the situation.

"Naturally enough," he explained, "I began by sending several wires to make certain of our ground. Then I ended up back at the front desk of the Hotel Metropole, where I implied that I was acting as Moulton's agent and the reason for my questions. As you know, there are one or two managers there who still recall the little service that I performed for them back in '83, when the Countess of Grantham, apparently suffering from some sort of emotional crisis related to her fortieth birthday the previous year, had placed herself in such a position as to utterly destroy her reputation. The Metropole management was quite grateful then, and to this day as well, and they had no hesitation in providing me with Mr. Abel Vernham's home address – in spite of their reluctance to do the same for Mr. Moulton.

"Their account of the theft of the letters was similar to that of Moulton's, although they did provide a bit of additional information. It seems that Vernham was already being watched after a few similar incidents where the shadows of suspicion had tilted his way – minor thefts occurred in rooms that were generally connected with him. He is one of the under-managers at the hotel, assigned to several floors, and on at least a half-dozen past occasions since his employment began just four months ago, other small items have gone missing – odds-and-ends that have personal associations to the victims.

141

"There has been no evidence to specifically point to Vernham, but he has been on the premises – and in fact on the very floors – when each minor theft occurred. And his antecedents have given the hotel managers some pause, as at one time long ago – and they only discovered this after he was hired, based on some hints that he dropped in conversations with some of the maids – he was an *actor*."

I smiled. "Scandalous."

"Exactly. And while we both know that being an actor in one's past does not automatically make one a criminal – for instance, it did me no harm! – it does still have a great deal of social stigma in certain quarters. The knowledge that Vernham had such experience in his past put him on thin ice – but that's not to say that in this case he was unfairly suspected. The evidence against him as shared by the managers is convincing, and he probably has been stealing. As I had arrived a bit too early this morning, I was prepared to wait and discuss the matter when Mr. Vernham joined us. Yet nine o'clock, when he was supposed to begin work, came and passed without his appearance. The managers were alternately irate and concerned, and it was then that they gave me his address, with the assurance that they would take no action until the heard from me, and that they would put Mr. Moulton off if he happened to arrive asking questions – in case leaving the matter in my hands wasn't enough for him after all."

He paused to take a sip of wine and continued. "Vernham's address is in Pocock Street, across the river in Southwark near Nelson Square. I hied myself in that direction to find that he actually lived just around the corner, in first-floor rooms above some stables, reached by a way of a poorly-kept mews. A word with his neighbors gave me to understand that he was at home, and that there was no landlord on the premises. I needed to convince him to speak with me – and I assumed that, if Vernham had chosen to abandon his job this very morning, coincidentally around the same time that the letters went missing, I wouldn't necessarily be welcomed. And I was right. At first he didn't answer the door at all, although I was aware from some slight sounds within the apartment that he was at home. Then, foregoing any attempt at deception, I identified myself and stated that I was there in regard to Mr. Moulton's missing letters. The resulting silence from that revelation was so emphatic that I began to fear that I'd made a mistake in not simply prevaricating. Then, after worrying that perhaps he'd skittered out through a back entrance, I heard the door unlock. Almost immediately a hand urgently gestured for me to enter the darkened rooms.

"There was a noticeable odor of neglect about the place, some of which was certainly from the various articles of unwashed clothing scattered around the floor. The room was dim, with the curtain pulled

142

across the only window, and the only light coming from the fireplace and a feeble gas fixture above the mantel. Vernham – for it was he – pushed the door shut behind me and then stood watching, awaiting my further explanation. He's about thirty years of age, lean and striking in a theatrical way, with high prominent cheekbones that throw shadows across his thin mouth. One can see the stage training in him by the way he stands, but unfortunately he also showed obvious signs of an incipient and detrimental opium addiction. All-in-all, he has the appearance of a skittish animal that would as soon bolt as remain, although I didn't know where he should have run this morning if the decision had been made to do so. Most important, the man was in fear.

"Normally an awkward silence is a useful tool for a man asking questions, but I could see that in this case, I would have to give way first. 'The managers of the hotel suspect that you stole the letters from Mr. Moulton's room,' I opened. He nodded noncommittally but didn't reply. 'When you didn't show up this morning,' I added, 'it rather sealed that belief.' Still no response. 'What made taking the letters worthy of such trouble, above other choices?' Then, in a flash of insight, I asked, 'Who hired you to retrieve them?'

"With that, his expressionless features devolved into something like a rueful sneer. 'I've heard of you, Mr. Sherlock Holmes. I thought that you knew everything. Well, you don't know what I've gotten myself into.'

"Here was something new, then. I had suspected that there was more to Moulton's letters than we had been told – why else should the man change his place of residence, and answer his door with a gun? But I seemed to have peeked under the very edge of something much more substantial. Affecting to have a bit more omniscience than was entirely true, I carefully replied, 'You've read the letters, then?'

"Of course I had no idea what was in them, but I gave the impression that I did. He nodded in reply. 'And I wish that I hadn't.' Then he frowned, as if just realizing that he'd made a mistake. 'Did Esher send you?'

"The name was familiar, but I shook my head in reply. 'The hotel is concerned,' I prevaricated. 'Too many guests have reported thefts lately. They've had their eyes on you.' I named off several of the items that had been taken, as based on what I'd been told an hour earlier. Vernham simply listened until I mentioned an insignificant ruby ring. Then he angrily reacted. 'I didn't take that! You can bet that one of the old lady's brats snagged that one, and is blaming the hotel!'

"'But you took the other things?' He nodded grudgingly. 'Those were all objects of demonstrable value," I continued, "but without enough worth to lead to police involvement. They might very well have been misplaced by the owners. Why change your method and take letters instead?'

143

"He shook his head as if I were a slow pupil. 'Esher! He forced me to. He told me just what to look for – he described the envelopes, and where they would be hidden in Moulton's luggage. He said that they would be in a secret pocket in the lining of the man's travel case. But he also wanted me to find something else, some other papers about Moulton's past, and they weren't there.'"

"'To be clear,' I asked, 'are we talking about Jack Esher, the swindler?'

"'Jack Esher the killer, you mean.'

"'I thought that he fled to America two years ago.'

"'He did, but he's been back for a week or so – at least that's what he said. He followed this Moulton – they came over on the same ship, but Moulton never realized it.'

"'And how did Esher convince you to help him?'

"'I knew him from . . . from before he left in such a hurry. He knows some things about me. When he followed Moulton to London, and to the hotel, he saw me working there. After that, he couldn't wait to have me nick those papers for him.'

"'Then why are you so frightened? Surely all that you needed to do was deliver the letters that you found, and report to him that the others weren't there. Then you simply had to return to work and brazen it out.'

"'You don't understand!' he snarled. 'I read the letters, and stupidly mentioned to Esher that I did it. Now *he* knows that *I* know!'

"'And what is it that you saw?' I asked.

"At this point he suddenly became cagy. 'Why should I tell you, Mr. Sherlock Holmes? How will you help me out of this mess?'

"'I'm not even sure about the extent of what this mess is,' I replied honestly, 'but if you feel that you need some sort of protection – '

"'I do,' he said. 'I certainly do need that.'

"So the long-and-short of it, Watson, was that I helped him get away from his meagre lodgings and into a place of safety that I maintain elsewhere in the city – one of my little hidey-holes where I keep disguises and other materials that I might need in the course of my work. I hated to let him know about it, and I told him that it belonged to an actor friend. Being a former actor himself, I think that he believed me, seeing the various items of clothing and the theatrical make-up on the mirrored table that is the main object of furniture in the place. After he was settled there, he told me the rest of his story.

"It seems that the letters that he was to retrieve were not – as you probably have realized by now – the innocent personal missives that Mr. Moulton tried to lead us to believe. In fact, they are a series of introductions promising substantial funds from a group of American criminals to be delivered to Bill Wayman of Bennett Street."

My eyes widened. "Bill Wayman, who has been making a serious play to replace Professor Moriarty's organization with his own?"

"The same. He doesn't have a chance, of course, but it's been useful for us to let him continue unhindered, as every resource that the Professor is forced to direct toward holding Wayman in check is one that he can't exert somewhere else."

"And if I recall correctly," I said, "Jack Esher was – at one time, at least – one of the Professor's lieutenants."

"Something like that," replied Holmes. "The Professor's chain of command isn't exactly laid out along military lines, but that description fits close enough."

I leaned back as the implications washed over me. "So Moulton has something for Wayman which will give him an advantage – a promise of American criminal support – and Moriarty's man contracted with Vernham to steal it before it could be delivered."

"That is how I read it as well," replied Holmes. "Somehow they became aware of the letters, even in America, but were unable to retrieve them while they were in transit.

"Well," I said, "why interfere? Let them settle it however they wish. As you said, everything that Wayman is allowed to accomplish for now diminishes Moriarty to some degree. Why not let Moulton complete his mission, so that Wayman can divert Moriarty's resources to an even greater extent?"

"It isn't that easy now. You forget, the letters have already been stolen and placed into Esher's hands, and surely Moriarty has them now. To get them back would be nearly impossible, even if we wished to do so. They're usefulness for Wayman is finished. And in any case, Wayman has been effective up to now because he functions at the same continuing level of success today as yesterday, and as he will tomorrow. To allow him a nourishing connection with American criminal resources would perhaps make him more powerful than would be healthy at present. There's always been the understanding that when Moriarty is ready, he'll kill Wayman and absorb his organization. If Wayman is allowed to expand his influence, he'll simply built a bigger resource for Moriarty to eventually control."

"And of interest from all of this is that Moulton is likely a criminal as well, and wasn't just delivering these documents as a favor for a friend?"

"Oh, it's quite certain. Vernham indicated that the other papers that he was supposed to locate contain evidence of Moulton's own crimes, which Esher – working for Moriarty – wishes to use as a way to control

Moulton. Having these documents in his own possession could allow Esher to force Moulton into Moriarty's service. As I mentioned, I took a moment this morning to send a few wires – all of them to some of my American acquaintances. You may be interested to learn that there is no record of an American named Francis Hay Moulton."

"But surely – " I began, and then checked myself. "To enter the country, he would have needed legitimate papers."

"Precisely, Watson. And someone that I know with a great deal of influence within the Foreign Office quickly checked the records of recent arrivals from America, confirming that no one named *Francis Hay Moulton* has entered the country, but one *Francis Harris Mason* did – a man of the same approximate age and description as our recent acquaintance, arriving ten days ago through Liverpool."

"*F.H.M.*" I said. "Still, traveling under another name is not evidence of a crime, or of a deep connection with a known criminal organization."

"This is true, but it turns out that Francis Mason, or 'Frank' as he's known in America and to his wife, has a long history of mayhem to his credit – theft, assault, fraud, and the odd murder or two when it was to his benefit."

"He sounds like a rough character – and too smart to have spoken with you at all."

"I puzzled over that as well. I unexpectedly intruded into their lives yesterday evening, having traced them from the Hotel Metropole to the Gordon Square house. They really had no choice but to visit Baker Street and let the matter with Lord St. Simon play out. For all they knew, I had the Gordon Square lodgings under observation in case they tried to escape, and might have complicated things much worse than they already were."

I took a sip of wine. "But again I have to ask, what is the purpose of your – *our* – continued involvement? Moriarty has the letters, and they are now as good as gone. This seems to be some sort of scuffle between two rival gangs, and any damage that they do to one another only benefits the greater good."

"Except that disrupting their plans is always good practice as well. Moriarty gaining some sort of ascendance over Mason – or Moulton, as I will continue to call him – is likely much worse than simply letting Wayman have access to American financial resources. The Professor would love to expand his influence to both the Continent and the Americas, and having the documents relating to Moulton's guilt would let him convince the American to change his allegiance, so to speak, from Wayman's team to that of the Professor. Then the Professor can make the American connections himself. And if nothing else, Mrs. Moulton needs to understand what sort of man that she has married, and be able to correct the problem, before it goes any further."

"And how will this bit of burglary that you promised do that?"

"I propose to find the papers relating to Moulton's guilty past, the ones that Vernham could not, and see him brought to justice."

"And what is your plan? Are we simply going to slide into their rooms – even as he guards them with his gun – and lurk behind curtains or the furniture until they go to sleep?"

"I have it on good authority that they are attending the theatre tonight."

"And how did you obtain that information."

"They told me so when I called upon them this afternoon."

I took a moment to ponder that before asking simply, "Why do that?"

"I visited on the pretext of being in the neighborhood on other business, making sure that they had arrived home safely last night, etcetera. I believe that Moulton was suspicious, but I didn't care. I was interested to observe that his wife is becoming impatient with being kept inside. I dropped a hint or two about some of the local theatrical productions which interested her greatly – the result of which is that they will be attending tonight's performance at the Haymarket, while you and I slip into the house in Gordon Square and search at our leisure."

I had a premonition – correct, as it turned out – that things wouldn't progress quite that smoothly, but I held my tongue as we paid our bill and found a hansom to carry us to Bloomsbury. We had the cabbie drop us at the corner of Gower and Keppel Streets, and then walked through the dark night until we entered Russell Square. Turning north, we paused on the steps of Christ's Church in Woburn Square, where Holmes raised his hand twice in a curious chopping motion. Within half-a-minute, a lad appeared from the darkness. It was Arthur Belling, one of his Irregulars.

"Something different from what you said to expect, Mr. Holmes," he said. "The lady left at the time you said she would, but there was no man with her, and she hired a growler. The driver helped her load a small trunk that was just inside the building. The lights to the rooms that you said to watch are still lit."

"Did you see which way they went?"

"To the south. Thad jumped on the back – he'll get word to us where they're going."

Holmes frowned and glanced at me. "I fear that I have been hoodwinked, Watson. This way!"

Leaving Arthur where we had found him, Holmes led me back down to the pavement, and so on along the eastern side of Gordon Square, and then straight to Number 226. Stepping off the street through the unlocked front door, he pounded up the stairs to the first floor, while I followed gamely behind. He reached a door as I stepped off the stairs and raised his fist to knock. Before he could do so, however, he sniffed, and then shifted his hand to push against the door. It opened, having not been entirely closed. He looked toward me. "Gun smoke – do you smell it?"

I did. As I took another step closer, his expression changed at whatever it was that he saw through the open door.

"Deviltry, Watson," he muttered, and then stepped inside.

From the doorway, I saw him approach the body of a man – Moulton – lying on the floor, his head lying in a thickening puddle of blood. The man's eyes were glazed in death, and his features were distorted, a result of the blackened wound on his left temple. A gun was tossed carelessly onto the floor at his side.

Holmes muttered to himself to a moment. "There is no attempt to fabricate a suicide," he finally said. "Moulton was right-handed – he wouldn't have fired into his left temple, and in any case, the gun is lying by his right hand." He leaned down over the weapon. "This appears to be the same gun that he had when I called up on the two of them yesterday evening." He stood and looked at me. "It would seem as if his wife somehow gained possession of it – probably without his knowledge, as there is no sign of a struggle – and she was likely able to approach him without arousing his suspicions. She killed him and then departed – probably for good, as she took a trunk."

He then turned and spent five minutes or so comprehensively searching the rooms, while I placed myself near the door, in case anyone should arrive with uncomfortable questions. I was struck by how solid the building seemed to be, and how silent as well. I couldn't hear anything from the neighboring flats – which was possibly why none of them seemed to have heard the sound of a gunshot.

Holmes returned and stood beside me. "She hasn't taken all of her possessions, but enough to indicate that she doesn't intend to return. And there is no sign of the documents related to the events in Moulton's past."

He raised a hand and rubbed his brow. "I have seriously erred, Watson. Something that I did today during my visit alerted them – alerted *her* – that I knew more than I was sharing. I thought that Moulton was the villain, but it seems that there was more than one viper in these rooms."

"You don't know that for certain," I said. "Perhaps Moulton was a brute, something that she never realized during the short time that they were previously married in the United States. We saw indications of it last night. Possibly he did something just today that drove her to kill him, entirely unrelated to the tale that you shared regarding Moriarty and Wayman."

148

"Possibly," he said. "But I can see from examining the rooms that her departure was efficient and organized. There was no panic here, no desperate attempt to flee from an emotional murder that came as the result of some sudden abuse. And the papers are missing . . . ."

There isn't much more to tell. One of Holmes's Irregulars, Thad Warren, passed the word to us that Hattie Doran Moulton's cab had deposited her at Victoria Station, where she had purchased a ticket and then entered one of carriages for the boat train to France. However, by the time the police could wire ahead and intercept it, she'd vanished from her compartment, abandoning her trunk in the process, long before reaching the coast. Holmes personally undertook to interview the lady's father, Aloysius Doran, still in England following her supposed wedding to Lord St. Simon. He had remained through the following week instead of returning to America, seemingly awaiting news concerning her disappearance. He claimed, as he always had, that he hadn't known where his daughter went after fleeing the wedding breakfast, and that she wouldn't have told him what she'd planned in any case, knowing his objections to her relationship with Francis Moulton. And yet, Holmes was certain after questioning the man that he had actually known all along where his daughter was during the week after the wedding, and more importantly, that he knew where she was now as well.

"I'm convinced that the old rascal helped arrange for her escape from the train," he said with great irritation a few evening later. We were sitting by the fireplace in Baker Street, Holmes with his pipe in hand. Old Doran had vexed him, and as Holmes cast more nets and obtained more information, it was clear that the American was a much more dangerous figure than we had first credited, based on the little that we'd previously heard of him.

"No great surprise there," I said. "A man like him who made a fortune in the western mines is surely ruthless and brutal."

"Exactly," said Holmes. "Just the kind of man who could parlay some sort of successful connection with Professor Moriarty, to their mutual benefit."

"You believe that is what's happening, then?"

"There is every indication of it. He hasn't been sitting idle during his visit to London. I've learned that he made several visits to Moriarty's Russell Square residence during the week that his daughter was missing."

"Then we have a rough idea of what is happening."

"But do we *really* know anything, Watson? It seems that these waters are even deeper and darker than we realized. Was Hattie Doran simply an innocent who found out the truth about her recently reunited husband? Or was there some newly threatened violence that prompted her to kill him? In either case, what made her choose to flee, rather than count on her father's money and influence to save her? Why walk away from her entire life – and in so effective and successful a manner? It might be easy for someone like her to do so – after all, she was ready a week ago to abandon Lord St. Simon and the security that life with him offered. Was she the woman that we saw the other night, talking too much while drunk and needling her new husband, or was she really pulling the strings all along?"

He set his pipe aside. "Thinking Moulton dead two years ago, did she then manipulate poor Lord St. Simon in search of a title, an entry-way into British society, only to abandon him when something better came along – a return to whatever life that she'd initially planned alongside a man with an extensive criminal history? I begin to think that the reappearance of the actual husband, while initially quite unfortunate for our saddened nobleman, was a rather lucky thing for him after all. The question now is where has she gone to ground – and why? Does it have something to do with her father's seeming association with the Professor? She and Moulton had already planned to go to France when I first visited them. Were they both taking direction even then from Moriarty? Is she still following that path laid out for her by the Professor, leaving behind her dead husband, her fortune, and even her identity? A striking woman like her cannot hide forever. Even under Moriarty's protection, if that's where she has taken herself, she must eventually be discovered."

And she was, but not until Holmes had a much greater understanding of the criminal enterprise which he faced, and only after the Professor had made one trip – only a little, little trip – which was more than he could afford when Holmes was so close upon him. From that starting point, Holmes wove his net around Moriarty, and all the little fish that encircled him as well. The final whereabouts of Hattie Doran, as I continued to call her, was one of the many mysteries that were cleared up to a small degree when Holmes's papers were examined in those dark days of May 1891, soon after he was believed to have perished at the Reichenbach Falls. I was with Inspector Patterson when he pulled the documents needed to convict Moriarty's gang from pigeonhole *M* – done up just as Holmes had described in a blue envelope and inscribed "*Moriarty*". Among them was a sheet telling how to find Hattie Doran, along with a long list of the crimes, some capital offenses, that she had committed since vanishing years before following the murder of her husband.

Holmes's notes were extensive, showing that he had found her just a few months after her disappearance. Rather than stay in that confining life of luxury, which she had apparently despised as her father attempted to marry her into the world of higher society, she had instead gone to work willingly for Moriarty's organization, a path that gave her some sort of satisfaction as she lived the dangerous life of an adventuress – and that eventually led her to the rope.

Holmes had gotten word of her activities in Monte Carlo, had set a watch in place, and then kept his eye upon her from that moment on, waiting. Sadly he wasn't around to see her arrest and conviction, as by that point he was using his presumed death to travel the world under the name "Sigerson" (among many others) while carrying out the nation's secret business under the direction of his brother.

I was allowed to speak with Hattie Doran in her cell the day before her execution, but she refused to answer any of my questions. She seemed to believe, even then, that somehow either her father's money or her association with the Professor's shattered organization would save her – the look of mocking and confident amusement at her plight was there in her eyes, and she made no effort to hide it. I understand that she became more frantic as the day progressed, and that she had to be sedated during the night as the hour of her execution approached. And yet, she took the truth of her relationship with Moulton with her, as well as whatever it was that had motivated her to kill him on that October night, just a day after our convivial little supper in Baker Street, sometime between the hour that Holmes had visited their apartment and when we later returned to burgle it.

I was at Newgate Prison the next morning when Hattie Doran was hanged, and I bore the brunt of the hatred meant for both me and Holmes as I tried to ignore the glare of her father. His blistering gaze was upon me instead of watching his daughter, even as the flooring beneath her feet gave away and we both heard her muffled and abruptly silenced gasp. He made it clear as I turned to go that he would never forgive, and he would never forget.

The Secret in Lowndes Court

It was the coldest March that I could recall, and I was glad that morning to have no requests for my attention. In those earlier days in Baker Street, my health was still somewhat precarious, although it was then approaching three years since I had been wounded in the Battle of Maiwand. Joining Sherlock Holmes on his investigations had done wonders for my recuperation, forcing me to set forth when I might otherwise have chosen to sit by the fire and sip whisky. My own brother had started down that path for far smaller reasons than a shattered shoulder and a grazed subclavian artery, and I was always aware that such snares could entrap any man before he knew it, and if he wasn't ever vigilant.

Having no regular practice of my own, I would divide my time between Barts as needed, and occasionally as a *locum* for various doctors whom I had come to know around the city. More and more I found myself participating in Holmes's cases, as time and health permitted, and early on he had made it clear that any fees that he earned which involved my assistance were to be shared. "If you were called in by another doctor to consult on a medical case," he had explained soon after I had assisted in the arrest of Jefferson Hope, "you would not expect to take your valuable time and offer your opinion – the result of years of training and experience – for free. Neither would you think it acceptable to pay from your own pocket any expenses incurred along the way – transportation, lodging, and so on. As a professional, you expect to be treated as one. You have earned that right. I, too, am a professional in my own way, and I demand the same. When I request your services, it is more than simply asking you to join me as a friend – although that aspect is not to be negated. Your presence and participation are part of that which is offered by my little agency, and as such, the client will be responsible for that payment."

Then he had dropped into his chair with a rueful smile. "Although I must admit that at times my professional charges, which I never vary except when I remit them altogether, do get remitted more often than they should. It has been my experience that sometimes the most challenging and interesting cases come from those who can least afford to pay for them." Then he sat up a bit straighter. "Nevertheless, we shall each of us, you and I, stand upon our professional dignity and demand proper remuneration whenever possible. We can but try."

Now, looking at Holmes's latest client, I suspected that this might be one of those instances when his fee might be remitted yet again.

Often in those days, Holmes's mornings were not very different from those of a general practitioner who opens the door to a steady stream of patients with a variety of complaints. The difference, or course, is that a doctor quickly learns that nearly all of the complaints fall into three or four typical categories, each requiring the same type of treatment, whereas Holmes's cases tended to be much more unusual. Of course, he would sometimes become weary of the tediousness of some of their stories, for as he'd explained once early on, "There is a strong family resemblance about misdeeds, and if you have all the details of a thousand at your finger-ends, it is odd if you can't unravel the thousand-and-first."

The amateur writer in me never tired of listening to the curious tales presented by Holmes's clients, one after another, and finding interest in their stories, as well as their diverse backgrounds. Holmes, however, with a thousand (or more likely ten-thousand) details at hand, would strip away all the frippery and froth in an instant and see the bones of the matter exposed underneath, in the same way that Sir Jasper Meek or Penrose Fisher, or any of the best doctors in London, could instantly recognize a disease – even a rare one like Black Formosa Corruption – because they had seen it presented so often before.

As I recall, that morning had been rather typical, with three or four clients already having come and gone. One was a young woman who had a bundle of her dead grandfather's letters, in which her recently acquired young gentleman seemed to have too great an interest. Five minutes of glancing through them, followed by a few questions about the grandfather's seafaring background and a look through the *Gazetteer*, was enough for Holmes to advise her to look behind a framed map (which she confirmed that she owned, in spite of not knowing how Holmes could have been aware of it) for a set of stock documents, hidden long ago, and now no doubt worth a fortune. (As she left, I added my own professional advice: Avoid the young gentleman in the future.)

After a couple of other similar consultations and a second cup of coffee, the morning continued with the announcement by Mrs. Hudson of one Ernest Wilson. He was a compact fellow of perhaps forty-five. His suit was well-kept, but not new. He had gray hair that was perhaps overdue for a trim, and it was pressed down in a ring-shape encircling his head, no doubt from wearing the cloth cap that he had clutched in his hands. He looked from one to the other of us rather nervously, but seemed to relax quickly – although not completely – when Holmes invited him to the basket chair before the fire.

"Thank you for your time, Mr. Holmes," he said, glancing my way with a bit of uncertainty. I had seen this before, but for the most part I no longer felt the need to apologize and offer to retreat upstairs to my bedroom, as I had done when Holmes and I first began sharing rooms, or even to the present when a client of recognizable importance professed a matter to be of the utmost secrecy. Usually Holmes indicated that I should stay – sometimes, it seemed, as a way to assert his authority over the client more than a wish for my presence – but there were still occasions when I *was* excused. In Mr. Wilson's case, there was no indication that I should leave, and thus I picked up my notebook to jot down a few points as the man told his story.

"You may not remember me, Mr. Holmes – "

"Of course, I do, Mr. Wilson. You're the manager of the messenger service in Regent Street, around the corner from the Union Bank in Argyll Place."

Wilson's eyes widened. "I am indeed. Thank you. Thank you." He paused for a second, as if some great honor had been accorded and had left him speechless. Then, in an effort to regain his train of thought that was visible to both Holmes and me, Wilson continued.

"As you say, I'm the manager, and have been with the company, at that location, since I was a boy. I started running messages when I was just a lad, a number of years before you two young men were born, I expect. It was a local concern then – we've since been absorbed by a larger organization – and as I came up, I took on more and more responsibility, so that when old Mr. Jeeter retired, I was given the reins. It's steady work, and necessary, and if one keeps an eye on all the moving pieces, there isn't too much that can go wrong.

"When I first started, I lived with me mum, not far out of the Seven Dials, and thank heavens I escaped from there, as many of my young mates did not. With what I earned, we were able to move to a better neighborhood, and there we stayed. Mum died a few years ago, but I remained there in our old rooms, by myself, until the middle of last February, just over a month ago, when we – that is, the other tenants and me – learned that the building had been sold to a nearby brewery so that they could demolish it and expand their building. Well, there wasn't anything to do but look for somewhere else.

"The same day that I learned I'd have to move, I was returning from delivering a package – as I've never risen so high that I don't still do some of that for myself – and I was quite fortunate to notice that a room had just become available near my place of employment – in Lowndes Court, just off Carnaby Street, not three or four blocks away from the service. It's an easy walk, and there are probably six or eight pubs a couple of minutes in any direction, should I wish for a little something at the end of the day.

"It's a small house, smaller than this one, and the lease is held by Mrs. Denbigh, a widow of about my age. It seems that her previous tenant, an

154

old man who had been a bank clerk, had dropped dead at his desk one morning a week or so before, and after his sister came and cleared out his things, she needed a new lodger. The rate is reasonable, including meals and laundry, and after I saw the sign in her window and knocked on her door, we had concluded the arrangements within fifteen minutes.

"I'm not one for change, you understand, but I had no choice. I'm satisfied with where I work, and I was happy with where I lived, until I had to find somewhere else. But this is definitely a satisfactory solution to my problem."

I could see that Holmes was becoming impatient, and to Wilson's credit, he perceived it as well. He hurried onward toward the meat of his story.

"I've lived there for just a month now – at Number 8 Lowndes Court. In all that time, there's been nothing unusual whatsoever, and I've simply picked up and carried on with my life the same as before – I just turn a different direction at the end of the day to walk home. But yesterday morning, as I was finishing my breakfast, Mrs. Denbigh knocked and asked to come in.

"That was a bit strange, as she usually waits until I've gone for the day to collect the dishes, along with any laundry which I've set aside. She seemed upset, and wanted to speak about something, but had a difficult time finding a way to start. I've seen this over the years with my lads at the service – when they've made a mistake, or something that should have been easy has had a complication, and they fear that they've handled it the wrong way. The best way forward is simply get them to tell it, and I urged Mrs. Denbigh to share what troubled her.

"'Have you heard any . . . noises in the night?' she asked.

"'What noises?' I asked. Truth be told, the house could burn around me and I might not wake up – it used to worry my mum something terrible.

"'Footsteps – that's how it started,' she said, as if she were embarrassed about it. I couldn't think why, until I suddenly understood what she might be thinking. She didn't mean a burglar. 'And then the knocking began.'

"'Do you think that the house might have a *ghost*?' I tried not to smile and make her feel foolish.

"She couldn't look at me then, as if hearing it said out loud, in the bright light of morning, made her too ridiculous. And yet, she'd decided to ask me about it, and she pressed on, instead of letting the matter drop.

"'Yes. No. Oh, I don't know, Mr. Wilson! I've never heard anything like these noises before, in the entire twenty years that I've lived here. For the last week they've happened every night – softly at first. Just a single knock on the wall outside my bedroom, as if a piece of plaster has

155

crumbled loose and fallen in the wall, or been knocked loose by the passage of a mouse. I'm a light sleeper, or I might not have noticed it – at least, when it began. But once I hear it, then in a few minutes – five or ten I suppose – there will be another, and it sounds intentional, as if someone had thumped a knuckle on the wall, and not as if the house is simply creaking as it settles for the night. Every night that I've heard the noises, they've begun the same way.'

"'Every night, you say. And you've heard them for a full week?'

"'Yes, although who can say when they started before I noticed them? They might even . . . might have started . . . .'

"Her voice trailed off then, and I knew what she was implying – that old Creech, the man who had lived there before me – was back somehow. I laughed aloud then, and her eyes narrowed. She didn't like being mocked.

"'You're thinking that it's your former tenant,' I said, trying to sound serious. 'But that's silly, Mrs. Denbigh. Surely you don't believe in ghosts.'

"That made her a little angry, I think. Her eyes narrowed and her nostrils turned white. 'I am sure that I don't know what to believe, Mr. Wilson,' she said tightly. 'I apologize for wasting your valuable time.' And she would have left in anger if I hadn't risen and asked her to stay, and to tell me more of what had happened.

"'Has it just been the knocking, then?' I asked.

"She shook her head. 'The first night I heard steps, somewhere in the house, but I couldn't tell from where, It was a sliding sound, with an occasional thump – the way that old Mr. Creech would walk around up here at night in his slippers.' She took a step forward, and put a hand on my arm. 'Have you heard him? Has he been up here as well?'

"I shook my head. 'But the walking was only the first night? After that it was the knocking?'

"She nodded. 'That started the night after I heard the walking – even last night. When I'm fully awake, it stops. Afterwards, I can't go back to sleep. It's a wonder the last few nights that I've managed to fall asleep at all, afraid of what I'll hear in the darkness, but when I do hear the knocking, I wake up, my heart racing. Are you sure that you haven't heard anything?'

"I shook my head and forcefully kept myself from smiling this time. 'I sleep so deeply that your Mr. Creech could be leaning right over my bed and I'd never know it.'

"I'd mistakenly made light of it once more, in spite of trying not to, and that only seemed to upset her yet again, but instead of turning to leave this time, a strange look came over her face, and she rushed on with her

156

story. 'But it isn't just the knocking and the walking around. Now . . . now, last night – he's written me a warning!'

"This, then, sounded more substantial. One might have thought that she was dreaming the other, no matter that she insisted she was awake. After all, I've only known the woman for a month, and while she's presented herself most sensibly during that time, I cannot really say if she might be the type to hear things that aren't there. But if there was actually a warning – something written down – well, now there was something to be going on with. As we say at the service, if it isn't written it doesn't exist, and this sounded like proof.

"Aware that the morning was getting away from me, I asked her to explain, but she said that she'd better show me instead. I nodded, and she led me downstairs – my two rooms are on the first floor, same as yours here, gentlemen – and then along the hallway beside the stairway to her own chambers at the rear. (The ground floor front is let to a key shop.) Of course I hadn't been to this part of the house before, but there were no surprises about it – She has a parlor with windows looking out over a small court, and a bedroom just beside it, and a small kitchen."

"And the basement?" interrupted Holmes.

"The door to the downstairs is underneath the steps going up to my rooms. It's located just outside of Mrs. Denbigh's sitting room."

"And who lodges above you?"

"No one – I'm the only lodger. Above me is just the attic, nothing more. It's a small house."

Holmes nodded for him to continue.

"In the parlor, she led me over to the fireplace. The wall there is papered – some sort of pink flowers, very small – and there, alongside the mantel, was the word '*Revenge*', written in soot."

Holmes glanced at me. Just two years earlier we had seen something of the sort scrawled on the wall of an abandoned house in Brixton. In that case, the same word – but then in German – had been inscribed in blood, located above the body of a dead American. It had been a most thrilling affair, especially to me in those early days of my recovery, and I wondered if Wilson's narrative might end up as another tale of vengeance spread across many decades and continents before coming to a grim conclusion in an old house in the heart of the British capital.

"Is the word still there?" asked Holmes, his features alert with interest. I knew that he would wish to examine it, and that he'd likely be able to glean a number of useful details.

Wilson shook his head. "Mrs. Denbigh washed it away later that day."

Holmes's eyes narrowed. "Describe it then."

157

Wilson glanced away for a moment as he reviewed the image in his mind. "The letters were even – none larger than the other – and each about a foot tall."

"All capitals?"

"That's right."

"And about how wide? Did they crowd together, or appear to get closer together at the end of the word, as if the writer had planned poorly and was running out of room?"

"No, they were evenly spaced – about six inches wide each, and an inch or two apart."

"Ah, a ghost who plans accordingly beforehand. What you describe would have been over four feet wide."

"That's right. It was at eye-level, and you couldn't help but notice it. There's plenty of room on that side of the mantel."

"And one would assume that the ghost – or whomever was responsible – dipped a finger into the fireplace to access this make-do ink."

"I thought of that. I looked in the fireplace, but Mrs. Denbigh had already built up the fire that morning. I did see some small droppings of soot across the slates in front of the fireplace leading off to the right, toward the message."

Holmes nodded. "A man after our own hearts, Watson! Possibly an important detail – for why would a phantasm need soot to write a message at all? Wouldn't such a creature be able to inscribe it with green flames, or with some sort of ectoplasm from 'The Other Side'."

Wilson nodded. "My thinking exactly, Mr. Holmes. Someone real – not a dead man – had been in those rooms. But even if it wasn't a ghost, it's still something that is a worry to Mrs. Denbigh."

"Agreed. And you say that this occurred yesterday morning?"

Wilson nodded.

"What did you do next?"

"There wasn't much that could be done. It was a bright morning as you'll recall, and the idea of ghosts seemed silly in the daylight. I mentioned that I needed to get on to work – Mrs. Denbigh didn't seem too pleased about that! – but I promised to think on it during the day."

"Does she not have anyone else that she can call upon for assistance?" I asked.

"It seems not. Her husband died fifteen years back – he was a brakeman for the railway, and there was some sort accident. She's mentioned that fact a number of times in passing. There were no children. If she has anyone else – a parent or brother or sister perhaps – I'm not aware of them. She doesn't have any photographs of family in her parlor, although there might be something of that sort in her bedroom."

"You've waited a day to approach me. What happened next? May I assume that there were developments last night?"

"Last night, and this morning as well. Throughout yesterday, I considered the problem, and decided that there was nothing to be done except hide myself last night and try to catch the person who was getting into the house. When I returned yesterday evening, I explained my plan, intending to settle myself in a little alcove near the front door, where I'd be out of the way when someone passed by – either entering somehow by way of the front door, or coming up from the basement."

"Is there a back entrance?" Holmes asked.

"Yes, but it's in the basement, so if someone were to enter that way, he or she would still have to climb the stairs and pass me in the alcove."

"Is there a separate entrance into the house by way of the key shop?" I interrupted.

Wilson nodded. "I thought of that, but I examined the connecting door in the front hall quite closely after I returned home, and it was locked and seems to be secure. The light wasn't the best there, but I could see that cobwebs across the doorway were too old to have been made since the night before, and they unbroken."

Holmes nodded appreciatively, and Wilson continued. "I also looked around a bit down in the basement, but saw nothing that seemed unusual. The rear door was locked up tight, and the door to the front areaway beneath Lowndes Court has a couple of solid locks, and while someone might be able to pick them, or even have copies of the keys, there's nothing there that revealed itself to me.

"After my little supper, I read for a bit and then went downstairs, knocking on Mrs. Denbigh's parlor door and letting her know that I was getting on station for the night watch. She seemed concerned that I'd be too far away, being near the front door, to know if anything happened, but I'd already arranged a comfortable chair in the alcove, and settled in to wait for whatever happened. However, gentlemen – and I hate to admit it – but . . . well, I fell asleep. I never heard a thing. This morning I awakened early, rather shamed that I'd been unable to stay awake for one night, and crept down the hall toward Mrs. Denbigh's parlor. She wasn't up yet, and the house wasn't making a sound. There, written in the same place as the morning before, and duplicating it as if traced in the same spot, was the word '*Revenge*', again spelled out in soot.

"It was quite early, and the fire wasn't built up yet, so I looked closely and saw where there were places in the soot where a finger had likely dipped in to be re-inked. I took the time to examine the letters more closely, and it was apparent to me then – and I should have noticed it the first time – that each letter would have taken a number of strokes to

159

complete, for a little bit of soot inked on each finger doesn't go far when writing seven letters that are each half-a-square-foot in size."

"What was Mrs. Denbigh's reaction when she saw this morning's message?" asked Holmes.

"Or more specifically," I amended with a smile, "when she learned that you had fallen asleep at your post?"

Wilson looked rather sheepish. "She said she'd heard the knocking again, and when I first spoke to her, she was a bit scared. When she saw the writing, she clung to me in fear. But then, when she heard that I'd slept through it all, she wasn't as upset with me as I would have thought. It seemed to please her in some strange way – proof that an intruder could enter once again, even with someone nearby. I believe that it further solidifies her belief that she has acquired a ghost."

"A ghost," Holmes added, "who dips a phantom finger into fireplace soot in order to physically convey his thoughts." He uncrossed his legs and straightened in his chair. "So you have now decided to consult with me."

Wilson rubbed his face. "I don't know what else to do. The woman asked for my help, and I could certainly hide again tonight, and this time make much more of an effort to stay awake, but then what? I want to stay in Mrs. Denbigh's good graces, and help her if I can, but I'm not sure just what I've gotten myself into. Suppose I do catch some fellow slipping through the house tonight. Do I try to trap him? Do I hit him over the head? Do I try and hold him until the police arrive, taking a chance that he'll do me an injury in the meantime?" He shook his head and sighed. "This is not my line at all. That's when I thought of you."

"And Mrs. Denbigh? Her thoughts about this consultation?"

Wilson shook his head. "I didn't tell her. I hadn't really decided when I left for the day. Instead, I simply said that I'd take care of things tonight for sure. That seemed to please her. Then, not long after I walked into work, I recalled you, Mr. Holmes – you were there last week, I believe – and my mind was suddenly clear on the matter."

Holmes tapped his lips two or three times, and then said, "This almost certainly falls into two or three likely categories. I'm aware of something like it ten or fifteen years ago in Saxe-Altenburg."

Wilson's eyes lit up. "That fills me with great confidence, Mr. Holmes! Although this matter has only intruded into my life for a couple of days, I'll be happy to have things return to normal. I don't like change, you see."

"Yes, I believe you mentioned that." He stood. "Doctor Watson and I will do a bit of research and let you know something before the end of the day."

Wilson and I rose as well, and he offered his hand, first to Holmes and then me. "Very good. I'll look forward to seeing you."

When the manager had departed, I looked at Holmes with an expectant raised eyebrow. "Pah!" he cried. "I shouldn't interfere at all."

"Indeed? Then why do so?"

"Because that messenger service is well-run and convenient, and I don't want to get on Wilson's wrong side. I fear that this will end badly for one of us." He glanced at the clock. "Nearly noon. Surely Mrs. Denbigh can be found at home. Would you care to accompany me?"

I did, and in ten minutes or so we were well-bundled against the cold and making our way by hansom toward the client's lodgings. We had held to our own thoughts down Baker Street and then into Marylebone Road, and it was only as we turned along Park Crescent, and so into Portland Place, that I sensed that Holmes was ready to speak.

"You indicated some familiarity with the matter."

"I did. It's as clear as if she'd pretended to fall into a stream so that he would rescue her, and then fall hopelessly in love."

I laughed at the image. "So that reference to some matter in Saxe-Altenburg . . . ?"

"That's real enough. The second daughter of Ernst I – the Duke – contrived something along the same lines to catch the attention of an aloof young man that she'd picked as a husband. The fellow was too dim to realize that he was being played like a fiddle, and set about trying to 'protect' her from the ghost that was following her about – that only she could see, mind you. I believe that they now have four children, and someone wrote a rather dull epic poem about it."

"I doubt," was my response, "that Mrs. Denbigh has read that poem. We must give her credit, I suppose, for coming up with the scheme on her own – if you're right."

"Oh, I'll admit it could be something else. Old Creech could have, in his misbegotten youth, stolen the Lost Fire Emeralds of the Yupik and hidden them within in the house, and now a vengeful tribesman, the last survivor of his people, has made his way on foot across the frozen wastes of the polar icecaps to chase Mrs. Denbigh out of her bedroom so that they can be retrieved. But the simplest solution is best: After a month, the widow has set her cap on the new lodger, who is too unaware to see the fate that she has planned for him. He did say, I believe, that she chided him for staying too far away from the parlor – and her bedroom – last night. I suspect that, in her own ineffectual way, she probably hinted that he should wait in her chambers for the ghost to arrive – a fact that probably eluded him, and thus he didn't feel the need to mention it. When he instead went the other direction, toward the front of the house, and in fact then fell asleep, it was easy for her to reload her guns with another message. Tonight, but for our intervention, the poor man might have been lost!"

"Holmes!" I said with mock surprise. "You hinted that this might end badly. I can agree that he might need to move if he finds this distasteful, which would be a bad ending for him – for you'll recall that he doesn't like change – but matrimony with the woman might end up being the best thing for the man! Don't disparage it, and don't charge in like wild bull and spoil something just because of your cynicism."

He glanced at me with a glint in his eye. "No promises, Watson. We'll see what sort of impression this woman makes. In the end, you might agree what saving Wilson is of the utmost importance."

And in fact the woman in question made a rather winning and pleasant impression after all. The hansom let us out in front of a small house, rather mashed between two larger buildings, as if in the past age when the city was being constructed, builders had started from either end of the court and worked toward each other, and when they met in the middle, their poor planning hadn't left quite enough room for a full-sized structure, and so the modest little house was built instead. The door to the residence was crowded to its left side, while the right held a modest little key shop – now dark, and with a sign on the door indicating that the owner would return by two o'clock. The entrance to the shop was reached by a little concrete "bridge" over the open space of the areaway below, and it had been added some years after the house's original construction, whenever the front ground floor was converted into a business requiring a second entrance. Those in the countryside might not have seen such an arrangement before, but in London it is rather common. A steep little metal stairway went down between the two doors to the areaway.

Holmes rang the bell of the residence door, and within a few moments it was opened by a slender and somewhat careworn woman in her middle-forties. The lines on her face, however, seemed more likely to have been caused by smiles rather than frowns – although when Holmes introduced us and explained our purpose, a frown was what presented itself.

"I had thought," she said, with rather tight lips, "that Mr. Wilson would be taking care of this matter for himself. I didn't expect that he would confer with outsiders."

"I understand," said Holmes smoothly. "But he had some legitimate concerns that whatever is going on might be more than he could handle – and he wanted to make sure that you didn't come to any harm along the way."

I glanced at Holmes to see if there was any sarcasm to his comment, but his face was open and without guile. When he then asked if he might

162

look around the house to see if he could determine what was going on, the woman allowed it, although clearly she still wasn't pleased.

After closing the door, she led us back along the hall to her parlor. I noticed the closed and locked door to the key shop on the right side of the entry way, and then the stairs on the same side, leading up to Wilson's rooms. The left side of the hall ran smoothly to the back of the narrow building, where it ended at a widened area consisting of four doors. One, directly in front of us and closed, presumably led to the lady's bedroom. A second, on our right, was well-lit by sunlight from the south-facing window, and was clearly the parlor. The third door beside it led into a small kitchen, and the fourth was underneath the stairs – leadng down to the basement, according to our client.

The parlor was small but pleasant. The papered walls, tasteful decorations, and comfortable-looking chairs made it seem like a good place to spend time, and the warm little coal fire was a treat after our cold journey from Baker Street.

I didn't venture too far into the room, instead leaving things as untouched as possible for Holmes. Although I'd only been accompanying him on his investigations for a couple of years, I'd long-since learned the correct way to behave when entering an area where interpretations of evidence might be possible – and crucial.

It was quite obvious that, unlike the previous day, Mrs. Denbigh hadn't yet wiped away the word which defaced the wall to the right of the mantel. Holmes slowly made his way across the distance between the doorway and the fireplace, while I simply watched. Our hostess noticed my gaze, and stated, "I have no idea why anyone would seek revenge against me, Doctor."

I was tempted to ask – simply making conversation – whether she had seen any vengeful Yupik lurking in the neighborhood, but I feared that my attempt to privately amuse myself would only make for an awkward exchange. Instead, I asked her how long she'd lived there, and she began to chat more freely, stating that she and her husband had obtained the lease nearly twenty years before, not long after their marriage, by way of a small inheritance combined with what he earned from the railway. When he was killed, a small settlement had given her a bit of financial security, and enough besides to remodel the larger front area of the house into a shop. With the income generated from that source, and also taking in a lodger to fill the space upstairs that she didn't need for herself, she'd maintained a comfortable-enough living.

Holmes finished examining the carpet, and then moved wider afield, still looking down as he criss-crossed the room, even investigating the window opposite the fireplace where it was unlikely the "ghost" would

163

have needed to venture. After only three or four minutes of this, he finally turned his attention to the sooty message upon the wall. This received less attention than I would have suspected, and he never looked into the fireplace at all – knowing that the day's new fire would have likely destroyed the signs that Wilson had seen where someone had dipped a finger into the ashes.

Murmuring something about with Mrs. Denbigh's permission he would now examine the rest of the house, Holmes briefly visited the kitchen and then opened the door to the basement – without actually receiving said permission – and vanished downstairs. He was gone for quite a bit longer than I would have expected, and my conversation with the landlady went from polite to strained to conclusion, and we stood in silence for an awkward long time awaiting Holmes's return. We finally heard him climbing back upstairs, whereupon he shut the door to the basement and, without a word, turned and went down the hall before then ascending to Wilson's rooms.

Mrs. Denbigh seemed about to object, but then she held her tongue – perhaps uncertain of her ground when she considered that Holmes was acting as Wilson's agent. Her dilemma was short-lived, as my friend returned almost immediately, joining us in front of the fire, which had remained quite pleasant to me, even in my coated condition.

"It's a very curious situation," he said, rather noncommittally, I thought, considering his earlier theory as to the source of the threatening message. Perhaps there was more to it than he'd let on, or possibly he simply wished to present his findings to Wilson, and thereby let the manager decide how to proceed. Additionally, he spoke rather quietly – or so it seemed to me – as if he didn't want to be overheard. It gave the conversation a seriousness that had previously been missing.

"We can see the writing on the wall. Can you tell us more of the noises on the first night?"

She nodded. "I described it to Mr. Wilson as if someone were walking, but that's not quite right, I suppose. It was a sliding noise, and it seemed to be all around – I couldn't say that it came from within this room, or the hall, or anyplace with certainty."

"And he also mentioned knockings."

It seemed as if she had momentarily forgotten that. "Oh, yes. There's that too. But the noises seem less important somehow than if someone – some *thing* – is inside the house and writing threats upon my wall." Her eyes pointedly glanced toward the fireplace. "Yet I'm certain that Mr. Wilson can manage this. I . . . I don't have money to hire a detective to spend hour after hour here trying to catch my ghost. In fact, you might scare him away."

"Wouldn't that be the purpose of the exercise?" asked Holmes with an innocent tone. Only someone who knew him would spot the humor in his narrowed eyes.

"Why, yes. Of course. But if the ghost does decide to leave, you will still keep investigating, day after day, to make certain he's gone, and I can't afford that kind of expense."

"I believe that Mr. Wilson took on that capital outlay for this matter when he hired me, madam, but I do see your point. In any case, I suspect that this matter will resolve itself rather sooner than later. Tell me," he added, "do you have a relative, or a friend, whom you might visit this afternoon? The doctor and I want to keep an eye on the house when it's empty, to see if anything unusual occurs."

Mrs. Denbigh frowned and seemed to want to ask a question, but then she nodded. "Anything to get this finished, I suppose. I can go see my old aunt in Norbury. I've been meaning to do so – it's been several months."

"Promise me that you will go? Excellent. Then for now the doctor and I will leave you, but we hope to have news for you by this evening."

She seemed puzzled, but also relieved that we were departing. After she shut the door behind us and we reached the pavement, I intended to stop and question Holmes, but he took my arm and led me down the street. Glancing back, I saw that the door had reopened, and the lady of the house was looking our way. Nearby, a stout man was unlocking the key shop, apparently having returned early from his errand, as it was still somewhat before noon.

When we were several blocks away, Holmes hailed a hansom and directed the driver to drive north along Regent Street. It was crowded, and we made poor progress.

"Your mood changed," I said. "After you had been downstairs."

He nodded, his face grim. "As you recall, Mrs. Denbigh told Mr. Wilson that the 'walking' sounds occurred about a week ago. I believe that those were real, even if she wrote the message on the wall herself."

"So that's established then?"

"Without a doubt. The pattern of her footsteps beneath the message tell the whole story."

"She might have stood there to examine it."

"No. The footprints shifted slightly from left to right, back and forth, as would someone who was carefully writing each letter, and then turning back repeatedly to the fireplace, bending down and obtaining more soot."

"And the knocking that she reported?"

"That was false, to gin up her story. She nearly forgot to mention it until I asked, and her facial expressions were clearly less sincere than when she described the initial walking sounds. I suspect that she truly heard the mysterious noises a week ago, and probably was made sincerely nervous. From that, she developed the idea of a full-blown haunting, intended to serve as an excuse to lure Wilson into her clutches."

"But back to my original question: What changed your level of interest after visiting the basement?"

"You recall that Wilson said he examined the basement to see if intruders had entered that way? What he failed to mention, no doubt thinking it of no importance, is that a portion of the basement under the key shop is walled off from the part used by Mrs. Denbigh – no doubt done when the shop itself was built following the death of the lady's husband. There is also a connecting stairway between the shop and their segment of the basement.

"There is a connecting door between the two sides of the basement, and it was well locked, with no signs of recent passage as Wilson said – which is likely why Wilson didn't mention it as a factor. Knowing that the key shop upstairs was closed, I had no hesitation at picking the lock to see what was going on in that half of the basement.

"Do you recall what happened just a week ago?" he asked, seemingly switching course midstream. I wracked my brain. Did he mean one of his own cases? Or something more generalized? Then it hit me.

"The Fenian bombing in Mayfair!" I exclaimed. "On the fifteenth, I believe. And they placed a second bomb at the offices of *The Times*, but it failed to explode."

"Precisely. And what do you think that I found in the basement of the key shop?"

"Good Lord," I muttered. "Dynamite?"

"Nine full cases of it. Enough to destroy several blocks in every direction around that woman's house should it go off – not to mention countless public structures if they have a chance to use it elsewhere."

"And she isn't aware of it," I said, half as a question, and half hoping it to be true.

Holmes agreed. "If she was a part of such a thing, she'd have no need to take in a strange lodger, just weeks before the plot was due to be executed. If she needed a lodger to complete the picture that she is just an innocent landlady, one of the Fenians could have filled the bill. I'm surprised that they didn't think of it – putting one of their own there when she advertised the rooms – but perhaps the timing was wrong. Possibly Wilson arrived right after she placed the sign, just in time to rent the rooms before someone else could present himself as another lodger. In any case, if she was in on the plot, she certainly wouldn't have started all this foolishness about having a ghost, and taking the chance on attracting

166

attention to the place, in the very week that the bombers were laying low and sitting on a deadly amount of explosives."

At that point, he spotted something and had the driver pull to the side and wait. Then he hopped down and danced through the crowd until he reached an idling lad of twelve or so – whom I recognized as Silas Thurber, one of his more steady Irregulars. They spoke for a moment and coins were exchanged before the boy dashed away and Holmes regained his seat in the cab, informing the cabbie to now take us to Scotland Yard with all possible speed.

"Gregson, I think," he said. "I believe that he's been involved in the formation of some sort of special branch to address the bombing problems."

The inspector was in a conference related to the very issue of which we'd been speaking, and when he heard that Holmes was there to see him, he immediately excused himself and led us along a hallway to an unused office. There, Holmes told him succinctly about our initial skeptical visit to examine Mrs. Denbigh's house for evidence of ghosts, and then what he'd found in the basement.

The inspector instantly perceived the gravity of the situation. "Are you sure that this landlady isn't involved? And what about this Wilson fellow?"

Holmes explained his reasoning as to why they weren't connected with the dynamiters. "No doubt this key shop was set up to appear as an innocent cover for the Fenians, right in the heart of London." Gregson nodded, and was all for immediately raiding the place, but Holmes had a different plan.

"I asked Mrs. Denbigh to get out of the house later today. One can only hope that she will do so as promised. If she doesn't, we can still proceed, but I'd feel better if she was gone. In any case. I propose that we get an anonymous message to the owner of the key shop – Randall, according to the name upon the door – that all is known. It should convey just enough to get him moving without really telling him anything. He may flee on his own, in which case we follow *him*, or he may assemble his men in order to move the dynamite, and we'll follow *them* – rather like spotting a single bee and marking his path until he leads you to the hive. We can try to take the whole nest of them. Granted, arresting Randall now and confiscating his cache of explosives will solve the immediate problem, and we might very well get some more names out of him – but then again we might not. I believe that in this way we can bag most, if not all, of the gang."

Gregson rubbed his face with one of his big hands and nodded. "I'll get some men around the place."

Holmes shook his head. "No – or at least not too close. I've already taken care of surrounding the building, as well as the neighborhood in every direction, with a veritable army of my Irregulars. Let them work in close to these men as they escape, so that no suspicions are raised. Have your men ready to arrest them when they've gone back to ground elsewhere in their other hidey-hole."

The inspector reluctantly agreed and returned to his meeting to quickly brief those who were waiting to learn why he'd been called away. Within a half-hour, we – along with the inspector – were on our way back to the area around Mrs. Denbigh's building.

We left our vehicle several blocks away, and Holmes stood patiently for a moment until Silas Thurber came out of a nearby alleyway to report. "The lady left not long after we got there," he said. "It's just the man in the key shop now."

"Good. And Dungiven?"

"We've fetched him. He should be here in just a few minutes."

And he was. Michael Dungiven was one of Holmes's agents that I'd met on a few previous occasions. He was from Ireland, and could lay on the accent so thick that he became nearly unintelligible when needed. Fiercely loyal to the Crown, he often provided information about Irish criminals when requested by Holmes. (Interestingly, he hadn't yet met Gregson, and after these events he was recruited into the newly formed Special Branch, serving with great heroism and distinction until his tragic death some nine years later, during the period following Professor Moriarty's death when the London underworld violently fought to fill the vacuum left by the destruction of that criminal's evil web of crime.)

Holmes quickly explained the situation, and Dungiven nodded. He really only needed to convey one thing to Randall, but his quick intelligence perceived the deeper aspects of the matter. He turned and set off for Lowndes Court, while we waited impatiently. He was gone for no longer than ten minutes, before approaching us from a different direction than that in which he'd departed.

"Any difficulties?" asked Holmes, while Gregson balanced impatiently from one foot to another.

"None," said Dungiven. "He was curious about who I was, but I dropped a couple of names he'd likely know, and that seemed to convince him. I was in and out in two heartbeats nearly. He's on the telephone, and he was starting to call someone as he watched me leave. I believe that things are in motion."

That proved to be correct. We strolled until we reached an alley, whereupon Holmes led us through to the Lowndes Court end, where we had a view of Mrs. Denbigh's building. Within half-an-hour, a dray wagon with a couple of draft horses drew to a stop in front of the key shop, and half-a-dozen men leapt down and pressed inside. Within a minute they were lugging crates to the back of the wagon like ants carrying cake droppings back to their hill.

"The question," said Holmes, "is whether Randall shall stay or go – Ah! He's locking the door and joining his fellow plotters."

"I'm glad that we listened to you, Mr. Holmes," said Gregson in a low tone. "That dray wagon could be followed by a man in a bath chair. We'll have them, and no mistake."

"You might want to hold off, Gregson – at least for a few hours – once you know their destination. You can pick off the ones that leave, and perhaps others might arrive in the meantime, even someone higher up in their organization."

Gregson frowned, considering whether it was worth taking the chance of possibly losing track of those that he'd just seen over the reward of a bigger catch. Then he nodded.

It was a gamble that paid off. The Irregulars followed the wagon as it crossed London to an old warehouse in Hackney, not far from Sutton House. There, Randall supervised the unloading of the dynamite, which was carried inside without incident. The Irregulars kept up a running contact with the police during the journey across the city, racing ahead on side streets and anticipating where turnings would occur. Later that evening, several other big fish did arrive as Holmes had suggested, and Gregson decided then to make his move. The raid swept up nearly a dozen men, including two who were definitely implicated in several previous bombings. More important, an additional quantity of dynamite was discovered in the warehouse that dwarfed that which had been moved from the key shop. We had found the Fenians explosives depot.

That night, Holmes and I knocked on Mrs. Denbigh's door. She answered with a surprised look, explaining that she had just returned a few minutes before from visiting with her aunt and was in the process of preparing Mr. Wilson's dinner. When asked if she could pause that and fetch him, she agreed, and soon we were in her little parlor, where Holmes was explaining the full details of the arrest of the lady's storefront tenant.

Both were shocked, and they glanced at one another as if they had just survived some great tragedy. "You've saved our lives is what you've done, Mr. Holmes!" said Wilson. "What if that dynamite had blown up during the night?"

"Or what if the police had caught wind of it on their own," added Mrs. Denbigh, "and arrested us without the benefit of your deductions that cleared us beforehand?"

"That's right," added Wilson. "You not only saved us, but you cleared our good names as well."

The two of them then chattered together, sharing remembrances of Randall that each recalled, indications that should have let them know what the man was really about. I waited for some mention of the knocking ghost and the warning of *"Revenge"* to be uttered, but they never seemed to get around to it, and neither Holmes nor I were inclined to remind them. In a very short while, we excused ourselves, and they seemed happy to let us go, as their conversation now was of the type that excluded all but themselves.

"Perhaps," I said, outside and pulling my coat tighter against the chill, "they'll recall in a few minutes that the question of the writing upon the wall wasn't adequately explained."

Holmes shrugged. "She'll likely concoct a reason that satisfies him – that Randall was somehow getting into the main house and trying to scare them away. It won't make any sense, of course, but people in love don't have any respect for logic."

"You saw it too, then," I said. "The dam between them has been breached."

"Indeed. Mrs. Denbigh's plan might have worked anyway without any of this, but the addition of a dash of danger in the form of dynamiters was just the extra ingredient to make Wilson gobble down the whole cake."

I laughed. "A curious metaphor. Perhaps it will be a wedding cake."

And so it turned out to be. Later that year I saw the announcement of their marriage in the newspaper. I mentioned it to Holmes, who was expectedly indifferent, but I found myself the tiniest bit peeved, as if we should have been invited somehow for helping them, in our own modest way, to complete the arrangements. However, after another moment's thought, I found that I was relieved that we hadn't been asked to attend. Perhaps, I realized with a start, just a bit of Holmes's antipathy was rubbing off on me – something that I vowed to resist with more effort than before.

> He turned into one of the district messenger offices, where he was warmly greeted by the manager.
> "Ah, Wilson, I see you have not forgotten the little case in which I had the good fortune to help you?"
> "No, sir, indeed I have not. You saved my good name, and perhaps my life."

> – Dr. John H. Watson, Sherlock Holmes, and Wilson
> *The Hound of the Baskervilles*

The Sunderland Tragedies

I do not recall the weather that day, the 17th of June, 1883. If asked, I'd say that it was dark, but perhaps that impression is influenced by the terrible events of the day before. While we were unaware at the time of what was happening, we would soon be involved in a peripheral matter that took precedence over all else, if only for a short while.

Holmes and I arrived in Sunderland on the 16th, located on the coast slightly southeast of Newcastle upon Tyne, looking into a question of an inheritance. What had appeared to be a simple but distasteful matter between two distrustful brothers had quickly devolved from an arrest into a serious matter of state when one of them was found to be under disreputable obligations to the German government. Holmes and I had been out all night and returned to our hotel at dawn, scraped and weary. Events had escalated quickly, and after treating our wounds, with both of us thankful that Holmes had managed to avoid a knife to the eye during an unexpected struggle, we separated in our shared sitting room and sought a few hours of sleep before the affair would recommence.

We had risen in the mid-morning, somewhat refreshed, but sore from the unexpected journey across the city on the previous night, followed by the ambush that had so nearly cost us both our lives. The miscreants were behind bars, but the job was only half-finished, and as we shared a meal that fell somewhere between breakfast and lunch, and then drank cup after cup of coffee, we discussed what must be done next to bring this seriously spiraling matter to a successful conclusion. It was then that a frantic knocking upon our sitting room door interrupted us, and Holmes rose to see who it was.

From my chair by the small dining table, somewhat behind the opened door, I couldn't observe who was facing Holmes from the hallway, but I heard a woman's tones, slightly high-pitched in an unnatural way, and breathless and hurried, as if she were restraining herself only with the greatest effort before collapsing into sobs. I stood and walked quickly to the door, uncertain as to whether my medical services would be required.

Joining my friend, I could see a woman who appeared to have dressed hurriedly. She was around thirty years of age, in expensive clothing that was unfortunately rather rumpled, reflecting her emotional state. She wore a fashionable hat, but it was cocked at an odd angle, as if it weren't properly seated on her head. She had a wedding ring, and while she seemed to be in overall good health, her color showed that she was functioning under a great stress. Her eyes, which would have been striking at normal times, were underscored by dark circles and red-rimmed from crying.

"Mr. Holmes, you must help me!" she cried as I came into view. "My daughter – he has taken her! I know it – when they didn't find her body last night amongst the dead, I knew it was him. He once threatened to take her. There were so many dead, and yet there's no sign of her. And if she wasn't killed last night, then where else could she be?"

Perhaps she would have rushed on with more of this confusing and urgent entreaty, but Holmes lifted a hand and said in a voice that surprisingly pierced her desperation and brought her up short.

"Dr. Watson and I would be happy to hear your story. Mrs. – ?"

"Barrhill. Mrs. Frank Barrhill."

Holmes nodded. "Mrs. Barrhill. Please come in. We can provide a cup of coffee, or perhaps something else to steady your nerves, and then we'll hear your story from the beginning. It's the only way to build an effective picture of what has happened, and what is required to effect a solution. No – not a word until you've settled yourself and had something to drink."

He spoke as a doctor would to a hysterical patient, and it seemed to be effective. I led her to a chair by the fireplace and asked what she would prefer. She wisely chose brandy – as I believe coffee would have been too stimulating in her condition, and she wisely indicated that waiting for tea to be requested from downstairs would take too long. Within a moment, she had the brandy in hand, and Holmes and I were seated on either side of her, in the same arrangement as if we'd been back in Baker Street before our own mantel, with the client in the basket chair between us and ready to relate an intriguing tale.

"Now," said Holmes, his voice still low and steady, infusing a calmness into the proceedings which otherwise might escalate at any moment when the woman began to tell her story. "You mentioned that they didn't find your daughter's body 'amongst the dead', and 'so many dead'. I'm afraid that Dr. Watson and I have been involved in another matter, and don't have any knowledge of what you describe. Has there been some sort of tragedy?"

The lady looked from one to another of us as if it was impossible that we could be so ignorant. It seemed that she couldn't speak. She took a sip of brandy and then whispered, "How could you not know? The . . . awfulness of it . . . ."

"I assure you, madam," said Holmes, "that we have no knowledge of any tragedy. We were out all night and – " He stopped as I rose, noticing the morning newspapers on a side table, left for us by the staff when our breakfast was served, but still untouched and unread. I recalled that the man who carried in the tray had seemed grim, but he had given no hint as to any terrible event. I stepped over and pulled the top paper from the stack. I needed to go no further than the front page – the story was emblazoned in all its terrible and graphic detail.

"My . . . *my God!*" I whispered.

"Watson?" asked Holmes, his voice rising. Beside him, Mrs. Barrhill sobbed and began to weep into a handkerchief.

The story is simply told. While Holmes and I had been dashing about, investigating the squabblings between two unadmirable brothers, we had been oblivious of the events that would tear the heart out of poor Sunderland. The previous day – the 16th of June – a pair of traveling entertainers, Mr. and Mrs. Fay, had presented their children's variety show as they had done countless times up and down the island. The Victoria Hall held over three-thousand seats, and the place was filled, mostly with children. Nearly half of them were upstairs in the gallery.

At the end of the performance, several things – all with innocent intentions – occurred, each combining to lead to disaster. It was announced that certain children with specially numbered tickets would be awarded prizes as they exited the Hall – one at a time. In order to ensure that the tickets could be inspected in an orderly manner, someone – it wasn't known who – had locked one of the stout doors at the bottom of the gallery steps so that there was a gap only wide enough for one child at a time to pass while showing his or her ticket for inspection.

In the meantime, a second set of general prizes was being distributed by the entertainers at the front of the auditorium, from the stage. The children in the gallery saw this, and – excited, ready to leave, and worried that they might miss their prize – they began to surge down the stairs, with the greater number of them pressing forward into the staircase that ended at the narrow passage beside the locked door.

It was estimated that as many as 1,100 children were in the gallery, along with just a few supervisory adults. What had seemed like a good idea by someone to keep order and allow for regimented inspection of tickets turned into a death trap.

To put it simply, 183 children were crushed or trampled to death by the slow-moving and inexorable human stampede.

Realizing what was happening, one of the building's caretakers, Frederick Graham, had valiantly tried to divert the children back upstairs. Finally he ran up another staircase to the gallery, heroically leading over six-hundred of them down a different way. At the bottom of the stairs where children were already dying, adults could not unlock or force open the door to widen the gap, and they frantically pulled child after child through the narrow remaining space and into the auditorium, even as more and more of them pressed downward on the other side. I could only imagine the screams of those trapped in the stairs as the weight from behind grew ever more steady. And then, when they could no longer scream . . . . It was found that bodies had slipped to the ground during the tragedy, to be trodden underfoot by the weight of hundreds of relentless feet above them.

Finally one heroic man was able to wrench the door at the bottom of the stairs off its hinges. I could almost imagine that I was he, sobbing as I pulled and pulled, to no avail, before giving one last desperate effort, causing the wood and metal to finally give way. But even so, that mass of people continued to overwhelm the wider door space as surely as they had the narrow gap.

I could not speak, and silently handed the newspaper to Holmes. Then I opened the other papers that had been left for us that morning, seeing much the same story. I filled a brandy glass for Holmes, and another for myself, and then refilled that of our visitor. When I'd settled myself back in my chair across from Mrs. Barrhill, I took a long swallow, holding it in my mouth and letting the burn seep slowly across the back of my throat. I closed my eyes, and kept them so until Holmes spoke, his voice tightly controlled.

"Your daughter was not among the dead."

Mrs. Barrhill shook her head. "No. I had dropped her off – it seemed safe enough, with so many children there. Betsy – my Elizabeth – is eight years old, and very wise for her years. It should have been a nice outing. I stepped down the street to do a bit of shopping, and took a cup of tea at a nearby shop. I was walking back when I saw everyone milling around outside the Hall. I started seeing the men carrying out the bodies. I thought that there might have been a fire, but there was no smoke. Some of the children were laid on the grassy verge before the men returned inside. Others were met by women – mothers like me – wailing as they recognized their children. One was crying pitifully and plucking at her little boy's coat. 'Make him breathe!' she sobbed, and the man holding him told her softly, 'He won't ever again.' The woman collapsed at his feet, and he lowered himself beside her, placing the child in her arms." Her voice drifted away as she recalled the horror if it. Her eyes rimmed with more tears

"How do you know that she hasn't been taken in by someone?" I asked, recalling her to the present. "A friend, perhaps, or another mother whom you know who led her to safety in the midst of all the chaos. Have you been home to receive word?"

"I have. I thought the same thing. When I couldn't find her among the dead, I rushed home, but she wasn't there either. When I went back out to search, I left instructions with the servants to find me, should a message arrive – but I didn't let on that Betsy is missing, or what I fear is the true reason. When my husband returns, I don't want him to know this has happened if it can be avoided.

I glanced at her wedding ring. "Your husband? He is away then."

"He is," she replied. "In South Africa. He has business interests there. That's where we met – I was traveling with my parents ten years ago when we encountered Frank in the hotel. My parents liked him very much. It was a short courtship, and we were married within a month. Soon after, we returned to England, and to his family home here in Sunderland." She recited the basic facts as if it was a story often repeated, and in doing so, she'd boiled it down to the bare bones. If there had ever been any romance to meeting and marrying her husband in a foreign land, she had long ago excised it from the telling.

"You said that 'he' has taken her," said Holmes, returning to the woman's initial statement, "a fact that I nearly lost sight of when overshadowed by this vast tragedy. Who is this 'he' to whom you refer?"

She took a deep breath and then a deeper draw on her remaining brandy. I raised an eyebrow and asked if she would care for more. She would. After it was poured, she took another breath and spoke.

"What I have to tell does not reflect well on me, gentlemen. I would never share it, except for the fact that my daughter has been taken. To get her back, I will do anything. I will share any secret, and destroy my reputation in your eyes. I only ask for your help."

We nodded.

"Before I met Frank, I loved another man – in a way that I've never felt for my husband. Altus Luckhof – It is he whom I loved . . . and he is the true father of my daughter. He's the man whom I believe has taken her.

"My late father had business interests in Cape Town during the years when I was growing up, and he often traveled there alone. But ten years ago, he decided to make a grand journey of his next trip, and to take both my mother and me along with him. I wasn't especially keen on going, but I was nineteen and had no choice in the matter, and so we set out.

"The journey was long and tedious, and I found the countryside hot and uninspiring – and nothing of what I'd been led to expect when picturing Africa. After our arrival, my father was often traveling around the countryside on business, and as soon as he would leave, my mother would take to her bed – she was always one for acquiring imaginary illnesses. Left to my own devices, it wasn't long until I became enamored with Altus, one of my father's business acquaintances, and nearly two decades my senior.

175

"I suspect that he'd seen his opportunity while my father was away. In any case, we were very close for most of a week, and again a few days later when my father set off again in a different direction. During that time, I came to love him. I was young and innocent, and knew no better. He was tall, with black hair and a matching beard, kept short. He had an old scar on his right cheek, quite white against his sunburnt skin, which he refused to explain. He was knowledgeable and dashing, and confident and assertive. I doubt that he felt toward me anything to the level of what I experienced, but I fully expected that he'd declare publicly that we were to go forward as one instead of two as soon as my father returned. But when Father came back, Altus became more distant and formal, and then he departed, telling me vaguely that he had business to the north and would be gone for several weeks, but would try to see me again before we returned to England.

"In the meantime, father had met Frank Barrhill, a man of much the same type as him – British with extensive South African business connections, moderately wealthy, and with good prospects. Frank was about thirty then, and very . . . typical. Nothing like the dashing Altus who had won my heart.

"It was all fixed up before I knew it, and I was so full of silent private despair from the loss of Altus's company that I willingly went along with whatever was proposed, knowing by then that my parents had chosen Frank, and Altus's absence indicated his true feelings – or lack of. Frank and I were married within a couple of weeks, and the four of us – two couples, my parents and Frank and me – returned to England together soon after that. Altus never returned before we left. Frank moved us here, to his family home, and we've remained ever since.

"Our marriage has been tolerable at best, but Frank seems to expect nothing more from me than that. I was content to live the life cut out for me. We tried half-heartedly to have children, but without success. Then, nine years ago, Frank informed that one of his South African clients, in England on business, would be stopping by our house. Normally this wasn't unusual – part of Frank's success is his willingness to open our home to his business associates, in spite of this location being rather out of the way. I was expecting just another South African business-man, and nothing could have prepared me for the surprise when our visitor arrived.

"As you've likely guessed, it was Altus Luckhof. I could tell from the beginning that he wanted to keep our past meeting a secret, with neither of us letting on that we'd previously known one another. Later, when we had a chance to talk, Altus claimed that he'd had no idea that I was Frank Barrhill's wife, and I almost believed him, but now I think that he sought

176

out a business connection with Frank just to find me, having learned of our marriage a decade ago in Cape Town.

"Frank was oblivious to the rising and sudden rekindling of interest between Altus and myself. Suffice it to say, we . . . carried on with a physical relationship for the short time that he stayed with us – discreetly, and quite without discovery. I didn't fear that Frank would learn anything, for he was already singularly uninterested in me by that point, but I did want to avoid giving the servants anything to speak of, and I thought that Altus and I were successful. Then Altus returned to South Africa, and I soon noticed that we hadn't avoided the consequences after. Nine months after our encounters, Betsy was born. There is no doubt that she is Altus's child, but Frank still seems to have no realization of this fact, as he's never questioned it, and seems to accept Betsy in a good-natured and vague way as his own.

"Two days ago – a day before the tragedy at the Victoria – Altus suddenly reappeared, after years of not making any effort to communicate with me. Somehow he'd known that Frank would be away in South Africa, and he timed his visit to see me alone. This time, he had no interest in resuming our romance – and neither did I, for he was quite a changed man. Before, he had been dashing and mysterious and handsome, and those extra years that he'd possessed had given him a rugged and intriguing character. But he must have had a hard life since those days, and the weight of his years seemed to be resting on him like the soil of a grave. There is something ill about him now – Though tall, he is now stooped. He is gray and sunken, and tired and querulous. His black hair and beard have turned white. But none of that mattered. He'd somehow worked out that Betsy was his daughter.

"From what I could gather – from what he told me – he'd arrived several days ago and watched us, Betsy and me. He checked the official records to verify the date of her birth, and discreetly questioned our neighbors, and calculated when she was conceived. But most of all, he saw her – from a distance he said – and knew without a doubt that she was his, for she is him all over again in coloring and features and height – the way he looked a decade ago – and nothing like Frank – or much like me, for that matter, although I certainly added some aspects of my own.

"He appeared at our house two days ago – I saw him walking up the drive and knew who he was in an instant. Rather than let him be seen by the servants, I ran out and intercepted him, leading him away into a copse of trees a distance from the house. I was filled with great trepidation – I hadn't seen him since our previous tryst, and I had no idea what to expect. I was ready to be defensive, and to let him know that our previous relationship would not be renewed, and when I saw him – the wreckage that he'd become – I knew that my resolve was equal to the task. In any case, he had no interest in continuing that aspect of our association. No, he demanded to have possession of our daughter.

"There was no polite conversation. He immediately jumped to his demand – and there is no other way to describe it. 'You've had her long enough,' he growled. 'Nearly halfway to adulthood. It's my turn now.' He said it as if it were perfectly reasonable – as if my daughter would be willingly entrusted to him, and taken away from the only life she's ever known, sent away with a stranger to a strange land for the rest of her girlhood. I laughed and told him he was mad, but inside I quivered with fear, for he had the look of madness in his eyes.

"He didn't waste time with any further argument. I suppose he could see that my mind was made up. 'So be it,' he said, rising. 'There are other ways.' And with a polite nod, as if we'd never met and as if we hadn't just discussed something so monstrous, he turned and left.

"Afterward, it was almost like a dream, and I sat and tried to imagine what might happen next. I suppose I always thought that he might be back someday, to threaten exposure of Betsy's true parentage to Frank, or that he might open some sort of legal proceedings. I puzzled over various possibilities the rest of that night, going without sleep, but it honestly never occurred to me that he might do something different – that he would simply take her and vanish."

"How do you know that he was the one who took her?" asked Holmes.

"Yesterday, after the . . . after the tragedy, and when I still believed that Betsy was at the Hall, I spent much of my time hysterically going from here to there – where they were laying out the bodies, or into the building itself and back out again, or scanning all of the thousands of children wandering around outside before they drifted away or were claimed by thankful parents. All the while, the screams of anguish where the bodies were being collected, as parents identified their own lost children, both repelled me and called me back, always afraid that Betsy had been added to the rows, but needing to know if she had been.

"Finally the word came that all of them had been removed – and she wasn't there, which lifted my heart, but it also left me with even more worry, as she was nowhere to be found. I ran across an acquaintance who said that she thought Betsy had walked away with a tall white-haired old man in a dark odd-fitting suit. I instantly recognized that it was Altus, and knew what might have happened. I regretted that it hadn't occurred to me that going to the theatre would place her within his reach.

"I tried to think – Where could he go? How could I find them? But it was no use. I went to the police, but they had no interest in speaking with

178

me or helping, being overwhelmed with the tragedy of dealing with the grieving families of nearly two-hundred dead children. Then, I saw your name in this morning's paper, Mr. Holmes, in connection with some arrest yesterday, and I recalled when you helped a friend of mine several years ago – Colleen Agutter – when she was staying at a hotel in Russell Square, and you were recommended to help her, since you lived just around the corner from there. She never told me what you did – only of the debt that she owes to you. She said that you believed her when no one else would."

Holmes glanced my way when Mrs. Barrhill mentioned that he'd been mentioned in the newspaper. Apparently he was displeased that our recent investigation had been reported.

When Holmes didn't speak immediately, the lady seemed to take it as reluctance to accept her case. She leaned forward, entreating, "I have nowhere else to turn. My husband is expected any day. I must have Betsy back before he returns."

"And can you offer any additional information as to where Mr. Luckhof might be found – assuming that he and your daughter haven't already departed?"

She shook her head. "I can only suspect that he would have been staying somewhere near the docks. He was always a rough man, and he could hide there. It's . . . it's a place where I wouldn't be able to follow him."

Holmes nodded. "We'll see what we can discover. Will you wait for us at your home?"

She nodded, and I asked for the address, which she provided.

"I hope to have news for you shortly. In the meantime, remain close, Mrs. Barrhill, should your daughter somehow free herself and manage to return to you."

She thanked us and rose, and yet she was still unsettled, as if she wanted to stay and talk more of her fears, while knowing that her departure would free Holmes to begin his investigation. Finally, with a nod, she left us.

As I shut the door behind her, Holmes returned my gaze with a frown. "I'm surprised that Colleen Agutter would have mentioned her little affair to Mrs. Barrhill," he said. "It was before your time, Watson. Her reputation was gravely at risk." He shifted, looking this way and that for his pipe. "Our client seemed most upset at the loss of life in the Hall yesterday."

"As anyone would be," I responded. "It's an unimaginable tragedy." As he began the process of filling and lighting the pipe, I asked, "Where do we intend to begin?"

He didn't answer for a moment, frowning into the rising smoke from the now-fuming pipe. I reached for one of the newspapers and read further of the tragedy.

One young survivor, William Codling, Jr., approximately seven years of age, explained that he was sitting in the front of the gallery when the performers began handing out toys from the stage far below. There was a great roar from the children up there when they perceived the unfairness of it all, but they were told that toys would be provided to them too, at the bottom of the stairs. He had joined the throng, and it had become tighter and tighter as he went down the steps.

He became aware that he was walking on someone who had fallen down, unseen beneath the pressed bodies. He yelled to tell someone, but no one listened. In spite of that, and the rising panic around him, he hadn't known how serious the matter was. In the midst of the screams and pleas, the people behind kept surging forward. It was only when a rumor that more toys were available back upstairs in the gallery that many turned back.

Codling recalled that the tightness of the crowd gradually loosened, and upstairs, he joined a group being led by a man to another stairwell. He soon found himself outside, reunited with his sister, who had been seated in the ground-floor of the auditorium. It was only then, as clutched him, weeping, and they wandered through the crowds and saw the dead bodies being carried out, that the true aspects of the tragedy made themselves clear.

It was then that Holmes rose to his feet. "Our options here are limited," he said. "I have no local contacts, and no Irregulars to send hither and yon for a stray fact, or to fan out like a small army, seeking Luckhof's trail. And yet, time is of the essence. The girl has been missing since yesterday. If he took her, they could already be gone – by land or sea."

"'If he took her'?" I asked. "You don't agree with Mrs. Barrhill's theory? You suspect some other explanation?"

"Let us say that I haven't accepted the explanation before us without certain reservations, until it can be adequately verified. But we'll know nothing until we make a search. I'll explore around the docks, as Mrs. Barrhill was unable to do so, and see what I turn up."

"And me?"

"I doubt that asking questions at the Hall would accomplish anything. We'll send a message to Mrs. Barrhill, asking which of her acquaintances saw the girl being led away – I should have thought to ascertain that before she left. When we have the name, we can speak with the woman and see if she recalls any further details. In the meantime, you can retrace her footsteps to the police station – although as she said, they have much more on their minds right now. Still, you might catch a sympathetic ear who knows something. I suspect that they have already become numb to worried and distraught mothers, but you can approach them with a different tone. Stay open to possibilities."

With that, he returned to his room, only to reappear in a few minutes in the guise of a dock worker. He was in a set of old rough clothes, which I knew he always packed for a journey in case they might prove necessary, but it wasn't simply those that changed him so much. He carried himself differently, and brushed his hair forward and over his eyes. He'd added some padding to his cheeks, and darkened the spaces under his eyes – more than they were already from our previous hectic day. With a nod, he was off.

While he was changing, I wrote a note to Mrs. Barrhill, asking for the name of her acquaintance who had seen Betsy led away by the white-haired man. After arranging with the hotel for its delivery, and instead of wasting valuable time sitting in our suite and waiting for a response, I set out into the streets of Sunderland.

Our hotel wasn't far from Mowbray Park, which lay alongside the Victoria Hall. I felt drawn in that direction, although Holmes had felt that making inquiries there would be a waste of time. Still, something within me had the morbid need to look upon the place.

The building itself was built like a small cathedral, rather than the theatre-like structure that I'd expected. It had tall windows – half-a-dozen of them on either side – lining the long side walls. Between each window was a protruding support column running all the way to the high terraced roof if I knew more of architecture, I could state what the supports were called, but they seemed to be attenuated buttresses, giving strength to the towering walls. Nearby, lying nearly at the foot of the building itself, was a decorative and well-landscaped lake, with paths designed for comforting and enjoyable strolls. Now, however, there was no joy to be found there.

Many people were standing around the building, and out away from it on the pathways by the water – some talking quietly in groups of threes and fours, while others meditated in silence, heads bowed and hands folded in prayer before a spot where a number of flower arrangements had been left. Here and there would be a husband and wife, huddled together, sobbing while lingering in that place where their child had been lost. All of them kept to the pavement, leaving the various grassy verges surrounding the building empty. One could almost picture how it had looked, less than a day before, with so many dead children laid out there, and more being carried out all the while to join them, while broken parents dashed about and sought to know the truth, hoping for a better outcome before locating their children with wrenching agony. The newspapers

181

reported that some families had lost more than one child, and in a few cases every child in the family had perished. And nearly a hundred others had been injured to one degree or another. The suffering was almost unimaginable, and I knew why no one was standing upon the grass: To do so would have been as if trodding upon and defiling a new grave.

I finally said a small prayer and turned away, making my way to the police station, but as expected, my endeavors there were unsuccessful. I found a harried and weary-looking sergeant willing to listen to my story – or as much as I wanted to provide – about a missing girl being led away during the confusion of yesterday's disaster. He understood the seriousness of the problem, but explained that they were simply too stretched just then to provide any meaningful assistance. He did offer to ask whether the officers there just then might know of anything, and I agreed. I also asked him to see if the officer who had spoken to Mrs. Barrhill the day before might be available, thinking she might have told him something useful, remembered at the time when the episode was much fresher in her mind, but forgotten a day later when she visited Holmes and me. I didn't have high hopes, and the sergeant returned in a very few minutes, saying he'd put the question to all of the officers that were currently present, and no one had any recollection of the incident, or of talking to our client. I had to accept that he had done his best, and thanked him.

Outside, I was at a loss of where to go next. It was too soon to expect a reply from Mrs. Barrhill, and Sunderland was simply too large for me to simply wander about with no plan, trusting to luck. Holmes was covering the docks. I decided to try the hotels.

Although it was something of a plan, it wasn't much better than simply wandering about, which I'd wished to avoid. I started in the area of the station and worked my way in an ever-widening exploration of the surrounding streets. At the first one I tried, there was no record of a guest called Altus Luckhof, and I was about to leave when it occurred to me that he might not have registered under his own name. I queried the desk clerk with the description given to us by Mrs. Barrhill – around fifty now, tall but stopped, white hair and beard, grayish coloring, and a white scar on his right cheek. The extra information didn't matter. The man wasn't a guest.

I had visited perhaps a dozen hotels with no success and was considering that my time might be better spent when I turned a corner and spotted Sherlock Holmes – now restored to his normal appearance. Apparently he'd been back to our hotel after what must have been a short trip to the docks. He hailed me and increased his pace. In a moment we were conferring to one side of the pavement as the crowds moved past us in either direction.

"I returned to change clothes, and to see if there was a reply to your message from Mrs. Barrhill. There was not. Then, based on what I discovered, I began visiting the hotels. I take it that you're doing the same."

I nodded and related where I'd already been.

"Good. We've each been working in different directions, and haven't crossed each other's paths. Have you been asking for Luckhof by name?"

"I have, and also by description, should he have visited under an alias."

"No, he is here, and under his own name. He arrived late yesterday evening from South Africa on the *Fuwalda*."

"Yesterday evening? But Mrs. Barrhill said he visited her home *two* days ago."

"She did. However, I definitely confirmed his arrival in Sunderland after that. He has been a passenger on the *Fuwalda* all the way from Cape Town. She docked in London four days ago, but he preferred to stay on board, rather than leaving the ship and completing the journey by train. He told the captain that he is meeting a business associate here who is also returning from London, and traveling by rail would place him in Sunderland too soon – he would prefer to simply travel as he had been for the remainder of his journey. He departed the ship yesterday after they docked, but I couldn't find anyone who remembered where he went next, or who would have transported him.

"I don't understand what is going on," he continued, "but I fear that we've been deceived. We must locate Mr. Luckhof and find what he knows."

We separated and continued visiting the hotels, occasionally passing one another with simple shakes of our heads to one another, indicating a lack of success. But finally, as I was about to enter a smaller hotel on a side street, Holmes hailed me. I turned to see that he was hurrying my way.

"I located his hotel. He checked in yesterday, not long after he departed the *Fuwalda* – several hours *after* the Victoria Hall tragedy, when he was supposedly seen leading away young Betsy Barrhill. And then, an hour ago, he hired a cab to take him southwest of the city – to the address provided by our client. I spoke to the cabbie, who had just returned, and is waiting for us now."

"Is there any sign of the girl?" I asked as we walked back the way Holmes had just come.

Holmes frowned at me, as I'd clearly missed the point, "I don't believe that Luckhof has anything to do with the girl's disappearance – if she's missing at all. No, there is something else happening here. We need to go to Mrs. Barrhill's as quickly as possible. I fear that there's some sort of tragedy brewing."

We were soon winding through ever-less-crowded streets and into the countryside. The cabbie informed us that our destination was no more than five miles from the city.

"You don't think that the child is missing?" I began when we were underway. "Surely Mrs. Barrhill's agitation and fear were palpable – she believes that her daughter has been taken."

"Does she? Or was she instead upset by the terrible tragedy and loss of life yesterday at Victoria Hall – as any mother would be when considering it – and did she then make use of those tears to convince us that she was also upset over her daughter's absence?"

"I don't understand," I said. "Why would she falsify such a claim? And what does Luckhof have to do with any of this?"

"I can't answer that yet. I sent a wire to Colleen Agutter, Mrs. Barrhill's friend, inquiring how much she had shared of her own situation, but there has been no reply. Likewise, I wired someone in London to provide information about Mr. Frank Barrhill, but those questions haven't had time to be answered yet either. All I can tell you is that Mrs. Barrhill has apparently lied to us about Luckhof visiting her two days ago, on the fifteenth – a day before he arrived here by ship, as verified by the crew of the *Fuwalda*, direct from South Africa by way of London – and if that portion of her tale is false, then possibly the rest of the structure is rotten as well."

I tried to see various explanations why the woman, so obviously upset, would contrive such a story, implicating a man who could not have done what she said. Holmes read my thoughts.

"If her story about Luckhof's visit to the house is a lie, as is the assumption that he led away her daughter yesterday afternoon, then one has to wonder if any of the other details so carefully and embarrassingly related – the account of her first meeting with the man a decade ago, and his subsequent visit so Sunderland a year or so later, resulting in the conception of the child – are true as well. And if not, what does she gain by creating this fiction –and by involving us?"

I nodded. I began to have a terrible suspicion what we might find at the Barrhill house, and I could see that Holmes felt the same way. I was tempted to urge the cabbie to greater speed, but we were already moving at a quick clip, and would be there soon enough.

The house was a pleasant-appearing structure, and much bigger than I would have imagined. Two stories high, and solidly built with an attractive mixture of brick and stone, it was set well-back from the road.

There was a loneliness to it, especially on that day, as there seemed to be no activity. Nothing moved, except for the lazy spiral of smoke rising from one of the chimneys standing above the rear of the house. My instincts were that something was wrong here, and I was grateful for the weight of my service revolver, which I had long-ago learned never to be without.

Instructing the cabbie to wait, we approached the door. Holmes pointed to a fresh-looking footprint, apparently made from a shoe that had stepped in a patch of earth nearby. I had accidently trod it in myself, and I put my foot down next to the print, creating a similar, though larger, duplicate.

Meanwhile, Holmes rang the bell, and again when there was no response. Finally, looking back to the indifferent cabbie who was already reading a racing sheet, Holmes put his hand forward to the doorknob. With a silent motion he turned it. The door opened, and we stepped inside as if we'd been welcomed to do so.

To one who has encountered it, the smell of burnt gunpowder, as produced from a fired gun, is unmistakable. There is nothing – burnt toast, or an extinguished candle, or burning wood or coal or oil – that quite resembles it, whether from a massive field piece in the heat of battle to a small gun in an otherwise plain room of a house. And it was that smell that we both recognized as soon as we stepped inside. The door was still open behind us, and while I withdrew my revolver from my pocket, Holmes stepped silently back outside. He was only gone for a moment, and I heard the departure of the cabbie even as he returned, pushing the door shut behind him. I didn't need to be told that Holmes had sent for the police.

We found them in a drawing room off the main hallway. Mrs. Barrhill was curled into a chair, weeping, and twisted to that she wasn't looking at the bodies stretched upon the bloodied carpet. Nearer her was the man who, based on the description we'd been provided, must be Altus Luckhof. He had a surprised expression on his face, almost comical if one had seen it displayed by an actor on the stage. But here, with his eyes glazed in death and focused on something far beyond the ceiling where they were turned, it was a tragedy instead of a comedy. A bullet wound had shattered his chest, and death must have been nearly instantaneous.

Across from him, nearer the unlit fireplace, was another man, younger than Luckhof, but still in middle age. His hair was dark, and if he'd been upright, it would likely have shown signs of needing a visit to the barber. He had a simple wedding ring upon his hand, and even in paleness of death, lividity causing the blood to settle within him, his coloring showed that he had been an active fellow, often outdoors. Now his otherwise handsome features were marred by a terrible wound in his

185

throat, along with another centered at his heart, matching the one in the body of the white-haired man across from him.

I stepped across to the weeping woman, saying her name softly, letting her know that we were there, and asking if she could relate what had happened. She didn't seem to hear me at first, and then Holmes quietly called for me to join him.

He softly asked me to examine the bodies, and while I saw no need – both men were clearly dead – I did as he asked, and quickly understood what he had already found. Meanwhile, he continued to look around the room, observing things that were beyond my seeing, likely otherwise hidden footsteps and such, giving him a clear picture of what had happened here, and also inspecting those things which were obvious even to me: The bullet hole in the mantel, almost certainly from the shot that had first torn through the dark man's throat, and the two guns lying beside each body, dropped there after their deaths – a Swiss ordnance revolver by Luckhof, and an Enfield Mk 1 by the other.

Holmes continued to inspect the room, at one point finding a decorative quilt folded over a chair at the far side of the room. He held it up and let it open, looking at it this way and that in the light from the window. With a noise of satisfaction, he replaced it, unfolded, upon the chair. Only then did he join me at the weeping woman's side.

"Mrs. Barrhill," he said in a firm voice, louder than I would have expected, and in a rather jarring manner. "What happened?"

She had jumped when he spoke, and then for a moment made no response, other than to continue weeping. Finally, with a shuddering sigh, she pulled herself upright and placed her feet upon the floor.

"My husband came home sooner than I expected. I . . . I didn't know what to tell him. About Betsy. I hoped that you would have news soon, and also that I could send you a message to make sure that you didn't visit, giving him a chance to find out what you were doing, and why." She had rigidly kept her gaze away from the portion of the room where the two dead men rested. Now she cut her eyes that way, just for an instant, before looking back in our direction.

"He was telling me about our trip when the doorbell rang. I answered the door, and it was Altus. He pushed past me, yelling for Frank. My husband looked out and they saw one another. Altus came in here, and they argued. I tried to stop them – to stop Altus from telling him the truth – but it was too late. Almost immediately, Altus bragged that he was Betsy's father, and that he was taking her back to South Africa. He demanded money. He said that he should be compensated for missing so much of her life before. Frank roared at him. He . . . he went to his desk where he kept his gun. In the meantime, Altus pulled out a gun as well.

They circled each other for a moment, and then both fired – several times. I screamed and closed my eyes. Then it was over, and when I looked, they were both dead. I . . . I don't remember what happened after that."

Holmes nodded, and then resumed inspecting the room. He looked in the dead husband's desk, and then nodded. "There is a gun oil stain, here on the wood of this drawer. Did your husband have other guns, Mrs. Barrhill?"

She nodded. "He has a small collection. He keeps it upstairs."

"And do you have one of your own? For protection, perhaps?"

She frowned. "I do. My father taught me to shoot as a girl. But I didn't have it with me this morning."

Holmes nodded. "How long ago did this happen?"

"What? Less than an hour, I suppose. I – "

"You said that you answered the door when Mr. Luckhof arrived," Holmes asked.

Mrs. Barrhill blinked. Then, "Yes. I sent the servants away when . . . when this trouble began. I didn't want them gossiping."

"And yet, you also mentioned that the servants were instructed to notify you if any messages arrived. When did you send them away?"

She frowned, and Holmes continued. "I had the impression from our conversation just a few hours ago that they were still here. But they were gone when Mr. Luckhof arrived. How curious."

He took a step back, and her eyes followed him. I had been sitting near her, and now I stood as well. I was aware that there were a number of decorative pillows resting near the lady. I wondered if a gun from her husband's collection might be concealed beneath one of them.

"That quilt," said Holmes, nodding his head toward the one that he'd examined and refolded a few moments earlier. "It seems out of place in this room. Can you tell me why it's here?"

She didn't reply. She didn't do anything except look at Holmes with a new wariness. I noticed that her tears had dried up.

"Perhaps someone used it in here while taking a nap – although that seems most unlikely. Unfortunately, it's now somewhat ruined. It has a bloodstain on it, you see."

Still no response.

"One has to wonder why that is – folded as it was and placed in a part of the room well away from the bodies. Perhaps, however, it *was* unfolded at one point, and used to cover one of the corpses – possibly so that it wouldn't initially be noticed by another man when he arrived."

I had been correct – there was a gun under one of the pillows. And in spite of how fast she moved, her arm shooting out with the speed of a striking cobra, I was faster, having expected something along those lines.

A single step and my hand caught her wrist, even as she knocked aside a pillow to reveal a small but deadly American Smith and Wesson Model 10 revolver. I scooped it up with my left hand and quickly shifted back a few feet, ready in case she came after me. But she did not.

"Dead bodies are consistent," said Holmes. "Not in everything, of course. *Rigor mortis* sets in differently for different people. But two bodies that died at the same time, not very long ago, in the same location and under the same conditions, should each lose heat at the same rate. However, your husband – as Doctor Watson can verify – is markedly cooler than Mr. Luckhof. Perhaps if there was a fire lit in here, your husband's corpse would have remained warm – as warm as the other – but you overlooked that. He was killed at least several hours ago, long before Mr. Luckhof's arrival. Should you wish to step over and touch the bodies, you can see for yourself. No? Then to continue . . . .

"We know that Mr. Luckhof traveled here by cab from his hotel less than an hour ago, as the same cabbie just brought us. So he has been cooling for less than that time – that is, we can fix the time of his death to a point not long before our arrival. And your husband's skin should feel the same – but it does not.

"Discussions with the captain of the ship that brought Mr. Luckhof from South Africa, and then from London to here, revealed that the ship was running somewhat late. It was supposed to be here a couple of days ago – the day that you claim Luckhof visited you and demanded your daughter. In fact, they only docked yesterday afternoon, *after* the Victoria Hall tragedy, and *after* he was supposedly seen by your unnamed friend leading your daughter away. If you had known that fact, that he wasn't actually in Sunderland, would you have adjusted your story this morning? Probably. But you contrived it on the incorrect assumption that Luckhof was already here, and that your story of his visit to this house, and subsequent abduction of your daughter, would be accepted.

"I think we can see what happened here. Your husband arrived home from South Africa – probably today. It's certain that you knew when to expect him, contrary to your earlier vague statement that he was arriving soon. He came in, and you shot him – missing the first time, in spite of your training, and only wounding him the throat. The bullet passed through and into the mantel. A fatal shot, but not immediate. You immediately corrected the mistake and put a second bullet into his heart. There are no close neighbors, and you had sent the servants away. We'll find out from them just what pretext was given. Then you found the quilt and covered your husband's body, so that Mr. Luckhof wouldn't see him when he arrived for his pre-arranged appointment with your husband, his business associate, and was brought into this room.

"Did he wonder what was under the quilt before you killed him too? I expect so – it's quite visible, and there would be no mistaking what it was – but there was no need to converse with him. You had him here, in the room, and you shot him immediately – with a different gun, another from your husband's collection. I'm sure that you picked one that the servants won't readily know. Then you removed the quilt and folded it, possibly unaware that there was a blood stain, or perhaps planning to clean and remove it later.

"What next? You had the props in your play arranged and your script ready. Did you plan to run to a neighbor's house, screaming for help about the mutual shooting you'd just witnessed? Whatever you intended, it was circumvented by our arrival. You were forced to leave the quilt – so out of place in this room – folded nearby, and then you pretended to be overwhelmed by what had happened, waiting for us to discover you."

"'Pretended'?" she snapped. Her tone was sharp now, and there was no sense that she was going to deny Holmes's interpretation of events. "Why should I *pretend*? Do you think me a monster? I've just seen two men die!"

"By your hand," Holmes reminded her.

"What of it?" she countered. "My husband was an evil man – vicious and abusive. Not the sleepy ineffectual thing that I described to you this morning. Our only peace – for Betsy and me – was when he traveled. It was only getting worse – and he was turning his . . . his attentions more and more to my daughter. I . . . I would not allow that. When he left this time, I decided to find a way to be free of him."

"You could have found another option," I said. "You could have sought help."

Holmes shook his head. "She is still deceiving us. Perhaps Frank Barrhill is as bad as she claims, but there must be more to it than that. Why else craft her plan to kill another man as well? An innocent man. Isn't that correct, Mrs. Barrhill?"

She glared at him defiantly, but didn't answer.

Holmes glanced toward the dead South African. "That man has never been a big strapping fellow, dark and handsome, but now much changed. Consider his frame, Watson. And if he wasn't the man that was described to us ten years ago, then the rest of the story is suspect as well. Perhaps, Mrs. Barrhill, you did meet Altus Luckhof during your journey to South Africa. More likely you first met him when he visited here nine years ago. That can be verified, but I'd be willing to bet that he was simply a visitor who stayed here a few days while he and your husband conducted business. When word arrived that he would be returning this week for another visit, you concocted this idea of shifting the blame to him, and

189

knowing that he would be coming out here to meet with your husband upon his arrival, you sent away the servants, and then killed both of them, one by one.

"What truly impresses me is how you were able to add on extra features to your plan, based on new events. The tragedy at Victoria Hall occurred, and you saw that as way to explain how Mr. Luckhof could spirit away your daughter. You read in the newspaper that Dr. Watson and I were here on another matter and, recalling your acquaintance with Colleen Agutter and how I'd helped her, you sought me out to give credence to your story. When the bodies were found, we could explain that you'd already come to us for help. After all, you said that I believed Mrs. Agutter when no one else would – did you think that I'd show you the same courtesy?"

"But her daughter?" I asked. "Where has she been during all of this mummery?"

"Oh, I doubt if she's too far away," Holmes replied. "She's too young to be sent away on her own, and leaving her with another person would mean that someone was out there who could tell the truth when the supposed story behind these murders was reported."

At that moment, we heard the return of our cab. We would soon be joined by a sergeant and constable from a nearby station. Mrs. Barrhill remained silent while Holmes explained the situation, but began to deny the accusations, still insisting that the two men had shot each other.

"There is one more bit of evidence," Holmes said. "Make note, Sergeant, when the bodies are examined. You'll see that the cuffs of each of the dead men are clean, and that they are both right handed. Mrs. Barrhill – if you would lift your right arm?"

She did so before considering that she shouldn't. Holmes took her arm and turned it for the policemen to see. "There are a number of small burns here – from burning powder expelled by one or both of the two murder weapons when they were fired. Preserve the guns, and this shirt, gentlemen. Test firings of the weapons will confirm that such markings on the clothing are evidence of who shot the guns, and that the dead men with their unburnt shirts did not."

Mrs. Barrhill wrenched her hand down and cursed Holmes with a low and vicious stream of colorful epithets. She was still promising her revenge when she was led away.

Before they vanished into the hallway, I stopped them.

"Your daughter," I said. "You must tell us where she's hidden."

Her mouth tightened, knowing that to do so would be the first crack in personally admitting her guilt – if one didn't count the fact that she'd tried to reach for a hidden gun resting beside her just a few minutes before.

190

Finally, realizing that the game was lost, she seemed to sag a little and said, "She's in the attic. I told her to hide – that bad men were coming – and to stay hidden until I came for her." She looked at the sergeant. "May I go up and get her? May I see her?"

With a gruff denial from the officer, she was led outside to the cab. It was then that she broke down, her wails being apparent until they had traveled a distance from the house.

Upstairs, there was only one entrance to the attic. We climbed the stairs, calling "Betsy" in calming tones, fully aware that the girl, fearing "bad men", would be terrified of our approach. Thankfully the attic was a large open space, covering the entire top of the house, lit regularly up and down on both sides by dormer windows. The plain wooden floor was drifted with dust, and there were only a few places where odds and ends from the house were piled.

Holmes indicated a path of footprints through the dust toward a side of the attic that was more carelessly piled than the other. He whispered that he would stay by the entrance, in the center of the great space, should the child bolt. He seemed to think that I would have a more calming influence on her.

I went toward the cluttered side with its more places to hide. There were boxes and piles of clothing, slowly being ruined by dust. Furniture was scattered here and there, some broken. It was near the back that the footprints vanished, behind a range of boxes that seemed to be stacked like a wall. It was quite telling that the dust around the boxes was also disturbed, indicating that they had been recently moved. Certain that I was in the right place, I repeated the girl's name in my most winning manner and stepped around the end of the barricade –

– only to be rushed by a shrieking creature, no more than three foot high, wielding a knife! With a scream and a thrust, she was upon me. Later I would find that my coat was slashed, but thankfully no part of the blade cut me. In spite of my initial surprise, I was able to grab her thin wrist and keep a firm hold, finally forcing her to drop the blade. By then Holmes was there, and he kicked it away. Meanwhile, I held the girl close, repeating her name and telling her not to worry, we were not the bad men that she had expected. But in my heart I suspected that in a way we were. We were trying to gain her trust in this moment, but we were taking her out of this illusion of protection into a changed life – one parent dead, the other soon to be tried for a brutal and coldly planned double murder.

We carried her out of the house without going into the room where her father's corpse still lay, and over to a nearby neighbor. There Holmes privately explained the situation, obtaining agreement that the kindly residents would keep watch over the child until the return of the police, who would make other arrangements. Then we walked back to town. I heard later that distant relatives had adopted the girl – possibly out of the goodness of their hearts, or so I liked to think, but my cynicism wondered if it was also related to the fact that Frank Barrhill was much wealthier than we'd thought, and that accumulated treasure went with his young orphaned daughter – for she was such, as her mother, sentenced to a life term, had died less than a year later in prison.

We stopped by the police station to make our statements, and to inform the police where Betsy Barrhill was now located. Apparently Mrs. Barrhill was already confessing in another part of the building, and what we provided was no more than corroboration to her statement. In truth, the entire matter was very distasteful to all involved, coming as it did upon the terrible events of the day before, and while it might have been a sensation in other more normal times, it was then something that seemed to be incidental.

We concluded what remained of our business in Sunderland that afternoon in time to make the late train south. I've recorded the events for the sake of my records – especially as I cannot do so in regard to the matter which first necessitated that journey – but Holmes and I have never returned there.

No Good Deed

I came up Baker Street that morning, April the twenty-fourth it was, dodging here and there between the people already thick on the pavement. Once I was obliged to step right off into the street so that a fine lady could get by, only to get a curse yelled my way from an omnibus coming up behind me. That's always been the way it's worked out, from what I could tell. No good deed goes unpunished, as my old mother used to say.

She had cause to know. She was the most charitable person I ever knew, and it never helped her at all that I knew of. At least not in this world. She may be fetching her reward for it now on the other side, for all I know – my dad doesn't believe it, and although I want to, I don't know that I do either. She wore herself out making the ragged ends meet, raising five of us kids, and putting up with her husband. She encouraged him to do the right thing, as often as he'd let her, and it lifted him up to being a better man for as long as she was able. But then she was gone, and he settled into different ways. Which was why I was making my way up that busy street, looking for a certain address and a man that I hoped could help.

It was late enough in the morning that the sun was starting to peek over the buildings on the eastern side, lighting up those opposite, where I was to be found, stepping from house to house. There it was, farther north than I'd supposed. I'd never been in this part of London before – I usually navigated along the river. I'd grown up there, just across from The Tower, but thanks to my poor mother, I hadn't had the chance to run that rat warren along the southern shore like the other children my age. She'd made sure that I'd stayed busy – idle hands and all of that – both around the house and on my dad's old boat. And along the way, I received a fairly adequate education, learned to read and write, and speak fairly well besides. I'd resented it at the time, but I certainly appreciated it now. Already, I'd been promoted twice since obtaining my current position – which would require my presence again by tomorrow night, so I hoped to get this business settled quickly.

I stepped up to the door, having the usual mixed emotions about whether I should even be involved in this, when – before I could knock – the black door suddenly flew open before me. Startled, I took a step back, almost stumbling. For a sailor, I've always been slightly clumsy, especially when on land. It always vexed my father to no end.

I started to mumble my excuses to the man hurrying out the door, but something caught in my throat. I suddenly felt, for no reason that I could

193

explain, a terrible feeling of fear, like a mouse under the gaze of a hawk. On the surface, there was no reason for it at all. He was just a middle-aged fellow, such as what I see on the ship every day. Tall and thin, with a high forehead, crossed by a few strands of whitish hair combed across. As he came out of the door, he was clearly angry, and muttering to himself while he reached up to place a tall black hat upon his head.

He was snarling to himself, something about "destruction" and "promise you one, but not the other!" when he saw me. With a hiss – and it was a hiss, it couldn't be called anything else – he raised his cane as if he meant to strike me. Then, he seemed to take hold of himself, and the rage twisting his face dropped as if covered by a falling curtain, replaced with a look of contempt as he flicked his eyes up and down, as if he was reading my very soul. His head moved from side to side, and I almost expected his tongue to flick out like a snake. He glanced up and down at my uniform and dismissed me, saying in a low voice, "You must be one of those d---mned urchins that he uses. Take heed, boy. You'll want to get far away from him!"

He brushed past me, while I tried to take the meaning of what he'd just said. Granted I was small, but surely I didn't still look like a boy. Obviously this was a smart man, but he didn't know everything. Maybe he'd just made a mistake because he was angry. My mother always said an angry man makes mistakes. As I wondered what other mistakes might be in store for him, I glanced up at the first floor window and saw that I was being watched. It was a man in a dressing gown, staring intently down at me. He had surely seen my encounter with his most recent visitor. There was a grim expression on his face, but when our eyes met, it softened, and he beckoned me to come in. Then he stepped away from the window.

Inside it was quiet, and with the door shut, the hallway was dark. Behind me, over the door, the fanlight let in some light, and I looked at it, with the reversed 221 showing as I waited for my eyes to adjust. Finally, I could see the closed door to the rest of the ground floor on my right, and the stairway leading up straight back from where I stood. I mounted the steps two at a time, rounding at the landing, and on up before stopping at the door that would surely open into that room looking down on the street.

I already had an idea what to expect. Just last year, I'd come across a copy of *Lippincott's* that contained a narrative about the tenant of these very rooms. I would have been interested anyway – I'd been following this man's career since I'd first met him over two years earlier. But to see the circumstances of that very meeting reported in the magazine was almost unbelievable. The article hadn't been specifically about my father and me, but we'd both played our parts, disreputable as they were, and I was even mentioned by name. It was the closest to fame that I was ever likely to get.

All of this flashed across my mind in just a few seconds, but it was apparently too long for the man inside. He called out, almost impatiently, for me to enter.

It was smaller inside than I would have thought. Only about fifteen feet from the door to the front windows, where he still stood, and about eighteen feet from side-to-side, with a fireplace over to my left. The two tall windows were facing east, and the morning sun was getting brighter. Mr. Holmes stood there, his right hand in the pocket of his dressing gown. I couldn't see his face with the light from the window behind him, but he seemed quite tense – not unusual, if he'd just had an argument with the man I met downstairs.

"I'm sorry . . . ." I began. "You've just had another visitor – "

He seemed as if he willed himself to relax, taking a step forward. His brow was knitted, but he made an effort to take a deep breath and straighten his posture, whereas before he had stood as if poised to defend himself. He removed his hand from the dressing gown pocket, and I was startled to see that it held a gun. He stepped purposefully toward the mantel, where he laid it amongst an odd collection of relics. Then he reached for a pipe, turned, and dropped into a chair facing me, stretching his long legs out in front of the cold fireplace. I was surprised to see how tired he looked. Careworn as well, as if he had been desperately overworked for too long. And yet, in spite of his obvious weariness, there was a tightness about him, rather like a coiled spring, with all that compressed energy simply waiting to be released.

"My landlady has apparently stepped out," he said, "which explains how my previous visitor was able to freely make his way in. I can't offer you any tea or coffee, but you're welcome to smoke." He gestured toward a basket chair beside him. Happy to have made it this far, and hopeful that I'd be able to tell my story and ask for his help, I gratefully sat down, fishing out the makings of a cigarette.

"I took you for a pipe smoker," he said, glancing at my pocket, where the shape of my pipe was obvious.

"I'm out of pipe tobacco."

He was packing his own pipe with shag from a foreign-looking shoe tacked to the side of the mantel. Although some unusual things had been described about him in last year's *Lippincott's*, including the syringe in the morocco case that I'd spotted lying about, nothing had been said about this unusual place to store tobacco!

"I can offer you some shag, although I'm told that my method of keeping it tends to dry it too much for most people to enjoy. You wouldn't have enjoyed what I smoke for my first pipe of the day, which had already been accomplished before my visitor. But if you'll notice over there – "

195

and he gestured toward the chair opposite him on the other side of the fireplace, " – there is some Ships. It's not too old, as my friend that uses it is still a regular visitor."

"Dr. Watson's, then," I said. "Is he not here?"

"The good doctor remarried a couple of years ago, and now has a practice in Paddington."

Replacing the cigarette fixings, I withdrew my old pipe, a friend to me both in port and on my travels, and stepped across for the tobacco. It was a bit stronger than what I normally used, but I felt that I would need the extra boost that it provided to convince Mr. Holmes to help me.

As we both finished the tedious process of getting our pipes lit, I settled back and started to speak. But even as my mouth opened, Mr. Holmes said, "Do you enjoy the London to Liverpool run better than plying up and down the Thames?"

I nearly dropped the pipe. I had seen a little bit of this for myself, during that short time I had been around him in September '88. And I knew as well from reading about it in the story in *Lippincott's*, called *The Sign of the Four*, that he did this type of thing all the time, the way that an old salt can tell the coming weather from the clouds, or judge the shallowness of the water just from the smells. But I somehow hadn't expected him to practice it upon me.

I glanced down. "I can see how you would know I'm a sailor," I said, "and this is the uniform of the Liverpool, Dublin, and London Steam Packet Company, out of the Albert Dock – "

"On the *May Day*, perhaps?"

I swallowed. "Yes. But how did you know about the Thames?"

He pulled his legs back and crossed them. "You were born in Southwark, and were raised in a brick house adjacent to the Thames, straight across from The Tower. It's since been torn down. You have four younger brothers, no sisters, and you are the eldest, twenty years of age. You are left handed, and walked here today, rather than taking a cab or some form of public transport. You are obviously a sailor, and have been on the Liverpool boats for two years, after spending your life assisting your father on his steamship, the *Aurora*." He closed his eyes. "Black, as I recall, with two red streaks. And a black funnel with a white band."

"Ah." I understood now. "You remember me."

"Yes," he nodded. "Sometimes hard facts make deduction unnecessary. You are Jim Smith, son of Mordecai Smith. You were but seventeen when Jonathan Small hired you and your father to wait for him while he retrieved the Agra Treasure, in order to transport it downstream to a waiting ship."

I nodded. "After we ran aground that night, you and Dr. Watson were quite kind to me. When the police took charge of the *Aurora* until it could be searched in the morning light, and my father and I were pulled onto the police launch, you gave me your coat."

He waved it away. "I was sorry to hear about the loss of your mother."

I raised my eyebrows in surprise. "How did you know about that?"

"Your little brother, Jack. He sometimes assists my Irregulars."

Ah, Jack. I feared for him. Since my mother's death, he had been in the care of my other brothers, who in turn were nominally under the protection of my father. However, as his situation had declined, so had their prospects. I was glad that Jack was likely benefiting from some association with Mr. Holmes, however remote. Strangely, I wasn't worried by it.

"I didn't know that Jack had found employment."

"That says a great deal about your brother's trustworthiness." A slight smile danced around his eyes. "I knew when the little scoundrel asked me for a shilling back in '88, and then another, that he was sharp." His expression changed, and he added, "I was also sorry to hear of the loss of your house and dock."

"Yes. When the building of the Tower Bridge was announced, we had no idea that it would swallow our little piece of property. We were given what was termed 'adequate compensation', but of course it wasn't. We, all of us that owned property around there, became amateur lawyers for a bit, learning about 'eminent domain'. My mother's insistence that I receive an education was useful at the time, but only enough for me to realize how little that I really knew, and how we never had a chance. It was disheartening when we finally understood that we had no recourse. I believe that my mother's broken heart was what led to her early death."

"And your father?"

I sat up straighter. "That's why I'm here, Mr. Holmes. It seems that my father has disappeared, and I need your help to find him."

Mr. Holmes's eyes narrowed, and a pained expression crossed his face. "I'm afraid you have come at an inopportune time," he said. "My previous visitor has been pushed right to the wall of late, and he has indicated that certain events are being set in motion that cannot be stopped. Things are quickly coming to a head, and all my attention and energy in the next few days will be occupied elsewhere."

"Perhaps," I said earnestly, seeing my chance slipping away before I'd even been able to present my case, "if you'll only let me tell you the circumstances, you might be able to at least offer a suggestion."

He closed his eyes and took a deep breath. Then, "Proceed. Perhaps an armchair investigation might be for the best today."

At that moment, I heard the street door open and close. Mr. Holmes immediately sat up, almost rising from the chair, glancing toward the gun on the mantel. Then, something in the sounds below must have seemed familiar, because he visibly relaxed. He stood and crossed the room to the door, which had remained open to the landing throughout our conversation. "Mrs. Hudson!" he cried before bounding down the steps. In a moment he returned, stating, "Excuse me. I had to relay some urgent instructions, as well as request for some tea. I had observed that you appeared to be thirsty before beginning your tale, and as you've taken the Blue Ribbon, I didn't want to offer you anything stronger."

"It's true. I took the pledge a few years ago, after my father's drinking increased. It had always been something of an issue, but my mother was able to keep it in check. Since her death, he has become much worse. I believe that is what has gotten him into this situation."

Returning to his seat, he waved. "Tell me more."

I settled back, relieved that I had this chance, but not enough to relax. "After we lost the property, we relocated to a house farther back from the river. My father found a new place to dock the boat, but it wasn't the same. Part of what gave him any success at all was having our house – and my mother – right there at our own dock to keep an eye on things, to manage the business, and frankly to keep my father out of trouble. Now that she was at the different house all day, and my father was left to his own devices at the dock, he quickly fell into the bad habits that had called to him throughout his life.

"As I said, my mother was heartbroken. As the shillings dried up, and she tried to accustom herself to the mean and nasty little house that had replaced our previous dwelling, she seemed to die a little more every day. My dad stayed away, drinking instead of earning a living with the *Aurora*. In the end, he lost it to the creditors, and my mother died, all within the same quarter.

"I had stopped working with him long before that. I had wanted to stay and try to help him find some sort of success, and frankly to keep him on the right path, but we simply had to have someone bringing in a steady wage. I was able to get on with Liverpool, Dublin, and London, and at least that kept food upon the table. But I was away for too much of the time, and there was simply no way that I could prevent my father's slow and steady slide.

"When my mother died, he seemed to rally for a while, for the boys. He stopped drinking, and he obtained a job with a merchant of some sort, who needed someone to manage his imports. My father had no experience with that sort of thing, but he did know the docks and the ships, so it seemed like a good fit. He was able to feed my brothers, and I began to worry less about all of them.

"It didn't take long, however, to see that something was weighing upon my father's mind. It took several months before I could get the truth from him, and even then the details were sketchy. The short of it is that his employer was involved in some sort of smuggling, which I suppose is no surprise, and with every week that passed, my father was more worried that he was being snared tighter and deeper.

"There was a sort of feeling growing within the groups that my dad had dealings with, an uneasiness that it was all going to come crashing down at some point, taking everyone involved with it. Once, when I was home for a visit, Dad broke down, worrying what would happen to the boys if he were arrested, or worse, and making me promise to take care of them. I calmed him, but the worry about it kept growing in my head."

"Who is your father's employer?" interrupted Mr. Holmes.

"Mr. Parnell. Abel Parnell."

His eyes narrowed. "And does young Jack know that any of this was taking place?"

"I'm certain that he does."

"He never told me about any of it."

"Apparently his trustworthiness and discretion run both ways."

His lips tightened in something like a smile, and at that moment, the landlady knocked on the door, bringing in the tea. Pouring a cup for each of us, she departed. I sipped mine gratefully, while Mr. Holmes left his cooling and untouched on the little octagonal side table beside his chair. He waved for me to continue.

"A week ago, I returned home to find the boys alone. My father had gone on some errand for Mr. Parnell several days earlier, and hadn't returned. Thankfully he had left them enough money, plus what remained of my wage, so that they hadn't run out of food. We're fortunate that a widow next door keeps an eye on things since my mother died, but in any case, it was of some concern that my father hadn't been home. I began to fear that either he had resumed drinking, or that his position with Mr. Parnell had led him into deeper danger. I asked around at his usual haunts, but no one had seen him. Then I crossed the river and went to Mr. Parnell's office, off Oxford Street, but I couldn't get past the clerk, who simply said that he had no idea where my father could be, and that if I didn't leave, he'd have me thrown out.

"I waited outside for several hours, knowing that it was unlikely that I'd see my father arrive just when I was on the scene – and I was right. He never appeared. Finally, I had to return to Southwark, making sure that my brothers would be all right for another week while I was off on my run to Liverpool and Dublin."

"And when you returned again this morning," said Mr. Holmes, standing, "you found that your father was still missing." He walked behind me, and around Dr. Watson's chair as well, to some shelves that were mounted on the wall beside the fireplace. They were filled with commonplace books.

While he pulled one down, I responded. "That's right. I asked at a few of my father's old watering holes, and around the docks, but it felt as if I was wasting my time again, as surely as I did last week. Finally, knowing it would be pointless to return to Mr. Parnell's office, I recalled meeting you a few years ago after the police chase and decided to see if you could offer any advice." I paused, and then said, with a lowered voice, "I'm afraid that I cannot pay what you usually receive."

He glanced up from the book, which had held his sharp focus, with surprise. Then, with an impatient shake of his head, he said, "My fees are fixed, except when I remit them entirely." Closing the book with a snap, he returned it to the shelf. "As I will in this case." He started to turn away, and then reached up and touched the book for a moment, looking from there to several other items around the room, almost with sadness.

"I have encountered Mr. Parnell before," he continued. "He is an agent of the very man that you met upon your arrival." I raised my eyebrows, and he correctly read my thoughts. "It is not so much of a coincidence as you might think. The man that was leaving today sits like a spider in the midst of a web that stretches across London, around and through it, with a thousand dirty threads in every direction. These days, it would be almost impossible to meet a criminal that isn't connected with the Professor, my earlier visitor, in some way or another. It really is becoming intolerable."

"Then why haven't you done something?" I blurted.

His lips tightened, and he turned toward the closed door behind him. Shrugging out of his dressing gown as he went, he answered, "I have."

He opened the door, revealing a small bedroom, barely lit by the tall window that looked out toward the rear of the house. I simply sat as he began pulling on a coat. I was afraid to speak, scarcely hoping that something I'd said had interested him, and that he was preparing to help me.

He returned and crossed the room while I stood. At the door to the landing, while he pulled on a Scottish caped coat and double-billed cap that would have looked more at home in the country than town, he asked, "What did the Professor say to you downstairs?"

"He warned me. He said I must be one those urchins that you use, and that it would be well for me to get away from you."

His eyes narrowed. "He must have recognized your resemblance to Jack. I'll need to get word to him and the others to stay out of sight for a while."

He held open the door and gestured me to precede him. "Let us go see Mr. Parnell."

Downstairs, he paused for a moment before opening the door. "I really do have some scruples about taking you with me. Just now, I'm under a rather dangerous cloud, you see."

I swallowed. "Mr. Holmes, I had no real hope of expecting any help today whatsoever. I'm very grateful, and I'll be happy to accompany you."

He nodded and opened the door. "Then we shall attempt to avoid the danger."

Outside, he paused, looking up and down the street, as if expecting something that didn't seem to be there. Right in front of us was a hansom cab. Having never ridden in one, it never occurred to me to think that I would now, and it turned out that I was correct. As if assuming that I'd meant to walk toward it, Mr. Holmes put a hand on my arm. "There are times when an urgency requires that one take the first cab that presents itself. Then, at other times, one should not take the first, or even the second. Today, if you have no objections, I think that we shall eschew horse-drawn transportation altogether – it has the disadvantage of trapping one in a box at the mercy of one's opponent, especially if the driver deviates from your chosen route. What do you say, Mr. Smith, to a ramble through London?"

I agreed, a little puzzled, and we started down Baker Street. My eyes met those of the cabman, and for a moment, it seemed as if his narrowed in anger. Then, I was racing to keep up with the much longer legs of my companion.

Mr. Holmes didn't cut a straight path. He led me down George Street and Thayer Street, and on into narrower William Street. He asked me a few more questions about by father, but he seemed to already know the answers, and while he listened intently, his attention was mostly turned toward keeping an eye on our surroundings. He looked toward doorways and passages and into mews, and upwards as well, towards windows and rooftops.

As we walked, I remembered a case that I'd heard about, sometime not long after I'd gone to work for the London, Liverpool, and Dublin. I asked him he recalled the facts related to Jim Browner's arrest. He nodded. "You worked with him, perhaps?"

"For just a bit," I answered. "It was he who informed me about the Blue Ribbon pledge. But we lost touch when he began to drink again. Then came his arrest, and then his suicide in his cell before the trial . . . ."

I trailed off, both at the sadness and horror of it all, and also hoping that Mr. Holmes would take up the slack. However, his attention had been distracted elsewhere.

While I had been talking, he had led me through Bulstrode Street, and so into Welbeck Street. As we walked south, he continued to scan our path. I was looking ahead down the street, glancing occasionally at Mr. Holmes, wondering if I could ask another question that might prompt a response, when suddenly we heard the sound of racing hooves coming up behind us. We were in the crossing at the corner which leads from Bentinck Street on to Welbeck Street when Mr. Holmes threw out his arm and pulled me back. It was a two-horse van, driven crazily by a man who was whipping his horses mercilessly. He took the corner into Bentinck Street on two wheels before racing down the short distance to Marylebone Lane. He turned there again and vanished.

I took another step back on my own and almost stumbled as the delayed fear washed over me. Mr. Holmes, still gripping my arm, steadied me, and said with a grim look on his face, "The Professor didn't waste any time. We'll have to be more careful."

I nodded. I had thought we were already being careful. But then again, we hadn't been killed, and that was something.

Keeping to the pavement, we soon crossed Wigmore and Henrietta Streets, and then made the short turn into Vere Street, which would lead us to Oxford Street. Somehow I felt that we would be safer on that busy thoroughfare than we had been so far.

I was soon convinced of several things – one, that possibly I should have taken Mr. Holmes up on his offer to remove myself from this situation, and two, that I was right to want to get to Oxford Street as soon as possible. We had barely started through Vere Street when Mr. Holmes gave a cry, pushing me forward at the same time. Thank goodness he had been looking up. I heard rather than saw the impact on the pavement behind me. I stumbled but kept my feet and, turning quickly, saw a shattered brick lying between us. Naturally, I looked up, just in time to see an angry rat-like face staring down at us for only an instant before it pulled back and vanished.

A constable was just up the street at the Oxford end, and Mr. Holmes called him over. Explaining in general terms that someone had intentionally dropped the brick from the rooftop above, thus endangering passers-by, he convinced the somewhat skeptical officer to investigate. A knock on the door and an explanation from the policeman to the landlady quickly gained us access to the roof. Mr. Holmes crawled about for a bit, looking here and there, while the policemen pointed several times to a pile of building materials piles nearby, explaining with some pride his theory that the wind – of which there was none whatsoever that morning – had blown one of the bricks over the side. Neither Mr. Holmes nor I mentioned that we had seen the man who dropped the missile, and the policeman became frustrated when his theory wasn't praised, or in fact even acknowledged. Finally, the detective straightened, thanked the constable, and led us back to the street.

As the irritated policeman wandered away from us, Mr. Holmes said softly, "I recognized the fellow on the roof. It was Parker, one of the Professor's men. Dropping stones is not his normal method – he usually prefers to carry out his killings much closer to the victims."

"If you recognized him, then why did you bother examining the roof?"

"To see if there was evidence of anyone else. It would appear that Parker is working alone. The Professor may have mobilized his troops, but so far they are rather disorganized. I believe that I owe you a debt of thanks, Mr. Smith."

"You do? For what?"

"You've done me a good deed. For getting me out and about today, after all."

I recalled what my mother used to say about good deeds. "But why? It has only placed you in danger."

"Not any more than I would have been in Baker Street. And if I had remained there, I would have been gradually surrounded and outnumbered and bottled up until there would have been nowhere to go, and no way to even summon assistance. No, by presenting your problem when you did, I was able to slip through their net before it was quite fixed. And I intend for that to remain the case. Shall we continue on our errand?"

And without waiting for an answer, he turned south again, and soon led me into the bustle of Oxford Street. Knowing that we were being pursued by assassins, and possibly even watched at that very minute, I recalled my earlier thoughts about the safety of the busy street and wondered at my idiocy. It would be nothing for someone to sidle up to us, here where so many were jostling each other, and slip a blade between our ribs. And while Mr. Holmes was certainly the focus of their anger, I would be marked now as well as one of his companions. I started to tell him just to abandon it. We would separate, and he could go find a place of safety, and I would return to Southwark. But then, I remembered my father, and knew that – in spite of his many failings – I couldn't abandon him until I found out what had become of him.

203

We had just reached the Berners Street corner when Mr. Holmes plucked at my sleeve. The noise was great, but he gave me to understand that he wished to cross to the other side, where Wardour Street turns south. I followed, looking around for killers on foot or in racing carriages, but we made the passage in safety. Crossing Wardour, we entered the Capital and Counties Bank, with the address, 125 Oxford Street, shown in gold lettering upon the door. I believe that this was the finest building which I had ever entered, and the fact that I didn't belong there was shown on the face of the doorman who let me in.

It was suddenly quiet inside, and I relaxed for a moment, realizing how fearful I had become on the street. While Mr. Holmes explained that he suddenly realized that he might need some extra funds in the upcoming days, before proceeding to speak to an approaching gentleman, I lingered near the door, realizing that very soon we would be back outside, facing the men sent by this mysterious Professor to kill us. Mr. Holmes had indicated that Mr. Parnell was working for this criminal, and therefore, by association so was my dad. It occurred to me to wonder if I was helping to save my father, or if I was going to get him into more trouble by linking him to this criminal organization which the detective was battling.

I decided to trust my guide, recalling what kind of man he had been on the night that Jonathan Small was arrested. The fat policeman that had been in charge, wheezing and crowing about his success, had only served to highlight even further the character and qualities of Mr. Holmes and Dr. Watson.

"Thank you for your continued trust," said Mr. Holmes as he rejoined me, slipping a now-fat wallet back into his coat. I suppose that I tried to look as if I didn't know what he meant. "You were pondering slipping out of the door while I took care of my business," he added. "Then you perceptibly chose to stay and see it out."

I nodded. What could I say to that?

We resumed our place in the street, crossing back to the north side, and then moving east until we reached Rathbone Place. Mr. Holmes knew as well as I did where we were going, leading me around the corner. I wondered what he could tell me about Mr. Parnell, and how much he'd found about the man in the commonplace book beside his fireplace.

Not far down on the left was a doorway opening onto a stairwell. I had been here a week before, and nothing had changed. We started upstairs, and I was very happy to let Mr. Holmes lead. I had the sense that my presence there wouldn't have made any difference one way or another, as he already had his course plotted.

We stepped into the room where I had been turned away before, told that I would be thrown out if I didn't leave voluntarily. The man behind the desk, the same as before, was lean and dangerous looking, and he half stood before sinking back down, a look of recognition and – possibly – fear on his face. He half-heartedly said something to the effect that we could not go in there, but it was too late, for Mr. Holmes had already opened the door on the other side of the room. He was, in fact, going in there. Rather than stay with the suddenly cowed occupant of the outer room, I followed him.

Inside was a fat man, rocked back in a chair beside a tall roll-top desk along one wall. There was only one high window behind it, apparently opening onto some court behind the building. I hadn't met Mr. Parnell before, but my father had described him, and I knew that we were in his presence.

He started to speak, but then collapsed into a rheumy cough, much like what I've heard the old workhouse men exhibit. I knew that if he tried to stand, he'd probably have the workhouse legs as well. How could a man like this have ended up in an office, carrying out important business for someone? For the Professor?

"Mr. Holmes," he finally wheezed. "I didn't expect you."

"I am certain of that. Has the word gone out that the inconvenience that I'm causing will soon stop, one way or another?"

"I have heard something along those lines, although there isn't any question about who will be the victor."

"That conclusion is premature. Tell me about Mordecai Smith."

Parnell's eyebrows rose like those of Punch – at least, the way they do on some of the fancier puppets I've seen. His surprise was sincere. Then, for the first time, he looked past the detective and saw me. His widened eyes narrowed in a scowl. "You're the son," he sighed. "I'd heard you were here."

"Why won't you tell me what has happened to my father?" I blurted, starting to step toward him. Mr. Holmes held up a hand – he would handle this.

"My friend's question stands," he said.

Parnell coughed and shook his head. "He had an attack of conscience. There is some important business about to take place, and he objected to it. He threatened to tell the police if we didn't desist." He laughed, and then collapsed back in his chair in a fit of wheezing. "If the fool felt like that," he said when he caught his breath, "why didn't he just tell the police? Why warn us ahead of time, as if his puny threat would make us change our plans?"

"I take it you are referring to the arrival of the *Lydia McGraw*, from China."

Parnell's eyes widened. "Maybe you really are as good as they say."

205

"I suspect my sources are better than yours. In fact, it was diverted in Marseilles four days ago, and the ladies held within have been freed."

That caused a reaction. "Impossible! I would have heard."

"You only knew what I wanted you to know. You wouldn't know now if I wasn't interested in Mordecai Smith's whereabouts."

"The Professor should have killed you years ago."

"Speaking of life and death, is Mr. Smith still alive?"

I cut my eyes toward Mr. Holmes. He had asked what I had refused to even consider.

Parnell waved a wrinkled hand. "He is. I hadn't decided yet what should happen to him."

"I have decided for you. Have him at Baker Street by 8:00 a.m. tomorrow. Unharmed. I assume that you're keeping him in the warehouse in Whitstable. By tomorrow morning should allow you plenty of time to retrieve him."

Parnell laughed. "And why should I do what you say, Mr. Holmes? You're a walking dead man."

"Need I remind you of Helen Silsoe of Stoke Mandeville?"

Never have a seen a man lose his color so fast. In fact, considering the man's condition, I'm surprised that Parnell didn't die on the spot. He swallowed twice, and then fumbled to open one of the tall drawers in the desk. He brought out a bottle of whisky and a glass, but then ignored the glass and drank right from the spout. He coughed, closed his eyes, drank again, and then set the bottle down.

Wiping away the tears that ran from his eyes, he said, "Eight, you said? I can have him there in four hours."

"Eight o'clock tomorrow is fine," said Mr. Holmes. "And in perfect condition. I have other business to attend to today." He looked around the office, as if memorizing its features. "I do trust that Mr. Mordecai Smith is still in pristine condition."

"He's well enough," said Parnell, a whiny tone now in his voice. If he wasn't too fat to do so, I believe that he would have slinked around on the floor like a starving cur.

"Good day, Mr. Parnell," said Mr. Holmes, turning to pass through the door. My eyes met those of Parnell, and for one brief instant, I saw the fire of hate flash, as when a stove door is opened and the air hits the embers, causing them to reignite. Then, just as quickly, it was gone. No doubt he feared that the power held over him by Mr. Holmes might also pass to me. Far be it from me to disabuse him of the notion.

On the street, I found myself somewhat shaken. Had it really been that easy? Of course, it wasn't over yet. My father still had to put in an appearance. When he did, I would explain to him his foolishness. If this

206

organization of which he was a part was clearly about to fall, then my dad would be a fool not to take this chance and escape completely while he could – especially as they had already nearly killed him.

I looked up as Mr. Holmes pressed something into my hand. It was his card, upon which he'd written a man's name, along with a well-known shipping company in the East End. "This fellow owes me a favor or two," he said. "If you think that you can straighten your father out, then take him there and let this man know that he needs a job. Show that card. It should be enough."

I didn't know what to say. I wanted to express my thanks, but before I could, he waved them away. "I'll see you tomorrow morning in Baker Street," he added, starting to turn away.

"But – " I said, then stopped. He turned, looking back expectantly. "But it isn't safe for you. Can I help?"

He smiled then, the first time I'd seen him truly smile since meeting him. Shaking his head, he said, "No, although the thought is much appreciated. You should make your own way home for the night, being careful, of course, that you aren't followed. You have, after all, spent a portion of the day with me, and that carries a certain amount of risk. Especially now."

He glanced around, as if to spot this very danger of which he spoke. "I'm going to spend the day with my brother at his club, and then possibly visit Dr. Watson." He frowned. "I believe that he's serving as a locum this week in nearby Mortimer Street." He looked up. "No matter. Thank you for your offer, but you should check on your family. I shall see you tomorrow in Baker Street."

And with that, he set off, back down Rathbone Place, and so into Oxford Street.

I watched him go, considering his advice only long enough to realize that I was about to lose sight of him. Hurrying, I saw him step abruptly into the street, hailing a passing growler. I recalled his advice about not taking the first or second cab, but assumed that this one, chosen at random on the busy street, was acceptable. I still felt that I needed to provide some sort of assistance, however insignificant it might be. I couldn't run after him down the street, wherever he was going, and I didn't want to try and follow in a cab of my own. Finally, hoping that I hadn't grown too tall, or that my uniform wouldn't attract too much attention, and trusting that my old skills hadn't completely deserted me, I dashed forward and secured a tenuous seat on the back of the vehicle.

We made our way south and west, winding through various side streets until we unexpectedly burst into Piccadilly Circus. Up to that point, I had been thoroughly lost. Now I was able to fix our location, but only for a moment as we again headed west. Soon, we turned into a quieter and more dignified street. Pall Mall, according to the signs. When I felt the cab start to slow, I jumped off as I had learned to long ago, dodging down into an areaway. Not a moment too soon, it turned out, as the cab stopped in front of No. 78. Mr. Holmes paid the cabbie and dashed up the front steps, leaving me to wonder exactly what I was doing.

I stayed there for several hours, and what occurred during that time isn't worth reporting, as nothing happened. But then, just I was considering whether to abandon my post, the detective appeared on the steps, pulling his gloves from his pocket. He had been there but a few seconds when he and I, from our different spots, both heard a cry. Mr. Holmes tensed. A man was running toward him from across the street, carrying a club, and bellowing to wake the dead. I realized that I was not suited for this type of work at all, as I had never even noticed the fellow. I was rising to pass through the areaway gate and render assistance when I saw that it wouldn't be necessary. Mr. Holmes had dropped his gloves and settled into a crouch. Even as the man reached him, a quick move that I couldn't precisely recall or even describe afterwards was all that it took to leave the attacker stretched on the pavement, rolling this way and that and clutching a clearly broken jaw. Mr. Holmes called for the elderly doorman to summon the police, while he shook his hand.

Turning toward where I was hidden, Mr. Holmes called, "You can join me, Mr. Smith."

I sheepishly walked up the street, where he was binding a handkerchief over two bleeding knuckles. "I suspect that the driver of the cab that brought us here – oh, yes, Mr. Smith, I knew when you joined us – told the Professor where I was. I suppose that I'm quite lucky that he only sent Devereaux to kill me and not a whole pack of them." He glanced up and down the street. "They must not have ready access at the moment to Von Herder's air gun," he said softly, almost to himself. "But they'll get it soon enough."

He finished wrapping his hand and said, louder this time, "I observed you start to join me just now. It is much appreciated, but I assure you that I can take care of myself. You should return to your family. I've finished making my plans with my brother, and I go now to inform Dr. Watson. I shall be safe enough."

I could tell that he wouldn't take no for an answer. And, as I was really uncertain as to what assistance I could provide in any case, and there was no way that I could follow him without his knowing, I agreed. I left him there, wondering if I would myself be attacked on the way home for simply having been in his company. However, I made my way without

208

incident, crossing the river at the Westminster Bridge and then turning east, every street becoming more familiar as I went.

The next morning, I was in Baker Street fifteen minutes before the appointed time. It was quite a bit earlier than when I had arrived the previous day, and it felt to me that there was less stirring now on the street. However, that idea was soon negated when I approached Sherlock Holmes's lodgings. There was a cluster of idlers standing in the street, and one of the fire wagons was nearby, rolling up a long hose while water was forced out the end of it, running it down the pavement.

I hurried forward and slipped through the loiterers without waiting to learn what had happened. There were faint smoke stains on the wall outside the windows of the sitting room. Had the Professor's men succeeded after all? Had Mr. Holmes been killed, in spite of his confidence and many abilities?

I dashed through the open door and pounded up the steps. The door at the top was open, and I lurched to a stop, seeing a couple of men standing there. One was a tall fellow with very blonde hair and large hands. Everything about him proclaimed that he was a policeman. The other, with his back to me, was some sort of priest. He was in a long black robe, and hanging from his hand was a wide round parson's hat of the sort that I've sometimes seen the Italians wear when onboard my ship. The policeman looked up and scowled when I entered the room. The priest turned more slowly, and I fear my jaw dropped when I saw that it was Mr. Holmes.

"Ah, Smith," he said. "The inspector and I were just discussing last night's fire. Luckily, the damage was only superficial."

The inspector's eyes kept looking at me with suspicion, something which has happened to me – and any boy growing up in Southwark – upon any number of occasions. Mr. Holmes noticed it and said, "Nothing to worry about, Gregson. This is another matter entirely. Just a bit of last-minute business before the game begins."

"If you say so, Mr. Holmes," replied the other man. He glanced toward a desk in the corner. "Will the papers be all right there?"

"They will. In pigeon hole 'M', and done up in a blue envelope, just like we agreed."

"I still don't know why you can't just give them to Patterson or me right now."

"We've discussed that."

The big man shrugged and put on his hat. "As you say, Mr. Holmes. We've discussed it. But I'm not sure that I agree with it. Luring him to the Continent? What will that accomplish?"

"It will serve to leave his train without a conductor, right at the most crucial turn in the track. With him distracted, the train will fly off the rails, and you and your men will be there to pick up the pieces."

"It sounds dangerous."

"It is."

They looked at one another, and then the big inspector stuck out his hand and shook that of Mr. Holmes. "God speed, then," he said with quiet sincerity, and then departed.

Before I had a chance to speak, Mr. Holmes turned away and began fussing with a case on his chair. He added some tobacco and, after careful consideration, an oily black clay pipe. Then he snapped it shut. It was then that I heard a cough. Turning, I saw my father standing in the door. Somehow he'd silently climbed the stairs. In the old days, when he was drinking, he could never have been so quiet.

I ran to him, feeling like a child in spite of my twenty years. He threw his arms about me and gave a sob. We stood like that for a moment, and then he took a deep breath and backed away. But he held my gaze and smiled. There was apology in it, but also an unspoken promise.

"They – " he began, and then had to clear his throat. "They told me that I'm free because of you, Mr. Holmes. How can I – that is to say, how can *we* thank you?"

Mr. Holmes clearly started to say that thanks weren't necessary. Then, he seemed to have a different idea. "If you don't mind just a little more danger, Messrs. Smith, I could use some camouflage."

And so, fifteen minutes later, we were in a four-wheeler, headed for Victoria Station. After we had agreed with Mr. Holmes's seemingly painless scheme, he had directed us towards the door. Then, placing the flat priest's hat on his head, he had picked up his bag and followed us. Turning, he looked back into the sitting room for a long minute. Now, after knowing what happened later, I wonder if he had a premonition, and was taking a last look around to say goodbye. But I suppose that I'm simply remembering it that way to make it a better story. In any case, he pulled the sitting room door shut, led us downstairs, and out through the back of the house.

We passed a lone plane tree in the yard, and then on through to the next street, and so on until we reached Dorset Square, where he hailed a cab. As we boarded, I hurriedly explained Mr. Holmes's card, with the name of a man who would give my father a job. My father started to thank the detective once again, but Mr. Holmes impatiently waved it away.

"They will be looking for me," he explained, changing the subject, "and I'm not certain that my disguise will pass muster. I wore something of this sort a few years ago, when I needed to fool a woman into showing me where she had hidden a photograph. I had hired a number of people to stage a fight in the street as a distraction, and some of them have also done work for the Professor in the past. They may very well remember that this disguise has been used before and be looking for it. However, in spite of the risk to all of us, it seemed like one of the best that I could assume in order to pass relatively unnoticed on the boat train.

"If they are looking for a priest, maybe it will be less conspicuous if I'm traveling with two other men. At least, that's what I hope. Both of you are known, one way or the other, to the Professor's people, and that could cause difficulties."

My father hung his head, looking ashamed for a moment. But then, remembering his new chance, he looked up with a new pride and determination that I was happy to see. I would do everything that I could to fan this new spark into a full flame.

As we made our way to Victoria, Mr. Holmes watched all sides from the cab windows. He seemed satisfied that we weren't being followed. We reached the station, and he offered to pay the cabbie to take us wherever we wanted to go, but my father demurred, stating instead that, if I didn't mind, we would prefer to walk and enjoy the new day. I found that I agreed with him. With that, Mr. Holmes thanked us again for our help, and then vanished into the crowds leading into the station.

My father and I stood there for a moment, breathing deeply amidst the bustle. We didn't seem to be too anxious to make our way home just yet. Inadvertently, we had fallen into an old habit of people-watching, an activity that my father had introduced to me when I was just a lad. He had rightfully pointed out that people make the best entertainment, and it's all for free. We watched men and women from all classes arrive in all levels of calm or panic, making their way inside the station. We were rather enjoying ourselves, now seemingly without a care and making low comments about this or that person, when I saw Dr. Watson arrive in a small brougham, driven by a massive driver in a dark cape and a scarf pulled over his face. No sooner had the doctor stepped to the ground and retrieved his bag than the driver whipped up his horse and vanished into the distance.

Dr. Watson watched him for a puzzled moment and then went inside. I was explaining to my dad who it was that we had just seen when another carriage arrived, also in great haste. Nearly causing an accident, it skidded to a halt, allowing its passenger to descend. I was shocked. Standing there, looking enraged, was the very man that had loomed so large in my thoughts for the last twenty-four hours: Professor Moriarty.

He turned his head this way and that, in that curiously snake-like fashion, clearly looking for someone – no doubt, Sherlock Holmes, or perhaps the doctor, whom he had apparently followed. Then, not seeing them, he began to make his way inside, cursing and swinging his stick as the crowd inadvertently blocked his way.

Telling my dad to stay where he was, I set off to follow. Inside, my eyes quickly adjusted from the morning sunlight outside, revealing that the terminal was just as busy within as it had been without. In the distance, over by the Continental Express, I could see Dr. Watson looking anxiously this way and that. Behind him, Sherlock Holmes, dressed as the Italian priest, was climbing into the first class carriage. Who could they be waiting upon? And was it possible that Dr. Watson was looking for Mr. Holmes, not realizing that the man was right behind him?

Even as I asked myself that question, the Professor saw Dr. Watson. He raised his stick, almost without conscious volition, and started that way. Not knowing what he intended, I moved without thinking. Dodging past a nurse pushing a pram and an old soldier with one leg, I circled back toward the Professor. He was still quite a distance away from the doctor and Mr. Holmes, and there was a surge of people between them, moving toward the train. The doors were starting to slam shut, whistles were being blown, and I could see that Dr. Watson was climbing into his compartment, still looking around. Then, he turned with a jerk, looking at the man in priest's clothing across from him. He said something. The train started to move.

At that point, the Professor gave a cry of rage. Several people turned his way, and I observed Dr. Watson look at him as well. His eyes locked with those of the Professor, even as the train gained a little speed. The Professor reached his hand into his coat. Fearing what he would remove, and what would happen when he did, I made a final lunge forward, knocking the man to the ground.

A gun fell from his hands and skittered across the platform. I had managed to keep my feet, and took another couple of steps forward as I regained my balance. Even as people around us stopped to watch, trying to determine what had just happened, I reached the gun. I had no intention of picking it up and using it, or even threatening anyone with it. I know my limitations. Instead, I simply kicked it, as one would a stone on a road, and watched as it slid the rest of the way across the platform and into the gap beside the accelerating train, where it disappeared from sight.

I turned back to the Professor, who was getting to his feet, assisted by two men around him. One handed him his cane, and he propped it on the floor, using it to push himself fully upright. Then he shook off the hands of those who had assisted him and raised the cane, pointing it accusingly in my direction. His eyes locked with mine, and then they flicked down toward my uniform. I knew that he recognized me from yesterday. He took

212

a step toward me, and then stopped himself. Seeming to make a decision, he cried aloud, "Bah!" and turned, making his way haltingly toward the office where one arranges to engage special trains.

I wanted to do something else to help, but I was at the end of what I could provide. If the Professor chose to engage a special, there was nothing that I could do. I prayed that Mr. Holmes and Dr. Watson, wherever they were bound, would be safe.

I looked around to make sure that none of the Professor's men were around, and that no one was taking an interest in me to finish what he hadn't, but the activity had resumed its normal flow. No one paid any attention to me whatsoever. I dusted myself off and made my way outside to thankfully find my father, waiting where I had left him. I realized that I was glad, as I'd almost expected to discover that he'd wandered into the nearby pub. Perhaps there was hope after all. Now all that I had to fear was that the Professor had marked me. That was quite enough to worry about.

Nearly two weeks later, on the seventh of May, I was on the run back from Liverpool when I happened to read the *Reuter's* dispatch, telling what had happened to Mr. Holmes when the Professor caught up with him in Switzerland on the fourth. The details were sparse, but it was enough, and it was absolute. I came to myself to realize that I was sitting down, although I'd had no memory of doing so. I couldn't imagine how it had happened. Mr. Holmes was the most capable man I'd ever met. He seemed to know exactly what was happening, far beyond whatever the rest of us saw. What set of circumstances had occurred that would let a man like the Professor win?

Still, I believe that, if the only way to defeat the Professor was for Mr. Holmes to sacrifice himself, then he wouldn't have hesitated. From the little that I'd seen during those two days, and all that I've read and heard about him during the two-and-a-half years since that day he and Dr. Watson left London, I cannot doubt that he knew what he was doing.

Just the other day, when I returned from the Liverpool-Dublin run, my dad handed me the newest *Strand* magazine. It had the account of what took place on those two days in April '91, and what happened after that as well. There was no mention of me or my dad – but then, there wouldn't be, as it's likely that Mr. Holmes never mentioned it.

I've thought about writing to Doctor Watson, to tell him of this, one of Mr. Holmes's last cases. Something keeps holding me back, but I really should do it, I suppose. Perhaps, now that I've written this account, I'll send it to him. He needs to know that, through Mr. Holmes's efforts, my father had the opportunity to change his life, and he grabbed that chance and has made the best of it. It's been a good year, and we had a good Christmas, all of us, including my wife and new child.

My mother would be happy, but she would shake her head when pointing out that, even though I now knew better, good deeds are always followed by punishment. "Look at what happened to poor Mr. Holmes after he helped you!" she would say, and no amount of argument from my side – that what happened to him was already in motion when he took time to aid us – would sway her, God rest her soul.

And God rest Mr. Sherlock Holmes as well. As Dr. Watson wrote, he was the best and wisest man – even if I only knew him for just a couple of days – that I've ever known.

The Dorset Square Business

We had rambled west that night after our return to London, ranging to Paddington and beyond, perhaps going a bit too far without considering the threat of rain. Our earlier arrival in Baker Street had been very late, as we'd had no wish to remain in the Hampshire village of Ecchinswell following the completion of our latest distasteful investigation. After paying the cabbie, we had stood outside our front door before spontaneously deciding to walk a bit. Leaving our bags just inside, we ambled back the way we'd just traveled, eventually crossing Edgware Road, and then down Praed Street and past the station, where we had only just arrived less than an hour before on a very early train. We didn't speak, our minds turning over the events of the previous day.

We'd been summoned to one of the downs three or so miles north of Litchfield, where a terribly mutilated corpse had been discovered near a rabbit warren. It was too beautiful a spot to have witnessed such a horrific crime, but the thought crossed my mind while Holmes made his initial investigation that there were likely stories at that site of similar viciousness from ages past, unknown to us and never to be told. At least justice might be found in this case for the young schoolteacher, cut down so tragically.

The details of the affair were straightforward, and yet so shocking that the full account can only be placed with those other records of a similar nature in my tin dispatch box, which is kept under lock and key, but I will never forget the long vigil that we kept by the warren as the daytime beauties of Watership Down faded and were lost in the creeping darkness of night. It was only in those very late hours, when the human soul's tenuous link to its clay is at its weakest, that the villain revealed himself. Inspector Dunleavy, who had joined as at the warren, had to be restrained from exacting an extra-legal vengeance upon the mad slayer. We hadn't known until then just how close were his relations to the poor victim, for the inspector is a man who keeps his emotions tightly in check. It was due to no concern for the murderer that we prevented the inspector from carrying out his own form of justice. Rather, it was to save him from himself becoming a killer – although he would never be the same, regardless of what happened that night, and I suspected that the murderer's final days in Broadmoor – for there was nowhere else that someone so insane might be placed – would end abruptly at the hands of another inmate.

At some point during our walk, Holmes and I each seemed to have independently found a way to move past the terrible events of what we had seen earlier that night. We had looped west, and then back again, returning to our door in Baker Street just as the sky was beginning to lighten with morning.

We entered and retrieved our bags. Upstairs, we paused upon the first-floor landing and wished each other a good night, having left Mrs. Hudson a note that each of us intended to sleep late that day. Holmes entered his room, and I continued up another flight to my own. My chamber, on the west side of the house, looked out upon the poor little rear yard where our little plane tree eked out its bleak existence. Beyond, on the back windows of the houses opposite, I could see a few reflected streaks of the sun rising in the east.

I had pulled off my coat and was reaching to undo my necktie when an urgent pealing of the doorbell filled the pre-dawn silence, followed by a frantic pounding upon the door – which marked the start of our involvement in what Holmes would later discreetly call the Dorset Square business. With a sigh, I turned, opened my bedroom door, and quickly descended, hoping to reach the street door before poor Mrs. Hudson was awakened – although that was unlikely.

As I passed by Holmes's room, he came out, a wry smile upon his face. He followed behind me, and then we were at the front door. I undid the locks and pulled it open to reveal a constable, about to pound on the door again. He arrested the motion of his upraised fist.

"Doctor Watson!" he cried. He was a young fellow, not more than twenty-five, and his eyes were wide. "Hurry, Doctor! Get your bag! Hurry!"

I made to return upstairs, but Holmes said, "I'll get it," as he pivoted and dashed toward the steps, belying that he was a man now in his mid-forties.

"And get my coat!" I called. He tossed a hand in acknowledgement and then rounded out of sight at the top of the stair landing.

I put my hands on the young constable's shoulders, trying to infuse him with some sense of calm. "What has happened?" I asked, giving him a small shake for emphasis. It appeared to work, and he regained some focus in his eyes, seeing less of whatever it was that had unnerved him. "It's Riley, Doctor. He . . . he was on fire, and then he jumped through the window! I was walking past on my rounds when I saw him come crashing through, and hit the pavement. He . . . I ran up and rolled him back and forth until the flames were out, but he's hurt terribly. I blew my whistle, and Ernest came running. He's with him now. I knew that you lived nearby, so I ran for you."

I could hear Holmes returning. I reached down and took the constables wrists, holding them up so that I could examine them in the faint glow of the street's nearby gaslight. As I'd suspected, his palms were burned from where he had taken hold of his fellow constable, Riley – whom I knew – in order to put out the fire. He would need treatment as well, and I feared that he would have scars for the rest of his life as a payment for his thoughtless act of selflessness.

Holmes stopped behind me. I turned and took my proffered coat, while he set down my bag and began donning his Inverness. When I was back in my coat, he held my overcoat, which I pulled on. Then he handed me my hat, placed his own fore-and-aft cap upon his head, and leaned down to pick up my bag. I led the young constable outside, and Holmes pulled our door shut, locking it, and then nodding.

The constable pivoted smartly and set off down the empty street. Soon he turned the corner, and we stayed with him. Within just a moment or two, he led us into Dorset Square, and around to one of the buildings standing along the north side. Even without his help, I would have known by then that this was the correct destination, for the house was lit up, with neighbors watching from a distance on either side, or out of their windows. There were several constables grouped before the house, clustered around a figure crumpled upon the ground. High above him, one of the tall second-story windows was shattered, the broken woodwork extending outward, indicating the direction that Riley had taken when he had defenestrated. I could hear muffled voices coming from the high window, although no one was looking outside.

I pushed my way through the men surrounding the figure lying in the street, calling for them to move aside so that I had more light. Kneeling, I nearly retched as I smelled the odor of charred flesh. And there was something else which made itself obvious just seconds later – the reek of lamp oil. The man's clothes were soaked in it. If the flames hadn't been put out, he would have been dead immediately from the fire, regardless of the injuries sustained after his great fall. And yet, there were still signs of life in him.

I carried out my examination, vaguely aware of Holmes questioning the men standing nearby. I gathered that the young constable who had summoned us was named Carrick. He repeated what he had told me – he was making his usual rounds through the Square when suddenly he heard a crash. He only had time to look up before Riley was hurtling through the air, a flaming nightmare arcing from the second floor window, screaming until his impact with the hard street silenced him. He continued to burn even as Carrick rushed forward, rolling him and trying to put out the flames. I didn't have the heart to negate the lad's bravery and quick thinking by pointing out that he could have squelched the flames just as easily by throwing his heavy coat over the man, sparing himself from his own injuries. Turning the injured man probably hadn't done that poor broken body any good either.

Riley was in terrible shape. Most of the burns seemed to be located upon his chest, and his clothing there was gone, burned away, as was much of the flesh. His ribs and sternum were terribly exposed in places, while charred muscle showed elsewhere. The pain would have been excruciating, but he had also suffered a number of broken bones when he impacted with the pavement, including an apparent skull fracture that had left him unconscious. There was no need to dose him with morphine – the time for that would come soon enough when he awoke. If he awoke.

The sound of the ambulance arriving was nearly concurrent with my awareness that I heard Inspector Lestrade's voice, mingled with Holmes's, in questioning Constable Carrick behind me. I surrendered my place at Riley's side to the attendants from the ambulance, giving a few quick comments to the doctor who had accompanied them. It was decided that the nearest and best facility was St. Mary's Hospital in Paddington. Riley was quickly loaded, and then I checked to see if Holmes and Lestrade had obtained all that they needed from Carrick before packing him into the ambulance as well, in order to obtain treatment for his hands. I could see that the shock of the event was passing, as was the adrenalin that had kept his pain at bay. The young man was in for a bad time of it.

I turned back to Holmes and Lestrade, who was explaining the significance of the house. "This is Donald Armilus's residence."

My eyes widened, and I could see that Holmes was suddenly more interested as well, for this particular building had been of some curiosity to the public for the past year.

In late 1897, about ten months earlier, Donald Armilus had unexpectedly bought the house and moved there from the United States. He was the grandson of a Bavarian who had emigrated to America long before, making his money in a variety of dubious enterprises, beginning with catering to the lowest base desires of men involved in the California Gold Rush. His own son Frederic had taken that small fortune and greatly expanded it through various questionable and seamy New York ventures. Frederic's son Donald had inherited the entire thing, and dark rumors had swirled for years that receipt of this legacy was rushed along by the curiously suspicious death of both Donald's older brother, and then Frederick after a short illness in which Donald allowed only one amateur nurse – a woman of little medical experience who was employed at one of the family's more disreputable business enterprises – to be in attendance.

Donald Armilus had been married several times, and had always tried to crack the upper tiers of American Society, but he was never welcomed. The old American nobility had recognized him for what he was: A tainted

218

and corrupt boor of low-class antecedents who would never be accepted as one of their class. Finally in disgust, and no doubt in connection with a growing myriad of accusations and likely criminal indictments mounting against him, he had unexpectedly and mysteriously relocated to London, taking an uncharacteristically small house in Dorset Square as his refuge. Not long after, mere days in fact, he was discovered in the middle of the night, sitting alone in his second-floor study, staring fixedly across the room at a blank wall, screaming unceasingly – deep within a madness from which he'd never recovered.

He had seemed to be broken and bitter after his flight from America, intending to burrow in and live the life of a recluse. His only servants, hired by his British agent who had bought the house for him, had been a housekeeper and a handyman who served as something of a butler and caretaker. It was this man who had been awakened by the screaming. He burst into the study to find that Donald Armilus had lost his mind. There was no apparent reason for his breakdown, and nothing could be done to abate his terrible shrieks. By the time that the police had arrived, his cries had already permanently damaged his throat. Only sedation caused the screaming to stop, and when he awoke, it began again, although by this point his vocal chords were so shredded that he would never make actual sounds again. Reports indicated that he was still screaming, locked away in an expensive institution in a fine London neighborhood, staring straight ahead and making all the urgent motions of a man howling in madness and pain – but never producing a sound beyond his labored breathing.

Afterwards, the house had remained empty. But just the week before, Donald Armilus's eldest son, a sly and spoiled young man named Nicky, had decided to visit London – his first time there, as neither he nor his younger brothers had bothered to make the journey the previous year when their father lost his mind, or at any time since for that matter. Nicky's solitary sojourn to the British capital, sans the company of his siblings, was widely reported in the press, and I saw him once, as I was passing through Piccadilly Circus on an errand related to one of Holmes's investigations. He was dark thin fellow, nothing like his obese and thoroughly unpleasant-looking father. He had shadows of a heavy beard on his face, and a dissipated and unhealthy aspect about his bruised-looking eyes. The rumor was that he was an addict to all sorts of detrimental sensations, and unlimited access to his father's funds had only served to ruin him that much faster.

He initially stayed at the Langham, but an incident with the staff resulted in his almost immediate move to his father's house in Dorset Square, which had been kept intact throughout the past year by the continued residence of the housekeeper and the caretaker, both remaining in the family's pay, as if no one had remembered to terminate their services as being unnecessary.

Young Nicky had moved in on a Tuesday morning, to great fanfare and under the scrutiny of the press. On Wednesday morning, he was found in the second floor sitting room, the same room where his father had gone mad, dead from blood loss. His unclothed body was covered in a multitude of shallow cuts, all apparently self-inflicted from his small pen-knife. He had used his own blood to draw various obscene sketches upon the walls, a task that seemingly took hours, based upon the number of them and their curious and unfathomable complexity. Finally, when the limits of his blood loss had been reached, he succumbed, collapsing in front of the fireplace. His head had been too close to the flames, and the hair was singed off and the skin of his face and scalp blackened and blistered – but by then he had been beyond any pain.

Lestrade had stopped by on other business the day after Nicky Armilus was discovered, and had casually mentioned the facts of the case, relating some aspects that hadn't been reported in the press. He seemed to be questioning whether Holmes had any interest in helping to establish a solution, knowing as he did my friend's interest in all things *outrè*, but Holmes shut that notion down quickly. "I've heard far too many stories of the Armilus family from a few of my acquaintances in the State," he said. "Their offenses against a few of the Vanderbilts, for instance, are unforgiveable. I have no interest whatsoever in being that agent that clears this affair up. Justice, however brutal, has been served."

"Fair enough," Lestrade nodded. "I wish that I had the luxury to take the same tack," he added, and then we moved on to other topics.

But now this curiously plain house seemed to have made an attack on yet another victim, this time one that didn't deserve it, and there was no question that Holmes would offer his assistance. Of course, mine was available as well, although I could never pretend to be as helpful or useful as Sherlock Holmes.

We made our way inside and up the stairs to the seemingly cursed study on the second floor. A grim constable was standing in the hallway beside the open door, and we passed him with a nod.

It was a fair-sized room, and with a curious open feeling, as there was very little furniture – a desk, a modest bookshelf, a couple of smaller chairs, and one big chair near the fireplace. There were a few small tables placed beside the three chairs. The two beside the smaller chairs were bare, but the one by the big chair had a book lying on it, and an ashtray.

The room was well-lit, with several gaslights spaced on both sides – two over the fireplace, and another pair near the door to the hall, which was the only entrance. There were several table lamps as well, all lit.

Conspicuously, another was lying on the floor, broken. A bit of lamp oil had seeped out onto the rug, its smell tinging the atmosphere of the room. I suspected that this was the source of that which had soaked Riley's clothing.

The wallpaper was a light tan with a small pattern that initially seemed innocuous, but upon further inspection appeared to suggest a much more subtle and objectionable image. I was unexpectedly reminded of the Ripper murders of a decade before.

There were two other aspects of the room that demanded one's attention. The first were the collected sketchings in blood that filled every available space along the walls, and even some spots of the great rug that covered most of the floor. They were obscene, and one had to wonder about what Nicky Armilus had seen in his life that could provide him such with fodder. In a few places above the desk, where he had stood during his artistic frenzy, Nicky had painted similar subjects on the ceiling. As a physician, I'm aware that a just a small bit of blood can seem like a great deal, and that they human body can stand to lose a sizeable quantity of it before expiration, but the amounts that had been used to decorate the room were simply astounding. It was now dried to a crusty brown color, but the coppery scent was still in the air, and I could only imagine how it must have looked when it was fresh, red and wet and shining in the gaslight.

While Holmes immediately set about his investigation of the room, Lestrade and I stood to one side, conversing softly.

"We were notified that Nicky Armilus had brought a number of important documents with him from New York, and that someone from America is coming immediately to take charge. I assume that these are the papers that are there in the desk. I glanced through them, but it's more than I can decipher. In any case, we didn't know yet what had happened here, so we've been leaving a man on duty. Riley's shift started last night at sunset. We've had men on similar duty since the last death, and no one has reported any problems. I wonder," he added, "why Riley chose to sit in here, rather than on a chair in the hallway. I'd hate to spend a moment more than I had to in this charnel room."

He drifted to silence and shifted his gaze to Holmes, now standing at the desk, and then paying careful attention to the tobacco jar on one corner. It was a tall thing, white Delft porcelain, with the word *Tabac* written on the side in complex and twining script. Decorating the jar alongside the word was a rather pudgy representation of the god Mercury, a rather sheepish smile on his face. I wondered just what he had to do with tobacco.

Holmes noticed me watching and said, "Watson, can you examine the book on the table? Lestrade, see what you can determine from the shelves."

The inspector and I separated, and I walked to the big chair, located near the fire. Examining the slim volume, I saw that it was covered with a thin layer of dust. Picking it up, I determined that it was written in French. My limited knowledge of the language revealed that it was of questionable nature – not surprising, considering whose house we were in. "Did Riley speak French?" I asked.

Lestrade, bent at the bookcase to look at the titles, said, "No. Why?"

"This book is written in French, although I don't think that he was reading it. The dust indicates that it hasn't been handled in several days. No doubt it was something that Nicky was enjoying before his death."

Lestrade grunted. "There's an empty space here – probably where it was shelved." He straightened. "I couldn't recommend any of these books, although I'm not surprised at their titles. The rich are interested in the most deviant sorts of things."

I glanced at Holmes to see that he'd moved from the desk to join me at the big chair, and that he was looking at the table before us. At first I thought that he was also looking at the book, but then he reached into the ashtray beside it, plucking something from it and putting it into one of the small envelopes that he habitually carries for the collection of evidence. Placing it in his pocket, he asked, "Did Riley smoke?"

Lestrade nodded. "He rolled his own."

"How many other men have stood guard here since Nicky Armilus died?"

Lestrade thought for a moment. "Two. Eckstien and Templeton. Riley was the third."

"Do either of those men smoke?"

"No, they don't. Why?"

"I have an idea about what has happened here, but there is more that must be determined. Can we speak to the man and woman who make up the household staff?"

"Certainly. I'll get them up here."

"No, perhaps downstairs would be better. I think you'll agree that this room is rather off-putting."

We moved downstairs to the large kitchen, located in the basement. Holmes indicated that he wish to speak first with the housekeeper. Her name was Lila Ring, and she was a big woman with long, dark, and unbound hair. She watched with a grim eye as we settled around the table. "This house is cursed," she began without prompting. "From the time the fat father arrived, I knew that he was doomed."

Lestrade raised an eyebrow. "If you knew, why didn't you do something to prevent it?"

"Why prevent it?" she countered. "A man like that – a family like that – they deserve to reap all that they have sown."

"Be careful, my girl," said the inspector. "That kind of talk will land you in chokey. It isn't just the father and son now. One of our own has been afflicted as well."

"I am truly sorry to hear that," she said. "They said that he set himself on fire and then threw himself out of the window."

"That seems to be the case."

"I warned him not to go in that room. He could have done his duty from downstairs, or if he had to be that close, he could have sat in a chair in the hallway. But when I went by last night, he was in there, sitting in the master's chair. Is it any wonder that he fell victim as well?"

"Fell victim to what?" I interjected.

"The curse. The evil that men do follows them like a cloud, and getting too close can destroy even a good man. And your constable seems like a good man. Will he live?"

"We're not sure," I answered evasively.

"Aye," she nodded. "I have that sense as well. My vision of his future is vague and uncertain."

"So you think that you have The Sight?" scoffed Lestrade. "If so, why didn't you see this coming?"

"Did I not say that I warned him? But he ignored me. There is only so much that I can do. Can I save all of them who has set their feet on a path to destruction? Should I? The threads of fate are woven already. They were fixed for the master and his son long before they arrived here, and well-deserved too. I'm sorry that your constable was caught up in that same net, and I tried to warn him, but it was his own path to choose and follow."

Throughout this exchange, Holmes had been silent. Now he spoke. "You are from originally from America, I believe."

She nodded, warily. "But not since I was a wee child. How did you know?"

"Certain aspects in the tonality of your speech. You have been in England for much of your life, but certain qualities of your American background are unmistakable. You were initially raised in one of the southern states."

She nodded. "My family was from Shooting Creek, in the mountains along the North Carolina and Georgia border, not far from Tennessee. We've lived there since coming over from England in the early 1600's. I'm named for my ancestor, ten generations back, who came over then with a large party and settled in the wilderness. She was a wise woman who was originally from Anglesey, of the Blood of Nial."

223

Welsh. That, I thought, explained her coloring and notable visage.

"Druids," said Holmes.

"She had The Gift," explained Lila Ring. "As do I."

"We're more interested in down-to-earth explanations," countered Holmes, and the woman scowled.

"You should have a care as well, Mr. Holmes," she said. "You also choose to walk a dangerous path."

Holmes ignored the warning. "Has your family in America ever have any dealings with Donald Armilus, or his children?"

She shook her head. "How would I know that? My parents came back to England years ago, and we lost track of our American kin. I'd never heard of Donald Armilus or his son until I was hired by the master's agent last year, when the master decided to move to England. After his madness, his living death, it seemed as if no one thought to close up the house or sell it, and so I simply stayed, continuing to receive my pay for keeping the place livable."

"And the agent continued to fund the upkeep of the house? To pay for the coal and the gas, and any other maintenance?"

"He did."

"What about food, and tobacco, and other daily staples?"

"We still receive an allowance for all of it – the food, and the laundry as well. Not tobacco, though. No need for that. Bill Kilbride – he's the caretaker – doesn't smoke, and neither do I. We both thought that at some point it would be realized that we were still here, keeping up an otherwise empty house, but we didn't want to disrupt a comfortable arrangement before we had to, and so we didn't say anything to anyone. Then, a few days ago, the agent came by, and it turned out that he hadn't forgotten about us after all. He knew all along that we were taking their money for doing practically nothing. That's when he told us that the son would be staying here soon. He made sure that the house was in good shape – which it was! – and soon after the son arrived. He was as much of a devil as his father."

"In what way?"

"It was obvious by the way he talked and the things that he said."

"Do you have any idea what happened to them both – the father and son – and now the constable, to cause such a result?" asked Holmes.

She shook her head decisively. Lestrade looked impatient, and Holmes, seeming to have heard all that he needed, stood and thanked her for her help. As she walked out, he asked for her to have Kilbride sent in.

Normally at this time, Lestrade would have asked several questions, but he seemed strangely subdued, as if putting the matter completely in

Holmes's hands. We remained in silence for the short time until Bill Kilbride entered the room.

He was a small man, about Lestrade's size, with the same lean quick energy about him. He had a full head of hair that was more salt than pepper, cut rather short. Whitish whiskers gave an ashy look to his face. He walked with a rather rolling gait as he crossed the room. When he was closer, I could see that his skin had a leathery tanned look, and his hands were rough, with enlarged knuckles. There were several old scars across the backs of his fingers, and a faded blue-black tattoo peeked from underneath his cuff, although I couldn't see what it depicted. He nodded and took the seat across from us that was indicated by the inspector.

"Mr. Kilbride," said Holmes, "I suspect that you've been interviewed by the police extensively following the death last year of Donald Armilus, and then again after his son's peculiar demise a few days ago."

The man nodded and swallowed. "No doubt about that. But I couldn't tell anything that seemed useful." He glanced at Lestrade. "Isn't that right, Inspector?"

Lestrade grimaced. "We're still considering it."

"Were you aware of Mrs. Ring's ideas that these men were under some sort of curse?" I asked.

Kilbride shook his head, a fond smile on his face. "She talks a great deal of that sort of thing – dark visions, and terrible destinies. She's warned me before, a time or two, and yet here I sit. Let the grocer forget to include an item in the weekly delivery and she's ready with a pronouncement of his doom. And yet," he added, as the smile drained from his features, "she has been right on several occasions – when old Mr. Whitaker on the next street died, she'd told me a week before – privately, you understand – that his time was nearly up, and that was just from the two of them having a passing conversation. The same for Lydia Striker on the next street – her with child, and Mrs. Ring knew when the girl's husband went to sea that he wouldn't be coming back."

"And the Armilus men?" asked Holmes. "How close to the mark were her predictions in those cases?"

"Well," Kilbride replied, leaning back a bit, "she said they'd come to no good end, right from when we met them, but that's no surprise, is it? I thought the same thing, and I don't have any special gifts."

"I know that you were interviewed after the events last year, and again the other day," said Holmes. "Do you have any new theories when considering last night's tragedy, and what happened to the unfortunate constable?"

Kilbride shook his head. "None at all. Mrs. Ring said it's because he insisted in going into that cursed room on the second floor. I know that

I've stayed out of it since then, but not just because of that. Since the younger Armilus died so peculiarly, the police have been here, keeping an eye on the papers until someone from America can arrive to take charge. The local agent didn't want the responsibility, I'm told, and it was him that summoned the police to watch the place. I was told not to leave, or to make any plans about a new billet."

"It's been a pretty nice one for you so far," said Holmes. "All told, the Armilus family probably didn't live here much more than a week during the entire time that you've been employed."

"That's right. It was much more normal for the place to be quiet as a tomb, with Mrs. Ring going about her own business, and me mine."

"And what is your business?" asked Holmes.

"Well, it doesn't take much to keep up the house, as you can imagine. With most of it standing empty, I hardly ever go upstairs at all."

"Not even to relax in the sitting room, for instance – smoking the master's cigars, or using his tobacco or brandy?"

Kilbride shook his head, a touch of anger apparent in the emphatic way that he did it. "We kept to the downstairs, Mrs. Ring and me. When my daily duties are finished, such as they are, I read, or take walks, or visit museums – I'm trying to better myself, you see. I went to sea when I was younger, and it was enough to convince me that I could do better. I returned to London late last year and happened upon this job, not knowing who was going to be living here. I thought that I was incredibly fortunate when I was hired – that is, until soon after, when Mr. Armilus moved in. I've never met a more objectionable piece of work – at least, until his son arrived. I'm not sure who was worse."

Lestrade started to say something, but then he shut his mouth and again deferred to Holmes, who asked, "During those times when the house was yours, so to speak, did you ever have visitors? Did your friends stop by? What about the tradesmen?"

Kilbride frowned. "I like to pursue my own thoughts, and I don't really cultivate many acquaintances. I suppose Steven Mullingar is the closest thing to a friend that I have."

"Oh? And who is he?"

"He works around the corner, at MacLean's, the tobacconist."

"Indeed. And how often does he visit?"

"Not all that often. I don't smoke, you see, so I suppose it's curious that we ever became friends. But he's a very smart man, and I enjoy our conversations."

"And how did you meet him?"

"Why, he delivered the tobacco that was originally ordered for Mr. Armilus when he moved in late last year."

"The tobacco that's upstairs in the jar on his desk?"

"Yes."

"And did the son, Nicky, smoke as well?"

"He did. Like a chimney."

"Was the old tobacco from last year replaced when he moved in?"

Kilbride's eyes widened in surprise. "No, it wasn't. We should have replaced it, I suppose, as I understand that tobacco gets old and dry, but I just never thought of it. You don't think – "

"I'm not sure what to think right now, Mr. Kilbride," said Holmes, "but you would do well to keep any speculation to yourself, even from Mrs. Ring. Do you understand?"

Kilbride nodded enthusiastically. "I do. Anything that I can do to help, sirs."

Holmes informed him that he was finished for now, and the man stood and left, pulling the door shut behind him.

"I would have thought," said Lestrade, "that there might be some vulgar intrigue going on below-steps between those two, disrupted by the arrivals of the Armilus clan."

"An affair between Mrs. Ring and Kilbride is actually quite likely," concurred Holmes, "but I don't think that they would need to murder the Americans to sustain it, or because it was somehow disrupted. After all, what happened to Donald Armilus last year should have resulted in the immediate closing of the house, ending both their association with it, and likely each other as well. The same factors make it unlikely that they killed the son."

"But what if either Donald or Nicky Armilus advanced some sort of objectionable action toward the housekeeper?"

"What if, indeed? Did it need to result in such a drastic action as whatever happened to each of them – father and son both driven mad, in different ways, and to different but no less terrible ends? And that doesn't explain Constable Riley's fate."

"The tobacco," I said. "You showed an interest in it upstairs, and it was on the edge of your questioning just now."

"Very good, Watson," nodded Holmes, reaching into his picket. He withdrew a couple of the envelopes wherein he stored evidence. "This," he said, "is a sample from the jar containing the year-old tobacco. Do you notice anything?"

He handed it to me, and I held it so that Lestrade could take a look as well. At first it appeared to simply be typical tobacco of some rich mixture, its dryness indicating that it had indeed been lying around unused for quite a while. I put my nose close to the envelope and sniffed it, perceiving a

227

slight sourness. As I had done, Lestrade did the same, and commented aloud confirming the observation. Holmes nodded. "Look closer," he said.

I did, and then saw what he meant. Mixed in with the various grains of tobacco were a number of smaller pieces of something else, each dark brown, also the same dark color.

"It looks like some sort of seed," I indicated.

"Now," added Holmes, "look at this sample from the ashtray." And he handed us the other envelope.

Within was the remains of a rolled cigarette, some unburned tobacco, and an equal amount of ashes. I pushed it around with my finger, showing that the seeds were also in the unburned tobacco, and a few burned seed husks were mixed into the ashes. I smelled it and perceived the same sourness, mixed with the burned smell of an old cigarette.

"The inference," explained Holmes, "is that Constable Riley sat in the study during his shift, and at some point rolled a cigarette, using the tobacco from the jar on Armilus's desk – the same tobacco that has been in there for a year, and was there when both father and son went mad."

"So the tobacco has been poisoned," I concluded.

"As a starting hypothesis, yes. But there is still much that still needs to be answered before we can consider the matter closed. Lestrade, what can you tell us about Kilbride and Mrs. Ring. I assume that you've already investigated them in relation to the two previous incidents."

"We have. Kilbride is what he told us he was – a former sailor, originally from Manchester, who came ashore late last year and happened to hear about this job. He has a sister who works for the agent, and she recommended him. It suited him, as he wanted to pursue his 'studies', which seems to mean reading books and visiting museums. I wish someone would pay be to do the same."

"And what about the agent, of whom we heard many references?"

"He's a man named Dennehy, long established in this type of work. He has connections with similar businesses in the United States, obtaining lodgings or offices for Americans who are coming over here without any previous associations. From what we learned a year ago, questioning him and examining his correspondence, the man has no other connection to Armilus than being requested to find this house and manage its upkeep. He pays the bills from an account funded by Armilus's New York office, and forwards the invoices, such as they are, back to America like clockwork."

"And Mrs. Ring? What is her story?"

"Well, she's actually never been married. Like most housekeepers, the 'Missus' is an assumed title to maintain authority. But in this case there's no one to maintain it over, as there is no other staff. Her family moved here from where she said not long after the American Civil War, when she was very small, and she's worked in domestic service since her teenage years. Like Kilbride, she found this job through Dennehy's office, as she had worked for one of his previous clients, also an American who moved here for a time several years ago. The files at Dennehy's noted that she had a sterling character from her previous employer. Neither she or Kilbride have ever shown a speck of dishonesty."

"In any case," I interjected, "I suspect that the question about the tobacco will lead us to MacLean's."

"Indeed," replied Holmes. "Perhaps we can determine if the two caretakers, both seemingly without a blot upon their respective copybooks, were responsible for the curious addition to the tobacco, or if instead it occurred at the tobacconists – either from the efforts of Mr. MacLean, or possibly Kilbride's friend, Steven Mullingar."

Lestrade announced that he would reopen the investigation into the caretakers' pasts, looking for some clue or connection that had been missed before, and that he would discretely see what could be learned about MacLean and Mullingar of the tobacco shop. In the meantime, Holmes announced that we intended to visit there in person.

MacLean's shop wasn't far, and both Holmes and I had previously stopped there upon occasion, although it wasn't our usual vendor of choice. It had always seemed to be a respectable and well-maintained little business, and I had to wonder about its possible association with the terrible events within the Dorset Square house.

Recalling the seeds, I asked, "Do you suspect ergot poisoning?"

Holmes nodded, but said, "Not entirely. Those were clearly something that very much resembled rye seeds. Their darker coloring could simply be from absorbing the moistures of the tobacco. But these symptoms – a man screaming from now until he dies, another painting with his own blood until his heart no longer has enough to beat, and now a third who has set himself on fire and then leapt from a window – are much too drastic for the symptoms of typical ergot poisoning, as bad as that can be. No, something else is happening."

By then we had reached the doorway to MacLean's little shop, which had seemingly just resumed operations for the day, as the owner himself was in the process of turning a sign in the window from "*Closed*" to "*Open*".

MacLean was a dour Scot, but friendly enough in his own way. He greeted us by name and asked what he could do for us. Of course, Holmes made no reference to the events related to Constable Riley, or the connections between the tobacco from MacLean's shop and that found in Armilus's study. Rather, he went through some complicated story about

229

having tried a tobacco blend, shared with him by a friend, that had many positive points. It had come from MacLean's shop, but he didn't recall the name. Could the owner help him?

MacLean nodded. I knew that he'd long coveted Holmes's custom, and I felt bad that my friend's attempts to gain information did not necessarily mean that he was on the way to becoming a regular customer.

MacLean showed us to a shelf where a number of jars were lined up, each with curious and intriguing names. "I don't recognize many of these," I said. "Are they special to your shop?"

MacLean nodded. "I have an assistant – originally trained as a chemist – who has created a number of unique mixtures."

"Indeed?" said Holmes. "And why haven't we heard of this before?"

"Well, he's only been in my employ for a bit over a year, and it took him some time to convince me to sell the results of his experiments. Only now is word starting to spread of 'MacLean's Special Blends', as I like to call them."

"And where is this Sorcerer's Apprentice of Tobacco?" Holmes asked. "I'd like to meet him."

"Alas, he's on a delivery. He's in and out all day long. He'll be sorry that he missed you both, I'm sure."

"Oh well. We shall certainly have another chance. Can I see some of his other blends?" And he turned away, back toward the rows of jars.

Having worked with Holmes for a number of years by that point, I recognized when he signaled that he needed a moment to investigate without MacLean's attention. I was only glad that he hadn't chosen to upset a whole shelf of jars – and this had happened before – in order to slip away while MacLean and I tried to clean up the mess.

Following Holmes's implied instruction, I walked to the other side of the shop, calling MacLean after me to ask about a few of the pipes that were for sale on a rack there. Out of the corner of my eye, behind MacLean's back, I could see Holmes slip behind the counter and into the rear of the shop.

I became truly interested in one of the pipes, and MacLean's enthusiasm joined mine as I convinced myself that I wished to buy it. When the topic could no longer be stretched any further, and the time had come for me to make my payment, I was relieved to see Holmes standing innocently by the opposite counter, having successfully completed his researches. I paid for my new pipe, and then Holmes requested a few ounces of three of the different blends, saying that he wished to compare them and then he'd be back. MacLean had a satisfied expression as he led us to the door following our transactions, and he wished us well before closing the door behind us.

We walked for a hundred feet or so before Holmes hailed a cab. In moments we were making our way through the awakening city to Barts, where Holmes still maintained privileges in the laboratories when he encountered something that was beyond the facilities of his own small chemical corner.

"I found where Mullingar carries out his tobacco alchemy," he explained. "Most tobacconists blend different strains – Virginia, Burley, or Oriental – and they add their own secret ingredients. I knew a man who added orange peel, for instance. But Mr. Mullingar has a chemical set-up that looks more like something one would find in the research laboratories at Woolwich Arsenal. I cannot tell if he synthesizes the various powders and liquids as additives to the tobacco, or he's up to something with far more sinister implications. But I did find a jar, hidden beneath the work counter, containing the rye-seed-impregnated tobacco, along with an adjacent bottle of clear liquid. As they were the only items secreted there, the implication that there is a connection cannot be ignored. I took another sample of the rye-tobacco, as well as pouring myself some of the clear liquid into one of the little empty bottles that he had stacked nearby.

"When we arrive at Barts, you would do me a great service by researching what you can find about ergot poisoning and lysergic acid in the medical library. Meanwhile, I'll make my way upstairs and attempt to determine what exactly Mr. Mullingar is keeping in that bottle, and what he's done to the tobacco, if anything."

Not long after, we were dropped outside the hospital, and we passed through the Henry VIII Gate before bearing right and through the inner court. Soon we reached the door which would lead to both the laboratory and the medical library. As always whenever I entered through that doorway, with its sign overhead proclaiming, *"Whatsoever Thy Hand Findeth To Do, Do It With Thy Might"*, I recalled all the other times that I'd read it beforehand, both as a student and young doctor, and on that New Year's Day in 1881 just before I was introduced to Sherlock Holmes, and then on so many other later occasions as well. They were good words, and seeing them yet again was always a comfort.

While Holmes proceeded upstairs, I entered the familiar and comfortable medical library. I didn't recall my way around with quite the same familiarity that I'd had as a student, but with the aid of a very knowledgeable and helpful medical librarian, I found what I sought rather quickly. My quick examination of the books didn't reveal anything new. Ergot poisoning is the result of a fungus that grows on rye, producing lysergic acid. Its hallucinogenic effects can have a profound effect upon humans, and while I had identified a number of case histories, nothing was recorded to the degree of what had occurred in the Dorset Square house.

After gathering several volumes from the library stacks, I wandered out and up the stone steps to the laboratory, where Holmes already had a complex system of piping in place. Always a careful scientist, he had a notebook open beside him, and he diligently made note after note concerning his findings.

I approached and set the library books nearby, with the relevant articles marked. He made no acknowledgement besides a short nod, and I turned to go. With no other task at hand, I planned to return to Baker Street.

I tarried a moment in the hall outside to share pleasantries with our friend Dr. Dickinson. He seemed to wish to draw me into a discussion about his latest research into the characteristics of blood, always a fascination for him, but I managed to extricate myself without offending him and then tread the familiar path down and out to the street. Not long after, I was in a hansom and on my way.

Considering that I was quite exhausted, having spent the previous day and into the evening assisting Holmes in his pursuit of the Watership Down killer, and then having had no sleep upon our return to London, I should have returned to Baker Street immediately. However, as I was out and about, I decided to carry out a number of errands. By mid-day I found myself near Charing Cross, and I impulsively entered the station, electing to get a meat pie and a glass of cider from a little vendor, set up in the eastern corner of the station, that I had met during one of Holmes's investigations. After that was finished, I ambled north to Charing Cross Road and the bookshops there, where I was fortunate enough to find a particular volume that I had long sought. Feeling that I had accomplished a great deal indeed, I hailed a cab and settled back for the slow early-afternoon journey to Baker Street.

I awoke with a start when we cabbie announced that we had arrived. Amused that I had fallen into a nap, and trying to recall exactly when it had occurred, I let myself in and went upstairs in something of a dream-like haze, having given myself over to the idea that as soon as I could gain my chair by the fireplace, I would resume my slumbers.

The house was quiet, and the sun, now in the west, had left the sitting room in shadows. I set my purchases down on the dining table and noticed that a package was already there, addressed to Holmes. Curiously, it had label reading *MacLean's Fine Tobaccos* pasted upon it.

I found that I was no longer sleepy, pondering just how it had come to rest there. Even as I was considering hunting up Mrs. Hudson and questioning her about it, I heard a the sound of a vehicle halt outside, followed by the opening and closing of the front door, and then Holmes's confident and energetic steps as he climbed the stairs.

232

Upon entering, he immediately glanced past me to the package. "From MacLean's," I said as he crossed the room. He leaned over the table, resting his hands on either side of the box, looking this way and that, and muttering to himself as he recorded various facts. Then, having seen all that he found useful, he walked to the chemical corner, retrieved a small knife, and returned, leaning over to cut the string. In moments, the contents were revealed – a package of tobacco, with an unsigned card that said "*With our compliments . . . .*"

I didn't need to be Sherlock Holmes to spot the darkened seeds that were interspersed throughout the blend. "Steven Mullingar must have heard about our visit this morning," I said.

"Now, Watson," said Holmes. "Perhaps you're slandering the poor fellow. Mr. MacLean himself could have brought this, although it's unlikely. But I expect that you're right, and that we can probably piece together what has happened. For some reason, Mullingar has adulterated the tobacco with his own concoction. This was aimed at the Armilus men, but caused the innocent Constable Riley to suffer the same effects when he used the old tobacco. No doubt Mullingar has heard about the incident and the constable's injuries, and then our involvement. The fact that we then showed up at MacLean's not long after, our innocent story fooling him not at all, forced him into this clumsy attempt to stop our investigation."

He stepped to the door and called for Mrs. Hudson to come up. In the meantime, I moved to my own desk, in order to obtain some of my own tobacco. "I shouldn't if I were you," said Holmes, suddenly quite serious. At that moment, Mrs. Hudson entered.

When questioned, she explained, "I had stepped around the corner, to the butcher's." She was suddenly concerned. "When I returned, the tobacco man was at the door, and he offered to take it up, as my hands were full."

"Did you see him leave?" asked Holmes. She hadn't.

"Was the page boy out as well?" I added.

"He was. His sister has just had a baby, and I let him go 'round to see her."

"Ah, well," mused Holmes. "He has had a few minutes alone, then. Thank you, Mrs. Hudson." She nodded, frowned, and departed.

I understood then why Holmes had stopped me from using my own tobacco. "I suppose we'll have to get rid of all of it," I said ruefully.

"And any bottled items as well," he added. "My research indicates that Mr. Mullingar has derived an extremely strong variant of lysergic acid. Apparently he discovered a way to add an amide group with two ethyl substituents to the original lysergic acid compound, greatly increasing the hallucinogenic aspects. It was present in the augmented tobacco in the seeds, and also in its pure form, poured into the leaves, matching the sample of liquid that I obtained. If Mr. Mullingar broke in to leave the tainted tobacco, is it too difficult to speculate that he also poured some of the fluid in our existing tobacco, or onto our cigars, or into our alcohol? For that matter, the liquid is easily dissolved in sugar, and likely other substances as well."

"I would advise," I said, "that we wash down our pipes as well, along with the silver and dishes, and anything else that might enter our bodies." A thought occurred to me. "Mrs. Hudson didn't see when he left. He was in the house alone – the *entire* house, and not just up here. Our food stocks downstairs might be contaminated as well! I must notify her."

I turned quickly, but not before seeing Holmes's expression as he pictured our usually very-patient landlady being told that she would have to throw out anything that might remotely have had a chance of being poisoned.

Later, when Mrs. Hudson had been mollified and promised reimbursement for the loss of most of the contents of her pantry, we summoned Lestrade for a council of war. It was then that I learned that he already knew just enough, by way of a telegram from Holmes before he'd arrived home, to have placed Mullingar under surveillance. He related that the report showed Mullingar traveling from the tobacco shop on a number of deliveries, and that among them was a stop at our rooms in Baker Street. The officer who had compiled the report, clearly a man of no imagination or gumption who simply recorded what he saw without further thought, had believed 221 to simply be another rooming house of no consequence. The constable had watched Mullingar disappear inside before returning a few minutes later, whereupon he completed his other deliveries before going back to MacLean's. Soon after, seemingly done for the day, he'd gone to his home in nearby Edward Street. "He's there now," added Lestrade, "if we want to pick him up."

"There's no reason to wait," agreed Holmes. "There's still a chance that he's innocent, but regardless, he has a story to tell us."

We found a cab and set off to obtain reinforcements. Along the way, Lestrade mentioned a curious fact. "I had a message from your brother, Mr. Holmes. About this case."

Holmes raised an eyebrow. "Indeed? And what is his interest?"

"He didn't reveal a great deal, but he asked to be informed of any developments."

"And have you related any of the specifics to him yet? About Mr. Mullingar's involvement, for instance."

234

"No, not so far. I didn't feel that we had enough to tell him. It's only now, after our conversation, that I have more of a sense of what's happening."

Holmes didn't respond, other than to nod and then sink into his own thoughts. We stopped at a police station to gather several other officers and then, in a few minutes, we found ourselves in narrow Edward Street. Men were dispatched to watch the various exits while we and a couple of brawny constables walked up the four flights, and so to Mullingar's room. Holmes knocked and, when a muffled voice from within questioned who it was, he replied that he had a telegram. Mullingar opened the door to find Holmes facing him. The man's eyes widened, and then, seeing the rest of us, he seemed to sag a bit upon realizing that he had been discovered. He submitted quietly when the handcuffs were placed upon his wrists, and he made no comments as our growler carried us south to Scotland Yard. Only when we were in one of the offices and his interrogation had begun did he say, with a half-smile and shake of his head, that perhaps trying to poison Holmes and me had been a bit too much.

"That's the least of your worries," snapped Lestrade.

"Yes," replied Mullingar. "I can see that you're upset about the constable, and for that I'm truly sorry. I had thought that I was remiss in not retrieving my special blend sooner, after it delivered justice on Donald Armilus. Still, I knew that Kilbride and Mrs. Ring didn't smoke, and I thought that it was safe enough. Time passed, and then, a year later, when Armilus's cursed son arrived, I could see that there had been a purpose in my leaving it in the house, for his punishment was enacted as well. Afterwards, with the police presence, I never had the chance to slip into the house and carry away the evidence."

"You refer to justice," said Holmes. "Then you feel that Armilus and his son needed punishment, and you were the hand of vengeance to carry it out?"

Mullingar nodded. "I never thought that I'd have the chance. But then, a year ago, the newspapers reported how Armilus had moved to England to escape the investigations overtaking his American enterprises, and that he was going to be living nearby. I took it upon myself to fix up my special blend and take it around, as if it had been arranged beforehand. I met Kilbride then, and he accepted delivery, along with all the other items that were arriving then to stock the house. It only took a few days for justice to be enacted, although I was uncertain as to what form it might take."

"I take it that you speak of the uncertain nature of the chemical that you've derived from the lysergic acid."

"That's right," replied Mullingar. "Reactions can manifest themselves in many ways, all hallucinatory, but not necessarily unpleasant. However, I made sure that what I added to the Armilus tobacco, both the poisoned seeds and the fluid, was guaranteed to result in a terror-filled death. Sadly, Donald Armilus didn't actually die, but what is left of him must be in a living hell, until his soul goes to the real place."

I stared at the man. "What did the Armilus family do to you that you hate them so much?"

Mullingar gave a sad smile. "Long ago, when I was a young man, I studied chemistry at a New York university. I was brilliant, and had an incredible future before me. One night, I was attending a reception to honor the various New York elite who had contributed in one way or another to the school, and Armilus was there, along with his daughter."

"Daughter?" said Lestrade. "I hadn't heard that he had a daughter."

"I suppose that it's little known now," replied Mullingar. "She was beautiful, but truth be told, she was just as scheming and devious as her father. However, I didn't see it then, and it didn't matter in any case – I would have sold my soul for her. In fact, I suppose that I have. We talked that night, just for a few moments, and my fate was sealed. She began to find ways to pay little attentions to me, although it was just a distraction for her, and those crumbs were enough to make me realize that I'd been starving before I met her, my life empty in ways that I'd never before realized.

"I was foolish enough to believe that we had a future – that *she* was *my* future – but I was nothing to her, although I didn't realize it then. I began to speak as if we were making plans, and she let me, for I suppose that it was amusing. I became more bold in my attentions, and soon there was a mention of the two of us in one of the New York newspapers, as if we were truly a couple. That brought it to the attention of Armilus and his sons. They had other plans for this girl, and clearly I needed to be discouraged. One night, thinking that I'd been summoned to meet with my love, I instead found myself facing Armilus and his sons, along with several of his bully-boys. The latter proceeded to beat me within an inch of my life. Only when I had been broken, literally and spiritually, did Armilus and his sons step forward to get in their weak licks as well, as I no longer presented any danger or possibility of response.

"As I healed, I became aware that a number of my friends would no longer associate with me. After I could get about, I learned that Armilus had gone to great lengths to destroy my reputation in a number of ways, all vile and irredeemable. I was dismissed from school, and suddenly my bright future was extinguished. A few weeks later, Armilus announced that his daughter was to be married to the son of a Russian nobleman of very dark reputation to fulfill some business ambition. I never saw her again, and as I understand it, she was carried away to Russia, where she later died under mysterious circumstances.

"I made my way after that as best as I could, but wherever I went, it seemed that the long reach of the Armilus family was still there to destroy me. By then, my association with his daughter was long in the past, but it seemed as if they took sport in constantly finding new ways to cause me harm. Finally I left America entirely and set myself up anew. Mullingar is not my real name, and my former identity isn't important anymore. I was prepared to live out my dull life here, without further incident – and then, I saw that Armilus was moving to London.

"As I said, I fixed up some of my special blend, made with one of the substances that I had discovered years before, and delivered it to the house, not knowing exactly what form the punishment would take. It seems that whatever horrors are in that evil man's mind have been released, to haunt him until he dies. Afterwards, I was satisfied, and seeing no urgent need to retrieve the tainted tobacco, I let it be. Then, as if it were a sign from the heavens, the son arrived as well. I knew that it was just a matter of time until the punishment would also fall upon him, and in fact it took less than a day. I'm only sorry that I wasn't able to destroy the other Armilus sons, and that the constable was injured before I could take away the tobacco."

"And yet," said Lestrade, "you had no hesitation in trying to do the same to these two men that you had done to Armilus and his son. They had never wronged you."

Mullingar shrugged. "I suppose that it was simply a reaction to the knowledge that my involvement was known. In an effort to preserve my life, I thoughtlessly attempted to shore up all the places where my plan was starting to collapse." He looked at Holmes, and then me. "Gentleman, I apologize."

At that moment, the door opened and a grim-faced constable entered, handing Lestrade a note. He read it and then angrily threw it on the table. "Constable Riley has died of his injuries."

Mullingar suddenly looked pained, and a haunted look entered his eyes. "I am truly sorry." And then he lowered his head, refusing to speak any further, before eventually being led from the room. He was found later that day in his cell, hanged from where he'd fashioned a noose out of his own shirt.

We offered our condolences to Lestrade and indicated that we'd be available later if he needed any further information. Then we stepped outside, where Holmes hailed a cab. I expected that we'd return to Baker Street, but instead he urged the cabbie to get us to MacLean's shop with

237

all possible speed. I wanted to ask what was so urgent, but the expression on his face indicated that he wasn't in a mood to converse.

When we arrived, Holmes was already out of the cab and in the door before I could disembark and ask the cabbie to wait for us. Stepping inside, I found MacLean looking shocked while Holmes disappeared into the back room. "Tell him, Watson!" he cried.

Not knowing how much to reveal, I simply stated that MacLean's brilliant assistant had been arrested for murder. The Scot was speechless, clearly wanting to ask questions, but not knowing where to begin. Before he could order his thoughts, Holmes had returned, carrying a large jar of tobacco, as well as another of a clear liquid. "Evidence!" he snapped to MacLean. "I'll be back later to tell you more." And then he was out the door, leaving me to apologize and follow.

Back at our rooms, Holmes asked the cab to wait, although he gave no indication to me for what purpose. We entered 221b to discover Mrs. Hudson, tidying the sitting room, her lips tight, obviously still peeved at having to re-stock her larder from scratch because of some activity related to one of Holmes's cases. She left without speaking, pulling the door shut firmly behind her. Holmes, typically oblivious to her mood, crossed the room and placed both the tobacco and the container of clear liquid on his chemical table.

"We'll need to be careful how we dispose of it," I said. "We can't burn it here, as the fumes would likely drive us mad, and the neighbors as well. We can't just toss it, as some trash-picker would doubtless retrieve it and come to a bad end."

"I agree," said Holmes. "Perhaps a trip to the Thames later today, where we'll sprinkle it in, a few handfuls at a time – although I fear that a fish might eat it and then end up in some poor soul's frying pan. But first . . . ."

He was still wearing his Inverness and, from a deep side pocket, he pulled a notebook – the same that he had been using to make notes in the laboratory at Barts. Stepping to the fireplace, he opened it, looked at one of the pages for a long moment as if committing something to memory, and then carefully tore out the sheet. Leaning down, he tossed it upon the fire.

"You heard Lestrade," he said. "My brother Mycroft is interested in this case. He has somehow dimly perceived what is going on, and I fear that he wishes to obtain this augmented lysergic acid for some devious purpose. I would trust Mycroft with my life, but the government not so much. One can only hope that Mullingar will keep the process to himself. I'll return momentarily to his rooms in Edward Street, and then again to the tobacco shop, in order to see if he kept any notes. But in the meantime, this tobacco, the fluid, and my own notes where I derived the formula as well, had to be removed from the board before Mycroft could snag them."

We watched as the sheet with Holmes's notes browned and curled before bursting into flame. Then, with an instruction to hide the poisoned tobacco and dangerous liquid until he returned, Holmes departed. He returned several hours later, with news that he had thoroughly searched both Mullingar's rooms and MacLean's shop, after explaining to the owner exactly what had occurred. The tobacconist indicated that no one had been by the shop since our previous visit who'd shown any interest in Mullingar or his experiments. Holmes had been unable to find any notes relating to the experiments at either location, and he hoped that the formula was now only known to himself and Mullingar. As he finished saying this, the doorbell rang, and in a few minutes the page boy delivered a note from Lestrade, telling us of Mullingar's suicide.

We never heard a word from Mycroft about whether he felt vexed upon being denied further knowledge of the dangerous substance, and of course Holmes was careful never to bring up the subject. Later that afternoon, we hailed a cabbie that we knew and made our way to Limehouse. There, after walking down a narrow and slimy alley, we stepped along the narrow shore. The tide was low, and we were able to make our way to one of the nearby sewer entrances, where a vile and odoriferous flow steadily joined the river. I was tasked with pouring out Mullingar's concoction while Holmes, wearing old gloves, scattered handful after handful of the tainted tobacco onto the surface of the greasy waters. We watched it drift away and gradually sink. After a few moments, we turned and made our way back to the street, and thence to our usual tobacconist. Then, once more in Baker Street, we warily lit our pipes and smoked in our comfortable chairs before the fireplace, each lost in our own thoughts for the rest of the day.

The Brook Street Mystery

Chapter I

T he rains of the previous night had left London washed and clean. The sky was a bright blue that morning as Holmes and I stepped out of 7B Praed Street, our business there successfully concluded. We had visited to hear details related to the death of Captain Brensham, which had a tangential connection to one of Holmes's own cases. We were just pulling the door shut behind us when a stout fellow stepped our way and seemed to recognize us.

"Mr. Holmes? Dr. Watson? As I live and breathe! I was just about to knock at this very door with a problem, but I'd much rather tell *you* about it. How fortuitous! You, sir, are the very man that I would have sought, but I understood that you had long since retired and no longer lived in London."

Holmes nodded. "Sir Percy. How do you do?" He turned to me. "Watson, you recall our old acquaintance, Dr. Trevelyan." I did indeed, although I barely recognized him in the figure before us. Holmes added, "Pray, let us not hinder you. I am, as you indicated, retired, but my Illustrious Successor inside will be completely satisfactory, I'm sure." And with that, he touched the brim of his fore-and-aft cap, worn city or country, warm weather or cold, and made as if to step around the fellow.

Sir Percy Trevelyan, however, was having none of it. He raised a hand. "Please, Mr. Holmes. I have a bit of a problem, and I believe that you are the very man who can help me, particularly with the insight you gained related to the events in Brook Street so long ago. Might I have a few moments of your time to explain the details?"

My friend's mouth tightened slightly in irritation, but I'm not sure that someone who hadn't known him for so long would have been able to spot it. Holmes relented, stating, "Very well. Let us adjourn to the pub up the street."

Sir Percy seemed as if he might object, possibly wishing to suggest a place of a bit better station, but he apparently realized that if he created extra difficulties, Holmes would slip off his line and be away.

We walked west for several blocks in silence, giving me a chance to observe Sir Percy in greater detail. I have to confess that when Holmes identified him, I was a bit nonplussed, as this man was quite different from the young doctor that I recalled, more than half-a-lifetime ago. He had gained considerable weight since that day nearly forty years before when he had visited our Baker Street rooms, enlisting our aid in the matter of his resident patient, Mr. Blessington. At the time, he was a thin, pale fellow in his mid-thirties, with a vaguely rodent-like face. He had been rather nervous and withdrawn then, but understandably so, and I had put it down to the situation in which he had found himself – namely, acting as a harried physician to the eccentric hypochondriac who bankrolled his medical practice, and whose behavior had been progressively deteriorating for a considerable period before the events which led the doctor to seek Holmes's assistance.

Now, I was hard-pressed to understand how Holmes had recognized the fellow walking beside us. He was certainly no longer thin or pale, with the features of his face filled out considerably. His rather thick hair had been replaced by a speckled pate, peeking out from underneath his hat, and in the morning July sunshine, I could detect a series of broken capillaries on his nose, as dense as a map of the vile alleys of Limehouse. His clothing was of the finest quality, and as we entered the pub, I could almost read his thoughts when he resigned himself to finding a seat upon one of the commonly used chairs which littered the place.

I knew that he was now in his mid-seventies, a few years older than Holmes and myself. Comparing the drastic changes in Trevelyan with the manner in which Holmes had retained his wiry strength and appearance was startling. I liked to think that I, too, had managed to keep myself somewhat in fighting trim over the years and, when measured against Sir Percy, I felt rather proud of myself.

The pub was quite empty that early in the morning. Holmes and I ordered tea, while the famous doctor asked for brandy. While we waited, he pulled out an antique Obrisset snuffbox and took a pinch, and then another for symmetry.

"I have kept track of your successes over the years," I said while he returned the box to his pocket. "Your work on nervous lesions has become world famous."

"And one must not forget your researches during the Boer War," added Holmes.

Sir Percy nodded graciously, with a humble and practiced and polished lowering of his gaze, belied by a proud little smile tightening his mouth. "I have been fortunate," he said, quickly raising his eyes. "I must admit that the events surrounding Mr. Blessington's death, and your brilliant solution, Mr. Holmes, were an opportunity for me."

"Indeed?" said Holmes with a raised eyebrow. "How so?"

"Why, simply because your explanation not only absolved me of any guilt that might have been associated with the crime, but it also gave me a certain amount of immediate notoriety that I was able to parlay into increasing opportunities. There was an initial curiosity about the affair that led new patients to my door. Word spread of my abilities, and the practice grew. What began as a nine days' wonder developed into a solid career. And it didn't hurt that I was no longer beholden to Mr. Blessington for the use of the house in Brook Street, or responsible for paying him a substantial portion of my daily income."

"Three-quarters of it, as I recall," said Holmes. "I would imagine that keeping the entirety of your earnings, rather than turning over so much of it to your patron, would help significantly. But I did wonder how you managed to retain the house. 403 Brook Street, was it not?"

Sir Percy looked surprised. "Why yes. I'm impressed, Mr. Holmes. That was a long time ago."

Holmes waved a hand. "I recalled your little problem for quite a while, whenever I happened to pass by that location, and I was curious when your name continued to remain upon the door."

"It is simply explained," said Sir Percy. "I was canny enough, in the original negotiations to reach an agreement with Mr. Blessington, to insist that I also be included on the deed for the house. I knew when I entered into business with him that he was in extremely poor physical condition and, in spite of my daily ministrations and examinations, he might die at any minute. If that were to happen, and if there was no arrangement in place for me to continue in the practice that I was endeavoring to build, I would be worse off than if I had never set up in Brook Street in the first place. After his death, I would be on the street and starting over from scratch. Blessington understood and agreed. Little did I know that, within a year or so, he would die in such a dramatic fashion."

"I suppose that it's a good thing that I never thought to question that fact during the investigation," said Holmes. "Such an arrangement might have been considered a motive for you to murder him." He glanced at me. "As I recall, Watson and I had some discussion at the time whether you had made up the story of the mysterious patients visiting your office out of whole cloth as a ruse to cover your own actions in the matter."

Holmes was being charitable – he chose not to mention that it was *I* who had posited such a theory, while Holmes was able to easily prove that the visitors had in fact existed, and had been in Blessington's house, and even present at his execution.

Sir Percy's eyes widened at Holmes's suggestions, and he appeared to search for words. I could tell that Holmes didn't like the man, and had simply chosen to rattle him – successfully, as it turned out. But my friend was already tired of this game.

"No matter," he added. "Clearly the evidence proved that Mr. Blessington was murdered by the men that you said visited the house in the days before his death – his former friends in the Worthingdon bank robbery gang. Tell us, sir, how may we help you today?"

"Ah. Yes." Sir Percy cleared his throat. "We've been visiting and I haven't yet told you my story. I would never have tolerated that sort of time-wasting while still in practice, and I know, from one professional to another, that you must feel the same way." He tipped up the remainder of his brandy, signaled for another, and then fished a fine leather wallet from within his coat. Opening it, he pulled forth several papers. From them, he selected a newspaper clipping. He then set the wallet and the other papers upon the table and handed the news article to Holmes. "Perhaps you noticed this a few weeks ago?"

Holmes glanced at it. "June 18th, I believe." He then handed it to me. Even without Holmes's special skills, I recognized it as a small item clipped from *The Times*, although I knew that I hadn't seen it before. Reading through it, I realized that, if I had noticed it, it would have taken close reading for me to understand its meaning, and by simply glancing at it, there would have been no reason for me to give it a second look – or so I thought.

LOST SHIP DISCOVERED

OPORTO – *The ill-fated steamer* Norah Creina, *lost decades ago with all hands upon the Portuguese coast some leagues to the north of Oporto, has been discovered wrecked along the coast of French Equatorial Africa, south of Libreville.*

It will be recalled that the ship sailed from London for Portugal in October 1881, but never made port. At that time, an intensive search was launched, specifically in the area north of Oporto, based upon the report of a local fisherman who had discovered and retrieved a life preserver from the missing ship. This was this sole piece of evidence that convinced authorities that the ship had been lost with all hands, although the witness's credibility was later put into question. The search was eventually called off, and no insurance claim was ever presented.

On its final fateful voyage, Norah Creina *reportedly carried three fugitives from British justice, who were being sought at the time for questioning in relation to a London murder known as "The Brook Street Mystery", wherein a former member of the Worthingdon bank robbery gang, one Albert Sutton, was killed in his home by the three surviving members, J. Biddle, P. Hayward, and S. Moffat. Following the*

243

1875 crime, in which £7,000 was stolen and never recovered, Sutton had turned informant, causing the other members of the gang to be jailed while the gang's leader was hanged. Sutton had apparently taken the name Blessington in intervening years, and some time before his murder had set up residence in the home of a Brook Street physician, Sir Percy Trevelyan. It was there that he was located and murdered by his former compatriots following their early release from prison.

Following the crime, the police determined that the men then fled on the Norah Creina, *but before the ship could dock in Portugal, where their arrest was planned, the ship was reported lost. Now it has been found upon the western African coast with no explanation as to why or how it came to be there. Local investigators report that it was beached in a small cove, surrounded by heavy jungle. It was discovered by another ship that had stopped there to make temporary repairs following a storm. No bodies were found on board, and the ship appeared to have been intentionally scuttled. The ship's bottom was partially blown out, apparently caused by an internal explosion from infernal devices found mounted in the lower decks. Some of these had not detonated, providing authorities with evidence that the sinking was intentional. However, the ship apparently grounded after being abandoned but before sinking.*

The ship had sailed with an abnormally small crew for a vessel of its size, further indicating that it was planned to be destroyed. None of the crewmen reported to have been on the ship when she sailed have been seen again following the initial supposed sinking. Additionally, there has been no further report of the men wanted by the British police for the murder of Sutton. The Norah Creina, *already one of the mysteries of the sea, will remain so, but with another tantalizing chapter in her story.*

I handed the clipping back to Holmes, who said, "I do recall seeing this in the newspaper, but I considered it irrelevant, as I doubt if, at this point, anyone feels that it's worthwhile to chase off to Africa to seek out the trail of any of these men, who must now either be dead, or getting very close. And after all," he added, "some might consider what Blessington received a form of rough justice."

244

Sir Percy nodded. "I would agree, if that's all there was to it. But you see, this notice in the newspaper seems to have stirred the matter up."

"How so?"

Sir Percy's second brandy arrived, and he took a sip. "I should explain. I have recently married," he said, with seeming irrelevance. "For the first time."

"I was aware of it," replied Holmes.

"Really? I should not be surprised, but how did you know? It was not announced in the press."

"The ring on your finger. It's fairly new – no recent scratches. Also, it isn't too loose or too tight. Most wedding rings end up fitting quite snugly as the finger within grows to fill them. While it's possible you had to buy a new one to replace an old one that became lost or damaged, the more likely explanation is a new marriage."

Sir Percy glanced at his left hand with a frown, revealing a moment of honest expression that seemed to peel away the puffed-up man before us and almost recalling the harried doctor who had first consulted us. "Well, you're correct, Mr. Holmes. My finger and I *have* grown a bit over the years. Which is why I consider myself fortunate to have found a bride at this stage of my life. Last year, I met my Emilie, and since then my prospects have brightened considerably. I feel twenty years younger." He ducked his eyes. "She is a bit younger than I," he added in a softer tone.

"Forgive me," said Holmes with a hint of impatience. "What is the problem that you would like to discuss?"

"Ah. Yes. I still haven't told you my story." He tipped up the remainder of his brandy, signaled for a third, and continued. The man behind the bar, now a bit busier than before, waved in acknowledgement.

"Even if you hadn't followed my career," continued Sir Percy, "you would likely have noticed long ago that I no longer maintained the practice in Brook Street. As my reputation increased, I became less involved with day-to-day patients, and refocused my attentions toward pure research, my first love. I worked at some of the major hospitals, and you are aware of the results. I've had some significant successes. In the meantime, I moved to a larger house, nearby and also in Mayfair, while continuing to retain ownership of the Brook Street building. For a time, it was rented to a middle-aged doctor who continued to maintain a general practice there, much like the one that I'd started. But he died unexpectedly of apoplexy in the nineties, and after that, I began to rent it as a residential property through a leasing agent.

"So my life continued, but at some point in recent years, I became restless. I realized that I was lonely, and to my surprise, I found that I had feelings for the widow of a former colleague. Our courtship progressed to the logical conclusion. My marriage, while very happy since then, has had one sour note. Emilie, through her union with her former husband, produced a son, Edward, now in his early twenties. I'll be frank with you – he is spoiled and of no account, but he is the apple of his mother's eye. And he resents me.

"We have quarreled from the beginning, and several months ago, when the situation was becoming intolerable, a solution presented itself. The house on Brook Street, which I still owned, became vacant, at just such a time as tension between Edward and myself reached a boiling point. It occurred to me that he could be moved to that house, which would serve to get him out of mine, while continuing to provide a very protected environment, as required by his mother. The two of them were agreeable, as the location is not so very far from where Emilie and I now live. The situation seems to have improved relations between the two of us, and even though Edward still visits our home regularly, we don't find ourselves in quite as many of the arguments that occurred so often before.

"It was in mid-June when the report that you just read first appeared in the newspaper. Edward was visiting for breakfast, as he is most mornings, even when he has been out late on the previous night, gambling at his club. He had no interest in joining the conversation, which suited me down to the ground. However, my wife was reading the newspaper – she is quite forward thinking in that and certain other ways – and she saw that my name was mentioned in the article.

"Well, I had already told her something of the matter during our courtship – an interesting anecdote from my youth, you understand – and so she mentioned it to me as a curiosity. But then she wanted me to tell the story to Edward. I was surprised to see that it caught his attention, so I related it in a rather dramatic way. And then I thought nothing more of the matter until a few weeks later. My wife and were coming in to breakfast – Edward wasn't with us that morning – when we spied a note, centered in the middle of the table. Picking it up, I read – well, here, you can read it for yourself."

He delved into the sheets held underneath his wallet, selected one, and pulled it loose, handing it to Holmes. I leaned over and read:

> *Reckoning is at hand. Sutton kept the £7,000. We have returned, and want what is ours. Leave it on the sundial. Cartwright will be avenged.*

It was signed: *Biddle, Hayward, and Moffat.*

"Curious," murmured Holmes. "They refer to vengeance for the member of their gang that was caught and hanged at the time of the robbery." He frowned and fell silent.

"Sundial?" I asked.

"There is an old one in the rear of the Brook Street house."

Holmes held the note up to the light, and then turned it this way and that. "Cheap note paper," he said. "Available at any street corner. Nothing obvious about the handwriting. Right-handed. Careful to appear featureless. Blue ink from a worn pen." He dropped it on the table.

Sir Percy cleared his throat and continued. "While we were still considering the note, Edward arrived with a puzzled expression, carrying a duplicate of the very same sheet that he had discovered the morning, lying upon the floor inside the front door at the Brook Street house." He pulled out a second note, which we saw was identical to the first.

"I called in the servants and, without revealing the specifics, asked if they could provide an explanation. None was forthcoming, and I believed them. These folk have been with me for many years, and have no reason to lie."

I glanced at Holmes, but he gave no reaction to this statement. He and I both knew that a new lady in the home could disrupt long-established routines, leading to resentment – and worse.

"A search around our house revealed that a small window on a little used rear door had been broken, allowing someone to reach in, unlock it, and then enter. That must be how they left the note. Subsequent investigation of the Brook Street house revealed something similar – a broken window at one of the lower levels." Sir Percy smiled. "I know what you're thinking, Mr. Holmes. We should have called you then, so that you could examine the clues. But I assure you that there were no footprints, and the glass was on the *inside* of the buildings in both instances, meaning that it was broken from the *outside*." He nodded my way. "Since that day many years ago when you notified me that you were writing up my experience for *The Strand*, Doctor, I've become a regular reader – not just of your stories about Mr. Holmes, but also some of these other detectives that have sprung up around London. I think I understand how you all work."

Holmes's lips tightened in a polite smile. He spoke to me instead of Sir Percy. "Watson, Watson! You have given away all of our secrets! Soon every criminal will know the correct way to break a window or to wipe away his fingermarks or to take care not to leave footprints." Back to Sir Percy, he said, "Did your stepson's servants in the Brook Street house hear anything in the night?"

"He doesn't keep servants at night. There is a cook during the day, and a few who come in to clean, but otherwise, Edward prefers to rough it."

"Had he been out the evening before?"

"He had, until around two a.m., and he is certain that there was no note when he came inside."

"And what happened next? I assume you did not leave the money on the sundial."

"No, I didn't leave any money anywhere. Emilie was quite upset, both at the thought that our own home had been violated, but also that her son might have been in some sort of danger. She has fretted ever since about what might have happened if he had encountered them in the night while they were leaving the note, and has encouraged me to pay. And it only worsened. A week later, last week, there was another note."

"Ah," said Holmes, holding out his hand in expectation. Sir Percy pulled one of two remaining sheets from underneath the wallet.

You must pay the debt. Sutton kept the £7,000. Leave it on the sundial. Cartwright will be avenged!

Again, the signature was *Biddle, Hayward, and Moffat.*

"This time, *avenged* is followed by an exclamation point," commented Holmes. "They are getting irate."

"That point was not lost on Emilie," said Sir Percy with a scowl. "If she had been worried before, this was worse. For you see, this time they only left the *one* note, at Brook Street, which places the threat more toward Edward than me."

"Surely," I said, "if these men, returned from wherever they have been for the last forty years, know enough to locate you, and to leave a note for you at your Mayfair home, then they would realize that your stepson in Brook Street is *not* the person to whom they ought to be focusing their attention."

"So I reasoned," said Sir Percy. "It doesn't make any sense, and I tried to convince Emilie of this, but she sees it from a different perspective – they are threatening Edward now as leverage against me."

"They apparently gave up threatening you very quickly," said Holmes, "before making Edward their sole target." He tapped a finger on the table and nodded towards the slip by Sir Percy's wallet. "There is a last note. Does it raise the stakes to the point where you decided to seek outside help?"

"It does. This morning, Edward was supposed to arrive for breakfast. He did not. Emilie called Brook Street on the telephone several times.

Finally, she was urging me to go there and check on Edward – which I had no intention of doing – when we in turn received a telephone call. It was from one of the day staff at the house. They had just arrived as usual to find Edward gone – or so they thought. It wouldn't have been unusual for him to have already departed, as he is at our house most mornings for breakfast – although I'm amazed that he can rouse himself that early after the late nights he spends about town.

"The staff, thinking that he had departed, had gone in to make up his bed and found him in his bedroom, unconscious, tied and lying upon the floor. He had a wound on the back of his head, but he awoke when the servants approached him. Emilie and I rushed over there, with Emilie in tears and reminding me that what she had feared had come to pass. Edward had come home at one or two in the morning to discover three men in the act of leaving a note – this note here, found on the floor beside him. They swarmed over him before he had a chance, and that is all that he remembers. He was attacked downstairs in the dining room, so they must have carried him upstairs and tied him." He handed the sheet to Holmes.

> Our patience is at an end. Put the £7,000 on the sundial.
> Cartwright will have justice!

Once again, the signature, consisting of the three murderers' names, remained the same as on the previous notes.

"I examined his wound – just a small contusion, and he will be fine. Emilie is not so certain, as you might imagine, and insisted that he be bundled back to our house. Both of them kept urging that I leave £7,000 on the sundial, but I still refuse. I was all for now calling in the police, because this has progressed from housebreaking to outright assault, but they are both afraid that will only increase the danger. Finally, I thought of you, Mr. Holmes, but knowing that you had retired, I decided to settle for the next best thing – your 'Illustrious Successor', as you put it, just up the way at 7B Praed Street. I was on my way there when fortune placed you in my path."

"The second and third times that Brook Street was invaded," said Holmes, ignoring Sir Percy's belief in fortune. "Did the gang break in the same way as before?"

"The second time, yes. The same window was broken, after it had only recently been repaired. I didn't think to check this morning, but I would assume so, since that method has worked so well for them before."

Holmes nodded. "You say that have no intention of paying the £7,000."

"Not at all, in spite of the insistence from my wife. I may have been successful in my career, but I do not throw around money so indiscriminately. And I know how this works – if you pay something like this the first time, they will simply keep coming back."

"I think that you could certainly expect that," agreed Holmes. He took the notes and the newspaper clipping, folded them, and put them into his own pocket. Then he glanced at his teacup, still full and now cold, and picked it up, drinking it in all at once as if he were very thirsty. Setting the cup down, he said, "May we now visit your wife and stepson?"

Sir Percy nodded, as if he had expected this. With clear satisfaction that Holmes was going to look into the matter, he said, "We can be there in just a few minutes."

At that moment, the waiter brought our client's next brandy. Sir Percy looked from one to the other of us, as if to observe whether there was any judgment on our parts. Seeing none, he stood and took it, drank it off quickly, and fished in his pocket for some coins, which he tossed upon the table. By then, Holmes was already halfway to the door.

Chapter II

Outside, the sun was bright on the entrance to St. Mary's Hospital across the street. We found a cab at nearby Paddington Station, and soon we were rattling down Edgware Road. Along the way, Sir Percy explained how he had transitioned from seeing patients in his practice into a career of pure research. He was describing some of his more notable successes as we turned into the streets of Mayfair. We stopped before a handsome house in Charles Street, just around the corner from Berkeley Square. Holmes asked the cabbie to wait. The front door was opened before we reached it by an alert butler, and inside we were led by the master of the house through a series of well-appointed rooms to a lounge in the rear. There, reclining upon a divan, was a young man with a bandage upon his forehead, while an attractive woman in her mid-forties stood by him, leaning forward in an attentive fashion.

Sir Percy introduced us, and both his wife and stepson seemed surprised. "How did you ever find Mr. Holmes and Dr. Watson?" asked the lady. "I understood that you were retired, Mr. Holmes," she added.

"I am," replied my friend.

"He was in Praed Street," explained Sir Percy. "It was good luck on my part. He and Dr. Watson listened to our story and agreed to look into the matter."

"What's to look into?" said the young man, with an unpleasant whine in his voice. "These brutes just want money. If you pay them, they'll go away."

"Often, it isn't that simple," said Holmes. "Those who resort to obtaining funds in this fashion will come back again and again if they are encouraged. £7,000 won't last very long." He glanced around, located a chair, and pulled it over near the young man's feet, so that he could face him comfortably. Seemingly embarrassed that he hadn't invited us to sit sooner, Sir Percy indicated that we should all join Holmes, who was peering intently the young man.

"Mr. – ?"

"Wilton. Edward Wilton."

"Thank you. Mr. Wilton, what you can tell us about your attackers?"

Wilton sneered. "Do you mean that you can't deduce their heights and shoe sizes from just looking at my clothing?"

While Holmes cast his eyes up and down the reclining pup, Mrs. Trevelyan looked aghast. "Edward!" she hissed.

Wilton seemed to recognize the implied rebuke, and he answered in a more direct fashion. "There were three of them. I had been out to my club, the Bagatelle. It was about two a.m. I let myself in the front door, and I suppose they didn't hear me. They were having a conversation in the dining room. I should have gone back outside and found a constable, but I crept forward instead. They were arguing, something about how to split seven-thousand three ways. They were suddenly silent – possibly they heard me – and then they rushed into the hall where I stood. They pulled me into the dining room, and we struggled for a moment before one of them, a big man, swung his fist at my head." He raised a hand and gingerly touched the bandage circling his forehead. "That's all I remember until the girl found me this morning, on the floor of my bedroom."

"Percy," interrupted the boy's mother, turning toward our client. "We must pay! I don't understand why you're being so stubborn!"

"Emilie," responded Sir Percy, "I've explained to you that I will not capitulate to these criminals!" He seemed set to continue, but Holmes raised a hand and asked another question of the injured man.

"You said one of them was a big man. Does that mean that the others were not? Or were they all big, and he was bigger?"

"I don't know!" snapped Edward Wilton. "It was dark – they hadn't bothered to light a lamp – and it all happened in less than a minute. I didn't have a chance to grab a piece of a coat, or scratch a face so that my attacker might be identified. They were simply three men in the dark."

"Were they talking in normal tones, or *sotto voce*?"

"What? Oh, normal, I suppose. I could understand them from where I stood in the other room."

"Hmm. That might indicate that they knew from observation that the servants did not stay overnight, and they felt comfortable making a little noise." He stood. "Thank you for your time, Mr. Wilton." He turned to Sir Percy. "Can you let us examine the Brook Street house?"

Apparently surprised that the interview had been so brief, the famed physician stood. "Of course." With a nod toward his wife, and no acknowledgement at all to his stepson, he led us from the room. I looked back toward the mother and son in time to see them each glance at one another in a worried way.

North through Berkeley Square and up Davies Street, we had turned into Brook Street in just moments. The home of the former resident patient was still as I remembered it, one of those somber, flat-faced buildings that line that block. Sir Percy pulled out his key, and as soon as we entered, Holmes began his examination. Sir Percy made as if to follow along, but I laid a hand upon his arm, indicating that Holmes would work best alone. We stood for quite a while in the entryway while listening to Holmes move throughout the house, once passing us to go upstairs – those same stairs where Blessington had challenged us with a gun so many years earlier – and then again as he came down and went to the back of the house. In a few moments, we heard a door open as he went outside.

I was to the point of suggesting that we find somewhere to sit, having realized that my admonition to Sir Percy about leaving Holmes alone had likely chastened the man to the point where he was afraid to step any further into the house, lest he destroy some vital clue. However, before I could make the comment, Holmes returned with a look of satisfaction upon his face.

"Will you be available later this afternoon, Sir Percy?" he asked.

"Why, yes. A message to my home will find me."

"Excellent. I should have some news in a few hours." He turned toward the door, and we followed him outside. At the street, he offered Sir Percy the use of the waiting cab to return to his home in Charles Street. With a promise again of a report later in the day, we watched the acclaimed physician drive away.

"I must be about some tedious business, Watson, but I thought that you wouldn't want to spend any more time with our unexpected client, even to the point of sharing a cab for a few minutes."

"True," I said. "I trust that you will be about your tasks alone?"

He nodded. "I need to do a bit of research, and speak to a few individuals who might offer additional perspectives. Do you have any questions?"

"Not many. I suppose the details have to be painted in, but I suspect that I'm caught up."

Holmes smiled. "Indeed. You have learned my methods well over the years, my friend. What tipped you off?"

"Oh, make no mistake, Holmes. I have seen, but undoubtedly I haven't observed, what you have. But I did notice that you had very few questions for Edward Wilton – your questions were almost perfunctory – and that you surreptitiously examined his shoes particularly while he reclined on the divan. There is one thing that you don't know." And I described the anxious look that had passed between mother and son as I was departing the lounge.

He nodded. "That, too, is helpful. Much must be verified, and there are facts that you don't know, through no fault of your own, that give me a fairly solid understanding of this case. What you've just described doesn't contradict my thinking, and it adds a nuance to be considered."

"Well," I said, knowing that he would continue to be cryptic until he was ready to lay out the finished explanation, "I look forward to hearing your report to Sir Percy."

With that, he nodded and turned toward the east, striding down Brook Street, looking no different than he did when he had retired nearly two decades earlier. I turned the other direction, moving in a more stately manner, befitting my age, and found a cab in Grosvenor Square. Soon I was traveling toward my home in Queen Anne Street, and I passed Holmes as he was nimbly dodging a boy playing on the sidewalk. Then he was lost to sight.

Chapter III

That afternoon, around three o'clock, I received one of those laconic messages that had been one of Holmes's most annoying habits over the forty years that I had known him:

> *Stranger's Room, 4 o'clock. If convenient, bring your journal containing Sir Percy's original problem. If inconvenient, bring it all the same.*
>
> *SH*

With a smile, I made my way to my study, where some searching and a bit of luck uncovered the journal to which Holmes referred. I flipped through it, a plethora of memories springing forth . . . The affair of the beleaguered Esquimaux and the singularly half-eaten meal. The dangerous matter of the Red Tincture, and the related ramifications to the very safety of the Capital. The service for Lord E----- and his odious bride of less than a week, whom it will be remembered was later found senseless at the last possible moment, locked in a sinking trunk in the center of the Serpentine.

I paged through the book and located the notes in question, using an old bill to mark my place. Then, somewhat before time, I made myself ready, retrieved my hat and coat, and found a cab, taking neither the first nor the second, but rather the third. The summer day was pleasant, with the wind from the south, bringing that unique and not unpleasant scent with just a hint of spice suggesting the river, along with something possibly imagined from the southern counties, and yet completely reminiscent of London.

As my cab made its way down Pall Mall, I spotted Holmes, waiting in front of the Diogenes Club. He was holding a small bag, similar in shape to a doctor's medical case. Even as I arrived from the east, a second cab bearing Sir Percy approached from the direction of St. James's Palace. We each alighted, nodded to one another, and then looked toward Holmes, who turned towards the unassuming doorway of No. 78.

Holmes didn't speak to the man at the front desk, but rather led us deeper into the building, and then upstairs and through to the Stranger's Room, the only place within the curious building where conversation was allowed. Sir Percy was looking around with curiosity, and when Holmes shut the door, he said, "I'm pleased to finally see this room. As I mentioned, I've followed your stories with great interest over the years, Doctor, and this room has always held special interest. Will Mr. Mycroft Holmes be joining us?"

"I'm afraid not," replied Holmes. "While my brother continues to spend quite a bit of time here – more, since his retirement following the War – his schedule isn't quite as rigid as it once was, and he is elsewhere at present. However, I did receive his permission to occupy this room for a bit. While I myself am a member of the Diogenes, and have found it restful upon occasion, it is Mycroft, as one of the founders, who has maintained this room almost as a second office, and therefore has the say-so of when it may be used."

"And why did you wish to meet here for a discussion?" said Sir Percy. "I must confess that when you suggested the Diogenes, I began to wonder how the problem might involve your brother. I'm relieved that it doesn't seem to require his participation, but you could have related your conclusions at my home." He looked around and then proceeded to settle himself into the wide red leather chair so often used by Mycroft Holmes. It dominated the room, as intended, but somehow Sir Percy, for all of his increased girth, failed to fill it in the same way.

Holmes's mouth tightened in suppressed amusement, and he and I chose the two facing chairs where we had so often found ourselves before.

It was here we had met to discuss countless cases – from the first time I was introduced to Mycroft Holmes, during the service for his neighbor, Mr. Melas, to the numerous discussions which soon followed related to the Ripper Affair. Through the years, Holmes and I had regularly visited here, sometimes summoned to assist Mycroft in a bit of work, and at other times to seek information. More than once I had visited this room without Holmes for one reason or another, and of course I would never know how often that Holmes had consulted his brother without telling me. The first time I met Mycroft Holmes, for instance, he mentioned that he'd expected his younger brother around during the previous week regarding the Manor House Case. Surely there were other consultations.

Holmes and I had been here often during the War and the years leading up to it. Our work had delayed – but not prevented – the terrible conflict. I pray that what we accomplished through foresight and planning in that very room helped to negate what could have been much more terrible.

While I reminisced, one of the club's staff entered to see if refreshments were required. Sir Percy requested a brandy, while Holmes and I had nothing. The servant stepped to a sideboard, sensibly poured a generous amount, delivered it into our client's hands, and then departed. Then Holmes began to speak.

"I will be blunt, Sir Percy. I did not want to reveal my conclusions at your home, because I wanted to provide you with the opportunity to consider your response away from your wife and stepson. This entire affair has been concocted by them, mostly likely to gain funds from you to pay the young man's numerous debts – funds which you would not otherwise provide."

Sir Percy's eyes widened just a bit, but he remained silent, taking a sip, and then another, before putting the brandy aside on a small table beside the red leather chair. Then he nodded.

"I suppose that I'm not surprised," he sighed. "After all, both Emilie and Edward wanted to pay the demands, rather than seeking outside help. They were quite insistent. I believe that I must have known the truth, deep down, but I didn't want to believe it." He closed his eyes for a moment, and then reopened them. "How did you arrive at your conclusions?"

Holmes reached into the case which he had placed by his feet and pulled out a blue-bound volume. "I purchased this at Hatchards earlier today." He held it forth so that Sir Percy and I could see it. I was rather surprised to find that it was a copy of *The Memoirs of Sherlock Holmes*, collected and published in book form by Newnes in 1893. He flipped it open, searching for a moment before finding the desired page. "Here we are – Watson's rather fanciful account of 'The Resident Patient'. If you

255

don't mind, I'll quote a few of the lines." He dropped his eyes and then began to read, changing his voice appropriately to fit each person speaking. His rendering was uncannily authentic, and I felt that I was back in our old rooms in Baker Street, listening to Holmes's explanation for the first time.

> Our visitors arrived at the appointed time, but it was a quarter to four before my friend put in an appearance. From his expression as he entered, however, I could see that all had gone well with him.
>
> "Any news, Inspector?"
>
> "We have got the boy, sir."
>
> "Excellent, and I have got the men."
>
> "You have got them!" we cried, all three.
>
> "Well, at least I have got their identity. This so-called Blessington is, as I expected, well known at headquarters, and so are his assailants. Their names are Biddle, Hayward, and Moffat."
>
> "The Worthingdon bank gang," cried the inspector.
>
> "Precisely," said Holmes.
>
> "Then Blessington must have been Sutton."
>
> "Exactly," said Holmes.
>
> "Why, that makes it as clear as crystal," said the inspector.
>
> But Trevelyan and I looked at each other in bewilderment.
>
> "You must surely remember the great Worthingdon bank business," said Holmes. "Five men were in it – these four and a fifth called Cartwright. Tobin, the care-taker, was murdered, and the thieves got away with seven thousand pounds. This was in 1875. They were all five arrested, but the evidence against them was by no means conclusive. This Blessington or Sutton, who was the worst of the gang, turned informer. On his evidence Cartwright was hanged and the other three got fifteen years apiece. When they got out the other day, which was some years before their full term, they set themselves, as you perceive, to hunt down the traitor and to avenge the death of their comrade upon him. Twice they tried to get at him and failed; a third time, you see, it came off. Is there anything further which I can explain, Dr. Trevelyan?"

Holmes looked up, a twinkle in his eye. "Is there anything further which I can explain, Sir Percy?"

The physician's eyebrows were pulled together in a frown, and I could see that he might become irate if he allowed himself to continue along that path. However, he knew Holmes of old, and was certainly aware that his patience would be rewarded. "You can explain everything, Mr. Holmes. I have no idea how your revelation that my wife and stepson have been attempting to defraud me relates to your identification of Mr. Blessington and the other bank robbers from decades ago."

"All will be made clear. Watson – did you bring the journal as I requested?"

I nodded and pulled it from my coat pocket. Flipping it open to the correct page, I handed the volume to Holmes. He glanced at the page where my notes for the affair commenced, and a smile crossed his face. I knew what had amused him. Long ago, I had considered calling the narrative "The Brook Street Mystery", but Holmes had reacted to my chosen title with the look of a cat encountering something inedible, and had suggested instead "The Resident Patient". I had already written "The Brook Street Mystery" at the top of the commencing page, but as I considered his suggestion, I had crossed it out and wrote "The Brook Street Patient", seeing if that was more appealing, and testing how it rolled off the tongue. Then, I had seen the sense of his idea and also drawn a line through that as well, writing "The Resident Patient" instead. And that was how it was eventually published.

Now, as Holmes looked down on the three titles at the top of the page, two rejected for the one that he had proposed, each word underlined with a wavy line in faded ink, I knew that he remembered that same afternoon when I had hoped to spend the day writing, only to return home with dismay as I found him practicing a difficult maneuver upon his violin. It seemed as if it were only yesterday.

Sir Percy cleared his throat, and Holmes looked up, the smile still upon his face. "My apologies. I was lost in thought." He turned his eyes back to the journal and flipped through the pages for a second before handing it to me. "Watson, please read the last paragraph upon the left-hand page."

I scanned down and saw that it was a part of what he had just read. *"You must surely remember the great Worthingdon bank business," said Holmes, "Five men were in it – these four and a fifth called Cartwright. Tobin, the care-taker, was murdered, and the thieves got away –"*

"That's enough," interrupted Holmes. "How is *Cartwright* spelled?"

"C – A – R –T – W – R – I – G- H – T."

"Exactly. With a *W*. And here in the published version?" He handed me the blue book.

I verified. "Also with a *W*."

"Exactly." He reached into his coat and pulled out several folded sheets. "And here, in these messages that we were shown this morning, each from the supposed criminals who had returned to England after all these years to seek the money that they feel is owed to them – how is the name spelled there?"

I took the sheets and looked. In all three written messages, *Cartwright* was also spelled with a *W*, and I so informed them.

"Finally," said Holmes, "will you verify how it's spelled in this news article from several weeks back, relating how the *Norah Creina* was discovered, with details about the fugitives and the old Worthingdon bank gang."

I quickly read through the article twice before replying. "The name *Cartwright* is not mentioned in the article whatsoever."

"Exactly." He sat back with a satisfied smile. However, Sir Percy and I looked at one another with puzzlement and what might have grown into frustration, if we hadn't both known that an explanation was forthcoming. I, however, was beginning to understand.

"There is," said Holmes, "one other piece of information that you require, and understandably do not have." He looked at me. "Watson, when you wrote up your version of the case all those years ago, do you recall referring to any of the official records? Did you do any research into the background of the bank robbery that had led to the arrest and conviction of the criminals Biddle, Hayward, and Moffat, based on the testimony of Blessington – as we shall continue to call him?"

"No, I didn't. I made notes while the matter was still fresh in my mind, based upon the events and our conversations."

"And you didn't ever consult my scrapbooks upon the matter, either then, or later, when you published the story in *The Strand* in 1893?"

"I did not."

"If you had done a bit of confirmatory research," he said, pulling a final piece of paper from his pocket, "you might have come across this."

He handed it to me. It was folded thrice, rather delicate and fragile-looking, and quite yellow. I opened it carefully and scanned through it, understanding his point immediately. Without comment, I handed it to Sir Percy, who did not reach the same enlightenment that I had obtained.

"What is this?" he asked, rather peevishly.

"An official Order of Execution. It was loaned to me earlier this afternoon from its official keeper, with the promise that I return it safely. Have a care, Sir Percy. It belongs to the Crown, and it's quite fragile."

"I don't understand. It has the name of the man who was hanged for the bank robbery in 1875. What does this have to do with anything?"

"Read his name."

Sir Percy squinted at the sheet. "*Marcus Cartright*."

"Exactly. And how is it spelled?"

"*C – A – R – T – R – I –* Wait a moment!" He looked up. "There's no *W* in this man's name!"

"Exactly. This is the *correct* spelling of the fifth member of the Worthingdon bank gang, who was hanged for the murder of the care-taker Tobin during the robbery. When Watson wrote the matter up in his notes, and then later for publication, he had no idea that *Cartright* was spelled *without* a *W*. I suspect that he was influenced by our acquaintance in those days with a lad named Cartwright, spelled *with* a *W*, and that he wrote the name accordingly."

"But . . . I still don't understand. How did this lead you to the conclusion that Edward was attempting to defraud me?"

"I believe that Watson comprehends."

I nodded and spoke. "The notes that were left demanding money each referred to *Cartwright* with a *W*. If the actual criminals had returned, they would have most likely spelled the name correctly. However, it was clearly written in the more common, but *incorrect*, way. Holmes must have immediately noticed the spelling – ?" I looked his way, and he nodded. "He saw the added *W*, and realized that the notes had been fixed up by someone who somehow knew the names of the other criminals, but *not* how the name of the hanged man was spelled."

Holmes continued. "I must confess that when I read Watson's account of the matter, years after the fact, I noticed that the hanged man's name was spelled incorrectly, but it was an insignificant and innocent error. However, when I saw it written that way in the notes this morning, I realized that someone was likely working from *Watson's published story* when preparing the demands, rather than first-hand knowledge. When relating to us what had happened, Sir Percy, you mentioned how you were prompted by your wife to tell your stepson the story of your involvement with Blessington, after the matter of the discovered ship appeared in the newspaper. Over the next few days, the idea must have occurred to him – or *them* – to see if they could work things to get some money to cover your stepson's debts, based upon your association with the very old crime.

"They found and read Watson's account, with the misspelled name included as part of its permanent record, and then fixed up the notes accordingly with the only data that they had. There was a great deal else that was wrong with their effort, and it should have occurred to them to check a few other facts before committing themselves. Besides getting the name of one of the men wrong, they also didn't take into account the factor of the ages of the others. When the criminals first came to your practice, Sir Percy, one posed as the son, while another as the cataleptic father. The man who portrayed the father, Hayward, was already elderly in 1881. There is no way he would have survived to the present. Biddle, who portrayed his son, would be feeble at this point as well, were he still alive. And yet your wife and stepson signed the names of all three, as if all three are still alive."

"And the third?" I asked. "Moffat? I had wondered at the time why he didn't participate more fully in the affair."

"He had been injured in his youth, and could not think clearly. Even during his sentencing in 1875, there was some question as to whether Moffat was competent at all, based upon his ravings and very odd ideas. Nevertheless, he was sent to prison along with the others, but it broke him completely by the time that they were released. He had some sort of family relationship to Biddle, which is how he was attached to the original bank robbery."

"So you knew," said Sir Percy, getting us back onto the main subject, "that Edward had written the notes, simply from seeing that the spelling must have come from Dr. Watson's account, rather than someone who would have actually known the correct spelling?"

"Not quite. I knew enough to realize that the notes didn't come from the original bank robbers. They could have been written by a family member of one of the original criminals. However, I suspected your stepson's involvement, based on your narrative of how he came to learn of the matter, and the timing of when the first of the notes appeared soon after. When we interviewed him, I still wasn't sure, but I took care to observe what I would need to know to further my investigation."

"Yes," I said. "When you took care to get a look at his shoes."

"Exactly."

"What?" asked Sir Percy. "His shoes?"

"Yes. I knew that, from his story, he would likely still wearing the same shoes that he'd worn the previous night, when his supposed attack occurred. He was tied up for the servants to find this morning, and it was very unlikely that he would have changed them upon being found and taken to your home and his mother's ministrations. I took care to note their size and whatever outstanding features I could see without being too obvious. Then, at the Brook Street house, I examined the house, and particularly the back, where the window had indeed been re-broken to simulate another intrusion.

"Your stepson's footprints – and *only* his footprints – were under the window, where he indeed took care to break the glass inward, so as to give the impression that someone had done so from the outside. Then, with slight bits of soil from the area under the window still upon the soles, he walked about downstairs quite a bit, without ever entering the dining room where he said that he was supposedly attacked by the three men, before heading to his room. There, he was tied and left for discovery in the morning. I found no indication of any attackers, but there *was* one other set of footprints in the bedroom, sometimes overlaying those of your stepson."

"Someone else was there? But who?"

"The person who hit him over the head, gently enough to cause a wound without truly injuring him. Then he tied him and left him to be found by the staff. Clive Edgerton."

I raised my eyebrows, for I knew the name. I imagined that most of London did, as he was often mentioned on the periphery of any number of ongoing scandals. Sir Percy shook his head. "He's a member of the Bagatelle, Edward's club. I had no idea they were acquainted."

"I went 'round there this afternoon," said Holmes. "Edgerton and your stepson are as thick as thieves – literally, it seems, since Edgerton was willing to involve himself in this scheme. Did you know that your stepson had been asked to absent himself from the Bagatelle in recent weeks, related to his increasing unpaid debts?"

"I did not," replied Sir Percy.

"In fact, in spite of his statement that he was there last night before returning home, he had been nowhere near the place. Instead, he was drinking with Edgerton in an establishment known as The Bow Bells in D'Arblay Street until nearly five a.m – one of those places that does not close its doors until the sun starts to rise. That was late enough that, when he returned home to break a window and then be tied after his supposed attack, he wouldn't have to lie about for too long, feigning unconsciousness."

Sir Percy seemed to be trying to comprehend the tale. "How did you discover this?"

"The cab companies have become more systematized over the years, and keep records of their travels. While I worked on other aspects of the investigation, a simple telephone call to a man who owes me a favor or two set things in motion, and it wasn't long before I had the name of the cabbie who took your stepson from The Bow Bells to Brook Street. I spoke to the cabbie, and he described your stepson perfectly, as well as the man with him – clearly Clive Edgerton. I had the same cabbie drive me to the club in D'Arblay Street and verified the rest."

Sir Percy rubbed his face in a curious washing motion. "And my wife? How do you know that she's involved? Perhaps . . . perhaps . . . ."

261

"Further examination of your stepson's life has revealed that over the last few months, he has made some small effort to pay a bit here and there on his debts – although not recently, I might add. Since he has no income of his own, he must have been getting the money somewhere. It is most likely that his mother is providing it. Although your wife has very limited funds, she *does* have the interest from a legacy established by her late husband. An examination of her bank records revealed that she has written small checks to your stepson, never more than a hundred pounds, and some of his debtors confirmed receiving similar payments near those dates. I believe that you'll agree with me that your stepson is responsible, most likely with the help of your wife."

Sir Percy raised himself in the chair. "Her bank records? You checked those? My God, Mr. Holmes – what resources do you have at your fingertips, to accomplish so much in a single afternoon?"

One might have thought that Holmes would make some effort to look modest, if one didn't know him so well. Instead, he simply stated fact. "This sort of inquiry demanded no great effort. I have established a number of contacts through the years. The system functioned smoothly by the time of my supposed retirement, and these men and women continued to serve quite well during the War. I've been careful to keep the machinery greased and fully operational in the years since. Through the help of an agent this afternoon, I was able to determine where your wife banks. A small service provided for that bank in the past made them amenable to opening their books."

Sir Percy nodded with a weary sadness. "I believe that you're right," he said. "She probably helped him. He is her darling baby boy. He is spoiled, and she won't hear a word against him. She seemed far too anxious to pay off the demands for money, rather than seeking help. What you say makes sense."

He looked at the empty brandy glass, then across the room where a refill was waiting, should he make the effort to get it. But instead, he pushed the glass back on the table and made as if to stand, shifting forward and saying, "I suppose that I should go home and confront them."

"Wait," said Holmes, raising a hand. "There is something else that we must discuss."

With raised eyebrows, Sir Percy settled back, even as Holmes stood. My friend crossed the room, retrieved the brandy decanter, and set it on the table beside Sir Percy's glass. Without a word, the doctor poured a tall refill and took a sip. "Go ahead."

"There is the unresolved question of the seven-thousand pounds."

Sir Percy set down the glass and cocked his head. "Seven-thousand pounds? Whatever do you mean?"

262

"The amount from the Worthingdon bank business in '75. It was never recovered. At least not officially."

"What does that have to do with me?"

Holmes settled back and crossed his legs. "There was always something rather strange about the original case. Blessington informed on the gang and was allowed to go free. Cartright was hanged, but the other three received fifteen years. Blessington, who had changed his name from Sutton, was allowed to get on with his life, believing that he had a good long time before he would have to worry about facing his former comrades. He probably hoped that they would die in prison. He bought a house. He bought *you*, Sir Percy, *né* Dr. Trevelyan, and set you up in practice. The question is – *how was he able to afford that?*

Sir Percy started to speak, but Holmes continued. "Possibly, in his role of informer, he convinced the authorities that the rest of the gang had the money. I have come to suspect over the years that Blessington had an arrangement with the bank, or at least some official connected with it, so that he could keep some or all of it. That bank wasn't the most ethical of organizations, and there was always something peculiar about the robbery. In any case, it was rather clear that Blessington had access to funds – substantially more than could be reasonably explained. However, after his body was discovered, his strongbox in his bedroom was examined, as you'll recall. It was in that big black box at the end of his bed, and it held nothing more than what would be expected from his share of the money that you earned for him from your medical practice."

Sir Percy took a sip, and then another. "What is your point, Holmes?"

"As I mentioned, part of my investigation today concerned checking bank records, in order to determine how your wife was able to help her son."

"Yes . . . ?"

"This afternoon, I also examined your banking records as well."

The heavy man sat up straighter. "My God, Holmes, this is really too much! What purpose could this invasion of *my* privacy serve?"

"If for no other reason, it helped me to decide that you were not telling me some complicated untruth as part of a larger scheme. Long ago, Sir Percy, I learned that clients *can* and *do* lie as often as anyone else. In this case, I determined there was no evidence that you were involved in some sort of action that required my participation to provide the illusion of legitimacy.

"But while I was looking over the records, I saw that you have banked with that same firm for quite a while. Since the late 1870's, as a matter of fact, several years *before* you were plucked by Mr. Blessington and set up in practice as his Resident Doctor. Your deposits throughout were small

263

and predictable, even after you moved to Brook Street and became his employee. But several weeks after Blessington's death, in the late fall of 1881, you made a deposit – a single and large amount of slightly over £6,000. I'm curious, Sir Percy. Can you account for the provenance of those funds? A legacy, perhaps, from a relative? Unlikely. Perhaps instead it was something like the discovery of a treasure – what was left of the Worthingdon bank loot – minus the original purchase by Blessington of the lease of the Brook Street house, along with the other expenses of setting you up in practice."

Sir Percy collapsed back into the red leather chair, his legs pushed out in front of him, with a look of bleary sadness washing over his face. Holmes continued.

"When Blessington died, I suspect that you worked out that there was the possibility that the £7,000, or a goodly portion of it, was still in the house, based on your new knowledge about the man. He wouldn't have been fool enough to keep that amount in his regular strongbox, where it could be carried away in an instant. The strongbox was simply a decoy. And even faced with his executioners, he refused to tell where he'd hidden the money, possibly hoping right to the end that his death would be avoided. Or perhaps he was too frightened to speak. In any case, the money remained in the house, and you found it.

"You were in an enviable position. Through Blessington's death, you inherited the Brook Street house, a contingency wisely included in the original partnership agreement. You were well on the way to building up a respected practice, and now you also had sudden unexpected and hidden wealth. It allowed you to set yourself up to continue those researches that were your 'first love', and which have so benefited mankind in general, and yourself in particular."

Sir Percy started at the rug for a long silent moment, and then raised his eyes. "You are correct," he finally answered, his voice soft and sad. "But what does it matter? As you said, there was something odd about the robbery to begin with. The matter was long settled before I ever found the money. If I'd given it back, what would it have accomplished? The bank would have just locked it away. The criminals had been tried, convicted, and punished. One was hanged, and their revenge was carried out upon Blessington. The rest were lost at sea on the *Norah Creina*. If I'd given back the money, I would have gotten a pat on the back, and could have continued to have a moderately successful life as a general practitioner. But with it I was able to accomplish so much more."

"That is all true," agreed Holmes. "But I still feel that there is something unfinished about the whole business." He shifted in his seat, sitting straighter. "All that you have accomplished so far has been of great

264

benefit to many. And yet, I sense that, even after all these years, you are not comfortable with how these events played out, and the way that you kept the money, rather than returning it."

"Holmes, what would you have me do?" snapped the doctor. "Return it to the bank? I don't even think that they're in business any longer."

"They aren't. Their own peculations sank them years ago. But I do have another suggestion."

Sir Percy simply looked at him, turning his head slightly the way a dog will when hearing a command that he doesn't understand.

Holmes continued. "You are known for your research, Sir Percy. What you have accomplished in the laboratory will never be forgotten. It has made you quite wealthy. From my perusal of your bank records, £7,000 is likely no longer an amount of money that can cause you to lose sleep. But your wealth is a cold thing, and you have become removed from the humanity which you serve.

Holmes glanced my way, stating, "It is my nature to operate within the realm of the theoretical. In my early years, a client was nothing more than a problem, a factor of no more relevance than X or Y in an algebraic equation. I elevated myself above the humanity of the people who sought my assistance. It was only through my association with Watson, here, that I realized that there was more to what I could offer with my own skills and gifts than simply cold reasoning without compassion.

"I have followed your career, Sir Percy, and have been impressed by it. But I've also seen someone who became less and less interested in the business of his fellow man with every passing year spent in a laboratory, considering causes and reactions to be more important than the patients themselves. Now, you are honored across the land, and I was happy to hear today that you had taken a bride. But it seems as if that particular voyage is about to go through some stormy weather.

"When you leave here today, you will need to settle things with your wife and stepson. Unpleasant, but manageable. If your stepson were a few years younger, I might suggest a year or so at sea to strengthen his character – but then again, I've seen in another case how that sort of advice can go terribly wrong. I assure you that Watson and I will not reveal that you kept the residue from the bank robbery loot, all those years ago. But *you will know that we know*, and I wonder if that won't motivate you, perhaps, to do something to improve our opinion of you, insignificant though that might be. *You will know that we know*.

"What I suggest is that you use the funds, the amount that you found hidden in the house in Brook Street so long ago, to set up some sort of clinic, to provide immediate patient care for those in need, rather than simply letting your legacy rest upon your research, which in the end will certainly aid many more people, but each of them unknown to you."

Holmes fell silent, leaving the doctor to consider his words. Then, with a last drink of the club's expensive brandy, he stood up. Holmes and I followed suit.

"I agree," said Sir Percy softly. "I'm not sure how to start, but I agree. And thank you, Mr. Holmes. For many things."

With that, he shook our hands, turned, and walked from the room, pulling the door softly shut behind him.

After a moment, I said, "He seems as if the revelation about the bank money has lifted some sort of burden for him."

"I think," agreed Holmes, "that several burdens have lifted – or at least shifted. I believe that his situation at home will be clarified and hopefully improved after this affair brings things to a head. He must have been aware at some level of the problems related to his wife and stepson. Pulling it into the light will undoubtedly provide some cleansing."

He made to depart, but I held up a hand. "I have another question or two."

Holmes raised an eyebrow, but nodded. Then he proceeded to fill two glasses from the brandy bottle, retrieved from the table by the red leather chair. We each seated ourselves as before, with Mycroft's empty place facing us.

I waved at the room around us. "Why here?"

"As I said, I felt that Sir Percy should learn this away from his family, so that he could plan his reaction." He took a sip. "I considered whether to meet at your home, but I felt that such a discussion would be an intrusion. The Diogenes Club occurred to me."

"But that leads to the conclusion that you spoke to your brother today. Is that correct? And if so, what would have his involvement been in this affair?"

Holmes smiled. "Good, Watson! You perceive that there is yet another layer to this matter. I wanted to ask Mycroft why the *Norah Creina* had been found after all this time."

I had known Sherlock Holmes for too long by this time to be surprised at this answer. I simply nodded for him to continue.

"If you'll recall the events of the investigation that you transcribed as 'The Resident Patient', the three men who executed Blessington in his own bedroom – Biddle, Hayward, and Moffat – all fled on the *Norah Creina* for Portugal. During the day following the murder, while you waited in Baker Street, I carried out my investigations, which allowed me to identify the gang and come up with an explanation of the events that satisfied me. As part of my efforts, I located the ships preparing to leave London. I

266

quickly ascertained that the three men were attempting to obtain passage on the *Norah Creina*, which was the only ship departing that day. However, what *they* did not realize was that that particular vessel was already earmarked for a different purpose – one of Mycroft's long-range plans."

A little more light began to be revealed. I had been aware of these "plans", as Holmes called them, for quite a while. Mycroft Holmes, who sometimes *was* – and maybe still *is*, in spite of his retirement – the British Government, a master at taking many different bits of information and seeing an overall relationship. His ability to perceive obscure connections unnoticed by others also gives him an additional advantage: He can see where to drop this or that bit of misdirection into the flow of events to nudge things in a way that he foresees will work out to British advantage.

"So the *Norah Creina* was one of his 'plans'. Presumably its disappearance was arranged. How was that of any benefit?"

"Who knows? He has a long history, as you know, of using ships to accomplish his mysterious tasks. The *Sophy Anderson*. The *Alicia*, and the *Fuwalda*. I didn't ask then, and whatever happened is ancient history now. But the *Norah Creina* was the next ship departing London, and when I saw some of Mycroft's agents on board, after I got onto Biddle, Hayward, and Moffat's trails and followed them to the ship, a quick word with a man I knew allowed them to go ahead and book passage. Then I popped around to see Mycroft – in this very room as a matter of fact – to let him know what was happening. Afterwards, I returned to Baker Street to explain to you, Inspector Lanner, and Sir Percy, what had happened – without telling the whole story. I'm sure you understand."

I did. In those days, I'd had no idea that Holmes *had* a brother – I had known him less than a year, and it wasn't until the early autumn of 1888 that Holmes even mentioned the man's existence, bringing me around to the Diogenes Club to meet him.

"This morning," continued Holmes, "I came around to ask Mycroft why the *Norah Creina* had been found again after all these years. He was reticent, and simply said that it was time, and those who needed to know would understand."

"And Biddle, Hayward, and Moffat? What happened to them after they sailed off on the ship? Its sinking was faked, and it's been . . . *somewhere* for the last forty years, but surely those men weren't with it the whole time."

Holmes shook his head. "After the apparent sinking of the ship was arranged, it continued on to Gibraltar, where it was refitted for its new mission. The three killers, based upon the evidence that I had provided to Mycroft, were tried in a secret court and executed."

He fell silent, and we each sat with our own thoughts for a moment. Then Holmes spoke. "What I told Sir Percy, about my own situation, was accurate. I owe you a great debt, old friend. Without your influence and insight, I fear that I would have been locked into the belief that the problem was all that mattered, without considering the very real people affected by it. I was reminded of that again this morning, when speaking with Mycroft. He, too, has more of a heart than one might realize, and some of the decisions he has been forced to make over the years will haunt him to his grave. It was he, those many years ago, who came up with the idea of how to handle Blessington's three killers, while also accomplishing his own business with the *Norah Creina*. I thought it a bit cold at the time, but I understood the necessity. Seeing how it played out was a valuable lesson in my own education. I hope that, even now, this affair will provide yet another lesson for someone else."

And it did. Sir Percy began to set his house in order that very day. I saw him socially several times after that, and his personal life seemed to find new levels of contentment after he revealed what he had learned from Holmes. Possibly of greater importance, he established a number of free clinics for the poor and indigent throughout Britain, at an expense far exceeding the original amount of the Worthingdon bank loot. Sir Percy himself became personally involved with the running of these clinics, and if he could have been knighted yet again, he would have been.

Only last week, I read of his sad passing, and was moved to add this account to that growing stack of Holmes's cases which must remain locked in my tin dispatch box until a point in the distant future. Some of the tales in the box are of great importance – governments might still fall if the contents were to be revealed, and the lives of great men might be shattered. This narrative is of much smaller scale – a matter of but a few hours to Holmes and me, a tying up of a loose end. But it was of great importance to Sir Percy, who apparently felt, on that day nearly five years ago, that Holmes's and my knowledge of his secret, along with our silent opinions of his character, was enough to send him down a different and far better path. His public accolades are many, but I wanted to record here, in private, his other great triumph.

Dr. John H. Watson
4 May, 1926

The Colchester Experiment

"Thank you for coming down, Mr. Holmes. I'm sorry about the weather."

So said Nicholas Nuneaton as he led us to the door of the old pub. He had just supervised the transfer of our bags from the cab that had carried us from the station to his own cart, tied at the side of the building.

I glanced up and watched the fast-moving clouds scudding west toward London. We'd been fortunate that there was a break in the rain while we traversed across Colchester. Otherwise, we might have been rather miserable, being that only a dogcart was available when we left the station. While Nuneaton finished up, tossing a tarpaulin over our bags, I wandered around to the front of the building.

The trip through town from the station had been fast, as the streets were rather clear. When we reached the High Street, I attempted to see the famed and well-remembered castle situated just to the north, but I only had a glimpse and then it was gone. I recalled our previous trip to the city, a little over a year before, when Sherlock Holmes and I, along with a local police inspector, had spent the better part of All Hallows Eve hidden in the eerie ruined grounds of St. Botolph's Priory, watching as a terrible rite was enacted. Our intervention had led to a mad chase through the dark streets in order to save the life of a golden-haired child. We'd been successful, cornering the self-styled High Priest at the Balkerne Gate, but not before he took his own life with a promise to return from beyond and take ours. I could only hope that Nuneaton's rather routine affair, as described in his letter, would prove to be a great deal more peaceful.

It was a few days before Christmas, and the pub seemed to have made a weak effort to decorate for the holiday, as there was a sprig of mistletoe tacked above the door. Or perhaps it was to honor some other celebration. As I had seen in the nearly three years that I'd known Holmes, the mottled and blood-stained skin of Christianity was sometimes very thin over a mass of other far older religions.

I glanced at a small placard outside the pub's door, indicating that it had been greatly involved during The Siege of Colchester in 1648, during the reign of Charles I and the battles between the Royalists and the Parliamentarians. It made reference to a number of bullets that had struck the building during the battle, the holes of which were still visible in the walls beside me. I looked and verified it, and then stuck my finger in a couple of them, pondering the men who had fired those shots two-hundred-and-thirty-five years before. They would have stood behind

269

where I was now facing, back along the river we had just crossed to get here.

Peering back to the west, across the low bridge that spanned the River Colne, I wondered what it had looked like in those days. Then, aware of the weather, I considered if this area might be prone to flooding. The bit I'd seen of the river as we crossed looked green and brackish, but perhaps it was a trick of the early winter light. Gaslights lit the gloomy day, and as the street vanished up the hill and in the darkness to the west, it seemed to be the work of some troubled painter.

I heard our host talking to Holmes as they came up behind me, and I turned to follow them inside. There was a low mutter of conversation throughout the spacious room, with its broad windows and attractive timbered ceilings, and it didn't diminish as we entered – always a sign that there was nothing suspicious going on, and that there was no concern among these patrons that strangers were now among them. Nuneaton seemed to want to direct us to a brightly lit table near the bar, but we would have had a number of people all around that could overhear us if they wished. Instead. Holmes indicated a quieter corner, dimly lit.

We settled ourselves and Nuneaton left us for a moment, returning with three generous glasses of whisky – most welcome on such a day. Then, with each of us having had a restorative sip, he began.

"Thank you for coming down, Mr. Holmes," he repeated. "I didn't know where to turn, and I didn't want to involve any of the local men who have set themselves up as inquiry agents – it's none of their business. Your name was recommended to me by my friend, Inspector Cowdray. He recalled you from that business last fall."

As well he should, I thought. The man had been prepared to make a completely mistaken arrest, and if Holmes hadn't seen a curious advertisement in the London newspapers, prompting us to travel to Colchester at all possible speed to identify the villain, another life would have been lost to the Boudicca Cult.

"How can we assist you?" asked Holmes. "Your letter indicated that this was a rather routine matter. I can see that you wouldn't want to involve the locals, but investigating the background of a man that you find suspicious is not all that difficult. Inspector Cowdray could have done it. I must confess that this sort of affair isn't something that I would normally undertake."

That was putting it lightly. When Holmes had received the letter, he'd snorted, tossed it aside, and lamented that his practice had devolved into seeking misplaced rings and checking on the resumes of foreign scientists. I thought that rather inaccurate, as the ring to which he referred had been that of the Baroness of Wolfsburg, stolen by her maid and hidden in a small loaf iced to resemble a pastry. And the foreign scientist that Nuneaton wished us to examine had been written about a great deal in the press, most recently when it was announced that he would be providing assistance to Nuneaton's uncle, Sir Samuel Bergholt, in relation to his curious scientific experiments.

"If Inspector Cowdray hadn't recommended me," Holmes continued, "I must frankly tell you that it's unlikely that I would have involved myself."

"I understand," said Nuneaton. "And yet, I hope that you can use your unique skills to provide me with a definitive answer, and eliminate my anxieties, and those of my sister. Right now, other than what I've seen of him in person, all that I know of Anatole Lika is what I read in the newspapers – after it was announced that he would be assisting my uncle with his electrical experiments."

I realized that I too knew very little about the famous but unusual scientist. A Serb in his mid-twenties, he'd moved to Paris the previous year to work for the Edison Company. Quickly making a name for himself due to some of his radical theories regarding electricity, he'd visited England on several occasions, giving talks that generated either praise or scorn. It was probably inevitable that he would end up assisting Sir Samuel, whose own theories in recent years had become rather radical – or so the press would indicate.

"Tell us about your concerns," said Holmes, elbows on the table above his whisky, and steepling his fingers.

"Well, first I suppose is that he's simply a bit . . . odd. I don't mean that because he's a foreigner. Rather, physically he's almost . . . *insect-like* is how my sister describes him. He's excessively lean, with the narrowest shoulders that I've ever seen on anyone. Yet his head is quite large, with a peculiar broad forehead, and his hair is kept parted in the middle and oiled down on either side. If genius is indicated by brain capacity, then he's the most genius fellow that I've ever seen.

"He seems to have a number of odd habits – many of them involving numbers. He has to reach the opposite side of a room, for instance, in a certain number of steps. Things have to be divisible by three – he requires eighteen napkins for dinner, for instance – Eighteen! – because it's divisible by three. He calculates the mass of his food so that he can determine the number of chews that are required to consume it. He only eats boiled food, and he fears contamination, wearing gloves much of the time, and always when there is a chance that he might have contact with another person. And let's see – oh yes, he fears earrings. When he arrived and saw that my sister was wearing them, he begged that she remove them, even before proper introductions had been made."

"A man's obsessions," I said, "don't indicate dishonesty, or incompetence. A fellow can't help how is mind sometimes tortures him. I'm certain that, if given the choice, Lika would gladly abandon these rituals in a heartbeat." Holmes nodded in agreement.

"I'm sure that you're right, Doctor," said Nuneaton. "I don't judge him based on that, but I did want to describe him, and the impression that he makes. He's lived with us now, in my uncle's house, for a little over a month, during the final installation of my uncle's apparatus, and we've learned to accommodate him – although I can only imagine the gossip and likely scorn about him that is tossed about below-stairs by the servants. I know that they have been discommoded by him in other ways. For instance, he claims to only need two hours of sleep per night, and when he's not working into the late hours, he prowls the house – which has given more than one other late wanderer a fright when they've suddenly come upon him. There have been complaints about this, but my uncle will hear none of it."

"What is your specific concern?" asked Holmes. "I must tell you that I'm unqualified to judge whether or not these electrical experiments – which have remained unexplained in the press – have any validity."

"I'm not sure that anyone can judge them," replied Nuneaton. "The experiments are unique – or so my uncle has said. I know that several of the finest scientific minds have been down to evaluate them, and to a man they all scoff. One of them, Dr. Percival Needham, is coming down today to observe the first phase of the process tomorrow morning. He has made no secret of his scorn, indicating that it's a waste of time. But my uncle cheerfully presses forward, sinking his fortune into the purchase of more and more equipment, and the expensive installation that goes with it."

"And you fear as well that it's all the merest moonshine and nonsense," I said, "and that Lika is ignorantly encouraging him at best, and possibly maliciously deceiving him at worst."

"Exactly," replied Nuneaton. "Any thoughts that you can give us will be much appreciated."

Holmes took another sip of whisky and said, "Tell us more of the household, and the upcoming experiment."

Nuneaton nodded. "My uncle lives at the family estate, south of here on the way to Wivenhoe, near the river. My sister and I have stayed with him since we were orphaned in our teens – about ten years ago. She serves as the mistress of the house, while I own a furniture store on the High Street – you likely passed it when coming here from the station.

"It's just the three of us, besides the servants, all of whom have been there for much longer than my sister and I. It's always been a very peaceful place – that is, until the last year or so, when my uncle became interested in electricity, and also the local geology. He believes that he's found a connection between them, somehow, and he's become rather obsessed."

"A connection?" I asked. "Between electricity and geology? In what way?"

"I'm still not sure that I understand it completely," Nuneaton replied. "Apparently there are fault lines in the earth beneath Colchester. He first became aware of them after becoming interested in geology. My uncle has had many hobbies through the years, and he throws himself into each of them with all his heart. For a while he was obsessed with the local history of the place – the Romans, you know, and Boudicca. He made frequent trips into the countryside, and at some point the geology of the place was mentioned, and he was shown some rocks that indicated something-or-other. So he lost interest in history and taught himself about geology.

"I don't mean to imply that he is foolish about it. He has the time and the funds to truly make a go of whatever catches his fancy, and he is a very smart man. He learns about his interests, and can talk on a level with true experts. As he studied the local geology, he decided that there is a very real danger in this area of a future earthquake, possibly causing a great deal of property damage, and even loss of life."

"An earthquake?" I asked, with raised eyebrows. "In Essex?"

Nuneaton nodded. "I know. Everyone disagrees with him. But now he feels that it's his mission to warn everyone to get ready, and to do what he can to prevent – or at least mitigate – the upcoming catastrophe if possible."

"And this has something to do with his electrical experiment," said Holmes.

"Yes. He believes that when the earth slips along a fault line, it's related to a massive amount of stored static electricity within the ground, and that when it reaches an excessive level, it can actually precipitate the slippage of the fault lines. My uncle feels that if there was a way to somehow control or manipulate this electricity, by overcharging it somehow before a truly large earthquake can occur, or bleed it off into the ether like lightning, the threat would be diminished exponentially. He has charts and graphs to prove his point, showing steep lines with 'asymptotic curves' and other such terms that are simply so much noise to me. He claims that the success of his experiment will vindicate him, but some of the country's finest minds are not so tolerant.

"In order to carry out his experiment – which is really much more than a simple procedure, as he describes it as something permanent, and is actually his ongoing attempt to manipulate the underground electricity – he has spent a fortune on building an electrical generating station next to the manor house. It's a tidy-enough looking building with generators and a tower and such, but instead of sending the generated power out through wires to the surrounding countryside as is typical, he has them running into the ground, into wells that he had specially dug, as deep as they could get.

"The servants are terrified that he'll electrify the ground and all the buildings, and the neighbors are afraid to take water from their own wells, fearing a lethal shock. But none of them have found a way to stop him, and Lika, his hired expert, simply encouraged him to build it all bigger and better, starting with their exchanged letters a couple of years ago, and then by providing detailed plans, and now in person."

"And you feel," said Holmes, "that if Anatole Lika can be discredited, this experimenting will somehow be quashed."

"That was the one thought that I had. My sister isn't sure that can help – quite frankly, she has stated that your visit is a waste of time and money – but I didn't know what else to suggest. I feel that if Lika can somehow be disconnected from my uncle, then the old fellow might drift away to some other interest – back to simply delving into the local history, perhaps."

Holmes looked at his fingers for a moment. Then, "I'm not sure what we can do. However, we can but try. Let us go to the house."

Nuneaton nodded, and a look of hope passed across his face. He led us outside, and I was glad to see that the rains were still holding off. Yet the angry-looking clouds in the sky were a sure indication that they weren't gone, and that it was going to be a dark, wet night, and likely stormy as well.

As we left town and bumped across the more rural roads, Holmes asked, "You mentioned that you own a furniture store. How did that come to be?"

Nuneaton smiled. "Before our parents died, my sister and I were raised in rather modest surroundings. My uncle made his fortune, while my father, though comfortably providing for us, wasn't quite so lucky. However, he owned a furniture shop over in Chelmsford, which he dearly loved, and I frequently assisted him when I was old enough. I very much enjoyed the work, and missed it when the shop was sold and we came to Colchester.

"When I was grown, Uncle Samuel sent me to university, and I was given to understand that I could be whatever I wished, but that I wouldn't be allowed to remain idle and useless, expecting to live on his bounty, or expecting an inheritance. That suited me to the ground, and as soon as I was able, I purchased a store in the High Street from a man who was retiring. The stock was adequate, although it needed some pruning here and there, and I had to build up a new clientele from scratch, as none of his old customers knew me at all, and one can't purchase good will when buying a business. But in the few years since, things have turned out rather well, and I think that I can say with a certain confidence that the store is now a success."

"And your sister? What are her prospects?"

Nuneaton's smile faded a bit. "I believe that she has less ambition than me – although if she had more motivation, I'm not sure where she would direct it. She's seemed content to be the mistress of the manor. And there's a fellow who is besotted with her – Rodney Fernworthy. I suspect that he'll be around tonight – he generally is – and that you'll have a chance to meet him, for what it's worth."

By this time, we were turning into a drive, bracketed on either side by two tall and ancient gateposts. It wasn't far from the road to the manor house, and I could see that it was a very handsome structure, parts obviously quite old, and with some relatively newer construction at either end – although the "newer" parts had been built long before I was born. It was a low building, with only a part at the back rising to an upper story – probably where the bedrooms were located. Otherwise, its square footage was spread over a great area, building wide rather than up, like so many other ancient houses.

The charm of the place, however, was rather spoiled by a new and utilitarian-looking building off to the right. Constructed of whitewashed blocks, and with a simple peaked frame roof, it resembled some kind of small warehouse of the sort springing up around the London docks. The windows were brightly lit by electric incandescent bulbs, some of the first that I had seen. They left a smear on my vision when I looked away.

I could just make out some sort of tower behind the building, apparently constructed from metal beams, with horizontal cross-pieces placed symmetrically to provide support. It narrowed as it rose from bottom to a narrow peak, and a heavy cable of some kind, no doubt an electrical wire, came out of the building and to the top of the tower, where it turned and ran back to the ground, where it then split into half-a-dozen or so segments. These squatted over and then entered several lighter patches of cleared earth like the legs of a giant spider. Undoubtedly this was where Sir Samuel's experiment to prevent an earthquake penetrated the depths of the geologic layers.

My attention was drawn back to the main building when the door opened, revealing a figure silhouetted against the more gentle and natural lamplight from inside. It was a woman, and as we pulled to a stop before the front steps, she walked forward. I could see that she looked nearly identical to our client. He hadn't mentioned that they were apparently twins.

275

"I saw you coming," she explained, even as Nuneaton was introducing her.

"This is my sister, Nancy," he said. Then he asked her to take us inside while he put away the cart and horse, explaining that he'd have our bags taken up to our rooms.

The entry hall was warm and cozy after the chilly ride from the pub. I asked about the age of the house, mentioning what I'd read of the bullet holes at the pub before our arrival, and wondering if it had been in existence at the time of the Siege.

"The house is much older than that, actually" Miss Nuneaton explained. "At least, the foundations go back to the fourteen-hundreds. Of course, that was long before our family came into possession of it. I believe that was sometime in the eighteenth century, by way of payment of a gambling debt. Our people are originally from Warwickshire."

She ushered us into a drawing room and offered something to drink. I chose tea, seeking something hot, and feeling that more spirits on an empty stomach might not be wise. Holmes declined entirely. As she went to arrange it, our client joined us, rubbing his hands. "Dinner will be soon, and you'll have a chance to meet my uncle. It occurred to me – "

" – that you don't want him to know why we're here," finished Holmes. "We aren't that much older than you are. Perhaps you can introduce us as old school chums."

"That's perfect," Nuneaton beamed.

"But," I asked, "where did you go to school? Perhaps we should know that."

"Oh, yes. I see. Durham."

"Well then," said Holmes, "I believe that Watson should keep mum, as I believe that you haven't visited there – ?" I shook my head. "I can speak about it on a limited basis, if needed," Holmes continued, "as I once passed through while tracking the history of a certain contentious land deed. However, it isn't likely that we'll be required to provide too much verification of our connections."

At that moment, Nancy Nuneaton returned, followed by a pleasant-looking older woman, apparently the housekeeper, carrying a tray with tea. When that had been distributed, Nuneaton informed his sister of our supposed Durham connection. She nodded in agreement. "I do hope that you can help. After you've had a chance to meet Mr. Lika, will you return to London and start your investigation, sending your little birds here and there to uncover the secrets of his antecedents?"

She asked the question with a most sincere expression upon her face, but I detected some little sour sarcasm buried within it, as if, as her brother had indicated, she thought that Holmes's efforts were a waste of time.

However, Holmes chose to take the question at face value, answering, "Mr. Lika's career has been rather well documented to this point. I have some associates that can investigate him in France, where he has been recently, and one or two others that might be able to tell me about his more distant past. However, I'm not aware of any chicanery in his previous behavior. His electrical theories are sometimes questioned, and even ridiculed, but no one so far has raised concerns about his moral character."

"But Mr. Holmes," said the lady, "there must be something wormy about him if he so willingly encourages our uncle to squander his fortune on that foolish and dangerous apparatus that has so ruined the grounds of the house. Oh, yes. Did Nick tell you? This folly has taken nearly all of Uncle's funds. About all that he has left is the house. If Mr. Lika was truly a man of good character, then he wouldn't have been a part of this at all."

"Then you don't consider it at all possible," I asked, "that there may be some validity in your uncle's theories?"

"No," she said resolutely, "and I'm not the only one. Sir Leonard Stokes of the Royal Society was down last week, and he said that none of his fellows agree with uncle's ideas. And then there's Dr. Needham, who feels the same way. He's here now, Nick," she added, turning to her brother. "He arrived not an hour ago."

"I'm halfway surprised that he came down at all," said Nicholas. "He had replied a week ago that it would be a waste of time."

"And so he still believes," said a hearty voice, as the door to the hall opened, revealing a smiling man in his sixties. I recognized him immediately, having seen a sketch of his likeness in the newspapers on a number of occasions: Sir Samuel Bergholt, our host. He was one of those men who, in spite of being less than five-and-a-half feet tall, looks larger than life. There was a certain Fezziwigian joy about him, but he was clearly no fool. The expression in his eyes conveyed it immediately. I somehow felt that he already knew the real reason that Holmes and I were there, in spite of the fact that nothing about us had yet been mentioned.

He was followed by an even smaller and rather bitter looking fellow, made even more so when held in comparison with Sir Samuel. He was introduced as Dr. Percival Needham. "This experiment has no scientific merit," he complained, his voice tinged with a perpetual whine. "I'm here to witness its failure, nothing more. Nothing personal, Sir Samuel," he added.

"Not taken that way at all, old fellow," replied the smiling man. "You'll change your tune."

He stopped when two more figures entered from the hall, a languid and rather slow-looking fellow in his late twenties, introduced as Nancy

277

Nuneaton's "friend" Rodney Fernworthy, and the other who could only be Anatole Lika.

He was even more striking in person. There was something almost inhuman about him, from the piercing and unblinking gaze to the unusually upright physical posture. He walked nine steps into the room, in a line away from other people, and stood with his uniquely thin figure facing away from all of us. I became aware that he was whispering something, but in a language that I couldn't understand. Then, having reached a point of meaning that he alone understood, he spun in place to face us, stopping with almost military precision. One of the Queen's Guards couldn't have executed the turn more flawlessly. His gloved hands were tucked together with fingers laced across his stomach. We were all introduced and he bowed. No move on either side was made to shake hands.

I didn't know what to say, and it seemed for just a moment that no one else did either. An awkward silence enveloped us until Holmes – who never felt awkward a day in his life – said, "Mr. Nuneaton has been telling us about your electrical apparatus. We saw it when we drive up."

"Ah," said Lika, "you have only seen the tower. It does nothing but support the transmission line. It is only the first of many. When each is constructed, they will run in various directions, to spread the current more effectively. The real device is located inside the building – generators of my own invention to provide the alternating current."

"Alternating?" I asked. "As in on and off?"

"No, sir. The simplest explanation is that the current reverses direction within the wire, countless times per second – in contrast to power from a cell battery, a 'direct current', in which the electricity flows one way through the circuit. By alternating at high speed, the voltage of the current can be boosted much higher by means of something called a 'transformer', which allows it to pass through wires while still retaining its high voltage without the losses that are experienced otherwise."

"And this will be useful when sending the electrical current into the earth?" asked Holmes.

Lika shrugged. "I cannot say. I wouldn't think so. I know nothing of geology, or the fault lines that so concern Sir Samuel. I am simply involved because he learned of my electrical advances and wished to incorporate them into his experiment."

The famed scientist's seeming lack of faith in his host's experiment didn't seem to bother Sir Samuel at all. He maintained a jolly *bonhomie*, even as Dr. Needham seized upon Lika's statement. "As we at The Society have said all along – this will accomplish nothing. Regardless of the voltage involved, the line will simply ground itself and the power will

278

dissipate, in the same way that electrically charged clouds equalize with the earth by way of lightning bolts."

"Of course it will ground itself!" countered Sir Samuel. "That's rather the point of it all, don't you see? I'm running the wire *into the ground*, for heaven's sake! It's the ground beneath us where the faults rub together, building up static electricity in the same way that silk rubbed on a glass rod can charge it. Then, at some point, it discharges – it has to – with the charge running out so that all things are equal again. I hope to find a way to nudge the earth into discharging and equalizing, but on a much greater scale, before too much is accumulated, in order to prevent even greater destruction."

"I can see why the locals are scared," said Rodney Fernworthy, speaking for the first time. "Imagine dropping a bucket down your well and a lightning bolt shoots out. Can't electricity run along water? Won't it charge the water table?"

"And don't you work at your father's bank?" asked Sir Samuel, now showing just a touch of irritation. "Stick with what you know, my boy."

"No, he's right," responded Dr. Needham. "It *does* run along water. And who knows how the electrical current will alter or interact with any minerals that are suspended in the water. The whole community could well be poisoned, and who would know until illnesses start to manifest themselves – sometimes months or even years after these experiments have occurred."

"Enough!" growled Sir Samuel, finally pushed to his limit. Then, he seemed to take hold of himself, saying in a calmer voice, "Enough. I believe that it's time for dinner."

"If you will excuse me," said Lika, "I am not hungry. I will instead go and check on the generators for the procedure."

"Of course," said the old knight. "We'll join you after dinner and let our guests have an early look."

We separated in the hallway, Lika turning toward the back of the house. I found myself somewhat disappointed, I'm ashamed to admit, that I wouldn't be able to observe his various compulsions manifest themselves as he ate.

Dinner was rather tame, and when asked about how we knew Nicholas Nuneaton, Holmes told a rather lengthy, tedious, and completely fictional story about a time that he and Nuneaton, while supposedly in college in Durham, had walked across a concrete beam that spanned a small fish pond in a college quad. It was a snowy night – according to Holmes's tall tale – and Holmes, the first person across the narrow span that was not more than three inches wide, had made it successfully because the accumulated snow served to pack down and provide traction. Then

Nuneaton had followed, now on the snow that had been compressed into ice, and it had been just as slippery as might be expected, sending him tipping into the freezing knee-deep water.

I didn't see the purpose of the story, as it added nothing and forced Nuneaton to agree to something that puzzled him more than anything else. However, it seemed to establish our *bona-fides*, and was dull enough that soon the others quickly lost interest in us.

Eventually the conversation turned, centering on local history. Sir Samuel indicated that if we stayed long enough, he would be willing to take us to a few local archaeological sites, where evidence related to the Iceni had been discovered, with some claiming a connection to Boudicca herself. I thought it promising that he hadn't lost interest in local history, in spite of his current fascinations. He enthusiastically instructed his niece to show us a small bracelet that she wore, seemingly of some type of iron beads on a simple string that he had discovered nearby. He was certain that they were Iceni artifacts. Then Nancy Nuneaton told a long story that somehow started in connection to a local group of women involved in the legendary uprising against the Romans in 60 A.D., but then it became rather muddled and seemed to become something of a defense of the suffragettes – although I couldn't be sure. In any case, the table gradually seemed to lose interest, except for Rodney Fernworthy, who watched the young woman with an insipid grin on his face, nodding with the steadiness of a slow-set metronome.

When Nancy's story petered out, Dr. Needham spoke up, obliquely referring to the upcoming experiment while mentioning the Edison Electric Light Company, which had opened the previous year on the Holborn Viaduct, using direct current. I had the sense that he favored that method over the alternating version endorsed by Lika, and I wished that odd scientist was here so that I could question him further about the difference.

Seeing that we were finished with our meal, Sir Samuel suggested that we adjourn to the generator building, where he could show us his prized apparatus.

I wasn't sure what to expect, but I admit to being impressed. As I had seen from the brightly lit windows earlier, the room was illuminated by incandescent bulbs, and the light seemed brighter than sunshine, especially when reflecting off the white-painted walls. The floor was painted white as well, and spotless. I doubted that this had anything to do with the process. Rather, it was simply an indication of the quality of the workmanship involved, and that Sir Samuel was willing to pay extra to make sure that it was done right.

A small electrical generator hummed nearby, likely powering the electrical lights in the new building. Nearby, two massive devices stood side-by-side, and each was connected to a small coal-fired steam engine which stood idle at one side. A massive smokestack rose from behind it, passing out through the back wall, although I didn't remember seeing it above the building as we'd approached the house.

Seeing the direction of my gaze, Nancy commented, "The chimney needs to be taller. When the steam engine is running, the smoke pours out and hangs around the house, five or ten feet off the ground, as if the building is on fire. I'm surprised that you couldn't smell it when you arrived. The smoke seems to cling to everything in the house – drapes, wall hangings, and even our clothing."

"Duly noted," replied Sir Samuel. "Plans are afoot to substantially raise the chimney. But first we shall begin the process of balancing the earth's electrical current. I fear to wait any longer."

"I understand something of how the generators work," said Holmes, "but what is that bank of objects stacked over to the right?"

"Those are condensers," responded Lika, taking three steps closer. "They accumulate the electric charge, so that while some goes directly outside and into the ground, a second amount can be diverted and stored here, and then released in a sudden controlled pulse, to 'punch' the ground with additional energy. Or so that is Sir Samuel's plan," he added, as if he too were a bit skeptical, but too polite or circumspect to bite the hand that was feeding him.

"That's it," agreed Sir Samuel. "Tomorrow will be the first round, and then we'll settle down to a steady schedule."

"Steady?" asked Dr. Needham. "What exactly does that mean?"

"It means that once we start, we cannot stop. A path will be created, in the way that a French drain, once built, diverts underground water flow. The electrical energy below will begin to accumulate in a different way. We'll need to continue to bleed it off every few days. My calculations indicate that every four-and-a-half days, or one-hundred-eight hours, we'll need to send a pulse through the apparatus, in addition to the regular continuous discharge."

"Continuous?" said Nancy Nuneaton. "One-hundred-and-eight-hours? What a curious number. I confess that I am lost."

"But," asked Dr. Needham, "if it changes the earth so that it has to be done forever after, why do it the first time at all? Why not leave well enough alone?"

"Because, my boy," he answered with a bit of good-natured exasperation, "I'm convinced that if we don't do something, this area will be rocked by an earthquake like we've never seen before."

"Or possibly," scoffed Needham, "you'll *cause* the very earthquake that you claim to be preventing. At least, that's the view of some of the Society members – unlike others, such as myself who think that nothing will happen at all. That is, in terms of geologic movement. And who knows what charging the ground and water will do to the people who live here."

Sir Samuel's gaze darkened. He had apparently come to a point where his inherent good nature was finally overcome by his guest's criticism. Without a word, he stalked to the large steam engine, where he bent, fiddling with this and that until it began to run.

"Uncle," asked his nephew uncertainly. "What are you doing?"

He didn't answer, and instead stepped to his right, pulling down what I believe is called a "knife switch". Immediately with a muted roar, both generators rumbled to life. Then he turned to us.

"There. Jumping the gun a little bit, but why wait until tomorrow? You'll see – nothing but good can come from this."

Lika and Fernworthy stood watching mutely. I myself made no move, not understanding entirely what the consequences might be. Our client and his sister gravitated toward one another, as if expecting to be blown up at any second, and wishing to go out of the world together as they had entered it. Holmes simply watched with a raised eyebrow and his typical scientific curiosity, while Dr. Needham moved to Sir Samuel's side, speaking words that could not be heard, and resembling a small yapping dog circling an indifferent bull.

After no more than three or four minutes, Sir Samuel came out of his reverie and shut off the generators, followed by the steam engine. The silence that descended over us only made the ringing in my ears obvious, where I hadn't noticed it before.

"Enough, enough," said Sir Samuel. "As you see, nothing terrible happened."

"But," replied Dr. Needham, "you said that running the current through the earth would *change* it. That afterwards you couldn't stop. What have you done, man?"

"It shall be fine," replied the old man. "Let's turn out the lights and get some rest. The experiment starts officially at six a.m. – that's when the press will be here – and I hope that you'll all be up and in here when it begins."

He shuffled us all out, including Lika, who seemed as if he wished to stay. Then, back in the main house, he said good night and left us. Dr. Needham, shaking his head while Sir Samuel walked away, announced that likewise he was going to bed, and Lika simply wandered off. Holmes nodded toward the drawing room and indicated that he wished to speak with the brother and sister. Rodney Fernworthy looked as if he wished to join us, but Nancy gave him to understand that we needed to speak alone.

"Well?" asked Nancy as soon as the door was shut. "Do you think that you can prove that he's trying to pull something over on my uncle?"

Holmes shook his head. "Mr. Lika is a well-respected scientist. It seems from first impression that he was simply hired to do a job, and that he doesn't have any more belief in your uncle's theories than the rest of you do. I can certainly spend more time looking into his background, but it seems unlikely that he's trying to do something dishonest."

Nicholas Nuneaton looked from Holmes to his sister, seeming to agree, but with a concerned expression on his face at his sister's reaction. As Holmes spoke, she became instantly angry. "I thought," she snapped, "that we could count on you to break this man's hold on our uncle! I see that he's fooled you as well! I warned you about hiring this man, Nick!" And with that, she stormed from the room, slamming the door behind her.

Nuneaton looked at us helplessly, but we had no comfort to offer. Instead, Holmes simply said that we'd see him at the six a.m. experiment, and wished him goodnight.

A servant showed us upstairs to our rooms. I paused outside my own door to ask if Holmes had any thoughts that he hadn't shared downstairs.

"Nothing, Watson. This was a waste of our time. I suppose we'll see the show in the morning and then go back to London." Then, wishing me well, he went into his own room.

As I settled in, I became aware that the weather outside was much worse than when we had arrived. Rain hit my window like waves crashing into shoreline rocks, and the smear of water down the glass was illuminated every few seconds by bright flashes of lightning. Sometimes it seemed quite close, and I was moved to wonder about the giant metal tower placed right outside the house. I had seen no indication that electrical wires had been run into the main building – which seemed curious to me, considering Sir Samuel's new love of electricity – but I feared that if lightning hit the tower and then into the generators, a great deal of damage could be done to the house simply by its adjacent location.

I slept fitfully, but managed to rouse myself sometime after five. I dressed and went downstairs, where some of the household had gathered for a light breakfast of rolls and coffee. Our client and his sister were there, as was Holmes and Fernworthy. In a moment, Dr. Needham wandered in, and almost immediately, we saw Lika pass by, heading toward the back of the house, where a short hallway connected to the generator building.

No one felt any indication to speak, and when Fernworthy made some comment about the night's storm and that it seemed now to have passed, no one replied.

We became aware that Lika was standing in the doorway, seemingly waiting to catch our attention rather than speaking directly.

"Yes?" asked Holmes.

Lika swallowed, his gloved fingers twisting nervously. "In the generator building. Sir Samuel . . . He's been . . . He has been electrocuted."

It took a few seconds for the information to register, and then, with a scream, Nancy Nuneaton ran past Lika and toward the back of the building.

We followed immediately and were in time to see her drop beside her uncle's body, where it lay in the center of the floor near the knife switch apparatus. She collapsed, draping herself across his chest, and sobbing mightily. Her brother and Fernworthy pulled her away, and I verified that he was gone. Meanwhile, Holmes immediately busied himself prowling the room, having instructed the others to stay back, except to allow Lika to ascertain that the apparatus posed no further threat.

It was clear to me that the old man had been electrocuted, most likely after coming back down to the generator building sometime in the night in order to check his apparatus. I noticed that one of the windows was open, where it had been shut the night before, and that there was rainwater pooled on the floor, even to where the body lay.

As we were so close to town, it wasn't long before the police arrived in the person of our old acquaintance, Inspector Cowdray. He quickly sized up the situation and pulled Holmes and me aside.

"We've been aware of this foolishness for a while," he explained. "The locals have been rather upset, you see. What do you think happened? He fooled about in the night, during the storm, and then lightning ran in on him?"

"So it would appear," replied Holmes. "I found no other footprints but Sir Samuel's after the rain came in the window. He apparently entered the room, stepped into the puddle, and was at that moment electrocuted."

"Well then," said the inspector, "that's that. The wind must have blown open the window. He came down to check during the storm, and the tower was struck by lightning. The neighbors will be happy to know that this nonsense was stopped before it started, and that's a fact."

I almost said something about how Sir Samuel had already run the generators for a few moments the night before, sending a charge into the ground, but held my tongue. It was almost certain that doing so had been the cause of nothing whatsoever, and mentioning it would only confuse the issue. Better that the nearby residents should now feel safe, instead of speculating about something harmful that didn't actually exist.

284

Sir Samuel's body was removed, and soon after Dr. Needham, having expressed his sorrow, left to catch the train back to London. Lika indicated that he would join him, intending to travel on from there to the Continent. Fernworthy volunteered to drive them both to the station. I had expected that we would depart as well, but Holmes made no effort to leave. After the front door shut, we were left in the front hall with the Nuneaton siblings. Holmes indicated the door to the drawing room, and though puzzled, they led us in, where Holmes shut the door behind us.

"I had a chance to look around this morning," he said, "after your uncle's body was discovered." Then, reaching into his pocket, he pulled out a small object which he held up for us to see. It was Nancy Nuneaton's little beaded bracelet, mentioned the night before by her uncle as an archeological artifact.

"I found this behind the large generators," explained Holmes. "Near the open window. You were still wearing it last night when we left the building. I saw it on your wrist. You must have dropped it when you returned in the night to damage the machinery."

Nicholas Nuneaton turned to stare at his sister with a shocked look on his face. The lady herself grew wide-eyed, and her mouth opened, but no sound came forth.

"There were several wires pulled loose from the back, dangling onto the floor," continued Holmes. "I spoke with Mr. Lika about it privately this morning. He likely has his own suspicions about what has happened, but I didn't elaborate for him, and in turn he didn't ask any questions. As he explained it to me, the pulled wires wouldn't have done much damage, and they were likely yanked out by someone who didn't know exactly what she was doing. As they were initially left hanging to the floor, nothing would have happened, and eventually they would have been noticed and replaced. But the rain coming in the open window created something of a circuit.

"When your uncle entered the room and stood in the puddle, the circuit was closed, and when he touched the knife switch, the accumulated charge from the condensers pulsed out, electrocuting him in the same way as if he'd been hit by lightning – which is how his death is being treated officially." Holmes patted his pocket, as if he thought to light his pipe, but then he refrained. "Lika explained that the condensers only held a charge because your uncle had run the generators for a time last evening, and that no one had thought to bleed it off. If he hadn't started his experiment early, walking through the puddle would have done nothing, as there would have been no accumulated electrical charge to run out when he inadvertently closed the circuit. In a way, he helped to kill himself."

Holmes walked a few steps toward the woman and held out the bracelet. She raised her hand and he dropped it into her open palm.

"What did you intend when you came down and pulled the wires, and opened the window?"

She looked dumbly for a moment at the ancient iron beads in her hand, and then slowly her fingers closed around them. She took a step backwards and sank into a chair. "I . . . I wanted to make it seem as if someone had entered from outside, one of the neighbors perhaps, and had fixed things so that the machines wouldn't work. I didn't know what I was doing, but I hoped that enough damage had been done to embarrass my uncle in front of the press, and that maybe he'd also realize that the neighbors truly didn't want this thing so close to their homes. He just needed to lose interest, and find another hobby . . . ." She sobbed then and began to weep, while her brother ineffectually rubbed her shoulder.

Later, on the train back to London, Holmes explained. "There's no question that this was an accident. I had verified before we came down that Sir Samuel's supposed fortune isn't all that much – nearly the last of it besides the value of the house has been used up on the construction of his generator building – so there was no reason to murder him on that score. A quick examination of the room found the iron-bead bracelet behind the generators underneath the window, and you saw that Miss Nuneaton never went near there later, after she entered and knelt by the body. Clearly she had returned in the night, as I saw the bracelet on her wrist when we all departed after Sir Samuel's demonstration, while it was missing this morning.

"While it was possible that lightning had struck the building somehow, a look outside showed no indications. The paint around the open window was still white and pristine, with no signs of damage, and the tower had a lightning rod attached to it, so that anything that struck it would be carried away – and isn't it interesting that every day, common folk use these handy devices to divert and run destructive electricity into the ground while fearing that Sir Samuel was simply going to do the same thing?

"It was most unfortunate, and Miss Nuneaton's actions certainly did contribute to Sir Samuel's accidental death, but I saw no need to expose her foolishness."

I nodded in agreement. It had been quite clear to both of us that she hadn't meant for this to happen, and that she would punish herself for the rest of her life.

Four months to the day afterwards, I was returning home from several wearying hours serving as a *locum tenens* for a doctor with a practice off

286

Fetter Lane when I heard a newsboy calling details of a most shocking event. I veered his way, nearly knocking down a scowling man and fishing some coins from my pocket. Then, stepping to the side of the pavement so that I didn't have to wait, I read the article, and then once again, before pushing myself into motion, hurrying home to share the news with Holmes.

He had already heard, and was reading a different newspaper account in his chair by the fireplace, his pipe held unlit in his teeth. Clearly, the news had rather shaken him as well.

Readers will recall the events of that day, the 22nd of April, 1884, when a considerable earthquake rocked Colchester at 9:18 in the morning. Major damage was caused throughout the city, as well as across Essex in a number of villages. It was later determined to be the most destructive earthquake to have hit England since the late 1500's. It seemed to be centered in Wivenhoe, not far from Sir Samuel's estate. It was described by those who experienced it that the ground seemed to rise and fall like ocean waves, and it was felt all around England, and even in northern France and Belgium.

Almost every building in Wivenhoe was damaged, along with many of the other surrounding villages, and several deaths were reported.

I re-read my own newspaper, and then Holmes and I traded, but his had no additional information, and it would be several days before the full extent of the tragedy was known.

We both sat in silence for quite a while, remembering the events of four months earlier. Finally, I voiced the thought that was in both of our minds.

"Sir Samuel predicted this," I said. "He felt that there would be an earthquake, and he tried to lessen the effects."

"Or conversely," said Holmes, "he *caused* it, somehow charging the ground with his generators, or at least accelerating the process when he ran the device for just a few minutes the night before he died. Dr. Needham warned that such might happen."

He reached for his pipe and began the process of lighting it. "Or his actions and predictions simply had nothing to do with what happened this morning whatsoever. Every day predictions are made, and most never come true. It's only the tiny percentage of those that coincidentally occur as predicted that are discussed and used to 'prove' that such prognostication is possible. The greatest minds all thought that Sir Samuel's ideas were foolish. I think that for now, knowing what we know, we'll have to agree. The future may reveal more, but for me it's simply an incredible coincidence."

287

I nodded, although in my heart I wasn't so sure. I intended to seek out Dr. Needham on the morrow and see if he had changed his mind – although I doubted it. Still, as night fell outside and the wind picked up, the precursor of a spring storm, I realized just how small we were, and how little that any of us – even my friend Sherlock Holmes – really knew about anything.

The Keeper's Tale

January of 1888 was a terrible time in my life. I nearly described it as "bleak" or "unsettled", but even now, as I write this nearly four decades later, I cannot use such reserved descriptions for that period. Following my own recent grief [1], I had returned to my former rooms in Baker Street, welcomed by Mrs. Hudson (who had already been so caring when I first moved there in early 1881 while recovering from the wounds I sustained at Maiwand), and by my friend Sherlock Holmes as well. His concern was more subdued, as one might expect, but he made valiant efforts to ease me through that period when my life seemed upside down.

That January, Holmes had involved me in a plethora of cases, as he was apparently putting his belief that "Work is the best antidote to sorrow" to good use. Very early in the month, we had travelled to the border of Kent and East Sussex and an ancient moated home at Birlstone to investigate the brutal slaying of an American, his head obliterated by the close blast of a shotgun. As was so often the case, the participants in the crime had brought their old feuds to our British shores. And like so many others, this affair had failed to provide a tidy ending – cleaning up the details of this one investigation revealed a thread to another, which would culminate, like so many others that we gathered in those days of the late 1880's, at the ledge above the Reichenbach Falls. There, Holmes paid a terrible price to rid the world of an evil scourge, sacrificing three subsequent years of his life to go into hiding, working from the shadows to finish what he had started, along with decoying danger away from my second wife, Mary and me.

Since the Birlstone case, there had been others, such as the terrifying matter of The Eye of Heka [2], when my own life was threatened on several occasions in a matter that was intertwined with events that could have started a global war, and the curious case of Miss V. Maitland and the seven surly mutes. It may be recalled, by those who would discuss the matter without shutting up entirely in disgust or embarrassment, that the initially simple commencement of Holmes's investigation ultimately led to the resignation of a cabinet member, the suicide of a prominent physician, and the arrest and hurried secret deportation of a band of Serbian acrobats.

That early winter of 1888 hadn't simply involved me in Holmes's ever-increasing caseload. He, in his attempt to distract me from my own often-dark inner thoughts, had taken to sharing many of his earlier cases. I'd heard of the Musgrave Ritual, and the Old Russian Woman. There was the Ten-Penny Whistle, used to send a message of fear through the superstitious residents of Lockerley, and the tale of when Holmes first decided to pursue the profession of consulting detective, following a consultation related to deductions concerning a former escaped convict who had built a secret life for himself in Norfolk.

Over the last few nights, Holmes had been going through the tin box where he kept the records and little mementos related to these past successes. Of course, he referred to some as failures, or as lessons learned, but even those, when he had related them, had sounded like victories to me. However, there was often some point about one or the other of them that stuck in his craw – a deduction that wasn't made fast enough, or an initial incorrect assumption that delayed the eventual solution – souring the taste of his triumph just enough to spoil the memory.

The previous evening, he'd once again dragged the box from his room while explaining how, earlier in the day, he had so quickly seen through a banker's elaborate attempt to fake his own death, as it had many features paralleling one of his early cases. "The old wheel turns," he'd said several times that month, comparing old adventures to new, "and the same spoke comes up. It's all been done before, and will be again." I believe that he would have pulled another example from the box if we hadn't heard Mrs. Hudson begin the steady ascent to our sitting room, with the slower and more deliberate steps indicating that she was bearing evening victuals.

Now our meal was long finished and the box was pushed to the side of Holmes's chair, near the small octagonal table that he had brought with him from his former Montague Street lodgings – apparently related to some past matter that gave it great sentimental value. Little did I know that the box would be opened again in just a few minutes.

Holmes had been in his bedroom and had just returned to his chair by the fire, the book he had retrieved in his hand. I sat across from him, reading one of the later newspapers to which we subscribed. Above and beyond the shared costs of the rooms, Holmes spent a small but fixed portion of his own income to maintain delivery of a representative number of London's newspapers, and this had proven to be a wise decision on countless occasions. He regularly butchered them to add seemingly unimportant or unrelated items to his scrapbooks, so I'd found that – with his permission – if I wanted to read them un-scissored, I'd best get to them early.

That night, the 20th of January, was apparently a day wherein nothing of importance had occurred. The paper was full of the usual bleats from the politicians, reports of matters that were already in progress, simple repetitions of past facts, and uninteresting news from other parts of the world, such as the few lines mentioning that it was the one year anniversary of the United States establishing a treaty port in Hawaii with the exotic-sounding name "Pearl Harbor".

With visions of wide beaches and swaying palm trees, I was about to turn the page from the international news when a small article caught my eye. The previous day – Edgar Allan Poe's birth anniversary as the newspaper described it – the mysterious man who appeared at his grave in Baltimore on that date every year and gave a solitary toast had once again been spotted. His business concluded, he had left the unfinished bottle of cognac on the late author's tomb and vanished into the darkness.

Seeing that Holmes hadn't quite settled into reading, I cleared my throat. "Amazing world," I opened. "An event can occur on the other side of the planet, and I can read about it here and now, the very next day, almost as if I had been there."

"Hmm?"

"Have you heard of this before?" I asked, my enthusiasm rising. "In America. About the mysterious man who shows up early in the morning each January 19th at Edgar Allan Poe's grave on his birthday, and raises a toast before slipping away? [3] I was unaware of it, but it's reported in this newspaper – apparently it happens every year."

I faded away, at first thinking that my conversational gambit had passed without interest. Holmes had initially appeared more inclined to follow his own thoughts when I began speaking, but the mention of Poe had pulled his gaze from the fire and toward me. After a moment, he raised an eyebrow and cocked his head. Then, with a smile, he surprised me by saying, "Many thanks, Watson. I had lost track of the date, and I'm glad that you've saved me the trouble of scouring the papers looking for that bit of information."

I raised a matching eyebrow – a skill I had always valued since I learned as a child that my unfortunate brother could not do it. "You were expecting this news?"

"I was. In fact, the toast, and its subsequent mention in the newspaper, is a message to me."

At that both eyebrows were raised. I knew that my friend had a high opinion of his own abilities and importance, an aspect that he had defended on numerous occasions as simply an accurate representation of his capabilities. As he often said, "I cannot rank modesty among the virtues. One should see things exactly as they are, and to underestimate one's self is as delusional as exaggerating one's own skills." With that in mind, I decided that he wasn't making a statement just for braggadocious effect. He clearly meant exactly what he said.

"How?" I asked simply.

He set his book onto the octagonal table. Then he unexpectedly rose while glancing at the clock on the mantel, no doubt ascertaining that there was time enough before bedtime to tell a tale.

"I seem to be a modern-day Scheherazade this winter," he replied, turning and kneeling beside his tin box. "This chest isn't bottomless, you know," he grinned. "I should space out the telling of these tales – perhaps one a month for maximum effect."

"Not a bad idea for a magazine, perhaps," I said, "but practically speaking, it seems wisest to relate whatever you have to tell me when it best connects to the current discussion."

"A good argument," he said, opening the lid, "if you were trying to wheedle me into telling the story. But since I'm already preparing to do so, it's moot."

He reached into the box and began to lift out various stacks of tied documents, little boxes, a scroll, a bottle, and a mummified ear. These were clearly related to other adventures, because they were set aside. When he had made enough room to apparently reach the bottom of the box, he wrapped the fingers about something and – with a bit of an effort – gave a pull. Whatever he had grabbed seemed to have great weight, for it resisted his effort, but in a moment he leaned back with a long slim object, about a foot in length, and wrapped in what appeared to be white silk handkerchief. Then he handed it to me before reseating himself and reaching for his pipe.

While he went through the tedious efforts that all pipe smokers will understand in order to get the tobacco satisfactorily fulminating, I examined what he had given to me. The wrapping was indeed a handkerchief, with the embroidered initials "*FJH*". There were a few small oval stains, possibly made by old fingers, that looked very much like blood. But the piece of silk wasn't what was of primary interest.

I could tell through the wrapping that the object was made of metal, but it was nowhere near the weight that had been implied when Holmes pulled had lifted it from the box. Loosening the wrapping, I found that it was a spear – or rather, the head of a spear. The metal was cold and quite dark, and it appeared to be some type of iron alloy. It was polished smooth and without any embellishing decorations. It was a functional thing, rough-looking, built to be affixed to the end of a spear and then to kill. It appeared to be discolored at one end, and I wondered if that was the remaining stain from the vital fluids of a long-dead victim. I found the thing unpleasant. I rewrapped the silk and handed it back to Holmes, glad to be rid of it.

By now he had his pipe lit, and he took the silk wrapping from the object and laid it aside. Then, leaning forward, he held the spearhead near the coal scuttle. With an unexpected motion of its own, the thing pulled from his hands and fastened onto the side of the metal bucket.

I frowned. "Yes, Watson," said Holmes with a smile, leaning back. The spear remained fixed halfway up the side of the scuttle instead of falling to the floor. "It has some type of magnetism. You saw that I had some difficulty pulling it away from the bottom of my box."

"But," I shook my head, trying to recall my schoolboy lessons, "the box is made of tin, and the scuttle is constructed from brass."

"With a tin insert," added Holmes.

"Then surely," I countered, "there must be some iron in the mix of both. I know that magnets are only attracted to iron."

"Yes. That is part of what makes this spear so unique. It is attracted to *all* metals. Let me tell you about it, by way of how it was revealed to me."

I motioned for him to continue. He would relate it in his own way.

"You may recall," Holmes said, "that in late 1879, I sailed for the United States with the Sasanoff acting troupe. At that point, I had been establishing my consulting practice for several years from my rooms in Montague Street, but it was certainly not so busy that I couldn't abandon it for a bit. While I never thought to become a professional actor, I realized that the opportunity that presented itself would be invaluable. It was a chance to explore America – while not extensively, still more than would be available to me otherwise – and I would also be able to hone my acting skills and practice making myself into another person, both through my actions and appearance, on a recurring basis.

"The life of a touring company is irregular at best. We settled in New York and began rehearsals. I had a great deal of free time, and I explored the city with my own agenda, eschewing those sites which might attract the casual visitors and tourists in favor of seeing the *real* New York, with all of its flaws, dangers, and raw details.

"Not long after we arrived, a small social affair was arranged for us in the home of a wealthy patron. Our attendance gave the New York elite a chance to mingle with us, and many seemed to be as skittish about it as if they were all Daniels walking carefully through the lions' den. It was amusing to watch them as they associated with the dreaded species *hominum histrionus*, little realizing that less than a mile away in the slums were much more dangerous creatures than they could ever imagine. Equally entertaining was the show provided by my fellow actors, who exaggerated behaviors for their richer hosts because it was expected of them – some who were reserved off-stage took on quite flamboyant characters. Additionally, the actors were making themselves quite at home, eating the provided comestibles with frank greed.

293

"That was their downfall, and my more ascetic habits saved me. Apparently there was something 'off' about the shrimp, and the next day the troupe, with the exception of myself, was completely defeated for the better part of a week. Seeing an opportunity, I received permission from Sasanoff himself, who waved me off from his sick-bed with an unsteady hand, and absented myself from New York for explorations farther afield.

"I only had a few days, so my choices were limited. I quickly decided that I should be make a fast exploration of that nation's capital, and so I entrained for Washington.

"My activities there can be told another time, but suffice it to say, after a day or so I unexpectedly found myself in nearby Baltimore. Following the arrest there of a particularly egregious example of the human race, I decided to range a bit before finally returning to New York on the morrow. I poked around the Inner Harbor, I helped expose a confidence scheme in a small restaurant on Calvert Street and, having heard it mentioned from an acquaintance acquired during that previous little matter, I decided to visit the grave of Edgar Allan Poe.

"By that time, there had been something of a revival of interest in Poe, who had died in quite dire straits. You may know that he had passed in 1849 under mysterious circumstances. He'd been found deliriously wandering the streets of Baltimore in someone else's clothing, and was never again well enough to explain how he had ended up in such a condition. He kept calling for someone named 'Reynolds'. This person was never identified. Four days after being found he was gone, and his final passing was attributed to any number of diseases or reasons, including alcoholism as the most likely factor. He received the equivalent of a pauper's burial and was laid in an unmarked grave in the Poe family plot of the Westminster Presbyterian Church. However, over the years, various efforts had been made to commemorate him, and the site of his grave was never lost, as family members knew of its location, and they would often conduct Poe's admirers to the spot.

"Just a few years before my visit, a local group had – after several previous failed attempts – raised enough money to construct a monument to the sad author. However, Poe's original grave was in the rear of the cemetery, in a crowded area behind the church, so the monument was built near the street where it could be seen, and Poe's remains were moved. The structure is an imposing thing, over six feet tall, growing wider toward the base and made of marble and granite, and Poe's face is carved into it. It's in the front northwest corner of the cemetery, at the intersection of Fayette and Green Streets, one enters the cemetery immediately beside it, at a front gate that passes through a tall brick wall – the bricks being of the same reddish black as those in the nearby building. The church itself – a newer construct lying atop much older foundations and crypts – stands close-by to the east.

"And so it was that I found myself approaching there on January 19th, the seventy-first anniversary of Poe's birth. It was already getting rather dark, as I had set out on this leg of my impromptu expedition late in the afternoon. I ambled down Fayette Street, aware that certain traversed neighborhoods were decidedly worse than others. However, I'd long ago lost any unreasonable fears of such places after my educational rambles through London, and I doubted that the American equivalents of our own home-grown slum-dwellers would present any different challenges.

"I spotted the church from several blocks away, with its high brick steeple looming over the houses on either side. I was invigorated by my walk, having made my way up and down several of the long sloping hills along Fayette Street. The air was cold and crisp, but I was warm in my Inverness and fore-and-aft cap, and I looked forward to a warm meal at my hotel following my return.

"The streets were thankfully empty, and at times I felt that I had the city to myself – at least the little portion that I saw. That's why I was rather surprised when I heard a cry of pain come from the direction of the church. Increasing my speed, I observed that several figures were just inside the street gate, scrambling near a large monument. I would later find that it was Poe's grave, my destination, but at that point it had no meaning for me. All that seemed to matter was that one man had his back to it while three others faced him, one with a raised club. The fellow under attack was gripping his left shoulder with his right hand, and I could see that he was injured and unable to adequately defend himself.

"Although I was taking a chance that the three men were in the right, I chose to stand on the side of the lone individual. As you know, I have some skill in the fighting arts, and while they were not so well developed eight years ago as now, they were not inconsiderable. My approach was fleet but silent, and before the man with the club realized it, I was behind him, grabbing the upraised object – which I was later to identify as an American baseball bat – and wrenching it backwards out of his hand. Sadly, he tried to retain his hold on it, and the resulting sound from his shoulder, rather like pulling apart a chicken wing, indicated that he had sustained some life-long and quite painful damage.

"Rather than waste time on questions or explanations, I took a firm stance and swung the bat toward the knee of a second attacker. With a solid crack from his patella, he gave a scream and collapsed. I straightened to see the third man skittering out the gate, indifferent to the fate of his friends. He rounded the corner into Green Street and vanished to the south and into the darkness.

"I shifted to the side of the man by the monument, the bat still raised, but both of the other attackers had barely regained their feet and were also making their way out through the gate. They would have been easily caught, their effectiveness quite nullified by their injuries, and I made to pursue, but a hand on my arm stopped me.

"'Let them go," said the man that I had protected in a strong Irish accent. 'It would do no good to arrest them, and I don't need the attention.'

"I took him at his word, asking, as any curious person would, 'What happened?'

"'They're not important, just low-level criminals that were hired by someone who is interested in something that I have. I was walking to keep an appointment when I passed the church a few minutes ago and I heard a cry for help. It sounded like an old man – I was stupid to fall for such a trick! I walked into the cemetery, but saw no one. Then, they rushed out of the crypt there – ' and he pointed toward the church, where I could see an opening into the dark vaults ' – and attacked me. I held my own for a minute, but then one hit me with that bat, and I was suddenly in real danger. I owe you quite a debt, Mr. – '

"'Escott," I replied, giving him the name under which I was traveling.

"'Franklin Joseph Hardy at your service,' he countered, and we shook hands. He was a big man with dark hair. His clothing was worn but not indicative of poverty. I could tell from his manner of speaking that he was born in America of Irish immigrants. I asked about his shoulder, and he said it already felt better. 'I'd best be on my way' he added. I wanted to ask further questions, for as you know, Watson, my curiosity can be insatiable, and this was clearly a situation that had any number of mysterious aspects. On impulse I gave him my card, which I'd had printed upon my arrival, indicating my alias, my temporary profession, and my lodgings at 39 E. 22nd Street in New York [4]. He glanced at it with a grin. 'Actor, eh? It seems as if you have a few other skills besides.'

"'Actually,' I added, 'I'm a detective, and my time as an actor is a temporary thing. If you should need any assistance . . . .' I made the offer rather hopelessly, as I didn't expect to ever hear from Mr. Hardy ever again, or to have my curiosity satisfied. His response seemed to confirm that.

"Pushing the card into a pocket, he said, 'I'll keep that in mind, Mr. Escott. And now, thanks once again, and a good evening to you.' As he started to turn, I offered him the bat, thinking that he might still need it. He smiled, took it, and, with a nod, he was gone.

"I spent a few minutes looking around the cemetery, including a period of pondering beside Poe's monument, while wondering how he – in Baltimore – ever came to be the literary agent for the anonymous fellow who wrote up some of Dupin's cases. Dupin wasn't pleased, you know, and I can't blame him. Then on a whim, I took a turn in the crypt, but my examination – carried out with a series of lit matches – only showed the jumbled footprints of the three attackers. There seemed to be no reason to waste further time trying to observe any useful data, so I departed. In the morning I returned to New York.

"I rarely thought about Poe or Hardy or the strange events of that January night until early July, when the Sasanoff Company traveled as a whole to Baltimore. Along the way, several members of the troupe shared various anecdotes about their previous visits to the city, some rather risqué. I knew a number of the actors well enough by then to consider them friends, but I wasn't inclined to relate my own adventure. I did wonder what had become of Hardy in the meantime, little imagining that I would encounter him once again just a few days later.

"We settled into our new temporary digs and began rehearsals. We were due to open in three days, and the time becoming accustomed to the new theatre is always precious – but more for the crew than the actors, as they have to determine the arrangements and placements of various aspects of the backstage area, in order to be familiar with the correct ropes to pull and lights to raise or dim. My part of the rehearsal done for the day, I exited the stage door to see Hardy himself waiting there for me, a grin on his face.

"I recognized him easily, in spite of the fact that I'd only seen him once before, in the twilit shadows of a grim winter cemetery. He seemed pleased when I called him by name. Then he asked if we might adjourn to a nearby bar and have a discussion.

"I noticed that he led me to the very rear of the establishment, where it was quite dark, and he placed himself with his back to the wall – a spot that I usually try to claim for myself, as you will have observed. We ordered whisky, and he seemed to be choosing his words carefully. Initially he asked about the tour, and how long we planned to visit Baltimore. Then, seemingly satisfied that no one was able to hear our conversation, or was interested in it, he finally began to speak of deeper things, but still approaching his topic from a sideways direction.

"'I've been to New York,' he said. 'I've visited your rooming house there, and asked questions, and I've seen you perform,' he said. 'You're very good.' I nodded noncommittally and asked which part he'd seen. 'Malvolio. It was incredible.' I acknowledged the praise, but didn't pursue it, as I didn't want the conversation to detour into a discussion of acting, and I was certain that he hadn't asked to meet me simply to discuss *Twelfth Night*.

"'I've done some research,' he continued. 'You told me that you're a detective, but I couldn't find anything about a detective named *Escott*.'

"I was amused. 'You conducted your researches in London in order to determine that?' I asked, rather facetiously. "Certainly it's obvious that I'm not from the United States.'

"'No, not London. Not personally anyway. But I have a . . . a friend there who was able to answer some questions for me. He confirmed that Escott doesn't really exist. But he *did* enlighten me about another fellow with a growing reputation . . . *Mr. Holmes.*'

"He didn't say it in any way as if to make it an accusation, or with any proud preening to display what a clever fellow he'd been to learn my name. Yet I was impressed. This fellow ran deeper than I'd first assumed. I had no reason to deny my identity – I was only using the alias *Escott*, derived from two of my names, *Sherlock Scott*, to keep my identities as actor and detective separate. I acknowledged what he had discovered. 'How,' I added, 'can I help you? And perhaps more important, why is my help worth enough to go to the trouble to determine who I really am?'

"'I initially sought to verify your identity,' he explained, 'because your appearance at Poe's tomb was a tad too convenient. For all I knew, you'd been sent to be a rescuer from the same man who hired my attackers, just to win my confidence.'

"'Worming my way into your good graces,' I added.

"He nodded. 'Exactly. If you'd simply been an actor, that could have been checked and confirmed. But you mentioned that part about being a detective. That sounded as if it were dropped into the conversation in order to gain my interest.'

"'It wasn't,' I explained. 'I was merely intrigued by your reaction to being attacked. You were willing to let the men go rather than seek any retribution – legal or otherwise. My professional instincts were alerted.'

"'As were mine,' he said, taking a drink. 'Failure to find anything about your existence prior to when you joined Sasanoff's company raised my alarms. I dug deeper, and learned who you really are. Any concerns about your motivations vanished at that point, but I realized at the same time that I might ask for your help.'

"'You refer to having professional instincts. Once must wonder what profession, exactly, we are discussing.'

"'I sometimes do work,' he said, dropping his voice even lower than it had been, 'for the British Government.'

"I was intrigued. 'You are a spy?'"

"He pursed his lips. 'Not in that sense. I'm an American citizen, and proud of it. I would never do anything against the interests of my country. But I have certain skills that came to the attention of a certain man in

London, and he convinced me that keeping my eyes open and relaying the occasional fact back to him as I encountered it could do both countries – and even the world – a great deal of good. This fellow has a number of little birds who bring him information.' And then Hardy mentioned this man's name.

"Suffice it to say, Watson, I recognized him immediately, as it's someone that I know very well. In fact, it would be an understatement to say that he is one of only two people on earth with whom I would trust my life. You are the other."

At that point, he paused to recharge his pipe, leaving me to silently consider his statement. I was honored beyond words, and by that point in our friendship I wasn't surprised, but it didn't need discussion. As would later be pointed out, in the most unusual of circumstances, Holmes and I were like brothers in bond, if not in blood [5] – more than I ever was with my own unfortunate brother.

At the time Holmes was relating this affair, I of course had no idea to whom he was referring. It was only later that year that I would be introduced to his brother Mycroft, a man sometimes referred to as being the British Government, and certainly someone with many strings in his capable hands.

Having reached a satisfactory balance with his pipe, Holmes resumed his narrative.

"Hardy took a drink and continued speaking. 'I came to the attention of this man in London because I'm part of a loose collective that has been recruited through the years – the centuries really – to protect a certain object. And there are indications that it's receiving just a little too much attention of late.'

"I found my interest quickening. I was in my mid-twenties, and no matter how I try to keep my mind focused along the paths of logic and reason, I was also raised on tales of lost treasures. 'And what exactly is this object?'

"He looked around yet again, but there was no one anywhere close that could eavesdrop upon us. "How well do you know the Bible?"

"Here was an unexpected turn. 'Well enough, I suppose. I received instruction like every child of my class. And I've read it in several translations since, both as a philosophical exercise, and for reasons of professional education.'

"He nodded. 'The answer I would have expected, based on our report of you. Do you know *John 19, Verse 34*?'

"I thought for a moment. 'Something about a spear. *The spear*, actually.'

299

"'Exactly. *"But one of the soldiers with a spear pierced his side, and forthwith came there out blood and water."'*

"I nodded. 'Yes. Following the immediate events of The Crucifixion, the Roman soldiers intended to break Jesus' legs to hasten his death, but upon examination they found that he had already passed. To confirm it, one of the soldiers pressed his spear into the body.'

"'Longinus,' said Hardy. 'That's the Roman's name.'

"'But I understood that his name was never confirmed – that it appears only in one of the apocryphal texts.'

"'Correct. *The Acts of Pilate*, which is itself just an appendix of *The Gospel of Nicodemus*. And yet, Longinus was real, and he is a saint of the church and was considered a Christian martyr. His body, and the spear itself, have traveled greatly over the centuries.' He took a sip. 'The spear wound was one of the five sacred wounds, the other being the two nail holes in Jesus' hands, and the other two in the feet, where Christ was nailed to the cross. The spear is traditionally believed to have pierced his right side, releasing blood and water, and it was into this wound that the Apostle Thomas – 'Doubting Thomas' as he's called – put his hand when Christ appeared after the resurrection.'

"'And this object to which you referred – surely you wouldn't have brought all this up unless it was the spear itself.'

"'Correct, Mr. Holmes. It has many names. The Lance of Longinus. The Spear of Destiny. The Holy Lance. The Holy Spear.'

"No doubt I looked skeptical, and I didn't bother to use any of my acting skills to disguise the fact. 'It's my understanding that the Spear has long been in the possession of the Vatican.'

"'They have *a* lance,' replied Hardy. 'As does Vienna, and Armenia, and Greece, and Poland. But the *true* lance has been guarded elsewhere, protected for centuries from those who would misuse it.'

"Holmes paused for a moment, working his pipe before finally saying, "I see your regular glances toward the spearhead affixed to our coal scuttle, Watson. I assure you that all will be explained – or at least, what *can* be explained. To continue . . . .

"I was uncertain exactly how to reply to Hardy's assertion that the real Holy Lance, if such a thing even existed, was under the protection of a mysterious band since ancient times. He noticed my skepticism and said, 'You fear that I'm some crazy fellow talking of magic beans, Mr. Holmes. I assure you that the Lance has power – if for no other reason than the force that it can command as a symbol. Symbols have their own strength, and can be used as tools, or weapons. There are legends that the army or nation that carries the Spear is undefeatable. In the right hands, it supposedly has healing powers. Other magic is attributed to it as well –

some even claim that it can raise the dead. Many seek it, but right now Germany is interested in it in a most unhealthy way. I would disparage their beliefs in the mystical and the occult, but for the equivalent reverence in England for such things as the Holy Grail, or Excalibur.

"'In a more prosaic fashion, Germany craves it for the political influence that it can provide. Bismarck continues to consolidate and unify the various principalities and fiefdoms, and such a tool in his hands, wielded before the disparate German factions, would do much to negate dissent – and while Bismarck has no interest in magical totems and fetishes, he sees and understands its power as a means to an end to implement his political policy. The German people would gladly fall in behind a belief in such a talisman. And therefore Bismarck is actively seeking the true lance.'

"I thought for a moment, and then said, 'By implication, you're indicating that it's here, in the United States.'"

"'I am. The men who protect it have a loyalty beyond borders – or at least they have had until recently. There was one among us, a traitor, who chose nationalism and his own pocket over sworn duty. That's how Bismarck learned of it in the first place. Now that man is here, trying to recover it for Germany.'

"'And the attack on you last January? Is it reasonable to conclude that you have very specific connection with the spear that made you a target?'

"'It is. Very specific. And not knowing whom I can trust within my own group, I'm seeking help from outside. *Your* help, Mr. Holmes.'

"I was silent for a moment, and then urged him to continue, with the *caveat* that I was committing to nothing.

"'I wasn't entirely honest with you last January,' said Hardy. 'I wasn't simply passing by on the way *to* an appointment when I was lured into the cemetery. Actually, the appointment was *in* the cemetery, specifically at Poe's tomb, with the man whom I've named as a traitor. We didn't know it then, and his attack – which he had every reason to think would be successful – was his opening move. When it failed, thanks to your intercession, the first cracks in his perfidy were exposed, and now we've had half-a-year to draw the lines and see where things stand – which is enough to convince me that I can't trust anyone – except now, *you*.

"'That night, we had barely separated when I read your card and memorized it. And then I burned it – I didn't want there to be any way to trace you. After that, I began to research your background, leading to this meeting now. I've made sure that I wasn't followed, and that no one here knows me. It wouldn't do for us to be identified as associates.

"'I won't waste time relating the strange path of the Spear – how it's traveled through various counties and continents, and back again. It ended up with the most unlikely of Keepers in 1830, when Edgar Allan Poe, then just twenty-one, entered West Point. He'd already been in the army in Boston and South Carolina, and had arranged a discharge in order to enter the military academy. While there, he met one of the instructors – a weary and bitter man, consumed by gout and anger, who had served in the War of 1812 – just an annoying skirmish to you British, as you were more distracted by Napoleon marching on Russia, but to us it was the Second War for Independence. It was somehow during this war that this sick old man had become the Keeper of the Spear. That's how it works – the Keeper always obtains it unexpectedly.

"'Now this man, a general with an honored career who resented being sent off to teach, realized that he was dying. With no easy way to reach out to others who understood his secret, he inexplicably chose young Poe as the new Keeper. He explained it to him, and what was required. No doubt it appealed to the young man – after all, his later literary works seem to have been influenced by his bleak responsibility. He was taught whom to secretly notify if needed, and then the old man died.

"'Poe seems to have been overwhelmed by the responsibility almost immediately. He became even more erratic, and within six months of his arrival, he contrived to get thrown out of West Point. He was court-martialed for disobedience and neglect of duty, and by early 1831 he was living in New York.

"'Protecting the Spear has never been an easy duty, but in those days it was likely easier, because the world was a different place then. Still, it clearly weighed on Poe's mind, because he became more unstable as the years passed. We know that several times attempts were made to take it from him, and that he was involved in affairs where his defensive actions ended up reflected in his stories. For example, he was forced to wall up one of his enemies, as would later be reflected in "The Cask of Amontillado". Another time he had to bury an attacker under some floorboards – later loosely referenced in "The Tell-Tale Heart". These actions, while necessary to protect the Spear, broke him.

"'We don't know what happened when he died. It was unexpected, and whatever series of events led to his encounter with the mysterious "Reynolds", or how he ended up in someone else's clothing, may never be known. But die he did, after arranging that the Spear was buried with him.

"Fortunately, the Frenchman who wrote up Dupin's adventures was one of us. He had met Poe long before, and when he heard what had happened, he hurried to America – no easy task in those days – and he recovered the Spear, just days before someone else went digging for it. And the new Keeper, who had seen what he had to do, even though he didn't want the burden, returned to Paris, where he kept it until five years ago. Then it passed to me. I received it as unwillingly as had all those before me, and now someone else is after it.'

"Suffice it to say, Watson, I was intrigued, but I didn't know why I was being told this information, or how I was supposed to help. Hardy sensed this, and he made to explain.

"'As I said, Mr. Holmes, I don't know now who I can trust here in America. I don't propose to cause you any difficulties at all. I simply want someone to know what's happening, and to ask that you be ready if I need your help in the future.'

"'You have it,' I replied without hesitation. 'But surely you know that my responsibilities to Sasanoff take precedence. And we will only be in the United States for a few more months.'

"'That's all right,' he answered. 'Whatever is going to happen will happen soon. We didn't realize that we had a traitor until my ambush last January. I thought that I was supposed to meet someone at Poe's tomb that I considered a friend, as the grave has become something of a symbol related to the Spear for those of us who know the truth. We were the ones who originally worked behind the scenes to raise the money to erect the monument. Knowing how being a Keeper destroyed Poe, and that none of the rest of us who serve will ever receive any recognition, it's something of a secret monument to all of us. My former friend had invited me there to discuss a perceived threat. Little did I know that *he* was the threat. He is a German, and pleasing Bismarck is more important to him than keeping his sacred oath.

"'I've become selfish,' he added. 'I settled down a few years ago, and since then my wife and I have had a daughter, Gertrude. I hope to have a son someday. Families aren't something that are denied to the Keepers, you know. Poe was married, and for many years he tried to live the life of a literary critic and sometime-author, hoping for something like normalcy. I know that I may face danger, and it's selfish of me to bring it on my family, but I want something more.

"'Additionally," he continued, "I'll soon become employed with the New York City Police Department, with a new band of brothers to walk beside me. But in order to accomplish this, I have to make an arrangement – a secret arrangement – with your help.'

"'Do you fear another attack?' I asked. 'I can help watch over you when I'm able.'

"He smiled and shook his head. 'Nothing like that. Rather, I hope that you'll assist me in a deception.' And then he proceeded to lay out his plan. It was simple, and I had some reservations. To be frank, Watson, I was rather resistant, but in the end, I agreed. After all, I was young and foolish, and the romance of it appealed to me, in spite of my lifelong efforts to follow the most logical path.

"A few weeks later, it began. The company had returned to New York, and I was in the sitting room of the East 22nd Street boarding house where I had had lodgings. There was a loud knock on the front door, and in a moment I heard the landlady call my name. Standing at the door was Hardy, with a grim smile on his face. I asked him to come in, but instead he nodded me outside. I followed, pulling the door shut behind me. He then led me down into the areaway, and I could see that he was moving with great effort. When we were in the shadows, he collapsed against the wall with a groan.

"'You have been injured!' I cried softly.

"'Only a minor beating,' he replied with a tight smile. 'I've had worse.' He reached into his coat and pulled out a long flat object – that very spear there, Watson, which you've been eying so suspiciously. That is Hardy's handkerchief, the same that was wrapped around it that night, and those are his bloodstains, left there when he pulled it from his pocket.

"Hardy handed the packet to me, saying, 'They only know that I got away with it. I'm certain that no one followed me here. They know that I'm hiding it somewhere, and that I'm prepared to reveal their crimes to the authorities and the press if I'm further threatened.'

"'And Poe's tomb?' I asked. 'Do they understand its significance as well?'

"'They do. As long as I appear there every year in the early hours of Poe's birthday and drink a toast, they know that their own secrets are safe. What they won't realize is that *you*, Mr. Holmes, will also see it as a message, recognizing that it's from me, and confirming my continued safety, and also their belief that I continue to hold the spear. You'll know that the bargain still holds, and that I've survived for one more year . . . as has my family.

"He urged me to put away the spear, and then he told me a name – there's no need to repeat it now – the man who had betrayed their cause, and who now believed that Hardy had hidden it where it couldn't be found – unless Hardy revealed how. Thus, a tenuous truce was formed between them, a bargain that would hold until this man found the leverage he needed. So far he never has. You'll have heard of this man, Watson, and I hope that we never encounter him. When the time is right, I'll share his identity with you.

"The packet was still in my hand, and Hardy urged me to hide it away. I placed it in my own coat, in an inner pocket, and then he fervently shook my hand, saying that he hoped we'd meet again. With that, he slipped away into the darkness.

"When I was quite sure that he was gone and that there was no sign of anyone following him, I went inside and up to my room, where I unwrapped and looked over the spear for the very first time. I quickly discovered the odd magnetic properties. As you might imagine, Watson, such a weapon might prove to be a hindrance in battle. It could attach itself to another weapon, such as a sword, at a most inopportune moment. The same would be true for any metallic armor that it might be thrust against. I suspect that it was more of a ceremonial construct than for practical use."

He leaned forward and pulled it from the coal scuttle, with no little effort. "You didn't examine it quite long enough to notice this," he added and, with a twist, he removed the tip from the spear.

He held the short end piece, about two inches in length, a foot or so apart from the main body of the spear. After demonstrating their separateness, he returned them together, where they rejoined with a little click. Then he handed it to me. I took it, rather unwillingly, and repeated the action myself. I could discern no indication of where they had joined. Then a thought made me frown.

"You see it then?" Holmes asked.

"I believe so. The broken ends shouldn't fit together like this, in such a clean manner."

"Correct. I have no knowledge how the tip was originally broken off, but it was obviously recovered and preserved with the rest of the spear." He set aside his pipe and stood, walking across the room to his desk, where he pulled some small object from the top drawer before tucking it into his waistcoat, and then fetched his small blackboard, where he sometimes outlined ideas as he explained them. Later that year, he would keep track of the locations of the Ripper victims and their commonalities on that blackboard, and in a decade he'd use it to puzzle out the curious meaning of the Dancing Men.

He propped the blackboard on a chair and leaned forward to sketch what I understood to be a magnet. "As you know, Watson, a magnet has a north and south pole, in which the fields are aligned, like this . . . ." And he pointed to the blackboard, where

N======S

"This represents the magnet. Now if it's broken, or cut, we have an arrangement where the separated segments form new north-south patterns, wherein each piece is now its own complete magnet. The ends at the separation take on new poles, like this . . . ."

N======S   N======S

305

"Since opposites attract, one would think that the new south pole at the separation end of one piece would be attracted to the new north pole at the other, but in fact, the magnetic field that surrounds the magnet is multi-dimensional, surrounding it in all directions, and it causes the ends to repel each other unless turned. Thus, the cut pieces of a magnet cannot be rejoined exactly as they were before – they will always try to shift to one side, or turn, before pulling together. Like this . . . ." And he made a third sketch.

N======S

N======S

"Here," he added, setting down the chalk and pulling the object from his desk out of his pocket. "Try it with this piece of broken magnet."

I took it from him and saw that it was a small iron bar, about the size of my thumb. It had been broken down the middle. The break wasn't straight across, but rather followed some weakness or fracture line within the metal. Therefore, the way that the two pieces fit together was obvious, and if when pressed together, they should have joined seamlessly.

However, the two segments that I received were instead skewed, with one only halfway aligned to the other. I pulled them apart easily enough, but when I tried to fit them together so that the two pieces would join exactly at the break, I felt considerable resistance. Eventually loosening my right-hand grip, I felt that piece turn quickly in my fingers before rejoining the other at the exact same shifted half-connection that it had held when I received it.

"I obtained that broken magnet years ago," said Holmes, who had resumed his seat, "to conduct that same experiment. One must be careful when cutting or breaking a magnet, as the alignment of the fields can be diminished if it receives too much of a shock."

I set aside the broken magnet and picked back up the spear. Then, for a minute at least, I took the broken tip off and replaced it, repeating it many times. I looked closer at the spear tip, confirming that in the dim gaslight I wasn't seeing well enough to know for certain, but believing that when the two pieces were joined, the line showing where they were broken was invisible.

"Based on what you've shown me," I said, "these pieces should not fit together like this at all. It's impossible. How . . . ?"

My voice drifted off, and I raised questioning eyes at him. He smiled but shrugged. "After Hardy left the spear in my care, I wrapped it up and hid it in my luggage. I took him at his word that no one had followed him, and that my existence was unknown to his enemies. Taking a leaf from Poe, I didn't go to extraordinary means to hide the spear, but rather simply took sensible precautions. I had already taken the time to exchange coded messages with our mutual friend in London to establish Hardy's bona fides, and that in fact my new possession of the spear was not an unexpected surprise. Then, I carried on with the tour and eventually returned to London, leaving Escott behind and resuming the mantle of Sherlock Holmes, Consulting Detective.

"Of course I'd seen by then the various unusual aspects of the spear – specifically the magnetic properties which defy our current understanding. I discussed the object at great length with that one other person in London who knew of its existence – until tonight, my dear Watson, when you have been made a member of the club. It was agreed that taking a sample of a sacred artifact for the purpose of scientific experiments would be unacceptable – even the slightest scraping."

"And the stains on the tip?" I asked, turning it back and forth in the light. "Blood, perhaps . . . ?"

He shook his head. "Again, we decided that we did not have the right to take even the smallest sample. We simply agreed that the metal is likely some unknown alloy, possibly from a meteorite that was found and forged into this shape. And so it shall remain, just as it was given to me"

"So for most of a decade," I said, leaning forward to hand it back to him once again, "you have effectively been the Keeper. And you've simply hidden it in the bottom of your trunk for that entire time, along with old case records, and objects like that withered animal paw, or the jar of some kind of pink crystals. Weren't you afraid that it would be stolen?"

"I suppose that I never gave it much thought," he replied to my surprise. "Once I'd seen what little could be observed, I felt no obsession to keep studying it. It's as safe with my records as anywhere else. It seems that the people harassing Hardy don't know of my existence, and if anyone else were to find it in the tin box, they wouldn't know what it was. Going to the trouble of placing it in a bank vault, or hiding it in a grave, as happened when Poe was the Keeper, would only serve to draw attention to it. And my contact within the Government felt that they have no business keeping it, as there are untrustworthy people there – our own equivalent of Herr Bismarck – who could do just as much damage with it. No, Watson, it's just fine where it's at." And he began to rewrap it with the old silk covering.

307

"But at least," I countered, "put it somewhere safer than the box. You have enemies – more than you did eight years ago, I'm certain. Someday someone may search these rooms and simply take the box whole, rather than spending time to open it, rummage through, and deciding, as you expect, to ignore the blade."

He didn't reply, but rather knelt by the box and replaced the spear, before recovering it with all of the other professional mementoes. Only after he had reseated himself did he reply.

"Perhaps you're right. I'll give it some thought. Just because it's been safe for so long doesn't mean that I should be complacent or careless.

Soon after he wished me goodnight and then, stooping to pick up the box, he carried it into his room and shut the door.

I can't say that I didn't think about it any further, for how could I not? I wanted to visit the British Library and request everything that they could tell me about the Holy Spear, but I pictured some nearby crone with big ears overhearing me, part of some global cabal similar to the mysterious band that produced Keepers when needed, roaming the cities and byways looking for hints of the spear's location. And so I forced myself to remain in ignorance.

A few days later, on a Wednesday, Mrs. Hudson was making her usual visit to her nearby sister, Mrs. Turner, when I returned home from an errand. Holmes was in a fine fettle, like a child who wishes to show off a new toy.

"I have taken your advice and hidden the spear!" he cried. I was in no mood for his enthusiasm, I'm afraid, and made that very clear. However, with twinkling eyes he persisted, so that I was then forced to look around the sitting room, trying to see where it might be concealed.

I discounted pulling open drawers or any such nonsense. I had some idea that it might be tucked in with the fire tools – possibly he'd put a handle on it so that it looked like a poker, resting alongside the one bent five years earlier by a madman who had stood at our hearth, making threats less than a day before ironically dying from his own scheme. I shuffled here and there, half-heartedly examining vaguely likely spots, but I perceived nothing. Holmes watched with delight – to my growing irritation – and I believe that if he had offered to direct me by saying "Warmer" or "Colder" based on my proximity to the relic, I would have stormed from the room.

Finally he understood that I wasn't going to find it, which was the object of the exercise to begin with, and he pointed toward the wall where he had patriotically – and most shockingly at the time – fired a number of bullets from his hair-trigger pistol, spelling out a tribute to the Queen, *V.*RI stepped closer, and saw nothing but the punched bullet-holes and the faded wallpaper. Turning my head with a querying expression, he nodded.

"I waited until it was Mrs. Hudson's day away, and then carefully lifted the wallpaper to expose the bare wall beneath. I've hollowed out a spot just large enough to hold the spear and its wrapping – to me the two shall always go together. It was a simple matter to re-plaster the void and then glue the paper back down."

I looked again to make sure that I could see no signs, and then agreed that it was as good a spot as any. It was safe, and would remain so unless the building itself were destroyed. And even though the best-kept secret is one that is known by a single person, this was almost as good. Holmes knew, as did I, and just one other – Mycroft Holmes, whom I would meet later that year when Holmes indicated that his amazing abilities ran in the family, and offered to prove it by taking me around to his brother's club where I could see for myself.

Occasionally in the years that followed, we would make some oblique reference to the spear, but it was never anything of day-to-day importance. When I learned that Mycroft Holmes was maintaining the Baker Street rooms during those years when Holmes was presumed to have died at the Reichenbach Falls, I suspected that it was in order to keep the location as a safe resting spot for it.

I never had any sense that anyone was aware of it and trying to take it, and I'm certain that Holmes didn't either. I did have occasion to meet Franklin Joseph Hardy over a decade later, when he traveled to London in relation to an investigation that he was carrying out for the New York Police Department. Holmes had warned me ahead of time to make no mention that I knew of the spear, and Hardy gave no hint as to its existence either. Later, Holmes informed me that, except for assuring Hardy of its continued safety, he hadn't told him where it was kept. I wondered what the man would have thought if he'd realized that he was less than ten feet from it when he sat in the basket chair before our sitting room fire.

Without fail, each year we've found indications, one way or another, of Hardy's annual toast at Poe's Tomb in the early hours of January 19th. This seems to be an indicator that Hardy's plan has continued to be was successful, although any reference or discussion of it is forbidden, in case there really is someone waiting patiently for any hint as to where the spear might be hidden, thus upsetting the delicate balance that has existed for lo these many years.

No communication about the spear was ever carried out – at least to my knowledge – between Holmes and Hardy about the spear, either in person or by other means. Our contacts with him increased in the following years in a natural profession progression, as the New York policeman with the ever-growing reputation conferred with the famous English consulting detective. In 1908, long after Holmes had retired to his cottage in Sussex, he agreed to foster Hardy's son, Fenton, for part of the year, taking the young man on as something of an apprentice. This wasn't unusual, as Holmes had trained a number of young detectives in like manner. The younger Hardy, in his early twenties by then, was planning to follow his father into a career with the New York Police when he finished college, and it was felt that Holmes's brand of practical observation and experience would be very useful to him. Holmes, it will be recalled, was at that time deeply involved in matters relating to the impending German War, and his supposed retirement to Sussex had mostly been contrived so that he could freely carry out necessary investigations for his brother Mycroft. Young Fenton Hardy was instrumental in successfully assisting in the conclusion of a couple of these before he returned to America, and he subsequently made quite a name for himself within the police force before retiring in his late thirties and becoming a noted private detective on his own, making his base of operations a pleasant-sounding coastal city.

Although the spear was never discussed between us and any of the Hardys, we had much besides to share over the years. I also became good friends with the family on my own, and only a month or so ago I received a letter from Fenton's two sons, named for their grandfather Franklin Joseph. Lads of sixteen and fifteen, they recently became involved in a mystery of their own, involving a theft from a nearby mansion, and proving the innocence of the father of one of their school chums. Their account of the investigation, including finding the treasure in a most unexpected tower, made fine reading. They mentioned that a fellow who contrives to produce a number of books for young people had approached them about publishing an account of the investigation, and they wished for any advice that I might give. I hope that I was of some help.

To my knowledge, when Holmes moved away from Baker Street, he left the spear there in its unique hiding place. For a number of years, and even through the War, he maintained the house at 221 for his own use as a base of operations when in London. Eventually, after the conflict ended, he settled into something that much more resembles a true retirement. I've never asked him if, during any of that time, whether he relocated to spear to a different location, closer to his current abode. As one of the few people with knowledge of its hiding place, perhaps I should.

I have prepared this document at the behest of Mycroft Holmes, now quite elderly (as are we all!) to preserve a record of the spear, in my own words, so that its provenance may be documented, should it ever be required. I understand that this account will be held by Mycroft until some future date, when its release may become necessary. I'm separately providing the name of the man who betrayed Hardy so many years ago, as revealed to me by Holmes during another investigation when that knowledge became important and relevant.

I have no further definite knowledge of the spear except for what Holmes told to me on that day in January 1888, and then I only saw it the one time. All that is attributed to it may be the merest of moonshine, or a colossal joke or distraction, but I suspect not. I held it once, and I saw for myself the unusual magnetic properties. More than that, I sensed something about it, something which I can't define or explain, and I saw the possible blood stain as well. It seemed . . . it *felt* beyond my understanding. Holmes would criticize any such thoughts, but I suspect that if he were to admit the truth, he has some of the same feelings about that piece of deadly metal that I do.

Over the years I've occasionally considered it one way or the other, as either an object of dangerous political influence, or perhaps something more. I can see why it would drive some, like poor Edgar Allan Poe, mad, and for the sake of the world, I can only be glad that it ended up in the possession of the wisest and most sensible man that I shall ever know.

Dr. John H. Watson
19 October, 1926

NOTES

1. This refers to the death of Constance Watson *née* Adams. Their marriage was short, lasting from November 1886 to her death on December 27th, 1888, just a few weeks before the framing events in this narrative. There are some who question the existence of Constance, insisting that Watson's first wife was Mary Morstan, whom he met in September 1888 during the events of *The Sign of the Four*. However, there are several clear Canonical references that indicate that Watson was married *before* he met Mary, and therefore the existence of a first wife, before Mary, makes a great deal of sense.

   Constance's identity was first revealed in William S. Baring-Gould's biography, *Sherlock Holmes of Baker Street* (1962). There are some who question Baring-Gould's facts, but it should be remembered that he had a family connection with Holmes by way of his grandfather, Sabine Baring-Gould. Sabine was Sherlock Holmes's godfather, as revealed in *The Moor* (1998, as edited by Laurie R. King), and as such, it's likely that he would have had access to much of the information regarding the Holmes family, including data about Watson's wives, and that he would have subsequently passed it down to his biographer grandson, William.

   While many aspects of *The Moor* and other documents presented by Ms. King's editorship are questionable, the matter of Holmes's godfather being Sabine Baring-Gould seems unassailable. (For more about the nature of the reliability of the stories edited by Ms. King, see "Necessary Rationalizations: The Overall Chronology of Sherlock Holmes and Dr. Watson (along with the Truth About Mary Russell)" by David Marcum, *The Watsonian*, Vol. 5, No. 1, 2017), and at my blog, *A Seventeen Step Program* (*http://17stepprogram.blogspot.com/*)

2. This is a reference to a (so-far) unpublished but fully edited Watsonian adventure *The Eye of Heka*. (The manuscript was located in London by me, David Marcum, in London on one of my Holmes Pilgrimages, and subsequently prepared for publication – hopefully in the near future.) It occurs in January 1888, during that period when Watson has recently returned to Baker Street following his wife Constance's unexpected death.

3. Sources indicate that the "Poe Toaster", as he's come to be called, first began his yearly ritual in the 1930's. He appears in the early hours at Poe's tomb in Baltimore, Maryland, makes a toast to the late author, and then departs, leaving the bottle of cognac from which he drank behind, and refusing to interact with observers. In spite of reports that he began in the 1930's or possibly 1940's, this narrative makes it clear that the ritual actually began much earlier, and that researchers should be looking in older news accounts for further discussion of this elusive figure and his descendants.

4. 39 E. 22nd Street, New York, where Holmes stayed during his time as an actor in the touring Sasanoff Company, is confirmed in the book *The Adventure of the Stalwart Companions* (edited by H. Paul Jeffers). Additional stories about this period include various segments of *Sherlock Holmes of Baker Street* (William S. Baring-Gould) and *I, Sherlock Holmes*

(Michael Harrison); "The Adventure of Vanderbilt and the Yeggman", *The Confidential Casebook of Sherlock Holmes* (Roberta Rogow); "The Old Senator", *Sherlock Holmes: The American Years* (Steve Hockensmith); "My Silk Umbrella", *Sherlock Holmes: The American Years* (Darryl Brock); "The Curse of Edwin Booth", *Sherlock Holmes: The American Years and Sherlock Holmes Mystery Magazine* – Vol 4, No.2 (Carol Bugge); "Excerpts From An Unpublished Memoir Found in the Basement of the Home For Retired Actors", *Sherlock Holmes in America* (Steve Hockensmith); "Cutting For Sign", *Sherlock Holmes: The American Years* (Rhys Brown); "The Stagecoach Detective: A Tale of the Golden West", *Sherlock Holmes: The American Years* (Linda Robertson); and "The Adventure of the Amateur Emigrant", *Sherlock Holmes: Before Baker Street* (Daniel D. Victor).

5.   The incident where Holmes and Watson are described as brothers in bond, if not in blood, was dramatized in the film *Sherlock Holmes* (2009).

The Village on the Cliff

"Watson – wake up. We're nearly there, I think."

I opened my eyes, never having truly been asleep, but rather drifting through one of those dozes into which one sinks while ill. I pulled myself straighter in my seat as I assessed my condition while reaching for my flask.

The soreness at the back of my throat was still present, and there was no denying now that I was coming down with something. My experience as a physician indicated that it was likely just a typical cold, brought on by fatigue and the recent abrupt change of season. I doubted that it was anything that I'd caught from a patient – like most who are involved in the healing arts, exposure to so many varied illnesses seems to provide an immunity of sorts. It's a phenomenon that seems to be matched only by teachers of small children, who regularly intersect with that veritable stew of childhood diseases that are carried by their students to the common locus of the school to be shared and blended.

My self-diagnosis was of very little comfort, however, as I took the smallest of sips of brandy, realizing that the flask was more empty than full, and that it was unlikely to be replenished anytime soon. I castigated myself for not inquiring as to a refill before we left the station and set off into this barren waste.

We were quite a bit closer to the small range of mountains that had been on the western horizon since we departed – less than an hour before, as I confirmed by checking my watch. Still, the sun was significantly lower in the sky than when I had closed my eyes. I had fitfully dozed almost as soon as Holmes had gigged the horse. Of course he was aware that I wasn't functioning at full muster. It didn't take someone of his abilities to observe that I should have probably stayed in London. Certainly I had slept most of the way down on the interminable train journey, awakening only at various stations of greater or lesser importance when Holmes would leap to the platform with his usual boundless energy to send or receive telegrams. The brisk autumn air would then rush into our compartment, and for a moment my sinuses would ache, radiating down the back of my throat along what seemed to be raw striations. If I had been well, none of this would have caused a second thought.

When possible we had found something to eat, although I had no interest in food, or when we were more hurried Holmes had obtained something hot for me to sip, and the heat of the tea or coffee had felt good on my throat. But those stations with a soothing beverage had become few and far between, and I had sipped my brandy instead, its heat offering a comforting but temporary cauterization for a few moments before I fell back asleep, rattling always westward, ready to assist when needed.

I'd been well the night before, retiring early and expecting Holmes's summons at any moment – although it hadn't arrived until the early morning hours. Two days earlier, Holmes had been alerted by his brother, Mycroft, that Lord -----'s diary had been stolen. The foolish peer had kept the journal against all common sense, as well as in defiance of the security dictates of his department. Explosive details of the behind-the-scenes maneuverings that related to the events at Fashoda and threatened to plunge us into war with France were recorded in the little book, an innocent-looking object of blue-dyed leather – and it had been taken by Lord -----'s valet, Edwin Byrnam.

The thief's identity was quickly established by Holmes, although his motivations were still uncertain, and Mycroft had set plans in motion to arrest the man and retrieve the dangerous volume before its contents could be revealed. But the affair was bungled when one of the arresting agents was himself revealed to be a German sympathizer. His own attempt to retrieve the diary spooked Byrnam, who vanished into the warrens of London with his son, Geoffrey. A widower, Byrnam apparently felt that he had nothing else to lose and a fortune to gain.

It took Holmes the better part of a day to get onto the man's trail, and word had arrived late that night that our pursuit must begin immediately. It had been decided that no chances could be taken that someone else might gain the diary – or even have the chance to read it – for after the incident of the German agent, who could be trusted? Therefore, Holmes and I would pursue Byrnam and his son alone, to take him into custody in person so that no one, not even an ignorant provincial policeman, might possibly see the diary's contents. Thus we traveled companionless, our only aid being uninformed watchers along the way who had no idea the identity of our quarry, or the reason for our interest in him. Their job was simply to relay where Byrnam and his offspring left the train back to Mycroft in London, who would then send coded messages ahead for us to collect along the way.

I knew when I awoke and quickly dressed the previous night that all was not right. At Paddington, we were able to catch the very next west-bound train after the one that Byrnam and his son had taken, and I immediately settled into my seat and fell asleep once more, rather than my usual practice of reading the newspaper or a book. There was certainly nothing to see outside as we flew through the night-darkened countryside.

When morning arrived, we were still making our way west, never quite catching up with the elusive valet and his son. As the sun moved across the sky, I began to feel that I had been on the train for days instead of hours. The morning passed in a blur of cold and uneasy dreams, rocking from our passage across the banks and turns of the line and the occasional points, or when passing another train hurrying in the other direction. Byrnam and Son seemed to randomly change directions, leaving the train at one station and catching another to a different quarter of the compass, and then doubling back, seeming to sense the pursuit, but always steadily working their way west. Slowly the sun overtook us, and by afternoon we began to chase it. Soon it outpaced us, and as it started to drop toward the far horizon, we reached a bleak and remote halt, somewhere in Wales, where Holmes leapt out to question the station master. In a moment, he beckoned me to join him, where he informed me that Byrnam and his offspring had arrived on the previous train, not more than an hour previous, and had walked out of the station. Somehow, we had managed to stay on his trail.

None of Mycroft's agents, nor any of the uninformed policemen conscripted into this scheme, were waiting at this particular location to verify the Byrnams' passage – for certainly there weren't enough of them available to cover every possible stop. I realized that the pursuit of the fugitives would continue, and that it was up to Holmes and me, on our own. The next phase of the chase commenced.

While I huddled in my coat, Holmes conferred with the station master, who related that the two men – one in his early fifties, the other about half that age – had rented a cart and left by a dirt road headed west out of the village. "But," he added in his awkward English with something of a wary tone, "he didn't follow my instructions. Do you see in the distance? There, where the road splits? I told him to bear right and run north along the mountain – he wanted to go inland – but he didn't listen. He kept going straight, toward that gap that rises up near the sea."

"And where will that take them?"

The station master mumbled something under his breath, and then said, "We call it *Cig* now. The road ends there."

"Cig? asked Holmes. He seemed to become sharper then, more especially alert somehow, as if that odd word might mean something – but only someone who had known him for so long would recognize it. "Is that a village?"

"It was once," came the reply. "Not much there now besides a few old houses and a church. It was abandoned years ago, when the fishing couldn't support them anymore. But . . . ."

He faded away, and Holmes frowned. "But what?"

"There are some other people there. They arrived back in the summer. They keep to themselves, and we let them. These men that you're after – they shouldn't have gone there. You shouldn't go there either."

"Why?"

The man shook his head and started to turn away, but Holmes stopped him, a hand on his shoulder, asking about obtaining a cart of our own. The station master scowled but directed us to a stable within site up the nearby dirt lane that served as the village's main street. Within a few moments, we had made our there, under the vaguely hostile gazes of a dozen villagers paused in their routine to watch a pair of strangers. We entered the ramshackle establishment and transacted with the owner, who seemed rather wary after learning our destination. "Bring the horse back safely," he warned, after demanding extra payment, but without further explanation. Five minutes later we were again following along Byrnam's track. Looking back over my shoulder, I could see the station master watching us, apparently with nothing better to do than see if we also took the left fork toward Cig. As expected, we did, and soon both the man and his ramshackle little village were behind us in the spreading darkness.

The sky was clear, with the promise that the night would be cold. The sun was hanging low in front of us, but glancing toward it didn't seem to hurt my eyes, and it didn't appear to lighten the blue metallic tints of the surrounding sky. Rather, something in the atmosphere, far out over the sea, looked to be occluding and muting the star's light to that of a full daytime moon.

I considered whether to take another pull at my flask but refrained, hoping to reserve my supply as long as possible. Again I wished that I had asked the station master about purchasing a fresh bottle before allowing Holmes's urgency to hurry me out of town. I knew now that my sore throat would only get worse as the evening progressed. And did I perhaps feel just the beginnings of a fever?

Beside me, Holmes was congratulating us on the successful pursuit of the Byrnams. He recounted the events of our journey that had occurred while I slept – the running series of messages between him and Mycroft in London, who had coordinated the various officials that had kept watch along the way to determine when Byrnam and his son changed trains, and in which direction. It really sounded like a masterpiece of modern cat-and-mouse. Holmes had confirmed that the two men had been left alone the entire time, and the diary, with its explosive contents, was certainly still in the man's possession. All that remained was to corner them and retrieve it, and if possible take them into custody – although that was of lesser importance. And I decided that I must ask the men a question: Why flee to this godforsaken corner of the kingdom? Sourly, I pulled my coat tighter.

Thinking of our destination, I glance at Holmes. "You seemed to be interested when the station master mentioned the name of the village. *Cig*. Does that mean something?"

He was silent for a moment, and if he hadn't been holding the reins, I suspect that he would have taken that time to go through the tedious process of lighting his pipe. Finally he spoke. "Do you recall Andrew Bradfield."

The name was familiar, but at first I couldn't place him, and I was irritated that Holmes would make me guess, rather than simply tell me. Then I remembered the fellow – small, earnest, and possibly a bit too willing to give credence to the impossible.

"He's the one that assisted Alton Peake for a time."

"That's him. Peake brought him up several days ago. He's disappeared."

"Hmm," I replied, noncommittally. My throat didn't encourage unnecessary discussion.

"Peake said that Bradford had followed some rumor or another west into Wales. And before he left, he had mentioned the word 'Cig' when he was trying to interest Peake in accompanying him."

"Well, why didn't Peake go, then? He typically chases after any rumor or legend that scurries across his path," I said grumpily, and rather unfairly. Holmes and I both respected Peake, even though we didn't necessarily agree with his perspective. Whereas Holmes had established himself as a consulting detective from the time he first came down to London in the mid-1870's, Peake had followed a parallel but very dissimilar track as an investigator of the occult. By the time that I met Holmes in early 1881, both he and Peake were already acquainted. I gathered that they had first run across each other in the reading room of the British Library – each of them then with too much time on their collective hands, waiting for clients, and attempting to educate themselves in their chosen professions. Although they have very different philosophies, they've always seemed to enjoy one another's company. Over the years, Peake has been both a casual visitor in our rooms in Baker Street, stopping by to share news and stories before the fire with whisky in hand, and we've also intersected with a few of his investigations during some of our own.

To be fair, he is never gullible, or willing to believe every outrageous tale that he hears, and in each instance that we've seen him in action, he's assisted in debunking a number of supernatural scams. But conversely, he's told us tales of cases that we haven't observed, of doings that are better shared around a dark fire in the woods than a quiet sitting room, relating things that cannot be explained away with logic and reason.

318

Holmes has always been politely interested, and his skepticism has sometimes been a bit more polite than mine, I'm afraid. He has explained to Peake on several occasions that "No ghosts need apply," further adding that if he allowed a supernatural explanation to be a possible option during an investigation, then he ought not even try to find the physical evidence which so consistently proves a more mortal motivation. "If I credit your ghosts and phantoms," he has said, "then I might as well be back in the Dark Ages." Peake usually smiles when Holmes says something along these lines, and then he takes a drink of whisky, but his eyes don't reflect his smile, for they always seem a bit as if he's seen horrors, and that he's still seeing them.

"Peake stopped by last week while you were away in Chelmsford," Holmes continued. "He wanted my advice on conducting a search for a missing person. Apparently waiting for a vibration through the ether wasn't doing very much to locate his former assistant."

I barked a laugh, and it devolved into a wheezing cough. Holmes glanced my way and continued. "Peake had taken Bradfield on as something of an apprentice a few months ago, but he found that the lad was simply too willing to believe every ridiculous story that he heard, without question. It was apparently useful at times – his sincere interest in what he was told encouraged a few mountebanks to become careless, allowing Peake to function quietly and expose them. But Bradfield's trust in one such swindler had been noticed by a young widow who took his apparent confidence as an endorsement, and she subsequently gave the man her savings. The scoundrel had absconded before Peake could reveal his methods, disappearing with all that the woman had. Peake was able to track the trickster down and effect arrest, retrieving most of the stolen funds, but he realized then that Bradfield had become a liability, and one that couldn't be adequately trained or trusted.

"They parted ways, but a week ago, Bradfield showed up at Peake's Charterhouse Square rooms, wild-eyed and frantic, reporting that he'd come across . . . something. He wouldn't say what, but he was in obvious distress, and he wished for Peake to drop everything and go with him at once – to Wales. To *Cig*. Peake couldn't get away just then – some bit of business was coming to a crisis – and he begged Bradfield to tell him more, and to wait a few days until he could join him, but the lad was impatient and left without further explanation.

"Peake consulted me about all of this, and I put a few lines in the water, but as you know, I was myself involved in that little matter of the Hucknall coffee poisoning, and I could do no more. I had to report that my sources had failed to identify a location in Wales called 'Cig'. Now I understand that the name is unofficial. How unusual that Byrnam would lead us there after all. Perhaps Peake is right, Watson, and there *are* lines and forces all around us, shining like a glowing path or a beam across the sky that our eyes cannot perceive, but yet resonating somewhere in our minds – possibly in that primitive hind-part at the base of our brains where the most basic functions lie. Even as our heart is kept beating, we are sensing what cannot be consciously perceived. What other reason could place the village of Cig in front of me twice in such a short period of time?"

I didn't even bother to comment, as this bit of metaphysical clap-trap was beyond the amount of energy that I currently wished to give it. I closed my eyes and pulled my coat tighter, certain now that I did indeed have a fever.

As Holmes realized that I'd failed to rise to the conversational lure that he'd tossed out, he ceased pondering and fell silent. I reopened my eyes and we both watched the track before us as it led, narrower and rougher but straight as an arrow, to a trio of small mountains standing near the sea. The slopes facing us were already deep in shadow, a dark and featureless blue. But as we pressed inexorably forward, a series of buildings along their base resolved into focus – a half-dozen or so small cottages of the sort often found by the coast, functional and built to withstand harsh weather. In the middle was a church, or what had been once, clearly the center of the small outpost, slightly bigger than the meager buildings surrounding it, and topped by a rather squat steeple. Behind this little cluster of weathered and colorless civilization, there was a rather startling gap between two of the mountains showing the line of the sea, lit bright gold by the setting sun, itself now invisible behind the dark rise of the more immediate prominence.

The mountains themselves might better be called hills, for as we approached, it was obvious that they were only a couple of hundred feet high, and no higher. However, in that area, where the rest of the countryside seemed to slope toward the ocean in gradual descents to the shore, or in others to drop abruptly in the form of cliffs formed by geologic collapses in ages past, these freakish anomalies, like jutting upturned fangs, stood out and appeared to be much more dramatically imposing than the dry intellectual measurements that their dimensions would otherwise suggest if only reading about them on paper.

The rises before us were dramatic and tended to focus one's attention to the church's steeple, now centering itself before the straight road toward the gap where the sea was visible. And as we moved closer, other details came into focus as well – unpleasant stains, dark and damp-looking, on the walls of the dreary buildings. The shingled roofs, and the darkened windows of the houses. A cart and horse came into focus before the church. There was a marked lack of trees, as if they had been cut

320

generations ago to burn for heat, and the cool wind rushing from behind us toward the vast empty horizon beyond the looming pinnacles only served to emphasize the loneliness of the place. I think that if there had been trees and the last remaining dead leaves of the season to brush against one another in that steady breeze, I would have been thoroughly overcome by the desolate emptiness. I shivered, and it was then that I perceived a sole figure situated before the door of the church, tall and painfully thin, and watching our approach with an unmoving patience, as if he had been carved from the last tree to stand in that godforsaken place and left as a sentinel.

I expected Holmes to make some comment, but he uncharacteristically appeared to be as daunted as I was by the picture that presented itself – the lonely and abandoned settlement, the dramatic placement before the steep and atypical hills, the mood of the dying day, and the single man who might have been an illusion for all the movement that he had made since coming into sight. The wind didn't seem to touch his garments whatsoever.

I myself had said nothing, due to the strangeness of what I beheld, and also because I very much did not feel like talking. My throat hurt now with every beat of my heart, and I was further convinced that I indeed had a fever – which only added to the dream-like feeling of this whole situation. I knew that I would not wake up and be in my chair before the fire in Baker Street – and yet, a part of me convinced myself that none of this fantastic setting could be true, and that any moment my eyes would open to reveal the usual clutter of our sitting room. But they didn't, and as Holmes pulled the horse to a halt, the mysterious man shifted into a smooth forward motion.

"Gentlemen," he said, his feet sliding oddly across the ground underneath a plain brown robe, his only raiment. He was arrayed like a monk of some order that had taken a vow of poverty, but like none that I have ever encountered before. His voice was low, with a curious vibratory quality, as if a bow were being drawn steadily along the lowest string of a *violoncello*, with no effort to change the note or offer any vibrato. "We rarely have visitors. Two others arrived not more than an hour ago – " He gestured to the horse and cart tied the church step's railing. " – and now yourselves. Might I conclude that you are following the former?"

As he spoke, I was able to perceive some sort of accent, eastern European perhaps, but nothing more definite than that. As he concluded his question, he stopped walking, having only taken a few steps in that peculiar slipping motion that placed him near Holmes's side of the cart.

It seemed that with his closeness, he intended somehow to prevent Holmes from stepping to the ground, but my friend had propelled himself with a sudden move so that the man had to take a surprised step back, his eyes widening. Now Holmes was facing the man, and I could see the two of them side-by-side, allowing me to realize that Holmes, himself somewhat over six feet in height, looked like a lad near the other man.

He was nearly seven feet in height, although he appeared to be even taller due to his excessive leanness. He was completely bald, with a rather knobby head perched on a thin neck. It might have been a trick of the fading light, with the sun now dropping behind the nearby mountains, but he also seemed exceedingly pale – quite gray in fact – except for his thin lips, which had an unusual purplish cast. They were pursed in irritation, apparently at having given ground to the shorter man.

I stepped down more slowly from my side of the cart and walked around to them, patting our horse on the nose as I rounded in front of him and coming to a stop behind the tall man, who was now forced to take another step back and pivot so as to face the two of us. I could see that his hands, with fingers laced, were long and thin, as might be expected, with ropy veins running along the backs and up under his sleeves. However, they had no color, and were obvious by their contour only. On his right hand was a ring supporting a garish stone, as black as night, a large oval running from knuckle to knuckle.

His feet were shod in simple sandals, further emphasizing his superficial resemblance to a monk. I observed that his long nearly prehensile toes were now rather curiously bent at the last joint, a condition known as "mallet toe", where the appendage cannot straighten – a most unusual condition for someone who wore sandals, as it was usually the result of wearing too-tight shoes. The great toe on each foot was much shorter than the rest

His only other adornment was a small silver crucifix centered on his chest, a couple of inches in length, held in place by a solid-looking little chain. It further gave the impression of some sort of obscure religiosity. I glanced past the man and saw that Holmes was looking at the small cross with unusual interest, leaning forward a bit, almost to the point of being rude.

By then we had stood there for most of a minute, and the silence had grown awkward, but that was always a useful tool. When Holmes didn't immediately reply to the man's question, and instead took a moment to glance here and there at the surroundings, the tall man was eventually motivated to the fill the silence.

"I am Brother Adămuș," he said, with a curious lilt to his name, implying that the vowels should be decorated with various and obscure punctuation marks as hints to the foreign pronunciation (and which I have reproduced as best I can, as based on details that I learned much later). He looked from one to the other of us, and then something about Holmes seemed to catch his eye. He squinted a bit before a look of enlightenment crossed his face. "You are Sherlock Holmes," he said, his low voice giving it an odd emphasis. Then inexplicably he frowned.

Holmes raised an eyebrow and he pushed back his fore-and-aft cap to better see the tall man. "I am. Do you know me?"

"Only by way of what I have seen in the press," he said, and then glanced my way. "We do not venture into the greater world, so the others here will not have heard of you – to them you will simply be as other men who arrive here – but as I must sometimes go forth to transact unavoidable business within the nearby village, and it is both my responsibility, and burden, to stay aware of outside events. I recognize you. I have seen mention of you before." Then he turned his head my way. "And thus you would be Dr. Watson."

I acknowledged it and cleared my throat, preparing against the pain there to speak, but he had already looked away, dismissing me in favor of my companion. "I repeat, you must be associated with the two men who arrived earlier, for we rarely have visitors present themselves so easily, and for two groups to appear in a single day . . . ."

"It is true," Holmes confirmed. "The men are fugitives, and we seek their return to answer for crimes committed in London. Can you take us to them?"

"Certainly," he said.

He started to turn, and at that moment, a light suddenly appeared in a window beside the door of the church, apparently a lamp placed there. Somehow its materialization made the rest of the village seem even more lonely, for none of the other windows were lit at all, not in any of the buildings that we could see stretching to either side of us. The cold wind seemed to blow a little more strongly just then.

Seeing the light, Brother Adămuș smiled – not an improvement – his lips pulling back into something like a smile, but with no corresponding warmth in his eyes. "Ah," he said. "The feast is ready to commence." He raised an eyebrow, and this time he looked directly at me. "Possibly you would care to be a part of it?"

Perhaps it was a trick of the fast-fading light, but his teeth, as revealed by that curious vulpine smile, had a curiousness to them, a dull greenish cast that gave the sense that the enamel had been polluted somehow. Then his mouth closed, snapped like a silent trap, and he was leading us toward the church. Holmes glanced my way, his look of warning quite obvious. He veered away from our new host, taking hold of our horse's halter.

"You mention 'others'," said Holmes, tying the beast's reins to the church rail – for there was no other place to secure him. The horse already

323

there nickered, and the two stable mates seemed glad to see one another. The stable man's warning to bring back our horse safely crossed my mind. "This spot appears to be quite deserted. Do you live here, or elsewhere, only gathering here at this location for your rites?"

The man paused with one sandaled foot on the single step leading up to the church entrance. Without looking back, he said, "Rites, Mr. Holmes? You assume, then, that we are some religious group?"

Holmes raised an eyebrow. "Forgive me. I'm rather used to make observations and drawing conclusions, and your clothing, as well as the crucifix that you wear, led me to interpret too quickly."

Brother Adămuş turned then, his hand rising even as Holmes spoke, and he stroked his finger up and down the tiny figure of Christ affixed to the long piece of the cross, almost sensuously. Another smile crossed his face as his fingertip continued to trace along the metal, but this time his lips never parted, and his teeth were not revealed. Finally he dropped his hand, I felt that I'd seen something obscene.

"We are not here because of a *religion*," said the man. "We are here to *exist*. We have journeyed to this place to be left alone. And still, here against the edge of the sea, we have . . . visitors. You say that you are here because you wish to remove these men that you seek back to London." It was not a question.

"Yes."

"That would be well, then. We prefer that no one intrude – especially any such as you. When we desire contact, we go forth and initiate it for ourselves, on our own terms. Is that so objectionable?"

From another man, the tone would have become strident, but his own voice maintained that curiously low and unnerving vibratory pitch. Apparently his question was rhetorical, for he turned without receiving an answer, and apparently not caring for one. He reached the door and went inside, preceding us without another word.

The building wasn't any warmer inside than out, but that came as no surprise. However, it was more quiet when we were away from the constant wind. I glanced through the door before it closed behind us, and met the eyes of our horse, tied in the creeping darkness. The old fellow seemed to be looking directly toward me, as if attempting to communicate some concern. I realized that I was apparently sicker than I'd believed.

The small anteroom to the old church was plain, with no furniture or decoration, except for a tall, thin, and rickety table underneath the window, where the lamp that we had seen placed from outside was sitting. I wondered who had put it there, and what exactly it signified. The yellowish light barely seemed to illuminate the room, and it effused a strong kerosene odor that I could almost taste, even with my oncoming illness.

The chamber had two doors aside from the one which we had just used – a set of double doors on a wider wall across from the outside door, and a smaller narrow door to the left side on the same wall. It was toward this smaller door that the man walked, before suddenly pausing, as if in thought. As he stood and the pause grew more awkward, the sudden silence, away from the wind, left me nonplussed. I wondered what was to happen next, as Brother Adămuș stood there, his back to us, as if making some sort of decision. Then, I was startled to hear a single rude laugh from deeper in the building beyond the double door – just once, before it ended abruptly.

That in some way this seemed to be what was needed to motivate the robed man into motion. He turned away from the small door and looked at Holmes. "But I have been rude," he said. "Night is coming, and you have traveled far. Your friend – " and he tossed an indifferent nod my way " – is clearly ill. Come – before you meet your prisoner, join us for some refreshment."

And then he turned aside toward the double door, striding with certainty while Holmes glanced to see if I'd heard it. I nodded. *Prisoner* – singular.

We entered a room that was probably twenty feet or more square, not excessively large, but certainly big enough for the sanctuary that it had once been when this had been a village church. The room should have been marginally brighter than the space where we had been. That had been lit by a single lamp, while this room had a half-dozen of them spaced around the perimeter on the same tall thin tables that were by the front window. However, the spacing of the lamps only served to make the center of the room a dark pool, made more obscure by the contrast with the brighter edges. It had seemingly been converted into something like a banquet hall, with two long tables running from another table placed on a slightly raised dais at the far end of the room, in a configuration resembling something of the symbol Π.

Yet there was nothing unusual about this. What was unnerving was that, as my eyes adjusted to the gloom, I could see that most of the seats at all three tables were filled – by thirty or so individuals who made not a sound, but rather stared ahead, as if gazing into an emptiness that I hoped to never experience. They didn't look up when we came in, and for a moment I feared that they were dead.

But there was one who was not that way. Sitting at the center of the head table, his motion drawing one's gaze by its contrast to the other corpse-like figures, was a fair-haired man in his mid-twenties. He had a couple of the transfixed men on either side of him, and I could see that they very much resembled our guide, Brother Adămuş. One of the lamps was placed somewhat behind the man who did not belong, serving to highlight him all the more. He was drinking lustily from an awkward and overly large goblet, and I could see that he had what appeared to be wine stains down the front of his shirt. His sloppy movements seemed to indicate that he was already drunk. As I watched, he laughed – that same braying tone that we had heard from the other room.

He tipped up the goblet to a nearly vertical angle to get whatever was left. Then, darting his tongue around his lips like a lizard peeking from a hole, he set it down with a clang that clearly left a dent in the tabletop before reaching for a short dark bottle placed near his right hand. As he carelessly poured a refill, Brother Adămuş spoke, as loud as he had been outside where the wind was blowing. It seemed thunderous in the otherwise quiet room, and I was reminded of when I had visited hospitals such as Bedlam, where the staff doctors would talk about the patients in their presence as if they weren't there at all.

"Here we meet when we have purpose," he explained. "We feast to celebrate."

"And what is that purpose?" asked Holmes.

"When we have something to feast upon."

A chill ran down my spine, and I somehow became aware then that the gazes of some of the men seated around the tables had shifted from their internal contemplations and had now focused on us instead. It was then that I understood what I must have already seen but not observed: Each of the room's occupants was male. There were no women present. Perhaps I hadn't found that unusual, as I am a member of several clubs in which women are never to be seen, and I've visited countless others while assisting Holmes on his investigations. But here, where we seemed to have found ourselves on the far side of the wall that separates the wild-lands from civilization, it seemed much more sinister.

As I looked around the room, my eyes sharpening in the dim light that reminded me more and more of the back recesses of an opium den, I could tell that each of the seated men were now looking our way without expression. All resembled the tall man beside us, with long bald heads and thin shoulders. Every one appeared to be shaped in the same mold as our chaperone, and from what I could see, they were all clothed in a similar robes. Unlike Adămuş, however, none had crucifixes around their necks.

The initial shock of the sight of seeing all these men was wearing off, and I was becoming more aware of my surroundings by the minute. I recognized that I had been smelling a familiar odor since we'd entered – the ketones produced by starving bodies. I had been familiar with this scent for more than twenty years, having first encountered it as a medical student, when working with London's poor. I had found it countless times since then – from the slums of India and Afghanistan to our own shameful Whitechapel, and even in the sitting room in Baker Street, where the occasional visitor would display signs of obvious hunger and neglect. Were these men so thin because they rarely ate? If so, it was no wonder that obtaining food was reason enough for a celebratory feast.

Meanwhile, the young man at the head table continued to drink noisily, with an occasional puffing belch. Those men beside him ignored him, and he in turn made no effort to engage them in conversation.

The scene seemed so static that I was more surprised than I care to admit when one of the men seated near us spoke, apparently addressing Adămuş while never taking his eyes from me.

"More?" he asked simply.

His voice was the same as that of Adămuş, that curious flat-toned buzz as if a thick string were being vibrated. And yet it was different. The curious accent that Adămuş evinced was thicker from this man. Adămuş snapped at him in some language that seemed to slide into one long word, broken occasionally by *sh*'s and *D*-sounds. Apparently we weren't supposed to understand the conversation, and the man had mistakenly spoken in English. In the middle of this flowing drone, I heard the words *Sherlock Holmes*. As he spoke, the man who had asked the initial question frowned, before saying something in reply in the same language. Adămuş gave a short incomprehensible reply, and the conversation seemed to be over.

"I was explaining your reason for being here," said Adămuş.

"Indeed," replied Holmes. "Croatian?"

Adămuş' eyes widened the tiniest fraction. "No, but similar. You speak Croatian, Mr. Holmes?"

"No, but I have been in some of the areas where it is used, and I have heard it before. Your people have migrated from that part of the world?"

"We have. A part of Hungary, southeast of Sibiu, in the Carpathian Mountains. From *Cetatea Poenari*, near the Arges River."

"You are far from home," said Holmes wryly.

"We came to feel rather . . . unwelcome in that part of the world. We moved west – rather like the Mormons described your book, Doctor."

I cleared my throat, having become rather used to being ignored by the man. "You have read it, then?"

"I have. It was entertaining. I find that as I grow older, my mind needs more diversions, and some of your English writing is quite . . . distracting."

"I'm surprised," said Holmes, "that you would go in for that sort of thing."

327

"Again, Mr. Holmes," said Adămuș, "you make the mistake of trying to equate us with a religion. We do not worship anything – at least not in ways that you could understand or tolerate, or that I wish to convey."

"And yet you wear a crucifix."

"Ah, this?" He raised his hand again and touched it, but thankfully he refrained from stroking it as before. "This was simply something that I recently came across and put on for my own amusement."

"You don't strike me as a man who goes in for amusement," countered Holmes. "In addition to being curious about your beliefs and practices, I have a special interest in that particular crucifix. You see, it had previously been described to me – do you see how one of Christ's feet has been broken off? – and the fact that it has appeared here, where its owner had announced an intention to visit just days ago, makes it even more fascinating."

Adămuș frowned. "You expected to find this here? But you said that you were following the two men who arrived earlier today. This trinket has nothing to do with those men."

"True. It's nothing more than coincidence. But I had been told that a man was headed this way, and he has since disappeared. Andrew Bradfield – is the name familiar?"

It was difficult to be certain in that dim light, but Adămuș' lips appeared to tighten. He seemed to catch his lower lip in his teeth for just a moment before replying, "He was here a few days ago. I met him outside, as I did the two of you. We gave him something to drink. Then he was gone."

"As simple as that, then," said Holmes, gesturing toward the seated men. "And now it's time for one of your celebratory feasts."

At that moment, the door on the far side of the room opened with a squeak, and a number of figures began walking into the room, one after another, each carrying platters.

Even as the smell of food wafted my way – boiled pork, apparently – I was shocked to recognize that the bearers of the meat were all women. Each of them wore the same style of drab robes, but otherwise they were much different than the similar-seeming men, a mixture of heights and colorings and weights. While the men all had the same tall thinness and grayish cast to their skins, these women – at least a dozen of them – could have come from anywhere in the British Isles. Blonde, brunette, red-head. Tall and thin, shorter and stouter, they ranged from girls barely out of their teens to more matronly figures nearing mid-life. None, however, appeared to be past their mid-thirties.

What they had in common was that they went about their tasks – setting the platters of meat along the different tables before the collection of curious men – without any expression upon their faces. In fact, each almost had a look in her eyes that resembled someone deep in the throes of *mesmerization*.

With the platters on the tables, the men all reached forward, without any urgency or ceremony, and began tearing off chunks of the flesh. Without benefit of plates or utensils, they used their long slim pale hands to convey the food to their mouths, wolfing great hunks that were barely chewed before being swallowed and replaced by more. Rapidly the feast, such as it was, disappeared. There was nothing else on the table – no vegetables or fruit or bread, no condiments, and nothing to drink. Apparently the only wine to be found was at the head table. I glanced that way and saw the fair young man tentatively chewing on some of the meat apparently taken from a nearby platter. He had an odd look on his face. Then, as if sensing that I was looking his way, his eyes met mine. I looked to find any hint of his thoughts, but I saw nothing but an inebriated greed, as if he were only living in the moment and interested in satisfying his primitive cravings.

The last of the women exited through the door, even as the food was consumed. One by one, the men around the tables lost their inward-turned expressions while they had chewed and swallowed, and refocused in our direction. Tearing my gaze away from their attentions, I looked back to Adămuş when he spoke, his tone now fractionally irritated while his hand grasped the crucifix, his already pale skin whiter across his tight knuckles. "I find your questioning offensive, Mr. Holmes. My brothers feel that you should stay, as we never turn guests away, but I think that it would be best if you depart as planned."

"And Watson too, of course."

Adămuş waited a fraction of a second before replying – a splinter of time that was just long enough to give the sense that the question hadn't been decided yet. Then, "Yes, the doctor as well."

There was danger here. I could feel it now. What I had thought before to be simply bizarre, or something generated by my impending illness, was very real. I had my service revolver with me, having long ago learned never to venture out unless it was in my pocket, and Holmes certainly wasn't defenseless, but there were many of these men around us, and who knew how many more that we hadn't seen?

"I believe," continued Holmes, "that you also indicated that we will be able to take the Byrnams – the men who arrived earlier today – with us."

Adămuş didn't immediately reply, as if he were recalling the conversation from a few minutes earlier, when he had first met us outside the church and recognized Holmes. Clearly he seemed to be weighing how much trouble would be brought upon them by obstructing our purpose. And even though he had already agreed that we could leave, I was certain that if he determined that we wouldn't be missed, or if he had any hint that our location was unknown to the greater world, the decision that we could leave would be rescinded.

As if reading my thoughts, Holmes added, "We were careful to leave word about our intentions to visit here, and to speak to several people when we passed through the village and obtained directions to this remote spot."

Adămuş relaxed a bit, as if he had reached some kind of decision. "You may return with the older man. He has confessed his crime to us when he arrived here, and he is being held elsewhere. But his son has chosen to remain." He raised his voice for the first time and looked across the room. "Geoffrey? Do you wish to leave with these men from London?"

The young man – really nothing more than a boy, in spite of his age – looked our way with a spoiled and drunken expression that could barely focus. In the sickly yellow light, the grease from the boiled flesh that he had consumed slicked his fat face. He resolutely shook his head and looked back that the table, finding the wine bottle right where he had last left it.

"So be it," said Adămuş. "He chooses to stay and become a part us. His celebration will occur in a few days. In the meantime, you may retrieve the father and depart."

He turned toward the door leading back to the small anteroom, and there was a low grumble behind us. For the first time, the men around us showed an emotion – something akin to anger. Two or three of them stood up, one of them not five feet from me. I could see that he was young, about the same age as Geoffrey Byrnam at the front of the room. But where Geoffrey was soft-looking, this thin man was lean and dangerous muscle. He was tense, as if he were about to spring like a dog rarified by hunger into a hunting machine.

Adămuş snapped something in his peculiar language, again using Holmes's name and the word *London*. The angry expressions didn't diminish, but no one else stood, and Holmes and I followed Brother Adămuş out. I shut the door behind me, as if doing so would be sufficient to lock away the occupants of that nightmarish chamber.

Without comment, Adămuş took the lamp from the window and then walked to the smaller door. It opened to reveal a set of narrow steps leading into a basement. The steps themselves were of stone, apparently cut out of the very ground upon which the church was built. The walls were stone as well, unevenly shaped, as if the amateur craftsman who had evacuated this chamber had stopped when the required volume was achieved, rather than taking any extra effort to make the area look finished.

There were two doors on the far wall of the basement both with ill-fitting doors. The one on the left seemingly opened into darkness, as revealed by the wide space at the bottom. A cold breeze was forcing its way through the gap, and I could only imagine what lay behind it. The cracks around the other door were lit, and the smell of the boiled meat was stronger there.

As if reading my thoughts, Adămuş said, "This door is to the kitchens, where the women prepare the feasts. There are separate steps leading up to the hall."

I nodded, but Holmes wasn't listening. He was looking over the other side of the room, which was divided from ours by a series of iron bars, placed about eight inches apart, stretching from the wooden ceiling of the old church above and down to fresh-looking holes chiseled out of the raw rock at our feet. A barred door had been hung awkwardly in the center of it all.

"You have installed a cell," Holmes said, a statement without any surprise.

"We sometimes require it."

"I believe that I understand why you were forced to leave Transylvania," responded Holmes.

"Ah. I shouldn't be surprised that you have perceived so much," responded Adămuş. "You know of that part of the world, then?"

"I read a great deal," said Holmes. "And additionally I happened to pass through there a few years ago, when it was believed that I was dead."

Adămuş now looked puzzled. Without further explanation, Holmes turned back to the cage, peering through the bars at a middle-aged man who was sitting on the floor, watching silently.

"Edwin Byrnam," said Holmes. "Get up. We are returning to London."

The man scrambled to his feet, but didn't approach the door. "Come out," said Adămuş, a stranger quality in his already strange voice. This new tone sounded compelling and commanding, and it seemed to resonate within Byrnam, who complied. "It isn't locked," added Adămuş. Holmes turned his head with interest and, keeping a curious eye upon Byrnam, he reached forward and pulled the door toward him.

I placed myself beside the man, giving him a quick examination, but always ready to reach for my service revolver. He appeared fit, though disheveled from his irregular dash across the country, as well as his more-recent imprisonment. He took no interest in my examination, and made no protest when I ran across a small book in his jacket pocket, removing it and handing it to Holmes. He flipped through it and nodded, and I knew that we had completed that portion of our mission. Although returning

331

Byrnam to face justice was secondary to securing the diary, I realized now that we had a responsibility to get him away from this place before yet another celebration could occur. Without waiting for any approval from the robed man, I took Byrnam's arm and led him carefully up the steps, Holmes close behind. I could sense from the awkward way that he ascended that he was placing himself to keep an eye on Adămuş below us while trusting for me to make sure the way before was safe.

I entered the vestibule half-expecting to find it full of the tall robed men, fresh from their feast, yet still hungry. "More," that one grim man had uttered. And yet, the room was empty. In seconds I had the front door open, and we were outside in the cool evening air. I inhaled deeply trying to rid myself of the sickening mixed stew of the stale mildewed building, the scent of starving men, and the terrible steam that had spread from the boiled meat. While I was helping Byrnam into the back of the cart, Holmes paused before Adămuş, whom I saw had followed us outside.

"Andrew Bradfield?" asked Holmes. "The man who arrived a few days ago?"

"As I said, he is no longer here." Adămuş reached up to the crucifix, wrapping his hand around it and giving a sharp tug. The silver chain broke with an audible snap and he tossed it in Holmes's direction. "Give this to his people if you wish."

Holmes caught it and then dropped it into his other hand, allowing the length of chain to coil upon his palm. Then he placed it in a pocket and untied the horse.

The air seemed to have revived Byrnam somewhat by that point. He looked around, as if waking up from a long sleep, confused at where he found himself.

"My son," he said. "Where is my son?"

"He is staying, for now," said Holmes softly. "We will do all that we can to retrieve him, but for now – "

Byrnam attempted to push his way past me, trying awkwardly to climb to the ground. "Geoffrey!" he called pitifully. "Where are you? We must leave!"

"Hold him, Watson," said Holmes quietly, untying Byrnam's horse and roping him to the back of our cart, so that they could pull in tandem. Then, after untying our horse as well, he stepped up and into his seat, picking up the reins. In an even lower voice, he said, "We will return, Mr. Byrnam, but we must be away now. There is danger here."

He had said it quite softly, so low that I was barely able to hear. And yet, from twenty feet or so away, Brother Adămuş spoke. "That is true, Mr. Holmes. There is danger. You are fortunate – more than you know. I would advise that you and your friend do not return. Ever."

Holmes made no response, and in fact did not deign to look in that direction. Rather, he turned the horse and sent us swiftly back the way we had come. But I was in the back with Byrnam, and I did meet Adămuş' gaze as we pulled away. It was as cold and dead as when we first saw him, and in a reversal of our arrival, he gradually disappeared into the surrounding darkness of the church's outline, as did the church as well a few moments later against the now-black mountains. Even the gap between them, where the setting sun had previously shown on the sea, was as nothing.

We reached the village where we knocked up the stable hand, returning both carts and horses. Then we roused what passed for the local innkeeper, obtaining a large upstairs bedroom and sitting room. Throughout our return, Byrnam had been somewhat catatonic. After finding that his son wasn't returning with us, he had sank into that same trance-like state in which we'd found him in the cell. I speculated on some sort of drug, but Holmes was of the opinion that it was something more like hypnotism, although it could be a combination of the two. In any case, it seemed that only time would reveal the truth.

In our room, we put Byrnam to bed, but without discussing it, both Holmes and I tacitly decided to refrain from dropping our guards. Somehow it seemed that the distance between the odd church by the sea and our rooms was not very far at all if Adămuş changed is his mind. With a word of warning, Holmes slipped out for a time to send a telegram to London. He returned, having been gone longer than I would have expected, explaining that he'd found and awakened the station master, only to be told that the telegraph office was closed and nothing could be sent until the morning. With that in mind, Holmes had then gone to the station alone, picked the lock, activated the lines, and then sent a message to Mycroft on his own. Knowing that no one would be there to wait for a reply, he'd remained until Mycroft responded, and they had made arrangements.

Upon his return, he enquired after my own condition, and I confessed that I had become worse as the night progressed. He assured me that he had the situation in hand, and encouraged me to sleep. He slipped downstairs and returned in a moment with a bottle of whisky, informing me where the landlord had thought it to be cleverly hidden. With a toddy to sear my throat, I allowed myself to fall asleep, service revolver in hand, in a plush chair that I'd pulled back behind the sitting room's outer door, so that anyone coming in that way might not immediately see me should they gain entry

I awakened to find the morning light spilling through the east-facing window, and a low conversation taking place across the room. There was nothing threatening in the tone, and more importantly, nothing like the unnerving drone of Adămuş' peculiar voice. I opened my eyes to see two men in chairs before the fireplace – Sherlock Holmes, and his brother Mycroft.

I believe that I have made mention of Mycroft's proclivity to remain fixed within his orbit when given the choice. However, that is by no means meant to imply that he couldn't move around when necessary. For instance, I had seen him away from his haunts at The Diogenes Club more often than I'd found him there. On the first occasion that I'd met him at the club, I had seen him not long after when he had beaten Holmes and me back to Baker Street to provide us with some additional information regarding a matter we'd just agreed to investigate. And just three years earlier, he and our friend Inspector Lestrade had visited our rooms yet again to set Holmes on the trail of some stolen submarine plans. Seeing Mycroft in Wales was not as surprising as it might have first appeared to those who didn't know better, but I was impressed with the effort that he must have made, certainly arranging for a special train to get him here so quickly.

I glanced at the clock on the mantel, seeing that it was somewhat later than I had expected, nearly ten a.m. I didn't think that I'd given any indication that I was now awake, but I should have known better, for Holmes said, "Watson, Mycroft and the soldiers have already been out to the church. There is no sign of Adămuş or his flock."

I realized that my breathing must have changed, alerting them to the fact that I was awake and listening. Mycroft continued, "Nor was there any indication of Byrnam's son. It seems that they have been spooked, and escaped through a set of ancient smuggler's tunnels leading out of the church's basement to boats they had concealed in caves at the base of the cliffs."

I cleared my throat, realizing that I was now in the full throes of my illness. Before I could speak, Mycroft continued. "Byrnam mean to sell the diary at Major Everless's estate to the north, but he took a wrong turning. We've had our eye in this direction for quite a while, but it's fortunate that Everless never got a look at Lord -----'s notes."

Mycroft's comments were interesting, but they didn't seem to matter. In fact, at that moment, none of the previous evening seemed real at all. I felt that I was awakening from some kind of vague rolling nightmare, and that in a moment I would roll over and go back to sleep, slipping into another story.

I heard Holmes explaining to Mycroft something about that I was sicker than he'd thought, and the response about it being obvious, and then I fell back to sleep.

Later that day, Holmes bundled me back to London, on the same train with Mycroft, Byrnam, and a small contingent of soldiers. I slept the entire way, and when we were back at our rooms in Baker Street, I went upstairs and crawled into bed. Mrs. Hudson looked concerned as I passed, but I assured her that things simply had to take their course. And they did – by the next morning, I was a great deal better.

I bathed and shaved, and then came downstairs, pausing to indicate that I was ready for a light breakfast. Then I entered the sitting room to find Holmes smoking his pipe in his chair before the fire, the morning light from the window at his back.

I nodded toward him, and within minutes Mrs. Hudson arrived with fresh provisions, including some much-welcomed hot coffee. Holmes's plate, abandoned on the table from where he'd already eaten, was essentially clean, and as Mrs. Hudson gathered it, I could see that she was pleased. As she departed, I finished the last of my eggs and, taking my coffee cup, moved to sit across from Holmes.

"What have you learned?" I asked. Of course he knew to what I referred.

"Not much," he replied. "Mycroft has traced Adămuş' people back to the location he named in Transylvania – it seems they felt no need to hide their origins when they arrived in England earlier this year. Mycroft's agents are thin on the ground in that part of the world, but he promises to have someone ask some questions at the earliest opportunity – whether their feasts and celebrations were the reason that they had to depart."

I nodded, thinking it likely. I doubted that I could eat boiled pork for a long time to come. "And so they came to England? How curious."

"I suppose so. One would think that they could find better places to hide if they had headed east – although rural Wales does have certain spots where one might left alone. In any case, one wonders where they will turn up next."

"I hope that Mycroft is keeping an eye out for that as well. These people are a menace to civilized society." I took a sip of coffee. "How is Byrnam?"

"Recovering. Grief-stricken at the loss of his son."

"One must assume that Geoffrey Byrnam *is* lost," I agreed. "Like poor Bradfield."

I pictured the women and their platters and the boiled flesh, and the silent and white-fingered hungry greed of the seated men.

"Indeed." Holmes reached toward the small octagonal table beside his chair, brought with him from when he'd lived in Montague Street, the relic of some long-ago case. Picking up the crucifix and broken chain that rested there, he held them up in the morning light, studying the object as it twirled back and forth. "It was just the merest chance that Adămuş chose to wear this after Bradfield forfeit possession. I saw that the broken piece met the description which I'd been given, and knowing that Cig was Bradfield's destination, it was easy to connect the pieces."

"Cig," I said. "What does that mean?"

"It seems that the original name of the village, before it was abandoned, was *Pen Clogwyn*, roughly 'Cliff-top'. Cig, I've learned, is the name that the locals gave the place after Adămuş' people arrived. I'm told that it means 'meat'.

I found myself suddenly rather queasy, thinking of poor Bradfield, and how he'd somehow stumbled upon knowledge of these people, only to go there and become the focus of their latest celebration. And then Geoffrey Byrnam, who hadn't wanted to leave . . . .

"I wish that Bradfield could have some sort of justice," I said softly. "These . . . these *cannibals* must be stopped."

"Ah, Watson. Data – we need data. You are making an assumption without full proof."

"But . . . Adămuş all but confirmed it! He *flaunted* it! I wasn't so ill yet that I imagined that."

"Oh, make no mistake. I agree with you, proof or no proof. And considering where they come from, and the stories that are told in hushed whispers about those from *Cetatea Poenari* in that remote are of the Carpathians, the possibilities are probably very much worse. I truly regret that they have been allowed to slip away – "

" – to set up shop somewhere else," I finished, adding, "and continue with their abominable practices."

"Ah, but perhaps not for long. You see, Alton Peake's interest has now been aroused – that, and his outrage. He has resources that we don't, and pathways that he can explore to find where in the shadows that people such as these hide and scurry. He will be here in – " He glanced at the clock. " – a quarter-hour, and we shall discuss a plan."

And so we did. Peak did indeed have contacts and channels of information that were unique to his own consultancy, and arrangements were quickly made which eventually led to a satisfactory conclusion – although not without cost. But that is another story. Suffice it to say that, on that day, while I recovered and alternately sipped tea or coffee, or brandy or whisky, Holmes and Peake discussed things for which the world is not yet prepared – and possibly one Dr. John H. Watson isn't either. But

336

I have no choice about it, really, and I suppose that I wouldn't have it any other way.

The Tuefel Murders

11 February, 1891

Dear Holmes,

I hope that this finds you well, and that your investigation is proceeding as planned. You've been away from London for at least two days longer than I would have expected. Do not hesitate to let me know if my service revolver and I can provide any assistance, and do not try to accomplish this on your own.

I'm writing this letter and sending it to the agreed-upon address, as the information within is too complex for a telegram. I met Gregson this morning outside Baker Street, as per your wired instructions. He was waiting when I arrived, both of us five minutes early for the arranged appointment. He had a separate unsigned wire from you, giving the message as to what I should seek inside.

He wondered why you simply didn't tell him the name of the man he needed to know, as identified by your current investigation, but I reminded him that there is some very real concern that one of Moriarty's agents is ensconced within Scotland Yard, and by this method – having me be the one to search your rooms for a document, based on a clue sent separately to Gregson that only I would understand – we can keep the actual written name from possibly being seen by the Professor's spy. Although the chance that this could happen is miniscule, Gregson seemed to understand, and passed me what you had wired to him: *W's 1st choice – Birlstone – KJ Ps 109:8*

Although initially obscure, it only took me a moment to understand.

I recalled the Birlstone affair of three years ago, but at first I was rather uncertain as to the rest. I immediately realized that *W* must refer to me – but what first choice had I made in the affair? Then I remembered the coded message that had arrived from Porlock, and our discussion that it must refer to a book – something large and in common use. I had cried out that morning that it must be the Bible. This must be what you meant by my "first choice". At that time, you said no, as there were too many editions of the Bible to think that we would be able to decode the message from the same one used by Porlock.

But you summoned us to Baker Street this morning to meet and find the answer amongst your possessions, so perhaps you meant *your* Bible! (Or so I reasoned – correctly, as it turned out.)

Explaining my thinking so far to Gregson, we entered, using my key. Greeting Mrs. Hudson, we then proceeded upstairs and to the bookcase where you keep various copies of the Bible. But which one?

Then I studied the message more closely. *KJ* – surely the *King James* edition.

Pulling it from the shelf, I flipped to *Psalms*, Chapter 109, Verse 8: *Let his days be few; and let another take his office.* And penciled in your handwriting beside it, as you well knew when we were given this task and directed this way, was the name that you needed to pass along to Gregson: *Dòmhnall Kallstadt* – the man that the press calls *Tuefel*: "The Devil".

We looked at one another in shock. This rich man who had been making such a strong political play for the last couple of years, appealing to the most base and narrow-minded populist instincts of various lower levels of the electorate, was one of Moriarty's tools? And yet, considering the crude way in which he behaved, and how he had quickly gained unexpected influence in spite of so many objections, meant that it was really no surprise after all.

I wonder how many other names are hidden in other books scattered around the sitting room, and what clues you would have used to direct us toward them, should any of those men have turned out to be one of Moriarty's agents. I only hope that, should we use this method again, I'll be able to decode those messages as easily.

Gregson nodded to himself, as if the idea of Kallstadt being the man he was seeking made perfect sense. "I have instructions from Mr. Mycroft Holmes to bring in the man – whomever it ended up being – immediately, and to keep it quiet. Would you accompany me, Doctor?" Of course I said yes, and we set out for Mayfair.

The cab drive was brief, and we each kept to our own thoughts. At the large and rather crudely ostentatious building, we were admitted without delay by the disdainful butler who went up to announce us. After a couple of minutes he returned, now quite flustered, and said that he couldn't get the master to answer. Gregson charged upstairs, followed by the butler, and I made my way as quickly as I could. By the time I reached the top of the steps, Gregson had forced a heavy door and was standing just inside. The butler was turned away, retching.

Inside, sitting at a massive desk, was Dòmhnall Kallstadt – *Tuefel*. The front of his head was caved in, and a heavy and bloodied walking stick had been tossed to the floor beside him. He was pushed up to the desk, as if he had been working on something, but there were no papers before him – the desk was empty. He had apparently been struck down by someone standing directly across and in front of him.

Somehow the man, in spite of the deadly injuries, had managed to write, with his own blood, a message on the desk blotter. It looked like *A440*, along with a symbol, also rather resembling the letter *A*:

$$A440 \; A$$

The investigation has commenced in earnest, but I wanted to place this information before you as soon as possible, to let you know what happened to the man whom you had named as one of Moriarty's agents, and also, at Gregson's request, to seek any guidance that you might provide.

I'll mail this immediately, and look forward to your response.

In haste,

Watson

* * * * *

12 February, 1891

Holmes,

I'm pleased to hear in your last wire that your own investigation has advanced in such a successful manner. I'm also glad that Dòmhnall Kallstadt's murder hasn't caused any appreciable delay in gathering the various threads.

To catch you up on the latest events: Following the discovery of Kallstadt's body yesterday morning, Gregson unleashed the Yard's full resources. While you have certainly been critical in the past of their efforts, in this case Gregson, seemingly having absorbed quite a few of your lessons, insisted that things be done right to the best of their abilities, and he frequently included me in his decisions, as if to confirm, through me, that you would approve.

I was present at Kallstadt's autopsy, and he was in far worse shape than anyone might have suspected. He was obese, of course, and as such his organs were sheathed in fatty deposits, and his heart would surely have given out sooner rather than later. The portion of his brain that hadn't been destroyed by the blow from the walking stick showed signs of damage related to dementia, as well as long-term destruction from syphilis.

The point of mentioning this is that, as you suggested, a man who had received such a destructive blow to the head could not have written the message in blood upon his desk blotter. A further examination of Kallstadt's hands showed that the layer of blood across his right forefinger tip was entirely smooth. I hypothesize that someone held his dead hand, dipped it into blood oozing from his head, and wrote the curious message upon the blotter, repeating the strokes as necessary until it was complete. This person then dipped the finger one last time, possibly intending to fill in a line but, seeing that no more blood was needed to finish the message, let the hand drop. If that last dip of blood had been used to write a final line, then it wouldn't have been so uniformly smooth upon the dead man's fingertip. Kallstadt would have needed multiple strokes of his improvised pen, with multiple dips into his own blood, in order to complete the message, and his brain was too damaged for that. He certainly didn't need to re-ink his finger one last superfluous time before dying.

Having seen Kallstadt's large desk, I also concur with your thoughts that it was too wide for someone to have leaned across from the front and given such a crushing blow with the stick – which proved to belong to the victim. Rather, the killer must have stood beside Kallstadt, on his side of the desk, in order to reach him. Then, Kallstadt was rolled up to the desk, as if to give the impression he was there when struck, and so able to write the message.

Furthermore, only someone whom Kallstadt trusted could have approached him so. All three of his children were in the house that day, while his wife, the former Countess Marya Zaleska, has left the country, having departed for the Continent several weeks ago, apparently for good, in order to return to the village from which she originated. Several of the servants – none of whom would have been trusted to approach Kallstadt behind the desk – confirmed that she was very unhappy and severely mistreated by her husband throughout their marriage, and that the three children, by way of Kallstadt's first late wife, were quite harsh and cruel to her as well.

We held brief interviews with the children, although to call them children is misleading. They are all three around forty years of age – older than their long-gone step-mother! Kallstadt didn't father them until he was in his early thirties. Aaron, the eldest, is a swarthy and unpleasant man who lives a very dissipated lifestyle, although in a different form than that of his dead father. (Kallstadt himself, as you know, is descended from a German who earned his fortune by way of most reprehensible activities, and it's a wonder with his ineptness that he was ever able to achieve any influence or maintain the wealth he inherited.) Aaron often travels, being gone for months at a time on hunting trips into the wilds of the Continent,

341

or even Africa. Rumor has it that it was he who was initially acquainted with the woman who would become his step-mother, and that he met her while hunting wolves near the village where she was born and raised, near the Poenari Citadel not far from Capatineni, the daughter of some minor nobleman of ancient lineage. He brought her back with him to London, whereupon she took up with Dòmhnall Kallstadt, with the eventually fulfilled goal of marriage.

The middle child, Etchison, is something of a dim flame. There is no gossip about him, except that he has never been in trouble because he isn't capable of thinking of any in which to involve himself. He mostly stays at the Kallstadt home in Mayfair, maintaining his "collections", which seem to be made up of uninteresting bits of rock, random animal bones, and stacks of magazines leaning heavily toward feminine illustrations.

The daughter, Idaia, is small and dark, with a vulpine expression that's more obvious when she smiles. It's very insincere, and her teeth are rather small for mouth, so that when she does make any expression, it curiously seems as if they aren't there at all. She is altogether rather cold and calculating, and seemed to carefully consider every question that Gregson put to her, as if examining it from all angles before deigning to answer – and then each of her answers was so vague that one had the sense that it had a double or even triple nuance about it.

None of the children could offer any thoughts as to who killed their father, but none seemed particularly concerned or upset either. And there the matter stood, until the next day – this morning – when your wire arrived, telling us to question Aaron again more closely, as he was implicated by the dying message – although I'm still uncertain as to what gave you that idea.

We returned to the Kallstadt home where the same butler greeted us. When we told him whom we wished to see. He went upstairs the same as yesterday – and then returned in the same harried and upset manner. We followed him up, this time to a different wing of the house, where Gregson and I discovered Aaron's dead body, apparently from suicide.

He was in a chair, and there was a half-empty teacup on the table beside him. The smell of bitter almonds from both the cup and upon his lips gave us the answer as to how he died, and the small bottle of cyanide on the table beside him was simply additional confirmation.

There was a note beside the bottle, written in pen. The paper and ink matched that found in a side-table, and the handwriting is uninformative and without feature – at least to Gregson and me. The message said:

A440: 880 – 988 – 1175 – 698 – 440 – 1175 – 1319 – 1760

342

There was also a little sketch along with it – apparently a piano keyboard with a star drawn on the *A*:

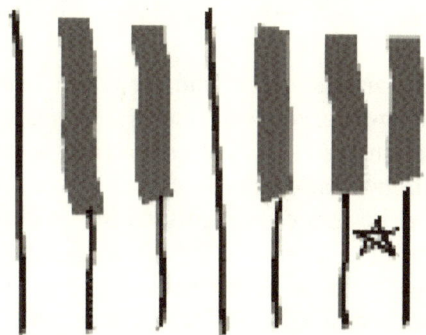

Any hints as to the meaning of the mysterious message, or the keyboard clue, or the multiple references to *A440*, or where to turn next in general, will be much appreciated!

Watson

* * * * *

13 February, 1891

Holmes,

Events are progressing, although I cannot speculate as to whether we go in a positive or negative direction.

Further questioning of the family and staff revealed no indications as to what lay behind Aaron's death. It was obviously supposed to appear as suicide, but there was no note indicating so, and no one can offer a reason as to why he would have done away with himself. If he had killed his own father, there was no obvious suspicion on our part that would have driven him to take that route to avoid punishment, and there is no indication at all that he felt any grief at the death of his father.

One of the servants, a valet named Earnshaw, offered an opinion. The man is sallow, surly, and sly, and having been here about six months, he feels that he's seen enough to "know what's what". Theoretically he divided his time evenly between Aaron and Etchison, but in truth, he explained, work for Aaron was usually the occasional storm of sudden activity when the man would appear after days away from the house, often hung-over and in rough shape, or when he suddenly decided that he was going out and needed to be made ready with no notice whatsoever. Earnshaw said that he mostly spends his time acting as something of an attendant for Etchison, who is rather indifferent to matters of self-care and personal hygiene.

In any case, as Earnshaw is around the house so much, he's picked up on gossip from longer-serving staff that Aaron was especially unhappy with his father following the older man's marriage to Marya – as he was the one who brought her back from whatever little duchy or demesne or exalted domicile that he found and acquired her. However, as useful as that fact might be, it gives a motive for Aaron to kill his father – which you'd hinted at already, based on whatever you perceived in the bloody message on Kallstadt's desk – but it doesn't help at all regarding Aaron's supposed suicide.

In the meantime, I also asked questions regarding the children amongst the various staff per your instructions. During their younger years, the boys were given lessons as might expected in various sporting activities – boxing, fencing, riding, and so on – and Idaia received some of this as well – shooting and riding – along with such training as a lady of her station might expect: Painting, and long-standing *piano-forte* lessons, as supposedly she has quite a bit of musical talent. She had a number of teachers, including one of long-standing named Mueller. (You didn't ask me to follow-up and question him, but I would have, although not knowing what I should seek, except that he is already gone – he returned to his native Vienna last year. I have his address if you need further information.)

Also as requested, I've placed the message that you wired to me in all of the newspapers – *The Globe*, *The Star*, *Pall Mall*, *St. James's*, *Evening News Standard*, *Echo*, and several others that occurred to me. It will run tomorrow. Just to confirm, as I can make nothing of it, this is what I advertised:

> *A440*
> *880 – 698 – 523 –932 –698 –622 –659 –1319*
> *494 –659 –440 –1175 –1319 –554 –1175 –659 –988 –1397 –*
> *1245 –554*
> *1245 –1109 –1397 –440 –1175 –554*

I begin to perceive your thinking, and although I don't know whom to expect, Gregson and I will carry out the rest of your instructions, and follow up with a report as to what we discovered.

Very best,

Watson

* * * * *

15 February, 1891 (2 a.m.)

Holmes,

Events have crowded fast and thick upon us, and I have no doubt that anything I'll relate to you in general will come as a surprise, but perhaps you will appreciate some of the specifics.

Following the instructions in your wire, Gregson came by about ten o'clock and we set out together in his hansom. We paid the cabbie some distance from our destination and then made our way by foot to the southeast corner of Charterhouse Square, which is dark enough that time of night, and with several deep doorways in which to hide in case our prey chose to enter through that narrow lane. Then we settled in to wait. Gregson was confident that his men, many former soldiers and handpicked for their stealth, and scattered in different locations around the Square, would remain equally unseen until our expected visitor arrived.

I'm still uncertain as to how you knew someone would be there at midnight, but it was almost exactly then that we heard footsteps, coming along the very passage where we were concealed. Pressing deeper into the darkness, we watched as a figure went by, moving at a steady pace, in no hurry and with no apparent agitation.

He entered the Square and turned right, up along the eastern side. At that point he stopped under a gaslight, fished out a cigarette, and seemed to wait for something. I was only mildly surprised to see that it was Etchison Kallstadt.

He seemed extraordinarily patient, and I wondered whom or what he might be expecting. After five or ten minutes he tossed aside his spent cigarette, and then he pulled a slip of paper from his pocket. He'd just raised it to his eyes when a single shot rang out, echoing around the Square.

As you know, the central garden there was a plague pit several hundred years ago. As we dashed from our hiding spot, with both Gregson and me drawing our revolvers, I had to wonder if the souls of the dead, tossed into that hole so unceremoniously long ago, were aroused enough to welcome Etchison Kallstadt into the afterlife – for even as we had rushed toward him, ignoring or forgetting the idea that we might be shot as well, I had seen him fall in the way that only dead men drop, and I had observed the single centered bullet hole that had appeared in in his high forehead.

345

There were no other shots, and we were able to examine him without fear of joining him. His eyes were open, and a look of simple surprise was predominant upon his bland features, in spite of the distorting damage done by a high-powered rifle bullet entering the enclosed confines of his skull.

Gregson grabbed the piece of paper that had dropped beside the poor man's hand in the moment of death. It was written in plain block letters, and curiously held the same message that was found with his brother Aaron's corpse just yesterday, and the sketch of the piano keyboard:

A440: 880 – 988 – 1175 – 698 – 440 – 1175 – 1319 – 1760

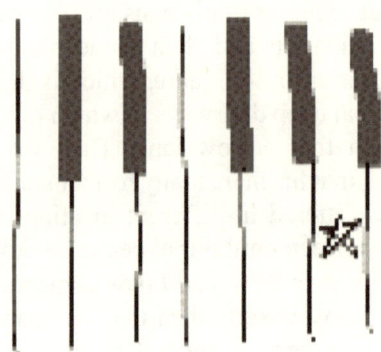

Before I could even ponder what it all might mean, there was the sound of a woman's scream in the northwest side of the square, opposite where Gregson and I had initially hidden. A man cried a warning, another cursed, and then, after another scuffling sound, we perceived the approach of several people. Stepping into the light was Lestrade, holding a cloth to his scowling face, and Constable Abrams firmly grasping Idaia Kallstadt by her thin arm. In Lestrade's other hand was a rifle. "We were too late to stop her," he called.

"You're supposed to keep away from her claws, Lestrade!" crowed Gregson.

Lestrade replied with an epithet that he didn't learn in Sunday School. Then he continued. "She wasn't even careful. She slipped out of the house a couple of hours ago, as Mr. Holmes told us she would, and walked toward Piccadilly before hiring a hansom. Then she came straight here, alighting several blocks to the west. She never even looked to see if she was being followed."

"Typical over-confidence," sneered Gregson.

That seemed to make her angry, but she looked at me instead of the inspector. "Where is he? Where is Holmes?"

I shook my head. "Approaching the problem of your master from another direction. The Professor is going to be unhappy with you tonight."

"Do you think so?" she hissed. "He will not take this without hitting back!"

"Settle yourself, Missy," said Lestrade, checking his handkerchief to see if the bleeding had stopped. I looked him over later, after what happened next, but then wasn't the time. "We've identified the Professor's man at the Yard," Lestrade continued, "so that branch has been pruned!"

I frowned, and Gregson started to chastise Lestrade, realizing that the woman might find some way to pass on this information to the Professor, in spite of our desire to keep it quiet for now.

Idaia Kallstadt gave her dark and peculiar smile, and I mistakenly thought that it was because she'd realized the same thing and planned to let someone know as soon as she could. But she had other intentions. She dipped her free hand into a pocket of her dress and brought it back out, clutching a small brown bottle. Popping the cork with her thumb with one smooth motion, she quickly raised her arm and drank from it before then dashing the bottle against the nearby building. I could smell the scent of almonds from where I stood.

She convulsed almost immediately, but had a little time left to speak.

"I thought that I could serve the Professor's ends and get something for myself too. We knew, through the man at the Yard, that my father was compromised and that it was time for him to die." She closed her eyes as a stab of pain hit, and her legs sagged a bit in the constable's grip, but he didn't let go.

"We were waiting for you to arrest my father. When it was apparent that you and the Inspector were on the way – you were watched in Baker Street – word was sent immediately, and I sprang into action. I killed my father then, just as the Professor demanded, and in addition to taking care of that part of the business, I wrote the coded message in blood that only Sherlock Holmes would understand. It was supposed to lure him there, away from whatever it is that he's doing now, worrying at the Professor's business.

"But it didn't work! He never showed up. So then I killed Aaron, and left another message as bait for Holmes. Still nothing!" She gasped and coughed. "Finally I saw Holmes's reply in the newspapers arranging a meeting here and I knew that he understood. I told Etchison to come here – he didn't know why, but did as I asked. Then I waited for Holmes to show up and find him – but still nothing. So I killed Etchison, certain then that Holmes would step into the light. And yet it was only you, Doctor –

you and these shabby policemen! – who came running. I was going to shoot you next, Doctor, before these men grabbed me. And now – "

Her legs collapsed then, and this time the constable released her. She settled slowly onto her back, foam now collecting on her lips. "The Professor – I failed him. Better to die by my own hand than face what he would have done to keep me from telling his plans . . . ."

Silence enveloped us. As far as I could tell, no one in the surrounding buildings had even bothered to light a lamp or look out a window at the sound of the rifle shot and subsequent disturbance.

There's little left to tell. Gregson blew his whistle, and the other constables who had been scattered around with instructions to man their posts until otherwise told differently, drifted out. The bodies were loaded into a wagon, and we all returned to the Yard, each of us vaguely unsettled, and hoping for explanations sooner rather than later.

I'm at home now, but I'll step out in a moment and mail this, in anticipation at your response and the unlikely expectation that I can sleep. In the meantime, I hope that these events have aided in your own investigation.

Watson

* * * * *

17 February, 1891

Watson,

I write in a moment of rare leisure, courtesy of the Professor, whose attentions were recently turned toward London, allowing me to complete my task unhindered at the last. I appreciated the letters, which I agree contained more detail than could have been included in a telegram. As to this tendency to dress up the matter with unnecessary decoration that would be more suitable to publication in some shabby monthly periodical – well, that's a discussion for another time.

To explain my thinking in the matter which led to the removal of both father and daughter, two of Moriarty's more important pieces from the board, I'll begin at the beginning – or at least *a* beginning. My current research showed that Dòmhnall Kallstadt, that most objectionable individual who had recently begun to spread his poison in a much greater scale by entering politics, was in fact an agent of the Professor – specifically carrying out duties that would aid our foreign enemies. I contrived the method you described of identifying him to the police

348

without sending an obvious and unguarded message by putting the names of various suspected agents in different locations within the sitting room in order to have the police go to you for assistance when each figure was identified and ready to be arrested.

When you discovered Kallstadt's body, the message written in blood was suggestive, but not conclusive. The symbol is actually one of four, those used by alchemists, to describe the basic elements, respectively fire, water, air, and earth:

The symbol for "air" – What could it mean? And beside it, *A440*. That meant more to me as a musician, for it signifies the A above Middle C, vibrating at 440 Hertz, or 440 vibrations-per-second. The French have used *A440* for years as the tuning standard for orchestras, and just a few years ago the Viennese began doing so as well. I recognized that whoever had written this "dying message" was sending some clue with connections to "Air" and music – but I didn't yet know what it signified.

I did suspect from your description that the message was unlikely to have been written by Dòmhnall Kallstadt – *Tuefel* – and that it was an attempt to frame someone. Your observation of the evidence of the blood on his fingertip only confirmed that. While I didn't know what the message meant or whom it was supposed to frame, the only faint indication was that the symbol "*Air*" sounded something like the name of the oldest son, "*Aaron*". Of course, your return to the house at my request showed that he too was murdered – and with another *A440* found beside him, and also a coded message and sketch of a piano keyboard, with the *A* designated for special attention by having a star placed upon it. I suspected that this was placed there in case I'd missed the significance of the initial *A440* written on Dòmhnall Kallstadt's desk. Now with a short message in hand, I then instantly recognized the other numbers in relation to *A440* and was able to decipher the code.

Each of the musical notes in our Western scale of tuning has a specific vibration. The A above Middle C (*A440*) is 440 Hertz, as mentioned. The rest of the letters (beginning with that A above Middle C and progressing upwards in half-steps – A, A-sharp (or B-flat), B, C, and so on – vibrate-per-second as follows in this table, which also shows a corresponding letter from A to Z across the alphabet:

A_4:	440	A
$A\#_4/Bb_4$:	466	B
B_4:	494	C
C_5:	523	D
$C\#_5/Db_5$:	554	E
D_5:	587	F
$D\#_5/Eb_5$:	622	G
E_5:	659	H
F_5:	698	I
$F\#_5/Gb_5$:	740	J
G_5:	784	K
$G\#_5/Ab_5$:	831	L
A_5:	880	M
$A\#_5/Bb_5$:	932	N
B_5:	988	O
C_6:	1047	P
$C\#_6/Db_6$:	1109	Q
D_6:	1175	R
$D\#_6/Eb_6$:	1245	S
E_6:	1319	T
F_6:	1397	U
$F\#_6/Gb_6$:	1480	V
G_6:	1568	W
$G\#_6/Ab_6$:	1661	X
A_6:	1760	Y
$A\#_6/Bb_6$:	1865	Z

The killer knew about these numerical tone designations – indicating a training in music, likely by someone French or Viennese who understands that convention – and also knew that I would be able to recognize the message. Thus, it was easy enough to take the message found with dead Aaron's body – *A440: 880 – 988 – 1175 – 698 – 440 – 1175 – 1319 – 1760* – and assign the numbers to corresponding letters, revealing that it said *Moriarty.* What better way to capture my interest? I sensed a trap, designed specifically for me.

I was certain that this whole scheme – while removing Dòmhnall Kallstadt from the board before we could question him – was also contrived to lure me away from my main attack upon the Professor. To let them know that I understood and was supposedly fooled, I had you put a similarly coded response in the newspapers:

A440
880 – 698 – 523 –932 –698 –622 –659 –1319
494 –659 –440 –1175 –1319 –554 –1175 –659 –988 –1397 –
   1245 –554
1245 –1109 –1397 –440 –1175 –554

Decoded, it reads *A440 Midnight Charterhouse Square*. That's how I knew to send you and the police there – not from something that I'd learned about the killer, but because I myself had lured the killer to that location. I already suspected that Idaia Kallstadt was the murderer, based on your information that she'd had the musical training necessary to think along the lines of contriving the musical code. I confess that I thought that she expected to arrive and find me waiting there – and then to possibly attempt to exert her noted feminine wiles before killing me – but I didn't expect that she'd send in her brother Etchison as a goat, holding a coded message reading *Moriarty* in his hand, and then – when I didn't immediately charge out to confront him – shoot the poor fellow in cold blood as a brutal attempt to force me out of hiding where she could also shoot me as I bent over his body.

Hearing that she also planned to do the same to you within a few moments – Well, Watson, I can only express my relief that Lestrade bravely stopped her beforehand, and once again apologize for putting you in such a position.

It's my understanding (by way of Mycroft, who keeps an eye on these things) that Marya Kallstadt *née* Zaleska is already returning to London, where she expects to take control of the family fortune as the last surviving heir. I can assure you that close eyes will be upon her – and the unborn child that she carries, rumored to be Aaron's instead of Dòmhnall's – to make sure that those resources aren't quickly funneled into the Professor's coffers.

I'm happy to report that, with my work now finished for this part of the investigation, I've seriously inconvenienced the Professor, and I'm eventually off to France – Narbonne to be specific. I hope that, as the nets are better fixed and this business resolves, that I can finally put the problem of Professor Moriarty behind me, possibly in just a couple of months.

In the meantime, I congratulate you on handling the matter most capably, and I wish both you and Mary the very best

Holmes

The Unpleasant Affair
in Clipstone Street

With each passing year, I'm able to look back and see connections that would have escaped me while in the midst of events. When I assisted my friend Sherlock Holmes on his notable investigations, it was only by way of his explanations – through his awareness of the bigger picture – that I was usually able to keep up with what was happening. In addition to his notable gift of being able to observe what others only saw, he had also cultivated a rare collection of friends and associates, and sometimes even enemies, who had either been able to instruct him in his youth as he prepared for his most unique profession, or to provide an important fact here or there in the course of an inquiry. His cases, and the individuals associated with them, formed threads in something of a "Great Tapestry". Some were self-contained and tied off neatly, while others twisted throughout the overall design, initially appearing for a moment, calling for attention before being subsumed back into the greater pattern, only to reappear quite far away – sometimes with no more than a quick bow or passing appearance, and others with much more serious and even tragic results . . . .

Our return journey from Ewelme had been something between quite tedious and rather unpleasant, first by way of an open carriage ride through the cold October mist, and then on a series of local trains. It could have been worse, I supposed, as we just made it into a small station in time to catch the departing train for the last leg into London. Holmes wouldn't have been happy to tarry any longer than necessary while waiting for the next train to arrive.

A couple of days before, a terse wire from one of his old school chums had resulted in Holmes's journey from Sussex up to London, where I joined him, before we continued together to that normally lovely part of Oxfordshire. The discovery of a hoard of Roman coins had resulted in an assault – a mysterious robed figure had violently stolen the collection and fled to Didcot. Holmes had initially been intrigued, but after reaching his solution following an examination of a nearby chalk pit and then a short interview with the wife of the man who managed the local almshouses, the culprit was quickly revealed, with the solution tawdry and seamy and embarrassing all at once. All told, Holmes's investigation, carried out with his typical skill, insight, and efficiency, had been remunerative and reputation-enhancing – none of which he needed at that age.

Because of the initial description of that problem, I had expected that we would be gone longer. Instead, it almost seemed that we had spent more time traveling there than what was required for the actual investigation. I wouldn't have minded rusticating in the countryside for a day or so, in spite of the autumn weather, but I could see that Holmes was only interested in leaving as fast as possible. It was only as we were stepping out of the inn where we had retrieved our bags that the local constable had stopped us, announcing that the thief had just been murdered – poisoned in his cell – and the cache of coins taken once again. I think that the solution, when it came, surprised even Holmes, and had left us both in a bitter mood – me with the realization that I'd never be able to share the truth of this adventure, and Holmes with a vast disappointment in his old school friend.

Upon our return to the capital, Holmes, having packed for several days, agreed with my invitation to stay at my Queen Anne Street home. Although my housekeeper was surprised to see us, as I had given the impression that we might be gone for a while, she was able to pull together a rather fine evening meal. Holmes was quiet for much of the evening, and soon after we ate he said good night and retired to his room, carrying with him a borrowed volume relating the history of the Romans in Britain. I read for a while before closing my own book, a recently published narrative regarding our friend Poirot's investigation concerning a murder on *Le Train Bleu* which had occurred the previous year. I turned down the gas and then made my way upstairs. As I grew older, I found that it was too easy to stay up late every night.

Back in the days when Holmes and I had shared lodgings in Baker Street, it was normal that he would receive unexpected visitors at all hours. I cannot count the dramatic entrances that ranged from the simply intriguing to the truly threatening, the initially innocent to the most portentous. Much less frequent were those occasions when a caller sought my assistance in some matter.

Thus, it was still a surprise, even after all those years that I'd been living in Queen Anne Street – twenty-six years by then, and several years longer than I'd spent in Baker Street – when a pounding at the street door sometime in the night resulted in the housekeeper being knocked up, causing her to climb the stairs to my room.

I'd already been awakened by the noise at the door and had glanced at my clock with a groan to determine that the hour had just reached six, meaning that I'd at least had more hours of sleep than I'd thought. For some reason in my half-wakened state, I'd expected that the housekeeper would stop at Holmes's bedroom, assuming that this was some sort of request for his attention. Even if that were the case, I would also soon be up and involved, regardless of the reason, but I certainly didn't anticipate that I would be requested first, or what followed afterwards.

With a solid knock upon my own door, I was informed that there was a man downstairs who wished for me to go with him, requiring my services as a doctor. I acknowledged this with something that resembled words. Raising my eyebrows to the empty room, I threw back the covers and looked out of my bedroom window. From that vantage, I could see that some of the neighbors were also already up, as evidenced by faint light thrown from their various windows. It was just enough to illuminate the ice that delicately limned the branches of the plane tree that grew in the bare little yard behind my house. An unseasonable plunge in the temperature had created a freezing mist, coating the surface with a thin rime of ice that resembled fairy tracery.

I could feel the cold through the glass, and the idea of going out was quite unpleasant. Still, I felt the obligation of my profession resting upon me and, having quickly made myself ready, I descended, stopping only to retrieve my medical bag. There was no sign of Holmes, so apparently he had wisely remained asleep. I continued on to the front door, where I found a tall man anxiously awaiting me, his hand on the door knob as if he were ready to bolt at the second of my arrival. "Doctor," he said, with a rather high-pitched whisper. "We need your help."

"Certainly. What's the problem?"

"It's our daughter, sir. She's taken sick in the night."

I had pulled on my coat during this short conversation and then reached for my hat and stick. Gesturing that he proceed me, I asked, "How old is she?"

I turned back to lock the door while he replied. "She'll be seven early next year

There was no sign of a waiting conveyance, leading me to understand that my caller was from the local neighborhood. We set off down the street, stepping carefully along the slick pavement. "What are her symptoms?"

He described a fairly common set of gastronomical complaints that had been spreading throughout the city for a few weeks. His wording was rather vague, in the way that some laymen use when describing the less pleasant aspects of an ill human body. In the case of his daughter, it sounded as if her condition might be a bit more severe than normal and that she could be dehydrated, and I indicated that he was wise to have sought my help.

Along the way, he introduced himself as Tom Birch. I could see that he looked to be around thirty years of age. He informed me that he and his

354

wife were caretakers at the house of a Mrs. Waltham, recently deceased. Birch's father had been one of the old woman's servants years earlier, when the lady's husband was still alive and the household had been much more vital. More recently, she'd spent her widowhood living quietly with only Birch and his wife Ivy to care for her. The Birch family consisted of just the father, mother, and one daughter, and they had their own apartment in the lower level of the house. When the old lady had died a month or so earlier, her attorney had asked Birch and his wife to stay on and look after the place until the estate could be settled, as there was some difficult in locating the heirs.

We walked farther than I would have expected, and it crossed my mind that in that neighborhood there were certainly other doctors much closer to where the Birch family lived. Why did he seek me out? I asked myself, but I kept those thoughts to myself. We hurried along Cavendish Street, and then for a short time north by way of Great Titchfield Street to Clipstone Street, where Birch led me into a mews, and so around to a set of steps leading down into the lower levels of one of the buildings that we had just passed. At the bottom was a solid-looking door with a small window at eye level, obscured by a curtain. The door was standing ajar. "That's not right," Birch muttered, pushing his way in. I followed.

Almost immediately we were in a little hallway, quite dark. There was a damp smell, as if laundry had been done recently and floors had been mopped. I sensed that my guide was moving deeper into the building, and I tentatively followed. Beyond him, I heard a door open, and then a light appeared ahead and to our right. Birch came to a sudden stop, and I barely avoided running into him. I was unable to see past him, but I heard a woman's voice. "Tom," she said. "He took her!"

Birch sagged and leaned a shoulder against the wall, allowing me to see beyond him. The hallway had several closed doors, and thus my eyes were drawn to the source of the light, a doorway that opened into what appeared – from my narrow view – to be a sitting room and kitchen. It was dimly lit, but I could see that there was very little taking up the space – not much furniture, and counter-tops that held only a few basic implements – a teapot and a few cups.

A woman was standing just outside the door, highlighted by the lamplight from within room. Setting down my bag, I laid a hand on Birch's shoulder, steadying his frame, and then stepping around him to face the woman.

"Mrs. Birch?" I said. "My name is Dr. Watson. Who has been taken? Your daughter?"

In the weak light I could see that she seemed to be around the same age as her husband – assuming that this was, in fact, Mrs. Birch. However, she seemed to acknowledge my statement, as she nodded. "Her name is Erin."

"And who took her?"

Her features tightened as she seemed to be trying not to cry. She covered her face and turned away. Apparently she had kept herself strong long enough for her husband to return, but now whatever had happened was overwhelming her. I sensed Tom Birch step up behind me. "Michael Whaley," he said. "It must be him – I don't know who else it could be."

The name sounded vaguely familiar, although I couldn't place him. Time enough to think of that later. I looked from one of them to the other, each showing a marked level of fear. "She has been kidnapped?" I clarified.

Birch nodded. "It seems so."

"But why?" I asked. "It sounds as if you know this man. What could he hope to accomplish?"

Birch looked at me. "You don't know Michael?" He ran a hand over his face and shut his eyes for a long moment. I shook my head, declining to explain that the name had triggered some vague sense of awareness. Then Birch continued. "It would be best, Doctor, for us to summon your friend, Mr. Holmes. We can explain it then."

"You know Holmes?"

"In a sense. Can you send him a message? Asking him to come up from Sussex?"

I considered arguing with him first. I wanted to press him for details, if only to satisfy my own curiosity. A part of me nearly said that we should summon a constable immediately, but I had known Holmes long enough by that point to realize that no one would be better able to help these people than my friend.

"There's no need for that," I said, and Birch immediately frowned, but I raised a placating hand. "He's in London now – staying with me. Are you on the telephone?" Birch looked toward his wife, who lowered her hands and shook her head sadly, so I added, "I'll go and fetch him immediately."

Mrs. Birch shook her head. "Please, no, Doctor. Stay. You've long been associated with Mr. Holmes – perhaps you can think of something while we wait for him to arrive."

"I can deliver a note," added her husband, eagerly. "It won't take long at all."

I could think of better alternatives, but I frowned and nodded.

After urging them to move into the room with the light, I followed and saw that it was indeed a combination sitting room and kitchen, with chairs and a sofa placed in the area behind the door, and a dining table

356

closer to the utilitarian countertop. There were unlit gaslight brackets set over the fireplace, and the room was instead illuminated by a lantern sitting on the table and a cheery little coal fire in the grate, its mood contrasting the tragedy that I had just entered. I could see that the room would always be rather dark, being mostly below ground level, with only a couple of small windows high on a far wall over the kitchen area. Near the door where we'd had entered were another couple of doors that opened into darkened chambers that appeared to be bedrooms.

I stepped to the kitchen counter, where I set my bag. I glanced around the room while I searched through it for one of the pads that I always carried, and then wrote a quick note, choosing my words carefully and succinctly. As I wrote, it occurred to me to see if there was a possible alternative to sending the message with Birch. When I finished, I turned and, to their surprise, told them that I'd be back in just a moment. I returned to the mews and walked briskly back out to Clipstone Street, lined on all sides by grim brick buildings, and where it was only slightly less dark than the Birch's doorway. The icy mist hung in the air without a hint of breeze, and I gave a shiver as it slipped between my neck and scarf. My breath formed and hung in the freezing air before me as stood on the street, looking left and right.

If there had been one of the pay telephones somewhere on the street, I would have called Queen Anne Street, but as expected, there wasn't, and I didn't know how far I'd have to walk before spotting one. Instead I was looking for a certain type of person – although the likelihood of finding such a one at that hour was uncertain at best. It had been years since Holmes had made use of those lads and lasses that he called his Baker Street Irregulars – and yet I didn't see why I couldn't do something similar. It had been nearly ten years since the war ended, and London had changed incredibly in that time, but one still occasionally saw those same rootless children of the type that Holmes had first started recruiting in the 1870's, when he'd lived in Montague Street and had decided to become a consulting detective. All of those original assistants had long since grown to adulthood and were now approaching old age. Even some of their children had served as Holmes's next generation of Irregulars before he left London in 1903. Yet, long after that he'd still made use of them, as his "retirement" was a rather misleading term, and he continued to carry out investigations regularly in those years leading to the war. But after the peace had been signed, he truly had retired, taking only occasional cases, such as the one that had led us to Ewelme the day before.

There was no one to be seen, and I kept walking, turning into Great Titchfield Street and thinking that this might not be the neighborhood or time of night to spot a potential messenger. I could very well end up going

357

as far as Queen Anne Street and fetching Holmes myself before I was through. Yet I was fortunate that in just a moment, I saw a boy of ten or twelve looking cautiously toward me from out of one the small alleys to the west. I raised an arm and approached this early-riser (or possible night owl) slowly, with the wry feeling that I was doing so in the same slow manner that one uses when trying to gain the trust of a stray dog. The boy made no move to turn away, and listened intelligently as I explained what I needed – without mentioning Holmes's name. I didn't know if he would recognize it, but if he did, I didn't have time to convince him that Holmes would truly be the recipient of the message.

I dropped the note and a coin in the boy's hands and sent him on his way, confident that it would be in my housekeeper's possession in mere minutes, and then into Holmes's hands soon after. Then I made my way back to the Birch house and through the mews, down the steps, and to the entryway. Once my eyes had readjusted to the darkness, I took a moment to look at the heavy door, but there was no sign of forced entry. Inside the dim apartment, I found Birch and his wife sitting at the table, heads leaned toward one another. Mrs. Birch had been whispering, but she stopped when I entered the room. I had the sudden sense that she seemed uncertain as to what could be said in front of me.

"Did you send the message?" asked her husband.

"I did. I found a lad to deliver it."

"I could have taken it," he continued, almost sullenly. Mrs. Birch laid a hand on his arm.

"Better that you stay here with your wife," I said. "Holmes should be here shortly. While we wait, Mrs. Birch, can you tell me what happened?"

She closed her eyes, and Birch spoke instead. "We should . . . we should wait for Mr. Holmes, I think. And just tell it once. No offense intended, Doctor."

I nodded, with none taken. There was silence for a moment, and I listened to the great house stacked above us, but heard nothing. Only the crackle of the coal in the fireplace broke the otherwise absolute silence. Even noises from the street were non-existent – not surprising at this hour, and on such a quiet byway.

I tried to see what I could by observing my hosts, but the light didn't reveal much more than what I already knew – a couple around thirty years of age, he rather brawny, and she petite and blonde. Her hair would probably have an almost-white cast in bright light – not the gray of premature old age, but rather that of platinum, with a shine that would definitely attract second glances. Her face was set in a frown – no surprise for someone involved in such a matter, but I could tell that such an expression came naturally to her, and wasn't simply caused by the current tragic events.

"May I see your daughter's room?" I asked abruptly.

"Why?" asked Mrs. Birch sharply, as if yanked back from wherever her thoughts had led her.

"To get a sense of her. When Holmes and I find her, she may need to trust us immediately. Knowing something of her likes and dislikes – a favorite doll, perhaps – may help win her over." It sounded feeble saying it aloud, but the woman nodded, took her hand from her husband's arm, and rose, leading me to one of the side doors after lifting the lantern from the table.

"Would you mind lighting the gas?" I asked Birch as I turned to follow. "For when Mr. Holmes arrives?"

Birch shook his head. "We generally do without. Ivy gets headaches from it."

I let that statement stand, considering whether to request that they light another lantern, but not wanting to disrupt what was happening, and wondering why the strong kerosene smell that currently hung about the lantern didn't also cause headaches. Mrs. Birch held the lantern just across the threshold to the bedroom, allowing me to see inside just a bit, but also blocking my way. When I made to move past her, she said, "I've heard of Mr. Holmes and his methods. Perhaps we should wait for him to go in – to see if there's any kind of clue. After all, Michael went in there in order to take Erin."

I hadn't been told that fact, but I nodded, although not necessarily agreeing with her reasoning. I could see a rumpled bed and some clothing on the floor nearby. The rest of the room was in darkness. I stepped back, and then Mrs. Birch reached around me and pulled the door solidly shut.

We returned to the table. I surreptitiously observed Mrs. Birch to adjudicate the state of her nerves, deciding that no offer of a sedative was required. They were both tense, but Tom Birch seemed to have turned inward, while his wife exhibited a brittleness that would bear watching. The silence between us grew, and I found myself quite curious about Birch's apparent knowledge of Holmes, and wondered again where I'd heard of Michael Whaley. I tried several times to recall something about him, but it wouldn't come to me.

There were any number of questions that I wanted to ask, but each seemed as if it would quickly lead back to whatever it was something that should best be told to Holmes first. Finally, however, I thought to quiz them more about the arrangements of the household.

"How long did you serve Mrs. Waltham?"

Birch's eyes took on a grateful look, as if this topic could help fill the awkward silence, and he had an answer to this question. As he spoke, his wife began to twist a handkerchief in her hands.

"About seven years," said Birch. "My father was her driver long ago, and my mother her companion upstairs. I grew up here – in these very rooms. Thirteen years ago – back in 1915 – Mr. Waltham passed suddenly. A terrible stroke they said it was, and the life seemed to go out of his wife. She released all of the servants and became a hermit. After that, my parents left to find another position – although they weren't nearly as happy as when they'd lived here. They were both killed nine years ago, in a rail accident.

"I was seventeen in 1915 when Mr. Waltham died, and long gone by then – serving in France. Lied about my age. After I came back, I found work at a hotel in Upper George Street. That's where Ivy and I met, a couple of years later when she started there as a maid." He reached over and squeezed the back of his wife's hand. She raised her eyes to his, but then looked away once again.

"Not long after, I heard from a grocer friend that Mrs. Waltham was in sad shape, living here like a hermit. I went to check on her, and found that it was worse than I'd heard. Her husband's death had fairly broken her. I started to look in more often, and doing little odd jobs around the place when I had time – repairing leaks, and cleaning the place where I could. It wasn't long before she perked up and offered me a position as caretaker, for lack of anything better to call it. With this opportunity, Ivy and I had a chance to marry, and then Erin came along."

"And you've lived here since then," I asked, and then, with possibly with less tact than I should have shown, I added "Below stairs, while Mrs. Waltham occupied all the floors above, alone?"

Birch looked at me without comment, and his wife replied for him. "She offered to let us have rooms upstairs, but we . . . we didn't want to be seen to be taking advantage." She glanced at her husband. "And this was where Tom was raised – here in the servants' quarters. It seemed right to stay down here."

"After she died," continued her husband, "her lawyer asked if we could stay on until things were settled. He didn't want the place standing empty, and he believes that it will be quite a bit of time before he can locate an heir. There were no children, you see . . . ."

His voice drifted off, and I felt as if I should do more to keep the conversation moving forward, but the awkward silence returned, and every question that occurred to me related to the couple's missing child and the involvement of the mysterious Michael Whaley. Mrs. Birch rose and made some tea, which we all drank in silence. I considered how long it would take for Holmes to receive my message, and then cross the distance from Queen Anne Street to Clipstone Street. Not long – assuming that I had chosen wisely when hiring my unknown messenger. Fortunately, it was only a few more uncomfortable moments before we heard the outside door open, and then footsteps along the dark corridor, stopping outside the living quarters where we waited. My directions had led my friend to this place. What would happen next?

Birch stood. "Mr. Holmes?" he said, as a tall thin shadow appeared in the doorway. Even as Birch spoke, his wife stood and pushed past him.

"It's Michael Whaley," she breathed. "He took our daughter."

Holmes stepped into the dim light, his face was grim, his mouth a tight straight line, and a deep *V* between his brows. He walked closer, nodded to Mrs. Birch, and pulled out a chair. He sat on the edge, leaning forward, concentrating intently – so different from how he sometimes listened to a client's story during those long-ago days in our Baker Street sitting room, where he would settle back with his eyes closed, fully engaged but seeing everything play out within his mind. He motioned and the couple sat back down. "Are you certain that it was him?" he asked.

Both nodded, and Mrs. Birch hurriedly said, "Not long after Tom went to fetch the doctor, I heard a noise at the door. It seemed too soon for him to have gone to Queen Anne Street and back, so I thought that he might have forgotten something. But it wasn't Tom – it was Michael. I gave a little cry, and he took a step toward me. I feared what he might do, but then Erin coughed in the other room. He stopped and smiled, and then turned that way. I knew then what he was going to do, and I ran at him, but he pushed me away, and before I could get up, he was back with her, bundled in his arms. She didn't wake up – she's feeling too poorly, I suppose. He told me to remain quiet, or that he would hurt her. How could he threaten that? A child – ? He . . . he left then, and . . . and I didn't know what to do. I just stood there, wanting to move, and yet afraid that I might anger him, or that he would hurt her if I chased him and he started to run, and maybe tripped and fell on top of her. And I needed to tell Tom, but . . . .." She broke off and put the twisted handkerchief up to her eyes.

Her husband spoke. "He must have been watching, and he must have known when I stepped out." He leaned forward. "What can we do?"

His tone implied that since Holmes had now arrived, all would be well. In truth, in the years that I've known Sherlock Holmes, I've seen that he is one of the most capable people that I've ever met. And yet, I knew that in spite of his many gifts and abilities, both naturally occurring and rigorously trained, he was capable of failure. I recalled the times that we had been asked to find a taken child – instances that sometimes ended in tragedy, such as the affair of the Salisbury bug-hole, and also in the much grimmer Amersham Substitution. Yet there had been triumphs as well – for instance, the shocking revelations concerning the Dunblane Bodach came to mind. But from what I had already seen, this matter was quite different.

Holmes looked at Birch. "I remember you from the old days, Tom. How did you know Michael?"

The man started to speak, apparently surprised, but found himself at a loss for words. It was his wife who answered.

"I was the one who knew Michael. During the war. Later, he would sometimes . . . he would come around to see me – after Tom and I married. He – " She looked at her husband. "He insisted that Erin was his child."

I glanced at Tom Birch, but he showed no reaction, keeping his eyes forward and onto the tabletop.

I thought that Holmes might ask her if it was true – such delicate subjects had never prevented him from doing so before, and any knowledge about the motivations of this Whaley fellow would certainly be welcome. Yet even as I pondered this, Holmes appeared to have already heard enough. Perhaps my short note had given him enough perspective before he even arrived.

He rose abruptly, causing Mrs. Birch to give a slight and surprised gasp. Then he set about examining the room, crossing this way and that, but without bothering to bend over, or drop to his knees and crawl, as he had done so often in the past. Then he returned to the table and took the lantern, expanding his investigation into Erin's bedroom. Mrs. Birch rose then, as if she meant to join him, but I raised a hand. I thought that she might argue the point – an angry look flashed across her face – but then she held her place.

I stood then and I moved over to the other side of the room, near the fireplace, as if to stay out of Holmes's way. Except for Holmes's own movements, there was silence.

Without comment, Holmes reappeared out of the girl's bedroom and then abruptly opened the door to the hallway. He paused for a few seconds as if listening, and then took the lantern with him, leaving us in darkness only opposed by the dim light from the windows and the red glow from the fireplace. I tried to imagine a child being raised in such a dark chamber. Birch said that he'd been brought up here, but somehow it seemed worse to imagine a young girl in these circumstances.

From my position somewhat behind the door, I couldn't see Holmes's actions, but I could tell by the movement of the lantern light that he'd turned away from the outside door and deeper into the basement. He was only gone for a moment or two in that direction before swiftly walking back down the hall and then outside. He was gone longer before returning,

362

and during that time, none of us that dark room spoke. However, I could sense some sort of tension arising between the couple, as if Mrs. Birch wished for her husband to do something. Yet he simply stood, pondering his own thoughts and looking toward the floor. Finally Holmes returned, leaving the door to the hallway open and replacing the lantern on the table. Everyone remained standing.

Holmes was shaking his head. "I found where he stood outside, watching this house." The Birch's glanced at one another, seemingly surprised. "The signs indicate that he was out there for several hours – likely since sunset. There's no indication of where the trail leads when he and your daughter departed. We cannot trace him physically, but instead will rely on what we can learn of his associates and habits." He took a step closer, his expression most sincere. "We will find your child."

Birch cleared his throat and asked, "How can I help? Shall I go with you?" His wife turned her head sharply toward him and frowned.

"No. Stay here. Await any messages that Matthew might send. I'll locate someone to remain nearby so that you can send word if you hear something." He glanced at the distraught mother, and then looked at me. "Watson, I'll need your help."

"Of course." I stood and, with a nod to the Birchs, walked over to the counter to retrieve my bag and then quickly followed Holmes outside. He led me briskly back along Clipstone Street, seemingly heading toward my home and practice. He was silent and set a pace that would have made conversation difficult, even if he was in the mood. I glanced from side to side, wondering if anyone was observing us. However, even though the first hint of false dawn was showing in the east, the icy mist perhaps a bit more pervasive, and there was no one visible on the street besides the two of us. We had just rounded the corner when he suddenly paused. "Slip back and watch the entrance to the mews," he said softly. "See if anyone enters or leaves." He reached for my bag. "I'll hold this for you. I'm going to use the telephone at the synagogue in Great Portland Street." He smiled. "I wonder if Rabbi Liebman still arrives with the sunrise."

I made my way back to where I could watch the entrance to the mews from an areaway across the street, hoping that no one had slipped in or out during the short time we were away. I stood there for ten or fifteen minutes, aware at some point that the occupants of the house behind me seemed to be waking up, and wondering what I would tell them should I be asked why I was trespassing ever so slightly upon their property. My concern was negated when I saw a man in a suit walk into the block and slip into a similar hiding place a few doors closer to the old house where we had interviewed Mr. and Mrs. Birch. At that point, I heard a distinct whistle.

Recognizing it as one of the long-established ways that Holmes and I communicated, I left my hiding place and joined him in the next street.

He handed back my bag and told me that the old rabbi had been glad to let him in, and sent greetings to me as well. I knew that the old man was fond both of us – Holmes more than me, for I had only untied the rabbi after Holmes discovered his whereabouts once long ago, while my friend had been responsible for taking down two of the captors to my one in the brawl beforehand.

We had to walk to Cavendish Square before finding a cab at that time of morning, pausing along the way to drop off my bag in Queen Anne Street. When we were settled inside, Holmes directed the driver to take us to an address in Chelsea.

"Latham was at home," Holmes said, referring to a high-ranking government agent with whom we'd worked closely during the war. "He answered himself – no surprise there. It was he who sent the agent to watch the house while we're away."

"I wonder that the Birches let us leave," I said. "Considering the effort to get us both there and into that spider's web."

"They didn't have much choice – neither of us seemed inclined to step together into the trap, and once they had us, they seemed most unwilling to take any additional steps to prevent us from leaving. I suspect that there is more to this than simply luring us into an otherwise abandoned house."

"I wonder what the original plan was. They clearly expected that I was to summon you from Sussex, and that it would have taken hours for you to arrive. They were surprised to hear that you were just a few blocks away – although they took care not to show it."

"I thought that after you summoned me, you might have been locked up when I arrived." He didn't add, "Or worse."

"I thought so too – I even gave them the chance, offering to look in the bedroom – but Mrs. Birch stopped me, saying that you should examine it first for clues."

"If they had locked you in there," said Holmes, " – assuming they didn't knock you unconscious or kill you – then you would have made noise which would have made it harder to incapacitate me, or they would have had to open the door to put me in with you. It was apparently easier to simply wait and trick us both into entering that windowless room – which I doubt ever was actually a bedroom – where they could then slam the door shut and lock it behind us. I appreciated that you didn't join me in there."

"I wonder that they didn't try to force me," I said.

"Perhaps they saw that you're armed."

364

I felt the weight of my service revolver. "I never leave without it."

"Still."

"Always." I shifted in my seat. "I had seen that new lock on the supposed bedroom door," I replied. "On the sitting room side. If there had actually been any signs of a child truly living in that grim basement, then I would have suspected they were cruelly shutting her up in that windowless chamber. When I heard that they wished for you to join us, I began to suspect a trap." I described what I'd found when I'd first arrived at the basement – all the signs that negated the couples' story of truly living there, and how rehearsed and awkward their actions had seemed. I particularly remarked how Birch had almost seemed to expect the news about the kidnapping before he heard it from his wife upon our arrival. "I assume that my note was clear enough?"

"Indeed. Your oblique reference to the Eastcote House matter was more than effective."

When I'd first entered the Birch's chambers, I had been struck how unlivable it appeared. The odor of recently washed clothes and mopping wasn't enough to cover the overall scent of abandonment about the place. And while the sitting room itself was clean enough on the surface, there was evidence in places – the back of the counter, for instance, where I'd stood to write my note – that showed indications of long-accumulated grime. That, and the lack of furniture and other accumulated possessions that one would expect to see, made it quite apparent that these people didn't truly live there, and if they were lying about that, then there were likely other lies as well. In my note, I had requested that Holmes come 'round at once, and to leave a note for Mrs. Eastcote that I would be unavailable. That reference, to a case that had occurred in Wrexham in the early eighties involving both of us being lured into a mine that was ready to collapse, had been enough for him to understand my warning.

"The bedroom – " I said. "Had it ever been occupied by a child?"

"Not at all. The bed had been slept in, but the form doing so was over six feet in height. It's probably where Birch has been sleeping."

"Not with his wife, then? Are they even married?"

"It's likely but unconfirmed. They were comfortable with one another, even if the situation itself was causing them tension. In any case, there was no sign of an actual child having been in that room. A few children's clothes had been piled beside the bed, but there was dust on them, and the same for an old rag doll lying nearby."

"So it was never meant to stand up to a real test," I said. "Just enough to look like a child's bedroom so that we would enter, and then the door would slam shut behind us.

"But I believe that there was some validity to the items, nevertheless," said Holmes. "Several of the pieces of clothing had '*E.B.*' marked inside them, and the name '*Erin*' was written on the bottom of the doll's shoe. The doll itself seemed to have been treated with a bit more respect."

"After they had locked us in – assuming we'd both willingly entered that room – what then? Would they have left us there to starve, on the assumption that we couldn't exit? Were they considering burning down the house around us? Did they plan to let some kind of poison gas under the door to asphyxiate us? Was there someone else in the house – upstairs – waiting to rush in and club us? I listened while we waited, but heard no indications."

"All good questions, Watson. There were a number of footprints that seemed to belong to Birch in the hallway dust, leading in and out of that sitting room and back to a closed door at the rear of the hall. While they were recent, there was no way to ascertain that they were fresh. That closed door was wider than the others on either side of it, and it certainly went upstairs to the main part of the house. I didn't hear anyone waiting on the other side, but just in case, I used one of my picks and quickly locked it before making sure the other rooms nearby were empty – all had been used in the past for storage, but are now long empty." He frowned. "It's likely that no one else was there. If it was assumed that I was still in Sussex – and no one had bothered to ascertain this ahead of time – other people may have meant to be there later when I arrived. Or this may be a little plot that the Birches have cooked up on their own."

"It certainly seemed to surprise them terribly when you came back after your search and announced that someone had been watching the house from outside."

"The merest moonshine. I knew that they feared that I'd walk in and dramatically denounce them – how could anyone not? There was no sign that anyone actually lived there – no clothing, no food. The rest of the basement hadn't even been cleaned. Maybe there wasn't any time to worry about being caught out – I'd arrived too soon, and we didn't cheerfully walk together into the trap.

"I wonder," he continued, "how they would have reacted if I had given away what we'd seen? Denial? More false tears from the lady? Some hastily fabricated alternative? Instead, I agreed with their claims, and elaborated upon them with a tale of a watching man. They must think me a doddering fool."

"I expect not. But you've certainly put them off-balance." I glanced at him. "I take it that you know them?"

"I know Birch – he was an Irregular once, but only for a month or so, when he was in his mid-teens during the war.

"He said that he fought in France."

"I have no reason to doubt it. When he worked for me, it was still early days – late 1914, I think. He didn't do very much, or last very long. You'll recall that there were always some that were like that – Irregulars recruited, never main players on the stage, only to drift away. What else did he tell you?"

I related what the two of them had shared with me sitting around the table. "Some of that may be true," judged Holmes. "The parts about Birch's parents, and Mrs. Waltham's history. He may have even worked for her for a time – but they certainly haven't been living there for years as they said. More likely when this plan was being concocted – whatever it turns out to be – they needed an empty house, and Birch remembered this one from his past association with it."

"And Michael Whaley?" I said. "He must have been an Irregular then, too. The name sounded familiar, but I can't place him."

Holmes pinched his nose as if he had an unpleasant headache, giving me a short biographical *précis* of the fellow in question.

"He was born in 1898 and raised in Lambeth," he said, as if reading from a document that only he could see. "Both his parents were alive, but he had little contact with them, and he was in and out of judiciary detention for various minor offenses throughout his formative years. Yet overall he never caused much trouble. Although I had moved to Sussex by the time he came of age, I still maintained my London network, as it continued to be most useful as I carried out those various tasks requested of me by Mycroft in the days and years leading to the war. Michael was a part of that little informal organization, still functioning in many important ways like the Irregulars of old.

"Having bought the lease to 221 Baker Street from Mrs. Hudson several years before, it was still known as a location where I could be reached if needed. As you know, I stayed there on occasion when I was in London, and it was during some small crisis, that I was introduced to Michael. He was just seven or eight then, and brought to Baker Street by one of the other Irregulars.

"Over the years, he was of some use, and I always found him trustworthy. But there came a time when something changed. I was following up on a little matter for Mycroft, and a few of the Irregulars had been sent to trail after a man named Lyons when he carried a stolen document from London to Reading – simple enough. While he was away, Michael's mother was struck by a carriage and killed in Berners Street. His father had died by then, and his older brother, his only sibling, had run away to sea a year or so before, so there was no one else left to him. He didn't find out about the tragedy until he returned to the city, having first

367

presented himself at one of my hidey holes where I was staying in order to make his report. He left with a few shillings in his pocket for a job well done. But when he arrived home, he learned the terrible news . . . .

"After that, something in him changed. I still used him when I needed that type of help, and he was always one of the brighter lads, asking questions about what I was doing – my methods, and the reasons for this-or-that assignment – but there was now a . . . a slyness about him. A darkness, as if he had acquired just the faintest hints of contempt for those things on the right side of that line that divides and defines legalities. I didn't realize it, but he was already being courted, so to speak, by some within the Kyle Gang. I only learned the truth when he was watching a witness named Cosford at my direction, in order to protect him, and he and his new friends sold Cosford's location to the man who was seeking him. I was able to pull the fat from the fire before Cosford was killed, but I knew then that my trust in Michael was at an end. Of course, withdrawal of my support only served to send him further into the embrace of the gang.

"I followed his progress from a distance, and that of the gang as well, but neither ever amounted to much. The Kyle Gang, still named that even though Kyle himself was killed by falling into a drain in 1909 while running from a dog, have tried to maintain themselves as a separate organization, never subsumed into the bigger organizations that pervade London, but in actuality they've never been anything but foot-soldiers for some of the more successful and better-run groups.

"One would have thought that a lad like Michael would have used his gifts to rise within the gang, providing it with a bit more success than it had over the years, but there was never any sign that he was more than a second-class lieutenant, doing the bidding of others who had no true vision or ambition – or so I thought. As the years passed, in spite of their public ineffectuality, they somehow – suddenly and right under everyone's noses – became the controlling force for a narrowly defined smuggling ring, specializing in certain rather rare French liqueurs. In spite of their sudden success, I still could detect no signs that Michael was adding anything of value to the gang's growing reputation.

"As the war approached, and my time was directed elsewhere, my activities in London diminished greatly. After 1912, when I left for the United States for my extended tour as that rogue 'Altamont', I lost track of a number of people, including Michael. I'll admit to having given him no thought for years, until his name surfaced in connection with a more serious crime. In 1921, he was one of the birds who slipped away following the Rothsay Street raid in Bermondsey, in which a great haul of smuggled goods was recovered. You'll recall that I was consulted regarding locating the cache, but I wasn't actually in attendance when the police invaded the smugglers' warehouse, as I was involved at the time with two other affairs of greater interest: The Brakebill Endowment, and that of the five Russian grandmothers."

I recalled the latter, and the ridiculous trail that was laid down for us both to follow through the neighborhoods of Hackney, but I had no memory of the former, and admitted as much. "You had other matters to attend to at the time," he said, explaining simply that the affair involved a message carved into a blackened mantelpiece of ages past.

"The raid on the smugglers' lair should have passed as routine," continued Holmes, "except that one of the Kyle Gang's lieutenants, a bruiser named Haddenham, cracked the skull of a policeman – most likely by accident. He was always a clumsy and lumbering brute. Whaley, in a case of split-second misplaced loyalty, threw himself into the fray. Some thought it was to help Haddenham escape, but I suspect it was because he wanted to injure an officer. Nevertheless, he was recognized in the process. He then fled himself, successfully escaping to parts unknown. The policeman lived, but has never fully recovered, and the law's vengeance was quick to declare that Whaley would certainly pay the penalty when he was eventually caught.

"And caught he was," Holmes noted. "He was quickly arrested a month later after he slipped back into London. He was sentenced to ten years, but was released after five. That was two years ago. He came to Sussex and looked me up. He truly seemed to have learned his lesson, and through some of my contacts, I was able to arrange that he find a job working for a little known government office in a house off the King's Road in Chelsea. I understand that in the intervening couple of years, he's gained a great deal of trust, and been quite useful on occasion as well. He lives not too far west of there, in that tangle of streets near the Ebury Bridge and the Grosvenor Canal.

That was the area that we had entered as Holmes finished his story, and the cab pulled smoothly to a stop in front of No. 85 Alderney Street, a narrow but rather handsome little structure of three stories. We parked behind a waiting police car and a man in a suit who was standing beside it, while two others – a shorter man also in a suit and the other in a constable's uniform, were just stepping out of the building. The second constable joined the first. I recognized the shorter man as Superintendent Cable, an old acquaintance. Even as we climbed from the car, another vehicle slid behind us and Latham, by then in his forties but still as fit as the college athlete he'd once been and exuding a sense of danger that he could never hide, sprang out to join us.

"I took the call from Mr. Latham," Cable said, explaining to us while nodding toward the man from British Intelligence. He bounced a bit on his toes and a very grim expression tightening his lips. "We mobilized immediately." His eyes cut toward the building. "It isn't pretty."

He was right. The corpse was in what had been a plain white shirt and dark trousers. He was sitting slumped back in a dining chair, itself pulled back two or three feet from the table. His throat had been viciously cut, and blood had shot outward, apparently in great gouts, soaking his clothing and landing as well on the floor and tabletop in front of him. There was nothing on the stained surface itself but an empty cup, heavy white ironstone. Inside were the dried dregs of what appeared to be coffee, while the outside was stained with dried and clotted blood.

The man himself – who must have been Michael Whaley from Holmes's grim nod in my direction – was around thirty, with a small paunch. He would have been rather unassuming in life. His sunken eyes were still staring straight ahead toward whatever he'd seen as his soul passed. His thinning hair was combed toward the back of his head, and it seemed to be gathered there into something resembling a short handle. Long experience told me that it had been held to jerk his head back by whomever had stood behind him and slit his throat. The cut was clean and deep, from left to right by a right-handed person. Whaley would have died instantly.

"Three days, Watson?" Holmes said after examining the body. I concurred. The man had clearly been dead at least that long.

"I wonder why they waited so long between killing him and this morning to set the plan into motion," asked Latham.

"Plan?" asked Cable. "Is this something that I need to know about, gentleman?"

"I'm not sure, Superintendent." Holmes went on to explain my early-morning summons, what I had seen to make me suspicious, and my subsequent message to Holmes. "While we think the intent was to trap us at the very least," he continued, "the rest makes no sense as yet. It seems that my already being in London, and ability to arrive within minutes instead of hours, threw grit into the works, and they were unable to adapt – or perhaps they simply got cold feet. I would wager that they didn't expect for us to be here in this room now, either. I doubt if many people – and probably not the Birches – knew that I was still in touch with Michael regarding his work or could make this connection so quickly."

"And what work was that?" asked the Superintendent. "If you don't mind me asking, that is," he added. He glanced at Latham, who was wandering further afield, looking at various objects in the room with a grim expression. "I know that if Mr. Latham is involved, it may not be any of my business."

"In the time since he was recommended our way," said Latham, glancing at Holmes, "Michael had discovered an aptitude for recruiting minor agents to fulfill small but necessary tasks. He went forth on a regular basis to establish connections with these people – gatherers of fragments of information for a small regular payment. Confirming whether such-and-such fellow made regular visits to a certain postal box, for instance."

He finished circling the room and stopped before us. "He was rather good at what he did, and had increased his responsibilities with every passing month. It was by way of a chance conversation that he became aware of a threat related to the introduction of Irish coinage later this year. I fear that something associated with that has blown up in his face."

Holmes frowned but didn't say anything.

Cable nodded, as if the murder by some espionage-related intrigue would lift the responsibility of the investigation from his shoulders. "Any idea who else might be involved?" he asked, almost hopefully, perhaps wishing it was some foreign agent who would fall under Latham's vengeance.

Holmes shook his head. "It's a mistake to jump to conclusions without data. We haven't even made an examination of the premises. The most telling factor is staring us in the face."

"He trusted his killer," I said.

"Exactly," replied Holmes. "Michael had become an experienced agent. Even if he'd allowed a meeting to take place here, in his own rooms, he wouldn't have let that person get behind him so easily." He pointed to the dead man, slumped in the chair. "There's no sign of a struggle. He just sat there until his hair was grabbed, yanking back his head and exposing his throat. Then the killer cut without any hesitation."

"What you say may be so," said Latham, "but we can't take the chance. I'm going to issue an alert. In the meantime, see what you discover otherwise."

He stepped outside while Holmes began to prowl around the dead man's quarters, first examining the area near the body, and then moving elsewhere, going through the man's papers, and then entering his bedroom. Soon he made his way deeper into the building. Meanwhile Cable and I were left beside Whaley's corpse, both having known Holmes long enough to realize that it was best that we not offer to help, and instead find a spot and stay there. I asked Cable about his two sons, both now at university, and he in turn got me talking about a trip I'd taken the previous summer to Edinburgh. Both of us made a point not to glance toward the gaping wound, covered in dried gore, that faced us from just a few feet away.

371

Holmes came back a few minutes later, a small stack of letters in his hand and a sad expression on his face. He seemed surprised that Latham hadn't yet returned.

"Some aspect of Michael's professional work may very well be the cause of this, but I think otherwise – that it's a much smaller and unhappy plot. Superintendent, will you join Watson and me as we return to Clipstone Street?"

Cable nodded and we went out to where the cars still waited. Latham was talking to several more men in dark suits who had arrived while we were upstairs. He turned to us, and then he and Holmes stepped to one side. Holmes let him read a few of the letters, pointing specifically to one in particular. Latham nodded, and then they separated.

"Latham is going to continue following up on his side of the business," said Holmes. "It would be unwise to do otherwise. But I think that we'll soon see an end to it."

We paid and dismissed our cab and joined Cable in his roomy official car, quickly traversing across London, now in the full throes of a typical mid-morning. Holmes explained what he'd found in the letters, and what he'd deduced from them. I shook my head for the thousandth time at the unhappiness in the world.

We parked on Clipstone Street and stood beside the car for a few minutes until the man whom I'd seen arrive and hide earlier stepped out. He and Holmes seemed to know one another, and it took but a few seconds for us to learn that no one had been in our out of the mostly abandoned house while we were gone. Holmes nodded, unsurprised, and then asked the man to move closer, keeping watch within the mews itself. "I'm not sure what to expect, but be prepared for anything, and protect yourself if anyone should suddenly emerge – especially if it's the woman."

The agent nodded, and then we walked through the mews and over to the basement door, which was now closed. Holmes knocked, and then again, but with no response. Looking at Cable and me, he gave a little nod and reached for the knob. It turned, and we walked through into the darkened hallway.

The damp smell still hung in the air, but now there was something else, all too familiar. I'd first been introduced to it early in my medical training. It was readily obvious and often encountered during decades of Holmes's investigations. And most recently, although somewhat different due to being several days old, we'd found the same odor hanging in the air of Michael Whaley's apartment: The coppery tang of blood. A great deal of it.

The door to the little sitting room was open, and while the fire had gone out, the lantern was still lit, and there was now more light coming through the windows over the kitchen counter. That actually served to make the room seem darker at first, as our eyes tried to adjust from the sudden glare and take in the other darker side of the room, where both Mr. and Mrs. Birch sat around the table. The woman was looking at us, her head turning as we moved from the door to a spot across from her. But her husband simply slumped in his chair. Unlike Michael Whaley who had faced eternity looking straight ahead, Birch had been met death staring at the floor. But even though his head was dropped forward, there was no mistaking the same type of wound across his throat. It was his blood that I had scented as we entered the building.

Mrs. Birch's left hand was lying cupped against her abdomen, while her right was on the table, holding a thin and rather keen-looking knife. It suggested something foreign, such as would have been used in ages past in assassinations of Italian nobles, being pulled out every generation or so to let it have another lick of misery. How it came to this dark basement was something that we would never learn.

"Tom was in the Kyle Gang, too, Mr. Holmes," the lady said, glancing toward the dead man beside her. "He thought when he became one of your Irregulars that it was the best thing that ever happened to him, but then you dropped him – you never sent for him, and he never heard a word from you."

Holmes cleared his throat. "I only dealt with a few specific lieutenants – usually members of the Wiggins family, brothers and sisters and cousins, who rotated in and out as leaders of the group. I remember Tom, but I thought that he'd simply lost interest, or had something else to do. It was one of the other boys who stopped using him."

She shook her head. "He always blamed you, though. Poor stupid Tom. It was only worse after he got into the gang. He wasn't ever very good at it, you know. He was arrested early on, just for being slower than the ones who outran him and got away. But he never peached on the rest of us. That was one good thing about him. He'd do anything for those that he cared about."

"Us?" Holmes asked. "Then you were a member of the gang as well?"

"In a sense," she said. "My father was Amos Sykes Kyle, who founded the gang. He died, you know. You killed him."

Holmes shook his head. "Not true. I was responsible for notifying the police where the warehouse containing the fenced goods was located. It was your father who took it upon himself to flee from the policeman's dog, abandoning his own troops, and then tripping and falling into the drains that were torn up in the adjacent street."

The woman sat up a little straighter then, angry now. "You lie! If you hadn't interfered, my father wouldn't have died, and things would have turned out much differently. Father was grooming Michael – without him, Michael was never able to get ahead. He never would have allowed things to get to the point where the gang was broken and he was arrested. It all goes back to *you*, Mr. Holmes!"

"If you still knew Michael after all these years," Holmes responded, "then you know that I was able to point him toward a better future after he was released from prison."

"A future without *me*!" she said, her voice breaking a bit. "That's why I had to settle for Tom." A sneer crept into her voice, a trace of contempt, and this time she didn't bother to glance toward the corpse beside her.

"We've read the letters," said Holmes, holding up the little packet that he'd brought with him from Alderney Street. "They were in Michael's bedside table."

She gave a little gasp, her surprise palpable. "He kept them then? Ever since he came back, he was . . . he acted so . . . so indifferent."

"He probably was," said Holmes, rather coldly. "Michael Whaley had a deficiency. Of character. People were never real to him – they were game pieces. It was useful in his new work, but for you to have believed otherwise, even as the mother of his child, was a mistake."

Ivy Birch sat up straighter then. "He loved me! In his own way! And he would have loved Erin too, if he'd had the chance to meet her. But when he got out of prison, she'd already died! He never had the chance!"

"I'm sorry for the loss of your daughter. I hope that she had a good life. Was it an illness that took here?"

Ivy Birch didn't answer. Instead, she glanced around the dark basement. "We have a place in St. John's Wood. Not so very different from here. Tom was never able to hold much of a job. He was in and of jail too, after the war." She looked at me. "That story about us meeting at the hotel was true, but he wasn't there for very long before he was fired for stealing. And his parents did work for the old lady that owned this house, but we weren't ever her caretakers. Tom just knew that she'd died, and that this house would be an empty place we could use for a while."

She shifted a bit, as if in pain, and then settled back and rubbed her abdomen again. "But Tom always said that he loved me, and when Michael was sent away, and I needed a father for the baby, he was willing enough to take us on. He even loved her like his own – or seemed to want to, on most days."

"And he didn't mind when you tried to resume your association with Michael Whaley after his release from prison?" He held up the letters again, as if to remind her that the whole sorry business was known.

"It was none of Tom's affair! Michael was still willing to see me sometimes, and Tom just had to live with it. He never complained."

"And when you became sick?" asked Holmes. "Did he mind that you approached Michael again – this time for help with your medical expenses?"

"What choice did he have? Tom said he loved me. To prove it, he had to take what came – including the fact that my heart always had belonged to Michael."

"And yet you killed him," countered Holmes. "That isn't quite clear to me. There's nothing in these – " He held up the letters. " – that explains why you would change your feelings so quickly, after so long."

"I'm not sure myself. I went to see him the other day. To ask for more help. You see, it's not just that the cancer is spreading. It's the baby – Tom's baby, this time. I'm three months along, and I wanted to tell Michael that this one could be his too – it could make up for the one that had died, and for what he missed while he was gone – if only he'd take me back.

"I waited for hours for him to show up, standing in the street, trying not to be seen. When he did come back, he said he'd been traveling for work. He looked more tired than I'd ever seen. He'd aged, and he didn't seem to want to talk to me. But he invited me up anyway, and he made a cup of coffee – I suppose to stay awake. He didn't offer me any. I guess he hoped that I'd speak my peace and go away.

"I told him about the baby – I hadn't seen him in several months, which was how he knew it couldn't be his. Otherwise, I would have told him that it was. I explained how he could be the father this time anyway, since he'd missed his chance before. But I needed money for the doctors – they want to do an operation, for the cancer. He drank his coffee and let me talk, but I could see that he wasn't even really listening – just waiting for me to finish and be gone. I got up and started pacing, but the more excited I became, the less he seemed to care, and he seemed to be getting ready to stand up put me out. He pushed his chair back, and that's when it snapped. *I* snapped. I was behind him, and I pulled out my knife – my dad gave it to me long before he died, and told me how to use it. I stepped up and grabbed his hair – that fine dark hair I'd always loved so – and pulled his head back. I'd made the cut before I gave it another thought – like I'd been taught – and before he could even raise a hand to stop me.

"He made a noise like a little puff of wind, and then it was done. And I walked out."

"But what of the rest of it?" I asked, barely staying even with what they were discussing. "Why lure Holmes and me here? Why contrive this ridiculous plot to seem as if you lived in this empty house, and that your child had been kidnapped?"

"It was Tom who thought of it. I knew it wouldn't work, but what else could we do? He'd always hated you, Mr. Holmes. You helped Michael after prison, but you never did anything for him. And you were the closest thing to a famous man that he'd ever met. He thought that if we could grab you, someone would pay to get you back." She looked my way. "It was me who thought of you, Doctor. I knew that you lived nearby, and that if we took you first, Mr. Holmes would have to come looking.

"After I . . . after Michael died, I came back and told Tom that there was no hope for any money from that direction. I didn't want him to see how upset I was, but I didn't want to see how secretly happy he was either. He tried to hide it, but his eyes lit up – him, a man never fit to wipe Michael Whaley's boots!" Yet even as she said it, she didn't waste a glance upon the corpse beside her. I wondered if he was listening somewhere, thinking of a life wasted as this woman cataloged her contempt for him.

"We thought to lure you here, Doctor, and have you then summon Mr. Holmes. Tom had remembered this place, and we spent a day moving in some things and cleaning enough to seem as if we lived here. We rehearsed our stories and decided that we couldn't take you outright – Mr. Holmes wouldn't walk in by himself. Instead, he'd have the entire police force at his back, searching for you. So we came up with the kidnap plan, because that would need to remain a secret.

"Tom was for killing you as soon as you'd sent a message to Mr. Holmes, but I thought different. I thought we should wait and lock you both up together. That's why I didn't let you go in there this morning with that talk of protecting clues. I thought that Tom might still rush over and lock the door, ruining everything. But then Mr. Holmes was already in town, and it was rushing by much faster than we'd thought – or planned. And then we both saw you had a gun, and you didn't both go in the bedroom together, so we couldn't lock the door behind you without first having to get into a fight. And then our chance slipped away and you'd both gone."

"And so you both sat here and stewed in your own failures," said Holmes, "before you eventually killed Tom Birch as well."

"I was tired of listening to him. He'd let you both get away, and how would we get another chance? Before, when we were planning it, Tom was full of confidence. He fixed up the room with the lock, and he was going to make up some gas by way of a recipe he'd learned in the war, using ammonia and bleach. When you were in the room, we would let it in under the door and finish you off so there wouldn't be any more trouble. Then we'd find out where to send a message and let them buy you both back – thinking that you were still alive, of course. But after you both left, he was the same failure that I've known for fifteen years. He just sat

376

around whining about 'If only' and 'What if?', and trying to reach and hold my hand. I realized that I'd be better off on my own – me and the baby. I walked behind him and finished it, and then I was resting here, trying to gather the strength to leave, when you came back."

She stopped speaking then. She carefully laid the blade on the table and simply continued to rub her abdomen.

The doctors somehow kept her alive long enough for the baby to be born. I made sure that it went to a good home.

Holmes looked upon the whole episode with distaste, and I couldn't blame him. After the woman's confession, he'd distracted himself by searching the house until he found the materials upstairs that would have been combined to make deadly chlorine gas. He commented that in that terrible basement, it was just as likely that Tom Birch would have also killed himself and the woman he loved.

Latham had stopped by Queen Anne Street that night to learn the details that he'd missed. He was quite relieved that whatever Michael Whaley had been investigating wouldn't be affected by the man's death, and pleased that the individuals whom Whaley had identified and cultivated on his last mission – enemies of the Government intent on as much mayhem as they might create – would be allowed a great deal more rope before hanging themselves, instead of being arrested for a seamy little murder.

When he was gone, I poured a couple more brandies for Holmes and myself, deciding that it wasn't unwelcome after such a day. I could see that Holmes had been bothered by the recent events.

"None of this was your fault," I said. "In spite of what she said, Events are too intertwined and tangled to be able to follow along a clear path back to the death of Ivy's father as some certain point where her life went wrong. The same for Tom Birch. I would venture to say that you didn't help him after his own time in jail because he never sought you out to ask."

Holmes sighed and took a long swallow of the brandy. Then pursing his lips for a moment, he replied, "I suppose you're right. Still, one is tempted along the way to feel responsible for things, and while I logically know that I cannot be the reason for Tom Birch's sad life, I still wish that I'd thought to make sure that everything was all right with him." He shook his head. "I keep seeing him, dead and defeated in that chair in a filthy basement – the inevitable culmination of a wasted life."

I set down my brandy. "Holmes, you are not God." I considered elaborating. I had done so in the past when he felt too much guilt for a burden that he had wrongly shouldered. I had sometimes realized afterwards that I'd hurt my argument by continuing to press it, always seeking some better way to say it that might, this time, find a way into his thoughts. But anything else that I might have said had already crossed his mind. I picked up the delicate snifter and took another sip.

Finally Holmes finished his own brandy and stood. "It didn't escape my attention that you seemed in the mood for a holiday when we set out for Ewelme." I nodded and he continued. "I find that I don't feel the immediate pull to return to my cottage. Perhaps we could set off on some other small journey the morning."

I raised my eyebrows. "No plans? No tickets or reservations?"

He nodded. "Wherever the wind takes us – or in this case, the exceptional British railway system. Right now, I think that such a trip would suit me down to the ground. Think of someplace you'd like to visit – any direction will do."

And with that he said good night, leaving me there with no chance of going to sleep anytime soon, a plethora of possibilities now spread wide before me, and the responsibility of making a wise choice. I stood up. Clearly more brandy would be required.

The Lincoln Street Minister

In spite of my careful attempts to dress accordingly, I couldn't help but sense that my clothes, as ragged as they were, were still too prosperous-appearing for this locality.

Sherlock Holmes and I stood back from the pavement, doing our best to appear as idle loungers while we observed the building across the street and a few doors to the north. While I had long ago taken to saving a number of my older garments for tasks such as this – those worn by age, out of style, or damaged during events of some of Holmes's investigations – I still felt that I looked too much like myself, while Holmes had managed – as always – to seemingly become another person entirely.

We were halfway down Lincoln Street, in Whitechapel, and the various efforts to improve the district following the Ripper murders of a decade earlier had not yet reached this thoroughfare. That short lane was uniquely located between the Whitechapel Union Workhouse to the west, the City of London Union Infirmary to the east, and a mortuary and the vast Tower Hamlets Cemetery to the south. The opening to Mile End Road at the north seemed to be the only way to escape what the rest of the surroundings implied – but there were, in fact, two other forms of figurative escape in Lincoln Street, both of a more inward-directed turn.

Near the north end of the street was a shabby public house, long a fixture here, where many locals congregated to numb their daily existence. And located just beside it was a new establishment in an old structure, the recently congregated Church of the Impoverished Souls, led by London's latest nine-day wonder, Reverend Philo Tate Simmons.

The man had first come to the public's notice several months before, when London was trapped in a hot and tedious summer. Mid-August had brought temperatures of nearly one-hundred degrees – tolerable to an old Afghan fighter like myself, but deadly at times to the average British citizen. In the midst of that, a man had begun to minister to those in need – serving cool water to passers-by in Trafalgar Square. At first he had been just another of several performing similar functions, and he would have passed unnoticed had he not also begun to perform miracles.

The word spread about him, dressed in black in the deadly summer heat. I had tarried once to watch him as I went from one place to another on an irrelevant errand. He was a big fellow, his graying hair rather long and frequently pushed straight back from his high brow, only to slip down again as he bent to assist the next person, and the next and the next. The stories began to be discussed and shared more frequently, along with his

379

name and apparent American origins, when the sick and lame would timidly approach, only to receive his prayers and touch and soft words, allowing them to rise and walk away, loudly proclaiming that they were healed of their afflictions.

I recall at the time taking the cynical view that the "healed" individuals were his cronies, hired to perform this little bit of dumb crambo for those who were gullible and susceptible to drama, and had money to lose, but one saw such every day, and it made no lasting impression. At some point around the turning toward cooler weather, I again became aware of Simmons, having read a short piece about him in one of the daily newspapers. Once more, I confess that I didn't pay too much attention, having encountered another one of his apparent faith-healing ilk long ago, during a boyhood journey to the United States. I did note that Simmons had now parlayed his new fame into obtaining a physical building in Whitechapel to be used as a church, seemingly by way of an enthusiastic patron. I recall nothing else from the account, and quickly passed along to other stories of greater interest.

I had no notion whether Holmes was aware of Pastor Simmons until one morning in late October of '98, when we had a visitor from Mr. Thaddeus Hellifield, the noted banker and Royal advisor. This, I would soon learn, was the pastor's reluctant and indirect patron, involuntarily by way of his only child, a daughter.

"I fear that I've been fleeced, Mr. Holmes," he said, settling himself in the basket chair before the fire, his leg stiff and apparently resulting from old pain, as shown by the wince of his eyes and the strong but well-used old cane that he kept by his side. He squinted slightly at my friend, who had the window beside the chemical corner at his back. It was always Holmes's custom, when he was able, to arrange things in this way, so that he could closely examine his clients while his own face was somewhat obscured, particularly in the mornings when the eastern light was on that side of the building. It had been of use to him on many occasions, including the affair of the Newby Bridge scandal, which had started with a small but deceitful conversation and had spiraled into an affair that threatened a half-dozen noble houses, and also the matter of the woman from Margate, whose awareness of Holmes's little trick with the light, and her ability to place herself in a different seat, had in itself been a clue as to her intentions.

Hellifield had arrived at the time indicated in his note sent the night before, asking for an appointment but declining to provide a reason. His position and standing were enough to gain him entrance, but if his case hadn't interested Holmes, he would have soon been invited to leave. I'll admit that I expected to hear some tedious tale of boardroom shenanigans involving comparisons of ledgers and serendipitously fortuitous identifications of discrepancies – which was not the tale Hellifield told us at all.

"You'll know of this minister chap, Simmons," he said, having accepted the offer of hot coffee. "He's been getting a lot of attention lately. I first heard about him from my daughter, Lydia, back in the summer. In the last few months she began to have an interest in that sort of thing – volunteering to help the poor, and so on. I've no quarrel with it, although Lydia seemed to think that I might when she first brought it up. We've always been at odds, you see. Rather surprised her that I didn't immediately forbid it. The truth is, after her mother died last year, I've really had no idea what to do with her, and when she found her way to this kind of thing, I was glad enough of it. Gave her something to do. I'll admit it taints her dinner conversation a bit when she starts floating those socialist ideas – she tends to get a bit shrill about it all – but thank heavens she doesn't seem to care a jot about being a suffragist.

"She could have worked with any number of organizations to help the sick, the poor, the lame, the lazy, and the downtrodden – far too many of them in London, as you're aware. The poor people, you know, not the organizations. No fault of their own, of course. At least not some of them. The poor veterans, for instance, and the ones who have no self-control – I pity them. I do. It's the ones who prey on them that I despise. I've heard tales of such things, and not just the sanitized versions of stories that Lydia brings home. After all, gentlemen, one would have to be a fool not to see the terrible underside of things. The Bank of England, for instance – settled in that little hub of ground that controls the richest parts of the Empire – is just a few thousand feet from Spitalfields and Whitechapel, for heaven's sake! The richest rubbing up against the worst of the worst. I was part of a group enlisted to take a look at these things five years or so ago. I know how things are. I'm not willingly blind like so many of my colleagues.

"That's why I've tried to help when I can – especially lately, based on Lydia's reports of where my resources can best be applied. I'm not foolish about it, though. I could give away my whole fortune to the poor tomorrow, and it would only be a bandage – and a poor one at that. There would be just as many of them needing help the next day. That's why I try to do what I do intelligently, and when Lydia said a good word for this American preacher, I was glad to help. It was little enough what he wanted – the funds to rent a broken-down building he's found for a small church. I provided them, for Lydia to pay the rent – on Lincoln Street, in Whitechapel."

I could see that Holmes was becoming impatient, and the fact was not lost on Hellifield, who hadn't obtained his position by being oblivious.

"Simmons has been there for just a month – since mid-September – and all reports are that he's settled in and is doing what one would expect: Giving sermons, serving up meals and medical comfort. Trying to provide opportunities for those who haven't had any and preach some sense to those who will listen. Something like the Salvation Army, I suppose – and it's no knock on Simmons to think that a better and established group like that might be more effective than he is, at least at present. There's plenty of work for all of them.

"But Lydia seems a bit too . . . involved with this one. At first I put it down to the enthusiasm of starting a new project and seeing it come to life. But it's more than that. I can see a gleam in her eyes when she talks about this American." He pursed his lips. His town lowered. He's reached his concern. "I think that she's in love with him."

Hellifield looked from one to the other of us, trying to elicit some sort of comment. I could imagine what Holmes might say – how this story appeared to be rooted in a father's disapproval of a man that his daughter might marry, and how this was nothing with which he could – or would – become involved. Hellifield's next comment seemed to confirm the direction of the consultation.

"The man is more than twice her age!" he erupted, his fists clenched and his face suddenly red at the thought. "He's quite likely around my age!"

Holmes uncrossed his legs and put his feet together on the floor, apparently preparing to stand. "Mr. Hellifield – " he began, but the banker raised a hand.

"I know what you're thinking. That I want you to find something about the man to convince my daughter he's not the one. I don't need you for that, Mr. Holmes. I have a dozen agents who are already working on that problem – quite discreetly. No, I came to you because I need a specialist. I need you to expose him as a fraud – so that Lydia will see him as he truly is."

Holmes shook his head, but he settled back into his chair. "I typically don't involve myself in debunking ministers – "

"But you do!" interrupted Hellifield. "I've asked around about you. You're right. You don't go after ministers *per se* – at least not that I know of – who are associated with churches, but you do stop those people who prey on the gullible. How many false mediums and spiritualists have you exposed? I've read about several in the newspapers, and I'm sure that for everyone reported there were three others that weren't. I recall that business on Great Wild Street last year, in which the Prime Minister's cousin was so nearly arrested after his affair with the ectoplasmic woman – it's common knowledge to some of us in certain circles, you see, in spite

382

of the PM's attempts to keep it quiet – and then there was the story your own brother told me about those girls kept prisoner by that supposed clairvoyant in the Waldeck Buildings in Ethelm Street. What makes them any different from exposing this Simmons and his parlor tricks?"

"The men you referenced," said Holmes, "didn't also found a church and feed the hungry and provide medical care to those in need. I keep an eye on things like this, and I've heard no reports of any questionable aspects of Simmons' ministry."

"So far," countered Hellifield. "Maybe he's as sound as the pound. Or maybe it's all a tactical maneuver to attract and wed a rich man's daughter – and my Lydia was the one caught in his net. Or possibly he never intended it that way, but in her fascination, she pushed herself into his sphere, and now that she's under his influence, perhaps he's changed his objectives."

"Have you discussed it with her?" I asked. "And have you met Simmons in person, and talked with him as well?"

"I have not," said Hellifield emphatically. "Lydia is headstrong. She's always been rebellious – natural enough, I suppose, but why give her ideas if they aren't there already? If she isn't in fact interested in this man, why suggest it as a possibility? And until I have all my facts straight, I'm not going to meet with Simmons either."

He turned to Holmes. "What I need is for you to investigate his claims to having this . . . supernatural power – this ability to heal the lame – in the same way you would one of these mediums who take money from the overcredulous and then put on a show in the dark with floating trumpets and knocking tables." He sat forward on his seat. "Don't think about it as me asking you to vet my daughter's suitor. Instead, consider if he's some American con-man who is taking advantage of those who don't know better, and can't afford it."

Holmes pondered for a moment, and I was wagering with myself which way he would lean. It could, I decided, go either way. Holmes had a marked distaste for charlatans, and had often gone to extra effort for no substantive reward when he perceived that one of them needed to be exposed. But as he'd pointed out, in this case the man seemed to be doing some good work – at least it seemed that way on the surface. I found myself wishing that he didn't dismiss Hellifield, as I suddenly wanted to know more about this man Simmons, and in spite of years of seeing some of the worst from people, I also hoped in a small and secret way that somehow Simmons's abilities would be confirmed – or if not that, at least not entirely discredited.

Finally Holmes nodded. "I'll look into the matter, with the understanding that I have no preconceived agenda."

383

Hellifield nodded and pulled himself to his feet. From what I'd observed when he walked in, and now as he braced himself upright with his old battered cane, that he suffered from some sort of hip dysplasia of long standing. It was reflected by the uneven wear of his shoes.

"That's all I can ask," he said. "Now that you're on board, I'd like to direct you to one of Simmons' services tonight. I have a little something in mind that might force the issue one way or the other."

Holmes raised an eyebrow and started to object. "I would advise that you let me make some inquiries before you begin changing the conditions of the test – " he said before Hellifield interrupted.

"No, no. I won't affect what you're doing, but it will give us something to think about. The service usually starts about seven." And then, despite Holmes's further attempts to elicit an explanation, he departed.

When we'd heard the front door close, Holmes looked at me. "You're features are all-too-obvious. You hope that Father Christmas will prove to be real."

I smiled. "Well, who couldn't use a little more goodness in the world? And magic as well."

Holmes wagged a finger. "Be careful, Watson. Some of these religious types don't want their magic to be categorized in the same way as a witch doctor's magic, in spite of the obvious similarities. And in any case, it's yet to be determined just how much of a con-man this Simmons fellow is."

"Now you're theorizing in advance of the data," I countered. "You've declared him guilty before proven innocent."

He stood. "So I have, which shows that even after decades of personal discipline, it's far too easy to be tempted into a lapse of thinking." He walked to the door, pausing to retrieve his Inverness and fore-and-aft cap. "Are you available this evening to attend tonight's performance at Simmons' church?"

I averred that I was.

"Excellent. I'll see some people and ask some questions, and send word about the arrangements." And with that he departed.

I spent the afternoon writing, making a record of our recent foray into Fynes Street, the dramatic rescue of Dr. Copper's daughter from the political vivisectionist, and the running battle that followed north into Westminster, terminating on that low wall separating the Victoria Tower Gardens from the river. The abrasions on my knuckles had nearly healed, but the politician's secretary – a killer of unusual stealth – wouldn't soon recover from the fall he took off the wall and onto the jagged debris standing in the mud beneath, revealed by the river's low tide. Whether he walked or was wheeled to the gallows was still an open question.

It was nearly five when Holmes sent word as to where we should meet in Lincoln Street, while advising that I wear old clothes to somewhat fit in. I complied, arriving at around six-thirty, where I joined my friend is a little-noticed doorway where we could see the relatively new church of Philo Tate Simmons, late of the United States.

"My afternoon was an exercise in futility," Holmes informed me as we watched men and women in various conditions of financial distress file into Simmons' makeshift church. Seeing that his clothing was so much different than what he was wearing when he departed Baker Street, I concluded that he'd visited one of his various hidey holes to take on a disguise. "I only found shaky confirmation of his 'miracles', and no argument to provide weight to an argument on the other side."

"Are you approaching the task as if you haven't looked deeply enough unless you find something negative to report?"

"Not necessarily, but one would have expected to discover something questionable. Through various American resources, I obtained a basic biography of the fellow. Born in 1853 in Johnson's Depot, in northeastern Tennessee. Worked for a number of years as a laborer for his father-in-law – yes, he was married once, apparently to a girl from the same small town where he was born. She died during childbirth in the early eighties – 1883 I believe – at which point Simmons underwent some sort of religious conversion, becoming an itinerant minister, slowly working his way north and east, until he ended up in New York City a couple of years ago."

"Your American sources were quite effective, considering the only had a few hours to assemble their report."

"I accept this information with a grain of wariness. Apparently after Simmons arrived in New York, he came to the attention of a newspaper reporter, attracted by the street-side healings that were being performed for the lowliest of the citizens. This reporter spent a few weeks last year researching Simmons' past, even going so far as to travel along the man's trail back to Tennessee, where he interviewed some of the early actors in the story. It should be noted that Simmons spent years moving from one place to another, sometimes serving as a minister at a church in a little town before abandoning it and taking to the road once more. The reporter found no indications of any questionable behavior, and was unable to verify when the healings first began. Simmons wasn't doing anything like that in his home town – no turning the water to wine at his own wedding, for instance – so it started sometime during his travels at an unimportant stop along the way. In the middle of this year, he unexpectedly announced the call to carry his ministry to London, and here we are."

"You mentioned 'shaky confirmation' of his miracles. Did that come from the reporter's story?"

"No. The fellow mentioned a few that he'd personally witnessed, but there was no apparent effort to speak with anyone who had actually been healed. I questioned some of my acquaintances who loiter around Trafalgar Square, seeing if they were familiar with anyone who had received a 'treatment' from the minister. For instance, Pete Byers' patch is set up near the location where Simmons' handed out water, and he didn't recognize any of the people who approached and asked for the minister's touch, before walking away rejoicing."

I knew Pete Byers of old, as he was one of the first people that I'd met in mid-1881 while becoming associated with Holmes's unique consulting practice. Those who knew Byers weren't fooled by his game, but visitors to the city were mightily impressed with his spurious artistic efforts and tossed substantial coinage his way, circumventing the begging laws in the same way that a street busker earns donations by offering an actual effort – although Byers' effort was in the wasted labor he spent each day rather than in actual creation. Early each morning he wheeled a covered barrow to a fixed spot in Trafalgar Square. Then, keeping the barrow's contents shielded by a tarpaulin, he moved what he carried to a fixed spot on the street. After crawling under the tarp and hiding under it for a few minutes, as if he were doing something important, he would emerge and, waiting for a moment where there was a lull in foot traffic, gently remove the covering to reveal a life-sized sleeping dog, seemingly sculpted from sand, as one would build a castle at the seaside. But in fact the tan-colored sculpture, meant to seem fragile and temporary, was cast as a solid and movable piece, easily transported to the Square in the morning and loaded up again at night for removal to Byers' lodgings.

I remember when Holmes had first introduced me to Byers. We had approached the fellow as he rested on his knees, leaning forward and gently smoothing the back of the sand dog with a cloth dampened from a nearby bucket of water, as if carefully shaping it toward some higher level of perfection. There were several buckets of sand standing nearby, apparently the raw materials of this ephemeral art. When Byers saw us he bounced up, and I wondered how he could kneel on the pavement for so long without destroying his knees. His eyes twinkled as I praised his mastery of the sand sculpture, and I tossed him a coin, for which I received a sincere and chipper "Thank you!" Holmes didn't see fit to tell me the truth of it until we were walking down the Strand toward Simpson's, where we intended to celebrate the recent conclusion of the Jermyn Street assault by spending some of Holmes's fee.

"He pretends to smooth it like that all day long," said Holmes. "Those who regularly pass by, including the constables, know the sculpture for what it is – it never changes – but for someone new to the city, watching for just a few minutes before impatiently walking on, or only visiting for the day, it seems to be a remarkable bit of artistry, and Byers regularly makes a daily wage through his futile pantomime of sculpting to feed a jolly wife and six fat happy children."

As we stood before Simmons' church that night in '98, it had been nearly two decades since I'd met Byers, and he still worked that same bit of pavement, six days per week. I suspected that he'd had to replace his sand-cast dog in the meantime, but I'd never bothered to find out for sure. I suppose there are worse jobs, but I had convinced Byers early on to set out some padding for his knees, although nothing could be done about the gradual curve of his spine that permanently formed from leaning over so often and continuing to lightly conduct his *faux* labors on the tan sculpted dog.

'It's a wonder," I said, "that Byers didn't rise up and ask for Simmons to heal him. I know for a fact that he's in constant pain."

"It never crossed his mind," said Holmes. "I asked him about this this afternoon. He did wander over to have some water, but a man in his profession simply doesn't give any credence to the possibility that Simmons' actions could be honest. But as I said, he did confirm that none of the 'healed' were people that he knew – those who would be likely to be hired to pretend to be healed and drum up interest in whatever Simmons might have intended. They seemed genuinely ill, and then genuinely better, and genuinely grateful as well."

I tapped Holmes on the arm, having observed a distinctly different visitor entering the church across the street. "I see him," Holmes replied.

It was our client, Thaddeus Hellifield, painfully approaching the steps leading up to the church's front door, slowly working his way forward with the use of his stout cane. Like me, he was wearing old clothes in an attempt to fit into the surrounding neighborhood, but he had done even worse than me in succeeding. The shine on his shoes was visible even where we stood, and his hair was too carefully barbered to fit in with those who passed him toward the entrance.

Glancing to make sure the street was clear, Holmes set out toward the church, and I followed. Hellifield perceived our approach and he turned toward Holmes, whom he did not immediately recognize. My disguise, however, was less successful, and the man smiled. "I'm glad you're here," he said.

"You mentioned," countered Holmes softly, "that you have 'something in mind that might force the issue one way or the other'."

"I do. I could have hired someone else to do it, but why pay a man to do what you can do better yourself?" He gestured toward the doorway. "It's nearly time for the service to begin. Shall we?"

We climbed the steps, and I could tell that Hellifield wouldn't appreciate any assistance. As we matched his slow pace, I was able to study the old building. It wasn't a house as I'd first perceived, but rather one of the old buildings constructed for use by the different guilds that had been scattered throughout Whitechapel in long-ago years. I understood how such a structure could be useful as a church, as it likely held some sort of larger space used for meetings.

And so it proved. Inside the front door, we were directed forward by a couple of ushers, middle-aged men in ragged clothes and pleasant expressions. Passing out of the small atrium, we entered a larger meeting room, with a stage constructed at the far end. Ranged before it were rows of folding chairs, all rather new, and likely paid for by our client by way of his daughter. We found seats together close to the front on the right side. The room was nearly full, and there were a number of low conversations, but by some mutual consent, none of them ever became loud or jolly – just an even hum that never ceased. There were always constant glances toward the stage, where there were three chairs placed in the shadows behind a worn and leaning lectern. On one of these, sitting slumped in seeming weariness with his gaze directed downward upon a Bible held in his hands, was Reverend Philo Tate Simmons, apparently in deep contemplation.

This continued for a moment or two until a tall well-dressed woman appeared from somewhere back-stage. She was in her mid-twenties, and carried herself with authority and grace. She glanced around the audience, and I could see when she recognized the man beside us – likely her father – although Holmes and I apparently caused no interest – just more faces in the crowd. She did not seem surprised to see him there, but she also gave no sign of acknowledgement. As she leaned down to whisper into Simmons' ear, the room fell silent, as if this was a sign that they recognized, and the only sound that was immediate to Holmes and me was Hellifield's somewhat sterterous breathing and the rustle of his clothes as he nudged Holmes to indicate that the young woman was his daughter, Lydia.

Meanwhile, on the stage Simmons was rising while Lydia Hellifield sat down in the chair that he had vacated, leaving the other two empty. Simmons had taken a couple of steps forward and paused, between his seat and the lectern, as if seeking strength to share his message for the evening.

Having seen something of the fire-and-brimstone ministers who preached a form of the Gospel in which only they could be certain to truly

388

avoid eternal Hellfire, I expected Simmons to open his performance with a crazed and foamy diatribe about sin and punishment and exclusion of those who didn't meet the levels of Godly requirement he'd constructed in his own head. I should have known better. This was the man who had provided water to the thirsty in the hottest part of summer, and opened a location to do the work of feeding and healing in one of the city's worst quarters. When he began to speak, I quickly forgot his curious Appalachian accent, so rarely heard here in London, and listened to his actual words.

He began with a quiet welcome, and a reminder that his message would be short, and food would be available after – "Unless someone needs that now more than you need to hear me," he added. A number of people laughed slightly – a sound that I can attest is not heard very often in Whitechapel – but no one felt prompted to rise and seek sustenance.

"Tonight I've chosen *Hebrews* 13:6," began Simmons. "'*Do not neglect to do good and to share what you have, for such sacrifices are pleasing to God.*'" He didn't bother to open and read from the Bible in his hand, but I was certain that should I bother to verify later, I'd find that he had quoted correctly. "You might not feel that you have anything to share," continued the speaker, "but God wasn't talking about sharing the coin from your pocket. It's just a piece of metal – man's construct to trade for a share of someone else's time or goods. It only means anything between us because we agree that it does – you and the baker agree that a coin can be traded for the loaf of bread that he baked with his own time, using the flour that he obtained from another man by trading another coin to him for what he had to sell. Remember, Jesus said, '*Render unto Caesar the things that are Caesar's, and unto God the things that are God's. The coin is Caesar's – and it represents what all of has to use to survive on this plane of existence. Some aren't as Christ-like in how they do it – they hoard their coin, or use it to deprive or speculate or overcharge and gouge others, taking more than they can ever use in a dozen lifetimes. We have to be part of such a system – we have no choice, trading our time and the sweat of our brows for food and shelter and a few moments of peace – but we can do so with Christ in our heart, taking no more than we need and finding a way to help those around us whenever possible."

There were nods of agreement around the room, and I found a way to glance at Hellifield beside us. Nothing in Simmons' sermon was specifically addressed toward him, but how could he not feel the tight pinch of some of the words about those who hoard and deprive? Even if he wasn't that way himself – and I didn't know enough about him one way or the other to speculate – he was certainly surrounded by such greed and constant conniving every day in the form of friends and associates. Such talk from a simple minister – con-man or not – was bound to be unpleasant. Nay, it could sound nothing less than dangerous and radical.

Behind the lectern, Simmons already seemed to be finishing his message, announcing for those who were new how the rear of the building could be accessed for the purpose of dining. There was a restless shuffle as people began to gather themselves preparatory to standing when Hellifield suddenly popped up beside us.

"When do you heal people?" he cried, his tone strident and confrontational. He half-raised his cane. On the stage, his daughter rose suddenly, a look of shock and embarrassment crossing her features. Hellifield was indifferent, stepping out into the narrow aisle that ran along the right of the building and awkwardly shuffling forward toward the stage. "My hip has been my cross to bear for half my life," he said. "I ache in places all the time, and other places have been numb for years. I've heard the stories about what you can do, and surely you've heard of me – you were willing enough to take my money to set up this church. Couldn't you have at least offered to use your gifts upon me in return?" He reached the end of the chairs and turned toward the short set of steps leading upward to the stage. "You never even thanked me!"

He paused once while climbing, and then reaching the stage, he began to walk toward Simmons, who towered over the smaller man. Around us people were leaning forward, and a low buzz of conversation filled the room – decidedly more urgent than what we'd heard before the service began.

On stage, Lydia Hellifield took a step forward, reaching for her father. She took his free hand in both of hers, attempting to pull him aside, but the small man gave a little cry, yanked free, and placed himself before the minister.

"Heal me," he demanded.

Simmons looked flustered. He glanced back and forth from daughter to father, appearing to have quickly lost the easy confidence he manifested when speaking to the attentive audience. Finally, coming to some sort of decision, he handed his Bible to Lydia and stepped forward, placing a hand on each of Hellifield's shoulders and leaning down, appearing to whisper in the other man's ear.

Lydia stepped back, and I took a second to glance at Holmes. He was at his most alert, watching what was happening with an unblinking gaze. His lips were tight and his nostrils flared, as if he needed extra air to encourage the hot combustion of his observational skills. I only thought to look back toward the stage when I heard Hellifield give a small cry, similar to that when he'd pulled from of his daughter's grip a moment before.

I was afraid that I had missed something – some flash of power, or indication that the miracle had occurred. I recalled once that I was so intent on watching an eclipse through a specially constructed box (so as to save my eyesight) that I completely missed the rippled shadow bands that seemed to wriggle across the ground during the moments immediately preceding totality. I was regretting that I wouldn't have seen the moment that Hellifield was healed – and clearly I was prepared to believe that he would be – when I was suddenly surprised (along with everyone else in the room, save perhaps Holmes) as the cantankerous man dropped heavily to the ground, as if the minister had turned loose of a large bag of potatoes.

My first thought, no more than a flash across my mind, was that the process had exhausted the older man. But possibly it was the sudden surprise and dismay that flashed across Simmons' countenance that alerted my medical instincts that something was amiss. I rose and was on the stage before I realized that had occurred. But it took no great medical skills to see that Hellifield was dead.

The look on his face was abominable. His color was pale, there was foam around his mouth, tinged with blood where he'd bitten through his tongue. As I stood, I became aware that Holmes was beside me. He quickly dropped and examined the body before rising again and turning to the crowd.

"There has been an accident," he said, his commanding tone somewhat silencing the chatter. "Can someone fetch a constable?"

One of the men standing at the rear who had earlier acted as a smiling usher nodded and dashed out. I looked back toward Simmons, who seemed to have shrunk inside his clothing. He was wringing his hands as he shuffled backwards, dropping heavily into one of the three chairs.

Speaking to Lydia Hellifield, still clutching the Bible, Holmes identified us. "I am Sherlock Holmes, and this is Dr. Watson." Although still wearing shabby clothes, he now looked remarkably like himself – standing straighter, his hair combed straight back with his fingers. "Your father asked us here tonight – and he said he had something planned to investigate Pastor Simmons' supposed healing powers." He glanced toward the body at our feet. "I gather that he intended to put the minister to the test."

The young woman nodded and swallowed, attempting to speak. Then, "Yes. He's – he had threatened to do something like this, but I never thought it would amount to anything. When I saw him hear tonight – I'm involved with several charities, and father is always – was always cynical about each of them equally. He's never tried anything like this before."

"He had suspicions that you and Mr. Simmons might be romantically involved," I explained.

She laughed – an unexpected burst that felt highly inappropriate so near her father's corpse. "What?" She looked toward the man seated nearby, who himself was suddenly looking back at her in surprise. "*Him?* Impossible."

Simmons stood then, looking possibly more broken than he had just a moment before. "Lydia – " he began, his unusual accent taking on an unpleasant whining aspect, but he was interrupted by the sound of footsteps arriving at the back of the church. I saw that it was a constable, accompanied by our old friend Sergeant Corby. He recognized us immediately, but glanced right and left to completely assess the situation before making his way toward the stage.

I glanced back at Holmes to judge his reaction at Corby's arrival, but he was focused intently on Simmons and Lydia Hellifield. Even when Corby arrived and spoke to him, he didn't turn away from them.

After greeting the sergeant, Holmes said, "Mr. Simmons, I believe you were about to speak."

The minister's initial shock at Lydia Hellifield's statement was now more controlled. Clearly he had been rocked back by the raw contempt she had conveyed toward him in just three short words. He shook his head, but Holmes pressed him.

"I believe that you were surprised that your feelings for Miss Hellifield were not reciprocated as you had believed. The expression on your face could have no other interpretation."

Simmons nodded and licked his lips. His fingers twitched, as if he wanted something to grasp – his Bible, perhaps, still in the young lady's hands, or possibly her throat.

"I thought we had an understanding," he said softly, his curious American accent giving his puzzlement an aspect of pathos. "We found this church building together. She believed in me – in the work we were doing. We had plans – a future." He looked toward the woman. "Lydia . . . ?" His voice trailed off.

Lydia Hellifield showed no hesitation, however, in conveying her thoughts. "A *future*?" The contempt in her voice was palpable. I heard a rustling behind me and realized that the congregation – momentarily forgotten – was still there, as if they were paying customers watching a play in which I was suddenly now one of the actors. I turned to look out at them. Everyone was still and quiet, and oblivious as several more constables quietly entered and placed themselves at the doors and up and down the rude aisles.

Philo Tate Simmons seemed to be collapsing in upon himself – a set of clothes that was emptying as we watched while the poor figure in them evaporated. Never have a seen a man emotionally crushed so quickly. He seemed to age in front of our eyes, sagging to a stoop and suddenly taking on an ashen tone to his skin.

With a sneer, Lydia Hellifield made as if to step toward him, raising the Bible in order to return it to him.

"Stop!" cried Holmes, surprising us all. "Why don't you keep that Bible for just another moment, Miss Hellifield." He said it with certainty, and she seemed to have no choice but to respond.

Glancing quickly toward me before returning his gaze to the young lady, Holmes asked, "How did he die?"

I turned toward the body. "One might initially think it was a fit of some sort – an apoplectic seizure of terrible strength." Holmes seemed to be waiting for more, and I obliged. "But he also shows every indication of receiving a massive, concentrated, and fast-acting dose of cyanide. But," I added, "there is no smell of it on his breath."

"Injected," was Holmes's reply. "Sergeant," he said, continuing to watch the girl intensely. "Would you and one of the constables stand on either side of this lady? But not too close!" he added quickly.

"Now, Miss Hellifield," he continued to the young woman, who watched him the way that a small mammal becomes frozen before a cobra. "Open the Bible."

There was no movement on her part. She continued to stare at Holmes, who took a step to one side, so that he was beside her father's body. Her eyes followed him, and did so again when he knelt beside the dead man.

"Your father asked us to see about debunking Mr. Simmons' abilities to heal by faith," said Holmes. "He visited us this morning, and I spent the afternoon researching the minister's background in the United States. I found nothing to indicate any falsity. But I didn't just spend my time examining that piece of the puzzle. I asked questions about you and your father as well."

At that point he gestured to the corpse, and the woman, hypnotized by his every word, involuntarily looked down. She seemed to see the dead man for the first time, and she gave a small shudder, as if understanding the reality of it all. Her tightly pressed fingers were white on the Bible.

Holmes stood. "Your relationship with you father has always been contentious – it's a well-known fact, and more-so since the death of your mother. And while he has left you on a long leash, you've been tied to him far more than you wished. That is no secret, either. Your constant demands for financial freedom and your 'fair share' of his fortune has been quite the talk of your social set. Fortunately I know a fellow who sits in a web and feels the vibrations of this sort along every strand, and he was able to give me a very sharp description of you – and what you might be capable of – and the fact that you are your father's only heir, and during recent arguments, he has threatened to disinherit you.

Holmes took a step toward Lydia Hellifield, bracketed as she was on both sides by the sergeant and constable. "You weren't surprised to see your father in the audience tonight. I suspect that he bragged or hinted about some plan of his to come here and test Mr. Simmons' abilities – to demand a healing of his afflictions, as we saw. So you came prepared as well." Once again he commanded, "Open the Bible."

Lydia Hellifield apparently realized that she had no alternative, or perhaps Holmes's tone was such that she was unable to do other than as he demanded. She held out her hands and let the book split open, revealing a shiny glass object, thin and long, pushed into the gutter between pages. I recognized it at once as a hypodermic needle, with a long thin needle and still partly full of some clear liquid.

"Hellifield said he had numbness over parts of his body – the location of these parts you would know," continued Holmes. "He possibly didn't even feel when you stepped up to him as he climbed on stage, taking his hand and pushing in the needle, using the plunger to inject him with a massive dose of cyanide. By the time he was standing before Mr. Simmons, it was too late – he was seconds from death.

"I try to observe everything," added Holmes. "It would have been natural to keep one's eyes on the main drama – the minister and the sick man. But I watched you as well. You reached out for your father, he grimaced and pulled away – certainly that was when you killed him – and then you stepped back, slipping something that glinted for the shortest second into the Bible handed to you by Mr. Simmons. Even as I approached the stage after your father's sudden death, I never took my eyes off of you. I'll testify that you were the one who slipped something into the Bible – the hypodermic – and that Mr. Simmons only touched your father for the briefest of instants on both shoulders. I have no doubt that an autopsy will show that a hypodermic needle entered your father by way of his arm – the same arm that you grasped when he came up here."

And so it proved, but the examination of the corpse didn't occur until the next day. That night at Simmons' church, Holmes reached and gently took the Bible and its damning evidence while a mute Lydia Hellifield was led away by Sergeant Corby – who only had the vaguest sense of what had happened, but knew from his past associations with Holmes that an iron-clad case existed nonetheless.

Simmons was bereft. I accompanied him to his bleak little room in a squalid house in Tilley Street, and several members of his congregation followed, anxious to minister unto him following the terrible shock he'd just endured. I understand that afterwards he never returned to the church, not even once, and soon after departed England entirely. I have no knowledge of his whereabouts, and if he does continues to minister, it is in such a way that has attracted no attention.

Later that night I returned to Baker Street to find Holmes smoking his pipe by the fireplace, cheery flames seeming to deny both the events of the night and the cooling October weather. I informed him that Simmons was being cared for, but the poor fellow seemed shattered.

"We may never know how things turn out," said Holmes. "We've intersected with these people for just a few hours – just enough to understand what happened tonight – but with no true knowledge of the overall picture."

"Such as," I added, "whether Simmons can really perform miracles."

Holmes nodded. "Events made that question irrelevant. And Hellifield tried to force an answer before I'd even had a chance to conduct a true investigation – typical of such impatient men."

"One might even be tempted to say that he accelerated his own death," I said. "Hiring you likely gave him the idea to go ahead and confront Simmons at the church, demanding to be healed. It's probable that his daughter had some inkling of what he intended to do, as you speculated, and decided to move forward with her own plan of killing him herself, and then framing the minister by putting the syringe into his Bible. But surely," I continued, a thought popping into my head, "she could have simply hoped that her father's death would be put down to a fit, with no autopsy performed. Why reveal the syringe at all by leaving it to be found in the Bible, which would be returned to Simmons. He would certainly discover it almost immediately, and more importantly, would know who had put it there, and what that implied."

"I suspect that her motivations were complex, but perhaps she wanted Simmons to know what she had done for some reason. Possibly she wasn't quite finished with him yet, and that tie, no reinforced with a secret between them, would be of some use. Or she could have intended Simmons to be murdered quite soon too, and wasn't worried about what he did or did not know. She may have just wanted a place to hide the syringe that wasn't on her person, and it was easiest to frame the minister by handing it over to him in the Bible as soon as possible. The ways of women," he summarized, taking a draw on his pipe, "are inscrutable. How can one come to any conclusions when attempting to build on such quicksand?"

A month or so later, I happened to pass through Whitechapel and took an impulsive turn into Lincoln Street. In most directions were poverty and death, and the public house was still doing a rousing business. But I was happy to see that in some small way, the church was continuing its mission, despite its loss of both minister and easy funding, open as something of a soup kitchen and doss house for the neighborhood's unfortunates. Remembering the gentle words of Pastor Simmons, wherever he might be, and even those of Thaddeus Hellifield when discussing the poor, I climbed the steps to see if they needed any help.

The Tea Merchant's Dilemma

I came down to breakfast that morning, aware that the weather had turned cold overnight. The distance between my room upstairs, warmed by its own little fireplace, and the sitting room on the first floor seemed longer when traversing the chilly stairs. Holmes's bedroom door leading from the sitting room was open, and I assumed, correctly as it turned out, that he had left early.

Just as I moved to ring for Mrs. Hudson, I heard the front door open and slam, and then my friend's unmistakable voice calling to our landlady. Hoping that he was arranging for breakfast, I went ahead and signaled my presence as well.

In moments Holmes had joined me, two red spots from the cold upon his pale cheeks and a gleam in his eyes as he shed his Inverness and fore-and-aft cap. He hung them up and stepped to the fireplace, where the blaze had already been started, rubbing his hands briskly.

"Have you been out all night?" I asked.

"Not at all," he said. "But a great deal of it. I popped awake with a flash of clarity at about four a.m., when I understood Reverend Mirehouse's secret agenda."

"Rather than the obvious one, I suppose."

"Indeed. It has been commonly thought that he had mailed the stillborn infant to the Home Secretary in order to protest the proposed closure of a cemetery, but he had another agenda, related to a housemaid under his nominal care – a position of trust that was sorely abused. When I understood what we had been told the other day by the cryptic groom, I dressed and made my way to Somerset House, where I was able to verify a few familial connections."

"You accomplished this in the middle of the night?"

"I have a connection who owed me a favor."

I shook my head. The matter of "The Home Office Baby" had been in the newspapers for a few days, another of those nine days' wonders that regularly filled the London press. "Will you notify the proper authorities?"

"I stopped on my way back to send a wire," was Holmes's reply. "Thus, our planned trip to Colsterworth later this morning is unnecessary – allowing us time to see Mr. Twickening after all."

I nodded, recalling the short note that Holmes had received the day before, requesting his guidance. Seeing the train of my thoughts, Holmes smiled and said, "I sent a second wire to Mr. Twickening, arranging to keep this morning's appointment."

Conversation turned to other topics, such as how young Vryland, who had visited the previous day, was faring since our dramatic meeting during the Colchester earthquake six months earlier, and the curious matter of the Cudham Dagger which, it will be recalled, was found on the altar of the village church, covered in what appeared to be blood. That already sinister aspect was found to be much worse when Holmes determined, at the outset of the investigation, that it wasn't blood at all.

With that grim conversation in progress, Mrs. Hudson brought our breakfast, and then the morning progressed. During that time, Holmes saw several of his "bread-and-butter" clients, as he liked to call them – individuals who made their steady way to Baker Street like supplicants upon a pilgrimage, trustingly laying their problems before my friend with faith that he would be able, by way of an incisive question or two applied with surgeon's skill, to steer them in the direction of a solution. These cases, while not dramatic, made up a goodly portion of Holmes's time in those early days, and were very much of the same sort that had occupied him when we first began sharing rooms. Only in later years did his practice – and the scope of his investigations – grow to the point that he was unable to advise clients from his armchair as he once did.

By the time the bell rang at eleven, I had returned to Baker Street, having been in and out several times throughout the morning on errands of my own. I was in the sitting room when we heard footsteps, and Holmes said softly, "Mrs. Hudson, and a man – our client, certainly. And someone else. A woman."

This was confirmed when our landlady introduced us to Mr. James Twickening and his companion, Miss Jane Tate, a lovely young lady in her mid-twenties. As we made pleasantries, his hand stole toward hers and gave a slight squeeze. She smiled toward him, and then they separated and found seats in front of our fire. Twickening placed a cloth satchel by his feet.

"Miss Tate is my fiancée," explained Twickening. "It was her idea that I consult you, and I thought that she should join us." He looked back and forth between us. "She is a clerk in the shop, where we met."

I did not raise an eyebrow, but I was a bit surprised. The Twickenings, while not royalty, had certainly risen over the last couple of centuries to be a highly respected family, based upon their holding of a Royal Warrant to sell tea. They were quite wealthy, and regularly mixed with the nation's rich and powerful.

I was certain that neither myself nor Holmes, who cared nothing for society's conventions, had given any acknowledgement by our expressions of the unusualness of Twickening's marital plans, but the man, a solid and dependable looking fellow who must be around forty, added,

398

"I knew from the moment that I met Jane – that is, Miss Tate – that she was unique, and that I would need her in my life for the rest of it, or I would regret it for all my days." The young lady smiled again, and I could understand his affection for her. I indicated for Twickening to continue, as I knew that Holmes had no interest in these details if they had no bearing upon the case.

"Right," said Twickening. "Well, as you know, our family have been tea merchants since the very early 1700's, having been located in the same establishment in the Strand the entire time."

I nodded, as I was quite familiar with the place. Just east of St. Mary-le-Strand, and across from the Royal Courts near the beginning of Fleet Street, the narrow shop, seemingly built as an afterthought in an alley between two greater buildings, was a Temple to Tea, and I had made a number of purchases there, both when I was in London receiving medical training, and then after my return from Afghanistan, always seeking new blends in the same way that a tobacco fiend looks for unusual combinations, hoping to hit on that exact and most-pleasing mixture.

"I had never thought to be involved in the family business," continued Twickening. "Having no interest in a life of leisure like my older brother, I trained in the law. However, having found a position with a firm in the Temple, very close to the tea shop, I discovered that the day-to-day activities there, producing endless documents to be filed away in teetering stacks of the same, was nothing much different than factory work – albeit under much better circumstances, of course," he hastened to add. "Then, when my uncle had a stroke nearly fifteen years ago, I was called back, so to speak, and I found myself running the family business.

"It was the best thing that could have happened to me. I found that I had a knack for it. And more recently, being there has allowed me to meet Jane, who came to work there last summer." He again turned his eyes toward the young lady. She lowered her head with a small smile.

Holmes cleared his throat and frowned. "Your note said you wished to consult me regarding a possible criminal matter."

"Ah, yes. Yes, indeed. I believe that Twickening's is being involved in something terrible."

"How so?"

"Last evening, I was in the shop, taking care of some paperwork. I'm often away, at our warehouses. You understand that the shop in the Strand is much too small to carry out the actual shipping and receiving, as well as preparation of the different teas in bulk after they arrive in England. It is used for public sales only, and I'm only able to visit there a few days each week."

"Excuse me," said Holmes. "I have been to your shop, and I'm aware of its Lilliputian size when compared with its neighbors. How many people regularly work on the premises?"

"Four, usually. A manager, old Mr. Bell, and three girls to serve the customers. Often, one of these will work at a separate counter, constantly preparing a fresh pot of tea in order to provide samples to the customers. Although the premises started simply as a tea room in the early 1700's, it had been quite a while since hot tea was truly served there. Serving samples to the customers was one of my own innovations. I've found that it often leads to additional purchases, as people who try something new will then take some home."

Holmes nodded and waved a hand for Twickening to continue. "Yesterday was the first chance I'd had to visit in nearly two weeks, as other matters have kept me at the warehouse. Since you know the building, you will realize that there is no first floor, but it does have a small basement, accessed from the back of the ground floor. Downstairs is some storage, as well as an area set aside as an office – a desk used by either the manager, Mr. Bell, or by me, when needed.

"Occasionally, correspondence for me arrives at the shop, and Mr. Bell sets it aside on one corner of the desk. Yesterday, I sat down and reached for the usual letters, only to find a box sitting on top of them." He nodded toward the satchel beside him. "This box. It wasn't addressed to me, but rather to my brother, Roger."

"And his position with the firm?" asked Holmes.

"He has none," said Twickening shortly. "He is my older brother, and should have taken over the business. However, he was involved in several matters in his early twenties that embarrassed the family a great deal, and there was a falling out. We have had no contact with him since – which makes it all the more puzzling as to why a package for him would be delivered to the shop."

"What was in it?"

Twickening glanced at Miss Tate, as if to see if she were agreeable to him revealing it. She nodded, and Twickening turned back to us while reaching for the satchel. "I was hesitant to force Miss Tate to view this again – she observed it yesterday afternoon, just after I opened it, and as shocking as it was for me, it must have been much worse for a lady."

"I am fine, James," she said. Her voice was firm, and had hints of the East End in her pronunciation, something that she had apparently taken pains to improve. Hearing her speak, I could believe that, indeed, whatever was in the box would likely not shake her as much as it seemed to have done to Twickening.

400

He lifted the satchel and removed a cardboard box, about nine inches square. It was unsealed at the top, and I could see shredded wood fibers, apparently used as packing material, peeking from the opening.

"It is – " said Twickening, but Holmes held up a finger and stopped him from speaking.

"I will see soon enough," he explained. "Let me discover it as you did."

Holmes reached for the box and then proceeded to examine it minutely. He lifted his lens from the small octagonal table beside his chair and held it this way and that, leaning forward, paying particular attention to the label. At one point, he brought the box closer to his face and sniffed. Knowing Holmes's methods, and how he would spend a great deal of time examining the box before moving on to the object – I had once seen him spend an hour-and-a-quarter on an envelope from a blackmailed Duke before reading the letter inside – I was not surprised.

Finally looking up, Holmes asked, "Did you save the string?"

Twickening nodded and reached into the satchel, pulling out a tangle of still-knotted twine. I saw with satisfaction that it had been cut and not untied. I knew that Holmes preferred to see whole knots.

Setting the box on his lap, Holmes then turned the string this way and that. He held up the cut ends and said, "You might want to sharpen your penknife, Mr. Twickening." Our client's hand stole halfway toward his waistcoat before he smiled and dropped it back to the arm of the chair.

Holmes tossed the string onto his table. "Sometimes a knot is simply a knot," he muttered. Then he took a pinch of the protruding fiber from the box and held it up. Apparently it, too, was just wood, for he dropped it onto the floor beside him, and then reached in to pull out whatever object the box contained, spilling more wood fiber onto his lap, the chair, and elsewhere. I leaned forward, eager to see what had moved Twickening to seek the detective's help.

With a further cascade of packing material onto his lap and the surrounding floor, Holmes pulled out a skull. I was surprised, both at the unexpectedness, and also because it did not seem as serious as I had been led to believe. Then, I recalled that seeing such an object, after our own varied and adventurous backgrounds and experiences, would be no shock to either Holmes or me. But to a tea merchant, opening such a box in a dark basement with no idea of what he was about to find, would likely be quite shocking – especially when associated with a prodigal brother.

Twickening and Miss Tate were silent while Holmes turned the collection of fused bones this way and that, using his lens upon occasion. Then, without comment, he handed it across to me.

It was clearly old, and severely damaged. It was a discolored and dingy brown, ironically looking as if it had been steeping in tea. The mandible was missing entirely, as was the left zygomatic bone and arch. The supraorbital margin above the right eye was broken and gone. There were no teeth.

Most peculiar was the shape of the thing. It was clearly that of an adult, but it seemed rather small and elongated toward the back, with hints that resembled animal rather more than human, and the maxilla protruded forward somewhat more than was usual.

I withheld comment, and handed it back to Holmes, who had thankfully been picking up the wood fiber and stuffing it back into the box. He replaced the skull there as well, and set it on the floor beside him. "I take it that you are concerned that your brother is involved in something questionable."

Twickening looked surprised. "I would think that it's obvious, Mr. Holmes – something of an understatement, as a matter of fact. Why else would a skull be sent to the tea shop? We've had no contact with Roger for years, and then such a package addressed to him shows up from out of the blue."

"What caused his exile from the family?"

"Gambling. Temper. Drunkenness. Living the life of a wastrel. A refusal to straighten out and assume his responsibilities. The same old story, I'm afraid."

"Do you know where he lives now? Where he works?"

"I had heard that he is in London, although that's really all that I know. We were very close once, but when I was chosen by the family to run the business instead of him, our paths diverged. Some terrible things were said, on both sides I'll admit, and I haven't seen him since."

"Do you have any idea why this object was mailed to the shop, instead of to wherever he now lives or works?"

"None whatsoever. I opened the box and was in shock. Jane came in just then and found me, and she saw the skull before I could cover it."

"James," interrupted Miss Tate, "I'm not as breakable as you believe."

"Nevertheless," said Twickening, "it isn't a sight for a lady." He cleared his throat and spoke to Holmes. "I put it back in the box, we discussed it. With no idea what it could mean, Jane suggested seeking your guidance."

"You were of assistance to my mother, once," interjected the young lady. "She was Helen Downs. The year before she died, you found her missing brooch."

"Ah, yes. She lived 'round the corner from me when I was in Montague Street. I'm sorry to hear of her passing." Back to Twickening, Holmes said, "I take it you want me to determine the facts behind this delivery."

"Indeed. I thought I didn't care what Roger was up to – he couldn't have embarrassed us any more than he did fifteen years ago – but if he's involved in something so . . . so seamy as grave-robbing, I need to know, in order to take steps to protect the business. Our competition, those fellows over in Piccadilly, would do anything to bring us down."

"It may not be as bad as you think," Holmes said. "After you put the skull back in the box, did you do any other work in the basement office?"

Twickening looked puzzled at this odd question, but answered, "No. We left, taking the box with us, and I haven't been back since."

"Excellent. And do you now return to the shop?"

"I'm afraid not," he said, glancing toward Miss Tate. "I have business at the warehouse in Hampshire."

"Will you be at the shop this afternoon, Miss Tate?"

"Yes. I plan to return immediately."

"Then Dr. Watson and I will call upon you there in a few hours." Holmes glanced toward the cardboard box and its unusual contents. "I will borrow this for a bit, if you don't mind."

Twickening nodded, and after a few pleasantries upon my part – as Holmes was already pinching his lip and staring into the fire – the tea merchant and his fiancée were shown out. After we heard the front door close, Holmes turned to me. "Grave robbing?"

I shook my head. "You know that it isn't." I sat back down. "Technically not, anyway."

He nodded and moved around and behind me to his shelf of scrapbooks. Selecting one, he carried it to the dining table and threw it open. "Bring the box over here, would you, Watson?"

Carrying it over, I placed it upon the table where indicated, beside the massive volume that was so much more than a mere scrapbook, with its pages stuffed with loose papers, clippings, and a hundred other things of curious interest. Holmes flipped until he found a series of pages with labels pasted upon them. "These," he explained, "are shipping labels from various companies. These particular pages contain labels provided by hotels, mostly within London, but some from the suburbs." He looked back and forth between the label on the box and those in the scrapbook, running a finger here and there while muttering to himself.

I leaned closer to look at the label in question. It was written in a distinctive style, sloping in a way to indicate left-handedness. It was simply addressed to *Roger Twickening, 216 Strand, London*.

"Charing Cross," said Holmes, placing a finger on one of the pasted labels in his book.

"The hotel, I presume."

"Exactly. It is their label. What do you make of the writing?"

"Distinctive. While the left-handedness accounts for the slope and also the ink stains as the writer pulled his hand across it, it also has a flamboyant style that will make it easily found upon the hotel register."

"My thoughts exactly. We shall visit there this afternoon, if you are free, after making a search of the tea shop's basement office."

"You expect to find something else, possibly hidden there, along the same lines?"

"Not necessarily."

He would say no more, and we proceeded to ring Mrs. Hudson for lunch. Soon after, Holmes picked up the nail scissors that had been found in the eye of Baron Trent's cold corpse, apparently intending to cut the label from the cardboard. Instead, he decided to remove it entirely and set up a steam kettle in his chemical corner, where he proceeded to steam the label from the box. Then, by one o'clock, we were in the Strand and entering the tea shop.

It was unchanged from my last visit several weeks earlier – indeed, as it likely was for nearly two centuries. It was extremely narrow, no more than eight or ten feet wide, although quite deep when viewed from the street door. On our right were various displays of tea, and a couple of young women were helping customers make purchases. We made our way to the back, where Miss Tate was talking with a wizened old man. They became quiet when we approached, and then the lady introduced us to Mr. Bell, the manager.

"I don't know what is going on," he said, rather peevishly, "but I know that Mr. Twickening is upset. Whatever I can do to help . . . ." His voice drifted off, as if hoping we would provide an explanation. We did not, and Miss Tate, standing behind the old man, smiled fondly at him. Rather than engage in idle conversation, Holmes immediately asked to see the basement office. Miss Tate led us deeper into the shop, where we found a very narrow and steep stairway leading down to a rather unpleasant little chamber, barely lit by gaslight.

There were numerous shelves around the wall, all loaded with tins, and the whole room had a curious smell, a combination of mustiness and tea. "I would imagine you cannot leave the stock down here for very long, or it might take on unpleasant odors," said Holmes. Miss Tate agreed, explaining that there was a quick turnover due to the always brisk sales upstairs. She watched Holmes as he glanced around the room, paying scant attention to the shelves, and then settling himself at the desk, where he began to shuffle through the papers, particularly what seemed to be the pile of correspondence described by Twickening.

Clearly Miss Tate was torn, wondering if Holmes had any right to be doing such a thing. To distract her, I directed her attention toward the steep stairs and speculated that moving the tea up and down them so often must be unpleasant and dangerous. She nodded, and related several instances where near and actual accidents had occurred. She was recalling another when Holmes abruptly stood up and thanked her, indicating that he was finished. She seemed puzzled. "I thought that perhaps you wished to search the shelves, or even the rest of the premises, to see if any other bones had been delivered or secreted here, unnoticed before now. Do you think that any of the tea tins might contain something . . . dodgy?"

"Do not fear, Miss Tate," said Holmes in that comforting manner he used upon occasion. "All will soon be resolved."

Outside, we began to walk west, in silent agreement that the day was too fine to make the short journey in a hansom. Truth be told, hopping into a hansom was not an option that we always automatically considered in those early days when funds were not as plentiful.

Our next stop was at the far end of the Strand. Holmes had done several professional favors for the manager of the Charing Cross Hotel, and it presented no difficulty at all to be allowed to examine the hotel register. Even I, with my limited experience, quickly saw that the handwriting on the label matched that of Professor Otto Krueg of Paris. The manager did not recall him, and called over a man named Leiter who was working the front desk.

"Small fellow," said the desk clerk. "German. Had several trunks. Yes, I did help him make up a package like you describe – about nine inches all around, and filled with wood shavings. No, I didn't see what was in it. He had the materials sent to his room, and then brought it down to the desk to ask for some twine and a label. I tied it myself. No, I don't recall who it was addressed to, but I did glue on the label. Oh, thank you sir. Thank you very much indeed."

The manager then confirmed that Professor Krueg had checked out over a week earlier, indicating that any mail received for him at the hotel should be forward back to his Paris address. Holmes copied this into his small notebook, and we walked outside.

"You might as well go back to Baker Street, Watson," he said. "I have some research to do at the Museum and the Reading Room, and you will find it tedious. Tell Mrs. Hudson I shall be home this evening."

And with that, he set off down the Strand, while I went the opposite way to carry out some of my own business.

That night, over a bit of left-over mutton, Holmes refused to be drawn, simply indicating that matters should be resolved one way or another in a few days. As I left the sitting room later that night to ascend to my own bedroom, I observed Holmes move to his chemical corner, where he lit the gas jet and lifted the steam kettle, used earlier that day to steam off the label. While I pulled the door shut, he was shaking it to see if it still held water.

No mention was made of the matter until three days later, when Holmes asked if I would be at home the following morning. I assured him that I would be, and asked why. "I believe that you will be interested in the resolution of the matter of the tea merchant." I agreed with his assessment, and made do with the knowledge that the matter would be explained on the morrow, as I knew full well that Holmes wouldn't provide any additional information before then.

At ten the next morning, the bell rang, and within moments James Twickening and Miss Tate were shown into our presence. "You have news?" said the merchant, but Holmes simply invited them to sit. Two more chairs than had been present during the couple's initial visit had been arranged before the fire. Before either of them could find their places, the bell rang again. Holmes went out, returning momentarily with a short man who was introduced as Professor Otto Krueg. I was curious to see the fellow, but Twickening and Miss Porter were clearly puzzled, and no immediate explanation was forthcoming.

While I helped Krueg remove his coat, the bell rang a third time. Again Holmes dashed downstairs. I heard low conversation, and at one point, Holmes's voice rose, saying, "Really, sir, you must!" Then, he and the other climbed the stairs to the sitting room.

Holmes came in first, followed by a tall thin man with a worried expression and sharp, intelligent eyes. Although he was physically quite different from James Twickening, there was a great resemblance about the structure of their faces, and it was no great leap to determine that this was brother Roger, separated from his family for a decade-and-a-half.

James Twickening took a step forward. I was concerned that he might erupt in anger, but instead he sounded like a small boy. "Roger?" As if forgetting any issues that had stood between them, a small smile danced around his lips. "Roger?" he repeated, and then, "You look . . . wonderful!"

Clearly Roger Twickening was no longer a wastrel. He was in a very fine suit, covered by a finer topcoat. He started to move toward his brother James, and then stopped himself, falling back on some inner reserve. "As do you, James." He glanced toward Miss Tate. "I was told by Mr. Holmes that you are to be married. Is this your fiancée?"

James started to introduce them, but Miss Tate had a peculiar expression on her face. "You've been in the shop before."

Roger smiled. "A few times. When I knew that old Bell . . . or James, or any of the others, weren't likely to be there. I . . . I wanted to look around."

James's expression darkened then. "Were you there to retrieve more of those boxes? What are you up to?"

Roger raised his hands. "It's not what you think. I was unaware that the skull had been sent there. I didn't know a thing about it until Mr. Holmes explained everything to me yesterday afternoon."

James turned to Holmes, rather coldly. "I think that I deserve an explanation as well."

"Certainly, but until Professor Krueg and your brother were both back in London, there was no point. If all of you will find a seat . . . ."

When we were all facing one another around the fire, Holmes pulled an envelope from his pocket. "This was on your desk in the basement, Mr. Twickening, in the pile of unopened correspondence. I found it the other day when Watson and I went to the shop and searched. As you explained, after you discovered the box with the skull, you left and hadn't been back. It occurred to me that there might have been a separate explanatory letter, also delivered to the shop, but unopened because you didn't bother going through the rest of the accumulated mail."

"That's true," replied James. "After I opened the box, and then tried to prevent Jane from seeing the contents, we left the basement, and I didn't finish catching up on my business there."

"So you took that letter with you following your visit the other day," said Miss Tate to Holmes, but with amusement rather than accusation.

"I did. Would you care to explain it, Professor Krucg?" And he handed it across to the German.

"Certainly." He glanced at the envelope. "Yes, this is the letter that I sent. I wrote it to explain the skull, and I mailed both from my hotel. I was in London on business, and had hoped to reach Dr. Twickening while I was here. I was called home unexpectedly, and didn't have time to determine how best to reach him. Not knowing that he was no longer associated with his family tea business, I sent the box and the letter there."

"And would you care to let Dr. Twickening read it?"

While the professor passed across the envelope to Roger Twickening, James said, "Doctor? I . . . I don't understand . . . ."

Roger tore open the envelope, starting to answer James, but then instead pulling out the letter and casting his eyes quickly across it.

Holmes spoke. "The separation between your brother and the rest of you has been more complete than you realized. After the events that led to him being ostracized, he picked himself up, went off to the Continent, and studied anthropology. He is now one of the world's leading experts on fossilized bones, particularly those of ancient human beings."

"Roger," said James. "I had no idea . . . ."

The older brother cleared his throat. "It didn't matter. What I did before really was reprehensible, and there was no excuse . . . and no forgiveness possible. But in a way, it was fortunate for both of us. You have made a real success of yourself here, and found your calling – I know you were dying a little inside every day while working for those lawyers – and I . . . well, I have found my own bliss as well."

"Be that as it may," said Miss Tate, "things won't be right until you've made up."

James's eyes widened, as if he had lived for so long without the presence of his older brother that he could not imagine him again a part of his life. Holmes, however, never one for sentimentality, interrupted with, "The letter, Dr. Twickening?"

Roger looked at the unfolded sheet in his hand. "Ah yes. From Professor Krueg. He wanted my opinion on a skull discovered a few years ago in Castenedolo. In Italy." He looked around. "I believe you said that it's still here, Mr. Holmes?"

"It is." He waved toward the dining table, where the cardboard box had been placed. "I shall deliver it into your hands momentarily. I believe that everything is clear now?"

"No," said James, rubbing his forehead. "No, it isn't. Not yet. How did you make these connections?"

"There was no real difficulty," replied Holmes. "Watson and I knew from our first glance at the skull that it was no modern bone, and certainly not related to grave-robbing – at least not in the sense that you meant it, Mr. Twickening." Both Roger Twickening and Professor Krueg seemed ready to take some offense at that statement, but with a placating gesture and a smile, Holmes urged them to relax.

"As I said, I suspected that there must be a separate letter. You, Mr. Twickening, indicated that you hadn't been to the basement office for several weeks, so the letter and the box could have been there the entire time. A search showed this to be true. The label on the box was easily traced to the correct hotel, whereupon Professor Krueg was identified, and a visit to the British Museum and the Reading Room confirmed his academic specialty. Further conversation with members of the staff there indicated the reason that such an object was sent to Dr. Twickening. I sent word to Professor Krueg, who agreed to return to London, and located Dr. Twickening's residence, only to find that he was away from home, but that he planned to return yesterday. I notified Professor Krueg that today would be best, and then made an appointment to see Dr. Twickening, explaining the situation as I understood it, and convincing him to come here this morning.

"And now," said Holmes, standing up, "the rest is up to you. As Miss Tate has indicated, it's time to make things up properly."

A silence stretched, and then James rose, his hand extended in front of him. He walked toward his brother, who stood as well. And then, just as Roger was about to grasp his brother's hand, James reached out and pulled the taller man into an embrace. Miss Tate smiled, Professor Krueg beamed, and Holmes looked faintly irritated before turning and retrieving the cardboard box.

Later, after they had departed, I was moved to comment. "The letter you handed to Professor Krueg was sealed."

"Hmm . . . ." He was involved in pasting clippings into a scrapbook.

"As it would have been when you found it, still unopened on the basement desk, from when it was sent through the mail."

"That is correct."

I smiled. "I feel that there is one aspect of the matter that you neglected to mention when recounting the steps that you took."

"And that would be?" he said, placing the glue brush back into the pot and giving me his full attention.

"The additional scientific examination that you carried out the other night, using the kettle that was still on your chemical table from earlier in the day, when you had steamed off the box's label."

Holmes raised an eyebrow. "You agree that, according to the procedure that you saw for yourself and then heard described, the matter was already settled by that point, in terms of the who's and the why's?"

"I do. You had identified the principals by then, and had found a reasonable explanation as to the presence of the skull in the basement of the tea shop."

"Then confirming or denying your implied hypothesis that I stooped to steaming open a letter in order to verify my own theory is quite unnecessary."

"Unnecessary, perhaps. But understandable."

"Nevertheless, I admit to nothing. You are welcome to draw your own conclusions, Doctor."

And with that, he returned to his task, while I smiled, rose, and walked to the sideboard to pour us both a bit of whisky – although I felt that upon this occasion, Twickening's Tea might have been more appropriate.

409

The Dowser's Discovery

"If you don't mind, sir," said old Fiedler as he finished pouring our coffee, "I'd like to go into the village this morning with the others. It's market day," he added.

Our host, Squire Boone, belched politely and raised a good-natured eyebrow. "Whatever could tempt you to visit that cackling circus?"

Fiedler looked sheepish. "It's not so much the market, sir, as what's happening nearby. There's been work going on at Mr. Retford's place, as you know, and today they're going to be using a dowser – he's that fortune-teller's husband – to find some of the buried pipes."

Holmes, sitting beside me and so far seemingly lost in his own thoughts, turned toward Fiedler with a sharp look of interest. "Really?" he asked. "So that's still being practiced out here, is it? Ah, these charming West Country superstitions."

Fiedler, unsure whether a response was required, stayed mute. Squire Boone, however, shifted in his seat with a smile. "Likely not just here, Holmes," he said. "Scrape any of the settlements from Land's End to John o' Groats and you'll find that our rickety civilization is only skin deep at best."

"A curious way of putting it," I said, "but true. To many, modern science is no more than a different way of trying to explain or justify those aspects of nature which just a few generations ago were credited to spirits and demons."

"And angels as well, Watson!" said Holmes. "We mustn't discount those advocates of the light!"

Squire Boone happily agreed that Fiedler could join the market party, and we were soon left with our coffee.

We were at the Squire's manor house near Sigford, on the eastern edge of Dartmoor, resting for a day or so after our recent exertions in the matter of the Down Ridge Circle, and the ancient blood ritual that we disrupted by the narrowest of margins. Holmes and I had journeyed there after receiving Boone's urgent wire two days earlier. Suffice it to say, the mood of the house was considerably more relaxed than when we had arrived – due completely to Holmes's masterful trapping of the madman Denton and the rescue of the crofter's daughter.

Seeing Holmes's apparent interest in the mention of dowsing, Boone stirred himself. "I wouldn't mind watching it myself," he said cannily. "Perhaps you'd both also like to make the journey?"

His offer was immediately accepted, and Fiedler was so informed. Not long after, the household departed in two wagons for the short journey across the moor. Along the way, the Squire told us about the man whose house we were going to visit.

"Reed Retford," he explained, "is the last of his line. The family made their money in shipping early in the century, and then diversified into other less risky investments. They came down from London and built a fine manor house on the moor, near the confluence of the three rivers – the high ground near the Sig, the Lemon, and Langworthy Brook. And there they've stayed, becoming more and more withdrawn and aloof as the years passed.

"Of the current generation, Reed was the older. Over a quarter-century ago, he married – a beautiful French girl who quickly became despondent after leaving the vibrancy of her native land for this brooding moor. Her only bright spot – and it was no surprise to any of us in hindsight – was Reed's younger brother, Stephen.

"He was always a wild one, vanishing for months at a stretch, traveling to London or abroad, or farther – returning in the winter with a deep sunburn and tales of bright places and colorful experiences that could barely be imagined. This had always been his way, but after his brother Reed's marriage to Célia, he stayed more than he wandered. As you might expect, they soon became devoted to one another – and Reed's dour nature only further served to make his younger brother seem all the more attractive.

"The marriage hadn't lasted much longer than a year when one day Stephen and Célia ran away together, never to seen again. Reed Retford only became more withdrawn, dismissing what little staff he'd kept, except for one scowling man named Dibrell, who has always seemed old and bent, even when he was young. The estate quickly declined into neglect.

"But six months ago, something changed. Retford has always been something of a philatelist, and that's the one subject to which he could still generate any interest. I dabble in it myself, so I'm probably the closest thing he has to a friend out here. I knew when he began corresponding with Sir Henry Winewall, the retired London barrister, about their respective collections. I was invited to the dinner, shabby though it was, when Sir Henry came down to visit. And I saw the fires – which I'd never believed could be rekindled – when Reed met Sir Henry's daughter who traveled with him, a widow named Helene.

"Well, the short of the matter is that Reed is now a man reborn. He found it in him to charm Helene, and she saw something that she liked too. She seems to be as attracted to this part of the world as she is to her fiancé

– for she and Reed are engaged to be married next year, in the spring. And Reed has dug deep to find the energy and resources to remake the manor from what he had let it become into a showplace for his new love."

"And," added Holmes with something resembling a sneer, "he is making use of a dowser."

Squire Boone made a rude noise with his lips. "The people here are willing to believe anything. The Hound, as you know. The will-o'-the-wisps and lights that supposedly lure people into the Mire. One of those traveling fortune-tellers set up a week or so ago, and I hear that she's had a steady stream of people willing to trade hard cash for vague assurances. It doesn't surprise me that her husband has a side-line in dowsing – but I *am* puzzled that Reed would make use of him."

"Perhaps," I said, "it's one of his contractors that asked for this kind of help."

"There are better ways," muttered Holmes.

I had to agree. While, as a doctor, I had seen some amazing demonstrations of the power of the mind in allowing the body to heal – belief in placebos for instance – I did not think that the holding of metal rods, or sticks from a certain type of tree, helped someone align with mysterious field lines running along the earth, or above buried objects or underground water flow. Still, even as these thoughts ran through my head, I realized that this was rather arrogant to believe that we pitiful humans could categorically state that this or that absolutely did not exist.

Holmes, as always, read my thoughts. "Many knowledgeable individuals believe in the power of dowsing," he said. "Some noted engineers use it to find water, claiming that it works when all other methods fail. Archeologists have been known to dowse to find tombs or graves – with some recorded success."

"Surely it's all chance," said the Squire. "When one of them is lucky enough to find what they seek, they trumpet the news everywhere. When they don't, it's shrugged off with feeble excuses and forgotten."

Our conversation was abated as we drew to a halt on the grounds of Retford's manor, Coleman Park. We were down the slope from a large brooding building, the stonework black and damp with age. Vines covered it from the soil to the roof peaks – but in places it was obvious that work was ongoing to reclaim the building, as great stretches had been cleared and exposed to the light, quite likely for the first time in generations.

There were already several dozen locals gathered in a loose semicircle, facing up the hill toward the house. Among them stood a woman in a loose garment, brightly colored, and augmented with garish handkerchiefs, necklaces, and bracelets. Her black hair was done up with more of the same colorful ribbons, with tendrils escaping wildly. The crowd stayed several paces away from her in all directions, as if she exerted some sort of force which might affect them without their consent. She was staring into the distance, swaying slightly as if to music that only she could hear.

A painted line ran along the ground from the house toward a low spot – clearly where the buried pipe was theorized to lie. A big hirsute man was pacing back and forth a number of feet away from the line around a medium-sized oak, carrying a Y-shaped stick, while two or three boys scampered around him, carrying their own recently obtained branches. They were careful to stay away from the man, who – like his wife – seemed to radiate something that inspired wariness. While not as colorfully dressed as the fortune-teller, he still had that same curious and unusual aspect – what one might expect to encounter deep within some Balkan forest where grim tales of supernatural creatures were still whispered around campfires.

At one side of the gathering a large grim-looking fellow stood alone, dressed in dark clothing like a vengeful preacher. "Retford," stated the Squire, leading us over to him. Introductions were made, and I had a chance to look at this morose man who had faced such a disappointment in his youth, only to receive a second chance. Perhaps, I thought, his countenance lightened when he was in the presence of his fiancé, but on this day he seemed as forbidding as he must have been throughout the previous quarter-century.

The day matched his expression. It was a typical October on the moor, dark and overcast, with a damp breeze that promised rain, and soon – nothing unusual. Stronger gusts occasionally whipped about us, blowing autumn leaves and other detritus before it. Low clouds scudded overhead, turning blacker by the minute. I lost myself for a moment, gazing across the distance at the far slopes where the cloud shadows raced across the ground like galloping moorland ponies. Intruding memories of other visits to this place distracted me until Holmes cleared his throat. I looked at him, realizing that, as ever, my thoughts had been obvious.

Looking around, I observed the rapt villagers as they tracked the dowser's performance, and I suddenly felt a kinship with our long-ago forefathers. The mood of the morning, combined with what the fellow was doing, seemed as if all our enlightenment and education had been stripped away, returning us to helpless small creatures fearing those elemental forces that had never truly vanished, but were only forgotten for a time. I realized that I felt as if I were in a place where the people could still see and do magic, simply because no one had ever bothered to tell them that such a thing didn't exist.

413

Even as an unexpected shiver ran up my spine, the brightly-dressed woman gave a sudden moan, closing her eyes and nearly stumbling. Then she shrieked, "*Murder!*" and collapsed to the ground.

At the same moment, before the stunned crowd could react, the dowser gave a surprised cry of his own when the stick in his hand made a violent twist toward the ground below him. A collective noise rose from the crowd, and a couple of watchers ducked as if instinctively dodging a threat from above.

Ignoring his wife the fortune-teller, the man with the Y-shaped stick stepped back. It immediately sprang back to a horizontal position. He moved again to where he had just stood, and it once more violently pointed toward the ground. He looked up, a terrible look on his face. "Dig here!" he said urgently, his voice low and rumbling with an unidentifiable accent. He nodded toward a couple of workmen standing nearby with the necessary tools.

She wasn't too deep, but she had clearly been there a long time. Wrapped in a soiled tarp, her exposure to the light revealed wisps of blond hair still clinging to her skull. Of course, Holmes had moved forward immediately, and I started to follow almost as quickly. I became aware that Squire Boone and Reed Retford were beside me. I heard a groan and turned to see that Retford was collapsing into a faint, while Boone tried to support him. I turned back and helped ease him to the ground, and was close enough to hear him mutter, "Célia!" with a sob.

"Watson," murmured Holmes from beside the body. Ascertaining that Retford was in no danger, I stepped to the tarp. Holmes pointed to the corpse's throat. Now a terrible wreckage of decayed flesh and exposed bone, I saw what he meant: The girl's hyoid bone was crushed – The years in the ground could not hide that she had been strangled, and violently.

Meanwhile, the fortune-teller had recovered, while declaiming loudly that this wasn't the whole story. "There is another here who cries for discovery!" she said. "A brother! Cruelly killed by the same man! '*Find me!*' he begs. '*Avenge me!*'"

The dowser had taken to quartering the ground beside the girl's body, while the boys that had shadowed him before had retreated to watch warily from behind the curious adults. He ranged in ever-wider lanes, becoming more frustrated as he moved. "Nothing," he muttered. "The other one must be buried somewhere else."

By this time, Retford had recovered and risen to his knees. "No!" he rumbled. "No! They ran away together! Stephen betrayed me, and he stole Célia. This cannot be!"

But it clearly was. The body was removed into Retford's manor house, leaving the crowds to be entertained by the continued incitement of the fortune-teller calling for justice, and the dowser, indicating that his rod was of the finest yew and would not lie – *Hadn't it found the girl?*

Inside, Retford broke down, confirming that the body was in all likelihood his lost wife. "She was missing the tip of her right little finger, you see," he said. "A childhood accident. She was ashamed of it, but I found it . . . endearing." He sobbed. "But I never told her! I should have told her!"

I recalled that the fingertip was missing from the body, but who could say whether it had been lost in life, or had simply fallen from the skeleton, to be located later within the tarp? As I considered it, Holmes asked softly, "And your brother? Should he also be found, is there anything that can identify his body as well?"

Retford shook his head and answered, "Nothing, really. He was a big man, like me. He had a tattoo of a sunrise on his right forearm, obtained on one of his journeys, but . . . if he is like my Célia . . . it is likely that it is no longer identifiable."

He put his hands to his face and rocked forward in his chair.

Squire Boone drew us aside. "I have authority in these parts, Holmes," he said softly. "May I have your assistance in clearing this up?"

Holmes nodded. "You needn't ask. Of course you have it."

"I suppose," said Boone, "that we need to take up the grounds to look for Stephen's body."

"If you like," said Holmes vaguely. "However, I have another idea that I'd like to explore before you go to the trouble." Then, with a glance toward the broken man, he nodded at each of us and abruptly departed.

Squire Boone, long used to Holmes's ways, gave a weary smile in my direction and turned back to comfort his friend.

I was at loose ends for much of the day. The local police had arrived within the hour, and explanations were given, such as they were, before the body was removed to Coombe Tracey. Leaving Dibrell in charge of the manor house at Coleman Park, Boone had rounded up his people and we had returned to the Squire's spacious home, bringing Retford with us. Barely had the carriages lurched into motion than the cold rain arrived from the south. Fortunately folk in that part are prepared for such conditions, and a variety of coats and umbrellas was quickly distributed. We soon reached our destination, where Retford was immediately put to bed in a guest room, and I kept a close eye on him, fearing a descent into brain fever. However, he maintained a level of shocked grief that became no worse, and he seemed to rally a bit when told that his fiancé Helene, had been summoned from London and would arrive late that night. Finally he agreed to a sedative, and within moments he was sleeping peacefully.

Meanwhile, a further development occurred, and as I heard it described, I dearly wished that Holmes had remained in order to adjudicate its importance.

It was an hour or so before dinner when the local constable came knocking at the door, saying that something was going on at Retford's place. Apparently the fortune-teller had continued to pontificate, even after she and her husband, along with the ever-growing crowd of locals, had been ordered off the Coleman Park property. They had gathered on the public lane outside the manor house's gateposts, where she continued to move in and out of "trances", as her husband described them. She seemed to be working herself up to making some type of prediction, and the constable thought that we ought to be present.

Checking that Retford was still asleep, we left him, telling Fiedler to keep a close watch. The rain had stopped during the afternoon, but the damp air felt much colder. A number of puddles revealed the low spots in the road, and several times the carriage dipped one way and then the next to avoid them. As we entered the moor proper, I asked about the fortune-teller and her husband. "I can't tell you much, Doctor," related the constable. "They showed up here a week or two ago, as their type often does, camping in the open and making it known that they were available for those seeking their services. There has been a steady stream of gullible folk beating a path to their campsite ever since, and when it got about that Mr. Retford was going to be digging to fix the drains, the husband, a man by the name of Ravni, piped up that he was a dowser, and could cut in half the time that they would take pot-holing around to look for the pipes.

"Ravni?" I said. "Sounds Croatian."

"Probably one of those gypsy names," replied the constable.

"He didn't seem very gypsy-like to me," said Boone, "except for those atrocious clothes. Give him a haircut and a bath, and he'd likely be as English as the rest of us. The same for his wife – if she really is his wife!"

At that point, we arrived at the gatepost for the manor, but instead of the crowd we'd been led to expect, there was no one. However, up the lane toward the house were lights, and we correctly assumed that the trespassers had been cajoled into entering the property illegally to see whatever it was that Mrs. Ravni, the fortune-teller, wished to reveal.

By the time we had stepped to the ground, the crowd of three-dozen or so were filing into the house, a mixture of both villagers and a few faces that I recognized from Coombe Tracey and even Exeter. They appeared to be quite orderly – there was nothing mob-like about them – but we could hear the cranky bleats of Dibrell, Retford's long-time servant, exhorting them to stay out after he had apparently and mistakenly opened the door.

We pushed past and through the crowd, the authority of the Squire and the constable cutting a path, to find Ravni and his wife standing in the front hall, facing the doorway with the group spread before them. Dibrell was dancing from foot to foot, whinging that they were not allowed and to get out. The constable agreed, stepping forward with raised arms to herd everyone back outside.

"Wait!" cried Mrs. Ravni in a raw voice that caused the muttering men and women behind me to fall immediately silent. "The dead cry out for vengeance against this man who has wronged them! My vision has led me here to this very room, where the evidence of his guilt shall be discovered, even as was the body of his poor cruelly murdered wife!"

The constable glanced back helplessly at the Squire who, with pursed lips, nodded to allow the matter to play out.

I had a chance to study both of the Ravnis more closely while the woman continued to make her dark and vague utterances. The man was a brooding hulk with long tangled hair. He and I were both about the same age, in our mid-forties. His skin was sun-darkened, and he worked his jaw in a peculiar grinding motion, as if something were caught in his teeth, but once when he pulled his lips back in a grimace, I could see that a number of them were missing.

While he was a tall broad man, something over six feet, his wife was much shorter, although of a round plumpness that suggested they didn't starve or lack from funding due to their odd choice of profession. Her hair was also a tangled mess, quite dark as well, but her features underneath were rather refined, if one could look past the unusual trappings surrounding them.

She had continued to ramble and rant along the same lines, but she was gradually turning toward a purpose, and she repeatedly made the point that a damning proof would be found within the room in which we stood. Then, after several iterations that were all much of a sameness, she finally added a variation: The proof could be found in the great clock standing to the side of the hall. It was a dark, dusty thing, nearly seven feet tall, and it was not working. Perhaps it hadn't run in years.

Her husband made a move in that direction, but the constable waved him away. He looked the clock up and down, and then – apparently deciding on the most obvious path first – opened the tall door that allowed access to the pendulum and winding weights. He removed his helmet, awkwardly positioned himself once or twice, and then inserted his head. With a small cry, he leaned back out, dropped to one knee, inserted an arm, and then withdraw a small sheet of what turned out to be notepaper, headed by the engraved name of *Célia Retford.*

He stood, brushed off the dust from his sleeve, and handed the page to the Squire. I looked over his shoulder at what was written upon it in faded ink. It was apparently the end of a longer note. It had a small "2" at the bottom, but the first page was missing. It said:

> *and I shall spend the rest of my life with your brother. That is the truth, and you must come to accept it.*
>
> *Célia*

Squire Boone finished reading and looked my way. While not conclusive, it seemed to confirm that his friend Reed Retford was not as innocent as he had indicated.

Even as murmurs arose demanding that the note be read aloud, I heard a familiar voice behind us. "Starting without me?" The group by the door parted, somewhat grudgingly, as Sherlock Holmes walked between them to join us. In low tones, we managed to catch him up on the latest developments. He nodded and asked to examine the note. Handing me a curious pair of *L*-shaped metal rods, he took it and held it up to the light, and then touched his tongue to his little finger, transferring a dab of saliva to one of the words – just enough to cause a small dissolving of the ink. He held it up again, turning it this way and that, before stating, "I would prefer a more accurate chemical test, but the dissolving of the ink indicates that it is likely from the 1870's, and therefore the letter is authentic."

"Of course it is," snarled Mrs. Ravni, pressing closer. "Do not doubt my powers."

"Ah, yes," said Holmes. "Our curious new acquaintances, the occult specialists." He held out his hand, taking back the metal rods. "How long," he asked the big man facing him, "have you had the gift of dowsing?"

The man looked wary, as if suddenly facing a threat he did not understand. "Since I was a boy."

"Indeed. And you use a *Y*-shaped branch from a yew tree?"

"I do," Ravni replied. "Some prefer hazel, or willow, but I learned that the yew serves me best, and is most attuned to my own energy."

"I see. And have you ever seen the likes of these?" And so saying, he handed the metal rods to Ravni.

"Not exactly. Some prefer witch rods that are shaped like those – like the letter '*L*'. The *Y*-shaped rod that I use is flexible – it bends and turns up and down. Those like yours are held in closed fists which allow them to rotate and align as they cross over water . . . or a grave."

"So I was told when I purchased them earlier today. But these are not the usual metal rods. In fact, they are specially constructed. Are you familiar with *aluminium*?"

"Yes . . . ." said Ravni cautiously.

"It is a curious metal for many reasons, and costly to produce. The process sometimes involves a great deal of electricity – thus infusing the metal with electrical energy. You may not know that men of your . . . 'profession', shall we say, are coming to rely more and more on this type of rod, rather than mere tree limbs, for a more accurate completion of their tasks."

"What does this have to do with anything?" interrupted Mrs. Ravni. "We have just discovered proof that a man committed murder, and you want to talk shop with my husband about witching rods?"

"But I left today especially to obtain these rods – for their unique properties also allow the user to identify *a murderer*!"

The crowd behind us, which had pressed closer throughout, gave a restive whisper.

"Madness!" growled Ravni. "The rods don't respond to that type of energy."

"But this is a new age," countered Holmes, "with new materials that have never existed before. Let me demonstrate." And he held the rods, one in each hand, with the horizontal segments bent at the top and facing away from him while he began to move aimlessly across the hall.

It didn't take long to see that something was influencing them. They seemed to have a will of their own, turning – no matter which path Holmes followed – to point back toward Ravni. When Holmes would suddenly change direction, the rods would quickly spin to point at the big man. The men and women pressed behind me began to mumble, and the word "Murderer" was whispered more than once.

Ravni had gone surprisingly pale, considering his dark coloring. His wife's teeth clenched, and several times she started to speak before reconsidering.

Holmes stopped moving and turned his head toward Ravni. "It seems that you are of interest to the aluminium rods, sir. Anything that you want to confess?"

Ravni swallowed audibly. "No." He cleared his throat. "No, nothing."

"Perhaps," said Holmes, putting both rods in his left hand and pinching his lip with the other, "it's a tattoo."

"What?" said Ravni, a puzzled expression now on his face. "What do you mean? A tattoo?"

"Yes," said Holmes. "Certain tattoo inks are made from ferric compounds – iron – and when they are applied, the iron is then

419

permanently etched beneath one's skin, creating an electrical field. Perhaps you have a tattoo of some sort that is attracting the rods – giving a false indication that you are a murderer." He took a step closer, a look of benevolent helpfulness on his face. "Could that be it? Do you have a tattoo?"

Ravni let out a breath in relief and quickly pulled up his sleeve, even as his wife tried to prevent it. But it was too late – we all saw the faded but unmistakable etchings of a sunrise – the same tattoo that had been mentioned to us earlier that day by Reed Retford when describing what we could use to identify his brother's body.

"Stephen Retford," said Holmes, the friendliness vanishing from his face. "I charge you with the murder of your sister-in-law, Célia Retford."

"It was an easy manipulation," said Holmes, tossing the metal rods onto Squire Boone's dining table. We were sitting around it, the same table where we had first heard of this matter only that morning, now having a late-night brandy. "Any conjurer knows how to make the rods turn as he desires, and with practice, anyone else can do it as well. It was how Retford learned to manipulate the Y-shaped limb when he and his wife conceived this scheme."

"Where did you find aluminium dowsing rods?" I asked with a smile.

"They are no such thing," he replied. "They are simply strands of heavy-gauge galvanized wire, bought this afternoon and bent for a one-time purpose."

"Never mind that," said Squire Boone. "How did you know to accuse him in the first place?"

"I took a short-cut. With the starting point that dowsing and fortune-telling and trances are the merest moonshine, I also began with the knowledge that the dowser and his wife were fakes. It was quite obvious to me from simply seeing them that they were in disguise – the clothing, the hair, and the man's coloring, obviously from walnut stain. Their assumed accents were easily spotted as well. Initially their performance was simply instructive and entertaining. Then the dowser located the body, and I understood that he must have done so because of prior knowledge of its location.

"When it seemed likely that the dowser and his wife were going to stay at Coleman Park and continue their performance, I decided to investigate their campsite. I quickly found evidence of Stephen Retford's real identity in the form of several letters and bills that he had carried down here with him, along with a few other telling items.

"Then I went into Exeter, where I spent some time sending and receiving wires. Knowing who he was, I quickly filled in a solid picture of the man. He and his wife live in Hythe, and have done so for over twenty-five years. That's where he ended up after leaving here – after strangling his sister-in-law and burying the body near a young oak tree – the same tree where he knew to locate it today.

"My sources in Hythe informed me that when he arrived there all those years ago, he obtained work in a pub, where he courted and eventually married the owner's daughter – our fortune-teller. Since then he's lived and worked there, taking it over when his father-in-law died, and has had nary a blot on his copy-book – but likely with the fear that his crime would one day be discovered. Then, a couple of weeks ago, he and his wife abruptly left town, leaving the pub in the hands of their grown son and telling everyone that they were going to see a sick relative. It wasn't too great a leap to realize that Stephen Retford had been keeping tabs on his brother Reed the whole time, and that he learned that the man intended to remarry. At that point, he decided to make a play for the fortune as the only living heir and frame Reed for murder by way of making sure that the body of Célia Retford was discovered.

"The letter in the clock," I said. "He took the last page of a letter that was written to *him*, breaking things off and stating that she had decided to stay with her husband, and used it as the evidence that Reed Retford had strangled her, rather than Stephen."

"Yes. That letter may have been what drove him to kill her. The first page, as well as several others to him from Célia, were hidden in the campsite. While the other letters could have been used if additional evidence needed to be found by way of a trance, this was the easiest to initially 'discover', since it was vague enough to implicate Reed. At some point today, one of them slipped away and gained access to the house and hid it in the clock, to be found in the most public manner possible.

"But," said the Squire, "if Stephen showed up to make his claim on the estate, a case could be made that *he* had murdered Célia and fled – which he had – and Reed would have gone free."

"Stephen and his wife had a longer game in mind. While searching their campsite, I also found a bottle of strychnine. With it were a number of other older letters from Reed to brother Stephen, along with more recent sheets where someone was attempting to use the old handwriting to craft a new letter – a suicide note. Clearly they meant to get at Reed in the next day or so, poison him, and leave the forged suicide note admitting his guilt. When you both brought Reed Retford back here today, it scotched their plan – but only temporarily, as sooner or later he would have returned home and they would have reached him.

"In the meantime, continued 'discoveries' with vague implications of guilt, as identified by the trances, would have turned public opinion against

Reed Retford to the point that his eventual suicide would be believed without question. Then, in a few weeks, Stephen Retford, the puzzled and innocent barkeeper from Hythe, would have arrived, having just heard of his estranged brother's death, and taken possession of the estate as the only heir."

At that moment, we heard conversation in the hall, and the door was opened to reveal Reed Retford, with Helene supporting him. "Thank you, Mr. Holmes," said the man who, in the presence of his fiancée, now appeared to be ten years younger than when I had first seen him that morning. "If you hadn't been here . . . ."

Holmes, looking rather embarrassed, waved his hand, but then he rose and shook Retford's outstretched hand. Soon after, with farewells to the rest of us, the couple departed for Coleman Park. As the front door shut, we sat down and Holmes said, "An interesting diversion, Squire. What do you have planned for tomorrow?"

Boone laughed, and then raised an eyebrow and pointed a canny finger at my friend. "I know you, Holmes. You're serious – lazy days of rest hold no interest whatsoever. Well, since you mention it, tomorrow night is the full moon, and if this month is anything like the past three, Richard Cabell's tomb will be visited by a pack of baying black hounds. I've seen it myself. Perhaps, since you're here, you could offer an opinion . . . ."

And the next night he did, although that is a vast over-simplification of what actually occurred.

The Triangle of Death

Every profession has its own challenges, but the ones that I understand best are those of a physician. Of those challenges I've had more than many, but one that I've always despised more than any other is *boredom*.

In 1878, I took my degree as Doctor of Medicine and tried for a while to set up my own humble practice in Southampton Street, just a few doors from Bloomsbury Square. But more often than not, despite my diligence, those in need simply chose to stay away, and regularly I would find my thoughts turning toward the nearby Alpha Inn. I resisted the impulse, and generally I was rewarded by visits from a few patients, giving me hope that my practice might grow. But eventually I joined the Army instead and set my feet on a different path.

It was just short of my twenty-eighth birthday when I was wounded at the Battle of Maiwand, leading to the cessation of my career as a military doctor. After barely surviving my wound, I was also nearly killed by my recovery, and when I returned to England at the end of 1880, I was quite honestly a broken man.

Whether it was luck or fate or Divine Intervention does not matter – Regardless of the reasons, I ended up finding better rooms in Baker Street than the expensive hotel off the Strand where my meagre wound pension was vanishing at an alarming rate. My new landlady, Mrs. Hudson, made it her business that I should recover absolutely, and my empty days were distracted early on by the activities of my new friend, Mr. Sherlock Holmes, who eventually revealed that he held the curiously self-invented profession of consulting detective. My recovery was only encouraged when he began including me in his investigations.

But that didn't pay the bills, and as soon as I was able, I began to take on the occasional medical responsibility – an occasional shift at Barts Hospital, and then more as I became stronger. When possible, I would serve as a *locum tenens* in a private physician's practice when he felt the need for a holiday, or had some other business to pursue. Which leads me to that day in late October 1881, when I found myself in the small office of Dr. Broughton in Little Harcourt Street, watching the clock tick and tick again, while my boredom seemed to increase exponentially.

I didn't know Dr. Broughton, but my name had been given to him by a colleague at Barts. I'd presented myself one evening three days earlier, after surgery hours had ended, as he intended to leave soon after. He was quite elderly, and resembled a bundle of long brittle sticks held upright by his constrictive old-fashioned clothing. He explained that he had some

423

business concerning his retirement that he needed to carry out "in the north" in order to "quell the machinations of a greedy cousin" (as he put it), and that he appreciated me filling in. (In truth, I'd jumped at the chance.) He'd showed me where the records and medicines were kept, as well as his day-book, and also his particular (and peculiar) way of recording payments for a consultation.

He let me know with something of a gruff aside that his practice had been quite busy once, what with the Marylebone Police Court just across the way, and the brewery, the Public Bath House, and Queen Charlotte's Lying-In Hospital all around the corner. "But there's a new practice down in the Seymour Buildings," he groused. "Glossy painted offices and bright-eyed young doctors – no offense taken. The patients like the shiny things, you see . . . ." His voice trailed off, and then he looked me directly in the eye with a sad smile. "That is to say, you won't be too busy, but I do want someone here for a few of my old patients, should they need seeing-to." With a few more instructions and a couple of pointed questions to gauge my knowledge, he seemed satisfied, handed me the keys, and departed with his single valise.

The next three days had been monotonous to an incredible degree. I'd unlocked the door the next morning and, expecting that it might be as quiet as I'd been warned, pulled a novel from my bag. When it lost my interest, I alternated with a medical journal, and that was how my morning passed. With no patients in sight, I hung a note on the door and walked to a nearby restaurant. I considered returning to Baker Street, not all that far away, but I did want to be as conscientious as possible.

Purchasing a magazine on my return, I settled in for the afternoon. There were no servants, and I was in the house alone. I was tempted to explore, but refrained from going any further than the kitchen to make the occasional cup of tea.

The second day was the same, and I was quite prepared with a variety of reading materials. However, I found myself simply standing in the open door of the small house, looking across at the comings and goings of the rear of the Police Court and concocting stories to fit the various characters that I saw.

By the third day, I was tired of everything that I'd brought to read, and I was looking forward to Dr. Broughton's promised return that evening. I felt rather embarrassed when I saw the day-book and the lack of any new entries in my handwriting. Still, there were many pages before I'd arrived that were just as clean and unmarked. I hoped that whatever he'd needed to accomplish on his journey connected to his retirement had been successful, as I couldn't imagine having to face this empty purgatory of an existence on a permanent basis.

424

I was nearly in a doze when the front bell rang. I started, confused for a moment as to where I was. Then I made the short journey from consulting room to the front door, where I found a short, sour-looking man in his early fifties, apparently some sort of servant, with his hand raised as if planning to re-ring the bell.

"Doctor Broughton?" He glanced at the small stained plate beside the door.

"He is away," I explained. "I am filling in for him. Won't you come in?"

"Not at all," was the reply. "I've been sent to fetch you. My master requires your assistance."

"One moment," was my reply, and I quickly retrieved my medical bag, hat, coat, stick, and the keys to the building. Then, locking the door behind me, I followed the fellow up the street, surprised that there was no carriage.

After being associated with Sherlock Holmes for a number of months, I had tried to train myself to notice things about my fellow man. I had seen that this chap was a servant from his clothing, protected against the cool weather by a loose overcoat. He had no hat, and he wore highly polished shoes which were not constructed for long walks. I soon understood that he hadn't felt the need to change his shoes or arrange for a conveyance when we reached our destination, a house in nearby Croydon Street that seemed much better kept than those around it.

Inside, a young fellow in livery took my hat, coat, and stick, and the older servant led me upstairs and to a dark door, where he knocked once and then entered without waiting for a response. I stepped in to find an elderly man in a broad bed. The room was well lit from a wide double window. The furnishings were old but solidly made, and probably expensive.

Stepping forward, I began to introduce myself, explaining, "I'm acting as a *locum* for Dr. Broughton – "

"Who?"

"Dr. Broughton." I was confused. "Did your man summon the wrong doctor?"

"No, but I wanted a second opinion, and told him to go and find me someone else – anyone. My own doctor, Kilburn, isn't helping me a bit."

His voice was a bit shrill, and I suspected that I was in the presence of that curious type of individual known as the *hypochondriac*, a valetudinarian who is either the bane of the medical professional, or his bread-and-butter, depending upon one's choice of philosophy. I'd met my share of them, and generally I was secretly amused by how they chose to worry away so many of their waking thoughts.

Mr. Clive Exton, as he introduced himself, had the typical litany of aches, pangs, and twinges to cause him cause him concern. In fact, these seemed to be normal discomforts that everyone experiences, but which some people simply cannot tolerate to any degree, having the idea that the rest of us are pain-free all of the time, and they deserve to reach that state as well. He was a nervous man in his sixties, pale and loose, and rather heavy. His nervous fingers constantly picked at the sheet pulled up near his pasty face.

He reiterated that his usual doctor wasn't helping him, so he'd spontaneously sought a random opinion, sending the servant, Beaton, out to seek a new physician. I conversationally complimented him on his approach and made an examination. He showed no symptoms of serious disease, and his vital signs presented as normal. He did have a number of patches of *acne vulgaris* on his forehead and cheeks, especially above and alongside his mouth. While unusual in a man of his age, these were likely caused by his penchant for staying mostly abed, and nervously touching and picking at his face, as demonstrated throughout our conversation.

I pronounced that I could find no obvious illness, to his undisguised disappointment, but I did offer a small bottle of a medicinal tincture, with instructions on how to have more made, a tube of salve for his face, and a recommendation for better diet and exercise. I could see that I'd already lost his interest as he rang for Beaton to show me out.

The servant paid me without question and I returned to Dr. Broughton's neglected office, entered my sole activity and fee into the day-book, and then waited the final few hours of my sentence before, upon the doctor's return, securing my parole with an exchange of his keys for what I was owed. He didn't seem surprised at all that I'd only had one patient, and he wasn't very interested either. I had no sense as to whether his trip was successful or not. We parted company cordially the doorstep, with his indifferent nod when I offered to fill in again as necessary, and I was halfway to the alley along the police court when I heard his door slam.

A week or so later, I seated myself at the table, feeling rheumatic and old, as the weather had turned damp and my wound, while more than a year in the past, was painfully reminding me of its existence. Holmes was in his chair by the fire, several newspapers already littered around him and another in his hands.

"Hmm," he said by way of greeting. "Didn't you fill in recently for a Dr. Broughton?"

"I did," more interested in listening for signs of Mrs. Hudson delivering my breakfast. "He's in the newspaper?" I asked, rather needlessly. I hoped that he hadn't passed away, knowing that he had some sort of retirement planned.

"Peripherally. One of his patients, Clive Exton, has died under unusual circumstances of a medical nature, and the doctor is nowhere to be found to answer any questions."

I started to speak, but Mrs. Hudson chose that moment to knock and enter, carrying a tray with my morning meal. She frowned at Holmes's untouched plate, previously deposited on the table before I'd arrived, and then left without gathering it up, likely hoping that he might graze upon it throughout the morning. It had been known to happen once or twice.

I took a sip of coffee, cleared my throat, and then spoke. "Exton wasn't technically Broughton's patient."

Holmes glanced my way.

"At least, not initially. I don't know if they met after I was employed by Dr. Broughton."

"You treated Mr. Exton?"

"I did." I went on to relate how I'd been summoned to Exton's residence in Croydon Street, the decided absence of any true illnesses, and how I'd left a couple of small nostrums with him before my departure. "How did he die?"

Holmes folded the paper and dropped it on the floor. "A sudden cyst on Exton's upper lip became massively infected within a short amount of time. It killed him. His servant mentioned that Dr. Broughton – though he actually meant you – had previously offered a treatment in the form of some sort of salve. As part of the routine follow-up – for it turns out that Mr. Exton was someone rather important in the banking world – attempts were made to confirm with Dr. Broughton in what sort of condition he'd found the patient during his visit, but when they went to interview him, he'd vanished. The man's regular doctor, Kilburn, had no information to provide, and now what was initially a matter of routine paperwork seems to have become a burr under someone's saddle, and they want answers."

I frowned, finding that I'd lost my appetite. Clearly Holmes could see the direction of my thoughts – there was no need to walk that ground with him. Whatever the nature of Broughton's disappearance, it was *my* treatment that was being questioned, even if my own name and involvement wasn't yet known. I suddenly had the sense of unknown forces moving around me, as if a rogue wave of great intensity was steadily building underneath my small watercraft, and I had no way of escaping it. I thought again of the very few minutes that I'd spent examining the now-dead man, a seemingly insignificant amount of time, and as my silence continued to spiral, Holmes interrupted me.

"After you've eaten, we'll walk around to Dr. Broughton's office and ask a few questions."

The short street was exactly as remembered, with a number of houses that might as well be deserted, something that wouldn't initially be noticed due to the constant activity surrounding the back entrances of the nearby police court and the brewery. As expected, a knock on the doctor's door produced no response, but Holmes did use our short time on the step to examine the lock closely – although to what purpose I didn't yet know. There was no response at either of the immediately adjacent houses, but two buildings to the north we found a rather surly woman who opened the door and looked at us with a grimace.

"Doctor left a week ago," she growled. "I always cleaned for him a couple of nights a week, and did the laundry. He told me that he was closing up – moving to Darrowby in Yorkshire, to live with his widowed granddaughter, a Mrs. Farnon, and her son."

"When did he leave?"

"Thursday of last week," was the answer. Two days after I last saw him.

"There has been a question about the passing of one of his patients," said Holmes. "Have you told anyone else that he's moved away?"

She frowned. "No one's asked. What is this? Are you the police?" Her stance changed as she prepared to slam the door.

"Not at all. We are simply trying to locate the doctor to see if his records have any more information about how the man died – when he was last treated, and so on."

"Well, I don't know about that. But I suppose if it's important, you can write to that woman in Darrowby." And with that she shut the door in our face – but without the initial emphasis that I'd initially expected.

Holmes nodded as if she were still there. Then he stepped away to a nearby lamppost, where he fished out his pipe. Then he handled it as if lighting it, although he never actually added any tobacco or lit a match. Instead, he ran his other hand into a coat pocket, where he felt around for a moment before nodding and then leading me back to Broughton's door, his hand still concealed. Looking to see that no one was paying us any attention, he pulled forth one of the rings of keys that he collected, one of them already apparently selected by touch, and deftly opened the doctor's front door. Then exuding full confidence, he stepped inside, stating, "Don't lag, Watson."

I moved without thought, feeling as if a dozen pairs of eyes were on me from the police court across the way. But there were no outcries, and shutting the door gave me some sense of security. Looking out through the small window revealed that no one had noticed us at all.

Holmes was already in the doctor's former office when I found him, having lit the gas lamp and in the process of examining a number of sealed boxes. "It seems that your services as a *locum* will no longer be required," he said. He puttered around until he found a box marked "*Desk*". "This looks promising," he said, and he quickly had it open. Then he looked to me. "Can you identify his day-book?"

It wasn't difficult, being stacked near the top. A quick glance showed that my entry was indeed the very last in the book. "I suppose," I said, "that he came back to London with his affairs up north settled. He spent a day or so packing what little he had, probably intending for it to be shipped later, and then he departed."

"So it's likely," Holmes added, "that your visit to Exton was the last professional call associated with this practice."

"Possibly. Of course, Dr. Broughton could have seen a patient, or been called out after that, and then failed to make a record of the visit. But somehow that didn't seem to be his way."

Flipping through the book, with the earlier pages filled with page after page of dense and cramped handwriting before the entries dwindled and ceased, Holmes nodded. "I agree. He has been fastidious in his note-keeping – a regular Pepys of medical records!"

An examination of the rest of the house revealed nothing else of interest, and soon after we locked up the building without molestation and located the estate office which managed the lease for the property. We confirmed that the doctor had indeed retired to Darrowby, and that he'd made arrangements to have the boxes still in the house to be shipped within a few weeks when he was settled.

Outside I asked, "What does any of this accomplish? It may have been your intent to keep me distracted with this quest, but the fact is we've only further established that I am the doctor who is seemingly under some sort of suspicion for providing poor treatment – a situation exacerbated by the absence of Dr. Broughton."

"We are clearing away the brush," Holmes replied. "Now to find out more about the actual death."

A cab ride brought us to Scotland Yard, where I had obviously become apprehensive enough that Holmes noticed it. "There is an advantage to knowing a man like Inspector Lestrade, who has no imagination – he will not jump to any unpleasant conclusions, and we will be able to learn some facts."

After we had reached Lestrade's office and told our story, I wasn't so sure. He looked at me with a wry smile, and as I didn't know him quite so well in those days, I interpreted it as the professional interest of a policemen who catches the scent of a crime. Yet even as I attempted to remind myself that I had nothing to fear, he said, "Looks a bit dodgy for you, Doctor. It hasn't been reported in the newspapers yet, but Mr. Exton's manservant is saying that *you* poisoned him somehow – although he thought that it was Dr. Broughton that had done it, as he hadn't quite recall that you weren't the doctor whose name was on the door. But we've already traced Dr. Broughton to Darrowby and confirmed that he didn't flee London to escape justice – and he also made certain to emphasize that he never even saw Exton. He told us that his *locum* had made the call instead, but he couldn't remember your name. We've got a man at Barts right now talking to the fellow that suggested you to him, so we would have come knocking at your door soon enough to get your story. It's a good thing that you came in on your own."

It sounded as if I were under suspicion of something after all. "Nonsense," said Holmes, seemingly thinking the same thing and sounding annoyed. "You make it sound as if Watson were a fugitive that had decided to surrender himself. What was the nature of the death?"

"Well, there wasn't any poison in the salve, as Exton insisted, but we do know that Exton died from a particularly nasty infection that started on his face – very soon after your visit, Doctor – on one of the sores for which you provided ointment. It got straight into his blood. He was dead within just a few days."

He searched left and right on his desk before his gaze settled on a particular sheet of paper. He handed it to me, and I examined it thoroughly before passing it to Holmes.

It stated that a large swollen area had formed suddenly on one of the small sores on Exton's upper left lip. Initially believed to be a cyst due to its size, it had turned hot and red, and within just a few hours the infection hidden within had poisoned the man's blood, sending him into septic shock. He fell into unconsciousness, and was dead within hours.

"The Triangle of Death," I murmured. Holmes glanced up from the sheet of paper, while Lestrade leaned forward.

"What was that, Doctor?"

I cleared my throat. "The Triangle of Death. It's an area of the face from a point between the eyes, running down along either side of the nose, and terminating on either side of one's mouth. Infections within this area have the possibility of turning quite serious – even deadly."

"I've never heard of it," muttered Lestrade, settling back in his chair. "Although it does seem like an area of the body where one would wish to avoid having an infection."

"Indeed," said Holmes, laying the report on the desk. "I see that my own medical education is still lacking – which is no surprise, considering the specialized areas that I've pursued. Tell us more, Doctor."

I elaborated a bit upon the nature of the rich blood supply to the nose and parts of the face in that area, and how physicians had long recognized that an infection there could quickly travel back through the sinus cavities and into the base of the brain itself, causing severe cavernous sinus thrombosis, meningitis, blood poisoning, or brain abscess.

"Well then," said Lestrade, "all of the questions have been answered. The fellow died of an unfortunate infection, and the mysterious question of which doctor had actually treated him turns out to have no significance at all." He stood, his mood more relaxed than it had been just a few moments before. "Thank you, Doctor, for clearing that up. There should be no trouble from Exton's man, Beaton, and his talk of poison. I'll see to that."

We found ourselves back on the street, walking north toward Trafalgar Square. My step was considerably lighter, but Holmes was frowning, his head turned down and his Inverness hanging from his shoulders, giving him the impression of some hunched bird of prey. Then he stopped as we reached the entrance to Craig's Court, straightening and looking at me from underneath the bill of his fore-and-aft cap.

"It wouldn't hurt to be certain," he said. He lifted a hand to hail a passing hansom. "What is Mr. Exton's address?"

Within a short time we had worked our way north and east and were back in Croydon Street, knocking on the dead man's door. The residence was decorated in mourning, and Holmes's energetic knock seemed excessive and loud. A surprised fellow, some sort of butler wearing a black armband, answered the door, and soon we were ensconced in a sitting room interviewing Beaton, who looked at me with open hostility.

Holmes introduced us, and upon hearing that my name was not Broughton, the man seemed even more hostile, but I quickly explained that I had been acting for the older doctor.

"We have just been to Scotland Yard," Holmes explained, "where we spoke to Inspector Lestrade. It has been established that the salve prescribed by Dr. Watson was untainted. The infection seems to have traveled quickly from the sore on his face to his brain."

Beaton considered this statement and nodded. "It did move powerfully fast, once it took hold."

"Was he visited by his regular doctor?" I asked. "Surely help was summoned when his condition turned so quickly."

"I did finally find someone, but it was too late."

"Find someone?" I pressed. "You mentioned a regular doctor when you visited me in Dr. Broughton's surgery – a Dr. Kilburn, I believe."

"Oh, he wasn't the regular doctor, either. Mr. Exton had quarreled with Dr. Ives, who had seen him for years, when he wasn't feeling any better. He went through a whole passel of doctors. Just before you, there was this Dr. Kilburn – he'd been here three or four times before I went to find someone else – you. He stopped by the next morning, after you had been here, and when he found out that Mr. Exton had seen another doctor behind his back, he was angry, but only for a little while. Dr. Kilburn calmed himself down, and then he looked at that salve you left. He said that it would do the trick, and even helped to spread it all over Mr. Exton's face. But something must have been the matter with it, in spite of what the police say, because in just a few hours Mr. Exton was terribly sick. He died the very next day."

"And did Dr. Kilburn come back after that?" asked Holmes, his voice having an edge of interest that only I would notice.

"He did not. When Mr. Exton became much worse, I went to him, but he said that he was too busy. So I then went back to Dr. Broughton's office for help, but no one was there. Finally Dr. Ives came back with me, but by then it was too late."

Hearing that story, I too would have believed that the salve was tainted, in spite of Lestrade's statement that it had tested pure. I wanted to ask further questions, but Holmes stood, signaling that the interview was over. Thanking Beaton, he led me through the house. We collected our coats and hats and returned to the street. The air was decidedly cooler than when we'd left Baker Street that morning.

"What did you hear?" I asked.

"Just . . . ." Then he stopped. "Return to Baker Street, Watson. I must do some research."

"But – " I realized that he wouldn't reveal anything until he was ready. With a wave he turned and departed.

I returned in time for a late lunch and wrote up my notes related to what had taken place earlier in the day. Since I was a lad, I'd been an inveterate keeper of a journal, and it had been quite useful on a few occasions when I'd recorded a few of my Afghan experiences in narrative form to share with some of my friends.

I was still at it when a four-wheeler clattered to the curb outside. I stood and looked out the window, but saw no one disembarking. This was due, however, to the fact that Holmes was already inside and dashing up to the sitting room.

"Ah, Watson, you're here. Good! I insisted that Lestrade swing by in case you wanted to be in at the kill. Bring your revolver." And then he

432

turned and went back downstairs, correctly assuming that I would join him.

In the growler, Lestrade's mood was grim, and I could see that it was due to the seriousness of our mission, and also a bit of embarrassment, as his earlier statement that the matter was closed had been proven false. As we negotiated the busy streets, Holmes laid out his narrative.

"The fact that Dr. Kilburn had returned, which wasn't part of the facts related by the Inspector here, seemed to be worth examining. From Beaton, we learned that not only had he smeared the salve on Exton's face, but made sure that the use of the salve would be noted. And as we saw, it was, when the man sickened and died, and Beaton was certain that it was poisoned. Later, Dr. Kilburn didn't see fit to return and check on the dying man. This physician interested me, and I decided to do a bit of research.

"I learned that Dr. Kilburn is thirty-one years old and was born in California – note that fact, Watson – although his mother, a widow, came to England soon after his birth and raised him here. She remarried just a few years later. She and her husband died three years ago when the *Princess Alice* sank in the Thames. Kilburn received his medical degree at the University of London that year – the same as you, Watson. Although he was considered a rather brilliant student, it took him a bit longer to graduate, as he's a few years older than you are."

"I have no memory of him," I said. "How do you know these facts?"

"Basic research led me to his school, and from there it wasn't a hard trail to follow. I learned about his family history from speaking to a couple of his professors, as it hasn't been so many years since he attended. They recall him not so much with fondness but rather vexation, for he blended his impressive skills and knowledge with a certain arrogant laziness. After receiving his degree, he opened a small practice in Nutford Place, keeping it going during the lean times using the small inheritance that he received upon the death of his parents."

"This is all very interesting," I said, "but how is it relevant?"

"Because," answered Lestrade, "Mr. Holmes also found out that the dead man, Exton, made his fortune during the California Gold Rush."

I frowned. Holmes had told me to note that Kilburn was born in California thirty-one years earlier – in 1850. "So Exton was in California when Kilburn was born?"

"When he was conceived," countered Holmes. "Or so I theorize. When I learned this fact about Mr. Exton's past – "

"Wait," I interrupted. "Why would you take the time to research Exton at the same time you were examining Kilburn?" This was asked in my ignorance, having known Holmes at that time for less than a year. As

433

our friendship grew, I came to realize that such thoroughness was only to be expected.

He went on as if I hadn't asked the question. "When I learned that Mr. Exton had been in California about the same time as Kilburn was born, I went back and checked the official records related to Kilburn. Obviously I found no record of his birth, since that had occurred in California, but I did find where he had been adopted by the man Kilburn who had married the baby's supposedly 'widowed' mother."

I saw where he was headed. "It's quite a leap to assume that one is the father of the other."

"True, but the connection had to be explored. With the help of the inspector here, I was able to verify a most damning detail from Mr. Exton's will: He makes the provision that his son – *whose location he does not know* – will inherit his entire considerable estate if he can be located. He goes on to state that this son was born in California in 1850, in the same month that Kilburn was born, and that he doesn't know the true name of the boy's mother, but that she was British and likely returned to London soon after the arrival of the child."

By then we'd arrived at Kilburn's rooms in Nutford Place, and as it was only late afternoon, we were admitted to his office immediately by a rather slouching page.

Kilburn was one of those men who exuded an initial confidence, but it became apparent that it was a brittle shell. He may have been a brilliant student once, but looking around his rather shabby consulting room, it hadn't translated into any kind of lasting success.

When we didn't sit, Kilburn stood to face us, looking from one to another, initially watching Lestrade because of the inspector's apparent authority. But as Holmes began to speak, explaining why we were there, the facts that he knew about Clive Exton, and the seeming connections with Kilburn's own history, he began to sweat, and after a minute he cracked, sagging into his chair with an odd little laugh.

"It's been so difficult, you see," he said. He looked at me. "You understand – we're both doctors. We swore an oath. But I was raised to hate him. My mother fled California soon after I was born, thinking that she'd be safer here, for he was a vengeful man, and she never thought that he'd leave America.

"They weren't married, so she was free to wed. She lied about being a widow, and my father – my adoptive father – never questioned her. He took me as his own, and gave me his name. They were good people, and . . . and I'm glad that they're gone so that they cannot know what I've done."

He covered his eyes with a shaking hand and told the rest of his story in that way, in a flat tone devoid of emotion.

434

"My mother first told me the truth about my . . . my real father when I was a lad. I hadn't guessed any of it. I wish that I'd never known. But all through the years, as she told me how cruel and wicked he was, we thought that he was in America, and that our paths would never cross. When my parents died, and her bitter words about him ceased, even after all those years, I lost interest in him. I opened a practice – this practice – and I tried . . . I tried . . . ."

After a moment of silence, he continued. "Then, a couple of weeks ago, his man Beaton came around, trying to find a doctor – any doctor – who could help his pain. I immediately recognized the name, of course, but I couldn't believe that it would really be him, here in London. But when I arrived, and as he and I spoke, I could see the resemblance between us, and I began to ask innocent-seeming questions about his past, implying that something in his history might help my diagnosis. Soon I knew for certain that it was he.

"I returned home and didn't sleep that night. I hadn't realized how much that I hated him – apparently as much as my mother had, this man I'd never met. When I went back a few days later, I asked more questions, including whether he had any family that also showed the same symptoms. That was when he mentioned having a son whom he'd never met.

"He seemed to regret it, but that wasn't enough for me now. He told me about the will he'd written, if he ever found the boy. It only seemed right by then that his estate should go to me. But I couldn't murder him. At least that's what I thought then. But as the days passed, and I visited him a few more times, I realized that I could poison him and make it look like an infection. I made a virulent concoction in the form of a medication that would enter the persistent wounds on his face and set up blood poisoning. I was taking a risk that it would be found in the medicine, but it turned out that I didn't have a chance to give it to him, for he had also tired of my lack of help and summoned you, Dr. Watson.

"As I continued to hear nothing from that quarter, I began to believe that I had been spared losing my soul by killing my own father. But then I was called back, at the time that the cyst had suddenly developed on his lip, and I heard that another doctor had been summoned in the meantime, and had left a tube of salve. Pretending to use that, I spread the concoction that I'd created over his open wounds, killing him as effectively as if I'd fired a pistol into his brain.

"A few days later, his man summoned me, but I refused to go. And while I should have been applying my thoughts as to how to obtain the inheritance in such a way that I couldn't be connected with the doctor who had recently visited him, I've found instead that all I can see is his face, looking at me and simply talking as he did, as if he weren't an evil man at all. Did I imagine that there was a look of affection in his eye for this son that he'd never met – the man that he didn't realize was standing there right in front of him? The man . . . the very man who killed him?"

Only at that point did his voice break as he ceased speaking, wracked with sobs.

Lestrade led the doctor away while the page and a housekeeper watched in shocked silence from the front doorway. A constable had been summoned and placed nearby for the time being, and he was explaining the little that he knew to them.

As we set out to walk back to Baker Street, my thoughts were racing in a dozen directions at once. Finally all that I could do was ask, "How did you know?"

Holmes looked at me and raised an eyebrow.

"From the little thread that Kilburn came back to visit Exton," I added, "you sensed enough to start tugging until the whole unseen garment unraveled."

He shrugged. "Experience? Despite my relatively young age in terms of years, I have been doing this for quite a while now, and studying the history of crime with a great intensity for much longer. It teaches one to see . . . connections."

"But Holmes . . . ." I wanted to express that it was more than mere study and familiarity. That he seemed to have a gift, in spite of his frequent assertions that anyone could do what he did if only they chose to observe rather than simply see. But I knew that he didn't want to hear it.

"What was it Shakespeare said?" he asked. "'*It is a wise father that knows his own child*'."

"True, but in this case perhaps Exton never had the chance. We only have the word of Kilburn's mother that he was an evil man. Her years of whispering poison into the poor lad's ear warped him – it aimed him straight to the fate that now awaits him. Shakespeare also said, "'*Hardness ever of hardness is mother*'."

Holmes nodded. "Truly it was a triangle of death. Exton and the woman and the child, stretched in different directions, but always linked." He shook his head. "We have referenced a pair of quotes about the father and the mother. Perhaps I might add a little maxim of my own about the child as well: '*When a doctor goes wrong, he is the first of criminals*'."

It would not be the last time that I'd hear him say so.

About the Author

David Marcum plays *The Game* with deadly seriousness. He first discovered Sherlock Holmes in 1975 at the age of ten, and since that time, he has collected, read, and chronologicized literally thousands of traditional Holmes pastiches in the form of novels, short stories, radio and television episodes, movies and scripts, comics, fan-fiction, and unpublished manuscripts. He is the author of over eighty Sherlockian pastiches, some published in anthologies and magazines such as *The Strand*, and others collected in his own books, *The Papers of Sherlock Holmes*, *Sherlock Holmes and A Quantity of Debt*, and *Sherlock Holmes – Tangled Skeins*. He has edited almost sixty books, including several dozen traditional Sherlockian anthologies, such as the ongoing series *The MX Book of New Sherlock Holmes Stories*, which he created in 2015. This collection is now up to 27 volumes, with more in preparation.

He was responsible for bringing back August Derleth's Solar Pons for a new generation, first with his collection of authorized Pons stories, *The Papers of Solar Pons*, and then by editing the reissued authorized versions of the original Pons books, and then volumes of new Pons adventures. He has done the same for the adventures of Dr. Thorndyke, and has plans for similar projects in the future. He has contributed numerous essays to various publications, and is a member of a number of Sherlockian groups and Scions. His irregular Sherlockian blog, *A Seventeen Step Program*, addresses various topics related to his favorite book friends (as his son used to call them when he was small), and can be found at *http://17stepprogram.blogspot.com/*

He is a licensed Civil Engineer, living in Tennessee with his wife and son. Since the age of nineteen, he has worn a deerstalker as his regular-and-only hat. In 2013, he and his deerstalker were finally able make his first trip-of-a-lifetime Holmes Pilgrimage to England, with return Pilgrimages in 2015 and 2016, where you may have spotted him. If you ever run into him and his deerstalker out and about, feel free to say hello!

439

440

Also by David Marcum
from MX Publishing

Traditional Canonical Holmes Adventures by
David Marcum
Creator and editor of
The MX Book of New Sherlock Holmes Stories

Sherlock Holmes and The Eye of Heka

*"Marcum could be today's greatest Sherlockian writer, and Conan Doyle
himself would be proud of this story."*
– Lee Child - New York Times *Bestselling Author*

*"David Marcum is the reigning monarch of all things Sherlockian, and his latest
long-form work,* Sherlock Holmes and The eye of heka, *showcases his utter
mastery of Watson's narrative voice, while at the same time entertains and
enthralls with his spot on descriptions of the characters and themes which
animate the world of the Great Detective himself. No mere pastiche,* The Eye of
heka *is a robust and creative novel in its own right, not to be missed!"*
– *John Lescroart - New York Times Bestselling Author*

*"Marcum assuredly handles multiple intriguing plots while plausibly adding
emotional depth to Dr. Watson . . . Marcum expertly balances deduction and
action as he more than meets the challenge of recreating the spirit and tone of
Conan Doyle's originals. Sherlockians will clamor for a sequel"*
– *Publishers Weekly* Starred Review

Edited by David Marcum
from MX Publishing
The MX Book of New Sherlock Holmes Stories
(MX Publishing, 2015-   )

"This is the finest volume of Sherlockian fiction I have ever read, and I have read, literally, thousands." – Philip K. Jones

"Beyond Impressive . . . This is a splendid venture for a great cause!"
– Roger Johnson, Editor, *The Sherlock Holmes Journal,*
The Sherlock Holmes Society of London

Part I: 1881-1889
Part II: 1890-1895
Part III: 1896-1929
Part IV: 2016 Annual
Part V: Christmas Adventures
Part VI: 2017 Annual
Part VII: Eliminate the Impossible (1880-1891)
Part VIII – Eliminate the Impossible (1892-1905)
Part IX – 2018 Annual (1879-1895)
Part X – 2018 Annual (1896-1916)
Part XI – Some Untold Cases (1880-1891)
Part XII – Some Untold Cases (1894-1902)
Part XIII – 2019 Annual (1881-1890)
Part XIV – 2019 Annual (1891-1897)
Part XV – 2019 Annual (1898-1917)
Part XVI – Whatever Remains . . . Must be the Truth (1881-1890)
Part XVII – Whatever Remains . . . Must be the Truth (1891-1898)
Part XVIII – Whatever Remains . . . Must be the Truth (1898-1925)
Part XIX – 2020 Annual (1882-1890)
Part XX – 2020 Annual (1891-1897)
Part XXI – 2020 Annual (1898-1923)
Part XXII – Some More Untold Cases (1877-1887)
Part XXIII – Some More Untold Cases (1888-1894)
Part XXIV – Some More Untold Cases (1895-1903)
Part XXV – 2021 Annual (1881-1888)
Part XXVI – 2021 Annual (1889-1897)
Part XXVII – 2021 Annual (1898-1928)
Part XXVIII – More Christmas Adventures (1869-1888)
Part XXIX – More Christmas Adventures (1889-1896)
Part XXX – More Christmas Adventures (1897-1928)
In Preparation
Part XXXI (and XXXII and XXXIII?) – 2022 Annual

. . . and more to come!

Edited by David Marcum
from MX Publishing
The MX Book of New Sherlock Holmes Stories
(MX Publishing, 2015-   )

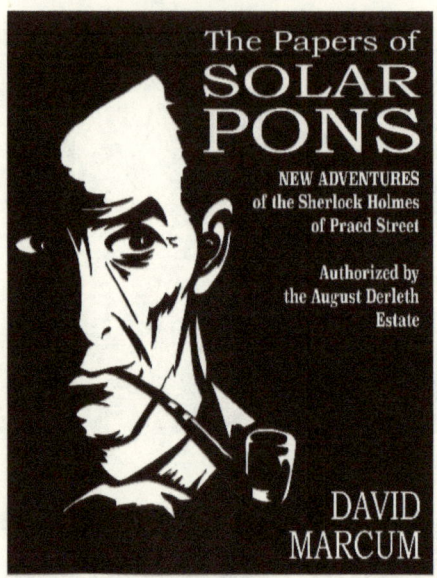

Edited by David Marcum
from Belanger Books

Sherlock Holmes: Before Baker Street

Sherlock Holmes and Doctor Watson:
The Early Adventures
Volumes I, II, and III

Edited by David Marcum
from MX Publishing

Imagination Theatre's Sherlock Holmes

The Further Adventures of Sherlock Holmes:
The Complete Jim French Imagination Theatre Scripts

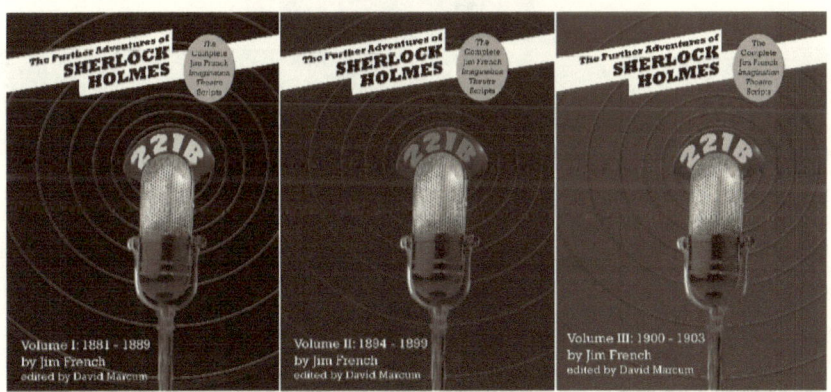

Edited by David Marcum
from MX Publishing

Sherlock Holmes in Montague Street
by Arthur Morrison
Sherlock Holmes's Early Investigations
Originally published as Martin Hewitt Adventures

Complete Hardcover Edition and Three-volume Paperback Edition

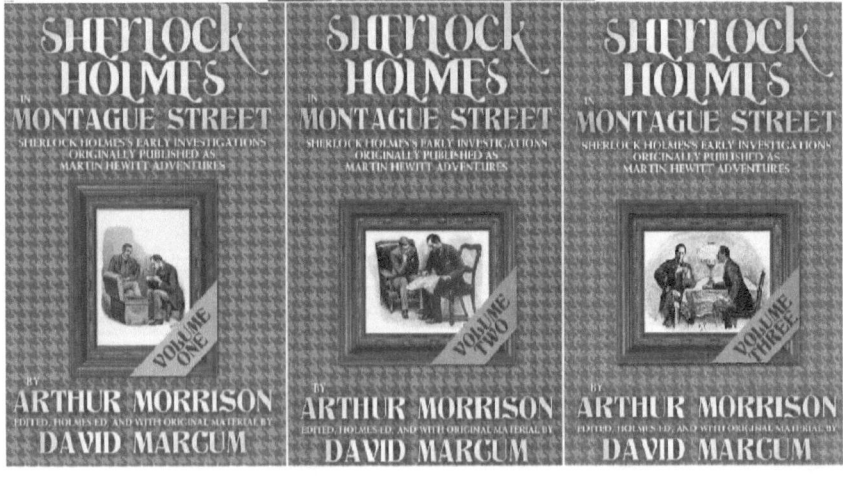

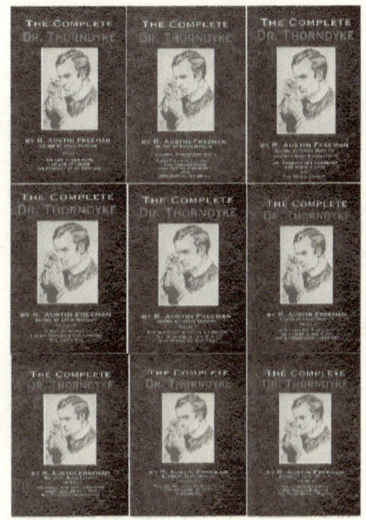
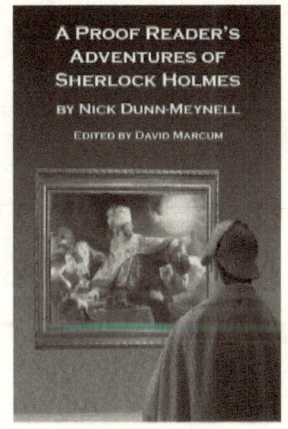
451

Edited by David Marcum
from Belanger Books

The Complete Solar Pons
by August Derleth

8-volume Paperback Edition

4-volume Hardcover Edition

The New Adventures of Solar Pons

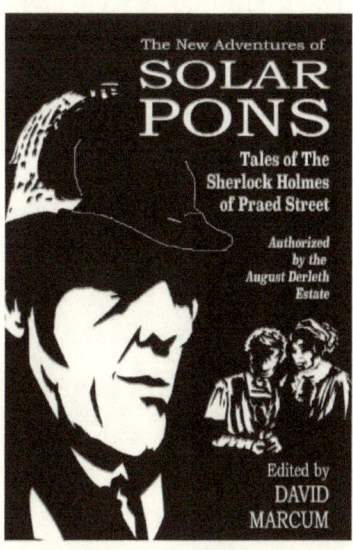

The Meeting of the Minds:
The Cases of Sherlock Holmes and Solar Pons

Edited by David Marcum,
Derrick Belanger, and Sonia Fetherston
from Belanger Books

Sherlock Holmes is Everywhere!

MX Publishing

MX Publishing is the world's largest specialist Sherlock Holmes publisher, with over five-hundred titles and over two-hundred authors creating the latest in Sherlock Holmes fiction and non-fiction

The catalogue includes several award winning books, and over two-hundred-and-fifty have been converted into audio.

MX Publishing also has one of the largest communities of Holmes fans on Facebook, with regular contributions from dozens of authors.

www.mxpublishing.com

@mxpublishing on Facebook, Twitter and Instagram

www.ingramcontent.com/pod-product-compliance
Lightning Source LLC
Chambersburg PA
CBHW020921020726

47495CB00002B/290

* 9 7 8 1 7 8 7 0 5 9 1 2 2 *